I0818358

WINGS OF LIFE

WINGS OF LIFE

MEGHAN LE FAY

Page & Vine
An Imprint of Meredith Wild LLC

Cover Design by Covers by Christian

Hardcover ISBN:978-1-964264-57-8

For ZuZu.
Without you, I would never have found my smile.

Content Note

For those readers who might have sensitivity to certain subjects, I'd like to warn you that this book is meant for adults and contains adult topics. For more detailed content information for *Wings of Life* as well as a look at my bonus content, please visit the Extras page of my website at meghanlefay.com.

THE RIHT

DRAKH

CAVENDAFFE

FETHERSEN

INGLETON

INRA

FÍON
N
W
E
S
VOLAACH

Jaeden Calendar

WINTER · SPRING · SUMMER · AUTUMN

1 TINMON
2 PATRIMON
3 GAYMON
4 INGOLMON
5 VALMON
6 JERRMON
7 MAYMON
8 TUSKIMON
9 BASMON
10 BEYMON
11 TALMON
12 FREMON
13 SHKALMON
14 YKATMON

Spring Equinox
Patrimon 21-22

Summer Solstice
Jerrmon 7-8

Autumn Equinox
Basmon 21-22

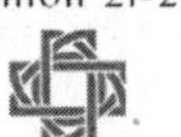

Winter Solstice
Shkalmon 7-8

28 DAY MON MOON PHASES

Day 1
Full Moon

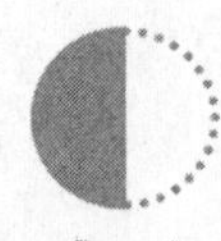

Day 8
Waning Half Moon

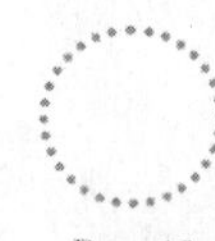

Day 15
New Moon

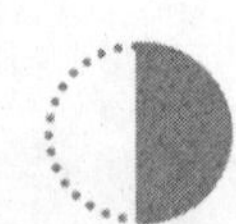

Day 22
Waxing Half Moon

Titles

Dana - *DAY-nuh*
The Rihtish title for queen.

Dane-*DAY-n*
The Rihtish title for king.

Dein - DEH-een
The gender neutral title.

Kish - *KISH*
The Rihtish title for the chefs at Drakh Keep.

Lanh - *LAH-n*
The Rihtish title for an artisan (particularly one who owns a shop to sell their wares).

Margrave - *MAR-grave*
A high-ranking noble who governs several lordships on a coastal province with prominent ports and answers directly to the king.

Margravine - *MAR-gruh-veen*
The wife of the margrave.

Marr - *MAR*
Old Rihtish for "master."

Rihtish Terms

"va draske" - *vah DRAH-sk*
lit. "let's get draked."
How the people of the Riht say: "let's get fucked (drunk)."

bab - *BAHB*
A round bun.

babi - *BAHB-ee*
The plural form of a round bun.

bierla - *BEER-luh*
Blessing.

bierlae - *BEER-lay*
The plural form of blessing.

choirsa - *KWAR-suh*
An oat drink packed with nutrients.

dowsa - *DOW-suh*
A dance or pattern the members of the Riht practice daily for body health.

dowsae - *DOW-say*
The plural form of dance or pattern.

ranng - *RAH-ng*
Crew.

reálta - *ray-ALL-tuh*
lit. "guiding light."
The title given to a woman devoted to the care and guidance of a prominent member of the Riht.

reálti - *ray-ALL-tee*
Plural or gender neutral form of reálta.

reálton - *ray-ALL-tuhn*
Male form of reálta.

Inraen Terms

bliaut - *blee-OH*
An elegant dress worn by women in Inra. Often laced like a corset.

cercle - *SAIR-kluh*
A simple crown worn by Inraen nobility.

chape - *SHAPE*
A hooded cape.

cote - *KOTE*
A simple overdress worn over a woman's base garment.

cotehardie - *koht-HAHR-dee*
A man's shirt worn as a base garment, buttoned down the front.

sollars - *SOL-lars*
Slipper-like shoes.

PRELUDE

I know a land beyond the sea,
Where all the live ones came to be;
I know a tide with waters deep,
Where all the monsters go to sleep.

I know a mountain, standing tall,
Where spirits hide from Death's dark call;
I know a hole within the ground,
Where small ones live without a sound.

If I could be the swirling breeze,
I'd sneak betwixt the swaying trees,
And fill my time 'til end of days,
With deep, dank night and leaf-masked rays.

Yet would I miss the blinding sun—
Her sparkling rays that banish dun?
Would I lament the crisp salt air,
Should I retreat without a care?

How little can my mind contrive,
The right things my heart needs to thrive.

PROLOGUE

BALE

MIDSUMMER, JERRMON 1036

Eleven months, two weeks, four days, and probably two and a half hours. It had been too fucking long since I had seen my family. There was no chance of making it home in the next month, let alone a week. The king's army did not recognize birthdays, so it did not matter that one week from today would be mine. It also didn't matter that I'd never before been apart from Serae on our shared birthday. We weren't twins. I was four years her senior and just lucky enough to share the day with my youngest sister—my little starling.

Not that Serae was little anymore. A few years ago, I'd returned home from school to find that she had grown taller than our mother—just a few inches below my own head. She was a full-fledged woman of twenty-one, soon to be twenty-two, with a temper as wild as her rust-colored hair.

Being sent to this hellhole was one of the worst turns my life had taken, not that it mattered to our jackass of a father. Everything with the margrave was posturing, and this time, it meant gambling my very life.

"Officer Cavendaffe, this way."

I mock saluted in the direction of the voice but did not glance over. It was Penderson, the senior officer in my section whose crooked teeth and superior-than-thou attitude were the last things I cared to play witness to today. I knew Penderson from school. Though he was two years my senior, we had the misfortune to cross paths regularly thanks to common clubs and overlapping interests. That wasn't enough to make me like the man, or even respect him. With an instinctual response one could only gain through countless hours of mind-numbing drills, I fell into line with the rest of the section—neat rows of four across—and marched.

As we walked, my mind drifted away from my sister and to a very different female who had been plaguing me. From the moment I laid eyes on her, I couldn't look away. It wasn't sexual, but I was drawn to her in a way I couldn't explain. Something about her sucked men in like a siren's call. The mere sight of her terrified me to my very core.

She had hair as black as onyx, complexion as white as burnt charcoal, and teeth sharp enough to tear through raw flesh. Her eye color was unremarkable. Her face, nothing to inspire the songs of minstrels. Her best feature was a nice, straight nose. And yet, to look upon her was to be consumed. I watched men and women alike get lost in her every move. If my sister was like a starling—full of song, mischief, and something just a little bit sweet—then this woman was a raven of Death, ready to trick you out of your soul, then rip you apart just for fun. She was Captain Qualin Henedew, leader of this regiment and destroyer of scores of men.

Everyone knew that Captain Henedew was in her position, the only woman of rank I'd ever heard of, because of her ruthlessness. She would sacrifice every last one of our lives if she had even an inkling it would benefit her standing. Luckily, more enemies died under her watch than allies. *Usually.* My only option was to keep my head down, work as hard as I could, and hope that I'd be released home soon—with duty to the crown fulfilled.

It had been close to two months since Henedew had led our regiment off course from our expected mission. Missives of our disappearance would have been sent home to our families by now. What we were doing here was anyone's guess. We were meant to meet up with a much larger host that secured the channel between Inra and Volaach. That was our task—routine coastal patrol. Not crossing the channel and wandering the barren lands of Volaach. But when the captain commands you to divert, you listen without question.

As if she'd been summoned by my thoughts alone, she appeared on my left. "Fall in," was all the captain had to say to send men scrambling into order. She never had to raise her voice.

I moved with the rest of the squadron to organize behind Henedew. Where she was taking us was anyone's guess. It wasn't my job to ask questions here. My rank outside the militia had little impact on my importance and influence within it. Cavendaffe was not a small province. It controlled a major coastline, and I was its margrave's oldest son. As the heir, I should be called Lord and treated at least as well as a Major. While I didn't mind the anonymity of a plain officer, I did mind the added risk to my life.

Our squadron split from the main group, setting a brisk pace to pass the larger part of the regiment. Periodically, Henedew would call out to one section or another to fall in—just like she had with mine. Once she had collected at least two entire squadrons, we split off and took a separate path east. If we were lucky, the captain would take pity on us tonight and share part of her plan. If not, as was likely, we would march blindly into whatever scheme she'd concocted. Whether it was toward something we had a chance at winning was anyone's guess. The only certainty was that Henedew would always walk away unscathed.

We marched at a brisk pace across the arid Volaachi lands in relative silence for hours, with only one short break. The weather was perfect for a midsummer day, but it was unreasonably warm for being dressed in mail with the sun beating down on us for hours on end. We kept to the larger clearings when not on the wide dirt roads. Every shambled town or cluster of huts we passed had long been abandoned. When the captain called to make camp, a collective sigh rippled across the lines. Tents were pitched, fires were stoked, and bowls of hot stew made their way into eager hands.

Penderson took a seat on the ground next to me, bowl in hand, and ate in slurping silence. After his last drop was drained—in half the time it would take me—he muttered, "What do you reckon?"

I wanted to feign ignorance, but I knew exactly what Penderson was asking. "Nothing," I replied. If I could speak freely, I would've said *nothing good*, but in camps like this, there were far too many open ears.

"Miloh thinks we're making a flank."

My stomach fluttered. "Maybe so. Hard to tell."

"I haven't seen signs of any other soldiers coming through here."

I nodded.

Penderson shot me a sideways glance. After a moment more of scrutiny, he stood and knocked his empty bowl against my half-full one. "Head down."

"Hold strong," I replied by rote.

A FULL DAY of marching was followed by another and then another. The land, as we progressed south, became increasingly dry and cracked. Rough soil gave way to packed dirt and scattered rocks. The sparse trees disappeared, leaving only scattered grasses and shrubs. Fresh water was scarce, making tempers flare. Our view of the rest of the king's forces disappeared after the first day. Our groups had entirely split apart. Perhaps we were creating a flank, after all. It was above my rank to be concerned.

On the third day, we stopped abruptly while the sun still hung high in the sky. Orders from Henedew filtered through the ranks: meal break, then begin fortifications.

"Fortify what?" Penderson grumbled at my side.

"You're the senior officer," I drawled. It was his fucking job to find out.

Penderson gave me a look that could've meant *wait here* every bit as much as it might've meant *go fuck yourself*, before he broke rank and advanced up the line.

The rest of us followed orders. Meal today was beans and flatbread. The beans were all right, but the bread was dry and tasteless. At least it wasn't another round of overcooked and under-seasoned stew. We were permitted a short respite after the meal, then preparations began. Our instructions: hold the line and give up no ground. I looked around. We were on Volaachi soil, if this dusty dirt could be called that. There was nothing but a few dry grasses and rocks. No castle, manor, or even a hill to call advantageous grounds. Just flat nothing in every direction. Judging by the slight breeze and sliver of sea on the east and west horizons, we were midway down the Andragori Peninsula—uninhabited low desert. If we continued south, we'd hit the open ocean. There was no reason any force would come here, friend or foe.

Still, we fortified. We built barricades, drove in cavalry spikes, and laid cover for archers and infantry. By nightfall, everything was prepared.

New orders came down: do not make camp. Stay alert, stay awake, and stay ready.

Henedew. Her name grumbled past every man's lips, alongside quite a few curses and gendered remarks that'd earn lashings if overheard by their superiors. Unlike most, I took no issue with following a woman's orders—especially *this particular* woman. I stayed alert, stretching periodically to keep loose. More than anything, I kept my eyes focused on the horizon.

"There!" I announced, just as Captain Henedew passed by. She turned, and with one nod, confirmed what I'd seen. She looked me up and down, and shivers coursed through my body.

"To arms," she ordered without looking away.

Shouts from senior officers rang down the line. "All men, up and to arms!"

Within minutes, the entire southern horizon turned black with approaching enemy forces. We were hopelessly outmatched—easily ten to one.

"What are they?" Miloh cried out. His shock echoed up and down the line. The mist that had clung to the army as it moved began to dissipate, revealing the black figures clearly. Grotesque reptilian beasts walked in formation on two legs. Short, flightless wings sprouted from their backs and extended outward. Black, leathery skin stretched over both wings, and scales covered their arms, legs, and faces—glinting in the sunlight like armor.

Penderson returned to my side, taking up point and drawing his sword. I looked away when his hand shook.

"Head down," I said to no one in particular.

"Hold strong," Penderson returned through clenched teeth.

"Fuck us all," Miloh whispered.

If these were to be our last moments, at least we'd face them with courage. My only regrets were a life misspent in obligations and the unshed tears of a sister leagues away—who would celebrate our next birthday, and all of her birthdays to follow, alone.

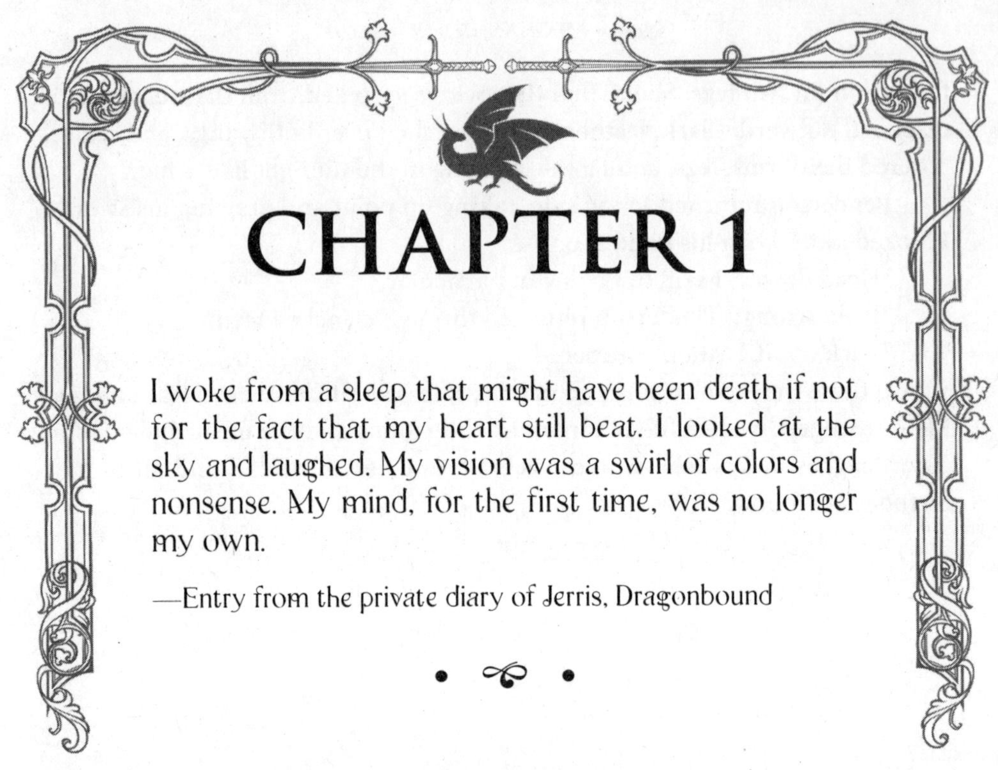

CHAPTER 1

I woke from a sleep that might have been death if not for the fact that my heart still beat. I looked at the sky and laughed. My vision was a swirl of colors and nonsense. My mind, for the first time, was no longer my own.

—Entry from the private diary of Jerris, Dragonbound

SERAE

EARLY SUMMER, VALMON 1036

"FASTER," I GASPED. Any faster and my heart might burst. Not to mention the bruising to my rear. But I needed to finish first. "Faster!" I urged again, louder this time.

"I'm coming for you," Tam shouted from behind. He was definitely gaining. "You don't stand a chance!"

"Nearly there, girl." I leaned in low over my mare's neck and urged her on.

Merria shouted something in the distance—I ignored it.

"Just a bit more."

Tam was right on my tail, his cropped brown curls flopping with each bound. If he wanted, he could reach out and slap my mare's rump. I had a bad feeling he might try to do just that, considering our last race, when he spooked her to steal the lead. I urged Copper on, leaning farther into the saddle. My rusty red mass of waves streamed behind me in the wind. In a last spurt of effort, we pulled ahead of Tam and his stallion, leaping across the makeshift finish line. I whooped and turned in my seat to flash him a victorious grin.

"All right, you may have beaten me this time, Cavendaffe, but don't think I'll let you off that easy. You're lucky I happen to like the view from second place." He pulled down the sleeves of his blue doublet, which he'd bunched to the elbow while riding. His mother would definitely have words to say about the wrinkles it left.

"You're the absolute worst, you know that?" I straightened my copper-wire glasses and ignored the heat in my cheeks.

"What? I was talking about Copper." He pulled up close and patted her flank.

I led Copper to the shade at the forest's edge, where trees lined the path like a natural barrier. Merria galloped by on Silvertail, the old family gelding. She brought him around and laughed merrily, her pale skin flushed with exertion. "Well done, Serae! I would never dream of riding that fast, especially not sidesaddle."

I heard the jab in it. I always rode astride, skirts bunched up in the middle, much to our mother's chagrin. It was one of Merria's many baiting points, but that was how our brother taught me to ride. Plus, it was the only way I had a chance at beating the likes of self-righteous, always-on-top Tam.

"Let's go, you lot, or they'll start luncheon without us. Serae's certainly had enough sun." Merria flipped her honey-blond ringlet curls over her shoulder and kicked Silvertail into a slow trot. She rode down the forest's edge, spine straight and curls bouncing.

Tam kept his eyes on Merria until she was out of earshot, then he turned back to me. "Her loss, never getting a proper ride in."

"You're rotten." I scowled down at my tan hands and forearms. Fair skin was the mark of a lady, who should spend her days indoors being demure and respectable—and bored to tears.

Together, we guided our horses down our makeshift racing track, this time at a calm, steady gait.

"Then again, it would take a lot of convincing to get any man between her thighs. I'd certainly never try it. I prefer more willing partners. Someone equal to the chase."

"Do you, now? You've always struck me as an easy catch."

"Oh, ho! You wound me. My eyes, like my heart, do not so easily wander."

"And here I was thinking we were talking about thighs."

Tam's voice dropped an octave. "I'd much rather be talking from between yours. When can I see you again?"

The heat in his warm brown eyes was more stifling than the afternoon sun. I almost had to turn away. "Have I left you begging?"

"And desperate, too."

I chuckled. Tam was certainly an attentive lover. Our betrothal had yet to become actualized by our parents, but I would still happily enjoy the benefits of Tam between my thighs. "Whenever you're next clever enough to find us time alone together, I suppose."

He winked. "Tonight, it is then."

"Tonight?" I pulled up short, and Copper whinnied. "How?"

Tam cocked his head. "Do you not know?"

I shook my head as we steered around the bend. The large white canopy housing our luncheon tables came into view.

"My family is to stay at the manor this evening. The margrave invited us and the Ingletons. He didn't tell you?"

"No, not a word."

"Hmm. Maybe he's caught onto us after all."

I laughed and tugged at my sage-green skirts, still bunched beneath me. "All of his grand designs are for Merria. I doubt I've even crossed his mind in the past month." That thought made me pause. Copper took the chance to nip some berries by the path. "Do you think he means to formalize things tonight?" A chill swept over me that had nothing to do with the afternoon breeze.

Tam was silent for a while, looking as if he were carefully considering each word before speaking. "Would that be so bad?"

I froze for a heartbeat. "Do you trust him?"

"Your father?"

"No, Naton."

"What does he have to do with us?"

My head whipped to Tam, who gave me that look—the one that suggested more than I wanted to hear. "Oh! I was thinking of Merria."

"A habit too many have. She would be well matched with that pompous twit. That would certainly serve them both."

"She *is* my sister." The clinking of silverware against china permeated the air. Luncheon had indeed started without us—but not without Merria, of course. "Bale won't be happy," I said as we reached the stables.

"Then he'll have to settle for one sister well matched." Tam smiled, holding my gaze as he dismounted. He handed his reins off to the stable lad and moved to my side.

I rolled my eyes but indulged him, kicking my feet out of the stirrups and swinging my leg over. He grabbed my waist and eased me down. As soon as my boots hit the ground, he pulled me flush against him.

"Serae." His voice was a ghost against the shell of my ear. "Would you not like to be Lady Fethersen?" He turned me at the waist, lips finding mine in an insistent kiss. "Would it not please you to run my home?" He trailed kisses down my neck. "Would I not please you in every possible way, again and again?"

Tam would—that was never the issue. How could I explain the way the boxed-in life of a woman grated at me? Marriage to my dearest friend was more than I could hope for, but marriage itself? I settled for saying, "I do look good in blue."

"To match your eyes."

I chuckled. "Are they not more green than blue?"

He ignored me and continued his trail of kisses. "Have I not demonstrated my devotion?"

"Why, Lord Fethersen." I flashed him a coy smile. "Do you mean to take advantage of me?"

"Of you, never." His grin turned feral. "Of every second alone with you, absolutely." He leaned in to claim my mouth again, but there was no time for this.

I pushed him to arm's length. "Later. Hold that thought for tonight. For now, it's luncheon, and I'm certain within moments we'll be missed."

No sooner had I spoken the words than Brig, Tam's youngest brother, popped out from behind the stable doors. Every bit of him, from his mop of light brown hair down to his yellow tights, was covered with leaves. Stick in hand, he whacked each piece of wooden railing he passed.

"Mam says you're supposed to be at the table."

"We're coming, you little menace. Where are your brothers?" I asked. Between Brig and Tam were two twin boys who were usually within a wooden sword's reach of each other.

"Mam won't let them up until they've eaten their full pie."

"And you finished yours?"

"'Course. Hiyah!"

Brig's stick cracked against the back of Tam's knees, eliciting a great yelp and leaving a dusty line across his navy trousers. I grinned as I turned toward the lunch table and the boredom it promised—or worse, considering Merria and her wagging tongue were there. I pushed my glasses up my nose, did my best to wrangle my hair, and set off down the pebbled path with Tam limping at my side.

The afternoon played out exactly as expected.

Merria's tinkling laugh rang out as she declared, "I wouldn't know what to do at an archery line. It's Serae who used to dress in trousers and play at shooting targets." There, she was wrong. The one time I'd tried to dress in trousers as a child, I was forced back into the house by Mother until I came out properly dressed in a skirt and bonnet.

Lady Fethersen smiled at me in apology with the same kind brown eyes she gave to her son. Her dress today was bright blue, veering away from the traditional navy of her house, and silver ribbons threaded the brown curls piled atop her head. "Lady Cavendaffe," she prompted, "do tell me about these gorgeous flowers in your hair."

Beside her, my mother beamed. Her *bliaut* was an elegant yellow trimmed with black that screamed Cavendaffe. As an extra adornment, black jewels dotted the yellow flowers pinned around the gold *cercle* atop her head. "I shall send Kiral to give your ladies a lesson. Even Lord Cavendaffe agrees her skills are unparalleled across the kingdom. Isn't that right, Tychon?"

"Absolutely, Constance, my dear." My father absently patted her thigh and returned his attention to Lord Ingleton at his other side. They spoke in low voices throughout the meal, both of their faces alight with eagerness. As a duke, Lord Ingleton outranked my father only slightly, but he liked to show it in every way. Unlike my father, who kept his hair short, he wore his in a silver tail at the base of his neck. Also, unlike my father, he dressed entirely in black from his collar to his short boots, gold embroidery highlighting his long velvet doublet. My father's doublets were all short, and he preferred puffed sleeves with no adornments, like the yellow and black one he wore today.

Across the table, Lord Fethersen was forced to lean in to hear. His serious face mirrored none of the excitement of his companions. Minus the mustache and girth of a middle-aged man, Tam was his spitting image. As an earl whose earldom separated Cavendaffe and Ingleton, he was the lowest ranking at the table and, likewise, stood the most to gain from an alliance with my father. His eyes drifted toward me, offering me a tight smile before returning his attention to the other two lords.

Later, Merria made a show of dabbing a dot of cream off the tip of my nose. "My *sweet* sister, you do so love your desserts." The entire table chuckled.

The only thing that came on faster than my blush was my scowl. Tam, at least, had the decency to look away.

At one point, our mother felt the need to recount the differences between her daughters for Lady Ingleton in a raised voice. After hearing that Merria was the slender one, the patient one, and the one devoted to constant improvement—a bald-faced lie—I'd had more than enough. I made no apologies as I rose from the table and left. If my footfalls sounded too heavy, or if my clenched fists were unbecoming of a lady, I didn't care one bit. My mind was full of petty rage. At twenty-one, I should have grown used to this treatment—from Merria and our mother. There was no reason for me to be off-kilter about it now. No reason at all. Yet here we were.

"Excuse me, miss."

I jumped. A stranger blocked my path. He shone bright with the colors of Inra—crimson and gold—not our province of Cavendaffe. A braided gold cord hung across his body, marking him as an officer of the king.

"I beg your pardon. I need the margrave as a matter of urgency." His eyes flicked down the path behind me as he shifted between his feet.

I took in his uniform again, from his red dragon tabard down to the mud-covered riding boots, and spotted the crossed arrows pinned at his shoulder. *A messenger.*

"This way." I hurried back down the path, barely in the lead at a near jog.

When we reached the canopies, the messenger found his mark and outpaced me with ease. With a few short words, he passed my father a note, then a footman led him away to rest.

Father cracked the seal and read. Then he sat. He passed the note wordlessly to Mother, who cried out and slumped in her chair.

In an instant, a flurry of motion engulfed them. Merria jumped up to fuss over Mother. Lady Fethersen called for smelling salts and a cool rag. Brig emerged from a bush shouting he was a Rihtlondish savage here to steal our jewels, then began lapping the table with Caper and Caddy, the Fethersen twins, in close chase. Lord Fethersen called for his wife to sit, while Lord Naton leapt to Merria's aid, all the while taking care not to upset his sleek black hair.

In all this, the letter lay forgotten on the grass. The world moved in slow motion as I stooped, gathered it up, and read:

Margrave Cavendaffe:

War Report—Fifth Regiment, under command of the late Captain

Henedew

With utmost urgency, you are informed that Lord Bale of Cavendaffe is reported missing in action. Last seen crossing the Inraen-Volaachi channel. Last report received two weeks prior. Presumed dead along with the rest of his squadron. Our deepest sympathies extended on behalf of the Crown. Creator keep his soul.

Sent on the order of Crown Prince Hammon of Inra—

The letter crumpled in my fist. *Missing. Presumed dead.* Only one enemy killed so ruthlessly and completely. My eyes flicked to Brig, happily playing at the very thing that had likely killed my brother—Rihtlonders. I only hoped his death was swift, considering their tendencies toward torture. Gravel crunched under my feet. I was halfway back to the manor before I realized what I was doing. My vision blurred, and my cheeks and neck were wet with tears. The next thing I knew, I was sinking into a mattress face-first, glasses thrown aside, screaming into the down. Soft hands pulled at my side, rolling me onto my back. I slapped them away. Then, I screamed and cried until everything hurt, not just my heart.

Eventually, my mind shut off, and I slipped into blissful sleep.

Hours later, I woke to the blurry face of my lady's maid hovering over mine.

Gerta eased me up. "Come now, you have to go down."

I shook my head then groaned at the pounding in my skull.

Her soft brown eyes were full of sympathy as she brushed a wet cloth over my face. "I'm so sorry, milady. The margrave demands it."

Her tight brown bun did nothing to hide the tear stains on her own cheeks. She replaced my glasses and re-pinned my hair.

I moved by rote, letting Gerta tug me along, but I felt nothing. Or rather, I felt the distinct lack of something. I was a tingling limb cut off from blood—screaming in silence as pins and needles stabbed at my soul.

"Breathe, milady. Just breathe."

I did. In.

Out.

In.

A sob racked through me.

"I know," Gerta cooed, caressing my back. Though only in her mid-thirties, she had always looked after me in a matronly sort of way, offering support and comfort when my mother did not. She led me down the hallway. "I know, I know. Just hold it in for a little while. Don't let the margrave see it."

Fuck the margrave. I didn't want to see any of them anyway.

We turned toward the family parlor at the base of the grand staircase. *Not the guest parlor?* The room was suited well enough for us, but the mantel was plain and unadorned. A single portrait of my father and grandparents hung above the mantel in an impressive gilt frame. The furnishings were comfortable, but the velvet of the cushions was worn, and the pillows had long since gone flat. The rug, at least, was less than a year old and still boasted a brilliant red and gold pattern with intricate dragons woven into the filigree. The best part of the room was the tapestry depicting the Creator—though at this hour, it was barely visible in the dim firelight.

The entire party, minus the small children, was gathered. All faces were grim. Merria's eyes were red, and she stood in the circle of Lord Naton's arms. The Lords Ingleton and Fethersen sat in identical chairs set before the fireplace. The three ladies were seated on one of the twin sofas that framed the mantel, separate from their husbands. My mother had donned a black shawl. They painted quite the picture of mourning.

Thrust into the room, a tempest amidst the gathered calm, I didn't know how to react. I stood there, trying to force the pieces of myself inward—trying to be small, unnoticed. Gerta ushered me to an open spot on one of the sofas, then retreated through the service door.

Father stood, brandy glass in hand, and paced the room, exuding detached authority that spoke nothing of the man who had just lost his only son. The other two lords rose from their chairs to flank him, identical glasses of brandy in their hands. After a moment, the margrave turned and addressed the room.

"We are at war with Volaach," he announced. The peppery streaks in his black hair glinted like steel in the firelight.

My brow furrowed. Was there more to the missive I hadn't read? Surely Rihtlond, our rivals dating back hundreds of years, was to blame for Bale's disappearance, not Volaach, who had not so long ago been our closest allies.

"This new threat makes our old enemy to the north pale in comparison. Today's news proves it. We've been summoned by our king to uphold our duty to our kingdom." He nodded to Ingleton and Fethersen. "We will answer it. We will each do our part."

Mother let out a wailing gasp and clutched her chest.

Father shot her a look of reproach, but it didn't last. For all his faults, he truly loved my mother. He paced the room, moving behind her and placing a hand on her shoulder. He cleared his throat. "We"—he nodded to the two lords—"and the king have had a plan in motion for some time now. Our purpose in gathering tonight is to ensure every person in this room understands their part and their obligations. Our alliances could change the tide of the entire war. Rihtlond's raiding proclivities against our borders are coming to an end. We must unite in the face of a new threat."

Naton and Tam nodded their assent.

"What threat?" Merria asked.

"The same one that's already claimed the life of your brother."

Tam's eyes locked onto mine—darker than I had ever seen them. He clenched his pointed jaw, and his eyes fell to the floor.

Father was speaking again, but my attention was lost to images of seafaring monsters burning villages and murdering innocents. "—by forging alliances that will best serve the kingdom." He motioned to Merria and Naton, still arm in arm. "Your union will be blessed by the Creator. Lord Ingleton and I have drawn up betrothal papers, which we will sign this very night. Our alliance with the Ingleton dukedom will bring trade, supplies, and strength against the encroaching enemy, benefitting us all."

Merria smiled, dipped into a curtsey, and said, "I am honored by you, Father."

Then, he turned to me. "My dear"—he *never* addressed me this way—"your part is the most crucial of us all."

My voice escaped me. I stared open-mouthed as my mind blanked of all thought. Finally, I managed, "I don't understand."

He nodded to Tam. "Your betrothal—" My heart squeezed as a thousand doubts pressed in. What was wrong with me? Being married to this man, who was both my friend and lover, should have felt like a gift from the Creator. "—must change. Think of it as a delay, nothing more."

The words rang around in my head, refusing to take shape. "Change?"

I glanced between them—my mother, the other two ladies, Merria and Naton, and even Tam. Every face in the room looked grave.

"A messenger will arrive within the hour. I will demand our arrangement be put in motion at once. Within a matter of days at most, you will be off, my girl."

"Off?" Merria gasped. "She's to leave?"

Out of the corner of my eye, I caught Naton placing a hand over Merria's shoulder. She fell silent.

"You're headed straight into the heart of our oldest enemy, for the greater good of us all." Father held my stare, but it was only the margrave who spoke to me. "You're to be betrothed to Eldreth of Rihtlond, the dane's heir."

"It's what the Rihtlondish savages call their king," Lord Ingleton added. In the firelight, his prominent nose and deep-set eyes cast an ominous shadow across his face.

I looked between the two men. My throat clenched, which was a good thing, as it kept the bile rising from my stomach at bay. Rihtlond was a land of brutality and death. Their danes rarely lived long enough to produce heirs before they were killed by usurpers. They were known best for the way they kidnapped and killed our border villagers for sport. And this is where my father wanted to send me—into the maw of death itself?

"You must be joking," I said at last.

The margrave moved. His steps echoed on the wood flooring, then muffled when he reached the rug. He stopped in front of me, his looming form filling my vision. His eyes were severe. "It's a betrothal in name only. There will be no wedding."

"I should say not!" I cried out, rising from my seat and forcing him back a step. "I won't marry a Rihtlonder, I won't."

His arm twitched, and I flinched. But he stopped himself, no doubt for the benefit of the other lords. He had never stilled his hand for my benefit before. Thanks to my rogue tongue, I knew all too well the sting of the back of his hand across my cheek. "You will do as your margrave commands."

I nodded. Anything else with this audience would only make things worse.

"Do not let yourself be ruined by them. I've done my part to ensure it, but you must do the same."

Every pair of eyes in the room turned to me with expectation. A strangled whimper escaped my throat.

"We must put that brain of yours to use. While there, you must learn their ways and become accepted by their people. As you gain their trust, you must document everything you see. Their ports, their numbers, their military actions, their ships—everything. We need to root out their weakness if we hope to stand a chance at surviving."

My mind was numb. His words oozed through me like hot wax.

"I'll teach you a secret code that will help keep your messages safe should they fall into the wrong hands. All your correspondence should be addressed to Merria. Tell them how dearly you miss your sister, and writing back and forth will seem natural. Anything you can't send by code you will detail in a journal to send back with your maid. We will have to work in secret, using what information you give us, to extract you. You must be ready in a moment's notice. There will be no warning when the time comes. Do all this"—he paused and glanced meaningfully at Tam—"and you'll earn your reward."

"You would sacrifice me just as you did Bale," I whispered and slipped back down to my seat. My legs shook, and I gripped my knees to still them.

"Play your part, girl," the margrave went on. "Remember your family. Remember your king. Do as you're told—and all will be rewarded to you tenfold."

I had always known the esteemed Margrave of Cavendaffe believed he owed no explanations for his actions, least of all to his daughter. So, I tried not to react. I did not bristle as he offered only commands, soft-spoken though they were. There were a great many of them—things that I should be listening to and remembering.

The conversation moved to speculation from the lords while the women remained silent.

"We'll use the extra manpower against the encroaching Volaachi..."

"Once we have the truth behind their newfound strength..."

"...trouble will be getting her out."

"How long?" I asked.

My words hung in the air, unanswered. Lady Ingleton appraised me with solemn scrutiny. Lady Fethersen looked at me with sorrow. My mother's eyes held only tears, as if I were already lost alongside her son. All three remained speechless while their husbands schemed and planned, ignoring the rest of us.

"How long?" I repeated more loudly.

My father was the first to turn at the interruption, his face hard and mouth pressed into a firm line. "Less than a year. A matter of months if we're lucky."

I shook my head. I had meant to ask how long he had been planning this treachery. It never occurred to me to ask how long I would have to endure it. Did it matter, when trapped with an enemy? Would not even one day be too long to stomach? Dread boiled in my gut as the fire of hope died away.

Play your part, girl. It echoed in my ears long after I was brought back to my room. The margrave had repeated my instructions until I could recite them all back. When Gerta returned, she stripped and bathed me while I was trapped in a trance. Even when she dressed me and tucked me in bed, I hardly took notice.

Bide your time. Tell him you'll give him a son.

At some point late in the night, Tam slipped into my room and bed. He said nothing as he reached for me beneath the covers. For a long time, he just held me close.

Keep your eyes open. Hide in plain sight.

When the room was thick with twilight, before the first rays of dawn, he finally moved against me. To my surprise, my body responded. I was desperate to feel anything besides this terrifying numbness. In moments, we were ripping off each other's nightclothes. Tam's mouth was everywhere on my body. He brought me to climax with the desperation of someone who feared this time might be the last.

Maybe it would be.

I pushed the thought aside as I straddled him and took him deep inside me. Still, I needed more. I slammed my hips down until my walls began to flutter and the tight coil in my core began to let loose. In a fluid motion, Tam flipped us and drove into me at a punishing pace. I bit my hand to keep from crying out as my final climax ripped through me, leaving me a boneless heap in his arms. With a great groan, he found his release, pulling out to spill on my stomach, then finally stilling above me. He stayed there, with his arms wrapped around me and my legs gripping his hips, until after I fell asleep.

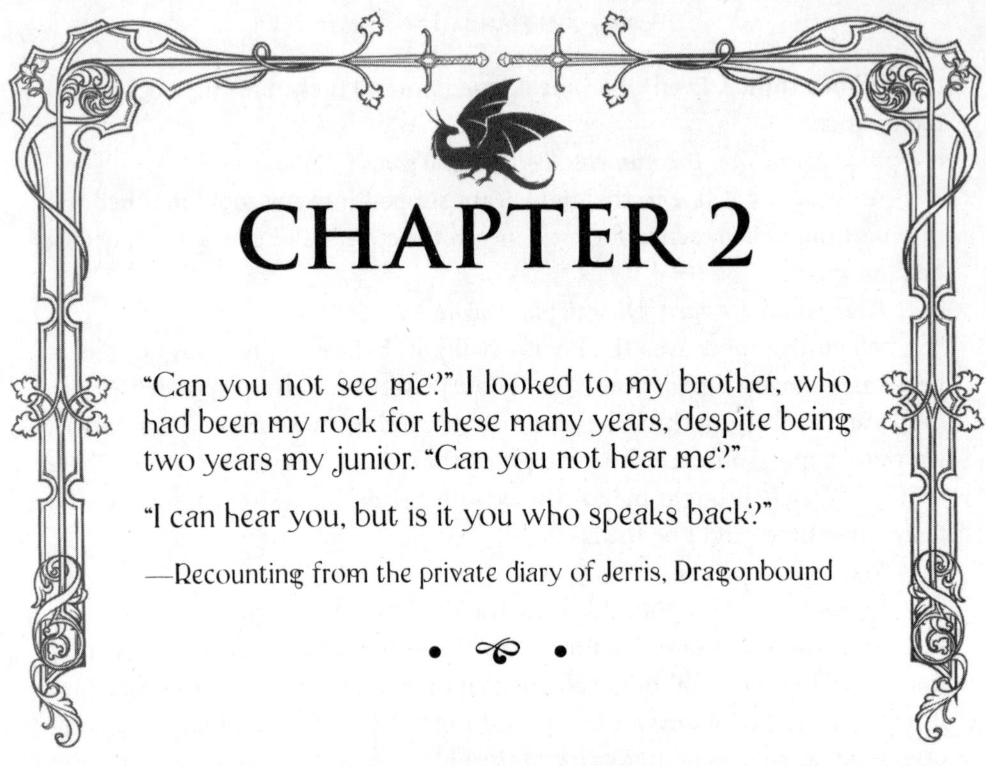

CHAPTER 2

"Can you not see me?" I looked to my brother, who had been my rock for these many years, despite being two years my junior. "Can you not hear me?"

"I can hear you, but is it you who speaks back?"

—Recounting from the private diary of Jerris, Dragonbound

ELDRETH

MID-SPRING, PATRIMON 1036

"ELDRETH, TELL ME this isn't true."

I watched her from three paces behind. She did not turn to me. Her platinum hair cascaded down her back, uncharacteristically loose. I memorized her hard lines as if it were the last time I would see them. Perhaps it was.

"Meralda, please—"

"Stop." She turned at last, raising a hand to silence me. "We're just having fun here. No reason to get attached." Her voice was a harsh mask, but I could hear the tremor underneath.

"You know that's not how I feel."

"Isn't it?"

"No."

"Yet, how easily I'm cast aside. I was never going to be your dana." I stepped toward her, but she pulled back. "No, I don't need your comfort."

"Perhaps I need yours."

The sternness of Meralda's face cracked. She cast her pale eyes back to the landscape—lush with the deep green that marked spring in the Riht. She hesitated for a moment, then took my hand and led me inside.

Neither of us broke the silence. After all, endings rarely needed more words.

MERALDA LEFT IN the middle of the night while I feigned sleep. There would be no rest for me. Once she was gone, I rose and dressed and headed straight for Dane Auldren's private chambers. The room was resplendent to the point of gaudy—and empty. Instead, I found him in the Receiving Hall.

"Call back your messenger," I demanded. "I can't go through with this. I won't marry an Inraen woman."

We were having this fight again. We fought for a full week the first time he suggested it. This bargain chafed from the moment I accepted it, but now that my life was changing, it was too much.

Dane sat on his throne, stroking his long blond beard and staring over my shoulder at the double doors I'd just entered. Looking up at him on the dais, waiting for him to meet my eye, I might as well have been a boy again—caught skipping lessons to wave around a wooden sword—rather than a man who had every right to question his liege's asinine orders. I was a commander of armies, master of blades, and named successor to the dane himself. I shouldn't have to remind myself. But in that moment, I was thrown back into the role of the child. I suppressed a wild urge to stamp my foot.

"I refuse," I continued when Dane remained silent.

"We've gone over this, son," he spoke at last, rising to his full, looming height. Dane's gaze was a physical weight when it finally fell upon me. "Nothing has changed. You'll marry her."

"Have you lost your senses? Why would you ever strike this idiotic deal?"

"Watch how you speak to your dane."

I bowed my head, half in deference, half to get command of myself. "How could she ever be my wife? We cannot make a woman like that dana of our people."

"She can learn." He lowered into his seat with a huff and flipped his long blond braid over one shoulder. He bent down to rub his knee and shin. The old injury bothered him more than he liked to show. "She's received an Inraen education. I'm sure they've taught her something useful."

"I'll be shocked if she has even two thoughts of her own in her head. How could she ever stand at my side when they're only taught how to be on their knees?"

The look in my father's eyes told me I'd gone too far. When he spoke, his voice was low and grinding. "She's the margrave's daughter, not some common Inraen whore. And you'll do as you're told."

I crossed my arms and grounded myself. I'd always had the good sense to leave my father to the politics and plots, but this time things had gone too far. Dane's machinations would destroy me. This was my future, my happiness, *my life*. I watched him closely—the way he stroked his carefully braided beard, the way the corners of his mouth turned down, the way he sat leaning on his elbow. I searched for any sign of relenting.

Dane Auldren stood again, but several long breaths passed before he continued. "You'll marry the girl," he said with uncharacteristic unease, then he looked away. "She need not know all the company you keep. She need not be dana forever. All we need from her is an heir."

I frowned. That was not the Riht way. Even if she was Inraen, this wasn't Inra. My father, more than anyone, knew that. There was a reason the throne beside him had stood empty for all these years after my mother... There was no point in rehashing her loss. It was mercy alone that told me to ignore his comments and change tactics. "You think this will work? That these people would accept a foreign heir when the time for conquest comes?"

"You're thinking like a Riht. Those people don't care who sits on their throne so long as they have food in their bellies. Inraen law will be on our side, and we have the strength of arms to back it. This step is crucial in winning over the people, nobles and commoners alike."

I frowned again.

"You wanted more peace, Eldreth."

I did. Despite the skills I'd dedicated my life to, I wanted the warring to stop. I wanted safety for those I cared about. Above all else, I wanted them to start making it home. But this wasn't the way to get it—this wasn't about peace. My father would fight until his dying breath to win back our ancestral lands. As if we didn't have enough. He would say whatever was needed to make me fall in line. After a moment, the fire in me went out. My brow relaxed, and I nodded. "I'll do it if I must."

We embraced forearms, and I lingered—long enough for him to remember why the arm he gripped was covered in scars—before I strode from the hall. There was much yet to be done.

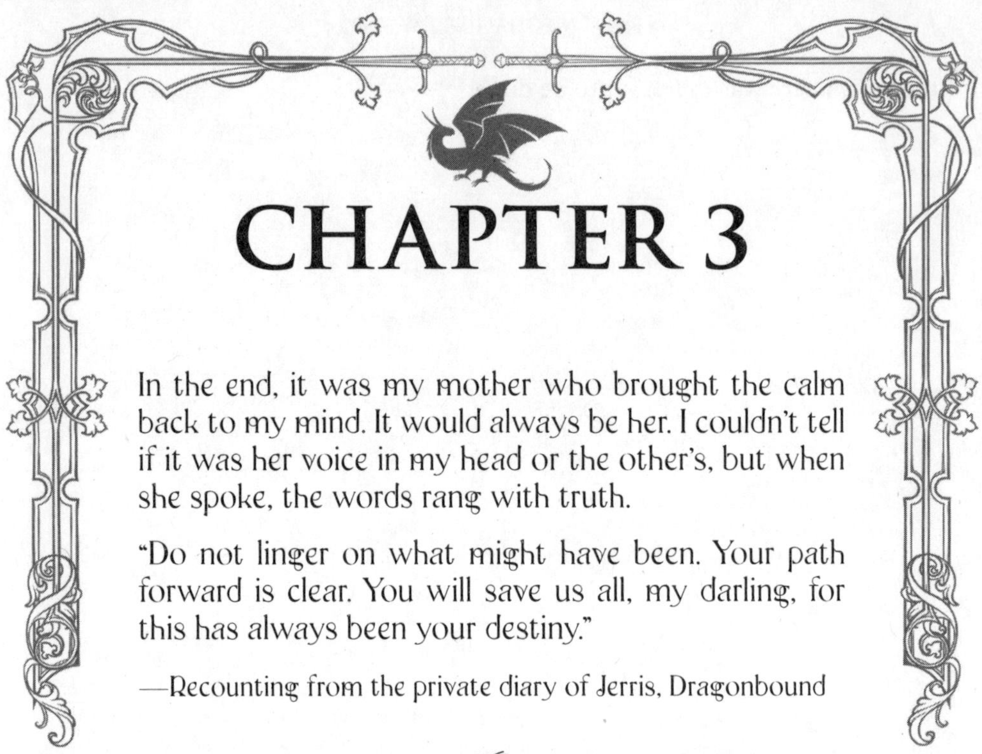

CHAPTER 3

In the end, it was my mother who brought the calm back to my mind. It would always be her. I couldn't tell if it was her voice in my head or the other's, but when she spoke, the words rang with truth.

"Do not linger on what might have been. Your path forward is clear. You will save us all, my darling, for this has always been your destiny."

—Recounting from the private diary of Jerris, Dragonbound

SERAE

MIDSUMMER, VALMON 1036

"SIT." MY FATHER'S voice held its usual sharpness, befitting a man of little patience. As the lord of a border province, I suppose it made sense. I crossed the library and took my usual seat at the round table. My legs were steady today, but my mind wavered from lack of sleep.

He placed paper and a quill before me. Across the page were gibberish lines and strokes that, at first glance, resembled Inraen script, but the closer I looked, the more nonsense it became.

"It's a phonetic cypher—the code you'll be using to send information back." He placed a second page beside the first. This one contained plain Inraen script.

"The translation," I clarified.

He nodded. A stack of fresh parchment and a full bottle of ink lay beside me on the table. "Do not get up until these pages are full."

"What should I write?" I asked.

"Anything you want. Fill them with your nonsense stories of dragons. Write letters to your friends. I don't care. Just make sure this cypher is in your blood before you leave this table."

"In one day?" I gasped before I could catch my tongue.

He stepped closer and leaned over my chair, taking up the entire space above me. I suppressed a shiver. "This is your task today. Tomorrow, you will have another, harder task." His breath held the sour tang of wine, unusual for him at this time of day. He must have more nerves about this plan than he let on. The thought brought me a new dose of dread. How would I survive in a country more interested in destruction than life?

"Yes, Father," I whispered. My voice quavered only a little.

His face relaxed. "You've been chosen for this task because, for reasons known only by the Creator, he bestowed on you the mind of a man. I'll not waste that gift by marrying you off to some nobody—not until I get my due. Mark my words, girl. Do this, or I'll find the richest lord desperate for a young wife to sire his heirs and be done with you."

I swallowed. Visions of last year's court ball swam before me—of lecherous Lord Penderson tracing his ancient hands down my backside. He was an early widower with only one son. Grief gripped my throat, and my vision blurred with tears as I placed my quill to the page. The younger Lord Penderson had been in Bale's regiment and, if the gossip Merria heard was true, had also been lost. The paths before me were turning increasingly grim, but as a woman, what choice did I have but to traverse them?

THE STAR JASMINE archway over my favorite garden bench was in full bloom. I sat in the summer sun with my eyes closed. My wrist ached, and I rubbed it idly while soaking in the day's warmth. My hand had morphed into a permanent claw from writing for three days straight, but today—my last day—I'd been given a break. I'd spent the morning proving my memory of everything I was meant to observe and report—along with all details of the code. With that done, my afternoon was free.

"I thought I'd find you here." I heard the smile in Tam's voice without opening my eyes. "Budge over."

I shifted for him, and he sat, pulling my hand into his lap to massage my abused fingers, palm, and wrist. I hummed with appreciation as his skilled hands went to work.

"How are you doing?" he asked.

My eyes opened, and I took in his navy-blue tunic and soft brown curls. His smile was strained, and there was pain in his warm brown eyes. "A loaded question."

He nodded. "Are you ready?"

I sighed. "No. How could I ever be?"

His fingers dug into the bones of my wrist, and a delicious pop relieved some of its tension. He traced his palm down mine and laced our fingers together.

"It's going to be okay."

I nudged him with my knee. "Don't lie to me."

He shook his head and turned toward me. "It is. I know it. You're brilliant, and you'll find everything we need. You'll come back with honors from the king and queen, and then our life can begin."

Our life. Martyrs, I loved Tam. I truly did, but the thought of a life with him terrified me almost as much as being sent to Rihtlond. I wasn't ready to take on the role of a wife. I was lucky, I knew, to be unwed in my twenties. Not many nobles could afford to keep one daughter at home for so long, let alone two. As harsh as he could be, it was a mark of my father's love that he had done this for Merria and me.

"Hey," Tam said, tracing a thumb down my cheek, stealing away my thoughts. "Come on, don't let it get to you like this. You can do this. If anyone can, it's you. This is just a blip in your life. A grand adventure, like the dragon tales you love to read."

I smiled. "An adventure—I like that."

He leaned in and kissed me. It was soft and sweet. His lips were feather-light on mine, giving me his support without staking any claim. I unlaced our fingers so I could instead throw my arms around his neck and pull him in closer. He deepened our kiss, sliding his tongue in slow strokes against mine.

"Serae," he whispered my name like a prayer to the Creator, "can I have you? One more time, please?"

"Yes," I breathed and recaptured his lips. We were no strangers to stolen moments. With our houses constantly full of families and servants, we'd learned to seize our chances. I smiled against his kiss at the thought of having him here, under the jasmine.

Tam sank to his knees in the soft dirt. He hiked up my skirt and spread my legs apart, settling his body in between. His fingers found their way to my tenderest flesh and began to tease. Pleasure awakened within me. I scooted toward the edge of the bench and spread my knees farther apart, encouraging him.

As one of his talented fingers slipped inside me, I reached between us and palmed his length through his trousers. Hard and eager, he thrust against my hand. I gripped his girth with one hand while the other worked the laces at his waist free. By the time I got them undone, two of his fingers were pumping in and out of me. We were both panting as I gripped his freed cock and stroked him root to tip.

"I can't wait," he whispered against my lips. "You're so flaming wet."

I guided him toward my entrance, and he sank into my warmth in one torturously slow thrust.

"More," I demanded. He pulled back and then pressed into me again. His pace was slow, but my need was rising. "Please," I begged, gripping him from behind and urging him deeper.

He held back for three more agonizing strokes before finally giving me what I needed. His pace quickened, and each thrust strengthened. That coil inside me was tightening, building, but I needed more. I gripped the hand at my waist and moved it to my center. His fingers—Martyrs, I loved his fingers—danced over my clit. My release rolled through me in waves. As my walls clenched around him, he groaned and thrust harder, chasing his own release before pulling out last second to spill on the earth beneath the bench.

"Fires above, Serae, you ruin me." Tam's voice was husky as he held my molten body against his. He kissed my neck and the shell of my ear, but his words had dragged me from such a beautiful high into a downward spiral.

"Creator above, what if they do ruin me?" I whispered, shaking in his arms.

"No." He gripped me tighter. "Nothing they could do would ever ruin you. Do you hear me? No matter what happens, you'll never be ruined to me."

"Do you promise?" I couldn't help the question. It was completely unfair, but I blurted it out anyway.

"Yes." There was no hesitation. This was what I loved most about him. His friendship and loyalty were everything to me. Even if it were just for a few months, it was what I would miss the most when I was gone.

Gerta flew around the room, packing with shocking efficiency. She said nothing, probably because she knew nothing would help. I watched her in numb silence, head full of cyphers and fear. She wore a thick traveling *cote* beneath her apron—long and stiff, unlike her usual short, lightweight servant's dress. It was only when my own traveling clothes were laid out that it hit me all at once. Tears flooded my eyes and dripped on the inside of my lenses, blurring my vision further. I hated crying. Never in my life had I been one to dissolve into tears, yet in the past few days, I had hardly stopped.

"Why is this happening to me? Why me and not Merria?"

"There, there, milady," Gerta tutted, fussing with her mousy brown bun. "It's not all bad. He may be a handsome lad, and you'll find something more than this arrangement between you."

Yes, a lovely barbarian ready for stimulating conversation and a deep emotional bond. I held in my scoff. "He's a Rihtlonder. Martyrs, I'll be lucky if I keep all my limbs."

"He's a prince, isn't he? That's got to count for something. You'll be a proper princess once you're married."

"Lovely. Princess of the heathens. What a treasure!"

My lady's maid, who had been with me as long as I could remember, sat beside me and patted my cheek. "We're invited in for an alliance, not as enemies. Even the most brutal people are kind to their own. And I'll be with you as long as I can be."

Images of thatched roofs in flames and a sea dotted with enemy sails flooded my mind—scenes from storybooks I'd read since childhood. "What would a maid know of forced marriage anyway?" I gritted out.

Gerta's eyes sharpened. "Nothing, of course." She bowed and stepped away, leaving me to sit with my words.

The trouble was, not even Gerta, who would be my only companion for a full month, could know the truth of my purpose in Rihtlond. I would have to fool even her of my sincerity. Knowing the truth would put her at risk, were anyone to grow suspicious. But she would be complicit, nonetheless. Father had given me four weeks to fill an entire journal with secrets, then send it home with Gerta. *Four weeks.* As if I could discover all that was needed in so short a time. I'd have to offer her my second-warmest gloves for the journey, and maybe my second-best *chape* as well, to make amends. Creator knew I should give her my best things for what she was about to endure on my behalf, but that would be questioned. Why would a servant be better adorned than her mistress?

My heart squeezed, and my head chose that moment to remind me that Bale would have understood me. But Bale was gone. Sitting with the news for a few days had not lessened its sharpness. Tam was gone as well, back to Fethersen with his family. Before he left, he had promised to stay faithful to me, no matter how long it took. Then, he kissed me in front of both our families and whispered in my ear, "I'll come for you when the time is right." It made me feel a twisting sort of hollow inside.

The door to my room burst open, interrupting my thoughts.

"Oh, Serae, how can this day have come!" Merria flopped onto my bed, gold and red skirts flying, and flung her arms around me. "First Bale gone, and now you. I'll be all alone."

I tried my best not to grimace. "It would have always been this way, no matter who I married." Except now, I might be headed toward my death.

Merria harrumphed. "You'll have to write me every week at least. How will I ever get along without you? Will we be invited to your wedding?"

I froze, scanning Merria's face, but she was all doe eyes and practiced pout. Was this one of her performances? If all went to plan, as Merria well knew, there would be no wedding.

"Ask Father," I said at last, aware of Gerta's keen ears. "Maybe he'll actually tell you since you're his favorite."

"Don't be bitter. Plus, his favorite was Bale. I'm only second because I'm the next oldest."

"Yes, and the rest of us are just backups."

"He's married you off well, hasn't he? I don't know why you're complaining."

"It's Rihtlond, Merria! *Rihtlond*." I couldn't voice more with Gerta nearby, but I glared my meaning just the same.

"Do you think they'll be as vicious as the stories?"

Gerta tutted, but Merria ignored her, as she did with all our household staff.

"I suppose they won't be raping the women or slaughtering the children in their own streets," she mused, as if the idea were a pleasant fancy, and not the very real horrors I would soon be facing. "I wonder if you'll have to live in huts and tents, or worse, a home at sea. What if you're never on dry land again?"

"They have cities," Gerta interjected. "We're not headed to a life of endless seafaring, milady. Don't you fret."

Merria snorted. "Maybe not, but that doesn't change the fact that their men like to destroy. Martyrs, are you worried your prince is going to try to destroy you?"

"Get out!" I shrieked. "If you're not here to help, then leave."

Merria's face softened to some measure of understanding. She sat back and arranged her curls. "It's going to be all right. I don't know all Father's reasons, but I'm sure he's got them. You'll be back before you know it."

Even if this was meant to be a temporary leave, everywhere I looked, I found reason to lament. I would miss reading in the gardens and the beautiful view from my bedroom window that overlooked them. I would even miss the way Merria flipped her honey-gold hair like a true-born queen. The way Father scowled and Mother dismissed me. Most of all, I would miss the way Bale grounded me, offering a secret smile or a wink when no one else was looking. But he was gone, and those times would never return. If only this day had not come so soon—but that was a useless thought. My days in this house, as a daughter and not a son, were always numbered.

THE SUN, EVER spiteful, continued its march across the sky. As it reached its zenith and began to fall, panic set in. I paced the length of the family parlor until my mother bade me sit. No fires were lit on the warm summer day, so I stared at the empty grate.

Mother donned her role as margravine and kept by my side, praising me for my dedication to the family and the kingdom. Father came next with repeated encouragements and hushed reminders. *Four weeks* rang through my head as he handed me a small brown journal. Between the two, it was more attention than I had ever received in my life. Only Merria remained the same, tossing me simpering eyes and a constant litany of nonsense advice. *You must always stand tall, but don't tower over your betrothed. If you can make yourself appear smaller without slouching, you must.* Bale was—

No, there was no point dwelling on him. I had spent a whole day wondering if people missing in action and presumed dead were ever found. Wondering if he would ever again be here to temper the family for me, to see me off with a grin and a kiss to the temple, or to simply remind me that I had value when no one else would.

The announcement came before anyone was expecting it. Even my mother flinched before rising to lead us to the manor steps. The gates were opened, and a retinue of Rihtlonders filled the courtyard. A striking man in a bold green cloak and a sharply trimmed blond goatee stepped forward and bowed. My father strode straight to him to clasp hands. He leaned in and spoke a few soft words, then stepped back and announced in Mayoran, the common tongue, "I present to you with pride and honor, the great High Dane of Rihtlond, Auldren son of Éalren, conqueror of Chancey, reclaimer of the rightful lands of the Riht, ruler of strength and passion, and now, bringer of peace and unity between our two peoples."

At the final word, every Rihtlonder placed a fist to their chest and bowed. To my surprise, so did Father. With brows raised, I turned to my right, Merria's usual place as the eldest daughter, but she was missing. I whipped around in confusion and had to tamp down my shock as I realized she was now standing *on my left.* She was slightly hunched and had changed into a high-necked dress. Her ringlet curls were gone, replaced by a thick braid tied with a large white bow.

Mother shot me a sharp glance, then led us in a graceful curtsey. She wore her best *bliaut* with her honey-blond hair—the exact shade Merria had inherited—pinned back in intricate curls. She donned her jeweled *cercle*, emphasizing her station. I lowered my head as I dipped into a curtsey.

"Dane Auldren, it is a pleasure to welcome you to our home," my father said in the common tongue, rising to his full height. "Won't you join me inside for a drink while we settle the final details?"

The dane approached. Though my father stood two steps above him, they were eye to eye. He held my father's gaze for a long moment. I locked my shaking knees and clenched my quivering jaw. I was no meek peasant who had never stood in front of a crowd. Why was I all jittery now? Annoyed, I clapped my eyes to the dane's retinue of men.

I gasped. *They're women?*

Looking again, about half of the stern warriors were indeed female. They exuded lethality from the set of their jaws, the bulge of their muscles, and the sharpness of their blades. The men and women alike donned long braids, shaved heads, or a mix thereof. I turned to my parents, a question on my lips.

"Margrave," boomed the voice of the giant of a man before us, breaking me from my thoughts, "I will take a drink with you. My messenger and two warriors will join, as will your daughter and future daughter of mine."

"Very good," Father agreed, nodding to my mother. He led the way to the first library, which we sometimes used to receive formal company.

Before I could enter, Mother grabbed my arm and whispered, "Go with and say nothing. *At all.* Do you understand?"

I nodded.

"You are the eldest now," she hissed through clenched teeth.

She shoved me into the library behind the men, and I moved to stand beside Father's chair. Its high back was carved to resemble the folded wings of the Creator. Shelves lined the walls, boasting scrolls and tomes of every shape and size. Father kept this room in perfect order, knowing the wealth and intimidation it projected.

I folded my hands in front of me and stared straight ahead. *I would probably hold more purpose as a statue.* The steward brought both coffee and whiskey, then he retreated to a corner of the room. Father spared me not a glance, so I remained still, neither sitting nor offering to pour. The Rihtlonder dane, however, watched me closely.

"Do you think you'll be a strong wife for my son?" he asked.

I opened my mouth to speak, but Father interjected.

"She'll be a perfect wife. She's well-educated, skilled in the arts, and very even-tempered. My darling girl is my pride and joy, and a model to her younger sister."

It was all I could do to keep my mouth shut. Mother's hissed words took shape as Merria's childish dress and change of order at arrival clicked into place. I steeled my features and focused on the conversation.

"Do you mean to tell me you don't even let your women speak?"

My brow raised at the challenge, and I glanced at my father. If the dane was goading him, it was working. My father glared at this beast of a man before him. "I'm not sure what you're implying, but we treat our women in Inra extremely well. I am her father, and I will protect her how I see fit, including from speaking in a situation that might intimidate her feminine sensibilities." He turned to me abruptly, looking at me for the first time, his face a mask of kindness. "My dear, would you care to answer a question or two from the dane?" he asked in a lowered voice, as if his words were for me alone and not a display for the gathered men. "You need not be put on the spot. That was not the intention for this day." His eyes were piercing in an alarming contrast to his kind smile.

"I could answer one or two, Father," I replied carefully.

He turned back to the dane. "Proceed."

The dane, however, did not speak right away. He stroked his long, glossy beard, every blond hair perfectly arranged in a neat braid.

"What do you think of living among the Riht, girl?"

The question caught me off guard. I was expecting to be grilled on my training as a wife, not on my feelings about living with these savages. He waited patiently, seated at our best table in black leather armor and thick boots.

"I will be quite happy there, I'm sure," I answered, hating how soft my voice sounded next to his. I adjusted my glasses, needing something to do with my hands.

"And what do you know of the Riht that you think will be pleasing to your...feminine sensibilities?" His grin was all teeth.

I racked my brain. Surely, I knew something positive to answer about Rihtlond. I would not be thought of as incapable of answering *two* questions. Where even was Rihtlond? Across the White Sea, north of us, but what was the land like? I remembered seeing a drawing in one of my old primers.

"The mountains!" I blurted, causing both men's eyebrows to raise. "Yes, I quite like mountains. And greenery."

The dane looked me up and down again, like he could flay me open with his eyes alone. "I see." He paused. "I assume you're packed and ready to be off with our company. Are you a strong rider?"

"Yes, yes, she's been riding since she was small," my father cut in.

My lip twitched as the lie registered. I had not received any instruction until my sixteenth birthday—by Bale. *Bale.* I had not meant to think of him again. I dug my nails into my palms, focusing on the pain before my eyes could mist.

"She is packed and ready, but I asked you here first to speak with you man to man, father to father, before that's settled. If you have no more questions for Serae, I'll allow her to take her leave and oversee the final preparations of her things."

"Aye, do allow her, Margrave."

My eyes widened as they darted between the two men. The margrave's face had gone ruddy, and the dane smirked back like a cat.

"Take your leave, Serae." My father's voice was clipped and cold.

A chill ran down my spine as I exited the room. Whether it was from the Rihtlondish men watching my retreat or from my dreading sense of the future, I couldn't tell.

Time crawled on as the valets secured my traveling trunks onto carts. At last, and yet far too soon, I was in my saddle, tears prickling my eyes as our party departed. I glanced back one last time at the stone-and-glass building. My mother and Merria stood waving from the steps. My father gazed after us with hands stuffed in his pockets. A tight ring of warriors formed around the dane as we passed through the gates. A moment later, another ring encircled me and my maid, closing off my view.

It's a prisoner's guard. I clenched my jaw. The flash of anger was short-lived. In its wake, there was only the long and boring ride ahead. Gerta, at my side, remained silent. We rode on, like two guarded pillars of stone.

LONG AFTER NIGHT fell, we reached an encampment dotted with fires and filled with at least fifty tents by my best estimate in the dark. Gerta and I were shown inside a large tent, three times the size of most and holding more furniture than we could make use of.

The tent flap rustled, and Dane Auldren appeared, filling the entry with his colossal frame. Standing side by side, he was a full foot taller than me, and I was tall by women's standards. His thick leathers were gone, replaced by a fresh brown tunic and black trousers.

My eyes flicked around the tent. Only two small beds, neither big enough to fit the dane's bulk. I let out a sigh, which the dane caught, making him smirk. Thank the Creator we'd not be sharing a tent with the likes of him.

"Daughter," he called me as if I were wed to his son already, "we will keep this encampment for no more than two nights, then we return to the Riht. A tray will be brought to you this night and in the morning. You'll be confined to these quarters from sunset to sunrise for your own safety."

I pursed my lips. It seemed I was a prisoner here after all.

"What am I to do during the day?" I asked.

"Do as you like. Enjoy your needlework or whatever you Inraens do to pass the time. I suggest you take advantage of it. Once we are home, your instruction begins."

"I have already received my education, Your Grace."

He snorted. "Your Creator's grace has not placed me at the head of the Riht. You call me Dane or Sire. And you'll not be learning your Inraen nonsense. You'll learn how to be a Riht, and you'll be expected to learn it well."

"What does that entail?"

Ignoring this, he turned and left as unceremoniously as he came. Gerta and I exchanged glances.

"Martyrs, they're rude."

"Tell me about it," I grumbled after the tent flap stilled.

"At least we have a rest on Inraen soil before we set sail. I expected to be carted off on a ship this very night!"

"But where are we? Surely Father would know about an encampment this size in Cavendaffe."

"The Creator only knows."

I sighed and ran a hand through my wind-blown hair. "I'd kill for a bath."

"You're in luck, milady." Gerta stood beside a small wooden tub, one eyebrow arched.

"No water?"

She shrugged. "I'll find some in the morning."

I turned my attention to the inside of the tent, which Gerta was already inspecting. It boasted two beds, a chest beside each, a standing mirror, and a table with four chairs. It was as well-furnished as the traveling tents I'd seen set up for King Ruper himself. Still, dents and spots of wear were visible on most of the furniture, matching my expectation of Rihtlonders and their more primitive lifestyle. The corner of my mouth quirked as I pictured how Merria would react.

Gerta bustled around, unpacking our necessities while I took a seat at the central table. Darkness had long since fallen, and we were closer to seeing the sun again than not. Oil lamps were mounted to the tent posts, casting more shadows than light across the room. A servant brought food and wine, laying out a wide spread before me. I picked at the food. I should have been grateful for a hot meal, but my stomach disagreed. Instead, I traced the table's intricate carvings with my finger. This piece of furniture was more ornate than the rest, inlaid with a shiny, rose-colored metal—an unusual design for a traveling piece, even in Inra.

Gerta joined me after a while to eat her meal. We sat in silence. The guards posted outside were speaking softly in Rihtlondish, but we were otherwise undisturbed.

Finally, Gerta whispered, "When do you think you'll meet the prince?"

I let out a heavy sigh, tugging my fingers through my tangled hair. "I wish I knew." For the better part of an hour, I had been dutifully *not* wondering the exact same thing. The burden weighed heavily on my heart, and doubt crept in. The one flaw in my father's plan was that I was not the sort of woman who distracted many men. I lacked the honeyed curls that made Merria look like some sort of Jaedan angel. I had none of her lithe, slender grace, that turned every head she passed in Inra—men with lust and women with envy. Instead, I had rust-colored, unruly hair and a tanned complexion marred with freckles. I was too tall to be called dainty, and so curved the dressmakers teased about needing extra fabric for my birthing hips. Then, there were my glasses. While the copper frames were expensive, and I kept them meticulously polished, they were a deterrent to everyone except Tam.

As if sensing my line of thought, Gerta reached over and patted my hand. "I hope he knows how lucky he is to be matched with you."

I smiled at what was now my only friend, but it quickly turned sour. A month with Gerta's support would be far too short. She would leave, and I would be alone.

Refusing to dwell on the thought, I rose to dress for bed, but even in summer, there was too much of a chill. Both beds had plush mattresses and thick quilts with vivid geometric patterns. I lay down wrapped in my *chape* and *cote* beneath the quilt, facing my back to Gerta's bed. Despite the considerable comforts, sleep was hard coming. A shiver ran down my spine as I snuggled deeper into the blanket. My insides twisted into knots. Perhaps tomorrow, I would meet my so-called future husband and find out how the rest of my time in Rihtlond would be.

Please, Creator, let him be different.

The prayer was hopeless, but what else did I have? I had no choice but to act the part, even with a monster for a betrothed instead of a man. Suppose his hands had been the ones to slay my kinsmen. Suppose he had led raids against the border villages that were now little more than piles of ash. Worst of all, he could be the type of savage who took pleasure wherever he wanted. Judging by the size of his father, what chance would I stand of fighting him off?

My mind raced and taunted me until the first pink light of dawn lit up the tent. Only then did my body finally give in to sleep.

CHAPTER 4

The biggest change was my dreams. I had always dreamt of things from my past, but now I also dreamt of a past that was not mine. I dreamt of a waking world that was like a dream, where nothing was as it should be, but everything felt right. And then there was the flying.

—Entry from the private diary of Jerris, Dragonbound

SERAE

MIDSUMMER, VALMON 1036

I WOKE WITH a groan. Soreness attacked my back and legs. I hissed in a breath as I rolled my hips and massaged my tight inner thighs. Clearly, short sprints around the manor had not prepared me for real travel.

Gerta was already up—washed, dressed, and humming while she prepared a steaming bath. My body ached to sink into it. My head was bleary, as if I'd spent the night drinking, and Gerta's tune was shrill in my ears.

"How on Jaeda are they heating the water?" I asked just to get her to stop.

"By campfire, milady," she said. "It's an interesting setup, I'll give them that. I'll go collect a fresh bucket now that you're awake."

Standing was harder than I expected on wobbly legs. I slipped out of my clothes and hobbled into the tub. It was cramped compared to my tub at home, but after Gerta added the last bucket, the heat worked wonders on my legs. My spirits perked up with each minute spent soaking. Even my appetite started to bloom.

I was loath to leave the warmth of the water, but Gerta produced a thick linen from the chest to wrap myself in while I dried. Just as she finished dressing me in a blue *cote*—this dress had a slightly shorter hem, better for walking the countryside—a man came in and laid a breakfast tray on the table. He bowed and waited just inside the tent flap.

"Thank you, sir," Gerta said with a short curtsey.

"Have you any other needs, my lady? I am at your disposal until my *reálton* returns." He flashed a bright, roguish smile. It was the first one I'd seen on a Rihtlonder that was halfway genuine.

"Your what?" I asked, not sure what to make of this man or the unfamiliar word.

"My *reálton*, Marr Wep."

More words I didn't recognize. Gerta and I exchanged glances, and I gave a little shrug.

"We have been able to see to our own needs. Thank you, sir," she repeated.

He bowed a honey-blond head, and I was struck by the similarity in color to Merria's. "Do enjoy your meal!"

I harrumphed in reply as he withdrew from the tent. My stomach growled, but my nose wrinkled at the smell. "Fish! Who eats fish for breakfast?"

Apparently, I did—well, choked it down, really. And though I would've killed for an egg or a slice of bread, I did enjoy the salty greens served on the side. Gerta ate her meal beside me, groaning in delight.

"You can't be serious," I spat. "You're enjoying that?"

"Mmm, I love fish. Even for breakfast." She winked.

"You're incorrigible."

"Won't catch me turning away a good meal, milady. I know what it's like to go without."

When finished, I shook out my hair, still slightly damp from my soak. "I suppose we ought to wander about today, however dreadful that sounds."

"As you wish, milady." Gerta gathered our plates into a neat stack, then retrieved our walking *sollars*. "Shall we?"

"Maybe we'll see something interesting while we walk, like a better breakfast than a slab of fish!"

That earned me a chuckle. I slipped into my shoes, but at the tent flap, I paused.

"Milady?"

"I'm fine," I said, clenching my fists. I couldn't get my feet to move.

Gerta's arm slid into mine. "Are you ready?"

No. How could I be? I was meant to find a place amongst these barbarians and somehow *pretend* that I belonged. I had to gain their trust and convince them to accept me.

Will they see right through me? Will they somehow know?

There were no satisfying answers, so I squared my shoulders and adjusted my glasses. Gerta remained locked to my side. We exited the tent like two women going to battle. In a camp full of female warriors, the irony was not lost on me.

In the light of day, my estimate of the encampment proved to be woefully short. Campfires and tents sprawled across a massive clearing, easily numbering double my guess from last night. *How had I never known this place existed?* Grass had begun to grow around the posts, and the thick fabric siding of each tent was weather-stained.

"How long have they been here, milady?" Gerta whispered out the side of her mouth.

"The Creator knows," I whispered back, making a mental note to share the location with my father the first chance I got.

Our tent sat in the middle of the encampment—close enough to be watched. We wove our way slowly around the tents. Most were simple green canvas, though the larger ones like ours were adorned with geometric patterns and variegated colors. People avoided us, showing no interest beyond the scowls and *many* looks at my hair. If red locks were as uncommon in Rihtlond as at home, I'd be in for a lot more gawking.

The air smelled of wet dirt, campfire smoke, and occasional wafts of roasting vegetables. Beside each fire, especially the larger ones cooking communal meals, stood a contraption for heating water. We paused beside one for Gerta to examine the metal drum and connected spigot.

"Efficient," she muttered, and I rolled my eyes.

The warriors around us were hard at work—pulling down tents, chopping wood, carting fresh water, and gutting enormous fish. Most were tall with muscular builds. And every one of them was some shade of blond. Their hair was tightly braided, mostly long, and many had stripes shaved on one or both sides of their heads. The braids were shiny and intricate, some adorned with silver or gold clips. Their leathers and gear were worn but clearly cared for—well-oiled and free from cracks or holes—much like the furnishings in our tent. It all spoke of a very different people than what I had conjured in my head of Rihtlond.

What will the townsfolk look like? Or the nobility? My ignorance of these people and their ways was painfully obvious the more I thought about it.

After walking a full circuit of the encampment, we paused to watch a group of warriors in the midst of some dance-like practice drills. They were aligned in neat rows, all facing the same direction and moving in sync. A woman nearest us caught my eye. She was tall and curvy, yet she moved with strength and surety. Each sharp slash of her arms and each pivot of her stance was mesmerizing. In an instant, I understood how Rihtlondish women could be viable warriors. I doubted a single woman in all of Inra could do the same. Yet, here I was, expected to live among these people and prepare to marry their prince.

They will never accept me. Another flaw in my father's ill-conceived plan.

"It's called a *dowsa.*"

I jumped at the rough voice in my ear. The dane was behind me, eyeing me over the brim of a large goblet of mead. He wore the same tunic and trousers as the night before, but his hair had been re-braided.

"I'm sorry?" I squeaked, detesting the shrill edge to my voice.

"A *dowsa*. D'you Inraens have proper training, or are you complete savages?"

"*Us*, savages?" I rounded on him. *How dare he?* "Inra is the peak of civilization! Our soldiers are highly trained and have many ways of practicing—"

"But you wouldn't know, would you?" The dane scoffed.

"I've seen my share of training drills. The Cavendaffe lands are hardly unguarded."

"Bah."

"*We* are not the savages! Our cities are clean and well-built. We have established trade routes and highways. Our women are highly skilled in—"

The dane slurped loudly from his goblet. "There is nothing worthwhile your women know."

"If that's the case, then why am I here? Why would you want an Inraen to marry your son?" It was a dangerous question, but in that moment, I was raring for a fight.

"Any woman can birth a child," the dane said with a lopsided grin. "You don't have to know anything for that."

A rush of heat bloomed over my cheeks. *Curse my flaming face.*

The dane laughed, pitiless. "Worry not, Daughter. You'll be learning our ways all the same." He clomped away on his uneven legs, a slight limp on one side—something I hadn't noticed before. His braided blond hair swung in a long tail across his back. A glint of silver flashed in the sunlight from a clip that gathered the hair at the base of his skull. It was shaped like a dragon, though it was not the Creator. It struck me again how little I knew of these people.

"And a man like that gets allegiance from all of Rihtlond," Gerta spat. "What your father was thinking when he made this match, I'll never know. Dane or not, he'd better be careful how he speaks to you in the future, or I won't be so courteous as to hold my tongue!"

I placed a hand on Gerta's arm. We were among enemies, showing any emotion put us at their mercy.

A horn sounded, slicing through the air and my thoughts. In an instant, everyone around us moved into action.

"What's happening?" I shouted, hoping anyone might answer, but no one did.

Gerta grabbed my wrist and hauled me off in the same direction as the crowd. She pushed through a throng of braided and leather-clad Rihtlonders toward what we had discovered was the front of the encampment. An army nearly as large as the already gathered warriors dismounted and flooded the clearing, doubling their numbers. Men and women clasped arms and embraced while horses were led away and horns of water and mead were pressed into hands.

"*The prince*," Gerta hissed.

I scanned the crowd but couldn't differentiate one man from another. I let out a strangled wail of frustration. He could be any one of them. Finally, I spotted the dane leading several warriors toward his tent. Just before they disappeared through the flap, he clapped his arm around one of them, but all I could see from this vantage was the trail of a blond braid, indistinguishable from the rest.

A sharp jerk at my wrist refocused me. Gerta yanked me toward the dane's tent.

"Gerta, stop!"

But she did not. In moments, she had dragged me in front of two guards blocking the entrance. Both had dark skin and blond braids and looked enough alike to be brothers.

"This is your future princess, Lady Serae of Cavendaffe," Gerta demanded in a voice far more confident than I felt. "She is here to see her future husband,

Eldreth, son of Auldren. Let us pass."

The guards cracked identical smirks but did not respond.

"You would do well to—"

Whatever Gerta had been about to threaten was lost as the dane himself stepped through the entryway. He barked something in Rihtlondish to the brother-guards, who moved at once to flank us.

"There's trouble," he said without ceremony. "Back to your tent, and do not move if you value your lives. Bracht!"

The same honey-blond man who served us our breakfast appeared behind the dane.

"Go with them."

"Yes, Dane." He hurried to our side.

The dane turned and retreated again. As the tent flap parted, I glanced through the gap and locked eyes with a man standing in front of a large table at the center of the room. He was handsome and well-built, with the straight back and steely gaze of a general. His sharp jawline, broad chest, and intense eyes rooted me to the spot. His gaze was clear and piercing as it met mine. A wave of his contempt crashed over me a second before the dane drew his attention away. I gasped. The turn of his head revealed copper hair tied back in a knot. The flap fell, and the guards stepped forward.

"Red," I whispered, unable to move my feet.

"This way, my ladies," Bracht said, as if there were nothing wrong in the world.

We walked briskly back to the center of the encampment, the two guards urging us on. My mind whirred.

"Why is there danger?" I asked the guard at my right. "Are we not still in Cavendaffe?"

He did not answer.

Bracht, ahead of us, turned as he walked. "Just a precaution. Nothing to worry about."

This was meant to be a sanctioned trip between new allies. I had studied the alliances of Inra at length—processions were common practice for foreign betrothals. In fact, if Father were a prince, or if Cavendaffe were a larger and more influential province, we might have paraded through Inra, announcing the betrothal before heading north. What could pose a threat less than a day into our journey? That beautiful, hateful general popped into my mind. He was standing over a war table. What could they have been planning?

At our tent, one of the brothers ushered us inside with a gruff, "Do not leave." Bracht shot us a smile that was more of a grimace before the flap was closed. The guards settled to their posts outside, blocking all exit or entry. The thick, dark canvas muffled the light of the sun, so Gerta set about lighting the lamps. Within minutes, with no airflow and the summer heat beating through the cloth, our space became a small furnace. I flopped onto my bed with a huff and every intention to sleep. Instead, my mind cataloged every comfort, every familiarity, and every bit of joy back home that I had lost.

"IT'S TIME TO move."

The same gruff voice from earlier boomed through the tent flap, jolting me awake. The space was empty of everything except the furniture and one tray of food on the table. I didn't recall falling asleep.

"Eat quickly," Gerta hissed as she scurried over with the tray.

"What's going on?" I croaked. My throat was dry and scratchy.

"There's plenty of time for asking questions later. Our things have already been taken to the horses. We're riding this night."

"Martyrs above, what time is it? Have you slept at all?"

"Well enough. Now eat."

I scarfed down the plate of greens and root vegetables in a brown sauce—surprisingly more satisfying than it looked. Within minutes, we were atop our horses and ringed by guards, back in our place in the procession. This time, I looked for the women. Everyone, skirts or no, rode astride like me—even Gerta. The path was dimly lit with lanterns, and the horses were alert despite the hour.

"Can you train a horse to be nocturnal?" I asked Gerta.

She shrugged.

The gruff-voiced guard at my left stifled a laugh, and I shot him a dirty look.

"It's a valid question," I shot back.

He nodded, a smirk plastered on his face. I shot Gerta a frown. Was this the sort of treatment I could expect from these Rihtlonders? Given what I knew of them, I shouldn't be surprised.

Soon, the line was moving, and I had to fight to keep my mare steady, unlike the ride during the daytime. No more than a quarter hour had passed before Dane Auldren's horse broke the guard ring and fell in beside mine.

"Have you been on the water before?" he asked.

"Do you think the Cavendaffes have no boats?" I scoffed.

"That's all well and grand, but have you ever been at sea?"

"I—No," I admitted, gripping the reins tighter. Something told me that the open sea might be different from the wide river journeys I was used to—and not in a good way.

"Take this." The dane held out a pouch. "It's *rubra* bark. For chewing."

"*Rubra*?" I took the pouch and peered inside. The reddish bark had been crushed into small chunks. The scent reminded me of cinnamon—good for nausea and indigestion. I looked back at the dane as he trotted off, back relaxed and braid swaying. He paused at each group along the line, exchanging a few words.

Less time passed than I expected when the procession pulled to a halt. The air was thick with the tang of salt and seaweed, the lapping waves a constant, muffled roar.

"We were this close?" Gerta asked at my side.

I shrugged, glad I wasn't the only one in the dark. Still, it begged the question, why the camp at all?

The line began to move slowly, and the trees parted to reveal a dozen masts set against the moonlit sky. I had expected to board a ship, but I could never have imagined the sight before me. A full-scale fleet of vessels waited, each carved with a dragon at the helm. The nearest dragons spewed wooden fire from the head of the craft while massive wings surrounded the hull.

"Do they think dragons still exist?" Gerta whispered, eyeing the next-nearest boat with similar carvings.

I could only shake my head, enraptured by the display.

"They do," came a gravelly voice beside us. The owner was the other dark-skinned, blond brother—tight-faced and bulging with muscles—who made up half of Dane Auldren's personal guard duo. "Anyone who thinks otherwise is blind."

"Really?" I asked, trying to hide my disbelief. Everyone knew the legends of the Creator, the last immortal dragon who saved humanity from evil, but even he vanished from Jaeda more than a thousand years ago.

He nodded, then jumped off his steed and motioned us to dismount. A young woman in a green tunic and trousers darted forward to collect the horses. There must have been room on these vessels to carry the people, the horses—one for every woman and man—and all the furniture and tents. The scope of it was astonishing. We climbed the gangplank and entered a small cabin that already held our chests. I looked to Gerta, who shrugged. We sat on our respective cots and waited. I looked out the porthole while Gerta tapped out a little tattoo with her foot. When the vessel finally lurched out to sea, it took my stomach with it. I locked eyes with Gerta, then we both reached for Dane's pouch.

TWO EVENTLESS DAYS at sea passed, surrounded by nothing but waves. The pace was slow and anything but steady. Sometimes, the water was rough, and sometimes, it was rougher. When it was what the captain called *steady*, we were permitted to walk around the ship, provided we could stay out of the crew's way. We both had to cling to the railing or risk falling over, and, more than once, I ended up leaning over the side to offer my latest meal to the sea. It was a miracle I didn't lose my glasses to the waves as well. When I wasn't heaving, I used the time on deck to track our general direction for my father, based on the position of the sun.

Aside from those *delightful* strolls, we were expected to stay in our quarters. In one tiny room, we slept, ate meals, and relieved ourselves—thankfully in a small closet-sized privy. Most of our time was spent taking turns yawning, lounging in our small cots, and saying, "Martyrs, this is dull." I spent some time adding the first entry to my journal—a rudimentary map of our ship and a count of the other vessels around us.

That third blissful morning, I awoke to find the Rihtlond shore stretching across the horizon instead of the endless White Sea. I no longer cared which land it was, so long as it was solid under my feet. My stomach emptied itself one last time, even though the waters had calmed. It was still a few hours before Gerta and I were hustled off the ship with our chests and left to wait on the docks.

As we waited, men carried crate after crate of supplies from the fleet. Women led horses and stacked large baskets along the docks. Others tied up sails, washed down decks, pointed, yelled, and in general played a part in an elaborate nautical dance that was entirely foreign to me.

"Are there fewer ships?" Gerta asked.

I turned to check, but a large figure blocked my view.

"This way," our gruff-voiced guard interrupted, motioning us forward. His brother, close behind, loaded our traveling trunks onto a cart. We walked from the docks through a small town of predominantly stone buildings. The smell of fish assaulted me from all sides.

"How can it stink worse than when we were at sea?" Gerta hissed through the cloth she held over her nose and mouth.

I wrinkled my nose and laughed.

Aside from favoring stone structures over wood, this could have been any Inraen port. The biggest difference was the height of the trees. They loomed over our heads, so high I had to crane my neck to see the tops. And everything was darker—the soil, the leaves, even the water.

Our destination was a small inn that had clearly seen better days. The stairs were slick with seawater, and white salt stains marbled the floors. But the fire in the room was warm, and the food was palatable. As a bonus, the large bed Gerta and I shared was dry and blissfully plush.

The next day, we were up on horseback again.

"When will we not be in transit?" I moaned.

Light danced in Gerta's eyes as she leaned over to whisper, "Perhaps they *are* nomads."

The thought made my stomach drop. I caught Dane Auldren's attention. "Sire, what's our destination?"

"Home, Daughter. Soon enough, we ride to Drakh. We have a stop to make first."

So, their home wasn't a port city after all. I tucked this detail away, along with the others piling up in my mind. I'd have to find a way to send my first missive home soon.

As we rode inland, I found myself replaying my geography lessons on Rihtlond's uninhabitable terrain. I had been no more than twelve, sitting in our lesson room back home...

"Why do we even need to learn geography?" Merria had complained, twirling a curl around her finger. Even then, her hair hung in long honey curls.

"Because you need to have something floating around in your head."

"Bale..." Our mother's tone held a warning.

I peeked over my book to watch the exchange. Merria and I were meant to be reading from our geography primers under Mother's supervision. Shortly before winter, our governess always returned to her family home to help with preparations for the cold months. She would return to us after the thaw.

Merria stuck out her tongue at Bale. "Why are you even here? Shouldn't you be off playing swords or whatever?"

"Why would I waste time training when my life's ambition is to make a fortune selling the sawdust from your ears?" He leaned back in his chair, lacing his hands behind his head, elbows wide. He didn't seem to care that his shirt rode up, exposing his sides to the cold. Mother gave him a pointed look.

"I'll show you sawdust!"

Thunk!

Merria's primer soared wide of Bale's head and crashed into a bookshelf.

"That's enough!" Mother roared. "Bale, if you want to stay, you'll sit correctly in your chair, fix your clothing, and partake in the lesson."

He grinned and let his chair fall forward.

"And Merria," she continued, "understanding the world is crucial for every woman, especially if you are one day matched to a foreign lord. Do you think a prince from Grathan or Volaach would accept a bride with no understanding of his lands?"

Merria sat up straight. I suspected the word prince was her biggest motivator.

"Now, we begin with Rihtlond—"

"Ech! I wouldn't marry a prince from there!"

"—our closest and most challenging neighbor. Bale, share what you've learned from your schooling, and let us pray our money was at least not wasted on your education."

Bale rolled his eyes. "If you want a verbatim account of what the great Professor Vernard said"—he puffed up his chest and continued in a pompous, nasal tone—"Rihtlond, as you all should know, is located to our immediate northeast across the White Sea. It is mostly rocks with sparse greenery. The land is full of snow and ice for half the year or more. The rivers come from glaciers and are frigid. The soil is mostly bedrock and difficult to till. Crops are small and sparse, spurring the Rihtlonders to raid their neighbors for want of food. You will learn more on this when we cover our long history of wars with Rihtlond, but for now, suffice it to say, they are a people as hard, cold, and fruitless as their lands."

Merria and I had laughed at his impression.

Now, standing on Rihtlondish soil myself, I saw nothing of bedrock or sparsity. The wind, once we made it more inland, was light, cool, and refreshing. The soil was dark and rich, and plants and greenery surrounded us.

At midday, it began to drizzle, so we stopped for a short reprieve. Our escorts were the same two maybe-brothers the dane had assigned to guard us since Cavendaffe. While we took refuge from the rain under a large oak, one of them plucked a fruit I didn't recognize from a tree beside the road. He tossed several to Gerta and me before picking more for himself and his companion, our gravelly guard. The fruit was juicy, succulent, and both sweet and tangy. Judging by how Gerta inhaled them and begged for more, eliciting buoyant laughs from the guards, she enjoyed them as much as I did.

We rode on for the better part of the day. The landscape remained lush, green, and beautiful in a new and wild way. By evening, just when I thought we would be riding through darkness, we came upon a cluster of buildings offering warm beds. We ate, slept, and were riding by morning with little spoken in between. Whatever business the dane had in the small town, he didn't reveal it to me. I spent most of the next day trying—and failing—not to fixate on my aching back and legs. Every time I broke down and asked the dane how much farther, he would just laugh and say things like "soon" or "you'll see." I scowled in response, which only made him laugh harder.

Just as I'd built up the courage to confront him for keeping me in the dark, we crested a large hilltop. My breath caught. The land sprawled out before us, a valley of rolling green hills, acres upon acres of crops, and an expansive city nestled at its center. The city's walls were vast and high, but I could still make out a large mound, atop which stood a formidable castle.

Trees dotted the landscape, as did patches of thick forest. Cavendaffe was a prosperous land, but nothing about it compared to the depth and variety of greens covering this valley. I could only stare in wonder.

"Welcome to Drakh, the high seat of the Riht." Dane Auldren winked and pointed a thick finger toward the south entrance of the city, where what I could only describe as a dragon's skull emerged from the walls. "This is our path. You may be the first Inraen to see it who lives to tell the tale."

I swallowed hard. I must never forget that I was an outsider here, a lone foreigner thrust into the heart of my enemy.

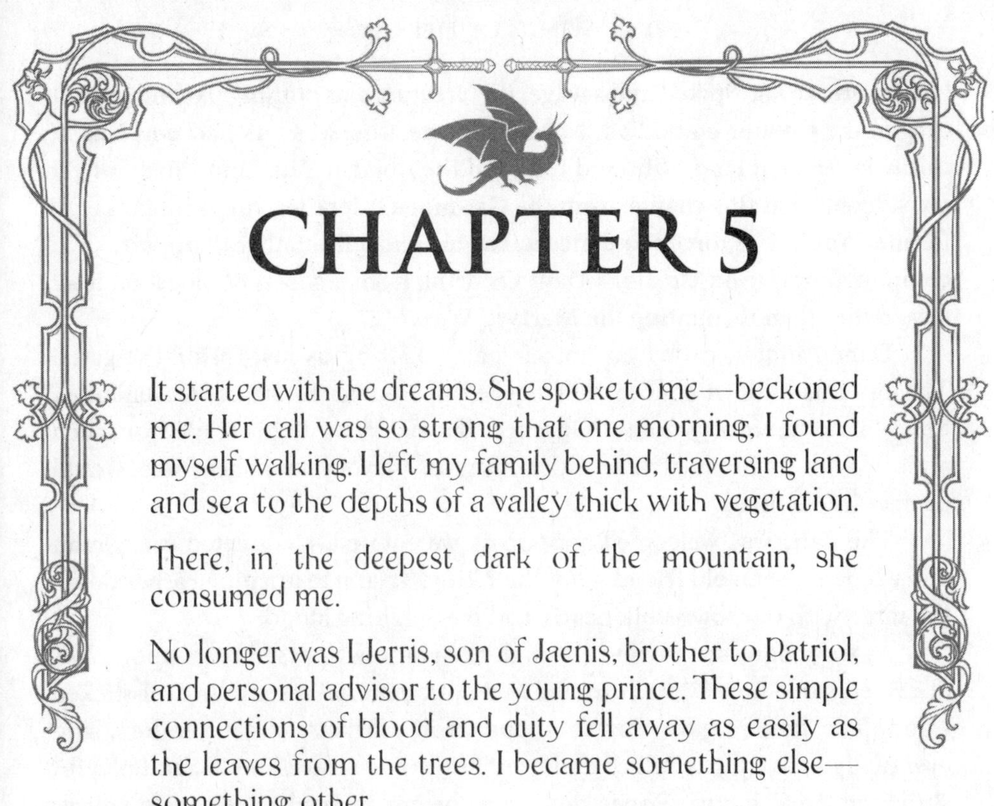

CHAPTER 5

It started with the dreams. She spoke to me—beckoned me. Her call was so strong that one morning, I found myself walking. I left my family behind, traversing land and sea to the depths of a valley thick with vegetation.

There, in the deepest dark of the mountain, she consumed me.

No longer was I Jerris, son of Jaenis, brother to Patriol, and personal advisor to the young prince. These simple connections of blood and duty fell away as easily as the leaves from the trees. I became something else—something other.

Something more.

—Entry from the private diary of Jerris, Dragonbound

• ⁓ •

SERAE

MIDSUMMER, VALMON 1036

Entering the city of Drakh was intimidating, to say the least. Great beams of iron and carved stone jutted from the front gates, twisting into the maw of a gargantuan dragon—the Great Dragon, as the Rihtlonders had taught me. I had at first assumed this to be their name for the Creator, but I couldn't have been more wrong. Spiked and savage, this creature was nothing like the elegant dragon the Creator embodied. No, he and the Nine Martyrs had no place in this wild, ancient land. Rihtlond followed the Ancient Path, and I had not yet considered what this change from the Carmine Order's teachings might mean for me. Would I be forced to dance naked around a fire rather than partake in communal prayer on Creator's Day? Or drink from a goblet of blood on feast days rather than recounting the Martyrs' Woes?

Dane Auldren called out to our party, halting us just inside the gates. The city was built in concentric rings, easily double the size of Cavendaffe's town—if not more. My stomach lurched. If it ever came to it, escape from such a place, with its impenetrable walls, maze-like layout, and sheer size, would be near impossible.

The dane was welcomed as soon as we entered. He greeted every man and woman like an old friend—not their king. Trying to imagine Father doing the same with our townsfolk nearly had me laughing aloud.

As we progressed inward through the rings, we passed rows upon rows of carved stone houses, each roofed in a dark material resembling oil-slicked wood. The houses gave way to shops, food markets, street vendors, and eventually schoolyards full of children. Peals of laughter, shouts, and playful shrieking drew me in. Ropes, logs, and beams formed an obstacle course in their play yard, and boys and girls alike scrambled over them, jumping and climbing. One boy, no older than Brig, had found a giant stick and was whacking it against every pole and stump in sight. *This* was something I understood, and I turned to Gerta to exchange smiles. I guess children were the same everywhere.

Our party wound its way toward the castle's thick retaining wall. A river surrounded it, splitting around the castle to form a natural moat, then continuing out the other side. Drawbridges spanned the river, all down and welcoming passage between the higher and lower rings of the city.

Once through the walls, we passed more rings of homes and shops. Less of a traditional castle courtyard, the interior was a fortified town of its own, with a keep at its center. Our procession halted before the mountainous keep, which threatened to overwhelm us—or Gerta and me, at least. Drakh Keep dwarfed our manor home, comically. Its towers touched the clouds themselves, and stone carvings of the Great Dragon dotted every crenellation and topped every window and door. Its sheer size was greater than anything I had encountered, and I had been to King Ruper's palace at the capital. How many lands must they have raided to fund all this? I frowned at the thought.

Before approaching the keep's portcullis, we were brought around to a nearby stable, which was an impressive building in itself. There, a young stable hand offered a mounting block to help us dismount. She pointed a finger toward the dane but spoke no words.

"She'll take the horses from here," the gravelly brother advised. "You're free to rejoin Dane."

Dane Auldren led the way inside the keep personally, giving Gerta and me little more than a sharp glance to indicate we should follow. A severe-looking woman stood waiting just inside the portcullis. She dipped her head in a quick bow before addressing him directly. I couldn't make out what was said, but the woman's eyes turned toward me and narrowed. She finished her conversation with the dane and approached.

"Lady Cavendaffe." She knelt into a deep curtsey. The contrast between this show of respect and the short bow she offered the dane was not lost on me. Had I not lived so many years with Merria, I may not have spotted it for the mockery it was.

"Please, call me Serae."

"I am Kahvrah. I will serve as your *reálta* until you are better acquainted with the Riht and able to select one for yourself." Her accent in Mayoran was thick, and her cadence was out of practice.

"My *reálta*?" I stumbled over the unfamiliar word. Hadn't Bracht used it, as well?

"A sort of guide. This way."

Kahvrah swept her long braid over her shoulder and proceeded into the keep. I scuttled after her, Gerta at my heels. The turns she took were nonsensical, so I kept my eyes locked on her golden braid and heather gray tunic until tapestries lining the stone corridors stole my attention. They depicted dragons of all different colors alongside people whose helms twisted upward with horns and spikes, some of which covered glowing eyes. Eventually, she led us up a staircase, down another hallway, and stopped abruptly. We faced a wide corridor with a set of doors on either side.

"That door leads to your future quarters. Beside it is a shared sitting room." Kahvrah pointed to the two modest wooden doors on the right. "This is the Training Hall." She indicated the wide set of double doors with iron ring handles on our left.

"Training rooms?" I asked.

Kahvrah narrowed her eyes. "Yes."

"What will I be studying?"

Her eyes sharpened even more as her brows drew together. After a while, she said, “How to be a Riht. Tests will follow. Come, I will show you to your temporary accommodations.”

My brow raised at the word *tests.* The dane had conveniently forgotten to mention anything about that.

“What about that one?” I pointed to the tallest door at the end of the hall that she hadn’t addressed.

“Off limits.” Kahvrah, not interested in giving out further information, led us back down the hall, taking several turns. I quickly lost track and stopped trying to memorize our path.

“Did they build this place to be intentionally confusing?” I whispered to Gerta in Inraen.

She only shrugged.

We halted at a long corridor lined on either side by many close-set doors, reminding me of our servants’ quarters back home. I glanced sidelong at Kahvrah, who selected one room seemingly at random, and ushered us inside. Calling the room narrow would have been an understatement. They had managed to squeeze in two cots abreast—barely. One small window at the far end let in a sliver of light, and a table with two chairs crowded the entrance. All in all, the room wasn’t much of an upgrade from the tent. In fact, the tent had been far more spacious.

“Exactly how temporary is this...room?” I glanced at the bare walls already closing in on me. I tried to breathe through my rising panic—that sense of being trapped.

“Tonight, Dane wishes you to stay here. In the morning, I will return and help you with your clothes—”

“I dress her.” Gerta stepped in front of me.

Kahvrah’s gaze slid down Gerta’s form, something baiting in her eyes. When she spoke, the corner of her mouth quirked up. “I could do with fewer assumptions. I am not a dressing maid.”

Gerta’s mouth tightened.

I shivered, only just noticing there was no fireplace. It may have been summer, but these stone walls held in the chill.

“As I was saying”—Kahvrah’s eyes flicked back to me—“I will come in the morning to *teach you* about the clothing worn in the Riht. They are different from your Southern nonsense. You will have no need for what you brought. If your maid has questions on how to dress you, I will answer them at that time, but you should know—we Riht dress ourselves.”

Gerta and Kahvrah exchanged stony glances.

"A server will bring you meals. Dane asks that you do not wander."

"Why?" I made the mistake of asking.

Kahvrah's hard expression did not alter. "For your own safety. You will be safe within these walls, but there are those who oppose admitting a foreigner to Drakh. Stay here, and Dane can guarantee you are safe. Wander, and you may find yourself at the wrong end of a blade."

I recoiled at the thought.

Kahvrah required neither thanks nor dismissal. She turned and left without a second glance, leaving us in confined isolation. The door clanged shut behind her.

Luckily, I knew the perfect way to spend my time. I rummaged through my trunk until I found my sack of quills and ink and sat down to encode everything I'd been storing up for the better part of a week—including the path to the elusive city of Drakh.

"BUT...THEY'RE *PANTS!*"

Kahvrah scoffed. "Of course they are not pants. They are leggings. What do you wear under your dresses in Inra? Nakedness?"

"No, we have underskirts."

Kahvrah burst out laughing. It was not a pleasant sound. "More skirts beneath your skirts? No wonder you can barely walk. Here, you will wear these. Later, I will teach you how to tie your skirt up into your belt when you need more range of motion."

"When would she need that?" Gerta asked.

Kahvrah shot her a look—hard eyes and one raised brow. She was fond of those. "You will both need it. I am here to teach you as well."

"I return to Inra in three weeks."

"Do you?"

Kahvrah glanced at me, and I nodded.

She shrugged. "There is no harm in learning."

Over the next half hour, I dressed in what Kahvrah called everyday Rihtlondish garb. For all her criticisms of Inra, Rihtlondish dress was still full of layers. It started with the dreaded leggings. The pair Kahvrah handed over were loose-fitting until a seamstress entered our already cramped room, measured my legs with a string, and altered the leggings on the spot with needle and thread—her fingers so deft they'd have put even Mother to shame.

Within minutes, I had a breathable fabric that hugged my legs obscenely. I might have been naked, except that my legs were now green.

"Lanh will make more leggings for you."

The seamstress left with a nod.

Next came the underdress, which went on like a man's *cotehardie*—front-opening, wrapping around my body, looping through itself, and tying at my waist. The sleeves fell halfway down my forearms.

The outer garment was a sleeveless overdress; its green fabric looked coarse, but against my skin was softer than the finest silk. It fell roughly six inches above the underdress' hem and was worn like an overlong vest. Last came instructions on affixing pouches to the belt, and the ensemble was finished with soft leather boots.

"This is for everyday wear?" I asked, presenting my boot-shod feet. "Not just riding?"

Kahvrah quirked up one eyebrow, then gave a nod.

I shot Gerta a look. I had a bad feeling I'd be adjusting to a lot more than life without *sollars* and layers of underskirts.

Kahvrah drew two pouches from the folds of her skirt and handed one to each of us. The larger pouch clinked as it fell into my hand, as did Gerta's smaller pouch.

"What's this?"

"Scale," Kahvrah said simply. At our puzzled looks, she added, "Money."

"What for?"

"For whatever you need."

I stared at her.

"You know how to spend money, yes?"

I bristled. As the daughter of the margrave, everything I needed had always been provided.

"She knows well enough," Gerta answered for me, "but we don't know what or where to buy anything here."

"This you will know as you learn about Drakh. Dane wanted you to be prepared, nonetheless."

Being finally dressed was not enough for Kahvrah. She forced me to strip and redress—including looping the money pouch through my underdress ties—until I could do it quickly and without aid.

"How do I—" I fidgeted with my overdress and the slight bulge from the money pouch. "How do I get to my pouches *underneath* my dress?"

Kahvrah erupted into laughter, which I did not at all appreciate. "You have pockets in your skirts and slits at the sides. You truly do not have this in Inra? We have all heard stories, but I never believed them." She moved aside some of the fabric and guided my hands to both pockets in my overdress—positioned on the side and slightly toward the front. Then, she pulled apart both overdress and underdress, revealing long slits down the left side. There were small ties on the underside keeping the fabric together, and the gaps between the ties allowed plenty of room to reach my hand through. When tied and fallen back against my body, the folds in the fabric made the openings effectively invisible.

"They will come in handy when you learn how to use a blade."

"A blade?" Gerta and I gasped together.

The air whooshed out of me. "You're going to make me fight?"

Kahvrah's grin was a little too pointed for my liking.

ONCE I WAS dressed, the next task was learning the way to the kitchens. This was more my pace. I loved being in the kitchens—either to help or steal food—back home. The kitchens in Drakh Keep were set off the Main Hall, which included a few private dining rooms and a side area with windows for ordering food on takeaway trays.

After the kitchens, Kahvrah led us through the same nonsensical halls back toward my future quarters.

"Mark this path," she advised, entering the doors on the left rather than the one leading to my mystery suite. They opened to a descending stairway, interrupted midway by a landing with four rooms, two jutting off on either side.

"Training rooms," she announced, then led us down to the double doors at the bottom of the stairs. Kahvrah pushed me through first.

I let out a squawk and stumbled, but just before I rounded on Kahvrah in protest, the dane's hulking form caught my eye. He stood in the center of a large room, with weapons lining the stone walls and padded mats covering the floors. The dane spoke in hushed tones with one of the most striking women I had ever beheld. She was tall, toned in every sense, and had an intricate platinum blond braid that fell to her waist. Her hair gleamed with such intensity, it looked white in places. Her high cheekbones and thin, painted red lips offset her angular features with a touch of elegance. But when she turned her pale eyes on me, there was fury in them.

My stomach dropped. I'd been in Rihtlond less than a day. What could I have done to deserve a glare like that?

"Come," Kahvrah whispered behind me. "We will wait over here."

I glanced in their direction, spotting one Rihtlonder I recognized—Bracht from the camps. He smiled and offered me a small wave.

Dane turned to me, his mouth pressed into a thin line. "Daughter."

The woman beside him sneered, tainting my initial impression of her beauty.

He beckoned me forward. "Your first of three trials begins now. This is your challenger—one of Drakh's most skilled *dowsae* trainers. She serves as the measure against which women in Drakh are tested. You have one objective for the next five minutes—stay alive." He raised an eyebrow in my direction, then stepped off the mat to join Kahvrah, Gerta, and Bracht.

I looked at this woman, my so-called challenger, at a complete loss. "Hello," I tried with a slight smile.

She grinned, and it was entirely feral. Then, she backhanded me across the cheek.

My neck snapped to the side, and my glasses went flying. The world turned on its axis, and pain exploded from my temple to my jaw. I gasped, vision blurring from more than just the pain. I covered my throbbing cheek with my hand and stumbled back, away from her, but she advanced after me. I retreated as quickly as I could, but she was faster.

"What the fuck was—" She struck again, a closed fist straight to my nose. I heard the sickening crunch before I felt it. It brought me to my knees, where I received a kick to my side. My ribs screamed in protest, and I recoiled, crying out, "Stop!" That got me another swift kick to the ribs. Pain stabbed through my side. On instinct, I sucked in a breath, sending more pain—sharp and sudden—down my shoulder and back.

She did not stop. Kick after kick landed. I screamed for Dane, to no effect. I curled inward, blocking what I could with my forearms and shins. I tried to roll away, but that only earned me more blows to my back. My whole body was pain.

Off to the side, Gerta wailed while Kahvrah shushed her.

"Dane, please!" Bracht's voice rang out.

"Enough," Dane's call sounded from somewhere in the room.

One last kick landed, but this time to my gut. The little air left in my lungs was driven out, and I began to heave.

Next came the crying. Sobs racked through me, making all the broken things worse, especially my pride. Heavy footsteps fell on the mat, and I knew it was the dane before his thick, leather boots filled my vision. Judging by the closeness of his voice, he was bending over me.

"We have more work to do than I'd hoped."

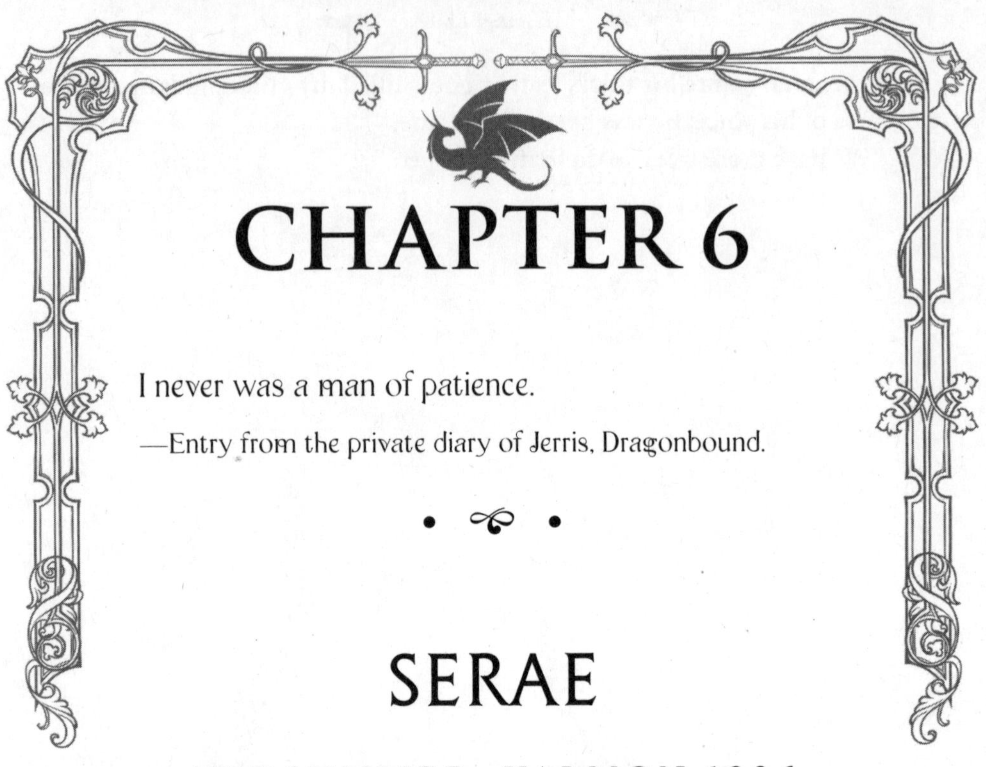

CHAPTER 6

I never was a man of patience.

—Entry from the private diary of Jerris, Dragonbound.

• ∞ •

SERAE

MIDSUMMER, VALMON 1036

I WAS NOT permitted out of bed, not that I had any desire to leave it. The sky was gloomy, my vision hadn't cleared yet, and I hurt everywhere. Worst of all, I couldn't rest my glasses on the bridge of my broken nose, compounding my diminished sight. Safe to say, my first few days in Rihtlond were some of the worst of my life.

Twice per day, an ancient woman visited to slather a hot paste over my wounds and wrap them in fresh linens. It made the room smell of pungent, bitter herbs.

"What is this?" I tried asking her.

She wagged a finger at me. "Don't touch."

On day two of bed rest, Kahvrah entered our little room to answer questions about my first test. Gerta had to step in for me, as the only question I had was, *Why the fuck are you trying to kill me before I even meet my betrothed?*

"Warrior's Initiation," Kahvrah said, as if that were explanation enough. "No one in the Riht would fall after a few seconds, but you are not of the Riht."

It was not at all reassuring to hear the test was designed to fail—or that most people walked away injured. The trial tested resolve, which did not bode well for what was to come.

On the third day, Gerta found a woman willing to send my first two letters home for a few scale each. It felt easier than asking for Dane's help with correspondence to my sister. I didn't know what he had in store for me next, but I had a few cracked ribs deterring me from seeking him out.

The fourth day started with sunshine. Sunlight streamed in through our single small window, bright and insistent. I decided it was time to get up. Everything ached, but I managed to stretch my arms above my head without blacking out. I even pinned the curtains back on their hooks with barely any shaking. Our room was still chilly, but I rotated the panes open for a bit of breeze. I had a bad feeling this was as warm as it got in Rihtlond.

Gerta greeted me soon after with our breakfast trays and a smile. "We've been told to report to the smallest training room as soon as you've eaten."

"For another beating?"

"Martyrs, I hope not. How are your ribs?"

"Lovely." Gerta shot me a look, and I rolled my eyes. "They're improving. I can barely feel any tug when I breathe." That much wasn't a lie.

"Milady, I'm sure you want to appear strong, but cracked ribs don't heal in three days."

That was definitely true, but poking at my sides wasn't as excruciating as expected. "Maybe Rihtlondish herbs are stronger than ours? Think I can get out of whatever's coming if they are still cracked?"

Gerta's next look was spectacularly doubtful as she held out both hands. When I gave her mine, she spread my arms wide and rotated my torso side to side like a ridiculous pantomime top. Crimson blossomed behind my eyelids.

I gasped, trying to tamp down the pain. My experience with pain mitigation was woefully insufficient. "Burning Martyrs, I don't have to go, do I?"

She nodded and let my arms drop. "We stop at the first sign of discomfort," she grumbled with her back to me, then, "Burning Martyrs, indeed."

I slipped into my boots. *Training.* What in the Creator's fucking bones was I supposed to do with that? Judging by the weapons lining the training room, it would be a bit more than target practice with a bow. Which I *might* be ready for if Mother hadn't stopped me from ever touching a sword. *A lady learning archery is bad enough*, she had bemoaned.

All too soon, it was time to make our way to the training rooms. Gerta had memorized the path in the days I was immobile. Inside the descending stairway, I froze on the landing, staring down at the double doors. It seemed the Creator had spared me when I noticed the first door on the right had been propped open. Kahvrah stood in the center of a small room with rug-lined flooring. She motioned us in.

"Good morning," I tried, dipping into a curtsey.

Kahvrah offered only a curt nod to each of us. "You will begin all lessons with a *dowsa*."

"Which is?" Gerta asked.

"A pattern of body movements, which you will memorize and repeat until you know each motion perfectly."

"So, like a dance?" I offered.

"Yes and no. It is better if I show you. Since you have no *dowsae* of your own in Inra, I will teach you our child's *dowsa*."

Gerta scoffed.

Kahvrah cracked a grin. "I doubt you could handle anything more."

With no warning beyond the tensing of a muscle, she leapt into action. She spun, kicked, and moved between stances with a speed that belied her grace. We stood entranced. Her movements were far more intricate and precise than what I had seen in the camp—those looked like synchronized drills. This was power, fluidity, and control. This was a woman who devoted her entire life to her body.

It ended as it began—abruptly and without ceremony. For a moment, I wondered if it had happened at all. I looked to Gerta, her eyes locked on Kahvrah with a new intensity.

"Now you!" Kahvrah shouted, then let out a bellowing laugh at our blank faces. "No? You cannot copy?"

What a delightfully fair task that would be. "You've been practicing this for, what, your whole life?" I asked.

She nodded.

"Does every Rihtlonder study combat?" Gerta added.

"No. This is not combat. This is body health, nothing more."

Not combat training? I looked anew at my memory of the warriors in the camp. If those sharp, strong movements were just maintaining their bodies, what on Jaeda did actual training look like? The thought was sobering.

Kahvrah's smile dropped, and she adjusted her stance—legs shoulder-width apart, spine straight, and arms relaxed at her sides. "Now, do as I do." She motioned for us to mirror her, pivoting one leg behind.

"You must be joking," I said. Call it health, combat, or anything in between, I wasn't here for this. I was here for one reason alone—information.

Kahvrah's body snapped to face me. "I am not. You are here to train. We begin now."

"No."

"No?"

"If there are lessons to learn about Rihtlond's governing, I will learn them, but I will not take part in warfare."

Her eyes sharpened. "You will learn what I teach. If you do not like it, take it to Dane— tomorrow. Today, you learn." She turned to face forward, and slow as molten glass, she began.

I scowled but followed her movements—arms sweeping in wide arcs, feet shifting, body bending and twisting. Every movement was slow and controlled. My glasses kept slipping with these movements, and I had to push them up my nose so often that Kahvrah began shooting me severe looks. Within minutes, I was drenched in sweat and vibrating from the pain in my ribs. Gerta beside me looked no better. The entire circuit lasted under ten minutes, and by the end, I was panting—hard.

Kahvrah tutted. "We will work on it. At least you are both still on your feet. Have some water"—she gestured to a short, round table with a pitcher and glasses in the corner of the room—"and we will try again."

"Again!" I shouted, earning myself another glare.

After an hour, my muscles were jelly, but as a small mercy, the ache in my ribs had gone numb.

Instead of giving us time to rest, Kahvrah made me recall the way back to the kitchens where we ate flatbread with bean paste. "This is fuel for your body," she said in that clipped tone of hers that could have been brevity as easily as annoyance.

When the three of us finally made our way outside the keep, it was well past midday. Every step was agony on my ribs, but having the sun warm my skin was a blessing. I thanked the Creator for being out of the dim lighting of the keep. It was no wonder it stayed so cold, with its thick stone walls and sparse windows. As we walked, I studied the plant life. Trees grew between buildings, bushes bordered homes and lined walkways, and numerous building sides boasted climbing vines. Most of the plants were thick with fruits, though some were still in blossom or barely starting to bud. It reminded me of harvest rotations back home.

"They're crops," I gasped, earning an appreciative nod from Kahvrah.

"Everything planted in the Riht has a purpose. Is this different from Inra?"

"I suppose. Crops are for farmlands, not city streets."

She nodded. "A wasteful approach, I think."

I bristled, turning away from the apple blossoms I'd been admiring with a frown.

"We are going to the closest market," Kahvrah explained as we continued on. "This is the only market you may visit until Dane says otherwise. When you are permitted to leave the keep, you must always be accompanied by one of the Riht. Your maid is not enough."

My frown deepened. *Prisoner is better than slave.* My mind drifted to my absent betrothed. Not a word about Eldreth had been uttered since our arrival in Rihtlond. I was not eager to ask why. I wished, not for the first time, that this was not my fate. Merria had always wanted the attention, the importance, and even the foreign prince—not me. How our fates had been switched, I might never understand.

The walk to the market was easy in these Rihtlondish boots. We crossed the length of the castle grounds on stone roads, and my feet were hardly affected. Clouds rolled in, and the sky opened up for a few minutes during our walk. In *sollars*, with soles barely thicker than indoor slippers, my feet would have been aching and soaked through.

Looking down the smaller alleys as we walked, I glimpsed pathways of dirt or heavily trodden grass. Any path wide enough for a cart was paved with flat, tightly packed stones—better joined than the cobblestone roads back home. I glanced over to Gerta, who was trailing one foot across the stones with a twinkle in her eye. *Great. Another thing she thinks is clever.*

"You can spend your scale here freely," Kahvrah said. "Everyone in this market will sell to you."

I adjusted my glasses. "Are there other markets where people won't sell to us?"

Kahvrah pursed her lips. "If there is anything you cannot find, tell me."

Anticipation prickled my skin as we walked the market road. Small shops lined either side, and a row of carts down the center left just enough room in between for a horse to pass through. I scarcely knew where to look. Most of the carts boasted a variety of foods in jars, crates, or overflowing sacks. Other carts displayed baskets of fresh fruits and veggies, but most were devoted to plants and cuttings of large leaves, whose purpose I couldn't even begin to guess. Men, women, and children browsed each stand, talking in the rapid Rihtlondish language.

The carts were portable, fitted with wheels and harness rods, while the shops were permanent, carved from dark stone. One had clothing neatly folded in stacks across narrow tables, another with a large sword mounted over the door, and another with waxy leaves as long as my arm strung up to dry in the window.

"What do you think those plants are for?" I nudged Gerta and pointed.

"Pathetic," a voice hissed behind me. *My challenger.* I'd recognize her sneer anywhere. "I heard stories of how sheltered Inraen women are, but you are worse. Weak *and* ignorant." Her accent was thicker than Kahvrah's.

"I'm...sorry?" I balked. Was she serious?

"You should be."

My challenger, whose name I didn't know, turned and walked away. Her every step was grace and purpose. It made my stomach turn. Beside me, Gerta's eyes smoldered with rage. I turned to Kahvrah and blinked—her expression mirroring mine.

"Well, she seems nice." I scowled at her retreating back.

Gerta's lips tightened into a thin line, but Kahvrah's frown cracked. "She has never been pleasant, but this time, she has her reasons. Come this way."

We visited the tailor who had completed a half dozen pairs of leggings for me, along with four complete everyday outfits. I was pleased to find an array of colors beyond green and brown, which dominated the rest of the market. The hues were more muted than the dyes of Inra, but the fabric was a downright luxury to touch.

I thanked her and paid with scale. The strange green coins were unlike anything I'd seen before. They were triangular with rounded corners instead of the round metal coins I was used to. They had a slight concavity to them, and they ranged in size and thickness. Each was marked with a rune I couldn't read. Kahvrah stood aside while Lanh explained their values and helped sort through the fees owed. When done, Kahvrah added a scale of her own to the pile, "For all the trouble."

"INTERESTING," GERTA MUTTERED, inspecting the tap in the private bathing chamber along our hallway, also permitted for our use. "I wonder how they keep the water warm."

I clenched my jaw and set my glasses on the counter. It would be a miracle if I had any teeth left to chew with by the time she returned to Inra. She had picked up a habit of marveling under her breath in every lesson and at random intervals through the day—especially when perusing wares in the market.

Each day, she found at least three things about Rihtlond to admire. That was all well and good for a woman whose trip had an upcoming expiration date. I, on the other hand, was stuck here. Nothing I looked at was novel or intriguing. It was foreign and uncomfortable and uninviting.

My new life continued in a similar, exhausting routine. Gerta brought our breakfast trays to our room each morning and dinner trays at night. Afternoons were spent learning from guest instructors about everything from leather tanning to the complicated values assigned to each commodity. That was the only part of the day I enjoyed. If given the choice, I would spend all my lessons working with the herbalist, the farmer—Martyrs, even the seamstress—who had all visited for guest lectures. But the most critical lesson was the daily hour I spent learning the Rihtlondish language. People switched to Mayoran only when speaking directly to me. Otherwise, I was at a complete loss.

I avoided walking as much as I could, considering the state of my ribs. We practiced *dowsae* constantly. Kahvrah, it turned out, was merciless with her corrections. When I attempted to sit out of training one particularly painful morning, the dane showed up in my room with gruff threats that there would be consequences if I skipped out again. I believed him.

Each night, I documented everything I could remember from that day's lessons in my journal. Luckily, it fit in my underdress pocket, as I no longer had a bodice to hide it under. It doubled as a reference book, helping me keep tabs on what we were learning. With Gerta's help, I sent another coded letter back to Cavendaffe. This one contained the few details about Rihtlond I had gathered—Drakh was huge, the castle was huge, the lands were vast and productive, and warriors were everywhere I looked.

After about a week of this routine, Gerta and I entered the afternoon lesson room and came face-to-face with the dane. He reclined in one of the high-backed chairs at the small table we used for tea and discussion. From what I'd gathered, each table lining the walls had a specific purpose: one slanted drawing desk, a workbench for multipurpose crafting, one slick black table whose purpose I had yet to identify, and our usual comfortable table in the corner, now set for two instead of three and occupied by my unlikely visitor.

"Dane Auldren," I greeted and swept into a short curtsey.

"Daughter Serae," he replied with twinkling eyes, a half-smile on his lips. "Send away your lass and sit with me."

Gerta retreated without a word. I frowned, then forced my face to relax.

Following Rihtlondish custom, I took a seat and poured a cup of tea for myself, offering none to the dane. Everyone served themselves in Rihtlond unless they were in the Main Hall—or so I'd been told, since we weren't allowed to attend. Dane was already sipping from his cup. I took the warm clay mug in my hands and inhaled deeply. One thing I had to admit—which I would never tell Gerta—I *loved* Rihtlondish mugs. They were larger and deeper than teacups with no handle, perfect for cradling between two hands.

"How are you finding Drakh so far?"

Foreign. Lonely. Unwelcoming. "It's a unique city, to be sure."

"Spoken like a diplomat," Dane chortled. "Pretty lies will not help you here."

I frowned.

He eyed me in silence. I focused on anything but his piercing gaze and sipped my tea. Instead of his customary braids, his beard and hair were left loose in wild blond waves. His heavy brow matched his deep frown, and a thin scar traced down his neck beside his ear.

"You've been learning your first few *dowsae*, I hear."

Unfortunately. I swallowed, nodding.

"Do you enjoy it?"

"No."

He nodded. "And your other lessons?"

"Well enough, Your... Sire." It wasn't a complete lie.

The dane pressed his lips into a thin line. "How do you address your father?"

"My...father?"

"Yes. At home, how do you address him?"

What kind of a question was that? "I call him 'Father' or 'my lord.'"

"Hmm."

"Is this what you wanted to talk to me about?"

He shook his head. "Titles matter in the Riht, but not honorifics. You earn a title through hard work. You show respect with actions."

I stared at him.

"You will understand when Eldreth returns home."

I adjusted my glasses and sat up straighter. "Is he expected back soon?"

"No. And yes. He is...well, you Inraen call it raiding." He barked out a short laugh, probably at the look on my face.

I knew dismay—or maybe even disgust—was splashed across it. My betrothed was a barbarian. Maybe a rapist. Maybe a murderer. That was the kind of thing they did on these raids, wasn't it? My throat squeezed at the thought of this man's hands touching me, when he had likely touched dozens of women by force. Not to mention, all the people he'd killed in cold blood. *No, not my betrothed.* My true betrothed was back home, not wandering distant lands and... *Tam.* A rush of guilt hit me. I hadn't even thought of him in more than a week. Then again, our visits in Inra were rarely more frequent than monthly. Enough time hadn't passed yet for me to begin missing him—that was all. *Wasn't it?*

"Enough of this." He waved one large hand. "Down to business. Two weeks have passed since you joined us, one in travel and rest"—I wouldn't call healing bruised ribs and a split face resting—"and one learning of life in Drakh. There are things you won't understand for some time. Important things. That's why I'm here."

I stilled, my mug halfway to my mouth.

"First, a dane or dana is always married before taking the mantle. The time for Eldreth to take the lead is not yet near, but he must be prepared. Among the Riht, we have a rite of betrothal, where you will earn your right to be betrothed to my son, as he will in turn for you. But first, you must complete your Sun Trial to be formally accepted into the Riht."

I clutched my hands beneath the folds of my skirt. If my knuckles were visible, they would be white as bone. *Creator save me, not another fucking trial.*

"What does that involve?" I asked, though there was nothing on Jaeda I wanted to do less.

"Kahvrah will show you... Daughter," he said, and for the first time, kindness laced his tone, "a Riht marriage is a real marriage."

I froze, not daring to move. I forced my face to relax. Did he know? Had I done something to make him suspect? *Breathe.* I needed to breathe and think. Choosing each word carefully, I replied, "How could a marriage not be real?"

"Marriages for the Riht are more than a political alliance—they are a match between two people."

"And yet you said I was only needed to produce—"

"I know what I've said," he snapped. "Listen to me now. In the Riht, the dane and dana lead together. If you want to become one of us, you need to understand this."

I nodded. *I didn't ask for this.*

"Focus on your lessons. Talk to the people. Prepare for your next trial. Think about an occupation."

Dane was beginning to sound a lot like my father. Lessons I could do.

The people might be a lost cause. And the trial? Thinking about that made me want to vomit. "What occupation?" I asked.

"An occupation."

My expression must have been blank. My mind certainly was.

"A way to spend your time. An expertise to give back to the Riht. Surely, you want to do something useful with your life."

"I don't know—" I bit off my last words. Dane already thought me weak enough. "I don't know what's expected of me."

"Very little." Dane's face was impassive. There was no sharpness to his statement, only fact.

"Then how am I supposed to know what to do? How do I learn what's acceptable?"

"What are your skills?"

"I— Nothing you would value."

"Oh, ho!" Dane's laugh boomed out of him. "Already adopting a Riht attitude."

I scowled. I picked up my mug, but it was empty. I set it down and ran my fingers through my tangled curls.

"Think on this." He stood, so I did the same. Rather than leaving, he loitered for a few moments. The muscles in his jaw jumped. I braced myself for whatever he was struggling to say.

"The dane and dana always rule as a united pair. If one dies, the other leads until it is time to pass on the mantle. You must learn what this means before you can agree."

I opened my mouth, then closed it. There was nothing for me to say. Things would never get that far.

"I will meet with you weekly," he added. "There's much to learn."

I began to curtsey, but stopped halfway down, scrambling to come up with the right protocol for goodbyes. *Is there even one?* Before I could work it out, he dipped his head and retreated from the room.

I stood there frozen, as everything Dane said hit me at once. He expected me to want a true marriage with a man I had never met—a man of brutality and hatred like the dane himself. He expected me to lead these people like he did, knowing everyone, listening to their complaints, yet accepting their tendencies to raid and conquer. Even if I were to be extracted before a wedding took place, I would have to prove my sincerity and acceptance of these people.

How could I ever do either of these things? And what about Tam, waiting for me while I—Martyrs, what *did* I expect to do when Eldreth returned?

This was nothing like the life my mother led as head of home, or the lessons I'd learned to prepare me for a marriage to a lord's son. I certainly never learned anything about leading from my father. Unless I counted his skills in leading people on. Even my mathematical and bookkeeping skills would amount to nothing here. I would've been better off studying subterfuge and hand-to-hand combat, neither of which would be practical nor *allowed* at home. On top of that, I could never condone the slaughter of the helpless towns these Rihtlonders conquered. I could barely keep a straight face when the topic arose. *Martyrs above, I'm going to need help.*

The weight of my isolation pressed in on me. Leaving the room at a half-run, I searched for my only confidant in all this accursed land. Gerta alone understood this pampered torture I'd been trapped in. Despite being the daughter of a margrave and honored by the king himself to fulfill this duty, I was just as caged as any animal—golden bars and all.

My stomach turned as I twisted the door handle to our room, which proved to be equally empty.

"Where in the blazes..."

I returned to the training rooms, throwing open the first door. Gerta stood in the middle of the small space. Kahvrah stood far too close to her, their faces inches apart. For a moment, she looked like she was caressing Gerta's cheek, but instead she tucked a strand of hair behind her ear. She stepped back and appraised her work.

"Braiding," Kahvrah said.

Gerta's usual bun had been replaced by a long plait that fell down her back. The intricate braid woven through her shiny, brunette locks was unlike any I'd seen. A soft smile played across Kahvrah's lips, but it faded when her gaze met mine. My eyes flicked between them as curiosity replaced my self-pity.

"This afternoon," Kahvrah continued, "we learn proper Riht hairstyles. The braids you can wear, and those you cannot."

"You have restricted hairstyles?" I raised an eyebrow, glancing at Gerta to exchange smirks, but she avoided my gaze. Her face was bright red.

"Not restricted, no. Braids have meanings in the Riht, just as your hairstyles do in Inra. You must learn the difference."

"Our hair doesn't mean anything."

"No? Then tell me, why have you not worn your hair up once since you arrived, as Gerta does?"

I drew back, and heat rushed to my cheeks. She was right—my hair might be pinned up, but it was never tied up in a tight bun like Gerta and the other servants'. I'd never even considered this difference in our stations, yet Kahvrah had seen it right away. *Martyrs, how had I never noticed that?*

"Indeed. Now, please show me whatever braids you already know." She motioned toward my rusty, red locks.

My assumption that braids could only have two or three strands turned out to be very wrong. Kahvrah demonstrated braids with up to seven strands, as well as several ways smaller and larger braids could be intertwined. She also demonstrated which were for children versus adults. By the end of the evening, I could see the logic behind the distinctions—with simpler braids or ones tied up in loops meant for youngsters at play.

As interested as I was in this new language of hair, it was nothing compared to Gerta. She held a hunger in her eyes with each new braid. Perhaps she planned to bring the unique styles back home. Lady's maids with special hair styling skills were highly sought after, according to Mother.

"Go on ahead," Gerta said at the end of the lesson. "I have a few questions to help me with braiding your hair. I'll be along shortly."

I nodded and left her to it. I wound through the twisting halls back to our room, where a letter sealed with my family crest lay on the small table. I froze, staring at the rose and dragon emblem while my heart raced. Then, I snatched it up, tore open the wax, and read. The letter was in plain Inraen, except for one hidden line written in our secret code—*Focus on their military strength and the layout of the city.*

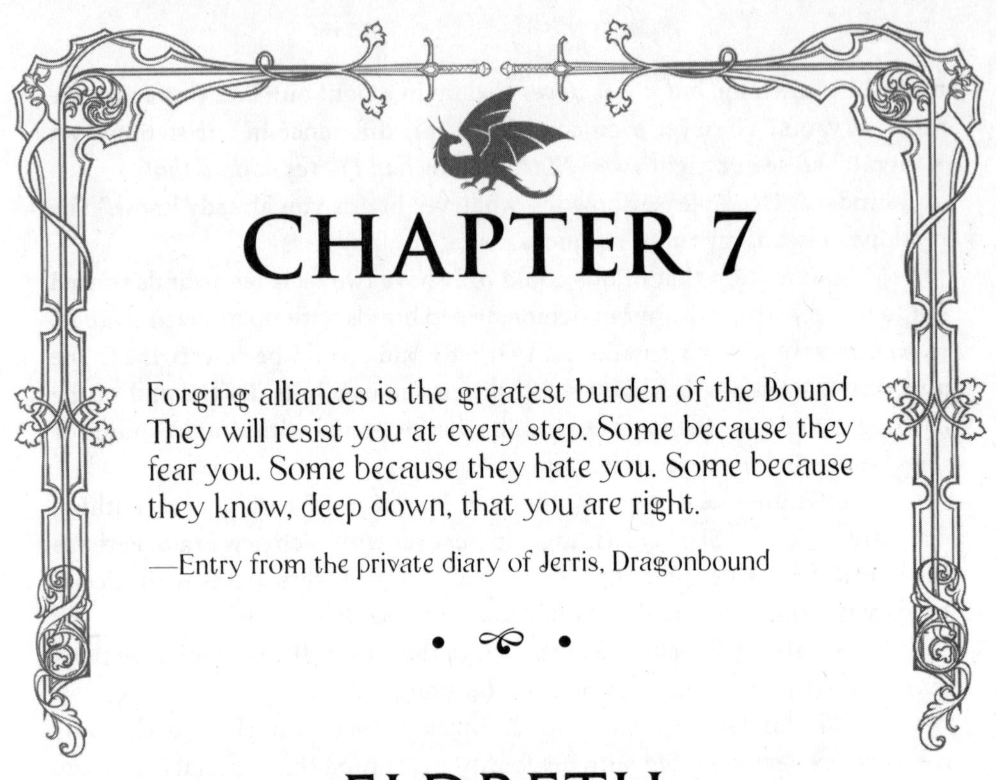

CHAPTER 7

Forging alliances is the greatest burden of the Bound. They will resist you at every step. Some because they fear you. Some because they hate you. Some because they know, deep down, that you are right.

—Entry from the private diary of Jerris, Dragonbound

ELDRETH

MIDSUMMER, JERRMON 1036

"Bring me that falcon," I commanded Sellan, who was my second in everything except height.

"Then up to the stempost?" he asked, handing over Fíon's bird and a scrap of parchment.

"Right, you are."

Thank the Great Dragon the Fíonai falcon found us when it did. Otherwise, the entire village would've been wiped out. Fíon was a small island of predominantly vineyards led by the tenacious Dana Ferngo—widowed two years prior from a similar attack—and her teenage son and daughter. No more than five hundred lived there, making them easy prey for attacks from the northern tip of Volaach. I diverted half our fleet from returning to Drakh just in time to catch the Volaachi crafts teeming with dragori, setting up to invade Fíon's southern port.

Fucking dragori.

If there was one thing I was sick of, it was fucking dragori.

Killing dragori was better than killing humans, but their sticky black blood, leathery skin, and reptilian limbs revolted me. Not to mention the smell. Up close, the half-human beasts were fucking vicious. Our best chance was to kill them from afar. Lucky for us, we had the superior archers. Dragori, with their useless, protruding wings, lacked the range of motion to master a bow.

Scribbling a note while flying across the waves made for rough lettering. I had to trust that they would be able to decipher it. I released the bird back to return to Dana Ferngo, raising my hand in a salute of safe passage. With luck, the Fíonai would have time to set sail and create a blockade while we positioned ourselves to the south, barring any Volaachi attempts at escape.

We hadn't set sail for warfare, so our ship was light on warriors and heavy on supplies. We had seven longships with twenty-five warriors apiece up against five of their carracks, each one carrying twice our number. But the skill of one Riht counted for at least three dragori. With the Fíonai warriors joining our ranks, we were certain to outmatch them.

"Yaego, what see you?" I called up to the crow's nest. Her eyes, like her scouting skills, were second to none.

"They've set sail. Three longships from Fíon, but they're undermanned," she called down.

It wasn't much, but it would have to do. I took up position at the sternpost. We were closing in fast.

"Get ready to turn starboard!" I blew three short blasts into the horn hanging from my belt. The signal echoed down the line. I gave them a minute, then shouted, "Now!" followed by a long blast of the horn. The rowers on half the ship continued while the rest of the crew rushed to the side railing, offsetting the weight to keep us from capsizing. I held my position at the steering board, guiding our turn. With winds like these, we would have one sweep, maybe two, before we were upon them.

My longship led our small fleet, and I steered us down the line as Sellan called the archers to ready. Dragori clambered on top of each other at their sterns, hissing and jeering—and presenting us easy targets.

They fell by the dozens.

I blew four short notes on my horn. "Prepare to approach!"

These travel longships weren't ideal for seafaring battle, but we could make chase, pick a few more off, and try for a fire volley on their sails. Ultimately, we'd need to board their ships and fight. Letting them reach land would be disastrous for the city.

All seven longships moved in tandem, each one turning about and closing in on our targets.

"Archers, prepare the oil," I called out.

BOOM!

Fire leapt into the sky. The central Fíonai ship lurched sideways, nearly capsizing. Its sail erupted into flames that licked up the mast.

"What the fuck was that?" Sellan shouted.

I looked up to Yaego who shook her shaved head.

BOOM!

A second longship was hit at the stempost. Wood flew in every direction. Chunks of debris riddled the water. Bodies of warriors, both dead and alive, fell into the sea.

"We've got a problem!" Yaego shouted, clambering her way down the mast. "I don't know what they are. Some sort of spiked balls that explode on impact."

"What about the water?" I asked.

"Nothing happens when they miss. When they hit, well," she gestured toward the wreckage.

"Fire!" Sellan shouted, and the tips of each archer's arrow ignited. "Release!" Our first volley soared, and most hit their marks—the billowing Volaachi sails.

"All to oars!" I called out, then turned to Yaego. "I need you up front." We made our way to Sellan, who I sent back to take over the steering board and command. What we needed now was speed, sparing only our two best archers to pick off as many as we could before our range disappeared. Yaego and I nocked arrow after arrow, letting them fly.

When our quivers emptied, we readied the ropes. We'd have to board by climbing, which was risky. Our longship pulled up, keeping pace with the outermost Volaachi craft.

BOOM!

I didn't have time to check which ship had been struck. Now was the time for action. Swinging my rope in a high arc, I sent the hook flying through the air. It embedded deep into the side of the Volaachi railing. I leapt from the longship and climbed arm over arm. The height difference between our ships was significant, but this was a skill I'd practiced since childhood. In seconds, I was over the railing, trusting that the next warrior would follow.

I drew the two short swords I kept strapped at my waist.

The first dragori, lost to bloodlust, didn't notice my approach until I had severed its wings. It turned with a screech. I spun my blade and severed its head. Black blood sprayed, and a putrid stench filled my nostrils. I didn't slow, piercing straight through the heart and stomach of the next creature in my path.

Sellan appeared at my back, and we moved forward in tandem, slashing through the beasts. I had judged the craft to hold about fifty, a quarter of which we had already slain. I hadn't counted on how many more they'd packed below. *No wonder their crafts were so sluggish.*

More dragori charged our way. My mind relaxed. I shifted from parallel strikes to singles, moving in a constant flow. My left sword came down, biting into a dragori's arm. I pivoted, and my right sword followed, opening the next one's gut. I reversed my grip and pushed forward, scoring hit after hit. With each strike, black blood oozed and sprayed, driving them into a frenzy and making it harder to take them down. They could block out all pain and fight through anything that didn't outright kill them.

But I had trained my warriors for this. The dragori were not human—there was no room for human tactics or mercy. They lashed out with monstrous, talon-tipped claws and lunged with reptilian jaws. They did not need blades when they could rip through human flesh. Sellan and I fell back, side by side, dodging their strikes and goading them into thinking they had the upper hand. Once our warriors were all on deck, we'd slice through their line, killing them in droves.

I glanced over my shoulder. A dozen Riht warriors gathered behind us. It was time to *push.*

"Fuck, Eldreth!"

I saw it, too. From somewhere at the front of their craft, a black spiky ball was lobbed over our heads. These were fist-sized, instead of the melon-sized ones they'd hurled at the Fíonai longships, but I had a feeling that didn't make them less deadly.

The creatures began to chant. "*Bahroi! Bahroi! Bahroi!*"

The first of these *bahroi* landed, blowing apart chunks of the deck. Half a dozen more flew overhead. We dodged easily enough, allowing them to blow holes in their own hull if they wanted to. But the last one they lobbed hit the side railing and found its mark. Everyone stilled when the explosive hit. I couldn't make out the face of the warrior who had just scrambled over the rope before they were taken in the blast. Chunks of flesh, sinew, and bone showered our rank.

The dragori hissed out cackling laughs, mocking us in their whispering tongue. The Riht closest to our fallen were covered in a mist of red blood and bits of matter, eyes wide with shock.

I broke the spell by cutting out the neck of the nearest dragori.

"*For Holin!*" someone yelled.

All took up the cry. Holin had two young girls at home, and I could not even bring them back a body to burn. I ignored the ache in my heart. Instead, I forced everything into my blades. I moved by instinct. With every slash, strike, cut, and stab of my swords, black blood sprayed, and death rained. I let go of Holin. I let go of Fíon. I let go of myself. I became an instrument of death, for through death, I would find a way for life to thrive.

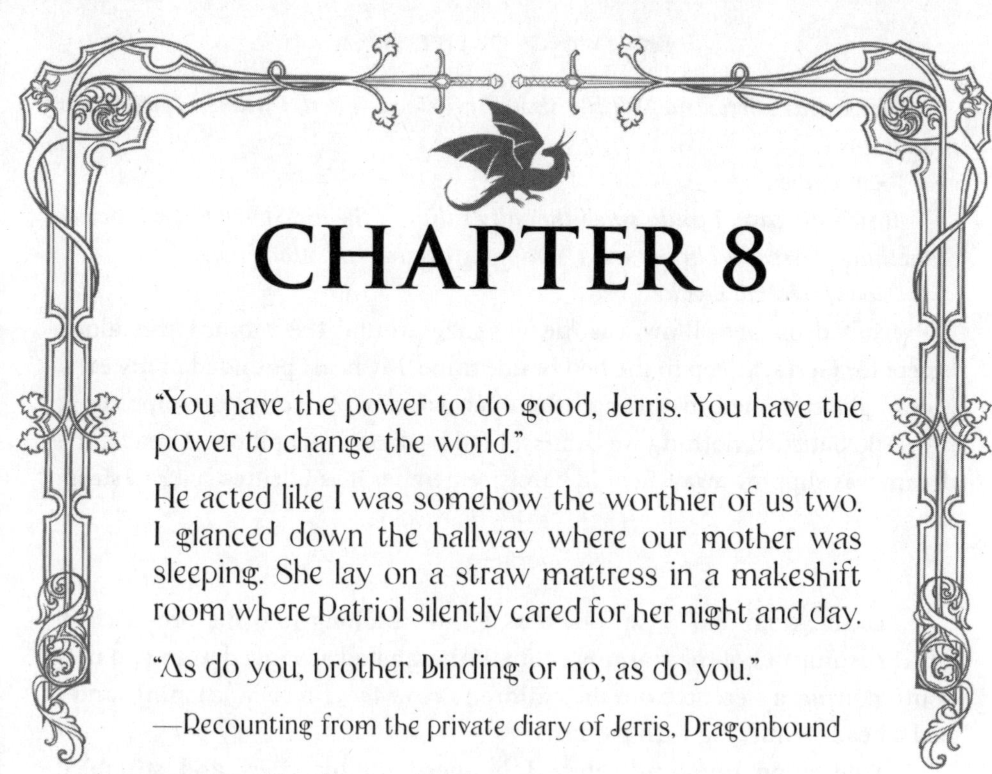

CHAPTER 8

"You have the power to do good, Jerris. You have the power to change the world."

He acted like I was somehow the worthier of us two. I glanced down the hallway where our mother was sleeping. She lay on a straw mattress in a makeshift room where Patriol silently cared for her night and day.

"As do you, brother. Binding or no, as do you."

—Recounting from the private diary of Jerris, Dragonbound

• ❧ •

SERAE

MIDSUMMER, JERRMON 1036

THE MOON SHONE bright overhead. I sat in the rich soil of the forest. It was night, and I was alone, but I felt no fear—only peace.

A breeze whipped through the trees, and the leaves chattered. They crooned and cried as their branches creaked. It was a noisy sort of music that tempered the quiet stillness of the night sky. I could sit here for hours. So, I did.

"I see you," said a voice.

I turned my head. There was only the night.

"I see you, and I will know you."

I did not reply because I did not have the words.

"Come find me. The time for sleeping has nearly passed."

Her words stirred me. With a thought, I stood. Then, I walked toward the mountains.

"Remember."

Inside the cave, I could smell the salty sulfur of the air. Sharp but not acrid. Something blessed hid in the scent, wrapping around me, filling me.

"Soon, we shall awake."

I jolted off my pillow, casting my gaze around the room. I was alone except for Gerta, asleep in the bed beside mine. My heart pounded in my ears. Moonlight streamed in through the open window, the crisp air nipping at my neck. Satisfied nothing was amiss, I fell back onto my pillow. Already, the dream was slipping away. I could barely remember it as I drifted back to sleep.

"Dane Auldren," I squeaked as I ran headlong into his broad chest while rushing out of the training room. Kahvrah had advanced us to two new youth *dowsae*, a step up from the children's *dowsae* we'd been learning, and I had a head swimming with patterns.

Dane stood unmoved while I bounced off his chest and stumbled backward. One of his long arms shot out and hooked my elbow just before I fell.

"Thank you, I mean—I'm so sorry, I mean—" I sighed and righted myself. My glasses had gone askew—something Kahvrah now loved to point out during drills. I checked my pocket to make sure my little journal was still there. "My apologies, Sire."

He snickered.

"Do we have a lesson today?" Dane's were the most enlightening, and I had filled half my journal with the things he'd taught me. Most of it was too complex to encode, so only a few details about their ships and seafaring vessels made it into my letters. But I had pages of diagrams, construction methods, and statistics on resistance.

"No, I came to tell you that Eldreth is delayed. He will not return this week as originally planned."

"This—*this* week? You never said he'd—" I narrowed my eyes at him. "When exactly will he return?"

"Next week at best. Or else, the week after. Don't worry, lass, he'll be home soon."

"And am I to actually meet him then?" I tried to keep the bitterness from my voice and failed. I leaned against the wall and rubbed my forehead.

Dane laughed. "I like when you're full of spirit. This will help for your First Sun."

"My what?"

"Your first morning as a Riht, after you pledge yourself to the clan during your Sun Trial."

Fuck. My next trial. I put my hand out on the wall behind me for support. Kahvrah had barely discussed it during *dowsae* training. For Rihtlonders, it marks the passage from childhood to adulthood. For me, it would decide whether they accepted or rejected me as a member of the Riht. I hadn't expected it to arrive so soon.

"Has Kahvrah not—"

"This week, Dane." Kahvrah appeared at his side, and I jumped. His hulking form had blocked her approach from view. "Serae has nearly mastered the youth *dowsae*. The sun *dowsa* is next."

Dane nodded. "I'll not interfere with your method." He nodded again and left.

THE SUN *DOWSA* was nothing like the others we had learned. All *dowsae* involved controlled movement, balance, and flexibility, but the sun *dowsa* used snapping muscles, quick jabs, and far too many kicks.

"Tie up your skirt," Kahvrah barked before beginning the lesson the following day. When I failed the correct tucking motions on the first try, she kicked out, hooking her foot into the loose fold and pulling me off balance.

I stumbled, my glasses slipping right off my nose. I caught them just before they hit the ground.

"This is why it must be right. Your skirt cannot be your weakness, only your aid." She knelt and helped me through the motions of retying them correctly.

We repeated the complex motions for hours on end. My muscles ached, yet we continued. Gerta and I had drained the entire pitcher in the corner, and still, we practiced. It was only when Gerta swayed on her feet that Kahvrah called us to a halt. She waved us across the hallway toward what I had affectionately dubbed the Relaxation Room. It was probably my favorite room in the whole keep. We plopped down on pillows that dotted the floor. I pulled off my boots and dug my toes into the plush rug. Tea was already set at the low floor table.

I studied the intricate tapestries lining the walls. Each was woven, not stitched, a skill entirely foreign to me. Tapestries just as detailed hung throughout the keep—in the rooms, the corridors, and the halls. The ones here depicted a legend of the Great Dragon, though I hadn't yet riddled out the whole story.

"The sun *dowsa*," Kahvrah began, breaking me from my thoughts, "is unlike the simple *dowsae* you have learned. It is meant to be done with a partner. Therefore, you must be perfect. If you are not perfect, you will be hurt. Maybe your partner too, but most likely just you. If your skirt is not tied up correctly, or if you are distracted in any way, it will be your downfall."

I cast aside my blue skirts and propped my feet on a nearby pillow. "Point taken. Enough with the doom and gloom." I turned back to the walls.

Gerta chortled, but Kahvrah just kept eyeing me. *Why were all Rihtlonders so sufferingly unreadable?*

"You may look," she said.

"Sorry?"

"No need for apologies. Go and look." She waved a hand at the walls.

Despite feeling like a child caught ogling the sweets table, I hopped up and studied the nearest tapestry.

"I suspected as much," Kahvrah added, and though her self-satisfied grin was aimed at the back of my head, I could still hear it in her voice. "Do you have an interest in weaving?"

"No." I shook my head. "I mean, yes, I'd love to learn about it, but I'm more interested in the story here."

"This is not a story. This is the truth of our past. It begins here—" She stood and walked to the far corner of the room, where four dragons swirled around a glowing orb at the tapestry's center. I trailed her. "—with all seven dragons working together to create Jaeda. The dragons of the four elements began first. The Earth Dragon and Water Dragon shaped the stones and seas. Then, the Fire Dragon"—she indicated the red dragon of the group—"built the hot lava that lives beneath the surface, while the white Air Dragon created the clouds and winds with its breath.

"Then came the Great Dragon, who breathed life across all of Jaeda." She moved to the next tapestry, which depicted a massive green dragon flying over a rocky expanse, leaving lush greenery in her wake. "Plants of all types sprouted from the deep soil. The dragons looked to each other, and in their unique genius, they conceived of all the animals that would fill their young world. The Great Dragon worked with her twin, the Spirit Dragon, to create these new forms of life." The next tapestry on the wall showed the green alongside a smaller purple dragon mixing their fiery breaths over Jaeda. "The world teemed with life, which thrived in its every corner. But there was no balance."

Kahvrah walked to the third wall, where a shroud of black and gray shadowed the tapestry. "The Dragon of Death took up his calling. When the lives of all creatures were well spent, he collected them into his fold. As time passed and humanity grew in wisdom and number, the Seven knew it was time for them to rest. Each dragon chose a champion, whose lifeforce they bound to their own." The next tapestry showed seven dragon-like figures, each a different color, holding hands. She paused before moving to the last wall and final tapestry. "There was peace for a time, until humanity descended into greed. The Dragonbound became too powerful and took control of the world, dividing it into factions. The Dragons, angry by our failure to honor their great gifts, withdrew their bindings and let the Dragonbound fall."

With a great sigh, Kahvrah returned to her cushion beside Gerta. "One day, it is said, when humanity has proven itself worthy again, the Dragonbound will return."

I scrutinized the tapestries, committing all I could to memory. Father had not asked for information about their beliefs, but something told me this was critical to know.

"After you pass your Sun Trial, I will take you to a weaver. That is to say"—Kahvrah held up a finger—"*if* you pass."

The truth was, as much as I hated the endless training, confusing language, and frustrating confinement, I wanted to pass this trial. I hated failure, even over something as insane as trying to belong in a place I couldn't wait to escape. I had nothing to prove to them, but perhaps I still had something to prove to myself.

"What happens if I fail?"

"You cannot live in Drakh or be betrothed to our future high dane if you are not one of the Riht."

"I'll be sent home?"

She shrugged. "Do not fail, and we will not have to find out."

I sucked in a breath, fear lancing through me. "I could be killed?" I had always known these people were brutal. Before coming here, I had worried for my safety. But until this moment, my mortality had never felt so real.

Kahvrah's lips pressed into a thin line. Her eyes tracked over my face, searching for what I couldn't tell. At length, she rose to her feet. "Come, let us continue."

We practiced the sun *dowsa* for the remainder of the afternoon. The following morning, we practiced again. And before lunch. And after. I lost all sense of time, as well as the feeling in my arms and legs. For more than a week, I lived, breathed, and ate nothing but sun *dowsa.* We only rested when I was reciting the vows I would pledge during the Sun Trial ceremony.

The night before my trial, I was a bundle of nerves. Gerta helped me dress for bed with extra care, even though I could long since dress and undress myself. Then, she pulled a tiny box from a hidden pouch in her pocket, revealing a small sweet. It was coated in chocolate and reminded me of home.

"I asked the kitchens to make it specially for you."

"Thank you," I whispered. "You are a treasure I don't deserve."

Gerta snorted.

"I was talking to the chocolate."

She swatted at me, but I dodged and stuffed the entire thing in my mouth.

When I finally tucked into bed, I rolled to my side, facing the wall. While my thoughts swirled and swirled, they dutifully avoided tomorrow. Confidence was the only thing that could settle my nerves, yet it was the one thing I lacked.

"Just breathe, keep your footing, and for all the Martyrs' blood, make sure you've tied your skirt correctly." Gerta giggled, but I bent and triple-checked the ties of my skirt. Then, I removed the journal from my pocket and tucked it beneath my mattress.

A knock sounded at the door. "Five minutes," the gravelly voice of Dane's guard called from outside.

I sucked in a breath as tension descended over me.

Gerta leaned in and straightened my glasses. "These must be a nuisance to practice in."

"You don't know the half of it," I deadpanned.

We walked to our usual training room, our gravelly guard trailing behind and offering me a small smile as we awaited my formal summons. The closed door mocked me. I wanted nothing more than for it to open, yet I dreaded the moment that it might. Gerta stood at my side—her words of comfort expired.

I should be productive. Prepare.

I tried to set my feet, placing one foot behind the other, but I teetered and lost my balance. The movements of the sun *dowsa,* which had been drilled into me tirelessly for days, did not appear in my mind's eye. My short life, my useless successes back home, and the entirety of my Inraen knowledge could not help me here. In Rihtlond, I would only ever be a failure. Or dead.

Unless I pass this trial.

But no, that wasn't my true purpose here. The thought twisted inside me. The reminder of my task, a cuckoo in a robin's nest, made my stomach clench. Nausea crept up my throat, and my mouth pooled with saliva. Unable to stop the heaves that assaulted me, I ran to the corner to retch. Bile and the small bit of food I ate splattered over the rug, barely missing my boots. That was when the door opened—and there stood Kahvrah, a frown etched into her face. Facing this fear, the consequences of failure, wasn't the worst part. It was having these unreadable strangers watch. *Would they be there at my death, too?*

So be it.

I wiped my mouth on the back of my sleeve, squared my shoulders, and marched out the door. We passed through familiar twisting corridors then turned into one lined with tapestries of warriors in single combat. At some point, we descended to a lower level, a damp chill permeating the air, and followed a long torchlit passage.

Kahvrah answered my unspoken question. "This leads to the pavilion, where most ceremonies are held."

I nodded, my useless stomach tightening again at the thought of how many Rihtlonders would be watching. I followed Kahvrah up another flight of stairs and through a narrow hall ending in a blur of white light.

Sunshine engulfed me as I emerged, waiting several heartbeats for my eyes to adjust. I stood at the entrance to a vast arena, not some small pavilion as I had imagined. Tiers of seating ascended on all sides, each packed with wooden benches, the rows just above ground level interspersed with low platforms. Kahvrah led us up to the nearest one. Gerta gripped my arm and gestured across the way. Her lips moved, but I couldn't make out her words over the hum of the crowd. I had no idea how many people the arena housed. *Surely thousands.*

Following Gerta's gaze, I found what caught her attention. Dane Auldren stood on a platform to our left, speaking with several men and women. I looked away, unable to meet his eye, and right to a familiar, piercing gaze. I recognized the grim set of his jaw as much as his unfairly handsome face—the general from the tent. There was no mistaking him. In the sunlight, I could see his coppery hair tied up in a knot. It was no trick of the light. Every Rihtlonder I had met was blond. Varying shades, yes, but all blond. Back home, hair color ranged from blond to brown to black, but never red. Aside from myself—and now this general. Shock flooded me, numbing my limbs and weighing me down.

"Who is that man?" I asked Kahvrah, desperation lacing my voice.

She smirked. "Well spotted. He has just returned from across the sea. That is our—"

Drumming drowned out Kahvrah's words. It came from every platform in the arena, and it was deafening. The frantic rhythm radiated through my chest. I could feel it in my teeth. Then, as swiftly as it began, it crashed to a halt. Every eye in the arena turned toward Dane. He raised his hands to speak. The general, or whoever he was, with his intense glare and perfect jawline, had gone. The platform was empty now, save for the dane himself, his chair, and a vacant chair likely meant for his absent heir at its side.

Dane spoke, and his voice boomed through the stadium. I tried not to gape at the sheer volume of it. Rihtlondish words flitted past me, until Kahvrah leaned in and hissed in my ear.

"Today, we gather to accept a new fledgling into our wing," she translated. "She will stand before us and ask that we take her into our fold, that we look to her as an equal, and that she may wear the mantle of the Riht as do we all." Dane paused as murmurs swelled from the crowd. Kahvrah waited in silence. When he resumed, she continued in tandem. "Being a foreigner, this is an action none should approach lightly. I ask you, brothers and sisters, to bear witness to this Sun Trial."

Kahvrah stepped away and spoke, not to me, but to the dane, in unison with everyone around us. Their voices resonated and clashed louder than the drums, jarring my senses. After the single, synchronized sentence, the hush returned.

I gaped at Kahvrah.

She looked me up and down. "It was a pledge to bear witness. Do you not do this in your homeland?"

"Do what?"

"Speak as one voice."

I shook my head slowly.

"Bring forth the challenger." Dane addressed the crowd, this time speaking in Mayoran.

Challenger. My stomach twisted, bile climbing up my throat. *Not again.* I tried to catch Kahvrah's eye, but she grabbed my wrist and dragged me down a small, covered staircase that led straight to the arena floor. Just before we stepped out of the archway, she pulled me to a stop. A woman was speaking

Rihtlondish, and the people responded with deafening cheers. From the archway, I couldn't see who awaited me, but I had a terrible feeling I already knew.

Kahvrah moved before me, taking up my view and holding my gaze. Her eyes were so intense, they cut through my panic. "Do exactly as we practiced when I opposed you," she commanded. "Do not misstep. Do not let your nerves take you. Breathe. If you fall, stay down until she has stepped away. Do not get up before she steps away. Is this clear?"

"Get up? What— I don't— Shouldn't we have practiced that?"

"You're ready."

Dane spoke again. "Come forth, attestant."

"Stay until I call you," Kahvrah hissed. She stepped out to the center, leaving me behind and alone. I craned my neck as far out as I dared while trying to stay hidden beneath the arch. Dane's platform was out of view, but I could make out Kahvrah's back, as well as the back of another tall woman with a long platinum braid. My heart sank.

"Dane, I stand before you, attesting the loyalty of Serae of Cavendaffe."

"Does Serae of Cavendaffe seek acceptance into the Riht?"

"She does."

"Does she wake each day with the light of truth shining upon her as it does upon the Riht?"

"She does."

"When she rises each day, will she stand with honor before the Riht?"

"She will."

"Let her stand for herself!"

At the dane's proclamation, the crowd erupted into cheers again. Hands clapped. Feet stomped. The ground shook, and for a wild moment, I thought the arena might collapse in on itself. Then, just as before, the cheering cut off in one swift instant, leaving a hollow echo in my ears.

"Come forth, Serae of Cavendaffe," Kahvrah proclaimed.

I stepped out to absolute silence. I could hear my footfalls on the soft earth. Just as easily, I could hear the shuffling in the stands nearest me as spectators shifted in their seats to get a better look at the Inraen freak.

Thankfully, the next part we had prepared for. I moved to Kahvrah's side and fixed my gaze on Dane, breathing deeply and remaining silent.

Dane's lip quirked as he let the moment stretch.

At last, he called out, "Serae, do you come before us in the name of truth?"

"I do."

"Have you prepared your body and mind in the ways of the Riht?"

"I have."

"Speak your truths."

This was the defining moment. I knew when I pledged these next words, in the eyes of the Riht, there was no turning back. My presence in their city, among their people, meant nothing before now. A part of me wondered if my father had prepared for how seriously they took this oath. I didn't want to think about what they did to traitors.

"High Dane Auldren, people of the Riht, I stand before you honoring my past as I step away from it. Tomorrow and every day of my life to follow, I will devote myself as a member of the Riht—holding the strength of one as the strength of all, the wisdom of one as the wisdom of many, and the pain of one as the pain of any. I pledge these words under the high sun for all to see their truth." My heart constricted, not knowing whether I meant it.

Dane raised both hands and called out, *"May your actions follow!"*

By some Jaedan miracle, the crowd began to cheer. They had accepted my pledge. But that was the easy part. Next came the actual trial. Despite our constant practice and Kahvrah's approval, my nerves jittered. But, a glimmer of hope shone through. The crowd continued cheering—*for me.* I turned to Kahvrah, allowing a slight smile to creep over my face. Kahvrah, however, was grim as she turned and walked several paces away, giving me and the challenger a wide berth. She nodded once, a sharp gesture meant for me. My signal to fall into stance and wait for the order to begin.

I closed my eyes, drew a breath, counted to three, and on my next exhale, I allowed my body to move—one foot behind the other, arms at the ready, core tight. It came to me easily now, thank the Creator. I paused at the end of my exhale, let my face relax, and opened my eyes with my next breath.

I stared straight into the hateful face of my challenger.

My body echoed with her last gift of cracked ribs and a shattered nose. I still didn't know the woman's name, but I knew her sneer all too well. Her mocking, hissing voice invaded my mind. *Pathetic. Weak. Ignorant.* The words did not need to be spoken again—they were written plainly on her face. She stood in a matching stance, openly appraising me. Her sneer morphed into a sharp, dark smile.

I was going to die.

My breath hitched, and my muscles clenched. Without moving, I broke into a full-body sweat.

"Begin," Kahvrah commanded, quiet and steady.

I hesitated. The first movement was mine. The challenger's were meant to be a complement to my own, provided that *I* got it right to begin with.

"Begin," Kahvrah repeated in the exact same tone.

My challenger snickered.

I breathed and began to move. I swept each of my limbs in clear, wide arcs. A half second later, the challenger did the same. These first movements established our distance and opened the dance. I lunged in with both fists, then retreated as the challenger mirrored. I spun and kicked forward, angling left, and the challenger's foot flew past me on my right. The dance continued, testing our accuracy and fluidity. Then, the moment of stillness came—the eye of the storm, as I thought of it. I collected my arms together, almost in prayer, for five blissful heartbeats.

The moment ended with a series of jabs, arcing punches, and rolling turns. I was a flurry of movement. Sweat dripped down my brow, but I clung to my inner calm. I kept my mind in a loose, unfocused state, and I ignored the surrounding crowd, made easy by the fact that they were pin-drop silent. My body moved entirely on muscle memory.

In a rare moment of clarity, I saw the end approaching, and I smiled. Success was in sight, mere seconds away. *I had done it!*

The finale of kicks began, and I braced myself on my dominant leg while initiating the first of several triple-kick combos. Despite the speed of each movement, I was flooded with peace. My eyes drifted to my opponent, as they always did in practice, searching for that familiar smirk Kahvrah always gave when the final bow was nearing.

But there was no smile. My challenger's face was screwed up in concentration, or perhaps anger, or more likely, disgust. I jumped, then ducked low for a sweeping kick. A moment out of sync, the challenger jumped to avoid my leg, then mirrored the low kick. I led the next movement, spinning to the side to create room, but something was off. The challenger should have been to my left, but instead, she was right before me. Had I mistimed my jump? Or missed a step, or maybe misjudged the turn?

It didn't matter. My challenger's kick swept me off my feet. I crashed down hard onto my back.

Stay down, said a voice in my head, but instinct had long since taken over. I popped my head up to see where I'd landed. My challenger kicked out again, and her shin collided with the side of my head. Pain exploded through my jaw, temple, and nose. A sickening crunch split my skull, and I collapsed flat on the ground. Red flooded my vision. I clung to the edge of consciousness.

Dane yelled something that may have been, "Enough!"

Someone was above me. Through the red, I saw a pair of eyes dark with fear. *Fear of what?* "I told you to stay down," a voice hissed.

I've never been a good listener, I tried to say, but the words wouldn't leave my mouth as the red turned to black.

CHAPTER 9

It was not the binding that hurt. It was the power. It burned through me, changing the very makeup of my soul. For several weeks, I stayed with her, allowing our binding to strengthen.

Not that I could have left if I wanted to.

"The pain will not last," she spoke into my mind. "It is the price of my gift, as it was for those who came before you, and as it will be for all who follow."

"There were others?" I asked.

"No one can live forever, Small One."

—Recounting from the private diary of Jerris, Dragonbound

SERAE

MIDSUMMER, JERRMON 1036

"Is THIS YOUR fourteenth birthday?"

"It's my sixteenth, as you very well know. Just give me a minute."

I eyed the stunning mare. Copper, as I'd named her, gave me a sidelong glance. I stroked between her eyes, cooing at my red beauty.

"Quit being a child and mount."

I rounded on my brother, poking him in the chest. "If anyone is being a child here, it's you."

Bale gasped, grabbing his chest in mock injury. "I, dear sister, am passing on my hard-won wisdom. From the generosity in my heart, I might add."

I rolled my eyes.

Three days before our shared birthday, Bale had come trotting back from school on a traveling mare, Copper lashed alongside. Our birthday coincided with Evenstone Academy's semester break. We were lucky we still got to celebrate together, even after he was shipped off to school. Unluckily, this gift came with the caveat that I learn riding skills not usually taught to girls. I had already been forced through lessons on how to interact with a horse and put them at ease, how to check and clean their shoes, how to groom and brush them, and, of course, how to saddle and unsaddle on my own. This was all without ever getting on the horse, hence this day's lesson of mounting without a block.

We'd readied our horses and led them to the empty stable yard. A couple of stable hands were busy mucking the now-vacant stalls, but we were otherwise alone. Copper nudged at my side as I checked the girth for the third time.

"Don't you start on me too," I said in an easy tone. We were still getting used to one another. "He may have brought you here, but I'm the one who gives you the best treats. What sort of a ride do you want for today?" I continued, focusing less on the words and more on keeping a steady stream going. "Something leisurely? A nice, brisk trot? Or, perhaps it's a day for you to run."

"Quit stalling and get up there," Bale interrupted.

"Don't mind him—he's just a grumpy old man."

A late summer breeze filtered through the stable yard. Copper and I lifted our heads, allowing the wind to ruffle our manes and cool our necks. The trees rustled around us, full of leaves that would not fall for another month. It was unseasonably warm for the month of Jerrmon, and my new equine companion seemed to agree.

"One day, you'll thank me." Bale flipped his mop of black hair out of his face, but it fell right back. "The easiest way to travel in a hurry is on horseback, but you have to know horses, and what you're getting yourself into. My training alone is going to save your ass one day. Now, get up."

"*You're* an ass," I grumbled, but reached for the pommel just the same. I'd ridden before—I just wasn't a very strong rider, and I certainly wasn't used to hoisting my own weight without help.

Bale sighed. "It's easier than it seems." His tone softened as he stepped behind me, gripping my waist. "You've got the lead. Copper's trained to stay for you. You have the strength between your arms and your mounting leg to lift your body. It's just an unusual position."

"Especially in a skirt."

"I'll take your word for it. Grip the pommel—good—and the back of the saddle with your other hand if that helps. Now, all at once, like you're taking a giant step." Bale's grip on my waist tightened, but he didn't lift me. As always, he was there to steady me, catch me if I needed it, but never take away my choice. It took three tries to figure out how to swing my leg over, but soon enough, I was up in the saddle, grinning down at him. My skirts were everywhere, half pinned under me in ways that bunched and pulled and entirely covered the pommel, but I was up.

"See? You're a natural." Bale's smile was brilliant. He mounted his horse with practiced ease. "Now, we ride!"

I turned Copper and trotted out of the stable yard and toward the forest path.

"Get up," a voice called from behind me.

"I am up!" I called back to Bale. "Don't be so slow. Let's go!"

"Get up," the voice called again, more insistent.

I turned in my seat. Bale was gone. The stables were gone. Behind me loomed a mountain cave that tickled the back of my mind. Had I seen it before?

"Get up, sleeping one."

"Who are you?"

"It's time. Awake."

I opened my eyes. Bright light flooded my vision, then it was blocked by Kahvrah's face. Her lips were moving, but her voice was muffled. Then the pain came crashing down. My head was splitting into pieces.

"You're awake." Kahvrah's words took shape.

"Maybe," I replied, a little relieved that I could form words despite the throbbing. "Did I pass out?"

"Yes."

"How long was I out?"

"Less than one day."

"What happened?"

"A kick to the head," she said matter-of-factly.

A door creaked nearby, then another familiar face was before me.

"Milady, thank the Creator!" Gerta cried with bloodshot eyes, deep purple shadows beneath them. "I was afraid you'd never wake."

"You'd never be that lucky." I tried to smirk, but pain shot through my temple and across my skull. I adjusted my nightdress and settled for a groan.

Nightdress? My eyes popped open. I'd been changed while unconscious. But my journal—where had I left my journal?

"Stay still," Kahvrah commanded. "I will call for the healer."

The healer, it turned out, was partly to blame for my time unconscious. Something about brain swelling and a sleeping tincture. I searched my memories—nothing after the trial. Unease crept through me. Was there something I needed to remember?

The ancient, matronly woman they called Marr looked into my eyes, massaged my skull, prodded down my spine, and gave me a bitter remedy to drink that dulled the throbbing within minutes.

Aside from bruised pride, a bruised face, and a suspicious twinge along my cheek, there wasn't much wrong with me. Marr set up a few more bottles of the same pain remedy, then proclaimed that I was still concussed and needed rest.

"Don't mess with that cheek." She waggled a crooked finger at me and left.

Kahvrah and Gerta followed with promises to check on me in a few hours. Once I was alone, I thrust my hand beneath the mattress. My fingers hit something hard, and relief flooded me. My journal was safe and untouched—thank the Creator for my foresight. I shuddered at the thought of how close I had come to being discovered.

Over the next three days, I rested. That was it. Between naps, I ate. After the first day, I was cleared for stretching and basic *dowsae*. No lessons, no tasks, no responsibilities—just pleasant, peaceful rest. I hated it. To combat my *extreme* boredom, I recited all the Rihtish words I knew. Then, the cities Dane taught me, as well as the names of the rivers, bays, and islands. I had no map for reference, but I copied out the names as closely as I could in the Inraen script and handed them to Gerta. I don't know what stopped me, but I did not include information about my Sun Trial.

By the second day, Gerta was more restless than I was, flitting in and out of the room every hour. That day marked the completion of Gerta's fourth week in Rihtlond. No word had come from my father or Dane about her imminent return. For distraction, she was only too happy to post my latest letter and join me in my practice of Rihtish.

I was spared from discussing my performance in the Sun Trial. For those brief few days, I neither knew nor cared if being knocked out counted as failing. If a noose or a chopping block waited around the corner. Martyrs, how did the Riht even execute their prisoners? The thought made the edges of my vision blur. I did my best to block it all out. Surely, if I was meant to die, there would be no point in healing me first. *Right?*

On the third afternoon, we wandered with Kahvrah through the upper city.

"Don't be so sour," Gerta chided. "A walk outside will do us good. We could buy some flowers or sweets. You'd like that."

I hummed in acknowledgment. I'd woken with a melancholy that I hadn't managed to shake.

"Walking is good for the body and mind," added Kahvrah.

"And another day off lessons," Gerta teased in Inraen, glancing sidelong at Kahvrah. "That's nice, too."

"I suppose," I replied in my mother tongue, which we'd barely used since our departure from the manor.

"You're missing someone today, aren't you?"

Bale. "I miss him every day."

Gerta slipped her arm into mine, and we continued walking. "It's hard to let go of the past, but you'll meet your betrothed soon enough. In time, he will just be a distant memory from your youth."

That swallowing guilt pressed in again, suffocating me. "Oh, you mean Tam." The truth was, I worried more about meeting my *false* betrothed than I did about being separated from my *actual* one. What kind of a person was I?

"I miss Bale too," she whispered, squeezing my arm.

"You mean to exclude me," Kahvrah said in Mayoran.

"Now you know how it feels," I retorted, switching back to the common tongue.

Kahvrah frowned at me, but Gerta, as always, came to the rescue. "It was just a sensitive subject, that's all." At Kahvrah's continued frown, she added, "A recent loss."

Kahvrah halted us. "Life and loss must always be in balance. We all know this, but it does not change the way it hits our hearts. There is no shame in sorrow. Come, let us go this way."

We turned down the first market street we had ever visited. People still stared, though I liked to imagine there were fewer with open hostility. My thoughts melted away when we turned a corner and stopped at a stand full of *books.* After a quick conversation in Rihtish, Kahvrah handed me a small hardbound book painted across the cover with leaves.

"Read this. When you finish, bring it back here, and she will give you another."

I flipped open the cover. It was a children's story, but I could already read most of the words. It was a simple story about a little green dragon who turned away from her dragon friends to help a small village that would not survive the winter without her gifts. I grinned.

THAT NIGHT, I dreamt of sweet grass as blue as the night sky. I spread great leathery wings and soared through the pink clouds with a red sun at my back. A lovely turquoise pool with golden fish called to me from below, and I made my descent. They chattered their small wants and dreams in my ears, and I swatted them away with my great, clawed feet. I drank my fill of the cool water, then swam to the shallows, finding a watery bed to continue my rest.

On the fourth day after my Sun Trial, Kahvrah appeared at my door holding a new set of clothes.

"Come, we must dress you," she said.

Dread flooded me. Since that first day, I had dressed each morning myself. "For what?"

"Your First Sun."

The relief hit so hard, I nearly toppled over. My First Sun—my first day as a Riht. They weren't going to kill me. Yet. But did that mean I'd passed the Sun Trial? Neither Kahvrah nor Dane had been explicit about what would happen during the First Sun, despite the many times I tried to ask. I had the sinking feeling the worst was yet to come. My arms shook as she handed over the bundle of clothes.

"So the Sun Trial is over?"

"It is."

"But then—"

"No more questions. Dane will explain."

The outfit consisted of an elaborate overdress, an underdress with half sleeves, and soft leggings—all in pale yellow. They melted around my skin like sunlight. It was the first thing I'd worn here that I truly loved.

Kahvrah then braided my hair and oiled my boots. When the process was complete, I frowned. Yellow was not a common color in this city of earthy neutrals and muted tones. It was also not lost on me that this particular shade of yellow mirrored the yellow rose insignia from the Cavendaffe crest. A chilling thought struck me—I was being sent home after all.

"If you have jewels, you may wear them."

I looked from Kahvrah to Gerta at a loss. Nothing from my previous life was welcome here. In fact, I had not seen a single Riht—man or woman—adorned with jewels, outside of the eyes on the dragon clips some wore in their braids or the occasional ring or pendant. But surely they wouldn't put me in jewels and a stunning new dress to face an executioner, would they?

Gerta crossed the room with eyes afire and thunderous footsteps, returning with a gold and peridot necklace. The gem was cut into a teardrop, the embodiment of joy and sorrow. This piece was one-half of a set, the other a single matching hair comb, which Gerta secured behind my left ear. Even I had to admit, the result was simple and striking.

"Head up," Gerta whispered, and I snapped my eyes forward from where they had slid to the ground. "Show them nothing."

I nodded, questions and fears warring within me. If Gerta knew more, she offered no explanation.

"It is time," Kahvrah announced.

"Time for what?" I tried.

She only pursed her lips. "Come."

I fell into step beside Kahvrah, Gerta close behind, and we marched swiftly out of the keep. We did not stop until we reached the castle wall, where Dane waited for us, but he was not alone. A dozen people were gathered just inside the towering portcullis that led to the lower city. Each person wore a stoic, expressionless mask.

"Lively crowd," I murmured to Gerta.

"Daughter Serae," Dane Auldren hailed, his voice carrying the same formality as during the trial. "Today, we present you to the Riht." He gestured across the moat where people lined the street, all watching me.

He motioned me toward a woman holding the reins of a regal blond mare. The creature watched our group approach, but she did not shy.

"Her name is Kappa. She'll let you ride her," Dane added more quietly. There was no taunt in his voice.

"She's magnificent," I replied.

"That she is. Let's go."

"Where are we going, Dane?"

"Around Drakh. You're to be presented to the people for judgment."

"Judgment of my trial?" I asked, trying to keep my brow from crinkling. I didn't understand any of this. Had I passed my Sun Trial or not? Was this judgment—the First Sun—a decider of whether I lived or died in Drakh?

Dane chuckled, perhaps knowing where my mind had gone. "You might say that."

I may not have been accustomed to riding long journeys, but I knew my way around a horse. As we approached, I stayed within Kappa's line of sight and steadily cooed her praises. It was easy to do, considering what a striking figure the mare cut. I tried not to think of my sweet Copper back home.

"What a strong, beautiful lady you are. Your mane is like silk made of sunlight. Do you like the sun, my girl? Would you like to ride in the sun today?"

The woman holding the horse's reins reached out and handed me a clump of crunchy oats. I offered it flat-palmed to Kappa, whose lips grabbed at the treat.

"Would it be all right if I rode with you today?" I continued. "Maybe if I'm atop someone as grand as you, the judgment will be a little less harsh. What do you say, will you help me?"

Kappa nudged me, which I took as assent. I moved to the saddle. Thank the Creator I had learned how to mount without a block.

Up in the saddle, I reached out for the reins, but instead, they were handed over to Dane.

He tutted. "Today, Daughter, I lead."

Thus, our procession began. We set off at a meandering pace, Kappa's languid gait jostling me back and forth. Ahead was only Dane. Behind me walked the same two guards who followed him everywhere, whose names I was determined to learn one day. They flanked the piercing-eyed general, another name I lacked, whose angry stare followed my every move. Behind the trio of men were Gerta and Kahvrah, alongside Bracht. Behind them walked two couples, each pair arm-in-arm, whom I had seen often around Dane but never formally met.

Calling upon my years of Mother's training, I relaxed my brow forcefully, then painted a placid smile on my face.

Walking through Drakh was an experience altogether. We began at the first ring of the lower city that surrounded the castle walls. The last time I'd even glimpsed beyond the wall was on the day we arrived. This time, there was no interaction between Dane and the people. Some nodded as we passed, but most just openly stared. I was an exhibit—meant for them to judge.

I had never felt more on trial, or more guilty, than in that moment. Parading through the city, an imposter on horseback, shining in the colors of my betraying house. *Perhaps this was the real Sun Trial.*

We rounded a corner and entered the next ring of the city. That was when the jeering started.

"Can you trust her on horseback, Dane, or will she fall off there as well?"

"Weak Inraen women don't belong in the Riht!"

They spoke in Mayoran to ensure I understood.

"Takes more than beauty to be our dana!"

I snorted, barely suppressing a laugh. *A beauty?* I recalled the two times I had been called that since arriving in this wet, dark city, and both had been by Gerta.

"Look at her face—as sour as her *dowsae*," spat a voice in the crowd.

I sighed inwardly. Had Gerta not warned me to give nothing away?

"And meek, too. How is she going to—"

"Enough!"

The voice came from behind me. I turned and saw Bracht red-faced, a snarl on his lips.

Dane cleared his throat. "Bracht." His voice carried a warning.

"Forgive me, Dane," Bracht murmured as he bowed his head.

Dane Auldren nodded, then looked out at the last woman who had spoken. "Enough indeed."

I scanned the crowd and saw her—my challenger—stomping off, her long platinum braid swinging behind her. It was too intricate for her to have done on her own. Whoever she was, she must belong to a prominent family. My heart sank as her sympathizers turned hard faces back to me. Though, thanks to Dane, no more spoke out. I couldn't help pivoting in my seat again, and my eyes immediately met Bracht's. The corner of my mouth turned up in a smile. He returned it with a wink.

Our progress continued, and similar insults were thrown on every street. I bore them with my head held high and an annoyingly pleasant smile on my lips. The hope that I had at least one ally in Rihtlond, outside of Kahvrah and Gerta, bloomed within me. It might not be much, but in that moment, one was enough.

By the time we reached the outskirts of the city, the sun hung low on the horizon. This was a different entrance than the one we'd used coming from the sea. It was guarded by a spiral of spikes that snaked back and forth overhead and ended in a long point. Passing beneath it was no less intimidating than entering the maw of the Great Dragon. When we made it through the short tunnel, we emerged into the deep, rich greens and browns marking Rihtish nature. Vast clearings spanned either side of the road, harboring fenced and sectioned crops. The road turned into a wide dirt path that eventually led to the dense forest.

My stomach growled, and my spine ached. Drakh was even larger than I remembered, and winding through street after street took most of the day. I shifted to dismount, but Dane turned and held up a hand, halting me.

"Is there something—oh!"

Dane wasn't just holding up his hand, he was handing me the reins. "You've been judged by the people," he said, failing to mention the verdict. "Now, you must be judged by the divine."

I stared at him, my mind providing me with absolutely nothing to say.

"Prepare yourself," he continued. "Above all else, stay calm. Any command I give you, follow without question. Do this, and there is no need to worry. Fail, and I cannot guarantee you your life."

"My life? What in the Nine Martyrs is going on?"

Dane scoffed. "If you know what's good for you, you'll leave your Martyrs behind."

At that, he withdrew to a beast of a stallion, large enough to bear his frame, and mounted with ease despite his favored leg. The party followed suit. Horses were provided for all, even Gerta.

We rode on as the sky darkened and began to drizzle. Raindrops dampened my hair and tickled my cheeks, refreshing me after a long day in the sun. The winding forest path meandered toward a mountainside. Bracht pulled up beside me and wordlessly handed over a flask.

"I couldn't possibly," I admitted, gripping the silver canister. The last thing I needed was alcohol muddling my senses, especially on an empty stomach.

"It's *choirsa*. Nourishment. Trust me." He winked, pulling out an identical flask from his belt. Apparently, winking was a thing he liked to do.

I uncorked the cap and put the flask to my lips. A rich, sweet, earthy scent wafted up. I took a long drink. It was thick and hearty, but it went down as easily as cream soup. The sweetness of oats and honey and a hint of something savory danced across my tongue. After one swallow, my body demanded more. I emptied the flask in moments, and when it was gone, I felt satiated though not quite full.

The path curved, revealing a bare patch on the mountain. Through the dim, I could just make out a crack between the rocks.

"We're headed to a cave?" I asked, turning to Bracht, but he had dropped back.

"Come."

I stiffened, and Kappa bristled. The voice was low, grumbling, and entirely inhuman. And yet, it was as familiar as a dream. I looked back at the others. Not one looked the least bit perturbed.

"COME." The voice filled every inch of my being. My body trembled. Still, no one reacted. Even Kappa was steady this time.

Are you a god? I thought back, but there was no answer. Turning again in my saddle, I sought out Gerta's gaze. *Where are we?* I mouthed.

Gerta shook her head once. Her eyes were blown wide. They snapped from me to something straight ahead on our path.

I whirled, but there was nothing before me except the approaching mouth of the cave—our destination. My skin prickled. A thick darkness filled the chamber. I couldn't see anything within. As we drew nearer, what had looked like any other cave entrance now loomed like a massive maw, not unlike the entrance to Drakh.

Dane, already off his horse, stalked to my side, motioning for me to dismount. "Walk into the darkness, Daughter. Do not speak. I know you're all questions"—he held up a hand, halting the one that was already on my lips—"and answers will be forthcoming. First, you must enter, face any truths that the cave gives you, and return."

"Walk into the cave and come back," I reiterated.

He nodded.

If it weren't for the deathly serious expressions on everyone's face around me, I would have thought this a bad joke. My eyes wandered to Gerta, who was still staring at the open cave. Kahvrah, next to her, was bowing her head and murmuring. *Was that a prayer?* Behind Kahvrah, Bracht stood stoically with the copper-haired general, whose stormy eyes, for once, were not focused on me. I turned away quickly before my gaze drew his attention, but not before noting the ridiculous amount of muscle in his crossed arms. Fuck, his body was inconveniently distracting.

A hand landed on my shoulder—Dane.

"Serae. It's time."

I nodded.

"Come," the voice echoed a third time in my mind, and this time, I was ready for it. It held a different note—alluring and seductive. It was nothing like how lovers call to each other, and yet it was every bit as enticing. My body responded to the beckoning, begging me to move toward the blackness.

So, I did.

Simple as one foot in front of the next, I approached the cave of un-empty dark.

"What are you?" I asked into the cave, afraid to know the answer.

Something beautiful and terrible wrapped around my mind, its warm fingers caressing my thoughts. Everything I thought I knew fell away, leaving me stripped bare in the ebony night.

"Let me in," it seemed to say.

So again, I did.

CHAPTER 10

"The fabric of this world has chosen you. It calls to you as I do, and you have come before me to accept its mantle of power.

"I bind you to me: body, mind, and soul. Receive unto yourself the fire of creation. All life lives at our command.

"When you go forth, you will be one of the Bound, and with this great gift, you will carry an equal burden. For, all bindings have a cost.

"Yet, worry not, Small One. One day, your debt and your sacrifice shall be repaid."

—Recounting from the private diary of Jerris, Dragonbound

SERAE

MIDSUMMER, JERRMON 1036

I WALKED BACK to the city in the growing dusk. Or, perhaps I rode. I remembered there being a horse. I remembered Dane looking at me with shrewd eyes and asking me questions. Did I answer them? I must have. I did not remember getting into bed, but I must have done that, too. All I remembered was one voice echoing through my mind.

"I bind you to me: body, mind, and soul."

The following day, I woke in my bed. Gerta's was already empty, so I rose and dressed in a tan underdress and my blue, sleeveless overdress. I wove my hair in a six-strand braid. There was a pressure in my head, but it was not quite painful. It strained like an overworked muscle—if the mind could be thought of in that way. Not knowing what else to do with myself, I sought out Gerta and found her in the Relaxation Room with our morning trays. Breakfast was a silent affair, anticipation preoccupying us both. The Sun Trial was over. My First Sun had passed. And Gerta's return home was overdue.

"I can stay with you, milady," she offered in a hushed tone, despite our solitude.

"Don't be silly."

"I would, though."

I took her hand. "My fate need not be forced on you."

As long as I could remember, Gerta had been there for me, supporting and guiding me. Somewhere along the line, her role as servant and caretaker had slipped into that of friend. I wasn't ready to let her go. Soon, she would return to Inra, and when I finally followed, we would be almost strangers to each other. We shared a new bond here, being the only two alike in this sea of otherness, but back home, she was just another servant, and I was just another lord's daughter. She would never be allowed to accompany me to the Fethersen estate. She was indentured to Cavendaffe, and unless Lord Fethersen decided to pay off her contract, there she would stay.

We both smiled, but there was only sadness between us.

We'd barely returned to our room when a knock sounded at the door. We both jumped. Gerta's eyes rounded as they locked on mine.

"Enter," I called.

The door swung open revealing Bracht, dressed head to toe in green. He swept into a bow, a boisterous smile on his full lips.

"Lady Serae!" he exclaimed. "Such a pleasure to see you today."

I startled. "Is it?"

"It is," he confirmed, maintaining his broad smile. His honey-blond shade again struck me for its likeness to Merria's. His braid was one of the shortest I'd seen, falling only to his shoulders. According to Kahvrah, hair was traditionally cut short as a sign of grief or shame. *What had happened to him?* "We've been barely introduced. Allow me to rectify that. My name is Anbrachten, but you may call me Bracht."

"And you may call me Serae."

"Not a chance, or Dane will have my head. May I escort you?"

I couldn't help but smile at his buoyancy. He looked like the sort of man who could flounce into any room and put everyone at ease.

"Where would you take her?" Gerta asked, dipping into a quick curtsey.

"If it pleases you, I will take her to her lessons," he replied to Gerta, then turned back to me. "That is, if you feel up to it?"

"Why has Kahvrah not come to collect us?" Gerta asked.

Bracht tilted his head and looked between us. "Ah." He smoothed his hands down his tunic. "No one has explained this. I'm sorry that it has to be me. Kahvrah has been called back to her regular duties and has taken over the position of Marr of *Dowsae*. Your training must continue, though, if my lady is to remain in the Riht."

I stood, willing my knees to stop shaking. First Gerta, now Kahvrah, too. "Who is to train me if not Kahvrah?"

Bracht put a fist to his heart and bowed. With his eyes on the floor, he said, "My *reálton*—"

"*Reálton?*"

"A dedicated companion, of sorts. Apologies, my lady. I have been devoted to Wep for so long, I forgot this is all new to you."

"Wep?"

He nodded. "Our renowned weaponmaster."

My stomach dropped. The last thing I wanted to do was train with someone considered a master of weaponry. I could barely control my own body, let alone hold a blade.

"Must I?"

Bracht looked up with wide eyes. "Do you not want to meet him?" His brow furrowed with concern.

"I'm sorry," I said. I couldn't admit that I was afraid of meeting a man I'd never even spoken to. Based on what, a feeling and my own imagination? I squared my shoulders. "Of course, I do. Please, lead the way."

Bracht nodded, and his broad smile returned.

"And what of me?" Gerta demanded, her voice harsh. "Can I not continue to learn with milady?"

Bracht cleared his throat and shifted from one foot to another. After a moment of thought, he announced, "Please, do come. I will speak with Wep."

As we walked, I wondered why my training would fall on the shoulders of a weaponmaster. Surely, his primary purpose wasn't teaching *weak Inraen women* the art of combat.

Bracht led us to the same stairway that held our usual training rooms, but this time, we continued to the double doors at the bottom. He ushered us inside and called out to a warrior at the other end of the room. "Wep, I have brought you both the Lady Serae and her lovely companion, Gerta."

Wep didn't spare us a glance, but I froze. I would recognize that copper hair anywhere. He didn't need to turn—I already knew the piercing eyes and their accompanying anger that awaited me. He stood at the far end of the spacious room, inspecting a rack of axes. Bracht darted to his side.

"You!" I blurted out.

The weaponmaster, *not* general, turned narrowed eyes on me. His gaze flicked up to my hair and lingered before trailing down my body. He turned back to Bracht, dismissing me.

I wanted to vomit.

"This room is nice," Gerta whispered.

Fire and ash, was she right. I hadn't properly examined it the first time I was in here, what with getting my ribs shattered and all. The mats were far thicker than the rug in the small training room. The walls towered above us, twice as high as the others in the wing. Weapons and tapestries covered the walls. And there were *plenty* of windows here. After training so long in such a dim space, this was a delight.

"By the Nine Martyrs, I hope you can stay here to train with me," I whispered to Gerta.

"By the Creator himself, I hope so too."

My eyes slid to a rack of long-handled weapons to our left, with heads of every shape and size. I didn't even know their names. "Do you think we'll have to use those?"

"Who knows, milady."

"This is how people lose fingers. Or hands. Or *who knows* what else."

Gerta chortled, and the two men's heads whipped toward her. She lowered her gaze, her face a mask of subservience. Once they turned away, she shot me a grin. "Suppose I can imagine what else one might—"

"Enough, Bracht," Wep hissed, the words carrying through the large room. "Please, go to Dane." He spoke in Rihtish, but it was simple enough for me to understand.

Bracht nodded and placed his fist over his heart. Wep caught him by his shoulder before he turned away, murmuring something I couldn't catch. Bracht's face split into a grin, and he walked back to us, one arm extended.

"My lady, if it pleases you, I ask that Gerta accompany me to speak with

Dane."

I looked to Gerta, who had gone very still.

"Can she not stay to train with us?"

Bracht shook his head. "Wep thinks it most appropriate that you spend this first day alone together. And...there is the matter of seeking Dane's permission."

My eyes whipped to the weaponmaster, who had taken up his favorite pastime of glaring at me. One word echoed through my head—*alone*.

Gerta nodded. "Yes, of course." With a tentative step forward, she took his arm, but her eyes flicked to me. After another backward glance, the two hurried out, leaving me at the weaponmaster's mercy. Just as he wanted.

I stood still and tried to relax. My mind swam with fears of what this man could do to me behind these heavy, closed doors. Had he been away on raids like Eldreth? Were his hands stained with the blood of innocent Inraens, too? Channeling Kahvrah, I steadied my breath. A voice echoed in my mind. *"Calm is key to survival."* I froze, my eyes widening. *What the fuck was that?*

Across the room, Wep's stare bored into me. His eyes were sharp, but his posture was relaxed. He wore a long-sleeved shirt, dark brown and stretched tight over his muscled arms, and plain black pants. He bore no tunic, tabard, or vest marking his house or station. Strapped to his wrists were well-oiled leather bracers that matched the leather of his boots. He shifted his weight then approached slowly. Watching him reminded me of the hunting dogs Father kept. And in this scenario, I was the fox.

I did not break eye contact.

Neither did he.

Wep stopped about two arm's lengths away. The silence of our twisted staring contest stretched. Of course, I was the first to snap.

"How shall I address you?" I asked in Mayoran.

He did not answer.

"Kahvrah has been helping me with your customs, but it seems I am without a *reálta* now."

He raised a brow.

"Is there a title I should use, like with Dane?"

"Yes and no," he said at last, shaking his head. From this distance, his steel gray eyes were more discerning than sharp. Or maybe it was a trick of the light. There was no denying they held more intensity than I could ever hope to mirror.

"He speaks," I quipped.

He pursed his lips. "Marr Wep. Most just use Wep."

"Thank you."

He cocked his head, looking down at me. He was a head taller, though not quite as tall as Dane. "And how should I address you?"

I smirked. "My name will do."

"No title?" He quirked that same eyebrow.

"None."

He kept me pinned with his eyes, like he was trying to see through my soul. The silence returned. I detested it, but for once, I didn't know how to break it.

"Do you have any other questions for me?" he asked.

It was my turn to look him over. I took in his muscular build again, his height, and his dark copper hair pulled tight in a knot. He moved to hold his arms behind his back, and a twisted part of me hoped my gaze unnerved him. He was the picture of a Rihtish warrior. He radiated severity and control.

But imposing figures had never stopped my wandering tongue before. "If I'm to be stuck with you, there will be plenty of time for questions." I knew very well it was not *me* who was stuck with *him*. "Where do we begin?"

We began, it turned out, with a review of my *dowsae*. Rather than lead, Wep planted his feet beside me, as Gerta would have, and followed my every move. When I faltered to fix my stupid glasses, he slowed his pace until I caught up, and our movements synchronized again. He made no corrections and gave no comments. I gritted my teeth. I didn't enjoy being patronized or tested, or whatever the fuck this was. When I completed almost all that I had learned from Kahvrah, he fell into stance opposite me.

The sun *dowsa*.

"Breathe," a voice commanded in my head. I froze, my heart slamming in my chest.

Silence.

I refocused on my breath, then I began. My muscles were already limber from the warmup *dowsae*, so I ducked and dodged with ease. Wep matched me step for step. The energy between us built, and my confidence grew. *This* was what should have happened in the arena. I had no fear of striking him—he was exactly where he should be. More importantly, he was where I *needed* him to be. My pace, I knew, wasn't perfect. I had a habit of rushing through the middle, but he kept up. He did not huff or stop me and make me start again, as Kahvrah would have. I jabbed in a controlled flurry, then it was time for the finale. I jumped, ducked, swept a low kick, spun to the side, dodged, turned back, and halted—hands raised in prayer. No blows came. I bowed. Across from me, Wep bowed low, and when he rose, his brow was furrowed.

"Why didn't you do this at your trial?" His voice was harsh.

"Maybe I was a little caught off guard by the stadium of people jeering at me," I snapped. This was what he had to say?

"No, you weren't."

"Oh? So, you know better than me how I felt?"

Wep paused. He frowned, eyes narrowed. "When you fell into stance, yes, there were nerves. Once you started, no."

I'd run over the trial in my head dozens of times. Had I misstepped? Botched my alignment? Missed a section altogether? The truth was, I *had* felt confident—until the end. "I don't know what happened."

"I didn't take you for a liar."

"Fine." I snapped. "The challenger wasn't where she should've been, not that you or anyone else would believe me. Happy?" My breath came out in huffs. Why was I so rattled?

He nodded. After a moment, he opened his mouth to speak.

"Listen"—I cut him off—"I don't need a lecture. I get it. I have way less experience, so I'm probably the one who was out of place." I took a moment to wipe my glasses on the soft front of my overdress. "Either way, I've already been judged and heard *plenty* of opinions about me already."

Wep strode forward, stopping right before me. "The only judgment you have to worry about is Dane's, the Great Dragon's"—his voice was low and hard—"and maybe mine." He smirked.

It was the closest to a smile I'd seen on his face, and Martyrs, did it suit him. Still, I scoffed at the sentiment.

"What of these glasses? They disrupt your pace. Can you not do without them?"

"Sure, if you'd like me to be in a constant state of befuddlement, no problem."

"It was just a question."

"It was unsolicited advice."

"Perhaps you need the advice of your betters."

I straightened my glasses. "Do point me to one when you find them." His eyebrow jumped. "What's next?"

"Next, we—"

The door burst open, and a young girl rushed in. She had twin braids swinging over her shoulders and wide eyes locked on me.

"Dane calls on you," the girl shouted.

Wep nodded and moved to follow. "Wait here," he commanded, voice sharp. No wonder I mistook him for a general to start.

"No!" the girl squeaked. "He calls her." She pointed at me.

I stiffened. "Me?" I choked out.

The girl nodded then ran out, the door slamming shut behind her.

I looked to Wep, but his face was a mask. He crossed the room and opened the door, waiting. Except my stupid, stubborn feet refused to move.

"Come," he snapped, gesturing through the door.

"Obviously," I spat.

One eyebrow raised dramatically. I couldn't decide if I liked his glare or his taunting brow the least. I looked away and stormed from the room, but Wep trailed me, staying a few stairs behind me.

"I know the way," I hissed over my shoulder, my temper rising to cover my embarrassment.

He didn't answer, and he didn't change his pace. His presumption grated on me. Dane had called for me—not him. What gave him the right to follow?

Though the castle was full of twists and turns, we arrived before Dane too quickly. I was still panting—from the sprint to the Receiving Hall and the *dowsae* before it. The moment I walked through the doorway, Dane's regular guard duo flanked me and escorted me directly in front of the imposing man, made even more daunting atop his dais.

"Daughter," Dane greeted. His beard was unbound, adding to his wild appearance.

I put my hand to my heart and bowed my head like he'd taught me. As I did so, I snuck a glance to the side and found Gerta seated next to Bracht on one of the many benches. My adrenaline spiked, blood pounding in my ears. Kahvrah sat on Gerta's other side. She clenched her fists around her long braid.

"What letters have you had from your Inraen family?"

My throat clenched, and I felt the blood drain from my face. "None," I sputtered.

Dane narrowed his eyes.

"Just one from my father, not long after I first arrived. I've had none since." The letters I'd sent to Merria so far had been unanswered.

"Hmm," Dane muttered, stroking his beard.

"Dane, if I may—" Wep stepped forward, but Dane shushed him. He waved a hand, and Wep moved out of my line of sight. I bit my lip, stifling my snicker. Served him right, imposing himself like that. I kept my eyes on Dane, waiting.

He had closed his eyes and hung his head. He might have been asleep, except for the furrow in his brow.

I pressed my lips tighter together and held my breath. Now was not a time to interfere. *Control your tongue*—Mother's favorite words for me. I could have sworn I heard laughter echo through my head in response.

After several moments, Dane raised his head, looking directly at me.

"Your maid has made a plea to stay in our lands and become one of the Riht." He kindly ignored the gasp that burst out of me. "She would like to put herself forth for her own trial. Kahvrah has come forward as her attestant. But she is not free. She is bound to the Cavendaffe lord, and he has written requesting her return. Unlike you, she has no promise of release from their servitude."

I cringed at the wrongness of those words, at the wrongness of Gerta's predicament. No woman in Inra was free. I knew this was the way of things. Even the queen was beholden to the king.

Dane turned to Gerta. Perhaps it was my imagination, but I saw in his eyes the same sorrow I felt in my bones.

I nodded, already knowing what was needed of me. "I will write to him. I'll ask him to permanently release Gerta to me, to stay with me as my personal servant here in Drakh. If he agrees, then I can dissolve the servitude myself."

"So be it." Dane nodded his dismissal.

I retreated from the hall—one foot out the door when Wep asked, "You would trust her already?"

My temper flared, and I rounded on him, not caring about the spectacle I'd make. "*Excuse me?* Since my arrival in Drakh, I have been nothing but compliant. I do whatever's asked of me. I've completed trials, given up my home, my life, everything—all to become part of the Riht. Gerta is my closest companion, and I would do anything for her happiness. You've known me for—what—an hour? Who are you to question me?" I crossed my arms and held his gaze. With no small measure of pride, I did not flinch. I may be a traitor to these people, but in that moment, I made my decision. Gerta's life in Cavendaffe would be one of servitude, but her life in the Riht, regardless of how long I remained here, would be one of her choosing. My father and his journal be damned.

"Write the letter. Go." Dane interrupted, waving his hand in dismissal. "Our rider leaves before last light."

I nodded. At home, a speech like that would've earned me a slap—or worse. I quickly bowed and spun on my heels, fleeing the hall before Dane could change his mind. I kept moving, tamping down the jitters that threatened to buckle my knees.

Thankfully, Wep didn't follow me out.

After putting several more paces between me and that damned hall, I broke into a full run back to our room. Behind the safety of my locked door, I finally let my guard down. My hands shook as I pulled out parchment, ink, and quill. I had not been discovered. Gerta had a chance to stay in the Riht. All was well—except for a pair of infuriating steel gray eyes that I couldn't get out of my head.

I cast more than a few sheafs into the fire before I was satisfied. The letter was equal amounts pleading, persuasive, and logical. I followed it up with a letter to Merria containing everything I dared encode. I didn't know what drove me to do it, but I held back about the First Sun and the mysterious cave. Instead, I added a coded explanation that I needed more time to complete my journal. In order for this to work, I'd have to come up with a different plan to get it home, and fast. When I was satisfied, I sealed both and brought them to the small lesson room, where I was meeting Dane for our weekly session. Voices carried through the door before I entered. Dane was speaking to someone in Rihtish, but I couldn't make out what was being said—until I caught my name.

I opened the door.

Wep stood across the room from Dane, arms folded in his favorite position and leveling Dane with a glare that put the ones he gave me to shame. The second he noticed me, his face relaxed, and his arms fell to his sides.

"Daughter," Dane said, too calm. "Please come in."

Wep put his hand to his heart, barely nodded his head, and made for the doorway.

"You can stay," Dane called before he reached the door.

Wep's eyes met mine in challenge. "I think she's had enough of me for one day."

I couldn't help my smirk, but Wep's expression did not change. His eyes lingered on my face for just a moment, then they flicked to Dane and hardened. He left, shutting the door behind him.

The desk today was arranged with papers, quills, and ink. Dane motioned to the chairs that were positioned side by side before it.

"Never mind him. Today, we learn the Rihtish script. You've had instruction on the lettering used in Inra. No doubt, you've also learned to write using the common tongue."

I nodded and moved to take my seat.

"You've been studying our language, and as dana, you'll need to be able to write letters of your own. We will start with greetings. Watch me."

Dane dipped his quill and began to write. From what I'd seen in their books, I expected the script to have the same harsh lines and even strokes. The flowing script Dane produced was an unexpected delight. Time flew as I copied each stroke, asking for the next and the next. Dane indulged me for two hours until he had to leave, but before he did, he stared at my work while smoothing a hand down his loose beard and said, "We may make a dana of you yet."

Something in me glowed as heat touched my cheeks. I bit back my smile.

That evening, as Gerta paced, I sat at the table with quill and ink, not caring that I was wasting an entire roll of parchment as I practiced. For the first time here, I had found something I could excel at.

THE NEXT MORNING, I woke from a dream. All I could feel was a nagging pain across my skin. My hands and forearms stung like a sunburn, but worse. I threw open the curtains, bristling at the touch of the fabric on my sensitive fingers and squinting against the harsh morning light. Glancing down, my skin was healthy and unblemished. In a blink, the pain faded. The room dimmed. The memory of my dream slipped away, leaving behind a feeling of unease in my chest.

I returned to my bed and sat on the edge of it. Judging by the bleariness in my head, it was still early, but Gerta was not in her bed. It was too dark to read my latest book—this one a basic introduction to the Seven Dragons of Jaeda and why the Great Dragon of Life was the strongest. Instead, I rose, dressed, and made my way early toward the training rooms.

That's when I heard the singing.

The walls were thick and strong, but, like water, sound had a way of seeping through tiny flecks and minuscule cracks. The voice was neither high nor low, but it was haunting all the same. I couldn't help but follow it. I crept down the stairs, with footfalls as soft as I could manage, until I was easing open the door to the large training room. A lone figure stood, eyes on the ceiling, arms extended to an absent audience. Their song was building, coming to a climax. I stood, enrapt by the spell they wove. What was this world I had walked into, where sprites sang to the proverbial rafters in the places where war was taught?

The door creaked behind me as it swung shut, and the music coming from this creature faltered. They spun around, and the entire melody fell away. I frowned. This was no faerie at all, just a person taking advantage of an empty room.

They grinned at me, a sheepish thing. "The acoustics are the best in this room, you know?"

"Oh," was all I could think to reply. "It was lovely."

Their hair was a shock of white-blond, cut short and sticking out in all directions. They wore a cream tunic with brown pants, though the pants were more like thick leggings. "I'm Teke, by the way. Well, it's Antekedora, but everyone just calls me Teke. Bit of a mouthful otherwise."

"Right. I'm just Serae."

Teke extended a forearm, which I grasped. It was the first time I'd been greeted as an equal.

"So, you're the Inraen one, then? What's it like?"

"Back home? Very different from here. What gave me away?"

Their eyes flicked to my hair. "The language."

"But you spoke first."

"Fair enough. Do they really lock women indoors until they're paraded around to find a mate?"

"Excuse me?" I bristled. I couldn't help it. I readied my tongue for a better retort when Teke's grin widened. "Ah, you're joking."

"Only half. I did hear that once when I was a youth! But Lex always was a liar."

"Excuse you, that's slander, and I won't have it," came a voice from behind me. A man shoved through the doors who could only be described as beautiful. He had sleek, buttery hair that cascaded down his shoulders and perfectly sculpted eyebrows. He smiled the grin of a fox and fixed all his attention on me as he purred, "Well, hello, and what do we have here?"

"Keep it in your pants, Lex," Teke snapped.

"Touchy." Lex plucked my hand into his own and brought it to his lips. "Ignore them. I'm delighted to meet an absolute treat like you."

The doors slammed, and I winced, bracing for whatever was coming next. My fears were only slightly assuaged when I turned to find Wep prowling toward us. As always, he was frowning.

"Behave, or you'll be paired with me for sparring today," he growled.

Lex dropped my hand with a yip like he'd been stung.

"I see you've met two of your *ranng*," Wep addressed me directly. "We're waiting on a few more, then we begin."

"My rang?" I asked, unable to place the Rihtish word.

"*Ranng*. There is no word for it in Mayoran. You'll have to get used to it." Wep eyed me, perhaps a moment too long, then added, "A *ranng* trusts each other above all else. You'll train with them during your morning sessions, plus private lessons with me when I can spare the time. The rest is for Dane to advise."

"I don't understand. Why am I in a *ranng* at all? Why train with others?" I glanced pointedly at the pair beside me, who had stepped away and begun a stretching *dowsa*.

"You don't like them?"

"No, it's not that. They're great, I'm sure. But I'm not a warrior."

"You're training with me."

"And you only train warriors?"

"Of course."

I gasped. "Am I expected to fight in battles?"

Wep appraised me. "You'll be dana," he said slowly.

"Oh, this is a knowledge thing. I need to be trained for the position."

He just shrugged. "Any other complaints?"

I wanted to ask more or to argue, but Wep had crossed to the other end of the room.

Got it. Conversation over.

There was a door on the opposite wall that I hadn't noticed yesterday. Wep removed two solid iron beams that were barring the door shut. He hefted each as if featherlight and set them against the stone wall. Then, he withdrew a key from somewhere under his shirt—black today—and unlocked the door. When he pushed it open, sunlight and fresh air spilled into the room.

A hand dropped on my shoulder, making me jump.

"Just me," said Bracht, warm tone and smiling as always. He must've snuck in after Wep. "You'll be fine. I hope you know that Wep would never put you at risk."

"Risk?" I echoed, trying to suppress the jittery dread that crawled down my spine. It hadn't even occurred to me that training with others might create risks.

Bracht's smile turned into a wince, and he trailed after Wep with a friendly nod.

The remainder of the group gathered in the next few minutes. I was relieved to learn that there were only six newcomers aside from myself, Wep, and Bracht. However, my addition left the class uneven for paired sparring, as one short, heavily muscled woman explained to Teke within earshot. Teke had only shrugged in response, and I decided I liked them already.

Wep cleared his throat, and the group closed into a circle without further prompting. I followed suit, regretting it immediately when he gestured to me. "A new member to your *ranng.* This is Serae. Don't fuck her up too much." A splattering of chuckles sounded. "And don't make me regret putting her with you." He looked at each one in turn, must have been satisfied by what he saw, then launched into our goal for the day. It was the strangest introduction I'd ever received.

As Wep turned away, a man with the darkest hair I'd seen in the Riht—fully brown—extended his forearm to me. "I'm Raif," was all he said. His eyes were night-sky blue. Between his downturned mouth and lowered brows, he and Wep could have competed for surliest man in the Riht.

Raif split us into groups of two—or three, in my group's case. Raif paired Lex, Teke paired the muscular woman, and the remaining two were stuck with me. From the corner of my eye, I watched Wep approach Teke's group. I couldn't make out what he was saying, but his face was a little less severe than usual.

"No, I don't know what he's planning," a deep voice rumbled next to me. He was a veritable mountain of a man with more bulging muscles than I knew a human body could possess. "He'll have figured something out, Helene, don't worry."

The slight woman, Helene, glanced toward me, met my eyes for half a second, then pulled her eyes to the floor.

What a thought. Was I, an uncoordinated interloper, a source of intimidation? *No.* Next to them, I moved like I belonged in a children's class—a bitter realization to swallow. After one day of private training, Wep had thrust me into a group that might mock or even despise me for holding them back. What was he thinking? What was anyone thinking, sending me to this confounded place?

I glanced at Wep, who was now talking with Raif's group. He cut an impressive figure, and Creator was it annoying. He was all perfectly honed muscles and looming height. Worse, everyone in this room looked at him with more than just deference—they respected him. Dane clearly had a high opinion of him, as well. Even the man beside me—who looked like he could rip a fucking tree out of the ground—kept glancing at Wep with open admiration. I bet it stroked his ego daily. He radiated strength, control, authority, and it made him insufferable.

As if feeling my gaze, Wep turned and met my eyes. I glared back as he approached. I may have been a lot of things, but I'd never been one to back down.

"You've done introductions?" Wep asked.

Neither Helene nor the giant man replied.

Wep sighed. "Helene," he said, pointing to the woman whose name I had already surmised, "Ivank,"—Wep pointed to the giant—"and Serae. There we are. Rotate through the strength *dowsae*. Serae doesn't know any of them, so you'll have to teach her. Start with the bear patterns."

Ivank nodded his shaved head, and Wep strode back to Teke's group. So much for him being an instructor.

I looked at my two newfound companions. "Sorry you're stuck with babysitting duty." I meant it to sound flippant, but it came out bitter.

"Teaching is much harder than doing." Ivank shrugged. "Stand beside me. Helene will lead."

Ivank turned out to be a patient teacher, and Helene was excellent at demonstrating. Perhaps it was a small blessing from the Creator that I'd been assigned to them instead of Wep. He spent the lesson focusing on the other two groups and shooting me covert glares. Helene, I quickly found, could hold any pose for ages, despite her slight frame. Her entire body, save for her mousy blond braid, would freeze the instant Ivank called for her to stop. My initial dread whittled away with each step of the strenuous routine. And, though I was holding them back from full practice, both made me feel included and welcome.

Had they been asked to? I tried not to think about it too closely or that hollow feeling would return.

After class ended, Wep approached our group. "You were adequate today. I have other matters to attend to. Take Serae with you when you head out." It was more words than he'd spoken to us all lesson.

Helene nodded, but Ivank pushed back. "I'm not going out."

A look passed between Wep and Ivank. It must've been some silent contest because after a moment, when Ivank didn't back down, Wep sighed, "Fine. Serae, go with Helene."

"Where?" I asked.

"Wherever she takes you."

"What does that mean?"

He waved a hand toward Helene. "Ask her."

Helene was staring at Wep with large, round eyes. At his returning glare, she squeaked, turned on her heel, and left.

I had to sprint to catch up. Sprinting was easier than ever before, but still tiring after the full training session.

"Where are we going?" I panted.

"This way."

A deep, rumbling laugh echoed through my mind.

I balked, glancing around. There was only Helene. I frowned. *That's it, I'm finally going insane.*

Once outside the keep, my heart sank as Helene continued toward the market. The jeers from two days ago were still fresh in my mind, and it's not like I had great experiences in the market in general. Helene led us straight through the rows that usually encompassed my permitted outings—and beyond. Before I knew it, we crossed a small bridge into the lower city, heading down one alley, then another. We stopped before a small stone building, a sign with a teacup swinging on a hinge just above the doorway.

I froze. The sign was *glowing*. The strokes of the teacup carved into the wood shone with soft yellow light, as if lit by fire from within. I stared, completely ignoring the door Helene held open. Was it a trick of my eyes? I craned my neck to look from another angle.

Helene glanced back at me.

"How is it doing that?" I asked.

Helene shook her head. "Doing what?"

I gaped, searching for a response. She beckoned inside. I was reluctant to pull my eyes away, but I followed.

The room we entered was downright quaint. The floors were covered with plush pillows, each boasting a unique pattern, and low tables, similar to the one in the Relaxation Room. Winding pathways spiderwebbed between the pillows, allowing barely enough space for one person to walk. In one corner stood a bar of sorts, with what I would have called a barkeep, were it not for the myriad of neatly stacked tins around him—and the distinct lack of alcohol. Behind him climbed ceiling-high rows of miniature shelves alongside stacks of different handle-free mugs. It wasn't until I took a breath that our location smacked me in the face.

"A tea house," I cooed, the strange sign forgotten. I was instantly transported back to the kitchens at home, where I would spend hours helping the cook dry herbs, flowers, and thin slices of fruit—mixing them to discover new flavors. The air was full of the warm scents of mixed spices, fruits, and floral notes.

"A tea bar," Helene corrected, the corner of her mouth lifting into a tiny smile. She led the way to one of the many open cushions.

There was only one other couple in the entire place, aside from the man behind the bar, whom Helene marked as the owner. This place was either not the most popular of haunts, or the hour was the culprit. Seated on my plush, orange cushion, I returned to eyeing the bar and noted the series of dark glass bottles mixed among the tins of tea blends. Maybe there *was* alcohol here. Drakh just got a lot more interesting.

Helene was the picture of comfort, lounging across three pillows in a way that claimed belonging.

A pang of jealousy flashed in my chest. What would it be like to feel so accepted—so at home somewhere? In Cavendaffe, I couldn't even sit like that in the privacy of my own bedroom. "What do you order here?" I asked instead of following that line of thought.

"You don't."

At that moment, the owner wandered over and set a drink down in front of Helene. It was a generous mug that steamed slightly, a small white flower floating atop the richly colored liquid.

"Who're you, then?" the man asked me in Rihtish. He had an open expression and a kindly look about him that brought to mind my father's steward, who often acted as family caretaker. Though this man was probably a decade his junior. His long, mousy-blond hair and beard were tied into several tight braids, and his eyes crinkled when he smiled.

Introductions were something I'd already learned. "Well met. I'm Serae," I responded in Rihtish, hoping he didn't ask other questions I'd have no chance of understanding.

He squinted as he ogled me from head to toe. He held his hands out, palms up. After a moment of staring incredulously at him, I took his hands, and...*something*...like a tingling warmth passed between us. Then, he tapped his nose and walked away without another word.

I was starting to understand why Helene, who'd spoken fewer than three sentences during our entire training session, liked this place. It took a few minutes, but the owner came back with an ebony mug. A single cinnamon stick peeked out the top like a stirrer. He waited, arms folded across his chest, staring at me.

What else could I do? With a silent prayer to the Creator, I drank.

My mouth exploded with a celebration of spices—warm and aromatic, dancing over my tongue in a way I'd never experienced before. There was the obvious cinnamon, but also nutmeg, pepper, anise, and several other flavors I couldn't place.

"Delicious," I purred, though I wasn't sure if I should be voicing my appraisal in such a quiet room.

The owner smirked in a self-satisfied way, reminding me of something much larger and more lethal than a house cat. He reached across the table, patted Helene's cheek, and returned to the bar.

I looked to Helene, who shrugged.

"My uncle. It's his gift," she said, raising her mug in cheers.

"His gift?"

Helene nodded. "Maybe that's not the best word. It's his *bierla*," she added, as if that were explanation enough.

"Blessing," the voice translated in my mind. I was getting used to its interruptions.

My eyes flew to the window beside the door, but I couldn't see that mysterious sign from here. "Are there other blessings?"

Helene nodded.

"Do you have one?"

She shook her head. "I haven't been presented to the Great Dragon."

Memory of the cave flooded me. My skin prickled as if I were being devoured by blackness again. I remembered a strange light. I had walked through and seen—*glowing*. Peridot green eyes that shone from within. A snout that loomed above me, and fangs, white and wicked.

"I'm not from Drakh. I haven't had my First Sun yet."

Helene's words tore me from my reverie. I focused my eyes back on her. "Did you have a Sun Trial?" Dane had told me all Riht went through one, but he was not forthcoming with details prior to my own.

"Yes, but I have not been called yet for the...blessing," she stumbled over the last word.

"From the Great Dragon?" I asked, breathless. She nodded as if everything crashing down on me was simple. At once, the world around me was too loud, too bright, too strong. That unfathomable cave towered over me. I had looked into the face of a living, breathing dragon—The Great Dragon.

No, it couldn't be. I recoiled from the very thought. There were no dragons left on Jaeda—no magic. My pulse quickened. Air rasped through my lungs. I gripped my mug with both hands as one thought pounded through my skull. *The blessings.* Had I not just seen their proof?

"Peace, Small One."

My mind stilled at the command. I sipped my tea, melting into its spicy warmth once more.

After that, we drank in companionable silence.

CHAPTER 11

"You're going to lose her," Patriol said. Tianna's shining chocolate hair swung behind her as she walked away.

"I've lost her already. What choice do I have, considering what my life will be?"

Patriol shook his head, mussing his auburn locks. "Brother, none of us are promised time on Jaeda. For all you know, you could die tomorrow, while Tianna lives on to be one hundred years old."

There was a truth to his words that threatened to give me hope. But hope was a dangerous thing.

—Recounting from the private diary of Jerris, Dragonbound

SERAE

MIDSUMMER, JERRMON 1036

SNOW FELL SOFTLY around the bed, but I felt no cold. A warmth enveloped me, and I knew that soft, delicious heat. A hard body pressed against me. Strong hands gripped my curves as his body snaked down mine, until his head was between my legs. He devoured me in a way that made me feel his lust just as vividly as his devotion. My body was something he wanted to worship, and he showed me with his tongue and lips and teeth.

"Wake."

No, I need more. He shifted, pulling me over to straddle his face, tongue reaching new depths.

"Wake. I cannot bear this."

I jerked and tumbled over the edge, smacking my head, shoulder, and hip against the stone floor. My bleary eyes opened as pain blossomed along my side. I'd rolled off my fucking bed. I lay there, tangled in my blanket, the evidence of my dream slick between my legs. I groaned at the ache it left behind.

"Fucking hell." Crawling atop my small cot, I willed myself back to sleep, ignoring the throbbing that begged for release. With Gerta only a few feet away, mercifully still slumbering, there was no flaming way that would be happening.

Over the next week, members of my *ranng* brought me to more new places in the lower city—some of which refused to serve *that Inraen girl*, and all with glowing signs. I saw color-changing garments, a shop for water skins that never emptied, and a stand advertising foolproof fire starters—though I had a feeling that last one was just a scam. Still, something inside me twisted. Believing my eyes was one thing, but blessings from a dragon?

It had been over a decade since I'd giggled with my siblings, pretending to be magic wielders from the days of old. There were many Inraen myths about the existence of magic in the wild lands before the Creator sent his devoted to rid the world of evil. The Nine Martyrs had sacrificed themselves in the name of faith, each dying horrible deaths at the hands of corrupt magic users. According to the Carmine Order's teachings, only the Creator's magic was true and pure. Yet, seeing such casual displays around me, none of which created harm or panic, opened my eyes to a new kind of magic. This wasn't the great magic of old—the kind that could shape a kingdom. This was the mundane, everyday magic of simple people helping each other get by.

Dane had permitted me to walk freely within the castle grounds, so between trainings, outings, and study, I found time each day to swap out my book for a new one from the small cart near the castle market. I'd been reading a series of short books, each highlighting the powers and personalities of the Seven Dragons of Jaeda. Oddly, none of the Dragons had names. They were only known by their colors—green for life, red for fire, orange for earth, blue for water, white for air, purple for spirit, and black for death.

At night, dragons and magic invaded my dreams. Night after night, I dreamt of the cave—of the great power emanating from it, taunting me with swirling colors, whispering voices, and that haunting pair of glowing peridot eyes. The worst was when I found only myself inside, but not as I was. This woman was older, regal, and thrumming with power. Yet I felt myself within her. When her eyes met mine, I woke—shaking and drenched in sweat—with a deep voice rumbling through my mind. It was the same voice, I realized, I'd been hearing in my head for weeks.

On the twenty-eighth of Jerrmon—the last day of midsummer—I woke with a pit in my stomach that had nothing to do with dragons. *Our birthday.* I was now twenty-two. Six weeks had passed since I left home, not that Bale would be there anyway. I glanced at the sky through the small window—still dark. Before long, the sun would rise, and it would be just another day to the rest of the Riht. But not to me. I needed to be anywhere but here. I needed to be alone. I dressed in silence, taking care not to wake Gerta, still asleep in her bed.

I made my way barefoot down the halls, holding my boots in one hand, toward the Relaxation Room. I had traveled back and forth from the training rooms so many times now that it was second nature. Halfway down the stairs, I paused. Soft thuds echoed from below. It was too early for Teke to be taking advantage of the acoustics. Plus, there was no singing. One door to the large room had been propped ajar, and a dim light shone from within.

I snuck the rest of the way down the stairs, keeping to the far right side, still carrying my boots. When I reached the bottom, I peered around the closed door, allowing it to block most of my body from view.

It was Wep, awake at this unreasonable hour and running through some form of practice. Whether it was a *dowsa* or another drill, I couldn't tell. I had never seen anything like it. Between slow, sweeping movements, his body snapped—legs whipping through the air. He spun. He flipped. Sometimes his hands touched the ground, and other times they didn't. I had seen juggling acrobatics before, and this was as similar to that as cats were to dragons. I watched for several minutes until his body stilled, his back to me.

I turned to sneak away, but Wep called out, "Come in."

Stepping into the doorway to reveal myself was a small type of agony. I tried not to look at him, instead examining the lit braziers that bathed the room in a soft, eerie glow. Weapons glinted in the firelight, sharper and more ominous than they ever looked in the light of day. Wep stood there, now facing me, drawing me in with his unnatural stillness. His copper hair was up in a knot, and he wore a simple sleeveless shirt and loose pants, both black. I'd never seen him sleeveless before. My eyes caught on the tattoos snaking down his right shoulder—and refused to let go. I couldn't tell what they were, but they suited him way too fucking well.

"An old injury," he dismissed with a shrug.

My eyes dropped to the red mottled scarring down his forearm, barely visible in the dim light. "You look good in black." *Fuck me, did I really just say that?*

"Do I?"

Laughter filled my mind. I turned on the spot, but we were alone. I whirled back around and straight into Wep's chest. I squeaked and darted to the side. How in the Creator's balls had he moved so fast?

He glowered into the dark stairwell, every muscle in his body taut.

"Why are you here?" he asked, turning to me with a frown and blocking the doorway.

I shrugged. He stared at me, his favorite pastime, so I stared back, leaning my weight against the wall.

"No shoes?" he asked, stepping toward me.

My traitorous body responded to him on instinct. He was one giant storm cloud wrapped up in a package designed by the Creator himself to bring me to my knees. The image of warm brown eyes danced through my head, and guilt settled low in my belly. *Tam.* I pushed off the wall and took a few steps into the room, distancing us. I needed to find some release soon, or I might do something I'd regret. I wiggled the arm holding my boots. "Too early," I said.

He leaned his back against the wall and shoved his hands into his pockets. The muscles in his arms flexed. He had no business looking that good before sunrise. "Did you need something?"

I shook my head. "Couldn't sleep."

"I know the feeling."

"Why are you up?"

He raised an eyebrow at me in response, letting the silence stretch, making me twitch. "Why are you here?"

"Does it sound juvenile if I say bad dreams?" It wasn't the exact truth, but how could I explain what this day had meant to me—and what I had lost?

His face cracked into a wry grin.

I adjusted my glasses, annoyed at how blurry they were.

"Training will help. That was a good thought."

"No, I came for the Relaxation Room."

"Come again?"

"The room with all the pillows."

He pushed off the wall, making it look like a thing of grace instead of a common, everyday action, and strode toward me. There was a heat in his eyes that scared me a bit. "Don't let me stop you," he growled. He turned away and crossed the room, back toward his million weapon racks. Martyrs, even the back of this man's body, with his broad shoulders and muscled back, was a sight to behold. Not to mention his—

All at once, his words and tone caught up with me. Was he mad at me? For wanting to sit in a fucking room before the sun was up instead of training with him? "Life is more than weapons training, you know."

He turned back with a scowl. I'd struck a nerve. I could practically see his hackles rise. "Training is a tool. It's a part of our station and responsibilities. Life is all the moments in between."

"Not everyone *has* a life."

"That's what's keeping you awake? Life in the Riht not exciting enough for you?" He stalked back toward me with the same lethality as the mountain cats native to this region.

I retreated toward the door. "N-no, I—" He followed me, step for step, until my back thumped against the hard wood. Panic struck. He'd closed the door. I was locked in with him. My head whipped to the side—the other door was still propped open, its exit less than a foot from me.

I snapped back to Wep, who had stilled. He looked me up and down, then he frowned. "What's wrong?" It was more than a question—it was a command.

I crossed my arms over my chest, in self-defense or maybe comfort. "Nothing."

He mirrored me, arms crossed, feet planted. The firelight flickered over his skin, casting every muscle into relief. "Have it your way," he said, voice stern. Everything about this man screamed barely leashed control. "I guess you forgot you're the one who interrupted me."

"Not intentionally!" My voice shook, though I tried to keep it steady. "I expected to be alone. It's not like I have my own room in this blasted keep."

That made his brow furrow.

I needed to get out. I was in no state to spar with him, physically or mentally. I was primed to buckle at any second. I inched toward the open door. His arm twitched like he might reach out and stop me, so I turned and fled up the stairs.

His footsteps followed undeterred.

A frustrated tear splashed down my cheek, and I flicked it away. With my hand on the handle to the Relaxation Room, I paused. "What?" I spat out, though it sounded suspiciously like a sob.

"Believe it or not, I'm not a complete asshole. I can see you're upset."

I dropped my boots on the landing and rounded on him, hands on hips. "Why would you care about anything I'm feeling?"

He crossed his arms. In the darkness of the stairway, his features were entirely shadowed. "I care when there's a problem I can fix."

"Typical." I turned the handle and pushed into the room. Predictably, he followed. I rounded on him again. "You're the big, strong man coming to solve all my problems, are you? Well, it was big, strong men who got me into this mess, so you'll forgive my skepticism." I glared at him with every ounce of haughtiness I could muster. I may not be Merria, but I could still channel the up tilt of her nose and *that look* that always made me want to throttle her.

Based on his glare and the set of his jaw, visible in the flickering flames, it had its intended effect. "I haven't done anything to you. Last I checked, you agreed—"

"Were you in here already?" I interrupted. A tall candelabra stood behind me, set up on the table with twelve candles burning. It had only just hit me that the room wasn't cast in complete darkness as I'd expected. The narrow window framing the top of one wall, which let in natural light, was still dark.

Surprise flickered across his face, just for a moment, before it relaxed. "Does that matter?" He asked in a neutral tone.

"No, I just didn't know you used this room."

"I created it, didn't I?"

"You did?"

"It's my Training Hall."

"Oh. Right." I don't know why that shocked me. This room, which was such a comfort to me, was created by this man who embodied the exact opposite. I struggled to imagine him sitting here, perhaps with his boots off, eyes closed, and head leaned back against the wall.

Wep scratched the jawline of his short beard. "Look, I'm doing my best here. This is new territory for me."

"Talking to women? I can tell."

His eyebrow quirked up. "She's got jokes."

"To the constant disappointment of my father. A daughter with a brain in her skull. Every lord's nightmare."

"I know a thing or two about fathers and expectations."

A smile ghosted across his lips, and something inside me shifted and settled. No part of me wanted to find him disarming, but—Martyrs' blood and bones—he was.

"I do care that you're upset," he went on. "I'm just saying, this is why we train. Healthy body, healthy mind."

"Of course it is," I sighed. Back to this again. "Training doesn't bring people back from the dead." I retreated to the nearest cushion and plopped down. "Or missing, or whatever. We got a missive from the prince. His whole squadron is missing, likely dead." I didn't know why I was confiding this in him. "My point is, today was... It doesn't matter. Either way, he's gone. He was gone before I even left Inra. No amount of training can fix that."

He stepped in front of me and knelt, forcing my gaze to meet his eye. One hand reached out and caressed down my arm. Despite the grief roiling within me, my shoulders dropped, and I leaned into his comforting touch. I was on the precipice of danger, but Creator above, it was exactly where I wanted to be.

"This man, he was lost fighting for your king?"

I nodded, and my eyes prickled. I rubbed the heels of my palms over them, forcing away unshed tears and trying to clear my head of this temporary madness. I couldn't let him—or anyone here—know my weaknesses. I shouldn't be letting him see me cry.

"You miss him."

"Yes," I whispered.

Something in Wep's eyes changed. A small pinch, a twinge behind his gaze. It was something akin to understanding.

"Do you love him?" he asked, voice low.

"Of course."

"That's why you hate it here. You were taken from the one you love." He breathed a sigh that could have knocked me over with its weight if I weren't already sitting. I'd never seen this side of him, and it made me wonder if he'd lost someone too.

"He was taken from me."

Wep's jaw clenched. He released it with visible effort. "What was his name?"

"Bale."

"How did you meet?"

Meet? "No, he's my—"

The door burst open. Wep stood and whirled around in one fluid motion. Somehow, he was always at the ready. The next second, though, his body relaxed, and he stepped aside, shoving his hands into his pockets.

Gerta stood in the doorway, panting, panic on her face, and holding my forgotten boots. "Milady," she huffed. "I didn't know where you were. I was hoping...but then the day and..." Her eyes darted from me to Wep, back to me, then back to Wep, trailing down his form, lingering on his bare arms. She dipped into a quick curtsey. "Forgive me, I'm interrupting."

She made to back out of the room, but Wep motioned her in.

"No need. I'm leaving." He pushed by her and was swallowed by the darkness of the stairway beyond. He didn't so much as glance back at me before he was gone.

It shouldn't have mattered. I didn't need him here. What reason was there for him to stay? When no answer came, I dropped my head into my hands. Training today was going to suck.

THE HOUR CAME upon me far too soon. I showed up to training with puffy, red eyes and a semi-permanent frown. When I walked into the room, I hardly recognized the place. Stands polka-dotted the mat, each displaying different weapons. My *ranng* chatted animatedly, pointing to different stations. I was the last to arrive.

"What's going on?" I asked Ivank, the only one whose attention I could grab.

"Assessment day." His brows did a little dance, and he pointed to a rack that held three different types of maces. "I'm going for the hammer first." Indeed, one of the maces had a box-shaped head like an overgrown blacksmith hammer. "What about you?"

"Burning Martyrs, I have to choose one of these?"

"No." Wep's cold voice rang out across the room. "You'll be trying everything you can manage to lift."

"I'm not using these. I never agreed to weapons."

"I don't care what you use, they're a part of training."

"But—"

"Non-negotiable. Let's begin."

Oh. Fuck. Me. It was by far the worst day of my life in the Riht. Wep went through the rest of my *ranng* first, all of whom selected one weapon to be tested on. Lispen was a wonder with two short swords. Ivank got to test with his hammer, though Wep disarmed him quickly. Raif, Lex, and Teke all went for longswords, and Helene tested with a slender sword with a curved blade

I'd never seen before. It suited her reedy frame and flowed with her graceful movements. Wep passed each one of them, even Ivank.

Then came my turn. I couldn't lift the two-handed maces, axes, or longswords. I managed to lift the short swords, but I didn't have the coordination to hold two at once without dropping one. I tried with one sword and a shield—that was a joke. The daggers worked just fine in my grip, but as Wep pointed out, they were highly situational and always required close quarters, which I couldn't even attempt without getting smacked by the flat of his blade. Between my poor performance and uneven balance, I wasn't even allowed to try the pike or spear.

"Come," Wep said once all stations in the training room had been exhausted. He walked out the open door and into the sunlight.

I followed, and he led me to a series of sprawling training pitches. There were grassy patches, circles of sand, and squares filled with small, reddish pebbles. He led me to the last area, which was covered in wood chips and set up with targets at the far end. On the stand nearest us were different types of bows, and another held quivers of arrows.

"Oh, archery." A small thrill bubbled up inside me.

Wep nodded, then plucked the smallest bow from the rack. He tested the string, then handed it to me. "Do you need a demonstration?"

"No," I said, eliciting a raised brow from him. This was one thing I had experience with. Mother had barred me from swordplay with Bale before I was six, and though she frowned when he brought me to the targets, she didn't intervene. According to her logic, I would never find opportunity to hold a bow outside our home, but swords were common. Especially in town where officers were abundant, she feared the easy access presented too great a temptation for me. So I settled for archery, counting it as a win to do something only allowed to boys. Though now, I was a year out of practice, with how long Bale had been gone.

I held the bow in my left hand and tested the string. It was slightly larger than what I was used to, despite being the smallest on the rack. I drew in a deep, slow breath. Plucking an arrow from the nearby quiver, I planted my feet and pulled back the drawstring. With my target in sight, I took three deep breaths. On the final exhale, when all the air had left my lungs, I paused for only a moment, long enough to relax my right hand. The arrow flew.

With a soft *thunk*, it embedded into the target. It wasn't a perfect center hit, but it landed. I turned to Wep, grinning, and bowed. Behind me, my *ranng* clapped, cheering my name.

Wep had a hand to his chin, eyes on the target. His short beard had been trimmed down to little more than scruff since I'd seen him that morning. I hated admitting it suited him even better. "You've had training."

"Only from my brother." My heart panged at the admission, but Bale would have been proud to see me like this.

"Good. I can work with this. Nock another, but don't release."

I did as instructed, back straight and arms spread. Wep moved to my front, repositioning my arms and hands, and showing me the lines I should be creating with my body.

"Your structure should give you support without wearing you out." He stepped around to my back, using his own feet to reposition mine.

"Can I touch you?" he asked.

What did he think he'd been doing? "Yes."

His hands smoothed over my spine from neck to base. "Good," he muttered. Then, they swept down my sides. He adjusted my ribcage slightly, then my hips. Finally, he reached around and ran his hands over my stomach. "Tighter," he whispered, his breath tickling my ear. I didn't need that advice—my whole body had already tightened at the contact.

"Your core is your stability. Everything builds from there." He was so close to me that he was practically enveloping me. His scent lingered in the air—eucalyptus and mint and something just a little bit earthy. I could barely focus on keeping the string taut.

He stepped back and appraised his work. "You sure you need the glasses?" he asked.

"I can take them off, but I can't be held responsible for whatever gets hit."

He nodded. "Release."

I relaxed, and the arrow flew true. My *ranng* exploded into hoots and hollers as it hit the target's center, but I barely noticed. My eyes were on Wep, drinking in his approval.

He nodded once, a small smile twisting the side of his mouth and reaching his silver eyes. I had never seen anything more beautiful.

I was well and truly fucked.

"TRAINING, LESSONS, MEALS, repeat. The life these Riht all think is so great is going to bore me to death." I flopped into what had become *my* chair at the small table in our cramped room and threw my arms over my eyes. Even my latest session with Dane, which covered maps of several regions around

Drakh, wasn't enough to keep my sense of boredom at bay. I ignored the way my gut clenched at yet more information I should be detailing in my journal to send back with Gerta. Information that could prove crucial when it was time to extract me.

Gerta tutted around as she rearranged this and that in our tiny space, a habit she'd developed to have things *as best prepared as possible* while we awaited my father's reply. It had been weeks since I'd sent that letter, but I hadn't remained idle. I'd continued to write home with one half-baked idea after the next of other ways to return the journal to him without losing Gerta.

My last letter to Merria included a suggestion to send it back with a trunk of my Inraen clothes. That plan was as weak as it was risky. The clothes were useless here, but there was no need for them at home—certainly not reason enough for an entire journey across the White Sea. My next plan involved secreting the journal within a selection of Rihtish goods, then begging Dane's aid in sending it to Cavendaffe as a gift for my beloved sister. The common issue with both plans, of course, was how I'd manage to hide the journal well enough to pass inspection. If he would have killed me for failing the Sun Trial, what might Dane do to me if I were discovered?

The trouble was, aside from my abysmal skills at planning and deception, my time was so filled with lessons and activities that I barely had time to think. Since our first visit, I had returned to the tea bar with Helene a couple of times for more earth-shattering concoctions, each drunk in absolute silence. I had stayed after training a few times to spar with Lispen—the short woman with cropped golden blond hair and a habit of kicking everyone's ass—when I was feeling particularly masochistic. And almost every day, I had private lessons that included strength-building with Wep. He had begun exercising alongside me in our evening sessions, and it was doing things to me that I didn't care to admit. Those left me in the worst mood, and not just from muscle aches.

If I were being honest with myself, his sessions weren't all bad. My lip quirked up at the memory of the prior night. Wep had me doing some ungodly balancing on a ball I swear was filled with sand. It was barely wide enough to stand on with two feet side by side, let alone balance. Of course, I fell a hundred times, cursed Wep up and down with every Mayoran slur I could think of—and a few extra in Inraen to boot—all while he stood there stoic and bored. Then, by the mercy of the Nine Martyrs, I finally found my balance and kept it. It was the first time I'd seen him break and flash an actual, full smile. The only praise he offered was, *Took you long enough*.

Still, the monotony of the daily activities chafed.

"This existence is pointless. Every bit as pointless as the one I had at home."

"Missing your needlework then, milady?" Gerta asked.

"No," I scowled. I hated needlework. What I craved was purpose. I wanted to feel like my life, my work, and my talents weren't just pointless nonsense. Yes, I could train my body and mind with Rihtish practices, but the Creator and I both knew I would never use them. If I stayed here, that would be one thing, but eventually, I would return to Inra, and all that I had learned here would be lost.

"Or maybe you'd rather be back in there with Wep, eh?"

What. The. Fuck.

Whipping around, I shot Gerta the sternest look I could muster. "Excuse me?"

She laughed. "Oh, shall I pretend not to notice what a handsome young lad he is, then?" She chuckled. "As you will."

"You've lost your flaming mind." I *did not* find that cold and merciless man attractive. Of course, I had eyes. Objectively, he had a body chiseled by the Creator himself. The muscle definition on that man was downright unseemly, and his tanned skin only served to highlight it. Seeing him sleeveless—fuck. Even the scars down his right arm did nothing to detract from how perfectly honed every inch of him was. Quite the opposite.

The problem wasn't his body. It was his face. Oh, he was handsome enough, with intense, steel-blue eyes, a strong jaw covered in just the right amount of scruff, and lips that were too inviting for their own good. But, he kept that beautiful fucking mouth in a constant scowl. That overall air of sourness was further pronounced by permanently drawn brows, making the whole package off-putting. I'd only seen him do anything resembling a smile twice.

The best part about him was his coppery, shoulder-length hair when it fell in his face, covering that constant bad mood. Except most days, he tied it up in a knot. I'd only *really* seen it down for the seconds it took him to re-tie it.

"Perhaps I have lost it, but my eyes don't lie. I've seen how you look at him."

I rolled my eyes. "Oh, for the love of the Nine Martyrs!"

"Fine, you don't like him, but you can't ignore the man's body. Even I can appreciate it."

A vision of his hard lines on top of me flashed uninvited through my mind. He had suggested sparring a few nights ago, he swept my legs out and pinned me to the floor with frightening ease. A flush of heat spread from the top of my head down to my chest. I needed to get laid, yet neither of my supposed betrotheds were around to help. "Fat lot of good that does anyone."

"Mmm. Imagine what Dane would think if he saw you mooning after Wep."

"I'm not mooning." I crossed my arms. "I do not moon."

"Of course not."

"And don't forget I'm betrothed."

"On my honor, I could never."

"Can we please get back to the matter at hand? Fire and ash, you're a gossip. What will you do when you're back home and don't have me to sew rumors about?"

Gerta froze.

I cringed. Blatant fear flashed across Gerta's eyes. My stomach dropped, and I sobered at the reminder of how soon she could be leaving me. "I'm sorry. I'm just sick of being useless," I muttered.

"Then talk to Wep. Maybe training doesn't have to be daily. We could ask Kahvrah—"

"Have you seen Kahvrah?" My interest piqued. It wasn't lost on me that Gerta disappeared most evenings. Dane had widened my reins to move within the castle grounds freely, but Gerta was still confined to the keep unless accompanied. The last time I had a tea date with Helene, she was missing all day and only returned to our room long after the dinner hour.

"Oh, I—uhm—yes. She's taken me to the market."

I sat up straight. "Without me?"

"Well, you have lessons and sparring sessions and...other plans..."

"What for?" I leaned forward in my chair. She was hiding something.

"For your basic needs, of course. Who do you think refills your personal items? And buys your favorite snacks?" Gerta's voice took on that sharpness from my childhood, like when I had painted flowers down the side of my dresser or ripped holes in all my stockings playing too roughly with Bale.

"She lies to you."

That burning voice again! Anger blossomed in my chest. I snatched up a comb and chucked it across the room. "UGH!" It cracked in half.

Gerta pushed a short breath out of her nose. "I suppose I'll replace that comb too when I next visit the market, shall I?"

I flopped back into my slump. "Don't be all high and mighty with me tonight. I'm not in the mood."

Her chair scraped against the floor, then her footfalls thumped across the room.

"You may not have chosen this life, but as a future leader of these people, one would think you'd see purpose everywhere you looked."

I opened my mouth to retort, but Gerta cut me off with a curt, "Goodnight," and closed the door behind her. I scowled at the ceiling and ignored the sting in Gerta's words. But Gerta didn't understand—didn't know—my true purpose here. I would never lead these people. The life chosen for me was that of a traitor. In every imaginable way, I was trapped.

"Any advice now?" I demanded of the empty room. "No? Silent now that you're not barging in on my conversations?"

"You have enough words for us both, my delicious little liar."

I clamped my mouth shut. Whatever it was that could hear me, whatever twisted part of my conscience was speaking back, it was really starting to scare me.

"BE READY."

It was the voice again, haunting my dreams. Why couldn't I just have a nice, simple dream for once? Just random regurgitations of the day and none of this commanding nonsense.

"The time draws near."

My eyes cracked open. The room blurred around me. I rolled over and smashed my face into the pillow. I didn't have time for dreams.

Gerta had returned at some point after I fell asleep. Her breaths were steady and even in the bed next to mine.

I closed my eyes and prayed for sleep.

"AGAIN," WEP COMMANDED, arms crossed and feet planted at the center of the mat. The calm in his voice was grating.

I huffed and took my stance, the wooden sword extended before me. Wep had decided that practice weapons would encourage my balance and coordination without the pesky worry of cutting off digits. The only problem was, fake sword or no, I sucked.

Lispen, opposing me, mirrored the stance. I lunged, and Lispen slapped my sword away with one sharp blow. My elbow rang with the impact, numbing half of the limb. My sword clattered to the mat.

"No," Wep said. "Again."

"What should I do differently?" I asked through gritted teeth.

"Not drop your weapon."

"Obviously!" I shouted.

Lispen's eyebrows raised. The room fell quiet, despite the other partnered pairs sparring with actual weapons.

"If you're going to teach me, you need to actually *teach* me, not expect me to just know what to change."

"You need to change your mind. You're thinking wrong."

"Thinking wrong?" I growled, snatching up the fallen sword. I fell into stance, and again Lispen mirrored.

Wep threw a glance over his shoulder, and the clanging of steel on steel resumed around us.

Lispen lunged, wood clashed, and my sword hit the floor. I shot Wep a look that would've made any other man wither where he stood. Wep, however, stared back, impassive.

I gathered up my practice sword *again* and fell into stance, unprompted. This repeated until my arm was vibrating with pain. I snatched up the flaming thing and flung it at the wall. A scream ripped from my throat as three other weapons clattered to the floor, scraping against the walls in their descent.

Everything went silent again, aside from my panting breaths and the jarring echo of metal on stone. I should have been embarrassed, but all I felt was the thick, hot pulse of frustration coursing through me.

"Feed it," the voice encouraged, utterly unhelpful.

"Enough," Wep commanded, snapping the tension. "Lispen, get a real weapon and take Teke or Raif. Serae, back to *dowsae*. Begin with child's."

"And then?" I shot back.

"I will tell you when to stop."

"Seriously?" I spat. I was itching for a fight. My blood pounded in my ears. "The child's *dowsa*?"

"More. Push your limits."

Wep's eyes held mine, then slowly, deliberately, shifted to the heap of weapons scattered across the floor. "Do you think something else more fitting?"

I growled but fell into stance. Wep took up beside me as I began. I gritted my teeth. I didn't need a reminder of how infinitely better Wep's honed body moved—even in this simple pattern—than my own. His every step was grace and power, balance and purpose. I was a fumbling idiot, every bit the child he'd insinuated. The worst part was my cursed self-awareness. I couldn't even escape into a meadow of blissful ignorance.

I had wanted to be accepted by this group, which had a casual camaraderie I envied from the first introduction. I had wanted to try my best, even when faced with an impossible, pointless task. I had wanted to prove—perhaps to myself—that I could do this, until my fucking temper got in the way.

Breath is for focus. Kahvrah's words echoed in my head this time, not *the voice*, and I obeyed. After a few steady breaths, my face cooled, and my heart rate slowed.

We continued the slow motions of the child's *dowsa* on loop for a dozen repetitions. Then, I walked to the wall and hung each weapon back in its original spot. I knew Wep was watching my every move. Fire and ash, the entire room was. When I finished, I stood beside him again and took stance, but he pivoted. He led me through the motions of the other *dowsae* I'd been learning—bear, fern, and even cat.

At the end of training, Wep touched my elbow. I looked up into his blue-gray eyes and, for a moment, they softened. He opened his mouth to speak but must have thought better of it. Instead, he gave me a quick nod that I hoped conveyed his approval and left.

"You don't dine in the Hall," a rumbling voice sounded behind me. It was Ivank, and it wasn't a question.

I scrunched my eyebrows. "No."

"Why?"

"Because I'm not permitted. I bring a tray to my room."

Ivank frowned. "We all eat in the hall, even Dane. All Riht may join."

My stomach soured. "Well, you've hit it on the nose, haven't you? I'm not a Riht." Several of the others leaned in toward our conversation. Whatever their opinions, I wasn't in the mood to hear them. I marched away before anything more could be said.

When I entered our room, I had expected to find Gerta waiting for me like usual for our midday meal, but it was empty—except for the chill. Everything in Rihtlond was cold, especially as autumn crept in. It was nothing like the dry, absent cold of Inra that made a house feel vacant. It was like a living entity, filling every hallway. The thick, wet chill pushed its way into every crack and crevice. It followed you down hallways and battered against windowpanes. It seeped into your skin, your bones, and your heart, and forced you to carry it with you through every step. I had expected to adapt quickly, considering winter had always been my favorite time of year. How very wrong I was.

"Let the tenth Martyr freeze to death," I hissed at no one at all. Then, I collapsed onto my bed. I glared at the wardrobe, weighing my options. I could strip this blanket off the bed and bundle myself up. But when Gerta returned, she'd tell me I was being childish. I'd had enough of that for one day. Alternatively, I could make use of the leather overcoat that had appeared in the wardrobe a few days ago. I had been avoiding it on principle. Or... something. It was heavy and unyielding and so very Rihtish. It was made to last for decades here, and I was not. I was a woman who wanted more pillows on her bed than any one person could use, enjoyed the look of elegant—if inconvenient—dresses and *sollars*, and missed being surrounded by frills and gilt trim. I was not someone who felt comfortable in leathers and boots or who could kick anyone's ass.

A knock at the door sounded.

"Enter."

"Your meal, my lady," a young woman said as she pushed through with a tray. She looked close to my age. She set the dishes, removed the tray, and stood to the side rather than retreating.

"Is there something else?" I asked.

"Yes, my lady. I have been assigned as an option to be your new *reálta*."

"An option?"

"Yes, my lady."

"And if I don't like you?" I knew the question was rude, but I'd lost my ability to care.

"Another option will be found until you are satisfied, my lady."

I growled at that, and my stomach echoed me. The smell of the food was taking its hold, and my traitorous body was acting as if it didn't know we were in the mood to hate all things Rihtish. I hauled myself off the bed and moved to the table. The meal looked as good as it smelled, piled with roasted veggies and a rich dipping sauce. I took a bite, and Creator above, they were spiced to perfection.

"What's your name, then?" I asked after half the plate had disappeared.

"Callagh, my lady."

"Will you be saying 'my lady' after every sentence?"

"Yes, my lady. Until you are Dana, of course."

"Of course." Bitterness and I were becoming fast friends. "And what did you do to get stuck with the likes of me?"

I glanced up in time to see Callagh's neck turn bright red.

"It is an honor, my lady."

That got a hearty, honest laugh out of me. "An honor? To be stuck with the Inraen bitch? Ignorant, prudish, good for only one thing. This is an honor to serve?" I gestured to my whole self.

The girl had the decency to look abashed.

"Sorry," I muttered, dragging my hands down my face. "I've had an awful day, but that's not your fault. If you don't want to be stuck with me, I'll tell Dane I want someone else."

"I'm not stuck," Callagh piped up. "*Reálti* can refuse any appointment. A match is required on both sides."

My heart sank. "I see," I forced out.

Several moments passed in silence. My eyes fell to my plate, appetite gone.

Callagh cleared her throat. "I yelled at my mom."

I raised an eyebrow.

"She's the one who assigns *reálti* to prominent families in Drakh. I may have told her to quit her bellyaching and just pick someone already. She thought she'd pick me as punishment." Callagh grinned with a wickedness that I would normally have found a delight, if not for the sentiment behind her words. I was a punishment. Callagh must have realized this too because her face fell, and she whispered, "Sorry, my lady."

"You cannot force these people to respect you, Small One. One day soon, they will all wish they had."

I blinked. Then, a laugh burst out of me. I laughed so hard that Callagh started chuckling too. I was a *punishment!* All this time, I had worried about being an inconvenience, being too weak or too ignorant. Meanwhile, the Riht had been avoiding me because I was a challenge. Maybe I was losing it, but soon enough, I was cackling, eyes streaming and stitches in my sides. Callagh was full-out laughing now, too.

Despite the awful morning, I decided to count the afternoon as a win. The food was good, and perhaps the company was, too. I made Callagh sit and tell me all about her mother and the other *reálti.* She never dropped her constant *my lady* addresses, but we'd work on that another day.

I smiled through my lesson with Dane—more maps, this time of Mayora—and even after I tucked into bed later that night. Perhaps I wouldn't be so alone after all. At any rate, it's not like I was going to be in the Riht forever. Even the voice in my head was oddly supportive.

"You, of all humans, owe others nothing."

I fell asleep to that notion, and for the first time in a while, I slept soundly.

When I woke the next morning, Gerta was still missing. Her bed was undisturbed, and there were no signs she'd come back during the night. A prickle of fear crawled up my spine. I dressed, pushed food around the tray Callagh brought, and invented a hundred reasons for Gerta's absence, each one more outlandish than the last. When I was nearly finished pretending to eat, a messenger arrived and spoke hastily to Callagh in Rihtish.

"We must away to Dane, as soon as you can, my lady."

I stood at once. As we hurried down the halls, I hoped it was a trick of the light—Callagh had turned quite pale. Instead of heading to the Receiving Hall, we ducked down a corridor I'd never noticed. The door was unremarkable, but stepping through it felt like crossing a magic portal to the king's palace. Floor-to-ceiling windows lined an entire wall, and every inch of the wall opposite was covered in vibrant, intricate tapestries. The chairs were so well polished that they gleamed in the scant sun rays. Every surface held a plush cushion, drapery, or carving with jaw-dropping detail. The room was a visual masterpiece.

Yet, there was no time to appreciate any of it. My eyes immediately fell to the back of Gerta's head.

Dane spoke, as always, with no preamble. "Your father is a right ass, Cavendaffe girl. Does he truly care so little for you?"

I stiffened. "I have rarely caught his attention, Sire."

Dane grunted and held out a single sheaf of parchment.

I snatched it, but as soon as I saw the writing, I already knew what it would contain. Gerta's eyes were rimmed with red. It was addressed to Dane, but I knew the words were meant for me.

Dane Auldren, Son of Éalren,

Your house has requested the permanent relocation of one servant from the House of Cavendaffe. Allow me to remind you that the terms of this return have long since been agreed. Before any transfer could be considered, payment in kind to buy out her contract must be received. As this has not taken place, I respectfully demand the return of my rightful property, as promised and without further delay. The initial four-week settlement period is past complete. In good faith, I graciously extend you this extra time plus reasonable travel without the need for compensation. I look forward to your agreeable response.

With respect,

Lord Tychon, Margrave of Cavendaffe

I choked out a laugh. This wasn't about Gerta—she meant nothing to him. She was primarily devoted to me while at the manor, and it was no loss to be without her while I was away. This was Father's way of telling me that my time had run out. The journal had to be sent home. Letters, plans, and bargaining would not be accepted. I was a fool ever to think, to hope otherwise.

"Time's up, lass," Dane Auldren said, voice low and brow furrowed. "We've no choice but to send her back. Keeping her would violate the agreement. You're smart enough to know what that would mean for you."

I nodded.

"We'll take a few days to wait out the inclement sea weather. I'll request your margrave's terms for her release. Best prepare yourselves, the both of you."

"Thank you, Sire," I mumbled. A glance at Gerta confirmed my worries. She had a steady stream of tears falling down her cheeks. Kahvrah stood off to the side, her face equally grave. A prickling sensation crawled along the back of my head at the sight of her.

As Callagh and I walked back to our room—soon to be just mine—a hollowness filled me. It was the sickly, twisting grip of loss. Gerta returned minutes after I did, and Callagh retreated with a short bow. I eased my shaking friend to a seat on her bed.

"I'll be all right," I offered, knowing it was useless comfort.

"Milady, I cannot leave you. I will not."

"You must."

"I won't."

I took a steadying breath. There was more to this than a maid reluctant to leave her charge. But there were no terms my father would agree to. If I were staying in the Riht forever, he might be tempted by a heavy profit. But leaving behind a woman who knew the intimate workings of his house? We stood a better chance of defying the agreement outright. However, the consequences would be steep—too steep. With a bit of time, I knew Gerta would see it too.

I gripped my friend's hands. "Staying would be seen as a betrayal by the Riht, not by you or me alone. There is no other choice. We both know this."

Gerta pressed her lips together so tightly, they turned white. "I'll return to you. I swear it."

"That would make me happier than you know, but for now, focus on your duty."

"Be clear by being vague," Gerta recited.

"Yes."

"Give inconsequential details."

I nodded. "Go on."

"Be honest about not meeting Eldreth."

"And?"

"Do not praise Dane too highly nor too lowly."

It was a mantra of sorts that we had worked out together over the past few days. She claimed it was to be sure she didn't betray me in my new life, but I had other suspicions in the form of a dark blond *dowsae* instructor, with whom she spent her final day. Another reason Gerta would have been more at home in the Riht, free of stigma. My motives came from a place of bitterness. I was expected to hand my father Drakh's secrets on a silver platter, and in return, he had offered me only two weeks of leeway for an impossible task and a threat.

We looked at each other, Gerta and I, and something passed between us. I had known her for so long, yet a new bond had grown while here. We were likely the only two Inraens in all the continent who knew the full scope of how different life in the Riht was. Being here together had forged between us something unique and irreplaceable.

Leaving this unspoken, I said, "The Riht should appear as neither a threat nor low-hanging fruit." They were Dane's words from one of our private lessons, and they had never rung so true.

Gerta nodded. "I'm ready."

But I'm not.

CHAPTER 12

Prince Charlog eyed me from his throne as I knelt before him. "The king is moving. His men-at-arms are mobilizing across the land."

"Your father, in his barren court, is fearful of the favor you carry," I said.

"Jealous bastard. I need a plan," he hissed and looked to me.

"Yes, my prince."

He held out a hand covered in rings for me to kiss.

Nobles fighting nobles, kings against princes, kin slaughtering kin. All trivialities. Something from the deepest magic of the realms was brewing, and it would rock this world greater than any petty war, regardless of which king sat on the throne.

—Recounting from the private diary of Jerris, Dragonbound

SERAE

LATE SUMMER, MAYMON 1036

In two days' time, I stood at the edge of the bridge, waving through tears as

Gerta rode away on horseback. Guilt lay heavy on my shoulders. I had failed to do more for her. She looked completely at home in her Rihtish clothes, surrounded by dark leaves and rich soil—unlike me. What a twisted fate that Gerta, who thrived in the Riht, was sent home while I was forced to remain here.

As my own small act of defiance, I kept my incomplete journal for myself. Instead, she carried my fattest letter yet, filled with sketches about Rihtish ships and details about the port city copied from its pages, plus a plea to open negotiations with Dane for her return. As long as I held the journal, there was a small chance he might relent. I just had to convince him the information inside was worth it. A risky move, considering it was equally likely he might consider me a lost cause and abandon me here, forever.

I stood frozen on the wrong side of the moat with Callagh at my side. My last tether to the girl I used to be trotted steadily out of existence. Now, I was truly alone in an enemy camp, expected to somehow get by. At least there was no suitor yet to fend off. Dane had stopped mentioning Eldreth's return date, and I'd stopped asking. It was a blessing from the Creator that I didn't have to feign interest in getting to know him, whoever he was.

The more time I spent in the Riht, the less sense I could make of being here. I had so many burning questions, none of which Callagh—or anyone, for that matter—could answer. My biggest one: *Why was I here?* The idea of needing an alliance was laughable now that I knew the wealth and reach of these people from my lessons with Dane. Perhaps equally important—how would I spend my life if I were to stay here? What if Father never came to collect me? What if I really did have to marry a stranger and become dana to these people? What was the point of all that I was learning? Of anything? Of me?

"Enough, Small One."

The voice was right. It was no good traveling down that line of thinking. Nothing about me fit in here, especially now that I was the lone Inraen in an ocean of Riht. What cruel irony, to have a fresh start in a new world and still be unhappy with myself. At home, I was the tall, buxom girl in a sea of petites. In the Riht, I was the weakling in a sea of muscles. My one constant—I was still the only redhead. Well, except for Wep. His rusty, copper locks stood out as dramatically as my own, yet somehow, his otherness fit.

It was with this mixed-up headspace that I went to my lessons. I entered the training room overwhelmed and ready to burst into tears. Lispen looked me up and down, then she kicked Lex, who was mid-gulp from his waterskin and promptly spewed it everywhere.

"Disgusting," she muttered, wiping the side of her face.

Teke approached and placed a hand on my shoulder. "I'm here for you," they said with a smile.

"Fall in," Raif announced.

I fell into stance along with the others and began warming up my muscles, following Raif's lead, focusing hard on his short brown braids to avoid catching anyone's eye. Halfway through, Wep entered from the outer door to observe before taking the lead. He spared one glance in my direction. Apparently, one was all it took. He froze mid-step, and I knew his gaze was on me—assessing, dissecting.

He was at my side in a moment. "Come," he said, voice low.

I scowled.

With a barked order at the rest to continue, he led the way out of the training area and up the stairs toward the Relaxation Room—assuming I'd follow him.

"Sit."

Receiving orders like a dog was low on my list of ways I liked being treated. Wep moved to the corner of the room and dropped onto one of the floor cushions, staring at me. Like he expected my obedience.

Seriously? Wep was not the talk-about-your-feelings type, as proven by our last encounter in this room. This was downright bizarre.

He huffed and had the gall to look exasperated.

"Fine." I selected a pillow of my own, but I scowled so spectacularly that even the great weaponmaster flinched. I took no small amount of satisfaction in it.

His lips thinned. He sucked in a breath as if to speak but then let it out. A muscle in his jaw ticked, and the movement caught my eye.

It might have been the dim light addling my senses, but I had to admit, he had a perfect jawline. A tiny, crazed part of me was forced to admire it against my will. It was purely physical. I hadn't been touched intimately in several weeks, not even by myself, and it was building up. My body was starting to feel desperate for release, making my imagination run wild.

Images of my last night with Tam flooded my mind, but I pushed them away. Thinking about Tam made me feel weak around the edges, like I might finally crack and let the despair over my situation in. I shoved it out and forced my eyes back to Wep and his stupidly chiseled jaw. I still wanted to throttle the man, but a girl could look.

And, looking I was.

I drank him in shamelessly, which was a big fucking problem, seeing as I was in Drakh to both entice and use my mystery betrothed while somehow keeping him at bay. I couldn't risk my tentative safety over some convenient sex. Still, I wondered what it would feel like to trace that immaculate jawline with my tongue. Not that he would let me.

Wep cleared his throat and shifted on his cushion.

Creator above, what had my stupid face just given away? "What?" I snapped, injecting defiance into my voice. It fell embarrassingly flat.

"You're upset," he replied matter-of-factly.

"Your perception is a wonder."

Wep smirked. I had expected him to frown. "You're no good for lessons today."

I sighed. *Were we really doing this?*

"Unless I'm misreading your obvious bad mood?"

Yep, we were. I had a hundred sarcastic comments waiting on my tongue. Instead, I asked, "Who are you?"

Wep's eyes narrowed. "Surely you know by now that—"

"The Wep I know," I interrupted, "is a tireless taskmaster. *Surely,* the best medicine for any ailment is drills and *dowsae*. Even an ailment of the heart."

Ah, there it was—that frown I'd come to rely on. "I didn't think you two were intimate."

The image of my tearful goodbye with Gerta hit me in a new light. "Martyrs, no!" I laughed, unable to stop myself. Wep's face hardened. *Shit.* I gripped his forearm. "No, I'm sorry, it's just—Gerta's been my maid since childhood."

Wep nodded. The muscles in his forearm twitched, and I withdrew my hand.

"Plus, she's so old!"

"She's not even forty. That's hardly *so old*." He leaned back, stretching out one leg and just barely grazing my knee. My body tingled in response.

"She's fourteen years my senior. Fourteen years!"

"I've seen couples in your lands with more years between them than that."

"Bleh."

A corner of Wep's mouth quirked up. Martyrs, it was a good look on him. He raised his arm to scratch his neck, and his wrist peeked out of his shirt sleeve. The memory of him sleeveless with those tattoos curling around his biceps wormed its way to the forefront of my mind. I shook my head. I needed to redirect this line of thinking. "How old are you?" I blurted out. Not the question I meant to ask.

"Twenty-six this autumn."

"And how do you feel about twelve-year-olds?"

Wep scoffed. "I think four years apart is a better fit for me."

The grin slipped from my face. I pursed my lips and gave in to silence. This was a place I absolutely could not go. His brain had clearly abandoned him as well. Wait, did that mean there was attraction on his end, too?

"Relax, it was a joke."

I ignored this comment and went for safe ground. "She was my only friend here." The words hit me harder than I expected when spoken aloud. I turned my head to the nearest tapestry, not sure what I might be revealing on my face.

"You're not the only one who gets lonely."

What the actual fuck?

I jumped to my feet. "No, you don't get to do that."

Wep held my gaze. When he spoke, it was a low rumble. "Come again?"

Rage from I didn't know where rose in me like wildfire. He couldn't possibly understand what it was like to be trapped, juggling two unwanted sides of the same ill-fated coin. I had no interest in this nonsense betrothal to a missing prince and no interest in this theoretical betrothal to my oldest friend. Above all, I had no interest in betraying these people, a few of whom showed me only kindness.

And there it was, my truth laid bare. Pulsing blood was ringing in my ears. Whether here or in Inra, I was barred from making my own choices. I was trapped by the will of men, and I needed to break free.

Rounding on Wep, I lashed out. "You don't get to pretend like our problems are the same. You are surrounded by admiration in the land you've grown up in. You know everything about this place. You are completely at home. You are accepted." I knew my voice was rising, but I could not bring myself to care. "You aren't sneered at while walking through the market. No one sidesteps you for being a stranger. You're not mocked for your hair, your body, your height, and everything else about your very existence. You know nothing of what it's like to be me. Nothing."

Wep stood. His jaw clenched, and this time, I only wanted to slap it. "I know a thing or two about being mocked for your hair."

I glanced at his coppery locks and rolled my eyes. Storming out would have felt blissful after such an outburst, but I only made it halfway across the room before I remembered myself. With a day of lessons ahead, I was not free to walk away. My mouth filled with bitterness.

"May I be excused?"

He scoffed.

"May I?" I repeated, wrangling the edge in my voice.

Wep sighed. "Go."

As fast as I could, I exited to my room. Despite the cramped space, it felt empty now. There was no one who could share this burden with me—no end to the depths of alone I faced. By evening, I would surely regret my outburst. My cheeks would burn to remember how the stoic weaponmaster had tried to connect with me, and I repaid him with harsh refusal. The rational side of me knew none of this was Wep's fault. But, for now, I gave in to my anger.

THAT NIGHT, MY dream of the cave was the most vivid yet. I approached the entrance with wide eyes and open ears.

"Come in," that now familiar voice beckoned in my mind. *"I've been waiting for you."*

I entered. Inside the cave was dark, yet it was permeated by color and light. Swirls of iridescence surrounded me, caressed me, and filled my very being. I was alight with it. Fire and ice and something I could only describe as vastness combined within me. I was ancient. Powerful. Perfect.

"I see you," I said into the light.

With my next breath, it consumed me. I screamed, whether from pain or ecstasy, I couldn't tell, and tried to move, turn away, or do anything to relieve this brilliance bursting through my skull.

Then, it was gone.

"Sleep," she said, and for the first time, I knew the voice was female. *"It is done. All is well. You are mine, and I am yours. Sleep."*

The next morning, I woke to the sounds of Callagh setting down my breakfast tray. I groaned without opening my eyes. The previous day came back to me. Before long, I would be faced with Wep again and would have to find a way to apologize. I just hoped my mood hadn't tainted things with my *ranng*, too.

"Dane wishes to see you after your meal."

I jolted upright. "Me?" I opened my eyes, and the room swirled.

"Yes, my lady." Callagh's face was soft. She understood too much.

"Why?" My voice sounded distant in my ears. I willed my mind to focus.

I was in my room, in my bed—that much I knew—but the air around me was swirling, sparkling light. I recognized it. There was something important that I knew, but I could not put it into words.

Callagh fidgeted with her skirt, and I fixated on the movement. "He didn't explain, my lady."

"Right, of course." I frowned. Head spinning, I got up and hobbled to the wardrobe. I stared at the clothes. The once-muted fabrics now shimmered with colors I had never imagined. A rainbow of iridescence poured forth, mingling with the vibrancy of the room. It was as if a veil of gray had been lifted from my eyes, and now the very breeze from my window swirled through the room in a thousand translucent colors. I gaped in awe.

"Are you all right, my lady?"

My jaw snapped shut, but I couldn't stop my wide eyes from darting around the room in wonder.

Dressing took time, and Callagh moved to help me without asking. I couldn't even form the words to thank her. When dressed, I sat before my vegetable plate and stared. I picked up the fork, but I couldn't bring myself to eat. Not only was my stomach on edge from all the swirling, but these vegetables just looked off. They were dark and ashen. I looked to Callagh, who was now eyeing me with wariness. I held my breath and managed four bites before my stomach threatened to expel everything.

"Let's not keep Dane waiting."

If my mind had not been in such a state, I might have noticed my glasses left behind on my bedside table. By the time I made it to the hall, my mind was a blur of fog and colorful mist.

I stood before Dane, who frowned while stroking the long braid of his beard. The floor tilted beneath me, and Callagh moved closer, gripping my arm to steady me.

"Are you ill, Daughter?"

My eyes jumped from person to person. Everyone in the room was glowing, vibrant lights spilling from their bodies. A rainbow of colors emanated through their skins. I gasped.

"What's wrong?" Dane's voice boomed.

I shook my head, and the colors swirled painfully in my vision. *Nothing*, I tried to say, but no sound came out.

"*Peace.*" She spoke, and I stilled. Everything quieted, and a small soft light beckoned me to a corner of my mind. I followed it, retreating into sleep.

"**Bow before me,**" she demanded through my voice, but it was all right.

I let her have it. **"I shall return to you soon to demand your promise be fulfilled. The time is nigh. Be ready when I summon you."**

A force *pushed* out of me, and everyone in the room toppled to the floor. Only Dane remained upright, though on his knees.

When he stood, I could sense the struggle and pain from his wobbling leg. He rose and looked straight into eyes that were not mine. "We stand ready to serve."

"You have done well, Small One. Now, sleep."

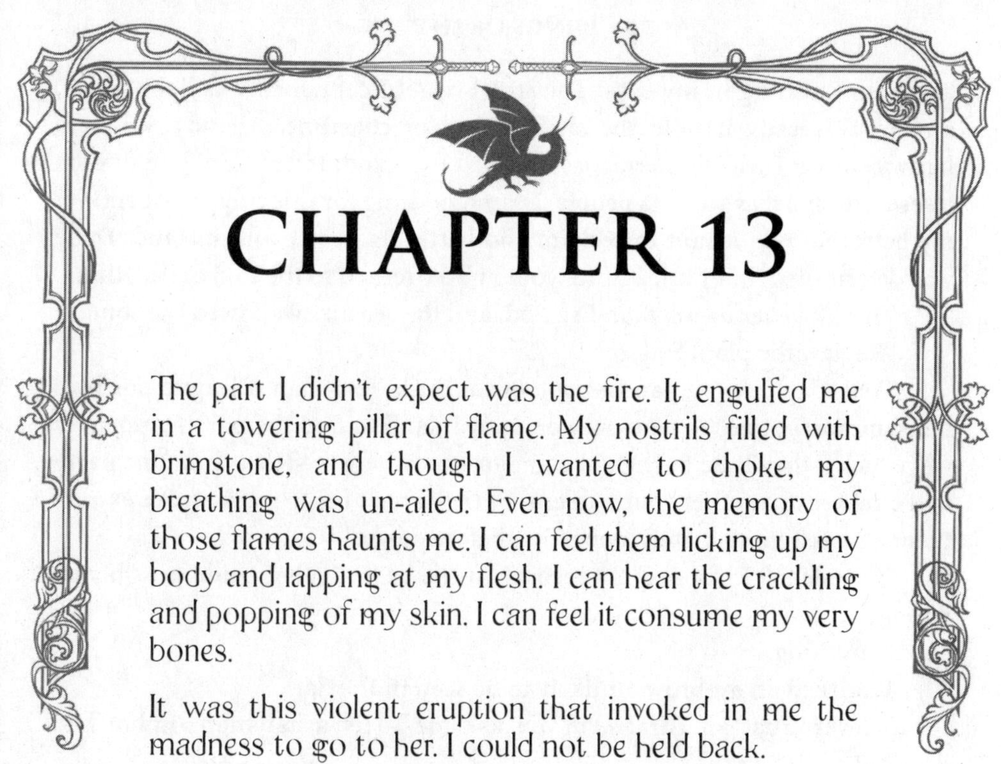

CHAPTER 13

The part I didn't expect was the fire. It engulfed me in a towering pillar of flame. My nostrils filled with brimstone, and though I wanted to choke, my breathing was un-ailed. Even now, the memory of those flames haunts me. I can feel them licking up my body and lapping at my flesh. I can hear the crackling and popping of my skin. I can feel it consume my very bones.

It was this violent eruption that invoked in me the madness to go to her. I could not be held back.

—Entry from the private diary of Jerris, Dragonbound

• ◆ •

ELDRETH

LATE SUMMER, MAYMON 1036

THE SEAS WERE rough, befitting the mission as well as the waning moon. Soon, it would be new, offering me the black night I needed for this fool's errand. I questioned my sanity for agreeing to it. Dane insisted it was vital for both my betrothal and the Riht. The latter I loved dearly, and the former, well, who knew what the future would bring. Not that there was any other choice now.

I welcomed the icy sea air against my face, the tang of salt on my tongue, and even the sting in my eyes. The small vessel I captained was light, quick, and would easily handle the shallow Inraen coastline. Already, we were halfway down Inra's western coast. I hated that land. It was hard and dry. Its trees were short, as were its people. I cared nothing for this tiny continent, yet my betrothal was meant to reclaim and better its people and its land. Dane was determined, but I knew Inra would never return to the fold of the Riht.

This all better be worth it. I sighed, and the sea air swallowed the sound.

"Review the plan, Sellan."

"Yes, Captain. We land tomorrow at dusk, less than a league north of the summon point. We take one company inland to find the missing *ranng.* If we're lucky, they'll be at the old campground where we left them. One party will circle east, another south, to ensure they aren't being tracked. We extract them and exit immediately, departing before dawn."

"Excellent." I clapped my second on the back. "What could possibly go wrong?"

"Anything."

I quirked an eyebrow, unlikely to be seen in the dark.

"Never trust an Inraen, if you ask me." His usual high timbre had dropped an octave.

"You think Dane was wrong to send us?"

"No. Dane had his reasons. He's playing some long game none of us can see. Always something turning in that great mind of his."

I grumbled my assent.

The sea tumbled, and the wind stayed strong through the following day. Each gust promised luxurious speed. We docked before dusk, to find our hidden camp nestled in the Inraen forest abandoned, tents empty, and only our permanent guard hidden in the trees. Fortunately, I'd allowed time to send an extra two groups to scout before the rest of the troop would start to move.

"Captain," Yaego called out, the swiftest scout in my contingent of warriors, "there's a party of soldiers making their way down the coastline. The rest of the area is clear."

"Thank you, my friend. Take some rest with the boat."

She nodded her fully shaved head, grasped my forearm, and turned back toward the shoreline. The plan was in motion. It was well-formed and well-practiced, as was everything with my *ranng.* Tonight was no exception. But it wasn't my warriors I worried about.

I watched Yaego depart, then turned to Sellan. "One party along the coast. Unusual."

Sellan nodded. "Perhaps scouting for something? Us?"

"No, Yaego would've marked them as scouts." I ran a hand down my short beard that had grown over the days at sea. "We keep alert. Spread the party's description amongst the troop. Let's hope we avoid them. I have no wish for bloodshed this night."

Sellan nodded and set off with his orders.

With night well underway, I led half the troop in small groups through the forest, the other half behind with the ship. We were no lumbering Inraen army, clomping around in noisy, even rows. No—we were a force of subtlety, stealth, and precision, at one with nature. Each warrior picked their way through the path in silence. Years of hard training, much of it under me, gave us our speed. Woe be it to any party not on their guard. A Riht force like ours could be upon them before they even thought to look up from their campfire, let alone draw a blade.

This was also how our sizable force came unnoticed upon a group of six men collected around a small fire. There was no sign of our missing *ranng*, but something told me we'd still found our quarry.

"I plan 'o take a proper bath an' get this grime offa me," one man announced in a thick accent. "Three months withou' un."

"Ye smell like i' too."

The other men surrounding the fire chuckled.

I raised a fist, halting the troop. I didn't recognize these men, but if I was right, there was only one among them that I would. They were hired men, speaking in Mayoran. Based on the accent, they were mercenaries, likely outcasts from Volaach, not native Inraens.

One slow step at a time, I circled the camp. With a single command, my warriors could plant arrows in every chest. They'd be dead before they knew they were under attack.

The youngest in the group jeered some nonsense across the camp, and the rest peeled into raucous laughter. Then, he stood—prompting more hoots and hollers—and strode toward the fire. He raised his arms, spun full in a circle, then bowed.

I rolled my eyes. Fucking attention whore.

"Gentlemen, our time here is finally at an end. Be at ease, my promised rescuers are here." He gave another annoying little bow. "Come, come!" he called out in Rihtish.

With a sigh, I rose and approached the fire. The rest of my *ranng* held back, ever cautious and in position.

"Brother!" At my approach, he held his arms wide as if he had just performed some great trick. More likely, he had noticed the soft bird calls Sellan was repeating to signal our arrival.

We clasped forearms before I was pulled into a swift hug. It was a ruse for my brother, slightly taller than me, to whisper in my ear.

"They're well paid, but toothless on your left has a strong allegiance to himself and is eager to find a way to double-cross."

I glanced over my shoulder and marked the man in question, grinning like an idiot, more teeth missing than present.

"We'll take them halfway up the coast and dump them," he added.

Here for less than ten seconds, and already giving commands. I sighed. "Nice to see you, too."

WITH THE HELP of the troop, dismantling their mercenary camp was a short affair. I grabbed one of my brother's sacks, wrapped in a thick tan cloth—almost white. I shook my head. Light cloth in a dark forest would shine like a fucking beacon, even at night. Any Riht should know better. I signaled to the two closest to me to collect the remaining bags. Within minutes, the fire was doused, and the half-dozen men were ushered in a single line toward the coast, flanked by my warriors.

The stars shone down on us, blessing our journey. I smiled at the black moon and focused on my steps. Within an hour, we would be at sea, making our way back home. I itched to get back.

The journey for these men would be much more difficult than it was for my trained group. I saw their eyes searching about in the darkness. We'd be better off just leaving them here. I stopped before my brother and handed him a length of rope, which I had looped through my belt for exactly this reason. One by one, we moved down the line, connecting all six men. Sellan took the lead. He guided our small contingent through the softest patches of earth, trying to minimize the clomping of the Volaachi mercenaries' feet.

As we neared the end of the trees, Yaego's earlier warning prickled the back of my mind.

I moved to the front and hissed into my brother's ear, "Step softly."

He answered with a tsk.

I turned as we walked, scanning the full perimeter.

The camp was far behind and out of sight when a clamber of metal rang out through the night, followed by men shouting. *Inraen men*. Yaego appeared before me.

"Trouble," she said, barely above a whisper.

"How long?"

"Minutes. The Inraen soldiers were headed straight for the campfire. We need to set sail immediately, or we risk being seen."

"Take the lead." I handed her the sack from my shoulder, and Yaego took Sellan's place. "We'll follow." I waited for Yaego's sharp nod before dashing toward the firelight. The clash of blades grew louder with each step. Cries sounded into the night. Cries of death.

I nodded to Sellan, not needing to explain my thoughts after years of battle and training together. Sellan nodded and slipped back into the trees. My face hardened into a grim mask as I took in the group before me, then I exploded out of the copse onto rough sand. The pommel of my sword met the first man's head with a sickening crunch. The man next to him was already on the ground, completely still. Three of my warriors were surrounded by the remaining eight Inraen soldiers, two of which wore officers' mail. From my troop, one man was bleeding, but the two women were unharmed. Three Inraens bled heavily. They would fall soon.

I didn't want to see more. I sliced at the nearest officer, a hulking brute. He brought up his sword in time to deflect the blow, but not the knife I sent flying at his companion. It buried into the shoulder gap of the second man's sword arm. He screamed, dropped his weapon, and fell to his knees. I could see the fear in the man's eyes—fear that was all too familiar. This was no seasoned soldier. This was an honorary officer, no doubt forced to fight in his king's army by some idiotic Inraen tradition. I had seen men like these—lordlings, nobility, and gentry alike—enough to turn my stomach. They were ill-equipped buffoons with god complexes. Still, the fight was unfairly in our favor.

I drew my second blade and attacked. The first brute fell in three blows. His lordling companion tried to rise, but I kicked him down, sparing his life—if he survived the shoulder wound. I turned to meet the third officer just in time, parrying his sloppy but powerful overhead strike. His eyes were wide with panic. I struck low, aiming to disable him. I had no interest in killing untrained men. This officer was quick and jumped out of range. I rolled, staying low and parrying three quick strikes from above as he swung at me in desperation. I swiped at his knee and scored a hit. He went down and, thanks to my mercy, would live to see another day. I glanced over my shoulder. My warriors had taken care of the last few Inraens, but judging by the blood, they had not left survivors.

The lordling tried to rise again, still clutching his shoulder. I locked eyes with him and said to my warriors in Mayoran, "Let's move." He stilled, and something like relief washed over his face.

I turned when metal rang out again. It sang, not in the way a sword cuts through the air, but in the way a blade sings when sharpened, sliding against a hard surface. The third one, who I'd spared, had a sword protruding straight through his mail-covered chest. His eyes bulged from his head. They were young, too young, as I watched them dim. The lordling screamed, ignoring his wounded shoulder to crawl toward his fallen companion.

I looked at my warrior responsible, standing behind him. "Branye," I breathed. "Why?"

Her hard eyes flicked to the right.

It was Praeth, her lover, clutching a side soaked with blood. Even in the dark, I could see the loss of blood was staggering. I grabbed the man around his middle. All I could do was hiss, "Run," to the pair of women as I hauled Praeth over my shoulder. My friend might live if we moved quickly, but he might yet die. Either way, we would all surely die if there were more Inraen soldiers nearby. This was meant to be a mission of stealth, not a large-scale battle.

My eyes flicked back to the lordling, helmet discarded, wailing the name of his dead companion. Something tugged at that familiar spot in my mind, but there was no time to consider it. We would have to add two to our crew for the journey home.

"Get up."

Hate-filled eyes turned toward me. "Die in a ditch."

"If you want to live, get up and follow. Otherwise, you can join your companions where they lie."

Sellan stepped forward out of the copse, shaking his head. No other soldiers were near enough to interfere.

"Bring him," I said to Sellan, switching back to Rihtish, "and see that he lives."

Sellan reached out with a length of rope to bind the man's hands. I didn't wait to see more with Praeth over my shoulder and bleeding steadily down my side and back. I took off toward the ship. We needed to get out to sea.

The sea was safety. The sea was the way home. The sea was hope.

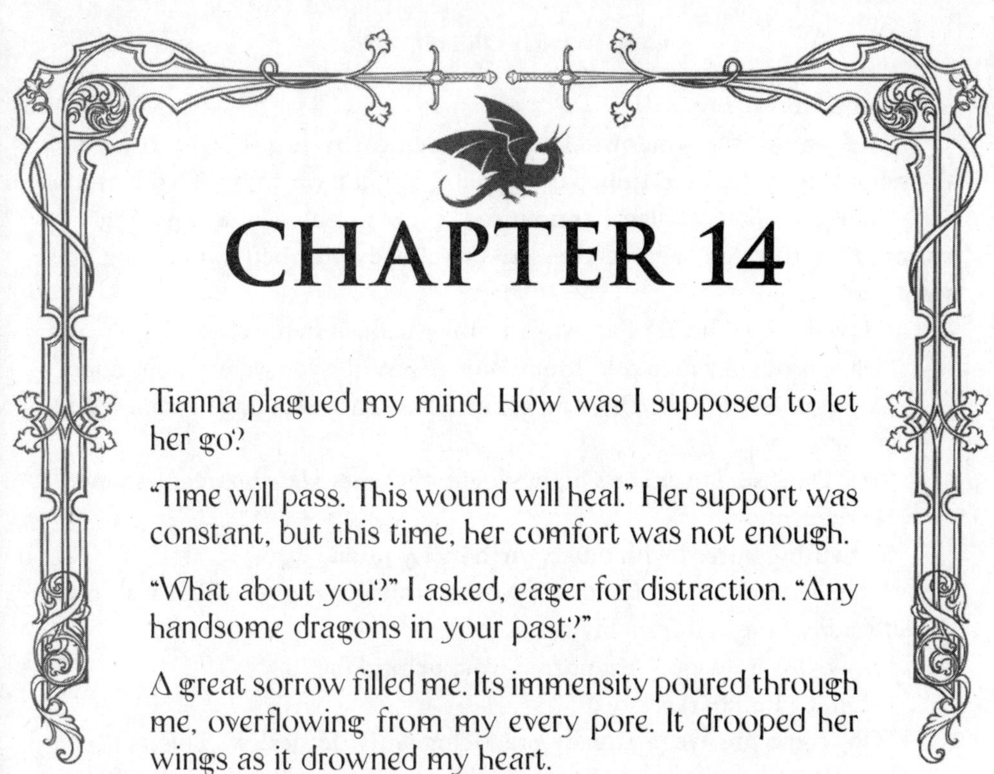

CHAPTER 14

Tianna plagued my mind. How was I supposed to let her go?

"Time will pass. This wound will heal." Her support was constant, but this time, her comfort was not enough.

"What about you?" I asked, eager for distraction. "Any handsome dragons in your past?"

A great sorrow filled me. Its immensity poured through me, overflowing from my every pore. It drooped her wings as it drowned my heart.

"In my past, present, and future, there is only Death."

—Recounting from the private diary of Jerris, Dragonbound

• ~ •

SERAE

LATE SUMMER, MAYMON 1036

MY EYES OPENED to a fire roaring in a nearby hearth, spreading its warmth over a spacious room. I was currently tucked into a large, plush bed, still in my overdress. It was a bedchamber. Tapestries of the Great Dragon covered the stone walls. Through the open door lay a sitting room with a table, a bulky wardrobe, and, unless I was mistaken, a separate door leading to a private bathing chamber. It was the antithesis of the tiny room I had become accustomed to.

And, oh my, the windows. They showered the rooms in light. If not for the pounding in my head from passing out, I might have appreciated it more.

"You're awake," Callagh announced a few minutes later, catching me rummaging through a large dresser. I'd already finished ransacking the wardrobe.

"How did I get here?" I asked, ignoring the flush in my cheeks.

"Dane brought you to your rooms, my lady. While you were unconscious."

"My rooms?" I looked around again. This space was huge compared to my last.

"Yes. Dane said to express his apologies that they were not ready sooner."

"Did he, now?"

Something purred with bitter mirth in my mind.

After a quick meal, I hurried to the training room, which was now directly across the hall from my suite.

"Now, this is a view," Lex purred from behind me.

"Shut it," Raif barked.

"Oh, come on. We're already practicing while leaderless. The least you can do is let me comment on the spectacular ass in front—"

"Nobody wants to hear it, lech."

"No fun." Lex's voice was still laced with seduction. "If you don't want to hear about Serae's ass, how about I tell you what the sight of that tight bulge between your legs is doing for me."

I groaned alongside the others.

"If you don't want to train," Lispen chimed in, "then by all means, come test your skills."

"Against you, spar-master Lispen? I think not."

She cackled.

"Though if you ever want to spar with a little less clothing, I'm your ma—*oof*!"

I turned to find Lispen flexing her fist, Lex doubled over and gasping.

"Next time, I'll aim a little lower." The grin on her face was feral.

Lex coughed a few times before muttering, "No fun," in a much more subdued tone.

"Where is Wep, anyway?" I asked. My tension headache had not yet lifted. My stomach growled, but I wasn't hungry. Was this my courses getting ready to start?

"Off on a mission," Raif piped up. He had been tasked with keeping us in line during Wep's absence. "Serae, with me. Pair up, we're back on disarming with swords."

For once, I leapt at the chance. I had been practicing extra with Lispen and Ivank, and I was finally starting to get the hang of it without jarring my arm off my body. I had even managed to disarm Ivank three times in a row, though never Lispen. No one but Wep ever managed to disarm her.

That afternoon, I stopped at the market to get my next book—I'd graduated from children's books and was attempting to read a text of the creation story that was depicted on the Relaxation Room tapestries. Then I returned to my room for lunch. The food looked ashen. The smell of it turned my stomach, and I rushed to my bathing room to hurl bile into the toilet hole. I begged off my lessons in favor of rest, and when Callagh brought my evening tray, the food looked the same. I sat down and examined it more closely. It wasn't so much that the leafy greens were black, but they shone with an odd, black light. I sniffed, and a bitter scent hit my nose.

"Callagh, come and look at this." I gestured to my plate.

Callagh had been lounging on the window bench in my sitting room, looking out at the forest below. At my request, she hopped down and padded over to me, peering at my plate.

"Does something seem off to you?"

She picked up my fork, prodded the food around, then sniffed. Her face twisted into a frown. "Well, it doesn't smell good. Let me get you a fresh plate."

I nodded, but as Callagh reached for the door, I called out, "Wait! Ask for a plate for yourself, as well."

"Oh, I've already eaten, my lady."

"I know. Just ask anyway."

She nodded, though her brow pinched with doubt. That was nothing compared to the way her eyebrows flew up when I demanded she fetch Dane after her return.

"To come see three dinner plates?" she squeaked.

"Yes."

Fortunately, she complied, though it took half an hour before Dane burst into the room. Just enough time for doubt to creep in.

"I hear you've summoned me to your quarters, Daughter," he boomed. "Is there something ailing you that prevents you from coming to the Hall?"

"If I had eaten my plated meal, yes, there would be."

With a glower, he crossed the room to examine the three plates I'd arranged on the table.

"Hungry, are you?"

"Poison," I corrected. "Or something like it."

"That's a heavy accusation, girl," but his hand went to his belt, withdrawing a pouch that contained a white powder that he sprinkled over each plate. The plate closest to him gave no reaction, but the next two fizzled when the granules came into contact with the food. I sank into the chair nearest where I'd been pacing. Worry bled from me, giving way to shock. *I was right.* I knew I would be, but seeing the proof rattled me.

I watched, mute and numb, as Dane rounded on Callagh. "Where did these come from?" He shouted, looming over her with fury in his eyes.

Tears spilled down her cheeks. "The kitchens!" she cried. "Dane, I swear, I just ordered a meal and brought it to her."

He lowered his voice to a growl. "Why are there three?"

Callagh's tear-filled gaze turned to me, pulling me back to the present. "That would be me. I suspected poison with the first plate. I asked Callagh to collect two more to confirm myself as the target."

"Aye, this was no accident. Do not touch these." Dane swept from the room.

Within the hour, three guards returned to collect the suspect trays, and one brought me a new tray, cleared by Dane himself. As soon as he set it down, my mouth watered. Fresh vegetables with a creamy dipping sauce and fresh fruits paired with a chocolate drizzle. The entire plate shone with bright golden light.

I dug in. As I ate, Dane's personal guards—the brothers—stayed behind to guard me throughout the meal. They stood stone-faced, staring at the wall.

"Will you have to stand there all night?" I asked.

"No, my lady. We will guard outside your door when you are ready to retire," the one with the gravelly voice replied.

"I see. If you'll be stuck with me for so long, I think I should at least know your names."

They both cracked smiles. Turns out they were twin brothers—Braethair and Braedur—and had been guarding Dane for more than ten years. It was easier than I expected getting them to open up and start talking, though I imagined with Dane, there wasn't much opportunity to chat.

That night, I opened my journal despite not attending my lessons. I had written no letters since Gerta's departure, but I continued to fill its pages with notes on what I learned. It helped me keep all the new information straight.

When I was done, I went to my wardrobe and prodded around the inner base. In one corner, there was a small gap where the base met the backing, just large enough to slip the journal halfway in with the spine facing up. The brown cover exactly matched the wood, acting as a convenient camouflage. With so much physical training, being knocked out multiple times, and now nearly poisoned, I could no longer risk carrying it.

Training sessions over the next several days, while Wep was away on his mission, were monotonous. Raif or Lispen, and once, Ivank, kept us on task with *dowsae* and sparring. Helene and I followed in relative silence. Lex groaned constantly and did his best to derail our lessons with a variety of nonsense. Teke just laughed and went along with whatever was said or done.

I had fully recovered from whatever-the-Creator-it-was, followed by my near poisoning. The swirling lights subsided, and instead, the plant life around me started to glow softly—*from within*. Alongside this was the equally miraculous healing of my eyes. I tried once to wear my glasses, but it turned my world into a dizzying blur. There was no denying it—this was magic. My own *bierla*, I suspected, though something told me to keep it to myself.

Nine days after Wep left, Raif drilled us for two full hours with practice swords. Then, Teke, Helene, and I split off toward the markets with Callagh for some much-needed time to let loose.

"This," Teke announced, holding up a nondescript round bun, "will change your life." They handed me the grapefruit-sized pastry, then bit a giant hunk out of their own. A thick, brown paste oozed in the center. I must've made a face, at which Teke grinned with a full mouth.

"Try it, my lady," Callagh encouraged. "It's better than it looks."

I took one small bite and forced myself to chew. The dough was light and fluffy and just the slightest bit sweet. On my second bite, I made it to the filling. I moaned, and Teke laughed in triumph. It was salty, sweet, savory, and packed with so much flavor and spices that it was nearly overwhelming. With the airy bun to tone it down, it was a masterful balance. All it needed was a dash of heat, and I would have called it pure perfection. I took another bite, savoring the mix of flavors dancing on my tongue, and closed my eyes.

Something slammed into the back of my head. *Pain blazed through me.*

I pitched forward, bun flying, and collapsed onto Teke in a heap. We went careening to the dirt. Laughter erupted around me. *Laughter.*

Air whipped my hair as someone jumped over me, and before my vision could clear, angry shrieks and the thuds of landing blows filled the air. The laughter on the street cut off, replaced by murmurs of disapproval. Turning my head throbbed. Focusing my eyes was worse. Helene threw punches and kicks, but her strikes were only glancing.

I tried to sit up, but the world spun, and I fell to the side. My fall was cushioned by a puddle of thick mud.

"Stop it!" someone shouted, and it took me a moment to recognize the mud-covered Teke as they jumped into the fray.

"Listen to your betters," a cold voice taunted. A voice I knew. *My fucking challenger.*

Protective instincts reared within me. She'd gotten the better of me three times now, but she would *not* hurt my friends. I blinked—and the world changed. Colors swirled around me. The mud on my hands morphed from dark brown to rivulets of red, green, purple, and blue. The wind itself whispered in my ears. Raw power surged through me, and I stood—pain gone—ready to face my attacker.

"Enough," I commanded, thrusting one hand toward her from several strides away. Vines erupted from the earth and coiled around her limbs. She struggled against them, one arm breaking free, until a thick root secured her middle and pulled her to the ground.

Around us, no one else moved beyond gasps and pointed fingers.

"She's been blessed," one woman hissed to her companion.

"A *bierla*? For an Inraen?" her companion responded.

"Truly, look!"

Calm washed over me. Then, *she* spoke through me, using words that were not my own. **"Threaten my Bound at your peril."**

I dropped my hand to my side, and everything around me snapped into motion. I swayed on my feet, but someone steadied me. Warm hands gripped my cheeks as Callagh peered into my eyes.

"Concussion," she said, then two sets of arms lifted me. I was sandwiched between them, one arm gripped by each of my rescuers.

"That was no concussion," Helene countered. There was a touch of reverence to her voice, making that thing inside me purr.

"This way," Callagh beckoned. "Let's get you back."

As we walked, Teke shouted rapid-fire commands in Rihtish behind us. The only thing I could make out was, "Get Dane."

I WOKE IN my bed, *again*, clean and dressed in a simple nightgown, with very little memory of getting there. I was getting sick of these gaps in time. I sat up and scanned the room. My head throbbed as the light from the fire stabbed my eyes. I squeezed them shut.

"She lives." Teke looked up from the book in their lap, grinning and sporting a fresh black eye.

"What are you doing here?" I croaked.

"Watching over you while Callagh gets a few hours' rest. It was the only way I could get her to leave."

"What happened?"

"Just a little tumble in the mud, nothing to worry about."

"And I hit my head?"

"Sort of."

Pain blazing from the back of my head. "She attacked me. Why?"

Teke shrugged. "She was stripped of her role as Marr of *Dowsae.* Dane gave it to Kahvrah—a thousand times more deserving, if you ask me—after that little stunt she pulled at your Sun Trial. She probably blames you."

I doubted it. She hated me from the moment she laid eyes on me. Flashes of food and Helene flitted through my brain next. "And Helene?"

"Fine, fine. Her pride's probably a little hurt, but everyone's good. You just rest."

I nodded, then winced. Going back to sleep sounded like a wonderful idea.

"Drink some water first."

A tray next to my bed was set with a glass and pitcher. My glasses had been pushed off to the side. I drank deeply, then sank into the pillows. I hoped morning was a long way off.

"IT'S LIFELIGHT, SMALL One."

"How can I see it?"

"You see it because I see it."

"And my eyes?"

"Your vision is my vision. You will see clearer than almost any human you meet."

"Almost?"

"Almost."

"What should I do with it? What is its purpose?"

"Life, Small One. Together, we will look upon all life and see their truths. To

control life is to first understand it. Our journey in this has begun."

MORNING BROUGHT WITH it an ache in my head as well as my heart. My back wasn't doing too great, either. My fingertips ghosted over the sizable lump that had formed on the back of my skull. The lump was the least of my worries. I had remembered a great many things as I slept. The attack, the jeering of the crowd, Helene and Teke jumping to my aid, and Callagh helping to clean and dress me before laying me in bed. Their care was touching, but it didn't erase the laughter. I was hated here. First poison, and now this.

"Don't get up," Callagh said, rising to her feet. Her dress was rumpled and her braid unraveling.

"You're still here? Did you get any rest?"

She chuckled. "Don't you worry about me. Just take your time. I've got a tray waiting for you. You're taking the day off."

She had no idea how much I needed it.

After eating enough to satisfy her and swearing I'd stay in bed, I forced Callagh to leave and get some rest of her own. But my mind wouldn't quiet. I moved my useless glasses to the small drawer in the bedside table, though I still reached for them every morning out of habit. I stood and dressed, trying to ignore the pain, rejection, and humiliation of the previous day. With nothing else to do and not yet feeling hungry, I moved through a few easy *dowsae* in painstaking slowness, careful not to jostle my throbbing head.

I was three movements from finishing when a knock sounded at the door. I had expected it to be Callagh, coming to check on her invalid, but instead, Wep entered. My heart clenched at the sight of him. His hair was loose, and damn did that tight shirt look good.

He smiled—*actually smiled*—at me. Or, more likely, he was happy to see someone practicing *dowsae* without being told. I couldn't find it in me to reciprocate.

"You're back," I said, flatter than I meant.

He nodded, closing the door and leaning back against it, arms crossed left over right. "You can't be rid of me that easily."

"Are we training then?"

His head cocked to the side. "If you're ready. I was told you're hurt."

"It's nothing." I rubbed the back of my head and winced.

Wep frowned. "What happened?"

"Teke can tell you."

He gave me a hard look. "And yet, here I am, asking you."

I groaned, not in the mood to rehash it all. "I just need rest."

His lip quirked up in that way I liked. No, not *liked*. There was nothing likable about this demanding grump of a man. "There is no rest for the Riht."

"I'm not a Riht!" I shouted. Pain exploded through my head. I clutched it as I staggered. Colors popped and swirled behind my eyelids. My body crumpled to the ground.

Power—I remembered the power.

Wep was staring at me, frowning deeply. He raised a single eyebrow in question. *And he was glowing.* I gasped. It was the purest, whitest light I'd ever seen. It was so white, it was silver. Wreathed in this glow, he was *stunning.* He pushed off the doorframe utterly unaware he was shrouded in a god-like light. He knelt in front of me, but he didn't reach for me. A war waged behind his eyes, and he searched my own as if he thought they might give him an answer.

The light dimmed. And I remembered how we had left things, with me walking away from him in the Relaxation Room. He must be here to make amends. I don't know why that made my shoulders dip.

"I don't remember everything," I whispered, trying to calm the storm whirling inside me.

"Tell me what you do," Wep said with his usual air of command, still kneeling before me.

"You wouldn't understand."

"Try me."

I held his gaze. There were a thousand things I could scream at him, like how awful his people could be and how it wasn't my choice to be here either, but no words came. I knew how pathetic they would sound given voice, and the last bit of fight in me was gone. "Never mind," I breathed.

Wep kept his eyes on me as he stood, extending a single hand. His gaze could have pierced straight through me if given a physical force.

I looked away, like the coward I was, as I took his hand.

He pulled me to my feet. "You need food, water, and rest." He didn't let go of my hand.

I rolled my eyes, though the motion hurt.

"The body feeds the mind. Take care of your body, and you will feel better."

"Spare me."

Wep's eyes never left me. His hand slid up my arm, ghosted over my shoulder, and softly cupped my cheek. I might have pulled away if I weren't so desperate for a kind touch. It was a chaste thing, almost tender, and so at odds with what I knew of this stern man. I'd sooner have expected him to slap me across the face than touch me like this. I looked up into his steel-blue eyes and wondered if maybe I did like his little smirk after all.

"I'm trying to," he said simply.

Some temporary madness overtook me. I turned my face up to him, and the next thing I knew, I was pulling him into me. My eyes fluttered closed as his lips met mine. The kiss was soft but lingering. That is, until it wasn't. Heat exploded through me. I was burning up with sudden, desperate need as flames licked through my every crevice. A small breath escaped me when our lips parted. Some crazed animal inside me was taking control—gripping his shirt and kissing him again like I couldn't live without his lips on mine. His hands gripped my waist as I threaded my fingers through his hair and moaned, deepening the kiss. The sun-scorching fire pooling in me was unbearable, and I was desperate for more, more, more.

The firmness of Wep's grip on my waist tightened, but instead of crushing me to him as I wanted, he slowly, deliberately, pushed our bodies apart.

"We don't have to continue," he said. His eyes were wild as he took a step back.

I had never hated a single step more in my life. One step forward was all it would take to get back to that blissful place where mouths and hands and hearts might meet. The Martyrs knew my body was calling for it, still aflame with need. But this was not a place I could go. Not when a ship bearing my betrothed was headed back to the Riht at any moment. Not when another kind-eyed man across the sea waited for me to take my place at his side. The thought of Tam should've been the bucket of ice-cold water I needed, but not even the knowledge of what I might have done—the mistake I might have made, would still be making if not for that one step—could dissipate this heat inside me. It was burning me alive.

I tried my best to force my head to quiet and my mind to focus. Nothing, not even this chiseled, magnificent man before me, should stand in the way of my true purpose. I was here for one thing—information—then I'd be gone. Even if I hated it, I meant to see it through.

I took a step back. "You should go."

"I didn't mean—"

"Go."

Wep scoffed. "Fine. Enjoy your headache." He turned and wrenched the door open.

The latch had barely clicked shut when flame engulfed me from within. The paltry heat of desire fled, replaced by something else entirely. A power as old as the sun and expansive as the sky. Everything around me erupted in a blinding blaze as magic surged through my veins. I was the beginning of all life, and through me, Jaeda itself turned. The fire consumed me, and I succumbed to it. It lapped at my skin, flesh, and bones until there was nothing left. The me I used to be was devoured, and in its place was something ancient, infinite, and new.

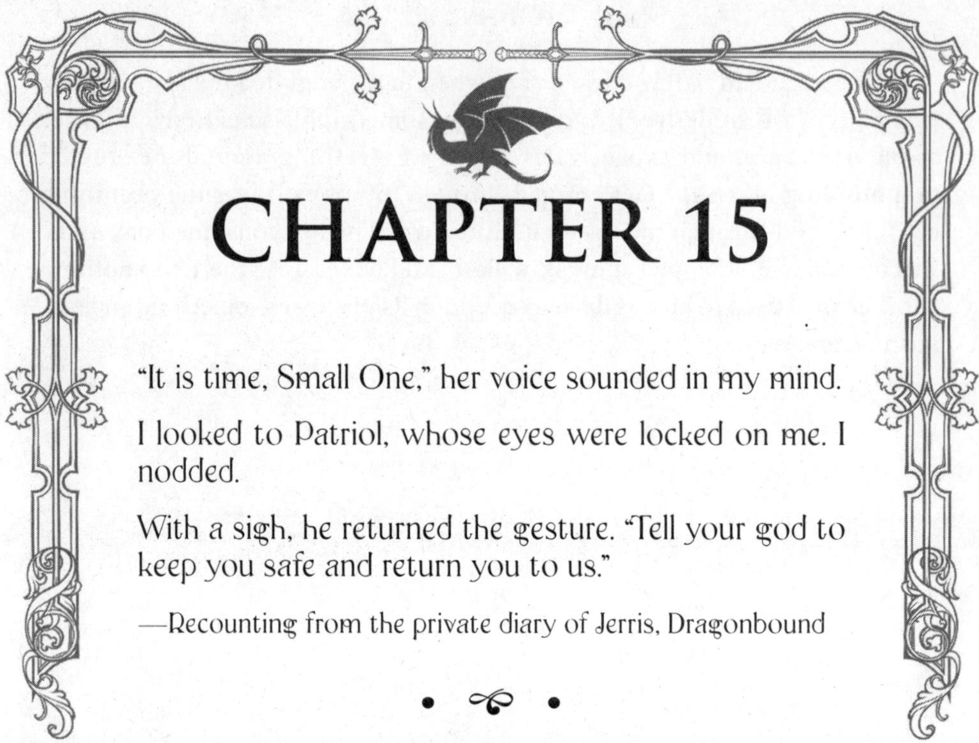

CHAPTER 15

"It is time, Small One," her voice sounded in my mind.

I looked to Patriol, whose eyes were locked on me. I nodded.

With a sigh, he returned the gesture. "Tell your god to keep you safe and return you to us."

—Recounting from the private diary of Jerris, Dragonbound

SERAE

LATE SUMMER, MAYMON 1036

"*Return to me.*"

"I cannot."

"*You must. You are bound to me. We must tighten and complete the binding.*"

"I don't know where you are."

"*You know, my child. Return at once, or the fires will consume you.*"

"They will never let me free."

"*They will. I have commanded it.*"

I opened my eyes. The dream flitted away from my consciousness, but a brilliant light still pulsed within my mind. No sooner had I noticed it than it dimmed. My head cleared. I threw off the covers, happy for the first time to be surrounded by the blissful chill in the air.

To say I slept poorly was the least of it. My dreams were twisted with fear and madness, leaving me thrashing in my sheets. Still, unrested as I was, a burning purpose hammered at me with every breath. There was somewhere important I had to be.

A knock sounded at my door. "My lady, wake up."

"Just a minute," I grumbled, shoving my face into the pillow. My tongue was dry and heavy in my mouth. I needed water, but I wasn't much inclined to move.

"No, my lady. We have to see Dane."

Dane? I shot up as pieces of my memory rushed back, moments I hadn't realized I'd forgotten. Power filling me. Collapsing in his arms. Dane carrying me to my new rooms. Wep, gripping my hips—I pushed that one aside. Then, the fire. I looked up to the black spot on my ceiling, a haunting halo above the place where I had burned.

"*My lady, please,*" Callagh hissed.

Clothes practically leapt from the armoire onto me. I inhaled a scant quarter of my vegetables and jumped to my feet—my feet! I hastily tugged on boots, then Callagh hauled me bodily through the corridors back to the Receiving Hall with many a "Sorry, my lady" between hurried steps. I was pushed before Dane with a speed and surety that I would never have done on my own. The benches around the dais held a dozen people I'd come to recognize as Dane's advisors.

He rose to his feet. "Daughter."

The door behind us creaked open, then shut with a dull thud. I whipped around to the familiar copper knot and closely trimmed beard that stood out amongst the Riht. His eyes scanned the room, then rested on me. There was something more in them than the usual harsh glare.

I held his gaze, breathing steadily until my shoulders dropped.

"Approach," Dane called.

A new fear overtook me as Wep walked slowly toward the dais, eyes flicking back to me with every other step. His brow furrowed. *Did Dane know?*

"Speak," Dane said simply.

It was Wep, of all people, who stepped forward. "My dane, I believe Inra means to betray the Riht."

"No!" I gasped, and all eyes turned to me. "Why would we?" My eyes flicked between Wep and Dane, then I clapped a hand over my mouth. If only I could shrink into the stone walls. I had no right to speak out of turn here. Even Wep, whom Dane held in high regard, did not interrupt in the Receiving Hall.

Dane's eyes snapped to me, blue, bright, and cunning. He held my gaze for a long, hard moment, then frowned. "Aye, the lady asks the right question." He stroked his braided beard. "The margrave sent his daughter to wed my son. The king issued a promise of peace. I hope you bring proof."

"I have—"

"Because we have gone to great lengths to make peace with the Inraens. A peace, I'll remind you, that you above all demanded."

My head snapped back to Wep so fast I nearly toppled over. He was the picture of control.

"We apprehended an officer traveling with a band of soldiers along the Inraen coast. Upon seeing us, they attacked without prompting or question. This was a violation of our peace pledge and defied our good faith agreement."

"What have you learned from the prisoner?"

"Nothing yet, but—"

"NOTHING?" Dane bellowed.

I recoiled, stepping back and turning away before catching myself. At home, a tone like that meant bruises. But I was not at home, Father was not speaking, and no blow would come.

"*No one touches you now, Small One.*"

My shoulders relaxed. She—the voice—was right. I was in Dane's hall. Ironic that I was safer trapped in a room of Rihtish warriors than standing before my own father.

Dane's head cocked to one side.

"I ask you again, Son. What can you prove?"

I shook my head, reeling at that word. *Son.*

Wep continued to speak, but the words lost their meaning. I began to sweat. My eyes went to Wep, then to the floor. I took another deliberate breath, but my heart rate skyrocketed. Chaos reigned within me, though I remained still.

"What do you say to this, Daughter?"

Dane's question caught me off guard. My mind raced through what had been said, scrambling for a response. "You were on Inraen soil unannounced?"

Behind me, the door creaked and thudded, admitting another newcomer. I did a double-take. The man was a near replica of the weaponmaster but with obvious mistakes in the copy. Mistakes that suited him perfectly. He was slimmer with a longer braid worn over one shoulder. His eyes were brighter, and his face held none of the severity and storm that I'd come to know. As he stepped into the light, I saw his hair was dark blond, not copper like Wep's.

"Father," he called. "What an austere welcome this is." He grinned and spread his arms wide as he walked toward the dais.

"Ell." Dane's greeting was flat. "You were expected to return a month ago."

My jaw went slack. *Eldreth.*

"I beseech your forgiveness, of course. I was delayed."

Wep snorted.

Ell turned an unwavering grin toward him, then moved forward and clapped Wep on the back. "Brother, you cannot begrudge a man one last hurrah."

My knees went weak, and Callagh stepped closer to me. My stomach threatened to upturn the small amount of vegetables I'd managed to eat. My voice had most certainly abandoned me, but I couldn't look away from the two men before me. Side by side, the resemblance was uncanny.

"Three days together at sea, and now you won't embrace me?" Ell asked.

Wep frowned severely but clasped forearms with his *brother* all the same. He glowered with clear reproach.

Over Ell's shoulder, Wep's eyes met mine. Ell turned, following his brother's gaze.

"Well, hello." Ell smiled at me. His face lit up, making his features even more handsome. "Aren't you a lovely thing?" He turned and approached with a casual confidence that was part of his natural gait. "I hear we're to be family."

I gawked. I didn't want to be a landed fish gasping for air, but here I was. He bent and kissed my hand—*when had he taken it?*—all the while keeping his eyes locked on mine. The warmth of his lips pressed to the back of my hand, followed by his thumb smoothing over my skin, sealing the kiss in place. I let out a breath, and my skin erupted in a body-wide blush. How could such an innocent gesture feel like anything but?

Behind his brother, Wep growled. *He actually growled.* I wanted to turn, to see what had the weaponmaster's blood aflame this time, but I could not for the life of me pull my eyes away from the man before me. Up close, I saw that he was muscular, despite his slim build, and slightly taller than Wep. His eyes were ice blue and playful. His lips quirked into a smile that I doubted ever left his face. This jaunty man was, at long last, my betrothed—returned from Creator-knows-where and looking at me like we were already fast friends.

I began to dip into a curtsey before catching myself. Slipping my hand from his grasp, I placed a fist to my chest and bowed my head. "Well met. I am Serae of Cavendaffe. I trust your journey was safe and productive."

"*Very.* Tell me, Serae of Cavendaffe, how have you been treated since you arrived? I imagine everyone's been downright brutish." He shifted, and I caught a glimpse of Wep with balled fists and a clenched jaw. *Was that an insult meant for him?*

My eyes darted between them. "Wep is your brother?" I blurted.

Ell chuckled. "Yes, indeed. You catch on quickly." He glanced back to Wep, then said, "What *have* they been telling you?" He grinned widely.

"Ell," Dane snapped, patience gone. "You owe me a report."

"Yes, all right." He let out a world-weary sigh.

Dane waved at me and Callagh. "We'll handle this other matter later. Dismissed."

I had no intention of moving, but Callagh grabbed me by the arm and pulled me back. I had a hundred things to say and a hundred questions to ask. But all I could think about was Wep and the storm in his eyes when they landed on his brother. Was that a good sign, or a bad one? Considering how little I knew of Wep, I honestly couldn't tell.

Callagh guided us back to my new rooms. Were it not for her steady hand, who knows where I would've ended up in the maze of corridors? I sank into a chair and stared at the wall. Beside me, Callagh watched in silence.

"My lady," she asked at length, "are you quite well?"

I did not look at her. "Was that him, Callagh? Was that really him?"

I felt more than heard her sigh. "Did you not know?"

"No."

"I thought Dane had told you after your First Sun."

"No." It was all I could think to say.

"I suppose it helps that he's terribly handsome, for all his other faults." Callagh chuckled, but the joke was lost on me.

I buried my head in my hands, whether from shame or this unexpected wave of sadness. Less than a day ago, I stood in almost this very spot kissing my betrothed's brother. Martyrs, I had wanted to do so much more, had he not stopped us. *No fucking wonder he did.*

"What do I do?" I whispered.

Callagh moved to my chair and knelt, bringing us eye to eye. "Continue exactly as you were," she said with a seriousness I had rarely heard from her. "This changes nothing. So you didn't know until today. So he has a brother who's a bit annoying."

I nodded, though I wouldn't call Wep annoying. Brooding—sure. Or frustrating? Absolutely.

"My lady, you are still meant to be dana. Your path is clear."

Path... The memory of my dream came surging back. *Return to me.* Urgency flooded me, and the call to move vibrated through my bones. My path *was* clear—not toward Ell or the future he promised. I stood, knowing with certainty where I needed to go.

"Callagh, do you trust me?" I grabbed her hands and held them tight. "Are you truly committed to me?"

I waited.

Hesitation flashed over her face for just a moment before she nodded. "Yes, my lady."

"Good. We need to ride."

CALLAGH WAS TRUE to her word. Slipping out of the keep and then past the castle walls was simple under her quiet guidance, though walking beneath the beastly gate was appropriately ominous. We saddled our horses, and I was happy to meet the same mare who carried me to the cave the first time. I had no horse of my own here, but I hoped Kappa wouldn't mind lending her hoof.

We mounted and set off at a slow pace.

"Speed draws attention," Callagh explained, "and suspicion."

I shrugged my assent as we continued. Something tugged at my breastbone, drawing me onward. There was no need to confirm the path with my *reálta*. I could feel it in my marrow, if not my soul.

"*I'm coming,*" I told the voice that had taken residence in my head.

A purr of appreciation rattled through me.

We continued down the wide path at a slow pace, affording me plenty of opportunity to look around. The deeper we got into the forest, the wilder the trees grew. Tiny mushrooms dotted logs and tree sides, moss-covered stones on the forest floor, and small burrows hinted at flourishing life. Yet the path had long since turned to well-trodden soil. How many others had been called to the mountainside cave before me? I had seen little of religion since arriving in Drakh, but a path like this made me wonder—could this be why they called themselves followers of the Ancient Path?

"Not long now," I said, as if I, and not Kappa, were truly in the lead.

Callagh glanced at me but remained silent.

We rounded a bend, and the cave mouth appeared. In the fading light, I had thought it was nothing more than a cave on the side of a mountain. Now, in the brightness of day, I saw it for its true nature: a looming volcano wreathed in clouds. At its peak, a heavy curl of smoke hovered, neither spilling over nor floating away.

I didn't stop. There was no hesitation as I dismounted and walked toward the entrance. I held up a hand to Callagh, who also dismounted and made to follow. I handed her Kappa's reins.

"My lady?"

"Don't fear. I'll be back soon." My voice held a confidence that I didn't know I could muster in a place like this. My senses stirred as a new awareness of my surroundings opened. I could feel each hair on my body tickled by the soft breeze. I breathed in the aromas of the forest—damp earth, woody bark, and crisp air from windblown leaves mingled with the musty sweet tang of decaying forest floor. Even the tiny, grinding sounds of insects digging through the soft dirt met my ears.

In a single step, the darkness consumed me. The light of the cave mouth winked out. I walked through pitch black, hearing every pebble shift underfoot and feeling every change in the pulsing winds that filled the cavern. I could do nothing but place one foot in front of the other and follow the pull that drove me ever onward. I trudged through darkness for so long that my limbs went numb, and I lost all sense of time—hours, days, perhaps weeks passing. When my body fell behind, I picked up and continued forward with my mind, searching for that ageless voice, or perhaps, searching for myself.

In an instant and yet an eon, my sight returned as the dark corridor opened into a monstrous cavern. Colors popped into view around me in blues, purples, and greens. Looking down, I saw my hands glowing with light from within. Where I expected dark stalagmites, I instead saw deep blues on one side and a dark green flickering on the other. I pressed my hand to the nearest one, knowing it was solid and yet needing to feel the cold rock to ground myself. Tiny bits of my golden light seeped into the calcified stone.

"It's me," I said.

"Very good."

"Where are you?"

"That is not the question you wish to ask, Small One."

I sucked in a breath. *Could she read my mind?* "What are you?"

"Come and see."

The pull to move onward was crippling. I was nearly there. I rounded another stalagmite and came nose to snout with magnificence. Scales as green as the forest and a neck twice the length of my whole body. My breath hitched. My legs locked. The nostrils alone came up to my waist. Massive overlapping fangs, each as long as my leg, poked out from her jaws, and horns like branches spiraled out the back of her head. Even her claws, relaxed as they were in sleep, could tear me in two with a single flick.

Fear slammed into me. My joints rattled uncontrollably, and I fell to my knees. My eyes welled with tears, and for once, I was not ashamed to shed them. I'd known where I was going, deep down—but seeing her still shocked me to my core.

A living dragon.

Emerald leathery wings draped over her scaled body, and patches of lighter scales lined her belly. As I reached out and touched her cold nose, peace radiated through me, banishing all fear.

"Say it, child."

"Say what?" I couldn't tell if I was speaking in my head or aloud.

"Say what you already know. Name me."

I met the creature's closed eyes. "The Great Dragon," I whispered.

"Good. To you, I am Vaya'la. Know this: you are bound to me. In this realm, I am yours, and you are mine. You are my conduit, and in you, I imbue the power of life."

"Are there other realms?"

"You will learn all there is to know in time. For now, remember only this... you are bound to me."

"What must I do? What does it mean to be bound to you?"

"Your world is at a tipping point. The balance between our realms has been upset. An unmatched evil has infected our kind and is spreading. Soon, it will cover all lands with its ichor. Together, we will find the power to return what is right to all realms. This is your task."

"I don't know what any of this means."

"You will."

A new thought bubbled to the surface. I should have been afraid to question this great beast, but I was not. "Why do you sleep?"

"Sleep is for the body alone, not the mind. I live in the Dream Realm, where the true monsters lurk. Heed my call, Small One. When I have need of you, you must come. When you most need me, I will be here within you, ready to come out."

"Why me?" I had so many questions. "I don't understand this burden you've placed on me."

A gust of dragon breath slammed into me, knocking me back several stumbling steps. Light and flames absorbed into my skin, and my mind blossomed with knowledge from the past, far beyond the reach of my own learning. I could feel it lurking under the surface of my thoughts, waiting to be tapped.

"Your eyes are open. All answers are within you. You need only ask the right questions. Leave this place, Small One, and heed what I have said."

"But what about—"

A loud snore rumbled the cavern, making the pebbles at my feet quake.

I fought back a smirk. *Message received.* Apparently, she was a surly dragon. I turned to leave, but after a few steps, a final thought came to me. "Vaya'la?" I asked. "Is that your name?"

"Of sorts. When you need to know more, you shall."

Excellent. Surly and cryptic. Just what I needed.

I left the cavern, walking in a straight line back through the darkness. Only this time, I began to recognize small patterns of deep colors on the walls and ground. The faint glow of my own body lit my way. My steps did not waver, even though my mind was swirling.

The light at the mouth of the cave blazed to the point of pain. I welcomed it, stepping through and bathing myself in the rays of the sun, obscured as they were by the surrounding trees. Everything turned into a wild explosion of colors, a thousand times stronger than before. I swayed on my feet. Steadying hands pressed against my shoulders, holding me upright. After a moment, my eyes adjusted.

"What is this?" I asked, closing my eyes.

"What is what, my lady?" It was Callagh's voice, but not the one I needed to hear.

"It is the power of my sight—lifelight. You will adjust."

I sighed. "Okay." I opened my eyes and saw Callagh. She was radiant and swirling with sparkling energy. Flickers of orange flashed through the white light emanating from her skin. Intuitively, I recognized it as *fear.*

I smiled at her. "Nothing to fear. I am well. Let's get back before we're missed."

"Did you see her, my lady?" She released my shoulders and gripped my hands in hers.

"See who?"

Callagh leaned in close. "The Great Dragon?" She whispered in my ear.

"Have you met her, too?"

"When I was sixteen. Many of us have. She has protected our lands for centuries. Where did she appear for you?"

That wasn't the question I expected. "Within. In the cavern."

"What, just standing there in the cave?"

"No, sleeping."

Callagh tilted her head. "Well, that's a first. Some say they met her on a mountain top or at a cliff's edge. My grandfather swears she rose from the depths of the sea to exact his pledge to the Riht. Did she give you a *bierla*?"

"A blessing?"

"Yes. A gift to help you with your passion and connect you to the Riht?"

"I—" What had Vaya'la said? *The power of life.* "I suppose so." I let go of Callagh's hands and stepped toward the horses. Kappa was munching berries that grew along the path.

As one, we mounted and guided our horses back toward Drakh.

We were nearly clear of the forest when Callagh spoke up again. "Why did she call you back?"

"I'm...not sure," was all I could think to say. The truth was much heavier than I knew how to voice. *You are bound to me.* Bound for eternity to the Great Dragon.

"Don't fear, my lady. If she's given you her blessing, then she's accepted you."

"Yes," I said, though a different command echoed through me, making my insides squirm. *Play your part, girl.* "I'm sure you're right," I managed.

But she wasn't right. Vaya'la asked no pledge of me—she claimed me as her own. She gave me no command beyond the calling of a task I barely understood. She told me that we were bound to each other and that through me, her power was imbued. Was I expected to become like the Dragonbound of old, straight out of Kahvrah's story, returned to prove humanity worthy? The thought was laughable. Did Vaya'la know that I was meant to be collected, removed from the Riht, and become a betrayer of these people forever?

If she did, she kept conspicuously silent.

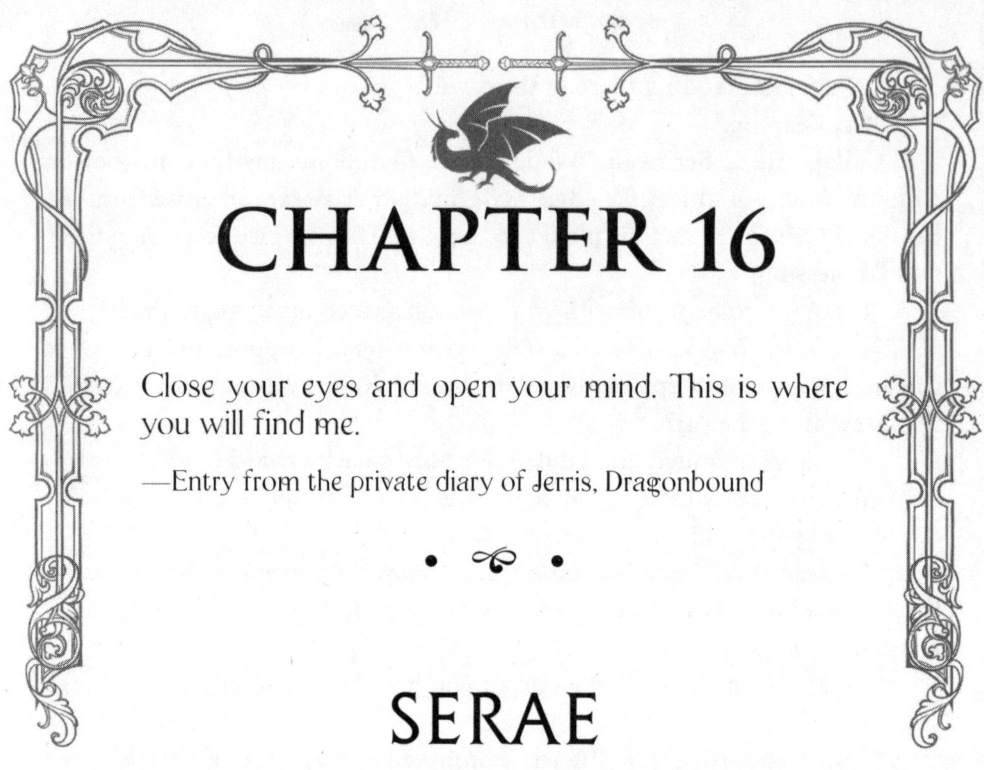

CHAPTER 16

Close your eyes and open your mind. This is where you will find me.

—Entry from the private diary of Jerris, Dragonbound

SERAE

LATE SUMMER, MAYMON 1036

Morning dawned with the same chill wind that brought the changing of seasons at home. Out the window, I could see the first few leaves on the trees had begun to turn. Little pops of orange and yellow dotted the treetops. The crisp, fresh air called to me, so I listened. I opted not to go to training, sending Callagh with my excuses. She came back with a message that all was fine. I suspected Wep was offering me a small mercy after being bombarded with meeting Eldreth. I ignored my twinge of guilt as I made my way to the gardens. Now that I had access to the entire castle, I was free to visit all kinds of new places on my own. Gardens in Rihtlond were nothing like those back home. Inraen gardens cultivated beauty through planning, pruning, and controlling nature. A statue or fountain, particularly one honoring the Martyrs, was never out of place.

In Rihtlond, gardens were about function. Even tiny plots held small crops and herbs. If there were flowers, they were likely from garlic and onions, or basil that had gone to seed. Then, of course, there were flowers like lavender and chamomile that were collected for teas. Even the rose bushes had culinary or medicinal purposes.

I grabbed a basket and wandered through the gardens, picking this and that under the pretense of helping the kitchens. As I looked at each plant, my new eyesight saw more than just the plant itself. Each blossom, leaf, and stem glowed with light, though it was different than what I had seen emanating from Callagh. A single color, unique to each sprout, shone through in steady beams. I hardly knew what they meant, but I could feel myself drawn to some more than others. Whenever a shade resonated with my hand, I plucked it and added it to my basket. I gathered parsley, cilantro, mint, a bushel of carrots, and a few beets with greens intact, then turned down a new row to examine the medicinal flowers.

"Well, aren't you a sight for sore eyes?"

Despite having only just met him, I easily picked out the sing-song quality of his voice. I turned and found Eldreth, my betrothed—or Ell, as everyone called him—making his way toward me.

"Tell me," he spoke with a lowered voice, as if we were coconspirators already, "how has my cantankerous brother been treating you?"

I swallowed the lump in my throat. Wep. *His heat against my body. His lips insistent against mine. The softness of his hair between my fingers.* I pushed the thoughts away. Of all things, why ask me this? I scrutinized Ell's white lifelight, swirling with forest green. *Content.* The smile on his lips was a bit too calculating when he offered me his arm. The bright iridescent lifelight emanating from me pulled back as my arm slipped into his.

"He treats me fair enough." It was the only thing I could think to say that wasn't dishonest.

"He's a bit of a bore, if I'm honest. This whole place can be."

"Is that why you were gone for so long?"

"Ah, that," he chuckled. "Well, I'm here now."

"It was a long wait to meet you." I meant it to sound light, but it came out chiding.

"Oh, ho! And I should've returned sooner to meet you, is that it? Trust me, nothing gives me greater joy than meeting my future dana." He said the words in earnest, yet they sounded anything but. Unease sparked within me. What was his game? "Besides, I had to return to defend myself against all the poison my brother undoubtedly spilled about me."

"Actually, he barely speaks of you."

"You mean never, but I appreciate the kindness. Now tell me, what are you doing in the gardens? Shirking your duties for the day?"

We turned a corner and continued down the path through a row of fruit trees. Ell plucked a small orange fruit, handed it to me, and then plucked one for himself.

"Is it terrible if I say yes?" I added the fruit to my basket.

Ell began peeling his own. "Not at all. Why do you think I'm here with you instead of up with my father?" He chuckled, and his smile was wide and bright. It was the sort of smile that could break hearts, and he seemed to know it.

"What did you have in mind?"

The light around him pulsed with lime green this time. *Excitement.* "I thought you'd never ask."

THAT AFTERNOON, I attempted to sneak out toward the market. Lunch with Ell was dizzying, and I barely managed three bites before making my excuses. He was curious, flirtatious, and forward in a way I couldn't wrap my head around. I needed a few hours on my own to think. The idea of finding those delicious buns again and stuffing my face in a quiet spot sounded like just the thing. But Callagh cornered me. One arm linked in mine, she led me toward the training rooms.

"You said training was canceled."

She gave me a heavy dose of side-eye. "No, I said all was well. Wep moved your *ranng's* training to the afternoon."

My mind had been swirling since the cave—Vaya'la's words now mingling with doubts over my father's expectations and Ell's intentions. I didn't have space in my head for any of them—Ell, my father, and certainly not Wep. I heaved a sigh and shoved my way through the double doors. My eyes threatened to bulge out of my head at the additions I saw to our usual group.

Kahvrah was there, for a start—talking animatedly with Lispen. Also in the room was Ell, speaking with a man I didn't recognize. A woman with a slick bald head stood idly, polishing a dagger she'd drawn from the sheath at her thigh. Bracht stood by Wep, looking as jovial as ever. He caught my eye and winked. Callagh slid into the room behind me, looking completely out of place and intimidated. It was the first time I'd seen cracks in her confidence. It was also the first time I would see her do any sort of training.

"Let's begin," Wep announced, taking his place at the front of the training mats. He wore lightweight fighting leathers and bracers instead of the usual loose shirts he favored for our regular sessions. Bracht moved forward, and

Kahvrah quickly fell in line beside him. Ell and the man I didn't know took up stances behind them. I tried to move with confidence I didn't feel, heading for my usual place in the back center. My eyes were weighted to the floor, which pissed me off, even though I couldn't convince them to rise.

"What's up with you?" Ivank whispered at my side.

A lie. Come up with a lie, quick. "I've just met Ell." *Shit.*

Laughter echoed in the back of my mind.

"Shut up, you."

The laughter continued, and I scowled.

"Ah, yeah, he has that effect." Ivank twitched an eyebrow.

"In stance," Wep barked. "We have a blended class today. Stick to your own *ranng*. There will be no cross-training."

"Kahvrah and Ell are part of the same *ranng*?" I whispered.

Ivank shrugged.

"Serae"—I jumped—"since you have so much to say, you can lead your *ranng* in the sun *dowsa*."

I scowled.

Wep immediately moved toward the other group. Ivank pushed me forward, and I stumbled to the front to assess my *ranng*. Callagh filled my vacated spot, still looking deeply unsettled.

In the other group, Kahvrah was speaking to Wep, looking completely at ease with his scowls. Behind her, Ell smirked at him—the exact same one I saw so often on Merria's lips. Bracht's eyes threw daggers at Ell, though his stance was calm and still. It reeked of Wep's influence.

"Pair us up," Helene whispered.

I shook my head. "Right. Lex with Ivank." Lex groaned. "Lispen with Raif. Helene with Teke. Callagh with me."

"C'mon, Serae, let me switch. I don't want to get kicked in the stomach when Ivank misses the third rotation."

"Fine. You can pair with Lispen." I grinned, all teeth.

Lex eyed Lispen with distaste. "That's okay." He turned to face Ivank as Lispen lunged forward and whacked the back of his head. "Ow!"

The rest of my *ranng* moved, and I couldn't help glancing toward Wep. He gave me a small nod, and I looked away quickly, hating the way something inside me swelled at his affirmation. My eyes slid to Ell. He was bouncing on his toes and stretching some muscle or other. I'd seen Wep warm up before, and this was nothing like it. Ell's movements were flashier. His lean muscles snapped with each sweeping motion, sharp and taut, but the movements weren't productive. The man next to him—maybe his *reálton*—was moving through the warmup I'd seen Wep use countless times. The two moved so similarly that I might have suspected he was Wep's brother, except that they looked nothing alike. He had dark eyes, dark skin, and a severe nose and brow.

I turned back to my *ranng* and found Callagh at my side.

"Thank you, my lady," she whispered. We began. Callagh was lithe and light on her feet, but she was not the most studied fighter. We completed the entire sun *dowsa* without issue, but the pace was a shade or two slower than even I was used to.

"Rest for two minutes," Wep announced. "Earth *dowsa* is next." He turned to the other *ranng* and gave different instructions.

"Why are we paired with that *ranng*?" I asked Callagh in a hushed tone.

She glanced over her shoulder. "It's Eldreth's *ranng*, I mean, Wep's *ranng*."

"Eldreth and his brother share a *ranng*?" I muttered to Callagh.

"They do now," she mumbled back. "They didn't always. I heard there's quite a story behind that, but I don't know it. Kahvrah is just filling in. It's one of her usual duties if Wep needs her help with training. I heard from my mother that Branye, a family friend of ours, is in the healing ward with her husband. They're both a part of that *ranng*, and I guess he was injured on their mission to bring home—"

"Continue," Wep called out.

We stepped apart. Callagh could be a fountain of gossip, especially when paired with her mother. I wondered if their blessings involved heightened hearing, with how much they seemed to know, but I hadn't found the right way to ask.

Earth *dowsa*, like all the elemental *dowsae*, was done individually. Callagh shuffled toward the back. I followed, sensing her unease and allowing Lispen and Raif at the front of the mat to take over the lead. I knew how it felt to be the newcomer and unprepared. Wep watched my retreat but said nothing. Guilt prickled through me, but there was no way to explain. I shouldn't want his approval—I didn't need it. My focus should be on my friend, who needed my support. Even so, my eyes kept drifting back to him.

We continued through the full set of elementals—earth *dowsa*, then water, then fire, which was performed from a crouching stance. By the time Wep called for another two-minute rest, my legs were sore and tight. I groaned and stretched my hands above my head, readying myself for air *dowsa*. I folded forward, relishing the burning stretch in my hamstrings and calves. Why did he have to change training today of all days?

"You're in quite the state today."

I shot up, overbalancing. Firm hands gripped my waist from behind. Reflex kicked in. I stepped, pivoted, and slammed my palm into a wall of chest.

"Relax," Ell chuckled, taking the blow in stride. He flashed a playful smile. "You sure do let him rile you. I'm not judging, though I do have to question your taste a bit."

"I'm sorry?" I blurted.

Ell waved it away with a hand. "No need—you didn't hurt me. Plus, it was a spectacular view."

"In stance," Wep shouted over the chatter. He moved into position with the opposite *ranng,* next to Bracht.

My cheeks heated as I hurried forward. This time, I made sure to place myself in the middle, surrounded by the protection of my *ranng.*

"Begin!"

Air *dowsa.* It was the newest to me, but we'd practiced it several times. Still, every movement was a nightmare. I fumbled, overcorrected, and at one point, flat-out forgot the next sequence and was forced to stand there like an idiot until my brain caught up with everyone else. Teke and Ivank both shot me glances.

Teke mouthed, *What's up?* when I turned left instead of right and ended up mirroring them.

Raif glanced over his shoulder, then repositioned himself directly in front of me. My face kept burning. I hated making mistakes, and the only thing worse was the special attention everyone was giving me. Everyone, that is, except for Wep. He kept his eyes trained on the back wall, leading the opposite *ranng* in a ridiculously complex *dowsa* with perfect fluidity and precision. He held long daggers in each hand, they spun and sliced with his every movement. A few times, one flew in the air as he flipped around. Every time, his hand ended up in the exact right place at the exact right moment to catch it and continue. Even through my embarrassment, I could admit that his movements were a work of art. His body was a joy to behold. I caught Callagh staring at him more than once, so it seemed I wasn't the only one distracted by him. Maybe Callagh's lean frame and shockingly blond hair would attract Wep.

Something unpleasant twisted in my chest. I forced my gaze forward, trying to banish that pointless line of thought, and stumbled again. I cursed aloud in Inraen and imagined the scolding look Gerta would've given me if she were here. Off to the side, Ell chuckled. I glanced his way, and he smirked.

My jaw hit the floor, making him laugh harder.

Fuck my fucking face. He spoke Inraen?

Mercifully, the *dowsa* ended.

"Take ten minutes," announced Wep.

I booked it. I lurched out of the training room and up the stairs that led out to the main hall. My intention was to run back to my rooms and hide, but Callagh would be on me in an instant. On impulse, I flung myself into the Relaxation Room at the last second, slamming the door behind me. It was all too tempting to collapse onto the pile of pillows and bury my face in them, but I was hot all over, my face burning more than the rest.

This was stupid. *I* was being stupid. Mistakes had never affected me this much before.

"What's wrong with me?" I pushed my memories of the afternoon at Vaya'la.

"Good, you're learning to use the binding well."

That wasn't the response I expected. *"What else can it do?"*

The door creaked open.

Only one person would look for me here first. I looked up, and for a second, I was relieved. Then, my breath hitched. A wry smile flashed at me through the dim light. My heart sank, even though I told it not to.

"Hiding away in here?" Ell asked.

"Yes." There was no point in lying.

"Do you mind if I...?" He pointed at the pillows beside me. I shook my head, and he plopped down. "What's this about? Surely, my brother doesn't put you this much on edge." He grinned. "Then again, he does have a way of intimidating people, doesn't he?"

I tried to smile and failed.

He nudged me with his shoulder. "You know, when we were kids, everyone assumed he was the older brother, even though I'm two years older and was quite a bit taller than him at the time." He looked at me with those ice-blue eyes. There was something kind and gentle that touched them. "It's because he was so serious, and I was always looking for fun."

Ell reached out and tucked a stray strand of hair behind my ear, then his finger traced down my jaw. I stiffened and willed myself not to pull away. I couldn't stifle my shudder.

"Do you like having fun?" he whispered.

He leaned toward me, and I became overwhelmingly conscious of how close we were. The entire side of his body pressed against mine, his face a matter of inches away and ready to close in. Warning bells rang in my mind.

"I don't—"

The door to the room burst open.

I jumped, flinging myself away from Ell. Perched awkwardly on the pillows, as I was, I went flying toward the floor. I threw my hands out, catching myself at the last second, but smacking my wrist against the table corner on the way down. I swore, sat up, and pulled it to my chest. Behind me, Ell's eyes danced with mirth.

Wep stood in the doorway, eyes like dark storms. However, he wasn't looking at me. All his fuming intent was focused on Ell, who bore it with an unwavering smile.

"We resume in one minute," he gritted out through a clenched jaw. His eyes never left his brother until he turned, leaving the door wide open.

"My, my, testy." Ell rose to his feet and offered me a hand.

I took it without thinking, then hissed as he pulled me up by my freshly injured wrist.

"Do you think he'll pout all week? Maybe he'll stay holed up in his training room and spare us all from his moods."

I just stared at him. He was not at all rattled by his brother. Then again, he had known Wep his whole life. It must have built up his tolerance.

"If he does, I want to take you out to the lower city myself and show you the real Drakh." He sauntered out, but not before throwing a tinkling, "Come along," and a wink over his shoulder.

"I don't like that one," Vaya'la said.

I wasn't so sure I did either.

Back in the training room, we were paired up for hand-to-hand sparring. The other *ranng* was in a semicircle surrounding Ell and Wep, who were warming up with blunted short swords off to the side.

"Ahem, eyes over here."

I looked to Lex, who was bouncing on his toes and quirking an eyebrow at me. I grinned. "Let's do this."

Lex was still far better than me, but I was improving. My hits landed more often than not. Each blow caused actual grunts from my peers, and I finally understood the need to pull punches. Even the *dowsae* movements were making connections in my mind. When Lex attacked high, I used pieces from fire *dowsa* to counter. When he reversed and kicked low, air *dowsa* helped me leap out of reach. I was beginning to feel the rhythm of a fight. Like the *dowsae*, there was a dance to it. I could see the elegance, and even though my body wasn't as strong as Lispen's or as graceful as Helene's, I understood my goal and could imagine how to get there.

A clash of swords, louder than the rest, drew my attention. Lex and I both turned, abandoning our sparring entirely.

"Well, fuck me sideways," Lex breathed with a low whistle.

I couldn't have agreed more.

Wep and Ell were a flurry of movement. Their arms and short swords were in constant motion, nearly impossible to track. How they managed to counter each other was a mystery, and judging by the others who had stopped to watch, I wasn't the only one who thought so. They moved in a way that only a lifetime of training could build. I couldn't tell who had the advantage. All I saw was snapping muscles and a flurry of blades.

"Wep has him," Raif predicted at my side.

"Maybe not," Helene replied. "Ell keeps driving him back."

"He's baiting," added Ivank.

"And to think, Serae, one day you'll have all that between your—ow!" Lex rubbed the back of his head.

I frowned, whether at that thought or the fact that my eyes had been glued to Wep this entire time.

Lispen's smile was sharp. "I'll smack you again if you can't control that tongue."

Silence fell except for the shuffle of feet, the clang of metal, and their grunts of exertion. Wep's face was calm. Even his consummate mask of annoyance had fallen away while he focused. I glanced at Ell, the one I should be watching. His face flickered between exertion and mirth. He said something I couldn't hear over the crashing of blades. Wep frowned, just a little thing, but it was more emotion than he ever let on his face during a match.

It was over in a flash. I didn't even see what happened, but one of Ell's blades clattered to the ground. He had fallen to his knees, and Wep had both swords crossed at his neck in an X.

Raif nodded. "Told you. He's not our weaponmaster for nothing."

There was a rumble of agreement all around, and one by one, we turned back to our pairings. I don't know what I expected of Eldreth, but considering what I knew of his father and brother, I shouldn't be surprised by that level of skill. The reality of his position as future dane hit me alongside a new fear. If I was bound to Vaya'la, would I be able to leave? And if my father's army failed to reach me, if I was forced to stay, could I really stand at Eldreth's side as dana? Focusing on my sparring progress suddenly held a new weight.

I ran my fingers through my mass of tangled curls, pulling out a stray dried leaf. Not expecting to have to train today, I'd skipped braiding it. I eyed the little thing as it crumpled in my fingers, dreading what it meant for my hair if it was stuck there all through training. Or perhaps I'd been holding back more than I realized. The simple thought refocused me, and I faced Lex, determined to give every move my all.

The following day presented me with another free morning. Training was to be held in the afternoon again, so I decided to visit the market. Callagh joined, and already I had learned this was an advantage. She knew *everyone.* And, while the people we passed mostly gave me sour looks, nothing more happened with Callagh at my side.

We approached a store with shelves of stacked jars lining the walls visible through the window. "Can we stop here?" I asked.

Callagh nodded. "You'll love Lanh Cergia, my lady. She was just telling my mother how she'd like to know more about Inra."

As soon as the shop door opened, the warm scents of clove, cinnamon, rosemary, and peppercorn enveloped me. My nose was so sensitive, I could pick out each individual fragrance plus a dozen more fresh herbs.

"I'll be right there!" called a woman in Rihtish. Jars clinked as she rummaged behind a counter. When she straightened, her graying curls bounced around her face. "Callagh, dear," she cooed. This was the same in every shop we entered, in every stand we stopped at, and from many people on the street.

"Lanh Cergia, so wonderful to see you again."

"Oh pish, you're too kind to an old woman like me, but I'm no sweet lady like this lass." She switched to Mayoran at the sight of me.

"Have you met my lady, Serae?"

She turned to me. "Hello, dear, it's just Cergia." She put a hand to her heart, leaving flecks of herbs on her shirt, which she brushed off with a little huff.

I couldn't help but smile. Something about Cergia tickled a memory and brought to mind Cook from my childhood.

"What brings you into my little shop?" the older woman asked, eyes flicking between Callagh and me.

"Oh, uhm, I'm so fond of bottles," I said.

Callagh choked behind me.

"For herbs, I mean! Not just empty bottles."

Vaya'la's laugh invaded my mind, and I groaned inwardly, fighting the urge to cover my face.

"Can you tell Serae a bit about the herbs and spices you make? She's got an excellent nose."

"Ah, a woman after my own heart." Cergia lit up at the request. "Please come and see."

One second, I was standing just inside the doorway, and the next, I was hauled behind the counter and had my face shoved into a bowl of greens.

"Smell! Smell! Isn't it wonderful?"

I took a tiny sniff. Holy Martyrs, it truly was. It was an herb I wasn't familiar with—narrow leaves growing on long stems. Beside it, another bowl overflowed with stems, and the next held just the stripped leaves. The scent was a bit spicy, fresh, and aromatic.

"Taste!" Cergia dropped leaves into my hand. "I bet you have nothing like that where you come from. It's called *savory*, or that's my best translation of it. Grows in heaps in the wild here, but these fools around us wouldn't know it from brambles." She cackled at her own joke.

I nibbled one of the fresh leaves. It tasted exactly as it smelled. I could imagine adding it to fish, vegetables, pies...

"It's good, yes? I have a great cookie recipe that uses it."

I raised a brow, but Cergia forged on.

"This batch I'm going to extract into an oil. But I do it dried, too. Lasts longer that way, though not as strong. What do you think it's used for, eh?"

"Fortitude of the mind."

"Excuse you?"

"Fine, don't tell her."

"Mental strength," I blurted. Then, to Vaya'la, *"Are you here all the time now?"*

"More of your memories come through to me as our binding tightens. The same will happen for you."

As if to prove a point, *I was in the air, wings spread broad. The clouds around me were pink against an orange sky. I soared, then dived toward a green lake.* I blinked.

Cergia gave me a sharp look. "Yes. Very good. Come, come, I know just what you need." She took my arm and pulled me around the counter toward towering shelves that lined the shop. Small jars, large jars, bags, and baskets were stacked everywhere, but she stopped at a section of wooden boxes. She plucked one up and set it into my hands.

"What do you think of this?"

I pried the lid open. The box was divided into a dozen little compartments, each one filled with a different spice. Some were ground into fine powders, others were whole seeds, and a few were partially crushed leaves.

"It's wonderful," I breathed. I wanted it to be mine. I was rarely the type to see something and covet it. That was always Merria—with dresses, shoes, parasols, ribbons. Martyrs, if she even looked at jewels... Back home, I wanted for nothing, but there was also very little that I might actually want. I reached for my scale pouch.

"Good." Cergia nodded at Callagh across the shop. "I'll send my bill to Dane, yes?"

"Please," Callagh confirmed. It was done before I could protest. The scale I carried came from Dane anyway, I reminded myself. I had never earned money of my own in my life, a detail that had never bothered me before that moment.

The spice box was not the only thing I brought back from the market. Toward the center was the flower stand. I chose carefully, remembering what Bale had taught me. Some petals crushed best when dried, others when soaked. I wasn't much of a painter, but I loved helping him prepare the paints. An idea was taking shape. With Callagh's help, we visited Lanh Migram, the tailor, who was happy to sell me a few bolts of pale neutral cloth. It was a thicker material than I'd been wearing, but she assured me they would be perfect when the chill came down from the mountains. She was curious in a polite sort of way about my intentions with the cloth.

"Bring it here when you're done, and I'll make it into anything you like," she said with a patronizing smile.

It took a lot of focus to stop my eyes from rolling.

"How *does* this all work, my lady?" Callagh asked when we were well clear of the shop.

"The spices are for tea, but *this*—I'll show you tonight."

AFTERNOON TRAINING JUMPED on me with fierce aggression, only I didn't possess the energy to counter it. Still, I entered the training room with my head held high. Wep, his back to the door, and the rest of my *ranng* were already in stance, waiting for me. Our little trip to the market had taken more of the morning than I'd expected.

"Sorry," I whispered to Teke as I fell into place.

Wep glanced over his shoulder and spotted me. "Good, let's begin." He rushed us through a warmup *dowsa* then assigned us sparring partners without once meeting my gaze. He looked right through me, sparking my anger. I glowered at him before turning to face Teke.

"You're off today," they observed, throwing a series of punches.

I dodged left and right, then ducked into a low kick. "Just rushed," I said, following Teke into a gripped roll. We separated and reset. "We were getting supplies."

"For?" Teke lunged.

I miscalculated and walked right into their strike instead of sidestepping it. "*Oof!* A... project... Damn, that connected good."

They grinned, and their guard relaxed.

I struck, still close enough to get inside their reach. One punch to the shoulder and one to the gut, both pulled.

"Fuck," Teke wheezed, and it was my turn to grin.

By the end, we'd each made enough hits to be blossoming a rainbow of bruises beneath our clothes, but that didn't dim the smile on our faces. Turns out, all I needed was to land a few good blows to improve my mood. The fact that I was able to land any was reason enough to celebrate.

"Dismissed," was all we got from Wep.

Right. Still a prick then.

I don't know why I did it, but I hung back.

"Hot springs? You've never been," Teke offered. "Lispen and Raif are going too."

I shook my head, glancing over at Wep.

They raised their eyebrows but didn't press. "We're headed to the Main Hall after. Catch up if you want."

I nodded, ignoring the way my stomach dropped. Not only had I yet to be invited to eat in the Main Hall, but I also wasn't sure I wanted to. I still attracted more than my share of glares and whispers when walking the streets. How much worse would it be if trapped in a room with it? Not exactly my idea of a peaceful meal.

It was a worry for another day. I steeled myself and turned to Wep, knowing we were alone.

"You need something?" All his ire was now directed at me.

"No," I blurted, forgetting myself under that gaze.

He tried to turn his back on me, but I surged forward, catching his forearm.

"Yes, actually. What gives?"

He glared down at my hand then back at me. "Something wrong with my training?"

I clenched my jaw. "No, but you're being an ass."

"Noted. Anything else you want from me?"

Martyrs, what did I want from him? I dropped his arm and backed away. "I—" I shook my head. This was idiocy. He was allowed his bad moods—it shouldn't affect me. At least, not more than anyone else in my *ranng*, but I didn't see them here confronting him. "No. Nothing."

I left. I hurried down the corridor in a daze back toward my rooms, but as I passed the Relaxation Room, a hand shot out and pulled me inside.

I squeaked.

It was Ell, looking at me with a catlike smile. "Been practicing with my dear brother again?" he asked with far too much mirth in his voice.

"No," I answered, moving toward the center of the room and putting distance between us. "*Dowsae* and sparring. He didn't join."

"Tsk, tsk, naughty brother of mine." He stepped toward me, blocking my exit.

I quirked an eyebrow. Something was off—his smile too broad, his attention too focused. I couldn't make sense of his lifelight, flashing green with flecks of umber.

"*Mischief,*" Vaya'la supplied.

"He always wants to stand back and watch, rather than make the right move." Another step.

"He didn't watch either." I stood very still. What was his game?

Another step closer. "Did that drive you mad, my sweet?"

Something unpleasant clenched in my stomach.

"Are you only happy when his eyes are on you, devouring you? Or, do you let anyone's eyes do that?"

Another step. One more and he would be close enough to touch. He must have meant to do just that, as with his final step, he raised a hand and crooned, "Do you let others touch you the way you let him?"

A tightness seized me as Ell's fingers caressed down my cheek. No, not a tightness—a tautness. I was a coil ready to spring, which is exactly what I did, smacking his hand away. "The only way Wep touches me is in sparring. What are you suggesting of me?"

His chuckle was a taunt. "Where has your mind taken you?"

I stepped back, right into the low table. I stumbled over it, my ankle smacking hard into the edge right on the bone. I tried to catch myself, but the joint rolled. I collapsed. Pain exploded through me. I swore in a way that would make my mother blush. I already had a purple bruise blossoming over that ankle from a poorly placed block during sparring. My leg from the knee down vibrated in anger.

Ell dropped into a crouch. He was surveying me with an odd look on his face.

"Don't touch me," I hissed through clenched teeth.

Ell rolled his eyes. "So sensitive." He stood and offered me a hand. "Come on, let's get you up."

The tone of his voice had changed entirely. Both the playfulness and mockery had vanished. It was stripped down, and I had a feeling this was the first I'd ever heard him—the real Eldreth—speaking. Only then did I recognize his attitude for what it was: a mask. I took his proffered hand, and he hauled me to my feet—foot. I couldn't put pressure on the right one yet.

"Can you walk?"

I nodded.

"Liar. Let's get you to a healer and have that ankle looked at."

"Fine." It probably would be fine, but it wasn't a great sign that the joint couldn't bear weight.

"You know, you're rather jumpy for someone who's supposed to be the future dana of the Riht," Ell said with a smile back on his face. It was friendly and lopsided and completely at odds with his usual sharpness.

"Fuck off."

His grin only widened.

CHAPTER 17

"There is a reason why the Bound do not take mates."

When she spoke those words, I wanted to deny her. I thought only of Tianna and her long hair, dark eyes, and flawless ebony skin. I would perform the handfasting ceremony with her in an instant if she would have me.

"You cannot have two bindings and fulfill them both, Small One. You are already bound to me."

Tears mottled my vision. Again, I wanted to deny her, but I would not. Never. It was a truth that broke me, but I needed to bear it all the same.

—Recounting from the private diary of Jerris, Dragonbound

SERAE

LATE SUMMER, MAYMON 1036

THERE WAS NO hot spring for me that evening and no training for me the following day. Luckily, it only took one day of rest for the swelling to reduce, allowing me to walk again.

"The mighty Serae, brought down by a table." Lex had laughed.

A day clear of Wep hadn't hurt either. Whatever happened over the past day acted like a reset for him. I wish I could say the same for me. I wanted to be nowhere near him, and yet, I couldn't get his hypnotic taste and scent out of my head. Wep, however, was back to leading the session with minimal surliness. The focus for the day was hand-to-hand, specifically breaking holds and redirecting momentum.

"This is the great equalizer," he explained. "You can take down a man bigger than Ivank with the right momentum and leverage. Serae, up front."

I groaned.

He crossed his arms over his chest, left over right. "That ankle recovered?"

"Mostly."

"Perfect, that's the best time to train. Up front."

He led me through the motions, adjusting my angles and showing me when to brace, when to shift, and how to take control. Shifting focus and staying out of the way was my *life* back in Inra. Within three tries, I had Wep flat on his back—well, he would've been if he didn't recover from every single thing with the grace of a feline.

"Good. Ivank, up front. Attack when ready. Serae, focus."

I bounced from foot to foot. "I'm ready."

"Twitchy little thing, isn't she?" Someone behind me laughed. It was sharp and unpleasant, and even if I hadn't recognized the voice, I would've figured it out by the darkening of Wep's face.

"Go."

Ivank lunged. Quick on my toes, I followed the motions to perfection. I barely felt the difference in weight, even though Ivank was at least half a head taller than Wep and twice as broad.

"Very good." Wep's mouth was threatening a smile.

"Oh, come on," Ell announced from the door. "Give her a real challenge."

"Get out of my class."

"Give me a go, and I'll leave."

"How about you just leave now?"

Helene cleared her throat. "It might help to have someone outside the *ranng* try."

Wep's head snapped to her, but his eyes softened. I couldn't blame him. It was impossible to be cross with Helene. She was the most disarming person in existence. He looked to me, and I shrugged. He relented with a grunt.

Ell moved through the center of the group toward the front. "Excellent," he said, shooing Ivank with a wave. "Ready, beautiful?"

I rolled my eyes.

He attacked, but I was ready. I gripped his arm, rolled into his space, twisted, and sent him to the floor. I turned back to Wep, eager to collect his smile, when something collided with my ankle—*that* ankle—taking it out from under me. The breath was knocked from my lungs as my back hit the mat.

"What the hell!" Raif shouted.

"It was one move, ass-wipe," Lex added.

Shouting echoed through the room, rattling my ears as my *ranng* flew to my defense, but Ell was already standing over me with that devilish smile on his lips. He extended a hand. "All in good fun," he said only to me.

Wep knocked his hand away, then everything happened at once. Wep shoved his brother off balance, jabbed him straight in the crook of his shoulder, kicked out his opposite knee, and socked him full-force in the stomach.

Ell dropped like a sack.

"Get out of my space," he growled, standing over Ell like he'd love nothing more than to deliver a few extra kicks.

"I like this one."

"Not now."

Ell wheezed. "Fuck...you couldn't have...pulled that last one?" He rasped between uneven breaths.

"I did. Get. Out. Before I do something you'll regret."

"I approve. He is worthy of you."

"Except the one on the floor is my betrothed."

"Pity. Bring him to me, and I'll eat him."

"You'd eat a man you already blessed?"

The snarling in my mind sounded an awful lot like confirmation.

I sat up. Ell stood, arched a brow at Wep, and muttered something too low to hear. Wep's eyes darkened as he watched his brother retreat from the room. The door thumped shut.

"I'll go for the healer," Raif offered.

"I'll go with," added Helene, and the two of them took off.

"A little space," Wep growled.

Ivank, Lispen, and Lex moved to the other end of the room. They made an excellent show of pretending to practice, but I could feel all three straining their ears to hear us.

Wep crouched before me. "May I?"

I nodded.

He took my calf in his hand and unlaced my boot.

"It's not that bad. It barely hurts at—*Fuck!*"

He had pried the boot off and was cradling my ankle. His eyes lifted to mine. "So, no pain?"

"None," I gritted out.

He huffed out a laugh. Fuck, if that wasn't the most inconvenient sound I'd ever heard. I wanted to taste it. The little quirk of his lip, the light dancing in his blue-gray eyes. I didn't know when it changed, but all at once, I wanted to climb into this man's lap and see how skilled he really was, broodiness be damned. I bit my lip, and his eyes tracked the movement.

"Serae," his voice was a low rumble, "you need to be careful with my brother."

An ice bath would've had less of a chilling effect on me. My face fell. "What do you mean?"

"He's not what he seems. Everything's a fucking game to him."

"A game?"

He nodded.

"Right. But not to you?"

A frown pulled at the corners of his mouth, and the loss of that little smile hit me like a blow. "I—"

The doors behind me opened.

"This way," Raif said, leading the same healer who had set my ankle just two days prior. In fact, she was the same elderly woman who'd been helping me since I arrived in the Riht.

"Delly," she admonished, Wep's grimace was spectacular, "you know better than to let someone train on an injured joint. Knees and ankles are no-goes. Say it."

"Knees and ankles are no-goes," he repeated flatly.

I turned, catching Teke's eye. *Delly?* I mouthed.

They shook their head and mouthed back, *Don't ask.*

I couldn't have asked if I wanted to, because at that moment, she took my ankle in hand and rolled the joint, testing my rotation. I gasped as pain like glass shards grated between the bones.

"Disgraceful," the woman tittered, then began layering a thick salve over my skin. She followed it with a bandage, then a stiff wrap, making the joint impossible to move. "There we go. Let's get her to bed. Come on, lift her up."

"Lift me what?"

"Sorry about this," Wep whispered, and in one smooth motion, he had me in his arms, carrying me like a baby.

"O-oh." *Brilliant.* I wrapped my arms around his neck.

He cleared his throat, and I felt the reverberation in his chest against mine. Thank the Nine Martyrs, my room was close. Wep took off, but his pace was careful and steady. I might have expected to be jostled on the stairs in anyone else's arms, but Wep was always perfectly balanced—perfectly in control. A loose strand of hair at the base of his neck brushed against my arm, and the intimacy of our situation screamed at me.

"You punched your brother," I whispered.

His eyes flicked to mine. His jaw flexed in that way I liked, and the images in my head—

"No, I don't want to see them. Keep your thoughts to yourself. You're shouting them at me."

"Sorry. You'll have to teach me that part."

"Preferably soon."

"First on the right," he said.

I turned my head as the healing matron opened my door and held it.

"My thanks, Marr Magda. I can take it from here."

"Right, you can." She turned a shaking finger on me. "No walking, lots of fluids, and you drink down the bottles I'll be sending three times a day."

I nodded, barely getting out a thanks before she shuffled out the door and let it thud shut behind her.

Wep stood there, holding me like I weighed nothing and dutifully avoiding my eyes.

I racked my brain and came up with exactly nothing to say.

"Chair or bed?" he asked, sparing me.

A question like that can do things to a girl. I swallowed that quip right back down. "Chair."

"Bed it is."

"What? No, I can...hobble around, I'm sure."

"No walking."

"That's impossible. What if I have to pee?"

He paused halfway to my bedchamber. "Do you?"

"No."

"Good."

He nudged the door open with his boot and entered, then hesitated. "Uh, which side?"

"Either is fine."

"Only monsters don't have a preference." His eyes met mine, and they were far too close. I could see every fleck of silver, the faint blue rims around his irises, and the widening of his pupils with perfect clarity. My eyes dropped to his lips as he wet them.

"He's got jokes."

His lip quirked.

"Right."

He moved, and before I was ready to let go, he had me settled on the patterned quilt and propped against my pillows. He looked around, finding my chair and writing desk covered with my paint jars, drying and soaking flowers, and the little practice sketches I'd made. The edge of my bed was the only option. He took my ankle in his hand again, as if it were the most natural thing in the world to touch me, and began inspecting the healer's work.

"Marr Magda is the master healer here. Lucky she came."

"I saw her two days ago." I didn't mention that I'd also seen her multiple times before his return.

His brows raised, and he nodded. "Good." He massaged my calf, soothing the sore muscle and sending tingles all over.

The silence between us thickened. All I could focus on were his rough hands kneading my muscles into relaxed submission.

"Why do you let him get to you?" I sucked in a breath as he reached the back of my knee. "Nothing else rattles you."

"Not nothing." He shrugged. His fingertips lingered at the sensitive flesh behind the joint, then he began working his way back down. "Too much history between us, I guess."

"Oh." That much I understood. Things were the same between me and Merria. My heart sank into my stomach. *Stop it*, I told myself. Wep wasn't my betrothed. Hell, *Ell* wasn't even my true betrothed. I was trapped in a game I didn't want to play.

"We can change the game, Small One."

I ignored her, busybody that she was becoming. "At least it was a good hit."

Wep laughed and pressed a thumb into the hollow of my foot. Creator, his hands were heaven. I bit back a moan. "It felt good, too." His smile turned wry. "And I *did* pull that punch."

"Sure."

"Got all his ribs intact, doesn't he?"

"Oh, that's the measurement? Whether you crack bone?"

He shrugged, a cocky little thing. "Maybe."

"I didn't kiss him," I blurted out. "I mean, I wasn't going to. I didn't want to." My face started burning, and I tried to wipe it away with my hands. "I'm sorry. I don't know what I'm saying. Forget it."

His hands stilled.

I examined the lines in the quilt. There was an ironic lack of florals for a place so in tune with nature.

"I'm not here to control you."

"I know."

"What you do doesn't have to be my business—"

"I shouldn't have said—"

"—unless you want it to be."

My eyes snapped to his. It was a monumental mistake, but one I was burning to make. His eyes were guarded, but they pierced through me all the same.

Instinctively, I knew I had to be the one to make this move. It was slow and awkward trying to inch my way down the bed without using my entire right leg.

Wep turned to me, tracing his hands up my thighs as I scooted toward him. He should have laughed. *I* should have laughed. The sight of me was surely ridiculous. When I made it within his reach, his hands scooped beneath me and lifted me the rest of the way straight into his lap.

"Your ankle," he whispered, devouring me with his eyes.

"Fuck my ankle." I'd been playing a losing game for weeks now. It was time for me to have a win. I wanted to crash into him. I wanted to push every inexplicable thing I'd been feeling into him, just to see if his control would finally break. But his brother had just snapped that control in half so easily that I knew another break wasn't what he needed. So, I took my time. I pressed my lips to his and kissed him slowly, letting him decide if he wanted this. We both knew it was wrong, but a kiss had never felt so incredibly *right*.

He deepened it, stroking his tongue against mine and igniting my whole body in fire and lightning. I was the charge in the air before a storm and the flickering blue precursor to white hot flames. His fingers delved into my hair, cradling the back of my head and angling our kiss even deeper. My hands wandered over his impossibly muscled arms. This man was all hardness wrapped up in soft skin that I was desperate to feel beneath his long-sleeved shirt. I ran my hands down his chest, and his breath hitched as I traced his taut abs, but he didn't pull away, and thank the Martyrs he didn't because I needed to touch every inch of him.

I raked my teeth over his bottom lip, sucking it into my mouth and teasing it with my tongue. He moaned, and I instantly needed to hear it again. That was, until he drove all thought from my mind, tracing his lips and tongue over my jaw and down my throat.

"Yes," I whispered, lost in this moment and never wanting it to end. I tried to rock my hips against his, but at this angle, I had no way of moving without transferring any weight to my ankle. I was completely at his mercy, yet there was nowhere else I wanted to be. His teeth raked over my neck, driving me wild with need, ankle be damned.

"Serae." My name was a prayer on his lips.

"Please don't stop." I didn't care that I was begging.

His lips returned to mine, and I couldn't remember why they had ever been apart, why they had ever spent a moment not locked together in this unimaginable heaven.

"We can't continue," he said, but his wicked mouth told me otherwise as his tongue slid back into mine, thoroughly exploring me and then opening for me to do the same.

A small voice in the back of my head sounded, and this time it wasn't Vaya'la. It was the absolute buzzkill known as conscience, logic, responsibility—take your pick. She was telling me that no good could come from following this path. This man would ruin me, and I would let him. And maybe, just maybe, when I was ripped away from this fantasy world I'd been indulging in, I'd run the risk of ruining him too.

It was that thought that brought me back to my senses. There were so many sinful things I wanted to do with him, but I did not want to be the reason for his pain.

The kiss slowed, and he ran his hands down my back like a sorrowful caress.

"I know you're right," I sighed.

"You need rest."

I nodded, the weight of this mistake, my father's deception, and my impending betrayal threatening to crush me as it came crashing back down.

Wep kissed me again, slow but firm, and it was the kiss of an ending. It was the sort of kiss that said goodbye without words. His strong arms lifted me and settled me back against my pillows. He looked like he might say something, but a knock sounded at the door.

Callagh's face peeked through. "Teke just found me and said—oh!" Her eyes rounded as they darted between me and Wep. "I'll come back."

"I was just leaving." He retreated from my side, and it took all my strength to keep my face neutral. To Callagh, he added, "Marr Magda is sending along a few remedies for her." Without quite meeting my eyes, he added, "I'll check on you tomorrow."

I nodded as he withdrew. Silence reigned in his wake.

Callagh eyed me, seeing too much and saying too little. "Are you all right, my lady?"

"Yes, of course." I knew she heard the quaver in my voice. "I just need a minute."

There was a bit too much understanding on Callagh's face. "I'll go to the healer's for your remedies. And I'll collect your tray from the guards." Dane was still having all of my food checked, though there had been no further incidents. In our last lesson, he told me the cook to blame had been dismissed, and he had assigned the most-trusted Kish to me, a round-faced woman I'd met on my first trip to the kitchens. I got the feeling there was something he was leaving out.

I sat there in my bed, ankle propped on a pillow I didn't even realize Wep had placed, feeling the ghost of his lips against mine and wishing everything about my life were different. White petals were strewn all along my bed. Something from Callagh—had I told her jasmine was my favorite? I had no space in my mind to consider it. Pity was a hollow, thankless thing, but self-pity was a whole different low. That was where I seemed to have taken up residence.

"We control our own fate, Small One. Sleep."

It was many long hours, plus the aid of Magda's nighttime remedy, before my mind stilled enough to comply.

Three days of bed rest at the behest of a very tender, very swollen ankle turned out to be one of the busiest times I'd spent in the Riht. Callagh spent most of the day with me, helping prepare and perfect the flower dyes. It was a long, tedious journey that left my room littered with petals. They somehow got everywhere—in my tub, on the bed, between my sheets, under every piece of furniture in the room, and even atop my wardrobe. I didn't remember setting anything up there, but that didn't stop them from tumbling down on my head one morning as I went to dress.

We began by grinding, grinding, grinding. The petals needed to be reduced to the finest of powders to be effective—otherwise the dye would turn out chunky and irregular. We talked while we worked about everything except a certain copper-haired man who had taken over every moment of silence in my mind. The first afternoon, Grinding Day, Teke sat with us after training, singing and teaching us songs. By evening, my arms were so exhausted, I could barely lift the spoon to my mouth. But I had three dozen small jars of powder to show for it.

True to his word, Wep visited in the evening. He kept distance between us, asked the same questions as the healer had about my ankle, then offered to play errand boy and collect anything I might want from town the following day. He raised his eyebrows at my request for the cheapest clear alcohol he could find, the palest vinegar, and an inquiry at the blacksmith about iron salts.

"You're not going to tell me what all this is about, are you?" he asked before leaving.

"Not a fan of surprises?" I smirked.

"No. The jars?"

"Sorry to disappoint you."

He lingered in the doorway. He'd worn a tight tunic that hugged his every muscle, which was completely unfair to come here looking so good. I, on the other hand, was covered in flower dust, wearing the most unflattering smock, and had more hair outside my unraveling bun than in it.

"See you on Mixing Day, then."

"Right." He tapped a fist against the doorframe and left.

On the fourth morning, I was right back to my usual routine, with one unexpected addition. Mornings were still spent in training sessions, afternoons in lessons—I was making drastic progress in my Rihtish—but my midday break now consisted of a short but pleasant walk with Ell following the midday meal.

After making amends for his idiocy with my ankle—swearing up and down he had forgotten I was injured—the elder brother was becoming less of an enigma. Since my recovery, his attitude had shifted. He stopped showing up at my training sessions, stopped trying to corner me in unexpected places, and instead started dropping his mask with me. At first, it was all too easy for him to bristle my hackles, until I realized he just wanted a different type of sparring partner than his brother. All it took were a few quips, letting my tongue be as sharp as it willed, and Ell was howling in delight. All in all, he was proving to be a playful partner. It was refreshing, in a way, to finally have eyes on my target, even though I had no idea what I was supposed to be doing with it.

I did write a carefully worded letter to Merria, telling her of his general appearance and disposition. I hoped that would serve to appease my father—an apology of sorts. I still had not resumed sending him coded notes. Every time the thought crossed my mind, something stilled my hand. Worse, I received nothing at all from home. I had no idea if he meant to punish me for defying him—or how. Would he still come for me? Or would he leave me behind, another child lost to their fate?

Intent on making any sort of progress, regardless of if I put it to use, I focused my attentions on Ell. Making him talk was no taxing task at all. With next to no prompting, he could prattle on about absolutely anything and everything, content to listen to his own voice uninterrupted. Every now and again, he would remember I was meant to be a participant in our conversation, not just a rapt audience, so he'd ask me a question or two. When he did, he was all charm, and it was easy to forget that everything about our interactions was a farce. Even so, the information Ell gave freely was fairly useless: bits about expeditions, which I already knew; details on the passing down of their leadership, which I also had already learned; some basic bits about their economy, which were interesting though not helpful; and so on. My ears only perked up when the conversation shifted toward their *bierlae.*

"Everyone has a unique blessing, of course."

"What's yours, then?"

"Ah-ah, that would be very telling." His lifelight flickered salmon pink. *Agitation.*

I was adjusting to this new dragonsight Vaya'la had gifted me, though I had yet to tell anyone about it. Almost all plants gave off unique hues of light that varied by species. People shone with different intensities of pure light that flickered, as far as I had discerned, by emotion. Stronger emotions elicited more dramatic light.

"Is it not polite to ask, or are you just holding out on me?"

He chortled. "Both. Do you have one?"

Unsure how to answer, I just shrugged.

"Don't worry." He patted my arm. "It takes time to recognize. It's a bit of a personal journey, discovering one's unique blessing. It took me ages to understand mine, but I was also abroad a lot when I was younger. Dane seemed to think it would give me world sense to tag along with various expeditions."

"Why would that matter?"

"The farther you are from the Great Dragon, the weaker your blessing becomes."

"You really won't tell me what yours is?"

He threw me a dashing smile.

"All right, keep your secrets, then. It's nothing to me."

Ell put a hand to his heart. "You wound me! Fine, fine. Let's just say mine helps me understand others better."

"So, like a language thing?" I asked.

"Not quite, no."

"Mmm." When Ell gave nothing further, I said, "Well, if you won't tell me this, then tell me instead about the best shops and stalls to visit. My view has been rather limited." That was a topic I knew could last him a while. His range of preferences was vast, but one thing about Ell was that he had an opinion about everything.

As invigorating as these early afternoon walks were, evenings had become my favorite time of day. Wep offered up the slick black table in the lesson room as a workspace, which meant I spent a couple of hours working on my fabric dyes before showing up to strength training. It also meant that, more often than not, I showed up with splotches of color covering my hands.

Once I had finished preparing enough dye, I fashioned a small paintbrush using a bit of my hair and a smooth stick. For the first week, I practiced patterns on the bolts of cloth Callagh and I had purchased. I made vines, several different types of flowers, and even geometric patterns—but my favorite by far was a melding of the geometric patterns of the Riht with organic petal shapes. The result was something I'd never seen on either side of the White Sea.

The biggest fan of my work was Teke. "I'm bringing you all my tunics," they announced one afternoon.

"No, you're not."

"Yes, I am. I'll pay you."

"These all need to be tested with multiple washes first. If the dye sets, we'll talk."

"Deal."

Teke's grin was infectious, and their encouragement made my heart soar.

More importantly, something new and wonderful happened every time I worked. I slipped into a trance of sorts, focused on the design as well as living in a world of memory. Vaya'la's memory, as she explained it. From there, I learned how to open and close my enhanced vision and control the passageway between our minds to block or engage her. The best part: this was only the beginning.

Every day, I woke feeling just a little bit brighter about the prospects of the day. However, every training session brought a slightly grumpier, more frigid version of Wep. It was like what happened between us had scared him off, which was for the best. That didn't stop my knees from going weak every time I remembered the feel of his body, his perfect lips, and—fuck, even his scent was hypnotic. Mint, eucalyptus, and something just a little bit earthy that I couldn't place. I wanted to drown in it.

One particularly dark and frigid morning, as I listened to the rain pelting the castle walls, I drifted in and out of sleep. While in dreams, Vaya'la took me to a cave in her realm made entirely of flowers. They were green and black and blue and the brightest violet. Each one was dotted with brilliant, sparkling gems that lit up the cavern like the night sky. Her jaws snapped appreciatively at my awe.

When the sun finally rose, it offered no heat. With limbs shaking from cold, I dressed and prayed to the Creator for a warm breakfast.

"Why do you pray to another dragon?"

"What?"

"You do know your 'Creator' is another dragon."

"Oh. It's just a habit."

"No, it's offensive."

I stopped short. *"Did you know him or something?"*

"I know all dragons, Small One."

Our connection dulled, and I recognized it as dismissal. Crossing the room, I examined my nest of curls. With a sigh, I began to wrangle it into submission. Today, above all days, I needed it under control.

No sooner had I finished a simple four-strand plait than Callagh's bright knock sounded at the door with four quick raps.

"Are you ready, my lady?" she asked as she let herself in.

"Yes," I lied.

Callagh's grin was as buoyant as a child's.

"Remind me why I let you talk me into this?"

"Because being cooped up in your rooms all the time is horrible. Because you have every right to join the rest of the castle in the Main Hall. Because no one will ever get to know or accept you if they never meet—"

"Yes, yes, okay."

Her grin morphed to a smirk.

I scowled. "You're sure it's allowed?"

She nodded.

"Then why have I always had a tray?"

"Idiocy," my *reálta* scoffed. "Let me assure you *again* that I'm positive you're welcome. I even asked my mother last night."

"You did?"

She hummed her confirmation.

With a deep breath, I said, "Okay." Callagh's mother was the formal trainer and selector of *reálti*. Riht protocol was her specialty. If she gave the stamp of approval, then it must be right. No one knew better than her, not even the Dane himself.

We walked side by side toward the Main Hall, moving through the maze of corridors far too quickly for my liking. I pulled my leather overcoat closer as if it could hide me from others' eyes as well as the cold.

"Ready?" Callagh asked again as we paused for a moment outside the ceiling-high double doors.

"No."

Callagh yanked one open before I could change my mind and flee. The Hall was warm and inviting and seemed larger, now occupied, than I remembered from my initial tour of the keep. Bright tapestries depicting foods and feasts draped the stone walls. Above them, long, skinny windows lined the room. On any other day, they would have been shining with light. Today, they revealed only gray clouds and steady rain. The ceiling towered overhead, higher than any other room in the keep.

A few heads glanced my way. That was it. I was given no more attention than a handful of frowns. Something deep in my chest unclenched.

Callagh led me toward two open seats at one of a dozen long tables. At the end of each, an attendant hovered, ready to clear dishes and serve newcomers. I couldn't see over the many heads, but I surmised the tables held at least forty seats apiece. Nearly five hundred in all...and our dining hall in Cavendaffe fit no more than twenty-two. The difference was rattling.

A bowl thunked down in front of me. "Drink?" the attendant asked in Rihtish. He was still a boy, perhaps mid-teens, with wisps of hair on his chin and an eager look in his eyes. Whether he recognized me or not, his demeanor gave no clues.

"Is there tea?" I asked, excited to use the language with someone new. He nodded and disappeared, returning in seconds with a steaming mug.

The bowl was a delight that I vowed to eat every morning for the rest of my life. I devoured spoonful after magical spoonful. What looked like simple porridge was chock full of fruits, nuts, creamy milk, and a drizzled syrup rich with warming spices.

"Enjoying yourself, darling?"

I could only moan my assent. I glanced up to find Ell across from me, eyes full of delight.

"Do go on." He gestured to my bowl. "The noises you're making are positively sinful. And enlightening."

I stuck my tongue out at him.

A tsk of disapproval sounded. I recognized the woman at Ell's side with sobering clarity. It was my challenger from the Sun Trial, the woman whose favorite pastimes included mocking me and breaking my bones. To say I didn't care for her was an understatement, and my face must have shown it.

Ell's eyes lit up with delight. "Serae, darling"—the woman bristled at the pet name—"have you met my dear friend Meralda?"

So, that was her name. I tried not to look at her, but her lifelight exploded with a shade of puce that confused me. Apprehension? Insecurity?

"Jealousy."

Schooling my features at that revelation, I shrugged and returned to my breakfast. I'd be damned if I let her ruin the best meal I'd eaten here.

"Oh, my mistake," he went on, delighting in every tense second. "I forgot about the Sun Trial. Such a pity I wasn't here to bear witness."

It was my turn to bristle. It was true, in addition to being humiliated—I suspected intentionally—by Meralda, my betrothed had not bothered to return to support me on a day the Riht considered sacred.

"You are my *chosen, Small One."*

That should have been enough. It *was* enough.

"You would have seen nothing but an embarrassment." Meralda's voice dripped with venom, as usual.

"For Cre—" A growl filled my head, and I cut off. "Just drop the act," I spat at her. "I get it. You hate me for coming to your city, for daring to walk my outsider ass down your roads and eat your food with my foreigner's tongue. You have a problem with it, go talk to Dane. Stop spitting your bile at me."

"Oh, ho!" Ell's face was sheer mischief and merriment. I hated this facet of his mask.

Meralda rose, towering over me as she placed both hands on the tabletop and hissed in Rihtish, "You will never deserve him. Filth." Then she left.

I just blinked.

Beside me, Callagh jumped to her feet and began shouting back. I understood only a handful of her words, but I suspected some were words I should learn rather soon. Meralda did not turn or respond, and Callagh left my side to follow Meralda out, scolding her all along the way.

When the tall doors blocked out their racket, all eyes in the room turned to me. I ducked my head and tried to finish my bowl, but all taste had gone from it.

"Why?" I asked Ell, fixing him with a hard glare.

He raised a brow at me and shrugged. "One should always know the competition."

CHAPTER 18

"What you use from our binding, you must replenish. The easiest way is through sleep. Dreams hold great power that can be consumed to replenish you. Find yourself a reálti, your guiding star, who can watch over you when your physical body needs rest."

"Who should I pick?" Patriol's face swam through my mind. I had been gone less than three weeks, but already I missed my brother fiercely.

"Whomever you trust. When you sleep, I will meet you in the Dream Realm."

—Recounting from the private diary of Jerris, Dragonbound

INRAEN PRISONER

EARLY AUTUMN, TUSKIMON 1036

As prisons went, this one wasn't too bad, not that I had much experience on the topic. The cell was relatively clean, there was a station for necessities and a window that let in light and fresh air. All it needed was an extra blanket, and a man could do just fine in a place like this.

Being captured was something of a low point in my life. The last thing I remembered was fire.

No—that wasn't right. It was a campfire, yes. A campfire in the distance.

I thought it would lead...somewhere. Somewhere important.

Before the campfire, the last thing I remembered was fighting. We were in a battle, and it was dire. We should've all died, but I survived. How? I must have escaped. Or been spared?

I remembered a blow to the head. It was scabbed over and healing now, tender to the touch and itchy. I tested it, shaking my head until my eyeballs threatened to wobble out of my skull. That probably accounted for the gap in my memory. My shoulder, on the other hand, I remembered well. The blade plunging in alongside that feeling, that deep knowing, that it was somehow a mercy.

They had yet to ask my name. Or familial connections, or homestead, or militia station, or much of anything of consequence. All they'd done so far was clean and bandage my wounds. I wasn't even quite sure where they'd taken me, other than the general impression that it was in Rihtlond based on the accents and dress of the medics and guards.

But this cell was fairly nice, as prisons went, and there wasn't much at home to miss.

A door creaked open, and soft footfalls echoed down the hall and stopped at my cell.

"Well, well, well, aren't you a pretty thing?"

I scoffed. No one had ever called me *pretty* before. I met the man's gaze—one of my captors—and rolled my eyes as dramatically as my head would allow.

"Come now, surely you have a wonderfully important name and station."

I shrugged.

"How shall I know what to call you, then?"

One thing I knew—keeping everything I could to myself would help keep me alive. If they thought I was important, I was only as good as the ransom. If they thought I wasn't, I was only as good as the information I held. Right now, with this fog settled over my brain, I had neither of those things going for me.

"Not a talker? What a pity. With a face like yours, I could spend all day talking to you."

"Rather forward with a man you don't know."

"Is it me being male or me being foreign that bothers you?"

I looked up at that. The stranger had a handsome face, hair that would probably be blond if it weren't cast in shadow, and a smile on his lips that was a little too suggestive.

"What's my incentive to talk? Isn't the first rule of imprisonment, keep your silence?"

"My, my, I don't want you to think of it like that. We're all rather civilized over here."

"And where exactly in Rihtlond is *here?*"

"You answer mine, and I'll answer yours." His smile spread as I pressed my lips together. "We'll start small. Give me a reason to trust you, and I'm sure I can do something about your current...*accommodations.*"

I got to my feet, despite the slight tremor in my head, and looked the stranger in the eye. He was a few inches taller, forcing me to angle my head upward at him. I couldn't tell if it was that motion or his piercing blue eyes that made me unsteady.

"I think you'll find that trust goes both ways."

He smirked, and the lock to the cell door clicked open. He pushed his way inside revealing a full package every bit as delectable as his face.

"Lucky for you, I've got all the time in the world to get us there."

SERAE

EARLY AUTUMN, TUSKIMON 1036

By training, my mood had turned from foul to worse. I'd been on the receiving end of undeserved ire before. Fire and ash, I had Merria as a sister, didn't I? But I didn't deserve having that venomous snake set on me first thing in the morning. Especially not from Ell. His playful banter and taunting comments were one thing, but this?

I was jittery and fuming as I took my usual place by Teke and Ivank.

"Let it go," Teke whispered when I stumbled for the third time during a simple earth *dowsa* warmup.

I shook out my arms and reset. I hoped we would spend the day outside practicing archery, the one thing where I needed the least guidance, but the weather made that prospect slim.

"Sparring," Wep announced. I could feel his eyes on me, judging me. "Pairs today are"—I cringed—"Teke with Raif, Ivank with Lex, Helene with Lispen, Serae with me."

Fuck.

Of course, he would pick me today. He usually paired with Lispen or Raif—the best in the class. Helene or Ivank might get selected if he was demonstrating how to overcome size. It was only my turn when Wep decided I needed punishment.

The room rearranged, and I moved to the front.

"What did I do now?" I snapped.

He stood there, arms crossed and towering over me. It should have been intimidating, but my body reacted to him in a completely different way.

"Guilty conscience?"

I took stance. "Should I have one?"

He lunged, locking me in one of the dozen holds we were practicing breaking—this one a simple grip of the wrists.

"I'm sorry," he said, low enough that only I could hear.

"For what?" *Blood and bones, he regrets the kiss.* The one I couldn't keep out of my mind. The one where, if I hadn't had a busted ankle, I'd have straddled his lap in a whole different way. I rolled my wrists, breaking his hold and jumping back to reset.

He grunted. "I heard about breakfast."

"Oh, that. Not your fault. She's had it out for me since I got here."

"Before, actually," Wep muttered.

"Before what?"

He lunged again, this time gripping me around the middle, my back crushed against his chest.

"Your brother," I asked instead, "he likes to make trouble, doesn't he?"

"Ell's a fucking prick."

I flung my head back, all but useless against him, though it did force him to loosen his grip. I stomped down on his toe. He sidestepped, but that second he was between feet gave me just enough leeway to drop and roll out of his grip. I threw a quick jab of my elbow to his gut, but he anticipated and tensed. I may as well have elbowed a wall instead of his abs, but I was still free.

"Good. Again."

"So, I'm not in trouble? We're still friends?" I asked, grinning like a cat.

The smile slid from his face, and he stilled. "Is that what you want?" he asked.

"I—" *What?* I clamped my jaw shut. My eyes flew to the others, but they were all focused on their own matches. My whole body began to tingle and ache. It was madness making me wonder if it would be wrong to fling myself into his arms right in the middle of training. A leaf tumbled out of my sleeve onto the mat, breaking my focus.

"Is that you?"

Vaya'la remained quiet. I focused on the connection to her mind, tunneling into that other world. *I lay in the blue-violet grass, basking in the glow of the red sun.* A deep sensation of peace washed over me.

Wep sighed. "Forget I asked."

"No, I—"

"It wasn't a fair question."

I swallowed whatever response I was trying to give.

"Your hold-breaking needs work. Let's continue."

"Fine," I said, a crooked grin spreading across my face. "So, you're saying today, you want us to fight?"

Wep arched one eyebrow, that wicked mouth of his mirroring my grin. "Yes."

We spent the next hour stepping through one escape after the next. Everything from wrist holds to being pinned down on the ground. Based on the smirks the rest of my *ranng* were shooting me, we must've been putting on a fucking show. When I couldn't understand how to use my hips to rotate out of a single-arm wrist hold, he gripped my hips from behind to guide me through the motion. He didn't need to follow up by pressing my backside into him, fusing our hips so I could feel the movement through his body, but I wasn't complaining.

We were the only pair to work on anything besides standing holds. The biggest problem? Having any bit of Wep's weight on me wasn't something I wanted to escape from. I practiced headbutting him from the less-than-advantageous angle and learned how to curl my legs beneath him to shove him off. I took it one step further and wrapped my legs around his torso, forcing him onto his back. Gripping my thighs, he shifted me lower, destroying my already frazzled composure—especially when I felt his arousal pressing into me through his leathers. While I was distracted by his touch, he shot up, flipping me beneath him to start again.

By the end, I was panting, sweaty, and nowhere near satisfied. The sky was still gray beyond the windows, but at least the rain had lifted along with my mood. I had every intention of staying back after training to do dragons-knew-what, when Bracht entered. He beelined for Wep, pulled him aside, and whispered something that had both men agitated.

Wep raised a hand and addressed the group. "Dane has assigned your *ranng* a mission. We leave before nightfall. Make sure you eat a hearty meal, pack a change of clothes, and bring the weapons you've been assigned. Meet at the east gate by sundown. Bracht can help with any specifics. If you have the chance, I suggest you rest this afternoon. You're in for a sleepless night."

Ignoring our questions, he marched straight for me, grabbed my wrist, and pulled me through the back door leading to the training field. His face, which moments before had been controlled and calm, was now livid. We emerged into the gray autumn chill, the last few raindrops tickling my cheeks. Out of habit, I turned right toward the training pitches, but his grip on my arm whirled me around.

"Where are we going?" I asked, seeing nothing but the boundary wall on our left.

"Out of earshot," he growled, tugging me toward it.

I had parted with my sanity, allowing myself to be carted off like this. We reached the edge of the training room's outer wall, and I pulled up short. Wep kept walking, and the momentum yanked my arm forward, breaking from his grasp. He rounded on me, but I ignored him, stepping past into a hidden alcove straight out of a fairytale. At the center stood the most stupendous eucalyptus tree I'd ever seen. Red and green strips of bark streaked between the brown, like someone had dripped paint all over it. Its canopy of leaves drooped in a wide arc. Wild mint and rosemary grew in beds around the walls, filling the air with an earthy, sweet aroma that calmed my senses. Underfoot, a plush leafy groundcover crept over the open space.

Three exterior walls of the keep, none of which held windows, met to create the alcove. Tucked away as it was, I'd never have known it was here without being led to it. I'd have to be standing against the outer wall to even see it.

"This place is amazing." I breathed in, intoxicated by the aromas.

Wep had not moved. He just stared at me with that intensity of his. My second sight opened, and his lifelight pulsed between pure white and bright gold. A wave of *passion* hit me, and a second later, Wep reached for my hand and pulled. It was a single, quick tug, but it sent me careening into him. He caught and spun me in one fluid motion, my back hitting the smooth bark of that stunning painted trunk. He captured my mouth, and in the span of a single heartbeat, every bit of his body pressed against mine. *Yes.* The hard planes of his chest, his strong arms enveloping me, and that kiss—Martyrs' bones. He kissed me like a man starved, and I was just as desperate for him. This was everything my body craved.

When he gripped my ass and lifted me, I wrapped my legs around his middle. His length pressed into me as he fused our bodies closer together, never breaking our kiss. That kiss was everything. It was hot and fierce and hard, and I needed it more than air in my lungs. Everything this man did with his lips and tongue—and fuck, even his teeth—was exactly right to drive me wild.

Too soon, he broke the kiss. "You can't fucking do that to me."

I didn't care what I'd done. I saw the same untamed need in his eyes and pulled him back, moaning into the next kiss and arching into him. His grip on my thighs was a vise as my fingers raked down his back.

"Fuck, I can't even. Control myself. Around you." He punctuated each word with kisses down my neck.

"Shut up and kiss me." I yanked his shirt, forcing our lips back together. I needed him to touch me like this and more for hours, days, weeks, even, but he gave me only minutes and never moved his hands from the backs of my thighs.

The next time his lips left mine, I wanted to scream. He hoisted his weight off me, set me back on my feet, and took several steps away. The front of his tunic was wrinkled where I'd gripped it. He dragged his hands through his hair and dropped them atop his bun.

"We're not here for this."

The fuck we weren't. "Then why?"

"Training."

I stepped away from the tree. Miniature white flowers scattered all around us. It should have been a fairytale, yet once again, Wep was pulling away from me. "You can't be serious."

"I am. Get the longest bow you can handle. Spend an hour, no more, honing your aim. Then rest. You need to be fresh and ready."

"What's this about?" I tried stepping toward him, but he moved back, keeping our distance.

"Dane. I think he means to test you."

Leaves tumbled to the ground behind me, but I ignored them. "Why? I thought you said I wouldn't have to fight."

Regret flashed through his lifelight. Three steady strides brought him back to me, leaving inches between us. His face lowered to mine, and for one wild second, I thought he would kiss me again, but he stopped short. His eyes swirled with emotion—raw and hungry—and his fingers caressed down the side of my cheek. "I just need you ready."

ELDRETH

EARLY AUTUMN, TUSKIMON 1036

"ELDRETH, COME." DANE's voice was grave.

I had just run into my brother, who delivered Dane's summons between curses over some mission our father had given him and refused to rescind. Good thing I was already looking for him.

I found him seated on a bench in the gardens beneath the same tree my mother used to sit at while she bundled her herbs for drying. I could almost see her sitting there, shallow baskets in an arc at her feet, long hair flowing loose down her back. I blinked, and the vision dissolved. I moved to stand at his side.

"Sit, lad. This isn't an easy talk."

I remained standing.

The dane took in a great breath, but when he let it out, only my father remained. I could always tell the difference. His eyes misted, and he rubbed a calloused hand down his face.

"The girl," he said at last, then paused.

At that, I sank to my knee in the soft grass.

"I think the Great Dragon has chosen her."

"As are we all. She's dedicated to the Riht, as you hoped."

"No. I think she'll be one of the Bound."

A lump rose in my throat. A pillar of fire burned through my mind. I stamped the memory down. "Why?"

"Something happened while you were away. You must give her your attention."

"Father..."

"Imagine it." He looked toward the heavens. He had always been a man devoted to the Riht but never overcome by reverence. "You could have a dana who is bound to the Goddess herself."

"You can't possibly know that."

"You weren't there. It's made me question everything. But you're right, she needs to be tested. Son, you above all understand this. We need to make sure."

My shoulders drooped. There would be no fighting him, but I hoped he was wrong. I needed him to be wrong. I had already lost enough to those flames. "What do you want me to do?"

"Go to her. Spend every minute you can with her. You know the legends. Only through an act of faith will all be revealed."

"You're speaking in riddles now."

"No, you're just not listening. Go. Strengthen the bond between you. Leave the rest to me for now."

"There is no bond. I barely know her yet." I kept my constant pull toward her unsaid.

Dane rose to his feet, and I followed. He laid a heavy hand on my shoulder. "Yet, lad. Yet."

He walked away, leaving me staring after him, shaded by the rustling leaves, haunted by memories of fire and death. My whole body tensed at his words. There was only one thing I knew for certain. I had to prove him wrong.

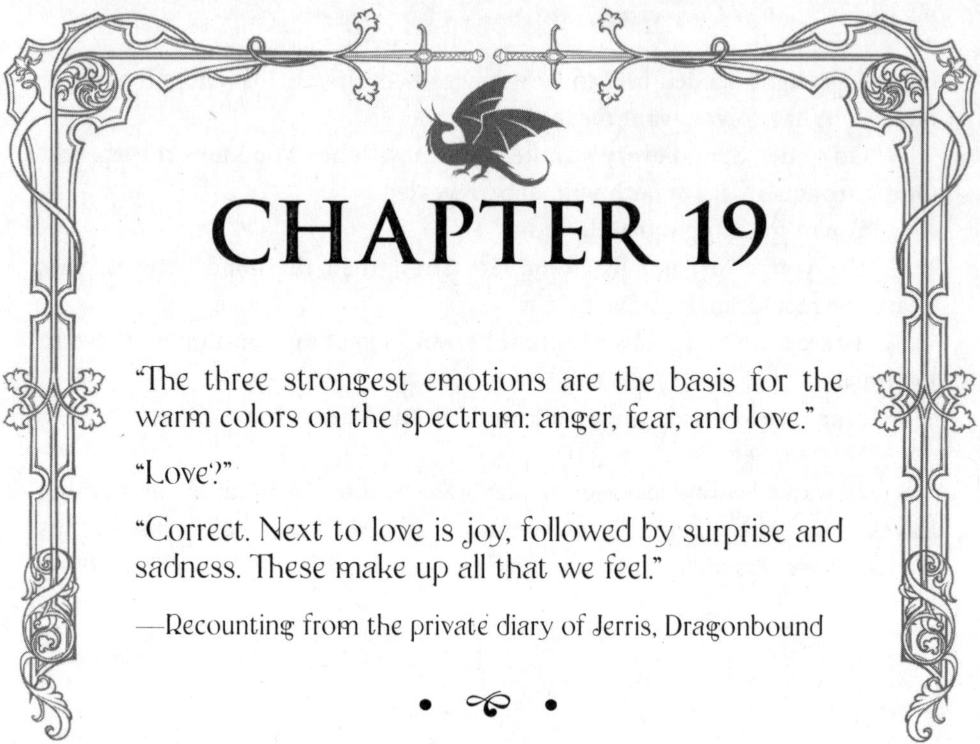

CHAPTER 19

"The three strongest emotions are the basis for the warm colors on the spectrum: anger, fear, and love."

"Love?"

"Correct. Next to love is joy, followed by surprise and sadness. These make up all that we feel."

—Recounting from the private diary of Jerris, Dragonbound

SERAE

EARLY AUTUMN, TUSKIMON 1036

THAT AFTERNOON, I tracked circles into my rug until my path left permanent marks. Callagh had left me hours ago after helping me prepare a traveling bag. I should have been resting. Instead, I paced.

Crunch.

I lifted my foot. *Leaves?* I'd long since relocated my fabric dyes and supplies to the lesson room. No bundles were drying on the makeshift line across the window. This was a mystery I didn't have time to solve. I brushed the fragments aside and continued my circuitous path.

Crunch, crunch, crunch.

An entire trail of leaves littered the path I'd paced down to the stone.

"Vaya'la! What is this?"

Only grumbling sounded in my head. I pushed into her mind. *A teal pool lapped around my body as I dozed in the red afternoon sun. The water rippled. I huffed, and a cloud of mist flew into the air, settling in glittering specs over the vegetation surrounding the pool.*

"Wake up, you useless dragon!" I shouted at her.

She snorted. *"Magic bleeding."*

"Is it bad?"

No answer. I pressed into her mind again, but all I could hear was snoring.

"Great. Now I have to worry about this, too," I said to the empty room.

The time to meet at the gates couldn't come soon enough. Except when it did, I was woefully unready. I donned a set of Riht seafaring leathers, soft, flexible, and something I had never expected to put to real use. The ensemble boasted leather pants, a long tunic, and a padded leather vest—all black. There was no skirt, and it was the first time in my life I was walking about bare-legged and feeling free. At the stables, Kappa waited for me. I snuck her two peppermint treats from the kitchen, and she allowed me to press my face into her long mane while she munched. Then, I lashed my pack behind her saddle, fastened a quiver of arrows at my back, and sheathed two new daggers at my thighs.

I mounted swiftly from the ground without a block. No skirts encumbered me, sitting astride. No hairpins scraped my scalp. No glasses to fidget with. I glanced down at my leather-wrapped forearms, remembering a very different day racing along the forest's edge with Tam and Merria. What a turn my life had taken—and yet I felt stronger and more in control of myself than ever. I nudged Kappa into a trot.

The eastern gate, like the other two, had been carved in the likeness of a dragon, but this time, the stone had been carved into a mighty dragon claw. Talons dug into the earth, made of sleek stone pillars that joined together at the top in a wide arc, forming the palm. The rest of the stone was carved with taut tendons, thick musculature, and scales covering the flexed claw. In order to exit the gate, we had to walk between the dragon's fingers. The effect was so realistic, I half expected the claw to clamp closed, crushing us all.

Just outside the gates, our party congregated. I scanned the blond heads surrounding us. No Eldreth, but my eyes snagged over one particular copper head. Wep wore his hair tightly braided instead of his usual knot. I made my way to him, watching the moment his eyes flicked to my own rusty braided locks. I was used to standing out in a crowd because of my hair, but I would never get used to the magnetism it created between us—the only two with red in an entire city.

"Your brother isn't joining?" I asked by way of greeting.

"Did you want him to?"

"No," I said before considering it, then saw my lifelight flicker with ultramarine. *Guilt.*

Wep smirked. "He was looking for you. Dane gave him another task."

"Where are we headed?"

"You'll see." He led his horse to the front and called out to the gathered Riht. He spoke in Rihtish, and I understood most of it. It was a call to assemble two across and begin the procession down to somewhere, the last being a word I didn't know.

Teke pulled up at my side. "Are you ready?"

I shook my head.

They grinned. "Me neither."

"Do you know where we're headed?"

"A hidden port east of the city."

"There's another one?" My brow furrowed. Dane had never mentioned a second port to Drakh in our lessons.

Teke leaned toward me and lowered their voice. "Only used in times of need. Whatever we're doing tonight, it must be too urgent to set sail from Port Drakha."

I swallowed the lump that rose in my throat and focused my sight forward. My anxiety over this mission was quickly festering into full-blown fear.

The path down to the hidden port began by crossing a small clearing until the forest overtook us, the trail growing rocky and steep. The horses had no issue navigating the trail, despite the trees blocking our view ahead. The sun had not yet dipped behind the mountains when we descended into a tiny village nestled in a nook between the cliff face and an inlet on the far side. A lone longship was docked at the pier. Unlike the cargo ship I had ridden to Drakh, this one sat low to the waterline, with no deep hull or cabins underneath. It was a ship meant for speed, carrying only warriors and their supplies—an instrument of death. Its sails had already been dropped and loosely tied. Within minutes, the craft would be ready to set sail.

Teke and I dismounted, and they showed me where we would stable our horses until our return.

"Have you been here before?" I asked.

"Not as a warrior."

"How long will we be gone?"

They shook their head with a shrug.

We caught up to the rest of our *ranng,* along with seven or eight other groups assembled along the pier. The air buzzed with speculation.

"They found a Volaachi ship," one man surmised to his companion, a woman with four braids long enough to tuck into her belt. "We'll be capturing it and bringing it home—mark my words."

I didn't understand her reply, other than the word *assumptions.*

Lex nudged my shoulder. Like most of us, he was head to toe in black leathers. The braids in his hair were tighter than usual and gathered into a single tail at the base of his neck. His face was alight with excitement as he scanned the gathered crowd.

"What do you think of them?" he asked, indicating the pair standing together. They were tall and slender with the same blond hair and tawny skin. When the woman turned, glancing up the pier, I saw her eyes were a rich, chocolatey brown.

"Are you asking for you or me?"

"Me, of course." He flashed a toothy grin.

"Way out of your league. Do you think they're siblings?"

"Dragons, I hope so."

"Not likely to take you to bed together, then, are they?"

He frowned. "Good point. It'll have to be two different nights then."

I snorted, and as the conversation continued, the weight on me lightened.

Lex pulled Raif into our game of conjecture on the purpose of our mission, and Teke joined too. After a few minutes, Helene was listening in but held her silence. Lispen was dutifully ignoring us, as was Ivank—until Lex proclaimed that our goal was to find a mountain troll large enough for him to bed. He made a swipe at Lex's shoulder, but Lex spun away with a laugh.

Instead, he fixed Lex with a glare and said, "Just because I refuse to bed *you* doesn't mean there's no one else. Ask Serae, she's met several women who have enjoyed my company."

"I have?" My mind exploded with possibilities. "Ohh! I *have.*" I had thought Ivank was well known in the town, but in hindsight, it was almost exclusively women who called out to him.

"Leave Serae out of this, or I'll tell Wep you've—" *Crunch.* Lex looked down, then up into the sky, then at my pack. "Did you bring leaves with you?"

Shit. My palms began to sweat. "Uh, why would I do that?"

He shook his head.

"Warriors of the Riht, attend!" Wep's voice sang over the crowd. He stood atop a stack of barrels at the end of the pier. He wore a mix of leathers and mail, strapped with weapons from his back to his boots. He looked out over the assembly waiting to board, meeting the eyes of every warrior and demanding our full attention. "We set sail by nightfall. Our task lies along our eastern coast. Word has reached us of a Volaachi ship that has landed along our coastline. They've made camp for as many as three days. Our latest messenger reported they are cutting down trees and beginning to erect shelters. Our task is to rid this blight from our land."

Cheers of agreement rose around us.

"There were no more than one or two dozen seen. We have the advantage of numbers and familiarity with our lands and seas. The Volaachi must be taken down swiftly and completely."

He paused, and the murmurs of assent this time were grave.

"How many of you have seen dragori before?"

Up until that point, I'd been following along well with the Rihtish, but this was a word I didn't know. I looked to my *ranng*, who all wore matching grim expressions. Raif alone raised his hand.

Wep continued, "They are monsters, make no mistake. For those of you seeing them for the first time, know that they are creatures of twisted magic. If they have a soul, it has long been consumed by their bloodlust. Show them no quarter, for they will show none to you. If given the chance, they will never spare a life. They deal only in death, so death is what we must give them."

Cheers broke out again.

"If any among you feel you are not able to take on this burden, stay back now. There is no shame in knowing your limits. Those who are ready to take up the mantle of protecting the Riht... BOARD!"

The crowd of warriors surged forward to tumultuous cheers. After about half had clambered aboard, Wep dropped off the barrel and disappeared into the throng.

"It's our turn!" Raif shouted, leading us forward.

I followed, keeping my eyes glued to Teke in front of me, thankful that Ivank took up position at my back. A stern woman with the sides of her head shaved ushered us into a row about two-thirds back.

Raif sat first and pulled aside a loose floorboard, revealing a narrow cavity beneath. I glanced up and down the benches, seeing others do the same. "Here, our packs," he called, stuffing his down and motioning for ours. One by one, we passed over our bags, and Raif tucked them beneath.

Stationed in the middle, rather than along the sides where the oar-ports were cut, our job was to sit still and wait. Behind me, Wep called out orders, answered questions, and checked in with *ranng* leaders. I focused hard on not turning around. Had it only been a handful of hours since he pressed me against that tree? To think, all these people were looking to him in deference, their leader, third in command after Dane and Eldreth. Women probably fell at his feet, yet it was me he pulled into that alcove. It was me he looked at with that wild intensity. It was me he kissed despite my betrothal to—

"What's this?" Teke plucked something out of my braids and handed it to me. It was a small, white flower. They laughed. "Is this one from your latest batch of dyes?"

I looked down at the white flower. There was no reason to use white in the dye-making process. They had no pigment to extract. "Probably." I forced out a laugh and tossed the flower aside. *White flowers underfoot beneath that beautiful tree, Wep's hard body against mine—*

"By all means, keep thinking of your weaponmaster. I'd love to see how this turns out. How many more flowers do you think you can grow?"

"How do I make it stop?"

"Use your magic, Small One. It's building up inside you."

"I don't know how!"

"You do. When the time is right, reach within."

The longship lurched forward. I forgot how horrible it was on the stomach to be at sea. Glancing back, Wep was at the steering board, completely in control. His eyes were forward, his slight frown was in place, and his attention was focused ahead.

"The moon is high," Ivank said up to the sky. "We'll travel fast this night."

He was right. The ship cut through the waves. I could barely think through the sting of the sea winds on my face. I now understood all the tight braids. *Thank the Great Dragon for Callagh's guidance.* The moon rose higher into the night sky, and a chill permeated deeper into my bones. We tracked the coastline on our port side. There was nothing but open sea starboard. After my joints began to creak, and my ass had gone numb from sitting, I heard Wep's voice behind us. He was pausing at each group and speaking in hushed tones. I couldn't make out his words, but they were stern and clipped.

Anticipation mounted, and I bounced my feet, hoping to get some feeling back into them. His scent wrapped around me before I saw him. That beautiful mix of mint, eucalyptus, and...

"Rosemary," I gasped. My second sight opened, and Wep's outline exploded with white light that flashed with green as fresh as a young fern. *He's pleased—to see me?*

There was barely enough room to walk between rows, but Wep did so with ease and dropped to a crouch before me. With my second sight open, I could make out every feature on his face. The side of his mouth quirked up. His eyes even held a faint glow to them. The warmth of his body near mine drew me in, and I had to grip the board of the bench to stop myself from crawling on top of him. When he spoke, he looked only at me.

"When we make land, the shields will exit first, then archers will follow. If we're lucky, we'll pick them off by arrow. If not, all warriors will be ready to move in on foot." His eyes flickered to Teke, then Ivank, then locked back on me. "Your *ranng* is untested, not unskilled. The dragori are unlike anything you've fought against, but a weapon is a weapon. A strike is a strike. You can cut them down just as you can any other. Take no risks. Stay together. Protect each other." He looked down the line at each of us, waiting for our nod before moving on to the next. When he looked back to me, something flashed behind his eyes as his lifelight flickered with warm yellow. *Desire.*

Wep leaned in, and I found myself doing the same, though I knew I should be pulling away. Giving into this thing between us was a madness for behind closed doors, not in front of a longship full of warriors. "Serae," he whispered. On either side of me, Ivank and Teke turned away, but I could feel their ears straining toward us. Both of them were pulsing with aquamarine. *Curiosity.* "I know this isn't the best time, but have you manifested a blessing?"

My heart sank. "I don't know," I lied.

"A *bierla* from the Great Dragon? Anything that might help you?"

I shook my head. "I'm not sure."

Teke glanced at me sideways but kept their silence.

He nodded and rose, and a single flash of dull blue shone out. *Disappointment.* "We make land in a few minutes, just on the other side of this cliff." I followed the motion of his hand. We were trailing the shoreline, but I hadn't noticed the looming cliff up ahead. It jutted out from the rest of the land, creating a makeshift wall blocking anything beyond from view.

Gripping Teke's shoulder, I rose to my feet. It was hard to make out in the darkness and distance, but there was something at the top of the cliff. It was dark—glowing with a light I could only describe as black—and pulsing with deep red. *Rage.* No, it was more than rage—it was *hatred.* The ship rocked, and I teetered, but Wep's strong hand gripped my arm, holding me up. I couldn't tear my eyes from that thing on the cliff and its absolute wrongness.

"*The cursed,*" Vaya'la hissed in my mind. Her fury seeped through our binding, surrounding me.

"Dragori?" I asked, though I hadn't meant to say it out loud. Wep whipped around, following my line of sight. His grip tightened around my arm.

"Yes."

Wep took off, running across the benches toward the stempost. Others were jumping to their feet in his wake. He climbed as high as he could, leaning out over the prow. We'd be underneath the cliff in minutes. I had no idea what he saw, but more and more of the clifftop was swarming with that awful red-black light.

"Up there!" A woman three rows in front of us cried. It was the same woman and her brother that Lex had been leering at on the dock. "They can't fly, right?" She turned to her brother. "Right?"

All heads lifted as the first creature leapt from the cliff.

"Vaya'la!" I screamed in my head. *"It has wings!"*

"They are abominations. Kill them all!"

It couldn't fly. Its horrific, twisted form flapped and extended wings that sprouted from its back, but they were too short to bear its weight. They could, however, allow it to glide slowly toward the water. It splashed down more than fifty yards ahead of us, but more were jumping now. I counted five, six, *seven* dragori jumping one at a time over the cliff. The first two would hit the water with their companion, but the rest would land right on top of us.

"Do we shoot?" someone shouted.

"No," Wep commanded in a tone that demanded obedience. "Raise your weapons. All blades pointed upward. Brace yourselves, and leave none alive!"

He whirled and drew the longsword from his back in one fluid motion. The first beast dropped from the sky with an inhuman snarl. Wep continued his spin, rotating around and slashing the thing in half. It clawed at him even as it fell apart at his feet. Its black lifelight faded, and death took it.

Another landed amid a group of warriors who cried out and stabbed the creature from every side at once. It died before it landed on its feet. Wep spotted his next target and tracked its fall. The third slashed at the forestay, partially severing the rope, before losing its legs, then its head, to the edge of Wep's blade. The next landed atop the yard, gripping the mast for balance. Three more landed after.

"Monserak!" Wep shouted.

A single arrow loosed. It pierced clean through one dragori, which plummeted down to the ship and into Wep's waiting blade.

"Climb," Wep yelled at a *ranng* at his side. Then, to another group, "Get them overboard!"

Warriors sprang into action, tossing bodies and severed limbs into the sea. I lost track of Wep but found him again as a cry sounded up ahead and to the left. A dragori had landed on top of someone. She had slashes down her face and neck, both of her blades embedded into the creature's rear. The tip of Wep's longsword jutted out between its wings. He yanked his blade free and helped toss the thing overboard one-handed.

My heart called out to him, thrumming with fear and pride and shock and I don't know what else, watching him defend these people and take every killing blow he could to spare them. Something deep within me reached out, wanting to help. As if I had called out loud, he turned and locked onto me. His lips moved in the shape of my name, but all I could hear was the flapping of wings.

"Move!" Ivank shouted at my side, reaching for me.

I looked up into the snarling maw of a dragori. Up close, I knew it for the abomination it was. Time stilled as I gazed into its black lifelight. Its head, wings, and claws were mockeries of a dragon's. It was covered in reptilian scales and hide that lacked the strength or protection of dragonhide. There was no magic in this thing, aside from whatever twisted magic created it. A small tail protruded from its back, but it was useless and cropped. Saliva dripped from its fangs, which were long and lethal. It was larger than a man, even a Riht, but not by much. I guessed about seven and a half feet.

Time snapped back. Ivank reached for me—just as something shot out from my back. He cried out, recoiling. I screamed and dove to the ground as three dragori landed on top of me. Thick, dark vines snaked around me, each one covered in outward-facing spikes. The dragori atop me clawed at the bramble growing thicker and thicker around me. One let out a hissing shriek, and black blood oozed through the cracks in my rapidly growing cocoon.

Gasps from the Riht sounded all around.

"Kill them!" Lispen shouted, accompanied by the metallic hiss of blades being drawn.

A ball of brilliant red-orange streaked across the cracks in my makeshift armor. *Terror.* In an instant, the weight of the dragori flew off me. My vines fell away, sloughing off like shed skin and crumbling to ash. Neither their creation nor destruction had been conscious, but I had no time to consider. I hopped up, finding my footing despite the rocking ship. Wep had killed one at my feet and dropped his sword to pry another off with both hands, leaving him momentarily defenseless. He reached for his sides and drew his short swords, but not fast enough to block the dragori's claws. In slow motion, it slashed out, straight for his chest. Its three-inch talons would gut him. Even his mail would do little to stop it.

"No!" I screamed, reaching for him. Something raw and ancient welled within me. Tingling heat raced down my arms as stakes, long and sharp, shot from each of my hands, embedding into the creature's back.

At the same instant, Wep spun, rolling with the dragori's strike and using his momentum to whip his blades around. One bit into its skull, the other into its spine beneath its wings—just a second after my spikes hit. With a horrifying shriek, its black lifelight winked out.

I sucked in a breath, fear crawling through me at what I'd done, but I didn't have time for it. Power still thrummed at my fingertips. With clenched fists, I focused on Vaya'la's peace, willing it to subside.

Wep yanked his blades free, black blood spraying in a wide arc, then turned to de-wing and stab the third dragori, who Lispen had engaged, straight through the back. It dropped, but not before its claws latched onto Lispen's forearm, leaving three deep gashes.

To my left, two more dragori had been slain near the stern, Raif and Helene among the group responsible. I looked up. We were out of range of the cliff. No more dragori until we made land.

Wep's intensity slammed into me, and I turned to face him. He was breathing hard and staring at me in a way that was all too intimate. His lifelight flickered juniper—*pride*—I might have craved it any other time, but not then. Not when my whole sense of self was changing. Not when I, Bound to the Dragon of Life, had turned into a bringer of death. Yet, I was trapped in his sights with no way to escape. All I could do was watch as he drove the tips of his short swords into the benches on either side of him, leaving the blades standing on end and covered in black blood. It took him three strides to reach me. He wrapped his arms around me, crushing me to him, heedless of the people around us and the armor between us.

"Living armor," he whispered in my ear. "Incredible."

Over his shoulder, I watched Teke rip one of my spikes out of the dragori's back before it tumbled over the side. They looked at me, eyebrows raised and pulsing with bright teal—*awe*—then chucked the spike over the railing. Raif pulled Lispen to the side, gripping her arm to examine the claw marks despite her protests. Ivank and Lex lifted the last dead creature and threw it overboard. I heard its thick splash before it was swallowed by the sea.

"Regret not killing the abominations. They should never have lived."

"You're the bringer of life. How can you say that?"

"I speak only truths. The abominations are creatures of Death, and to Death they must return."

"Marr Wep, we need you!" the man Wep had called Monserak shouted across the ship.

Wep released me, squeezing my arm for a second longer, though he had already turned to answer the call.

My knees buckled, and I sank to the deck. Rough hands directed me to the nearest bench.

"Was that your first time using your blessing?" Ivank asked.

I shrugged, looking at Teke, who shook their head. Shooing Ivank, they knelt in front of me and gripped my shoulders. "What I can't work out," they said in a hushed tone, "is how you called upon roots in the market but made vines and spikes today. It's unlike any *bierla* I've ever seen." Their eyes were a warning.

"Do I need to hide our binding from them?" I asked Vaya'la. I had been hiding it on instinct, not instruction.

"All will be revealed soon enough."

"I couldn't say," I told them.

They pulled me into a fierce hug and whispered in my ear, "You need to work it out. Wep is perceptive. He should hear it from you first."

"How long have you known?" I whispered back.

Teke held me at arm's length again. "You told me, remember?"

I nodded, though I hadn't told them. *She* did.

We made land minutes later. Scanning the coastline, I saw nothing of that corrupted black light. Wep sent three *ranngs* out in scouting parties while commanding the rest to follow him. My *ranng*, being the least experienced, remained with the ship.

We waited in the darkness. I readied my bow.

"Do you think there'll be more?" Lispen asked Raif.

"Wep said two dozen max. We've already killed half that," he replied.

Teke stepped up at my side, shield in hand. "Keep your eyes on the tree line. We want to see them before they're upon us."

"We need to assign sections." Raif walked in an arc, making six divots with his boot. "We each take a slice extending out to the trees. Call out anything you spot. Serae," he turned to me, "you're our best archer. Get in the longship so you have the advantage of height."

"Do me a favor, love," Lex begged. "Don't hesitate. If they get too close... well, you're a good shot, but you're not *that* good." He grinned and ducked as

Lispen's hand flew harmlessly over the back of his head. He popped up with a great, "Aha!" and leapt away to his divot.

From my post on the longship, it was easy to watch the trees. The stempost had dips in the carving to accommodate bows, and I positioned myself behind one. I kept my second sight open. The soft white glow of my companions comforted me as I lay in wait, ever watchful for that horrible black light. Occasionally, flickers of periwinkle—*boredom*—would flash through one of them, though we all remained at the ready. It was an exercise in patience, to be sure.

The night was still thick around us when I caught black and crimson glowing between the trees. "Helene's quadrant," I called out below and watched every one of them stiffen and turn. I waited for it to break the tree line and present a better target for me.

"Do not hesitate. All dragori must die."

I loosed an arrow, eyes trained on the creature. It kept running. When I loosed my second, its corrupted lifeforce winked out.

"Ivank's," I called as two dragori barreled toward us. Three of my arrows took one down, but the second ran at Ivank with alarming speed. Raif rushed in to intercept. He slashed at its side, but the creature's claws clamped around his blade. With arms distracted, it couldn't block Ivank's mace crashing down on its skull.

By sunrise, my kill count had climbed to seven. Fifteen corpses littered the beach, and rank black blood clung to my *rang*. My vantage alone spared me.

The other *rangs* began to filter from the trees with Wep at their rear, black blood smeared all over his armor.

"Were there more?" Raif asked after giving him our report.

"Dead," was all he offered.

He walked straight into the sea, soaking every inch of him and even submerging his head. He left behind a dark pool that floated like oil on the surface. Dripping wet, he directed the rest of the *rangs* back to their places, rotating out those stationed at the oar-ports. Ivank and Teke were both assigned to rowing, so I found myself sandwiched between Helene and Lex on the trip back.

"He looks good wet," Lex whispered in my ear.

I elbowed him, but Martyrs, was he right. Wep stripped out of his soaked leathers and mail. His tunic and pants clung to his body in a way I shouldn't be appreciating.

The strong winds shortened our return to the small inland port. Most *ranngs* were ordered to mount and ride directly for Drakh, mine among them. Drained, we departed in relative silence, heading home to rest and prepare for afternoon training. Nothing, not even this mission, could stop Wep from training.

When I was back atop Kappa, Teke pulled their horse up to my side. "Do you want to talk about it?"

"Nothing to talk about. Everything's fine."

"Liar."

I whipped around, finger extended, ready to give them a piece of my mind, but I pulled up short. Their shoulders shook with suppressed laughter.

"What's so—"

They pointed. Behind me, a torrent of reddish-green leaves blew in the wind. The *ranng* behind us had gone hoarfrost white, all gaping at me. Behind them, more were leaning in their saddles, craning their necks.

"It is past time we begin, Small One."

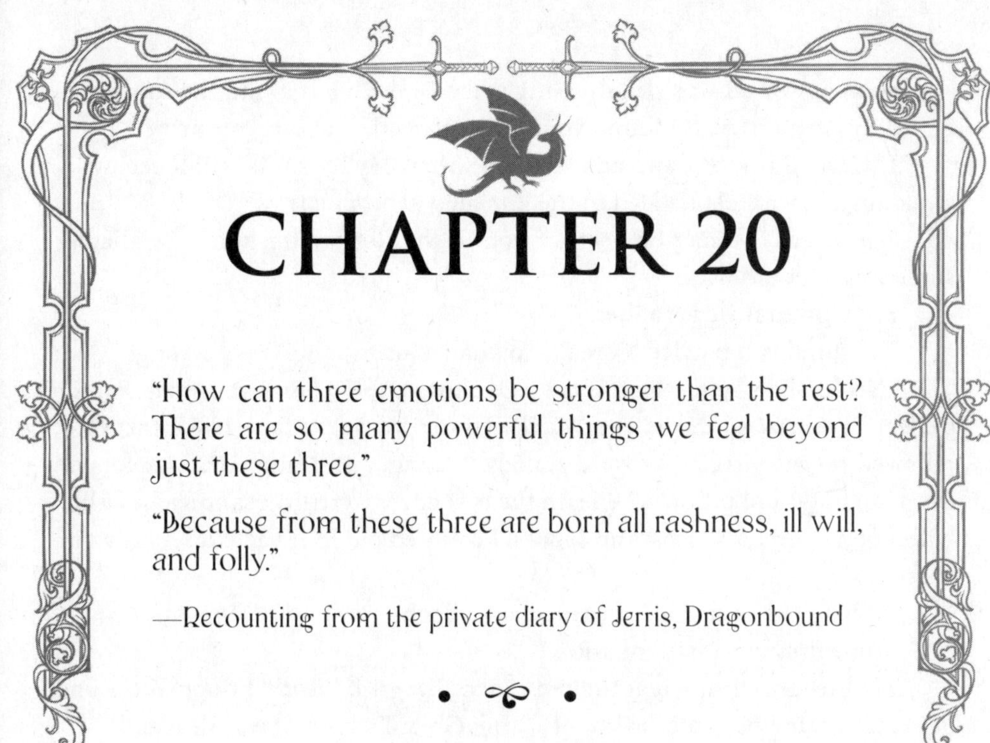

CHAPTER 20

"How can three emotions be stronger than the rest? There are so many powerful things we feel beyond just these three."

"Because from these three are born all rashness, ill will, and folly."

—Recounting from the private diary of Jerris, Dragonbound

SERAE

EARLY AUTUMN, TUSKIMON 1036

Back in Drakh, I bid Kappa farewell at the stables with promises to bring her more peppermint treats tomorrow, then headed straight to my room for a hot soak. I unbraided my hair and washed it, luxuriating in the heat of the bathwater. When I got out, little white flowers floated on the surface. Their soft scent wafted toward me. *Jasmine.*

"You will learn to make them at your command."

"When?"

"When you're ready to begin."

"I'm ready."

"Sleep first."

I did need sleep, but with the sun streaming in through my windows, I only managed a few hours before I was up again. I would have training that afternoon anyway. I was still dressing when Callagh burst into the room.

"My lady, I'm glad I found you," Callagh said, grabbing my arm.

I fastened my vest and adjusted my skirts. My hair was still loose, wild, and damp. "I was just headed to the kitchens to order a tray."

"No need, I've had one set for you in the Relaxation Room." Callagh's smile was a bit too wide.

I narrowed my eyes at her. "Why?"

"I figured you needed a break. You had a long night. Was I wrong?"

"No." I slid my arm into hers. "Of course not. Thank you, that sounds perfect." We crossed the hall and ducked into my favorite tapestried, carpeted, pillowed respite. Two trays were already waiting, and I immediately plopped down on a stack of pillows. Beneath the tray cover were thin sandwiches filled with veggies, creams, nuts, and sauces. I counted out four varieties, plus a pile of fruits.

"What's the occasion?" I smiled at Callagh.

"Your first successful mission."

My lifelight dimmed at the reminder. *Bringer of death.* I popped the end of the first sandwich into my mouth, and, Great Dragon, it was heaven.

"I appreciate the effort," Vaya'la offered at my oath.

"I'm glad you noticed. Maybe now you'll stop whining."

"I do not whine."

I laughed in her direction, and a great harrumphing sounded in my head. I had to stifle a real laugh.

I took another bite, and the walnut, apple, and sweet, creamy sauce took over my senses. I could eat this sandwich all day, every day. The door opened, and Wep walked in with that intense look in his eyes he could never get rid of. His hair, too, was washed, damp, and loose. His shirt was askew, with wet spots on his shoulders from his hair. My eyes darted to Callagh, who was smirking like a cat. Her tray was untouched.

"Hungry?" she asked him, all sweet and innocent. I saw right through that. "Bracht set you a tray in here."

"Me?" Of course, Wep was confused. He was probably tricked into coming here, same as me.

"Obviously. Who else gets trays besides the two of you recluses?"

"Ah." He looked like he needed rescuing, but I was very much staying out of it.

"I was just leaving anyway." Callagh rose to her feet and tossed me a not-so-subtle wink. "Have fun, you two."

I gawked at her. *So, Callagh and Bracht were in this together.* My world tilted as I reassessed the covert looks I'd seen Callagh throw at Wep, where Bracht was always a step behind.

"This room is for *relaxing*, not fun," I called after her.

She ignored me and left. She could escape from me now, but later, we'd be having words.

"I thought you wanted to be alone with this one. You seemed to enjoy him last time." Now Vaya'la was laughing. *"And the time before."*

"Whatever," I grumbled.

Wep was still standing in the doorway, arms crossed left over right, staring at me in a way I couldn't handle. "That's for me?" he asked.

I nodded, then thought better of it. "Don't ask me. Callagh dragged me in here. Your tray was already waiting." I wished he'd do something—sit down, leave—rather than just looming in the doorway. Either way, it didn't matter to me. Or so I told myself.

He must've heard my prayers, because he crossed the room and sank into the pillow across from me, the low table between us. Under his tray cover was the exact same array that had been prepared for me. I had no idea what had gotten into Bracht to plan something like this, but Callagh should know better. Wep may be inconveniently attractive, and we may have shared that one—two—okay, three glorious, invigorating moments, but that didn't turn him into my betrothed. Nothing could turn him into his brother.

Wep eyed his plate, then mine, putting pieces together.

"They're plotting if you ask me, but who knows what."

He hummed in non-acknowledgment, keeping his thoughts to himself.

Fine. I'd have to push.

I layered on my most gregarious tone and leaned toward him—just a bit. "Tell me, what does the great weaponmaster do when it's his turn to relax? I've never seen you use this room before."

He shrugged. "Not much opportunity."

"You brought me in here once before."

He swallowed a bite of his sandwich. "I did. Where's the usual crew?"

I shrugged. Off gallivanting somewhere, celebrating the previous night's victory, no doubt. I had hoped to spend my time before afternoon training alone. Vaya'la and I had an important date—expanding our connection and beginning to learn control. After last night, it was only a matter of time until he started asking questions that I wasn't ready to answer.

His mouth opened, then closed. He took a deep breath.

I needed to redirect to anything else. "Should we talk about it?" *Fuck, fuck, fuck! Anything but that!*

He looked up at me. "Your *bierla?*" he asked at the same time I said, "That kiss."

His eyes darkened, gaze dropping to my lips and continuing down. It gave me hope that he was every bit as affected by this as I was. But it had to stop. We needed to establish that it would never happen again. No matter how good he tasted and felt and smelled and...I was in so much trouble.

"Should we talk about ground rules or something?"

"Do you want them?"

"Maybe," I whispered.

His wandering eyes traced down my lips, my face, my neck, and it burned in a way that threatened to consume me. He drank me in, and I would be putty in his arms if he moved even an inch closer.

"Wep..." I breathed. I knew it was wrong, but I couldn't make it stop.

He leaned in, like he might take the chance to taste me—if only I would let him. Great Dragon, I wanted to.

No.

I couldn't keep making this mistake. "That look is what got us into trouble in the first place," I said, trying to ruin the moment.

His eyebrow quirked in that way I liked, and fuck, that beautiful smirk. Everything about this man was entirely unfair. "Trouble, huh? So, you don't want more of it."

My core clenched at the thought of exactly how much trouble we could get into. I tried to swallow a moan, but it escaped as an idiotic squeak.

"You don't want my lips on your neck. My hands in your hair."

I couldn't stop myself from leaning into him. Yes. That was exactly what I wanted.

"You don't want to let those wandering hands of yours roam free over my body."

Yes, I wanted to touch him so badly that my hands were shaking.

"You want to keep this table between us, then?" He reached for me, tracing his thumb down the side of my face.

Yes, yes, yes. His fingers continued down my neck, resting at the hollow of my collarbone, but I wanted more. I wanted his touch absolutely everywhere. I *needed* him to keep going.

"Yes," I encouraged him, leaning in to give him more access.

His hand didn't move.

I opened my eyes, fearful of what I might see there. Maybe he'd woken from this madness. Maybe he'd realized that, even if his brother was an ass, he was still family.

"I need to know what you want," he said, voice raw with hunger.

"Fuck, Wep, you know what I want." We both knew exactly what.

"I need to hear you say it."

I want you to take me right here on this table and don't stop until I'm screaming your name. Is that what he wanted to hear? A vision of Tam flittered through my mind of the last time we were together. The last time I was with anyone. Regret twisted in my gut. I wanted to give in, throw every scrap of duty and expectation away, and just fall into his arms. But what kind of person would that make me?

I pulled back. I wouldn't be staying in the Riht, or maybe I would be. The fact that I didn't even know was bad enough. Either way, I couldn't do this. I was not about to leave this trail of destruction in my wake. Steeling my resolve, I stood. "This is a mistake. I can't—*we* can't keep doing this."

Before I could change my mind, I booked it to the door. Wep huffed out a sigh, the air forced from his lungs like I'd delivered a blow straight to his chest. I couldn't stop now. I had to do what needed to be done.

"I need space," I said to him with as much finality as I could muster and left.

DESPITE VAYA'LA'S PROTESTS that we begin training immediately, I sought out Callagh. With one look at my face, she offered up a visit to the market with no questions asked. We left the keep in silence. At the market, we bought root vegetables, waxy greens, and berries so dark black they might have been made of the night itself. I gave them to the rotund woman at the kitchen window—Kish, my assigned cook—who made me a special dish that I took on a tray to my room.

Callagh returned after my meal to sit with me. Though I would have preferred time to myself, I didn't have the heart to tell her. I collected a few dyes and a fabric swatch from the black table in the lesson room and set them up in my chamber. My mind wandered as we worked. So much had happened in the past day and a half. It was strange to think that only yesterday morning I had been upset over a few harsh words from my challenger.

"Do you know much of that Meralda woman?" I asked while plotting out a test pattern.

"No," Callagh answered, giving me a look. "She's a bit older than me, and we don't revolve in the same circles."

I nodded, but I could tell there was something she wasn't saying.

"She's been rather nasty to me," I tried.

Callagh nodded. "A streak of malice in her, to be sure. I heard Dane asked her to return to Cról, where her family lives."

"Any particular reason?"

"Great Dragon, you've heard the rumors, haven't you?"

I hadn't heard anything, but she was now vibrating with the effort to keep whatever it was in. She just needed a tiny shove. I shrugged with what I hoped came off as nonchalance and said, "I may have."

The dam burst. "Resorting to poison! I would never have imagined. And with her station and former title—no wonder Dane stripped it from her. He probably doesn't have the evidence to charge her, or she'd be in a prison cell already. I wish she were."

"It was her?" I asked, unable to stop myself. "*She* tried to poison me?"

"It looks that way, but I don't think we'll ever know for sure."

Silence fell again. After a few minutes, I tried a different tactic: bold straightforwardness. "What do you think of Eldreth?"

Callagh looked away. Perhaps she was expecting a telling-off. "Why do you ask, my lady?"

"No opinion? I assumed you'd have one after that little stunt earlier."

"I don't see anything wrong with planning you a little alone time, my lady."

"Ah, is that what they're calling it now?"

"Oh, well," Callagh made a show of rearranging my dye bottles and inspecting one of my brushes. "I can't claim to be sorry for doing something kind for you."

I swirled my brush in some of the alcohol Wep brought me from the market to cleanse it and selected a new color.

"Did it go well, at least?"

"Callagh, it's not meant to be."

"Don't say that, my lady. There's clearly something between you. I can see it, Bracht can see it—"

"Now *there's* something to talk about. Spending a lot of time with Bracht lately, hmm?"

Callagh's face bypassed red and went straight to fuchsia. I didn't need my second sight to read her feelings. "I don't know what you mean, my lady."

"Oh, don't you?" I grinned. "Tell me, while you two were scheming this little plan, where were you both? A bit of free time?"

"Serae!" she hissed.

"Spend it in any way you'd care to share?"

"Okay, okay!" She jumped from her chair and paced the room. "Your point's taken."

I cackled as Callagh's scowl deepened. "You like him, though, don't you?"

"The lives of humans are dreadfully dull."

"Hush you."

"I'm restless. Send her away. There is much for you to learn."

"Patience."

"Fine, keep shedding greenery. Or worse."

Callagh sighed. "I do. Don't take this the wrong way or anything, but *reálti* rarely marry. It's just easier to remain unattached in our line of work. As your *reálta*, I've pledged myself to you. Forming lasting attachments to others can lead to a lot of...difficulties."

Guilt crept through me and settled low in my gut. Callagh had pledged her life to me, meanwhile I had been planning to run back to Inra the first chance I got. Something in me shifted. I had already failed in securing Gerta the life she wanted. I would not let that happen again. "We'll change the rules, then. We'll make sure that you can have both."

"Do you mean it?"

I nodded.

Callagh flung herself into me, spilling dye all over my practice square and nearly upending us both. "Thank you, my lady. Thank you so much."

"Right." I straightened. "If I'm going to be dana, I'm making some changes around here. First, knock it off with the *my ladies* in private. If you need to use the title in public, fine, but when it's us, my name is Serae."

"Got it." She beamed at me.

"Next, I need you to arrange a meeting with the tailor. We have things to discuss."

"Lanh Migram? Not what I was expecting, but okay."

"And third, no more plotting between you and Bracht. I want you to spend time with him because you want to, not as some excuse."

Again, she nodded. "I'm sorry about that. I truly thought you two got on."

"We do. We get on a bit *too* well," I admitted, rubbing my face in my hands and probably getting dye all over myself. "That's the problem."

THAT NIGHT, I lay in bed sleepless, sinking deeper and deeper into my wallowing. My bed was threatening to become a pile of leaves.

"Enough," Vaya'la commanded. *"Get up. We begin now."*

I rose and sat at the end of my bed.

"Close your eyes. We start simple. Imagine your favorite flower. See it in your mind's eye. Then, hold out your hand, and make it."

What utter nonsense.

"Try," she chided.

I closed my eyes and thought of the little star jasmine that had riddled my bath water. They grew along the archway in the manor gardens. There was a bench beneath them where I could sit in the sun and read, surrounded by their beautiful scent. Those were rare times of peace for me. I focused hard on those tiny blossoms. I held out my hand and pushed *something* into it.

I opened my eyes. My palm was empty.

"Try again."

With a sigh, I closed my eyes and began visualizing again. And again. And again. I tried for several hours. I thought of every flower, herb, and plant I could remember. I tried standing, sitting, lying down.

"We will figure out a way. Do not be discouraged."

"Haven't you done this before?" I shot back at Vaya'la.

"It's different for each of you, Small One. Open your senses and feel. Claim your emotions. Many first touch the power through fury, but not so for you, I think."

"I'm fucking sick of being different," I said aloud.

My mind flooded with images. *"Is this you?"* I asked, but they pushed everything else away. It was Wep, standing on the dais at my Sun Trial, looking radiant. I gasped. It was the first time I'd seen for certain the red of his hair. The first time I hadn't been the only one in a room with locks of flame and fire. It was Wep, smiling at me after strength training, when I finally learned to balance. It was Wep, sleeveless in the flickering firelight, moving like a force of strength and grace and perfection. It was Wep, shining with pure, white lifelight before he kissed me in my room, in my bed, against my new favorite tree. It was Wep, smiling at me like *I* was the one made of pure lifelight and engulfing me in his strong arms.

Warmth, like sunlight on a summer day, filled me from the inside out. It started in my chest and spread through every inch of my body. When it reached my fingertips, heat surged from my palms. I opened my eyes. Jasmine petals littered the floor and bed around me. They were falling from my hair and tumbling out of my palms. That feeling of pure, unhindered joy burst through me, and I laughed aloud as more flowers cascaded from my skin. I opened my second sight, and each one shone with a tiny bit of starlight.

"Good." Her praise was everything. *"This is the key."*

It was Wep. Wep was the key. Not Tam, not Eldreth, Wep. My heart cracked into a thousand shards of glass within my chest. The flowers decayed to dust before my eyes. I fell to the floor in a puddle of my own misery. Tears pooled in my eyes and rained down onto the ashes of my ruined happiness.

"Do not despair, Small One. The future is ours for the making."

I only cried harder, for she could not have been more wrong.

THE NEXT DAY, after two sleepless nights, I didn't rise with the sun. Callagh brought me meals, which I told her to leave on the table and then ignored. My stomach was in knots. Eating felt impossible. Callagh tried multiple times to entice me out, but all I did was withdraw further into myself.

"Should I get Wep?" She asked that evening, desperation in her voice.

"No. Not him."

How could I ever face him again? It was one thing to want him, but knowing that he alone brought me more joy than any other, that *he* was the key to tapping into my source—it was more than I could bear. My life would never be bound to Wep's, and yet, in a twisted, gut-wrenching way, it already was.

I sent her away and wept.

When most of the following day had passed in solitude, I rose, sick of sitting with my thoughts. I had nothing to do, so I washed, collected a clean shirt, and made my way to the kitchen. I clutched my little spice box under one arm. Bypassing the Main Hall, I went straight to the side entrance where trays were ordered. Kish peeked at me through the window, then leaned all the way out.

"You've not been eating."

"I know, I'm sorry."

She thumped a meaty fist against the counter. "I'll make you anything you like. A nice roll with jam? I've got an elderberry that'll suit you nicely."

"Just tea?"

"Hmm...how about chamomile?"

“Perfect. Could I throw a few things in the mug before you pour?”

That earned me a healthy dose of side-eye, but Kish stepped away and returned with a mug. I threw in a pinch of lavender, some dried, crushed rose petals, and a small sprig of lemon balm. She eyed me again, but this time, with an unmistakable glint. A few minutes later, she came back with a small steaming pot and three plain biscuits on a tray.

“Eat all three.” She nodded at me. “It’ll settle the stomach.”

“You’re a dream. How can I thank you?” I took the proffered tray.

She chuckled. “I like you. Come back anytime. And, if you bring me more osage, I’ll make us something nice to share.”

“Osage?”

“Those little black berries—you know.”

Ah, so that was their name. “Thanks, Kish.”

She tutted. “No more Kish. You call me Dallah.”

“Dallah.” I nodded.

The following day, a messenger arrived with a letter in Merria’s script. I set it down and turned to my project for the day. I wasn’t ready for Merria’s inanities, flippant attitude, or simpering words. No doubt this letter was filled with nonsense about her betrothal to that horrid duke’s son. Instead, I flattened out my newly purchased sage green tunic, collected a few shades of green and indigo ink from the lesson room, and got to work in the privacy of my chamber. There was a beautiful stillness in the repetition of a pattern. It needed focus and precision, but it was also rhythmic work. My mind wandered as I created leaves, flowers, and spirals of wind. The embellishments were concentrated on the cuffs and hem, then wound upward like trailing vines. They needed to be dried, set, re-dyed, and set again. It would take me most of the day to complete.

All the while, another scene played in my mind’s eye:

I was standing on the blue-violet grass, my legs planted into the earth. My tail swayed behind me, and I tucked my wings in tight. I needed to shift. It was a simple thought. Simple, but not easy. My shoulders cracked, my wings folded in on themselves, my snout broke, and my teeth retracted. I pressed in on myself, again and again, until I was small and insignificant. I reared up on my hind legs as my forelegs reshaped into arms. Last to go were my scales, which flaked off into a pile on the floor. I shook the last few loose.

The nakedness in this form was inconvenient. I stepped into the glow of the red sun, warming my flesh. The grass beneath my feet was buoyant, and the blades tickled as they tucked between my toes with each step.

"Feel the life in each blade," I said to my Bound One. "Then, dig deeper."

I knelt and dug my fingertips into the soil. It was soft, black, and wet.

"Feel the pulse. Slow your heart and match it. Ask, don't take."

I tugged, just lightly, on that taut string that connected me to all life, and it responded, flooding me with purpose. I was the conduit. The go-between. But I was also the shaper.

I held out my palm and willed that sweet, intoxicating power to gather in my hand.

"Just a thought is all it needs. Be specific. Be precise."

An image of a vining plant common to these parts came to me first, then the spiny white flowers they created, and finally, the succulent pink fruits that grew from them. I focused my will. From my hand, vines tumbled stem after stem, stretching down to the ground. I poured more into them, and flowers sprouted down their length. Harder and harder I pushed, willing the flowers to blossom and propagate until, finally, bulbous pink fruit swelled, weighing the vines down until they snapped apart.

I shook my hand, and the vines fell away, leaving my skin pink and new.

"It takes intention and listening. Emotion is your conduit, but this is your goal."

The lesson was learned. It was time to shed my skin and return to my natural form. I harnessed my magic through a single thought. My bones cracked and lengthened. My skin tore apart as scales grew through, covering the softness beneath. Wings sprouted from my back and unfurled in sweeping arcs. My nails elongated into talons, and my spine stretched long. When the agony had ended, I felt right and strong and free. With a great leap, I took to the sky.

I returned to myself, gasping at the echoes of a pain that was not mine. Dark was descending over the keep. I regarded my finished tunic hanging on the line by the fire. It was dry. Petals littered the floor around my feet. With care, I swept them up and cast them to the fire as kindling. Then, I wrapped myself in the tunic and tied it snug. From my wardrobe, I took the heather green skirt that I had already finished, patterned in a matching forest green overlay.

I beheld my completed work in the mirror. It was a subtle masterpiece, similar yet contrasting to anything I had seen on anyone in the Riht. It was as intricate as the finest needlework I'd ever done in Inra, but without all the flaming needles and thread and squinting and headache. It also lacked the telltale Inraen gold, boasting instead the natural pigments of the Riht. Like it, I stuck out in either place, matching both and belonging to neither. I was a woman of both lands and nowhere.

With this in my mind, I marched my way down to the hall for my dinner, trays be damned. Every head that turned along the way was a private victory. At least now, the attention was a choice—*my choice.*

Entering the Hall doors was nothing dramatic. I might have been anyone else walking in the room, but as heads glanced up to check the newcomer, the double-takes could have been counted like popcorn kernels. Wep was among them, and I felt his slack-jawed stare most keenly. I ignored them all and sat at a table alone. The server brought me a plate. Eating in the Main Hall was not so different from eating in my room. The biggest change was that the Hall was filled with noisy chatter, but I was still isolated and silent.

A mug of spiced ale plunked down in front of me. Inside, there was a whole cinnamon stick. I looked up.

"That's from Cergia," Callagh said with a wide grin. She nodded toward a corner of the room.

"The spice lady?"

Callagh nodded.

I glanced over and indeed saw the owner of the lovely herb and spice shop raising a mug in my direction.

"She says she picked the right night to join the castle mess."

I cracked a grin, but it didn't last. I was not ready to fully let go of my dark mood from the past two days. Callagh was downright giddy at the heads still turning my way. She kept up a running commentary with her thoughts on how jealous each person was likely to be, who was looking with lust versus admiration, and who was gawking in contempt for my outlandish break with tradition. In short, there was no staying mad with Callagh at my side.

"Was it too much?" I whispered, stuffing the last of my roasted potato into my mouth.

She crossed her arms, leaned back in her chair, and looked me up and down. "If this is any indication of how you'll be as dana, you're going to shake these people to their cores and look fucking phenomenal doing it."

"Anything fucking phenomenal is something I need to be a part of." Lex plopped down next to me and raised his hand at the server. He was in black again, this time just a loose tunic and very tight pants. His hair was braided in a single plait, unlike his usual array of braids, ties, and ornaments.

"Do your balls still work with pants like that?" I asked.

Callagh coughed into her tea.

Lex grinned and gripped himself. "Do you want to test? *Ouch!*"

Lispen arrived and smacked him across the back of the head.

"Every time," he grumbled. "How do you do that?"

"I've got a bullshit meter that can spot you from a mile away," she deadpanned, then raised her hand to the server just as Raif sat down at her side with two mugs of ale.

Teke plopped down on my other side and gripped me tight around the shoulders. "Gorgeous. Stunning. Turning heads and breaking hearts. Serae, have I told you that I love you?"

"You sound like Lex," I admonished, but I grinned just the same.

"I like it better when you're here. You should join us every evening," Lex said.

Callagh and I exchanged smiles.

"I just might."

ELDRETH

EARLY AUTUMN, TUSKIMON 1036

FROM THE FRONT of the Main Hall, I watched Serae with magnetic efficiency. She was fierce. Poised. Her talent with the dyes in those little jars was staggering. I had seen patterns like that in Inra, but hers were different. They were undeniably and uniquely her. She was a sight to behold.

She walked into the room and commanded the eyes of every Riht in the entire fucking Hall. The only problem was she didn't look back at me—not once. *Fuck,* did I want her to? I needed to know that she was all right, that we would get past my idiocy. I knew that I'd pushed things with her. I also knew it would come back to bite me in the ass. I just didn't know how hard. And I couldn't seem to help myself. With her, I lost all sense of right and wrong.

Dane wanted me close to her. My *reálton*—wherever the hell he was—wanted me to spend time with her. Everything was pushing me in her direction, except for her. That was the problem. *She* had pushed me away.

It was testing every last ounce of my resolve to hold back.

Instead, I watched her with her *ranng,* who had undoubtedly become her friends while I was away. She smiled at them, and I wanted to steal it for myself.

Across the hall, my brother's eyes lingered on me. I met his brooding stare. I wasn't usually a violent man, but lately, I wanted to punch through his fucking face. Somehow, he had snuck into her inner circle and become her confidant. I didn't want to know what else. I prayed to the Great Dragon that there was nothing else between them. I had never been the jealous type, but when it came to her, my heart didn't listen to reason.

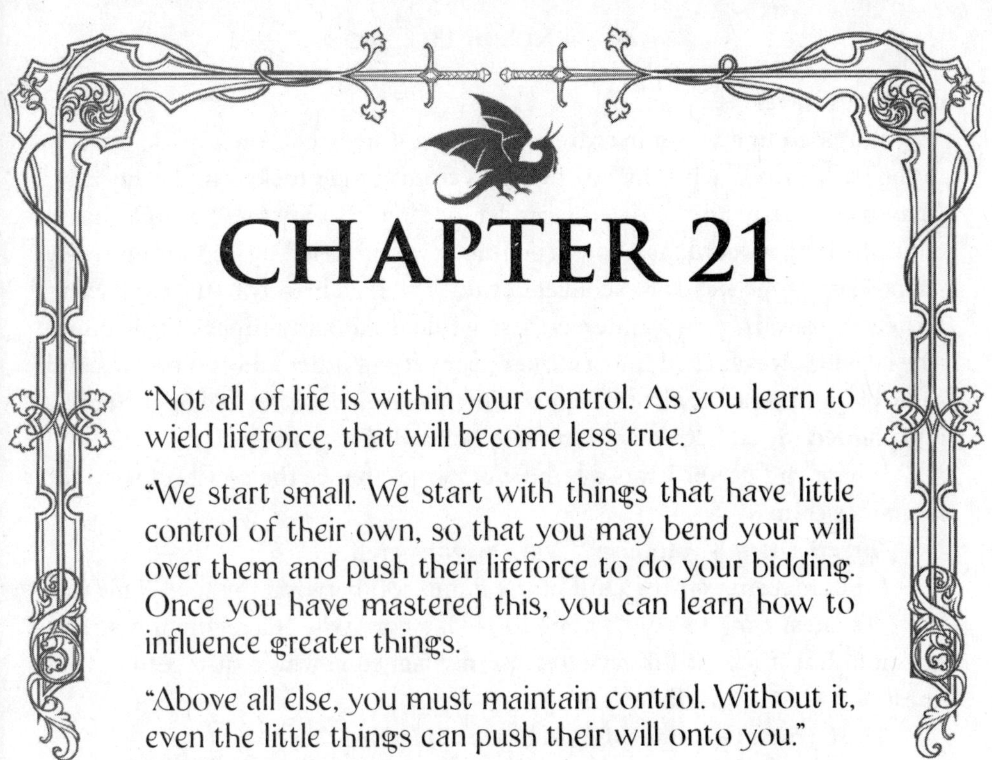

CHAPTER 21

"Not all of life is within your control. As you learn to wield lifeforce, that will become less true.

"We start small. We start with things that have little control of their own, so that you may bend your will over them and push their lifeforce to do your bidding. Once you have mastered this, you can learn how to influence greater things.

"Above all else, you must maintain control. Without it, even the little things can push their will onto you."

—Recounting from the private diary of Jerris, Dragonbound

SERAE

MID-AUTUMN, BASMON 1036

I DIDN'T BOTHER with training the next day or the day after that. It was independence I craved and time to be on my own. I had some very explicit instructions from Vaya'la on work that needed to be done. The sun had just begun to peek over the horizon, scattering pink rays through the windows and across the stone floors. It cast a warmth over the castle, contrasting the early morning chill. Outside my window, red and orange streaked across the land, lighting the forest ablaze with color. Patches of evergreens dotted the mountains, enough that they would still look lush and green after all the deciduous leaves fell.

I dressed in a warm overdress and fleece-lined coat, then made my way to the back garden with the box of spices from Cergia tucked under my arm. I had used nearly all the dried lavender, adding it to my tea. Lavender grew naturally in these gardens, though not much would be left by mid-autumn. My purpose this time was not to collect flowers. I walked briskly to the spot where I knew it grew, having wandered these gardens so many times at this point. The lavender was tucked into a corner near several other edible blossoms and some blooming garlic, all at the ends of their season. I sat, kicked off my boots, and planted my feet directly in the soil. I closed my eyes.

Where do I begin? I was a bundle of nerves, hence the constant need for lavender's calm.

"Breathe, steady your heart," Vaya'la whispered.

I did, focusing on the chill of the damp soil between my toes. This was Vaya'la's latest trick to connect me to Jaeda's core without relying on strong emotion. But it meant I'd have to wash my feet somewhere discreet to avoid questions when I was done.

"Push your other thoughts aside," she chided me.

"Right, sorry."

"Feel for the connection."

I dug my toes deeper. Then, remembering my last vision, I sank my fingers into the dirt. My breathing slowed, and I allowed my mind to still.

"Listen..."

Thump-thump... thump-thump... thump-thump...

It was my own heart.

"Deeper."

I pushed lower, past my heart, past my center, down, down, down into the earth. At some point, my eyes closed. I stilled, except for my slow, steady breaths. Something hummed beneath me. It was an ancient rumbling. It was deep and earthy and so, so powerful.

"Can I touch it?"

"Yes."

I reached out, not with my hands, but with myself, down toward that pulsing core. Glowing strands of light, shining in every color of the spectrum at once, crisscrossed my mind. They begged to be strummed like the strings of a lyre, each vying for my touch. My fingers, still thrust into the soil, closed around the nearest strand, plucking it from the mass and pulling it into myself.

"Direct it, Small One. You must tell it where to go."

I held out a hand, palm up. The power filled me, flowing and flowing inward. I started to sweat. The more the power flowed, the hotter my skin grew. It itched and burned.

"Direct it."

"How?" I panicked. I couldn't stop it. It just kept filling me, until I was bursting with overwhelming light. *Make it stop.* I needed it to stop!

"Open your eyes."

They snapped open and locked onto the lavender in front of me. I thought of its smell, its taste, the way the tiny buds felt—soft on the plant but firm as rice when dried.

"Focus the energy out."

I lifted my hand and tried, but nothing happened.

"Your right hand, Small One. Left is for in. Right is for out."

I switched hands, plunging my left back into the ground and extending my right. I channeled the energy through me, becoming the conduit. My hand burned, but I pushed my will into the texture, smell, taste, and sight of the lavender. I became the lavender. I imagined it sprouting from me in tall fronds, until the entire surface of my hand was nothing but pale purple blossoms.

"Close the connection," Vaya'la urged, pushing an image of a pond into my mind.

I yanked my hand from the earth and rocked back on my bum until my feet hovered in the air. Everything in my mind went still.

I looked at my hand. Like some freakish pincushion, lavender sprigs sprouted from every inch of the front and back of my hand, wrist, and forearm.

"Get it off!" I shrieked.

Vaya'la's laughter filled my head. *"Just let go."*

"I'm not holding anything!"

"With your mind. Let go."

I screwed up my eyes and thought of a stone dropping into that pond. As the stone plunged in, ripples spread across the surface, touching every corner of my mind.

A rustle, then a cool breeze covered my hand. I opened one eye, then the other, and I breathed a sigh of relief. My hand was my own again. My skin was unharmed, though it was a little tender to the touch. At my feet lay a heap of lavender, far more than I'd ever cultivated.

"Ah, shit," I said, gathering the lavender into a giant bushel. I'd have to figure out what to do with it all. This much lavender in full bloom would be conspicuous.

"Well done, Small One. Tomorrow, we try vines."

I didn't like the sound of that.

THE DAYS PASSED. I kept to my *dowsae* in the privacy of my room. I practiced growing vines and blossoms from my hands for Vaya'la—as insane as that sounded—when alone in the gardens. Soon, she said, I'd be graduating to fruits. For long hours each day, I painted shirts, skirts, and leggings for Teke, Callagh, and myself. Wep never showed up demanding I return to training. Ell never came by asking for walks or conversation.

I missed the activity, but I didn't regret the time away from either of them. Whenever I thought about either one, my blood boiled for all the wrong reasons. I hadn't gotten over Ell's calloused sense of humor, and Wep...I hadn't gotten over *him* at all. Thinking about him threatened to send me back into that place of despair. Everything with him was a mind fuck. He kissed me and touched me and said things I couldn't burn out of my soul—not with all the magic I pulled from Vaya'la or Jaeda itself. All the while, he knew I was betrothed to his brother. What would Dane say, I wondered, if he knew how his two sons acted?

Callagh constantly encouraged me to let it go. She attended training in my place, allowing me time to wander the gardens in semi-peace. She didn't seem to mind my aloofness, even if her lifelight dimmed to a dull blue—*disappointment*—each time I made my excuses to leave. No one, except Vaya'la and the insides of my boots, knew the real reason I spent so much time hiding away.

That morning, though, she looked irritated when I parted ways with her to head outside. The marjoram had gone to late blossom, thanks to my influence and Vaya'la's latest lesson. Each flower had a curiously blue lifelight that made the tiny pink blossoms look violet. I didn't pick any, though I did sit and practice reproducing single blossoms in the palm of my hand.

"Control is the most important lesson you will learn," Vaya'la said by way of praise at my success.

The tart scent of orange hit my nose, and I looked up. There were no citrus trees here, so I expected to see Callagh with juice from the kitchens, or perhaps a belated lunch tray.

Instead, standing over me was a very irate Dane, distinctly sans juice, but not without a hefty scowl.

"So, this is how you spend your days, is it?"

I frowned and got to my feet, hoping he wouldn't mention me being unshod. "I suppose so. What else is there for me to do?"

"Your duty would be nice." He didn't bother to check the edge to his voice.

"What duty is that?" I spat back. "I'm learning plenty about the Riht from Callagh and my lessons, I study these gardens every day, I'm making excellent progress with your language, I've continued my morning *dowsae—*"

"You never struck me as one to shirk your responsibilities. What of your training?"

"That's on pause." I didn't miss a beat, but neither did he.

"Then un-pause it. What are you doing to learn more of your blessings?"

I swallowed the lump that rose in my throat. "I'm keeping myself open. Everyone tells me these things take time."

The red light around Dane pulsed ominously and darkened. *Fury.* I'd pushed him too far. "It's been weeks since you visited the Great Dragon again." It wasn't an accusation, just a statement, but he planted his feet and crossed his arms.

"It has." Well over a month, in fact, but I wasn't aware he knew, let alone was keeping track.

"What have you to show for it?"

I had *a lot* to show for it. I could produce vines, leaves, and flowers. I was making progress with fruits, and I could also influence things to grow.

"What does it matter to you? Any *bierla* I manifest is my own."

Dane eyed me. He had a knack for making me feel minuscule with nothing but a look. "There's no point in keeping anything from me, Daughter. I know what goes on in my own home. Get yourself back to training tomorrow, and if you're going to skip, you need to be spending your time communing with the Great Dragon."

It was an effort to keep the shock off my face, and not one I succeeded at. "Is that something required of me as future dana?"

To Vaya'la, I added, *"Does he know?"*

"It is not yet time."

What in the Nine Martyrs' bones did that mean? The truth was, we *had* been communing daily, and our binding was stronger than ever. Each time I called upon her power, her light rushed into me with more force and brilliance than the last. I had disguised my time in the gardens as a distraction—an indulgence, even—when it was really a careful misdirection for the training

Vaya'la demanded of me. Returning to training with Wep and my *ranng* meant moving ahead with my purpose in the Riht and returning to that place where I was trapped between what I wanted and what was expected of me.

"There's something else," he said, interrupting my thoughts. "You have a letter."

He pulled it from his pocket and handed it over. I saw Merria's script on the front. I'd forgotten about the last one she'd sent, probably discarded somewhere on my desk. I looked up—the red pulse around him had dissipated.

"Have you read it?"

He shook his head. When he handed it over, the seal was intact.

I nodded, neither thanking him for the trust nor allowing my own guilt to creep in. My path in the Riht might not be clear, but my past with Inra was. My growing connection with Vaya'la was slowly erasing all doubt.

Dane sighed, probably seeing the war on my face. "Do you not realize by now that you're one of us? You've been blessed by the Great Dragon herself. There's no going back."

I kept my silence and watched him walk away, knowing that, yet again, my life going forward would have to change, no matter the course. I already had perhaps the most valuable piece of information anyone could hope for from their enemy—I was bound to an actual dragon, and there were more dragons in the world living today. Knowledge of this scope was likely beyond what even my father hoped his gamble would garner. With this information, he and the king could turn the tides of the entire war between Inra and the Riht. A distinct rumbling filled my mind.

"You are safe with me," I said to Vaya'la.

"I know, Small One."

How trivial my small woes of mortal life and love must seem to an endless creature like her.

THE NEXT DAY, I gave in to Dane's command and returned to training. I did miss practice with my *ranng*. I even missed honing my body. More than anything, a very large, irrational part of me missed seeing Wep. Just looking at him—nothing more, I told myself—would have to be enough.

"You're back, then?" were the only words Wep spoke to me. He turned away before I could come up with an excuse. I had no right to complain, he was giving me the space I'd asked for.

We went straight into drills.

"You're sloppy," Lispen scolded after I dropped my spear tip so many times that she started kicking it away with minimal effort.

I nodded.

"Figure your shit out." She turned and left me, joining Lex and Raif instead.

Ivank dropped a hand on my shoulder. "She's been worried about you." I snorted, but his grin was rueful. "Come on, join in with us."

The spear was not my forte, not that anything was yet. I hit the mat so many times that my shoulders and hips were throbbing before our training was even halfway through.

"Switch groups," Wep called out. "Alternate weapons." He walked to each group, replacing spears with axes, swords, and daggers. When he got to me, he did not meet my eyes as he ripped the spear from my hand and thrust long daggers at me.

"I haven't been trained for these."

He smirked. "Tough."

These daggers, it turned out, required an excellent grip. I had neither the gripping power nor dexterity with the longer blades to be of any use with them. I struggled to hold my guard, keep the weapons in my hand, and stay on my feet until Teke took pity on me. They abandoned all pretense of sparring and began adjusting my grip.

"Your grip is too tight."

"I hardly think so. I'm dropping them every fucking second." I gritted my teeth.

"Yes, but you're using your arms like spikes. You need to be reeds."

I gave them my flattest look.

"Have you ever been whipped by a reed when the northeast wind is heavy?"

I shrugged, bracing myself for a fresh dose of humility.

"No? I've got scars that look like dagger slices down my legs from them."

"Clearly, you weren't wearing the right gear."

Teke grinned. "I was buck naked and getting ready to have my way with three other people in a lake, so yeah, you could say I was a little underdressed."

I stared.

"Oh, now you're listening?" They flashed me an all too suggestive grin. "Good. Your grip is *too fucking tight*. Would you fist a dick like that?" Thank the Great Dragon, they didn't want an answer.

"Agreed," Vaya'la butted in.

"You need to be loving with your daggers. Grip them firmly, not tightly. You need the fluidity in your wrist to make them effective. Try again."

I'd be damned if I treated those daggers like cocks, but I shook out my wrists, stopped caring about the weapons being knocked from my hands, and started mirroring Teke's movements. Something clicked, and I relished the thrum of energy between us. They turned opposite me, and the dance continued. It was the eagle *dowsa*, but also not. It was our very own unique choreography that we each knew instinctively. As we moved, all else fell away. I heard their eerie song, haunting me from the first morning we met. Teke was strong, agile, giving, and demanding all at once, and I was their exact opposite, countering with each complement in turn. I didn't notice when the rest of the room stopped to watch. I didn't even feel their eyes on me, so lost in the trance of our bodies and minds moving in tandem.

What finally distracted me was my second sight opening on its own. Teke exploded with a beautiful yellow-green light, the exact shade of my peridot necklace. Their skin radiated pure sunshine between the pulsing waves of *euphoria*. I was awash with their lifelight and overwhelmed. My arms dropped as I stared, my daggers falling away, forgotten.

"You're incredible," I gasped.

Teke grinned and engulfed me in a giant hug. "Welcome back," they whispered into my ear. I squeezed them tight. "I was starting to miss you."

Over Teke's shoulder, I locked eyes with Wep. His hands were loose at his side, and his face held a new serenity and openness as he appraised me.

Teke released me, and their bright smile filled my vision. "Enough of that. After training today, we're drinking."

Behind me, Ivank and Lex shouted, "*Va draske!*"

Va draske, it turned out, was a Rihtish phrase meaning something along the lines of, "Let's drink," though by the looks Helene was giving, I gathered it was somewhat cruder.

The whole *ranng* gathered at a nearby tavern, which I hadn't known existed. Even Lispen came, though she grumbled about it still being light out. This tavern, aptly named The Dragon's Maw, had a colossal wooden carving of a dragon head, mouth open and teeth gleaming, hanging from the central wall. Each scale was individually carved using a variety of wood, giving it variegated colors. The overall effect was so lifelike that it could have passed for real if not for the size.

"Everyone loves me," Vaya'la drawled.

I jolted. She had quips now?

"You're up." I thought back at her, hoping the flatness of my tone carried through the binding. She'd feigned sleep each time I tried to question her further about Dane.

"Naturally. Our binding requires energy to strengthen. You've barely been sleeping, so I had to regenerate all on my own."

"Liar."

A glass plopped down in front of me. Vaya'la's snark would have to wait. I had some drinking to do. I couldn't say exactly what I was expecting from Rihtish alcohol, but it definitely wasn't the drink Lex selected. He paid for our first round, which was a rich red-gold liquid that tasted like berries and vinegar.

"It's tea-based," Helene whispered in my ear when she saw my expression. The first sip made my jaw ache and my whole face pucker, but as I kept going, it mellowed out and went down far too easily.

As the dinner hour approached, the tavern filled. I tucked into the center of my group, not wanting to create a scene. The outbursts of hatred had lessened as people got used to my presence, but going someplace new always presented a risk.

"More!" Raif shouted and rushed to the bar. He came back with a scowl and seven small glasses. "They wouldn't give me doubles," he grumbled as he passed them around. They were warm to the touch and held a clear, thick liquid.

Ivank downed his in one gulp, then shoved his tongue into the glass, licking the sides. Teke did the same but used their finger, swirling it around the side and sucking off the last drops.

"Scales and talons, do that again," Lex crooned, reaching for Teke's waist, but they batted him away.

"Purified elderberry liquor," Helene said at my side.

Sniffing the small glass, I detected floral notes, but mostly, I was hit by the pungent strength of the drink. Just the scent made me lightheaded.

"You don't sip this one," she explained, then tossed hers back. Unlike Ivank and Teke, she set her empty glass on the table, remnants unmolested.

Drinking this concoction went straight to my head. I had the immediate sensation that I was floating. Lex was at my side, snaking his arm around me. He whispered something that made me giggle, but a moment later, I couldn't remember what. Then, he was tracing his fingers down my cheeks and begging to kiss me.

Lispen came up from behind and kicked him in the balls.

He dropped my waist, doubled over, and began shouting at her in Rihtish. I sat down in a nearby chair, my head spinning pleasantly around the room. After a while, it could have been minutes or hours, Helene and Lispen flanked me as a third drink, this one a deep purple, clunked down before me. I wasn't sure I would make it through the night.

We drank, and we drank, and we drank. Rihtish drinks had different effects than Inraen ones. What I hadn't expected was the peppery drink we had last, which significantly cleared my senses. I still had a nice buzz, as if I'd had two glasses of wine back home, but nothing like my befuddlement from moments before. The drink looked like black sludge, but it had a heavy mint undertone and was, on the whole, rather pleasant. We chased it with a glass of water, then parted ways. Lex threw an arm around Teke as Helene and Ivank followed them toward the lower city. Lispen and Raif wandered off in the opposite direction, while I headed back to the keep.

I made my way back to the training room. I was in no state to train, but I had an unreasonable amount of courage, a dangerous lack of sense, and a bone to pick with the weaponmaster.

The door behind me opened. I turned, already expecting him.

Wep let the door swing closed. His sleeves were rolled to the elbow. His shirt and pants were simple. There was nothing to mark him as second in line to become dane.

"No training after drinking," he said. His voice was flat and too loud for the echoing room.

I exhaled through my nose. This man was on my last nerve. "Obviously."

"Rough day, then? Being forced back to training is so awful?"

I ignored him, sucked in a breath, but then hesitated. Whatever I had wanted to say to him flitted from my mind.

"Just say it." His jaw clenched. When I didn't respond, he went on. "Whatever's on your mind, out with it. You're good at telling me exactly what you want."

I reeled. He did *not* just go there.

"Fuck. *You.*" I could barely speak through clenched teeth. "He's your *brother*, Wep. Did you forget that?"

His brow furrowed.

"Have any other older brothers you want to tell me about?"

Wep's mouth pressed into a thin line. "No. Just the one."

I huffed out a laugh. "Lovely." I began pacing. I wanted to scream and rant and rage, but I couldn't tell how much of it was the alcohol. Everything between us was so much more real than I expected. I should have known this was always where things were headed—back to Wep and me. Regret bubbled to the surface. I was drawn to him from the first time I laid eyes on him in that tent. I couldn't stay away. I was a fool to think just looking would ever be enough.

The silence stretched across the room until it was tense and taut. I released it. "How could you?"

Wep cocked his head to the side.

"You could have warned me."

"That my brother's a self-inflated ass? You may recall that I did."

I shook my head.

Wep took a few steps toward me. "Is it my age? Does that matter so much in Inra?" His voice softened.

"What? No, I don't care about that." Or rather, I did care. I cared immensely that he wasn't older. Or that Ell wasn't younger.

"Then what's the problem?"

How could I possibly answer that? How did he not realize that he was driving me insane? I couldn't handle these stolen moments that would never last. I wanted my betrothed to be *him*, but that was the last thing I could say.

"Serae..."

My eyes snapped up to Wep's. He was right in front of me now, looking down at me with that furrowed brow and storm-gray eyes of his.

"I've been trying to give you space."

I nodded.

"Was it enough?"

I nodded again.

He growled, "Fuck yes," before capturing my lips with his own.

My mind went completely blank. My body froze, but my mouth sure as hell took over. I matched his kiss with every stroke of my tongue. He kept his arms firmly at his sides, so only our lips were joined. We were locked in a battle to see who would snap first, though whether I was meant to push him away or crash into him, I couldn't tell.

Dragons' flames, he tasted fucking amazing.

I never wanted the kiss to end. Suddenly, the reasons why his body wasn't pressed to mine were nonexistent. I wanted to rake my fingers through his hair and pull him into me until he crushed me against the wall, the floor, whatever. Need for him pooled in my core so quickly and violently, I could barely contain it. If he touched me, even once, I'd be stripping out of these clothes right then and there.

At that sobering thought, I jumped back. He was my betrothed's *brother!*

"You keep kissing me," I gasped like an idiot.

"Is that wrong?" His eyes fell to my lips, and he frowned as if he too, were questioning the sense of ever having them apart again.

"Why?" *Stupid brain! What the fuck does it matter why!*

"Is this not what you want?" he demanded, gesturing between us.

"It's not about you."

"So, it's someone else?"

I scoffed. "Everyone else be damned. I don't care what others think."

"Then what do you want from me?"

I couldn't answer. I didn't know. At that precise moment, Tam's face flashed behind my eyes, and I squeezed them closed. Nothing back in Inra mattered anymore. My path, my life, my freedom all lay here in the Riht. Was kissing the future dane's brother really so bad an offense? It's not like we were married yet.

Wep dragged his hand down his face and grumbled, "At least I know what I want."

"What *you* want?" I shouted, finally snapping. "What about what *I* want? I arrive here, and I'm treated like I'm nothing for weeks. You show up, belittle me, drill me like I'm a child because I didn't grow up with your ridiculous *dowsae*. Then, out of burning nowhere, you kiss me. You *keep* kissing me. What do you expect me to think of that? What do you think that does to me? Have you ever thought about my side of things? I was betrothed to a man I didn't even know, solely to fulfill family expectations. I didn't get to agree to it. I was sold away, like a prize calf meant to seal an alliance with my body. You think that's a life? You have no idea how that sits in your stomach and turns your insides to rot, having no purpose besides breeding and the posturing of men."

Wep took three steps away from me and muttered something that sounded an awful lot like "fucking blind." When he turned back, eyes wild and raw, his words exploded out of him. "All I think about all damned day is you! I can't just—" He ground his teeth. "You think you're the only one with restrictions? With family expectations?"

My heart constricted. It was too much.

"Yes, poor you." I crossed my arms. "Beloved by all, skilled and perfect, and born into Riht royalty to boot."

"Yeah, let's focus on you and all your misfortunes. Wealthy family in Inra. Pampered your whole life. Never had to do anything hard. Here in the Riht, you have to work, but you'll be dana, and you'll have the means and opportunity to do anything. Any interest, whatever passion, all of it will be yours."

A whine escaped my lips. My arms fell to my sides. There was truth in what he said, but his words ripped me bare. "You don't get it. I have nothing. I *am* nothing." My voice dropped to a whisper. "I'm just a tool for an alliance. Who would ever care to see *me*? To want *me*?" The words hurt to speak, but he had his truth, and I had mine. My reality, whether in the Riht or Inra, was that my primary function was not my own. Here, I was bound to Eldreth. And once my father came for me, I'd be plucked from Drakh, placed at Tam's side, and never thought of again. I was meant to follow orders, be a good daughter, and be a good future wife.

"Serae." He held his arms out wide as if presenting himself for sacrifice. "I'm right here."

Something in me cracked. I flew into his arms, and he caught me easily. Our lips fused together, and in that moment, I knew only that I had to have him. I didn't care if it was wrong. My father and his father be damned. Our kiss deepened, and Wep's hands began to roam the curves of my body. *I needed more.*

I inched backward, pulling him with me until my back met the stone wall. He pressed me against it, and the wall gave me just the right leverage to rock my hips forward. He let out a delicious moan and gripped my waist, encouraging me. *More.*

I ran my hands up his chest to the nape of his neck, desperately wishing his hair was loose so I could fulfill my recent obsession with raking my fingers along his scalp. His hands responded in turn, and I gasped when he cupped my breast and ran his thumb across my nipple. These Rihtish clothes were *amazing*. I could feel everything through them in the best way. Our kisses turned frantic, doing little to sate my hunger for him. *More.*

My hands wandered the planes of his back. I needed to feel all of him and wasted no time untucking his shirt so I could slip beneath and rake my fingers across his soft skin. Martyrs, the feel of his hard muscles beneath was everything. He mirrored me, pulling my underdress loose enough to give his hand access to trace up my stomach. For a moment, he ghosted along the side of my breast as if asking permission. I arched into his touch, and he immediately moved to fill his hand with my heaving chest. I broke our kiss with a moan as lightning ran through my body and straight to my core, drenching me at his touch. *More, more, so much more.*

My hand moved to his cock, completely ignoring the logical side of my brain telling me this was a bad idea. Still, my hand moved, driven by my own need and desperation to feel him. He was impossibly hard already, and his breath hitched as I squeezed his length. Then, his hand at my waist moved to my ass and pressed my center firmly against him. Another moan escaped me at the pressure and friction. He recaptured my lips, dipping his tongue into my mouth in time with the thrust of his hips. Fire and ash, this man was unfairly hot.

"Well, well, well, what have we here?"

We jumped apart, but as I was already against the wall, my awkward jolt made me smack my head against the stone. Wep's body leaving mine, aside from making my body protest the sudden cold, only served to further expose the evidence between us. I ached for his heat to return, but over his shoulder, I locked eyes with the absolute worst person to catch us in this state—Ell. He stood in the doorway with a brow raised and a mischievous grin on his lips.

Wep tucked in his shirt, cleared his throat, and looked away. I had no doubts that every inch of me was still covered in lust. I couldn't stop myself from drinking in Wep's disheveled clothes and broken composure. A flash of pride ran through me.

"My, my," Ell chuckled. "If I'd known there was this much excitement at home, I would've never stayed away. Carry on." He winked at me as he backed out of the door.

"I'm—I apologize." Wep's voice cracked, and he wouldn't meet my eye. "I shouldn't have— I didn't mean to—" He cleared his throat again, then walked briskly out of the room. Ell's taunting voice resounded from the stairway.

Propped against the wall, vest and underdress askew and alone, the wave of shame finally crashed over me. More poignant still was the sting of Wep's rejection. The unsaid word that hung in the air had sucker-punched me in the gut. To him, this was a mistake.

For me, this was another lesson to remember. A few stolen kisses were one thing, but this was something else entirely. This could *never* happen again. This time, I had to mean it.

That night, I paced my room fretting over what to say to Callagh, who would know the moment she walked in that something was wrong. My fears were needless. Callagh never came. I collected a tray from the kitchen and ate mindlessly, just to satisfy my growling stomach, which I'd abused by all the alcohol and nothing to soak it up.

When I tucked myself into bed, I thought about the irony that I was the second-born daughter who could have been betrothed to a second-born son. I played the scene over and over in my mind, obsessing about every little detail. It could have gone so many ways, but I had made all the wrong choices.

I was so caught up in the things I had done that I hadn't stopped to think about the other end of it. Ell's mocking laughter and taunting words echoed in my mind. That was his reaction to finding his brother entwined with his betrothed? That was the man I'd be bound to?

"You are bound to no one but me," Vaya'la growled.

My blood ran colder than the chill trapped in these castle walls.

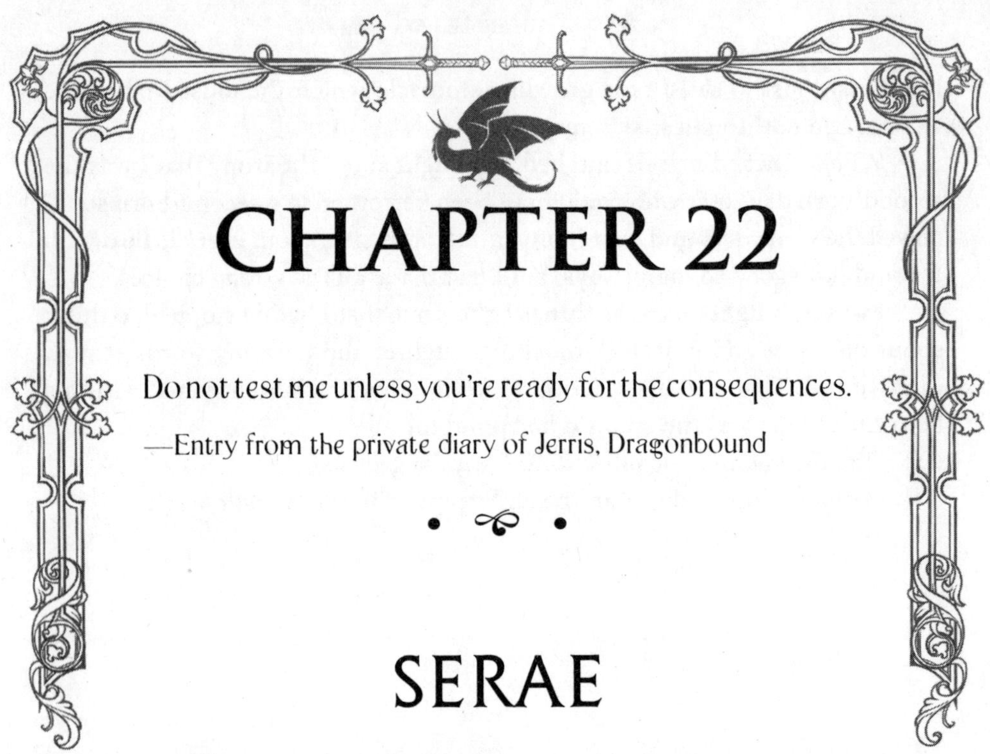

CHAPTER 22

Do not test me unless you're ready for the consequences.

—Entry from the private diary of Jerris, Dragonbound

• ❧ •

SERAE

MID-AUTUMN, BASMON 1036

My head was splitting in two. That Rihtish alcohol packed more of a punch than I anticipated, even with that peppery little sobering remedy. I sat at my writing table, Merria's letter in hand, and rubbed my temples. What in the name of the Great Dragon was this?

The few letters I'd received from Merria were all nonsense about new dresses and parties she'd attended. She never responded to the letters I sent her or inquired further about the scraps of information I *did* give her. I had made it a habit to write nearly weekly, though I had lapsed lately. Now, she wrote a letter with no less than ten questions about my life here—many centered around Eldreth. *What is your young prince like? Is he handsome? Is he gone much leading their expeditions? Does he ever take you with him?* It didn't feel right.

Merria must be desperate for entertainment if she was stooping so low as to write to me *about me*. Especially when a certain duke was hanging around as much as I suspected. Or, more concerning, my lack of useful information of late was noticed.

A small tap at the door rattled my brain like a gong. A moment later,

Callagh peered in.

"It's time, my lady."

The frown on my face was threatening to become permanent. My afternoon lesson with Dane yesterday had brought news that my *ranng* was being sent on reconnaissance. I would continue training alone with Wep.

I wasn't sure if this would be better or far, far worse. There was nothing for it. Delaying would not improve my lot in this life, so I gathered my skirt—a completely unnecessary habit from a time when the skirts I wore were voluminous burdens—and moved to the door.

Callagh stepped aside and trailed behind me. We reached the bottom of the Training Hall steps in no time. I didn't need an escort to walk across the hall, but I knew Callagh did it as a show of support.

I steeled myself outside the door for only a second. I had to enter the training room with my head held high, even though my stomach was churning at the idea of being in his presence again. *I am in control*, I reminded myself. Never mind the feel of his lips, his perfect jaw, or that little smile that did things to my heart. No. He may be physically perfect, but the logical part of my brain still recoiled at letting him in.

"When the head and the heart are at war, you should listen to your gullet."

"Humans don't have gullets."

"Pity," Vaya'la laughed.

I sent a few choice curses in her direction and opened the door, scanning the room.

Holy. Fucking. Muscles.

Wep was in the middle of the mat running through a *dowsa* that apparently required him to be shirtless. All I could see were muscles and tanned skin with tattoos covering his back. I couldn't make out the details of the ink with how fast he was moving, but every muscle of his torso, arms, and back was on full display. His pecs, his abs—dragons, did the man have an ounce of fat on him? His arms were nothing but corded muscle, and the way he moved was power, speed, strength, and yet also grace and fluidity... He was a force to be reckoned with, and in that moment, I lost all sense of my mental barriers.

So, yes, I was staring. Ogling, if I were honest.

The door thumped closed, stifling Callagh's giggling.

Wep altered his lethal dance enough to glance my way, then the rest of him came to a stuttering halt. Dragon snout and scales, I wanted him to keep going, but he turned away and began walking toward the far side of the room.

This put his full back on display, and I gasped. He paused mid-step. His entire back was covered with dragons.

The green one in the center I recognized immediately, and not just because it was the largest. It was Vaya'la, though she was awake rather than slumbering. The red dragon on his shoulder looked remarkably like the Inraen iconography of the Creator. The others I had seen before on the Relaxation Room tapestries: a blue dragon across his other shoulder, a white dragon by his hip, as well as an orange and a purple. The colors, except for Vaya'la's, were minor accents within the black ink, but Vaya'la was full, detailed color. A piece of it snaked over his shoulder and down his bicep, which must have been the tails I'd noticed before. I wanted to grab him and inspect every last inch of it. Instead, he reached the corner, bent over, and snatched up a bit of fabric. Then, he was walking back toward me, fully clothed.

"We need to test your blessings," he announced.

I blinked, still processing the loss of that spectacular view. "Excuse me?"

"Dane has tasked us with further testing your blessings as soon as possible. Your *ranng* has been given other responsibilities for the next several days."

The reminder hit me like a weight. "Oh, right," I managed. *Him gripping me close, overflowing with pride, and whispering into my ear. "Living armor."* Fuck, he didn't know the half of it.

"What do I tell him?" I asked Vaya'la.

"This is the one you trust, yes?"

"I don't know." I trusted Wep, but did I trust him with this, considering what it might mean for him, Dane, or the Riht? I'd never allowed myself to consider what would happen once they learned I was Bound. It might make things better—or far worse.

"You will know when the time is right."

Perfect. Unhelpful as usual. I settled with, "How do we start?"

He eyed me. "We don't know enough about manifesting multiple blessings, so we'll test what we can."

"Who said anything about multiple blessings?"

"Dane."

"He's wrong. I only know of the one."

Vaya'la snorted.

"What's changed in the past few months for you?"

I raised an eyebrow.

"About yourself, not about your life," he deadpanned.

"An excellent point of clarity. Otherwise, we'd be here all day."

"Don't get smart—"

"So, you think I'm smart?"

Wep paused and looked me up and down. "I think you're uniquely brilliant when you decide to apply yourself. It's your motivation that's lacking."

My jaw fell open.

"Back to the point, it could be something about your body that's changed, like feeling faster or stronger. Or, you might be pulled toward an interest you never had before, like a sudden desire to weave or fish or—I don't know—metalwork."

"No metalworking going on here, I promise." I tried for a smile and failed.

"You're not wearing your glasses anymore."

Dragons' balls, he noticed.

"What do you know of dragon balls? You seem rather preoccupied with this one's—"

"Finish that sentence, and I'll make all my dreams the kind you detest."

"Is that punishment for me or you?" My mind shook with her laughter.

"Has your vision improved?"

I forced my focus back to him. "No."

"You just prefer to be in, how did you call it, *a constant state of befuddlement*?"

I smirked. "I'm just taking the advice of my betters."

Wep pursed his lips. *Point to me.* "Fine, if it's not your vision, then we should talk about that night."

His hands on my skin. His teeth on my neck. His length pressed against my core.

I cleared my throat and walked toward the nearest weapons rack, pretending to inspect the axes. "What night?"

He followed, and his warmth at my back beckoned me to lean into him. "The night you saved yourself from the dragori."

Oh. That night.

"Have you summoned the armor again?"

"No," I answered honestly. I moved on to the next rack bearing short swords. He trailed me.

"Had you done it before?"

"No." On to the daggers.

"So, that was your first time."

"Yes." I rounded on him, and he stepped back. "How is this helpful?"

He scratched his jaw. His short beard was freshly trimmed down to stubble, and his copper hair was loose today. "I'm trying to stop this from being trial and error for us."

"Meaning?"

"Meaning, if you haven't figured anything out on your own, we'll test everything. I'll observe, and you'll be honest with your experiences." His stare was a challenge.

My instinct was to decline, but that would probably get me thrown before Dane to explain myself. I had to come up with another option. I'd always been a sucker for a good experiment, and this could be exactly that. I was aware of the ways I was changing. There was Vaya'la's vision and overall heightened senses. There was the work with plant life. We'd even started on minor healing.

Aside from that, my body felt stronger each day. Part of it was physical strength. Three months training with Wep had toned my body in a way I hadn't dreamt possible before joining the Riht, but it was more than that. If I had to put a word to it, I had more vitality. I wondered what else might be changing in me, and I was *definitely* curious about what other blessings were out there.

"This is all to be reported back to Dane?"

He nodded.

"You'll be documenting our findings?"

"I...suppose so."

I could make this useful—if I could keep my findings separate from Dane's. Sharing all I'd accomplished with Wep made my spine tingle, but the thought of Dane knowing churned my stomach. I thought about my abandoned little brown journal, filled to the last page. Perfect for cataloging everything I had learned over my first few months in the Riht.

"I accept."

He sighed as if reading my mind. "I guess we need a ledger."

"Two."

"Why?" He narrowed his eyes and crossed his arms.

"I need one for myself."

"What for?"

"Does it matter? Can I have one or not?"

He eyed me for several moments, no doubt trying to find a crack. I kept my face steady and firm. "Fine." *Point two to me.*

"Great. Lead the way."

I collected my fleece-lined coat, twisted my hair into a quick four-stranded plait, and met Wep back in the main hallway. He'd tied his hair in its usual knot and donned a leather overcoat that was nothing short of a work of art on him. It was open at the front, braided strips running down the collar and sleeves. The layered panels of leather doubled as flexible armor, and the sleeves cut off at the elbow, allowing room for his matching bracers, keeping his range of motion free. They had to be a set, and with that level of craftsmanship and how perfectly it fit him, every piece must have been custom-made for his body.

He turned to me while hanging a pouch and dagger to the belt at his waist, his longsword already strapped to his back. Either I'd been in the Riht too long, or this look was far too good on him.

I swallowed hard. Maybe this wasn't such a good idea after all.

We walked side-by-side in silence through the streets, but my mind was anything but quiet. Everyone we passed nodded to Marr Wep, and not a single person scowled or jeered at me. A few even offered smiles just for being in his company, which I tried my best to return.

"Figures," I muttered as we rounded a corner down an empty side path. After months here, the most I'd managed were a few trips to the market where I was generally ignored. Turned out, all I needed was to stand at Wep's side. *Yet, it was the one thing I couldn't do.*

Wep's head turned to me. Out of the corner of my eye, I saw him frown, but he didn't comment.

"We control our own fates, Small One."

I ignored her.

The shop we entered was down a street I already knew well. It was close enough to the stall where I'd been trading Rihtish books back and forth that it was a wonder I'd never noticed it before. Crossing the threshold, that giddy, childish anticipation hit me. I might have been eight again, waiting on Midwinter Eve to open my holiday chest. Bookshelves lined the walls, and standing shelves created aisles across the room. Each one was filled with stacks and rows of books. Rolls of paper, binding cords, ink, and feather-tipped quills—made from metal, wood, and glass—covered the tables capping each row. At the back was a counter, and I could just make out an array of gold and silver stamps beside blocks of colored wax.

Wep walked straight down an aisle to a specific bookshelf, selected a thin ledger with black binding, then looked at me.

I needed no further prompting. That row held three shelving units, each six shelves high, displaying journals and ledgers in different colors, sizes, patterns, and thicknesses. There were some with lines inside, some blank, and some with special decorations. I would have liked to pry open every cover and pore over my options for hours, but huffs from Wep directed me otherwise.

In the end, I settled on a green cloth-bound journal stamped with a metallic rendering of Vaya'la on the front. It was significantly thicker than the ledger Wep had selected, but he said nothing as I handed over the book and allowed him to pay the shopkeep, a kindly man who offered up five different additions—all shot down by Wep—before he gave up. The entire time, his eyes twinkled and darted to me, likely knowing his true customer. I vowed to return here on my own with a full pouch of scale and plenty of free time.

On the way back, my nose brought me to a stand of those same sweet and salty buns Teke had introduced me to.

"Can we stop?" I blurted out.

Wep glanced at the cart but kept moving. "There's plenty of food in our kitchens."

Just the smell of them had me hanging back, but when I saw they were sliced in half and drizzled with hot sauce, a desperate whine escaped my throat.

He studied my face, and whatever he saw was pathetic enough that he relented and circled back. He ordered one and passed me half.

I sank my teeth in immediately, relishing my luck. This time, with him at my side, I was guaranteed to enjoy the entire thing without the threat of a blow to my head.

Wep ate his half far too quickly, then ogled me. I couldn't blame him. My taste buds were having a heyday with the complexity dancing over my tongue. The sweet, the salty, the spicy, the richness, the fluffiness—it was all too much. I may have moaned more than once, earning a raised eyebrow from him and scandalized looks from passersby.

"It'sh 'eally goo'," I managed through a stuffed mouth.

He shook his head, but his eyes never left me. Not even as he ordered another bun and wordlessly passed me half. Clearly, I was putting on a show, but I couldn't be bothered to care as I took bite after bite of incredibleness.

"We could've stopped earlier if you were hungry," he muttered.

"I wasn't." I was partway through my second half and already eyeing the third in his outstretched hand. I didn't exactly cut a convincing figure. I swallowed a huge bite and licked the salt from my lips. "These are just so fucking good."

That earned me both raised eyebrows.

The walk back, with my journal in one hand and the lingering taste of bun on my tongue, was far more pleasant. It had the added benefit of Wep's silence, which was uniquely bereft of his usual raincloud.

Back in the training room, testing began. We started with weapons, obviously.

"Do we have to?" I asked, holding up a throwing dagger dubiously.

"You could end this now by telling him the truth."

"I thought you said it was not yet time."

"Open your eyes, Small One. Do you trust him or not? You know the answer."

My lips pressed together. I hated it when she was right.

"I'm always right."

"No," Wep replied. "If you've got something else in mind, we should start there."

Despite Vaya'la's goading, part of me did want to tell him, but unease stilled my tongue. I shook my head.

"Fine. Weapons are the easiest thing for me to gauge any change."

"So, not because you prize weapon skills above all else?"

His eyes narrowed and darkened. "You have no idea what I prize and what I don't."

"I don't know about that. I'd say I have a pretty good—"

"Stop stalling and throw."

I scowled, took the rest of the throwing daggers from his outstretched hand, and aimed at the target. Then, I spent half a second imagining Wep's face instead of the wooden dummy's. I threw and missed wildly. This was *nothing* like archery. He made a note in his ledger. We repeated this with hatchets, throwing axes, which were somehow different, and balls—literally apple-sized spheres made of some ridiculously heavy wood. The results didn't vary.

"Maybe your vision hasn't changed," he muttered after making more notes with a frown.

"What's that? Something to say?"

He glared at me. "I said, your aim fucking sucks," he retorted, louder than he needed to.

"It's harder than it looks."

He dropped his ledger, plucked all four balls from my hand, and chucked them in tandem, two with his left arm and two with his right, at the target. Every one hit its mark.

I scowled. "It's not like I have your muscles."

Wep exploded with laughter, catching me off guard. He dropped his ledger again, which he had just picked up after his unnecessary display of show-offery, and doubled over, laughing to the point of wheezing.

"Stop," I commanded.

Wiping his eyes and collecting his ledger, he choked out, "We use these for children."

I wished my looks could kill.

"*Small* children."

At the end of this first day, all we had established was: Wep was a fucking prick, I was not at all stronger than before, and I had no sense of aim or coordination with anything other than a bow. I, on the other hand, had concrete proof that my taste had heightened—the sight and smell I already knew. I suspected touch as well, but I wouldn't be running any tests on that for a long, *long* time. Hearing was a big question mark, but I was drawing a blank for how to approach that one.

"You don't need to test what I have already told you. You now share my senses, which are all superior to human ones."

"You telling me something is different than me knowing and understanding it," I reminded her. We'd been having this conversation in pieces all day, as she reminded me repeatedly of the time I was wasting in this *charade with the weaponmaster.*

Aside from the general senses, I had also spent a decent part of my time in the market seeing if I could sense the earth through my boots to make the connection. I hadn't made much progress there yet, and Vaya'la unhelpfully assured me it might take years of practice, but I was determined to see that change. What good was having all this power if I had to stop and take off my boots to use it?

That evening, after a delightfully Wep-free meal with Callagh in the Main Hall, I sat at my table and documented the progress of my powers in my new journal. When I was done, I glanced around my room, wondering if I needed to hide this journal as well. Scraps of Rihtish writing practice littered my desk. A bit of white beneath the desk caught my eye, its red seal identifying it as Merria's ten-question letter. I snatched it up and returned to my seat at the table.

"Do I answer it?" I asked Vaya'la. I had been asking myself the question for days and had not yet come to a conclusion. Answering it, even without divulging any information, felt like a betrayal of Vaya'la—and those I cared about in the Riht. Not answering, though, would confirm what I feared my

father already suspected. It could spark him to come for me and might even prompt a war.

"Let them come," Vaya'la hissed. *"When my body wakes, I will eat them all."*

"A lovely sentiment, but let me remind you that the last time you woke in the Mortal Realm was centuries ago."

"Only because your powers must grow. It is not yet time for my kind to wake."

I sighed and tossed the letter aside. It would have to be a decision for another day.

A knock at my door sounded, then Callagh hurried in with two plates of berry tart. She glowed with bright olive green. *Eagerness.* I hadn't realized I'd opened my second sight.

"Just me, and I brought dessert. How was it?" She glanced down at the letter, then set the tray atop it.

"Every letter from my sister is a headache."

Her tinkling laugh rang out. She sat down in the chair opposite me and pulled a plate toward herself. "No, silly, your day with Wep! Did you figure out your blessings?"

I narrowed my eyes. "He told you?"

Her lifelight dimmed. "Of course not. I, uh, talked to Bracht for a while." Her cheeks flushed.

"Did you, now? That's a story I'm much more interested in hearing."

She giggled, blushed even harder, then told of the day they spent strolling through the forest picking berries and trading stories about life as *reálti*. "All good things, I promise!" As she talked, I did my best to keep a true smile on my face. Hers was turning into a perfect love story, and she glowed brighter and brighter with yellows and golds in rapid succession. *Fondness, affection, caring, desire.* From what she described, and the extra little things I picked up on, Bracht was a perfect match for her. I ignored my aching, jealous heart.

When the subject was well and truly spent, she turned back to me with guarded eyes. "Was today no good for you?"

I sighed and took a bite of my tart. "No luck today."

Her smile morphed into one with a bit too much understanding. "Give it time."

THE FOLLOWING DAYS of that week found me in constant proximity to Wep. We completed the array of weapons testing, then we eliminated all manner of jumping, twirling, and whatever else Wep could dream up. I half suspected he put me through it all just to make sure I knew how incompetent I was next to him. Trust me, I knew.

At first, each failed test was a small victory, but I had underestimated Wep's thoroughness. For every one crossed off the list, he added three more, many of which involved my sight in one way or another. Keeping track of what might reveal my heightened senses wore me down, as did the little frowns that tugged at his mouth when I intentionally underperformed. Even more pressing, I'd started shedding small yellow petals that dried as they fell to the floor.

"Make it stop!" I begged Vaya'la.

"I cannot stop what you create."

"What can I do to stop creating them?"

"You've gone too long storing up my magic. Stay calm, and you won't bleed out the excess lifeforce."

"That's a bit hard right now."

"Well, by all means, tell your weaponmaster and be rid of this nonsense so we can work on expanding what you actually *need to know."*

Absolutely not. Instead, I practiced steady breathing for the rest of the session, but that didn't stop Wep from glancing more than once at the crushed petals, both of our boots, and the barred outer door.

After a while, we ventured out into Drakh again to see what other skills might call to me. I only agreed after extracting a solemn vow that we'd return to the bun cart. I finally learned they were called *babi*, and burn me if that wasn't the most beautiful word I'd ever heard. We visited a metalsmith as well as a blacksmith, a clothier, three different bakeries—besides the bun cart—a jeweler, and some sort of perfume shop filled with hundreds of little bottles, where I almost vomited from the onslaught of scents.

"Has your sense of smell changed along with your eyesight?"

"No," I said, still gagging. At that, he eyed me closely and made a lot of notes. I begrudgingly conceded a point to him.

Then, we visited what Wep called a companion shop. Inside, there were caged rabbits, birds, cats, and even snakes. The owner demonstrated which pets we could hold and how. She was rather put off when he said we weren't here to buy anything. As I looked, my eyes refocused, and I saw each animal as they truly were. They glowed with inner lights, and instinctively, I understood them. They spoke no words. It was nothing like my connection with Vaya'la. Still, I could tell by looking at the rabbits that they were hungry and hadn't yet been fed. The snake was sleepy and did not appreciate being handled by the owner. The birds were all restless and wanting to fly, except one large bird that sat in the open, strapped to a perch. The poor thing radiated misery.

"That one," I blurted.

Wep's head snapped to me.

"I want that one," I repeated.

The owner perked right up, then she saw the bird I was indicating. "Oh, that old thing? He's a sourpuss. I have lots of lovely songbirds over here."

"No, I want him."

"We're not here to buy." Wep was at my side, his fingers barely grazing my forearm. My skin exploded into tingles, and I shifted toward him.

Our eyes met.

He hesitated, his hand now loosely grasping my arm. He seemed inclined to pull me in closer, and an impractical, stupid part of me wished he would. In the middle of the shop. With the owner eyeing us closely.

"Please," I whispered.

He cleared his throat. "How much?" he asked, eyes still searching mine. After a moment with no response, he stepped back, glared at the owner, and repeated, "How much?"

"Oh! If you're sure..."

We both nodded.

"Three hundred scale."

Wep scoffed. "You really want this one?"

I'd seen plenty of haggling in the markets to catch on to what Wep was doing, but the few things I'd bought with Callagh had been billed to Dane without discussion of price. I had no idea if this was an outrageous sum or not. I looked at the bird, who turned away from me. "No, just leave him. It's not like she'll ever sell him."

"Two-fifty scale," the owner called out.

I turned to leave, knowing the bird would be there tomorrow to try again.

"One-fifty. It's the lowest I can do. Any lower, and I'll be at a loss."

This time, Wep nodded. "I'll send a runner today with the scale and a cage to collect him."

"Absolutely, Marr Wep."

"We're not taking him now?"

Wep eyed me again, a flat look on his face. His lifelight flashed plum. *Irritation.* "You want to carry him around with you? What, on your shoulder?"

"Why not?"

"He won't perch there," the owner interrupted. "He doesn't like people."

She grimaced at the admission.

"He'll be fine," I said with a confidence that I didn't feel. I shrugged on my coat, which I'd been holding as we walked in the afternoon sun.

She muttered something like, "On your own hide be it," and untied the bird.

His eyes opened fully for the first time. I nodded to him, hoping he could understand my intentions. I jerked my head toward the door for good measure. *This way*, I thought desperately. He bobbed his little black head and flew to my shoulder. For a moment, pride bloomed in my chest, and my own lifelight danced with juniper. His wings stuttered through the short flight, barely making it, eclipsing our moment of triumph.

"His wings are clipped," I gasped.

"Yes, of course." The owner smiled.

I frowned, opened my mouth to give her a piece of my mind, but this time, Wep gripped my arm firmly.

"We'll be off. Look for Anbrachten before the end of the day. Dragon's blessings on you."

At this, the owner preened and offered many thanks and well wishes as Wep shoved me bodily, bird and all, out the door. He turned a corner, tugging me along. The bird squawked in my ear, nearly bursting the drum, and dug its talons into my shoulder.

"Slow down, you maniac!"

"Can't."

He tugged me again. The bird gripped tighter, and I yelped. It might have punctured the coat's leather that time. At that, he glanced back at me, then my shoulder, then sighed and pinched the bridge of his nose.

"Just move quickly."

Wep released me, and I hurried after him. Within minutes, we emerged into a clearing just beyond the castle walls, inside the lower city.

"Where *are* we?"

"It's a park."

"A park?" I gawked.

"Never heard of a park before?" The drawl in his voice was grating.

"You're in rare form today. Of course, I've heard of a park. I've just never seen one so...wild."

This piqued his interest. "What are parks like in Cavendaffe?"

I began to walk a slow circle around the clearing. "Well, manicured, I suppose. Paths for walking, benches for sitting."

"So, a garden."

I ignored the irk in his tone. "No, no crops." Completing the circle, I spun in place, taking in the sheer variety of trees lining this little haven. Rough paths intersected them that I imagined led to other hidden secrets just waiting for me to peruse.

There were no benches, so Wep seated himself right on the grass. He shrugged out of his coat and leaned back on one forearm. Opening his ledger, he unwrapped a piece of hard charcoal from a pocket I hadn't even known existed in his shirt and looked up at me.

"Why the bird?"

"Martyrs' flaming bones, do we have to?"

His eyes said, *obviously*, even though his mouth remained shut.

"Fine." I plopped down on the grass away from him. If we were really doing this, I might as well get comfortable. "It looked sad and lonely."

"Remind me not to bring you to the orphanage," he muttered.

"What!"

"I said, they all did. Why *this* bird?"

"I don't know. He just called to me."

Wep scribbled some notes. "When you say called—"

"No, not *actually* called. I just looked at this bird, saw he was miserable, and knew I had to help him."

"I see."

Glad that made one of us. I waited while he finished his next notes. "So, is that it?" I asked when he looked at me. "My blessing is a dumb pseudo-connection with this bird?"

"Second blessing," he corrected, tapping his chin. "I can't see how this relates to the thorns. Don't you know what type of bird that is?"

I sighed, not wanting to give him another thing to lord over me. I patted the bird's head, more blue-gray than black in the sunlight, then took the bait. "What is it, then?"

"A sparrowhawk."

"And?"

"They're meant to be trained."

"To do what, run messages?"

"Doubtful, but you could try. They're hunters."

"Great."

"And they mostly eat other birds."

I eyed the little beast, who puffed his feathers. He looked distinctly content as he settled his head into his fluff and closed his eyes. A savage pride filled me at the thought of him soaring over our tomato patches, picking off the finches that kept eating the little yellow ones I liked before they ripened. "Good. As soon as he can fly, I'll put him to work."

That's when the questions really began. I thought he was being exhaustive before with the physical training. I was So. Very. Wrong.

"Can you talk to him?"

"No."

"Can he talk to you?"

"Isn't that the same thing?"

"Could you sense him from across the room?"

"No."

"Can you give him commands?"

"Sleep and ignore me. Wow, he listened!"

"Can you see through his eyes?"

That one startled me. "Is that a thing?"

"Can you beckon him? Does *he* beckon *you*?"

"No. Are we done yet?"

"No. Do you feel a kindred connection to him?"

"Do you? You both seem to be the same shade of grump. Maybe I'm cursed to be attracted to the surliest things on Jaeda."

Wep sat up straighter. "You're attracted to me?"

I balked. "N-no."

His smirk was as delicious as it was infuriating.

"Don't make me sic Sprakt on you," I warned.

"That's his name? Did he tell you that?"

"Dragon's scales, no."

"Where'd you learn that word?"

"It's a name, idiot, not a word."

"Hmm." I hoped I would finally get a break, but he continued, "Can you share thoughts?"

I glared. "You asked that one already."

"Fuck, it's like you're not even trying. It's obvious there's an understanding between you two." He tossed his ledger aside, got to his feet, and began pacing.

"This is exhausting." I poked at Sprakt. He hopped off my shoulder and glided to a boulder a few yards away.

"You're telling me," he groaned.

"You're the one putting us through this."

"Trust me, I'm not."

Not for a second had I forgotten that little ledger of his would find its way back into Dane's hands. I kicked out my feet, fell backward, and lay there flat against the grass. It was thick and long, plush as a cushion. I closed my eyes. Through the earth, I could feel him claim the patch of grass beside me. I imagined him with his ankles crossed and hands laced behind his head, lounging like he owned this clearing—and, maybe he did. Or his father did, rather. The details of land ownership in Drakh weren't clear to me yet. In Cavendaffe, we owned the entire province, and everyone who lived there leased the land from us. Of course, there were many contracts ensuring rights of tenancy that passed through generations. We also paid hefty tithes to the king each year, whether in coin, crops, or militia, as did all lands across the kingdom. We were owners in name and title, so long as the king willed it.

"Who owns these lands?" I asked, needing to sate my curiosity.

Wep shifted, and I imagined him examining me. "They belong to Drakh."

"So Dane owns them?"

"Hmm." He paused. "No. Dane's responsible for them."

"Who gives him the responsibility, then?"

"The last dana, his mother."

"Not his father?"

"No, Éalren was the chosen leader, so he bears her name, not my grandfather's."

I lapsed into silence. I knew women had more freedom in the Riht, but I hadn't connected the extent of it. Freedoms I would lose if I were ever forced to return to Inra.

"How can you own land?" he asked, interrupting my thoughts.

I opened my eyes. Turning to him, my breath hitched. He was lying in exactly the position I'd imagined, but with his head to the side, eyes locked on mine. He was a lot closer than I had thought. Our faces were barely three feet apart. If he moved, his elbow could brush my shoulder.

"You control who lives on it," I breathed.

His brow furrowed. "You can't keep animals from living where they please."

"Animals don't count."

"Oh, don't they? Today suggests otherwise."

"You know what I mean."

"No, I really don't—"

A horn blared in the distance. Then a second. Then a third, so close the ground rattled.

Wep was on his feet in an instant. "Get your bird. We have to get to the keep."

"What?"

"Now, Serae."

I jumped up and called to Sprakt, who flew back to my shoulder. I'd need to figure out something about his death grip, or I'd be permanently bleeding from my clavicle. We ran back to the keep, twisting through alleys to get there more quickly, and I relied solely on Wep to know the way. As we sprinted, I held a steadying hand behind Sprakt to keep him from being jostled off. He couldn't fly alongside us with clipped wings.

That thought boiled my blood.

We were just outside the portcullis when Wep turned to me and gripped my arms. His eyes were intense. "I need to go to Dane and get orders. Stay inside. You'll be safe within the keep walls. Don't leave for anything unless Dane himself tells you. Don't go outside."

"Okay..."

"Please, Serae." It was the second time I'd heard my name as a plea on his lips in a few scant minutes, and it pulled something in me. "I have to trust you to keep yourself safe. Can I?"

"Safe? What's happening?"

Instead of answering, he released my arms, surged forward, and kissed me. Sprakt squawked and fluttered on my shoulder, but Wep's hands stole my attention. One cradled the back of my head while the other slipped to the small of my back, pressing me into him. The kiss was hot and firm and igniting, but it was over just as fast.

"I will answer all your questions when I return." Then he left. The entrance to the keep swallowed him before I regained my wits. I was standing in the bustling courtyard where people ran back and forth with supplies of every kind—cloth, grain, swords, leathers, bags, crates, and baskets. Not one person glanced my way. Not one person seemed to care that Wep had just kissed me in the open, in the middle of the most jam-packed courtyard I had ever seen.

Sprakt shuffled on my shoulder, grounding me. "Sorry, bud. Let's go in." I'd barely turned three corners inside the keep when I ran into Callagh.

"Thank the Great Dragon, you are here."

"What's happening?"

"Ships were spotted. Unfriendly ones, but that's all I know. They're hours away from our ports. I'm sure Dane thinks they mean to attack."

"But we won't make it to the docks in time!"

"We aren't going anywhere. The company stationed at the docks has already set sail. Dane is conferring with Wep. They'll be sending reinforcements to arrive before sundown."

A thought struck me, locking my limbs and stealing the breath from my lungs. *They're coming for me.* "Who are they? Is it Inra?"

"Inra?" Callagh's brow furrowed. "I sure hope not. Do you know something?"

"No, no, of course not."

"Do we need to go to Dane?" she asked, her voice low and even.

"Callagh, no. I don't know why I thought that."

She eyed me, unconvinced. "Let's get to your rooms. We're just in the way here."

My rooms, however, were a massive mistake. I had nothing to do but pace back and forth, despite Callagh's repeated pleas to *sit down*, *stop pacing*, and my personal favorite, *you're making* me *dizzy*. It was a credit to her concern for me that it took until the evening meal for her to ask, "What's with the bird?"

Sprakt perched atop the back of one of the empty chairs, snoozing. His blue-gray head was tucked into his orange-striped breast.

"It's a long story."

"Did Wep buy him for you?"

"Reluctantly, yes."

Callagh cackled with glee. "Only you could bend that man to your will."

I rounded on her. "Meaning?"

"Oh, come on. He's the most stubborn person in all of Drakh, even more so than Dane. The only reason Dane ever gets his say is because Wep bends to him. But you come in with your sharp tongue and big teal eyes, and that man turns to a puddle."

"He does not!"

She laughed again. "He does, and you know it."

I didn't know it. I had no idea how to respond, so I clamped my mouth shut, which only made her laugh harder. I crossed my arms and turned away from her.

"Oh, Serae, please. I'm sorry. I didn't mean to laugh. It's a good thing! It means you two are well-matched."

"Fat lot of good that does me," I grumbled, but Callagh only smiled and rose to clear away the dishes.

Alone in my room, I looked at Sprakt, still asleep on his makeshift perch. "It better not be my father," I whispered to him. "I'm never going back."

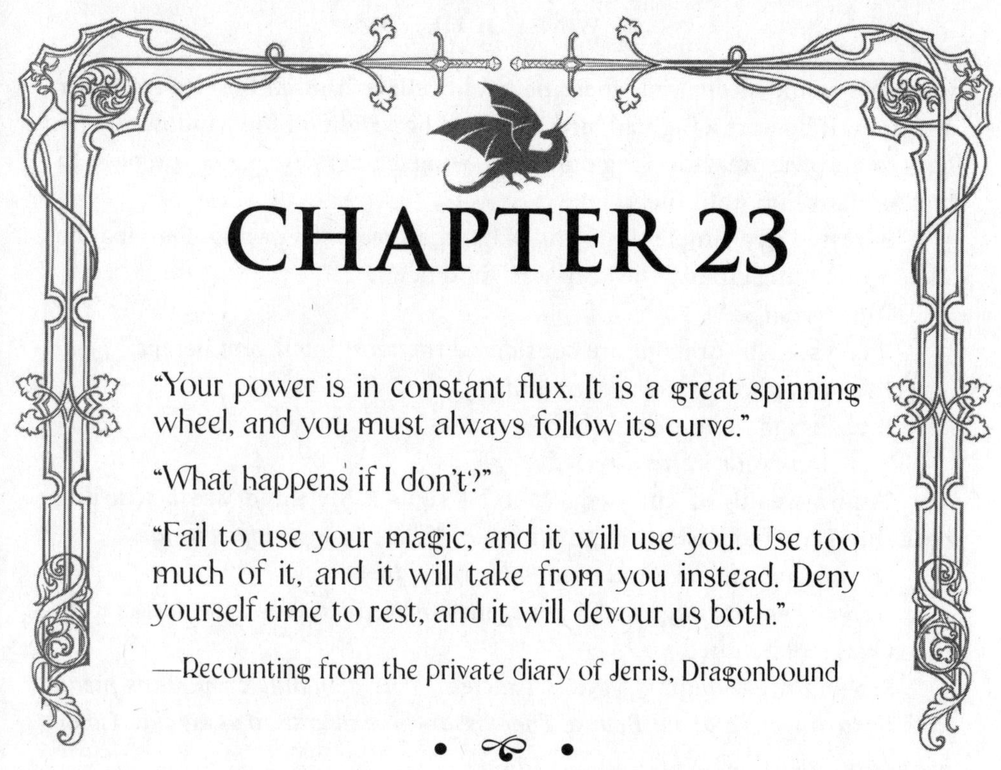

CHAPTER 23

"Your power is in constant flux. It is a great spinning wheel, and you must always follow its curve."

"What happens if I don't?"

"Fail to use your magic, and it will use you. Use too much of it, and it will take from you instead. Deny yourself time to rest, and it will devour us both."

—Recounting from the private diary of Jerris, Dragonbound

• • •

SERAE

MID-AUTUMN, BASMON 1036

THE MORNING DAWNED with a red sky. The sun shone deep umber until it cleared the horizon. Sprakt and I spent the sunrise staring out the window in stoic silence. The stones were cold as ice beneath my forearms as I leaned against the windowsill. I was trapped inside, wrestling with my conscience, even though the morning stillness beckoned me to the gardens. My feet itched for soft earth again instead of the unforgiving stone, but something in Wep's urgency held me back.

So, I paced.

It was too early for a breakfast tray, even if I went to the kitchen to request one. Yesterday, in the tumult of returning to the keep after buying Sprakt, I forgot about the very real practicalities of caring for him—like what he ate, where he would sleep, and where he could relieve himself besides my chair and floor. If he were a flighted bird, he could hop right off the windowsill and hunt to his pleasure. How long did it take wing feathers to regrow? I'd need to find food for him until then.

I dressed in a simple tunic and skirt, then resumed pacing. Perhaps the silence that hung around the keep was good news.

"You're restless."

"I can see why dragons are considered the most intelligent beings."

"We are. Speak to me in your mind."

"I can't right now, obviously."

"Just think your words directed at me."

"And a wealth of knowledge, too." I sighed. My mind was a whirling mess, but I tried to push through it for her. *"I hate being trapped inside."*

"Good. Come to me if you need to be free of those walls."

"I can't. I have to stay here." The urgency in Wep's tone and the desperation in his kiss still haunted me.

Sensing my thoughts, Vaya'la snorted. *"The demands of humans mean nothing to dragons and our Bound. There is nowhere safer than at my side. Come to me, and we will walk between dreams."*

I was tempted, but there was no way for me to get a horse on my own at that hour. I could try to wake Callagh, but she would never agree. She also still lived outside the keep, though within the castle walls, with her mother.

A knock startled me out of the morning quiet, but when I opened the door, Teke was smiling at me instead of Callagh. Their arms were piled high with cloth.

"I knew it," they announced. "Already moping about being stuck inside. Lucky for you, I brought us a project." They pushed their way inside, dropped the pile on a chair, then tossed a pouch onto my table that clinked suspiciously.

"No arguments," they said at my sharp look. "I'm paying, which means you need to get to work."

"Fine," I conceded, a smile tugging at the corner of my lips. "Help me get my supplies."

Teke and I did more than just gather supplies. We dragged the black table up the Training Hall stairs and into my room, along with extra pillows stolen from the Relaxation Room. I was going to question this, but when Callagh showed up partway through rearranging the space with Lex and Helene in tow, my questions died away.

While I worked, they poked through my bottles and designs, asking questions and feigning interest in my overlong explanations. After a while, they left me in peace to collect breakfast trays. I considered protesting that I was confined to the keep, not my rooms, but it gave me the perfect opportunity to expend some of my built-up magic. So much time among friends in my room reminded me of the weeks I'd spent cooped up with only Gerta. I latched onto the raw emotion her absence elicited and used it to bloom cherry blossoms by the dozens, then push them all into fruit.

"I'll never go hungry again, will I?" I asked Vaya'la, examining my work in the form of a tub full of cherries.

"Did you ever go hungry before?" she mocked. She was right, I hadn't experienced that sort of hardship. A new way I could be of use to the Riht blossomed alongside the tiny pink flowers as they shriveled and turned to fruit.

Chatter outside the door announced the return of my companions—Lispen now among them—and I took care to latch the door to my private bath as I rejoined them.

"Where'd the bird come from?" Lex asked as we ate from our trays scattered around my sitting room.

Callagh's eyes lit up. "A gift from Wep."

"Not a gift," I shot back, but the damage was done. The rest of the meal was spent with food turning to ash in my mouth as Lex, Callagh, and Teke gushed about the love they imagined between us. Turned out, I was worse than I thought at keeping my eyes off him during training. They devolved into tales of sweeping romance rife with looks of longing and passion. In another life, their show of support would have meant the world to me, but I couldn't ignore reality. In the Riht, I was betrothed to Ell. In Inra, I would be trapped with Tam. I had no other options.

When the topic turned to the murky waters of planning our future, the walls of the room threatened to close in on me. I set my tray aside and returned to my work. My heart ached hearing the happiness they imagined for me. Perhaps they thought I could change Dane's mind, swapping a marriage with his heir to his second son. If a marriage between a dane and dana was a real one, surely Ell would be better suited with someone else anyway. Could I approach Dane, admit to being a second-born daughter, and beg him to adjust the betrothal alliance? Would Wep even want that with me? My mind spun until my fingers clutched my brush, and my usually smooth lines wobbled.

After a while, Helene came to my side and offered to help me work.

"Thank you," I breathed, flexing my fingers and handing over the brushes

I'd been alternating between in this three-color pattern. "They're a bit much."

Her soft smile was filled with mischief. "They can't speculate about your life when they know nothing about it," she whispered.

I looked at her in a whole new light. "You sly thing."

Her smile turned to a full-on smirk.

They spent the day cooped up with me without complaint, except for Lex, who whined about everything. Eventually, a deck of cards made its way out, and the four of them, excluding Helene and me, took up some game I'd never heard of that involved a lot of shouting and throwing of cards across the room. The game was mostly friendly until Lex announced, "You're worse at leading cards than you are at leading the *ranng*. No wonder Raif won't hand over command!"

Lispen jumped from her chair. "We are *not* fighting over command, you ass!"

"But you're fighting about something?" Teke asked.

Helene and I looked up to watch. I'd never talked about Lispen and Raif with her, but I guessed she had picked up on the tension between them, too.

"We're not fighting," Lispen repeated through clenched teeth.

"Then you're fucking." Lispen kicked straight for his gut, Lex lunged to the side just in time to miss the brunt of it. "You can be as mad at me as you want, but it's one of the two. I'm never wrong where a cock is involved."

"Don't be so crass." It was Callagh who spoke up, earning raised brows from the other three. "What? I like sex as much as the next, I'm just tired of him always talking about it."

I glanced at Helene, whose lips pressed together, but her eyes dropped away from my gaze.

A knock at the door dispersed the subject. Teke jumped up to answer it.

"A letter for you." They held out the familiar white wrapping and red crest. *Another* letter from Merria?

"Just leave it on the table," I said. The last thing I needed today was stress from my idiotic sister. A smile twisted my lips at the thought that both Wep and I had an older sibling we could rarely stomach—though it quickly soured. That older sibling was my betrothed, and deep down, I knew trying to change that wouldn't work. That feeling of being trapped settled over me, drooping my shoulders as I turned back to my work.

When the sun sank in the sky, restlessness won out, and the group trickled away one by one. Each left with a promise to return tomorrow. I cleaned my brushes and tidied my bottles of dye and cloth while Callagh set the rest of my room back to rights. She tutted as she tackled the mountain of papers strewn across my writing desk, then gaped when she peeked into the privy and discovered my fruit-laden tub. I'd forgotten she carried a copy of my key.

"You can make fruit?" she asked. Then, ignoring my stuttering, "Does Wep know?"

I sighed. "He will. I just need time."

"Well, let's just leave this here for him to see. Or maybe, you prefer the one-on-one time with him?" Her smile widened.

The room was suddenly far too hot. "I don't know what you mean," I lied, pretending like the entire afternoon's conversation hadn't revolved around me and Wep.

A stillness crept over her face as she regarded me. Whatever she was searching for, she only asked, "You care for him, don't you?"

If only anything were that simple. Had I been sent here as his future bride instead of Ell's, there would be no question. With my father's deception, my complicity, and the impending betrayal of Inra hanging over my head, the better question was whether I'd be allowed to live, let alone worry about which brother held my heart. And now, there was Vaya'la to consider. Whatever she had in store for me, I had a feeling it would one day take me far away from Drakh and the Riht. There was zero chance Wep could pick up and go with me, abandoning his duty to his dane and the people. *If* he even wanted to. Tears pricked my eyes, but I blinked them away and said, "It's not meant to be."

After bringing me a dinner tray with a bowl of seeds and berries for Sprakt, she left me in peace. I picked at my food while the sun slipped beneath the horizon. I considered writing more in my new journal, but I was too fidgety to write. I'd been sitting in stillness the entire day, but unable to fully slip into my trance-like state with Vaya'la, not with so many people in the room.

Instead, I paced.

"This restlessness is grating," Vaya'la chided. After keeping her silence for most of the day, this comment irked me.

"You would be too if you were trapped in the same room all day."

"Then come to me."

I huffed. *"Not this again."*

"Fine. Go to the garden where the sacred tree grows. Sit beneath it on the bare earth, and we can begin."

Technically, I'd made no promises, I reminded myself, and the gardens weren't outside the castle. It was hardly a risk to go mere feet outside the keep walls, especially under the cover of night. Without another thought, I grabbed a thick cloak and tossed it over my shoulders. I picked up my boots but did not put them on, preferring to pad down the hallways barefoot. Sprakt jumped onto my shoulder. There were few moving about the keep at this hour, but still, I sidestepped the common stairways and hallways. With a bit of luck, I made it to the garden unseen.

"Now what?"

"Close your eyes and feel for the tree."

"How?"

"Use your feet."

My feet? *"That doesn't make—"* Seafoam green exploded from my lifelight as *astonishment* gripped me. A thread of magic pulsed beneath me, untangling from the rest and latching on, linking me to the essence of the tree. The little strand tugged, compelling me forward—not quite through my feet, but through my connection to Jaeda and all of her sparkling threads. I followed it to a section of the garden I hadn't visited before, tucked in a private corner. Soft pink and white blossoms floated to the ground and bench beneath a wide canopy. I sat directly on the earth beneath the tree's shelter. Sprakt hopped from my shoulder to the bench and eyed the tree, looking for a low branch to jump toward. I tamped down a flicker of guilt at being outdoors and focused only on Vaya'la.

"Deep breaths, Small One," she whispered to me. *"Settle your mind; steady your heart."*

The chill air whipped around me, prickling my face, though most of my body was warm under the cloak. The ground was damp but forgiving. The last rays of the sun's purple light had disappeared below the horizon. The moon and stars twinkled overhead, lighting my surroundings with the softest glow. I closed my eyes and focused on my breath.

"Relax," Vaya'la breathed.

With every exhale, I focused on relaxing a part of my body, starting with my toes, then ankles, then legs and knees, then hips, and up my body until I reached the top of my head.

"Connect to me."

I let go of myself, slipping into Vaya'la's mind. I fell from consciousness and tumbled into sleep.

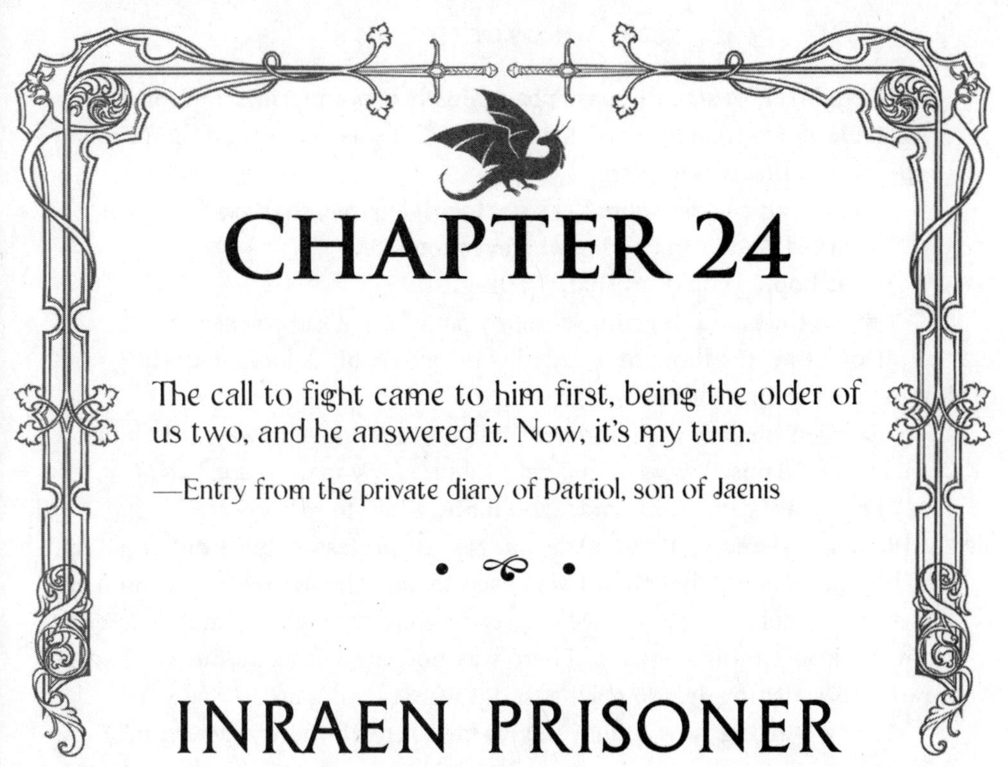

CHAPTER 24

The call to fight came to him first, being the older of us two, and he answered it. Now, it's my turn.

—Entry from the private diary of Patriol, son of Jaenis

INRAEN PRISONER

MID-AUTUMN, BASMON 1036

THIRTY-SEVEN DAYS spent with my ass aching on the hard cot of this dungeon. Or was it thirty-eight? Maybe forty? It was hard to tell, with how much of the daylight hours I spent asleep. Sometimes, it was because my shoulder was still healing after being stabbed through by that fucker. For the first week, I could barely use my arm. Other times, I wondered if entire days had passed without me ever truly waking. The boredom between visits was crippling.

"Back again so soon," I said without looking up. I'd heard that telltale shuffle of poorly concealed footsteps. Looked like it was a visiting day after all.

"Did you miss me?" A crooked grin peeked in.

"Do you want me to have?"

The door clicked, and my visitor—no longer a stranger—entered, closing the cell behind him. It might have been intimidating, except this same thing had happened half a dozen times already. I raked my eyes over him. It was strange having my body react this way to one of my captors. We'd been locked in this dance, neither saying too much, and both saying too little.

"How's the food been?"

"Delightful." It actually wasn't bad. Mostly oats and fruits, but sometimes a vegetable stew with a hunk of day-old bread. It was better food than I'd had in the camps, that was for sure.

"It could all be over soon. Let's start with a name, shall we?"

I smirked. "You can call me whatever you like."

"I was hoping you'd say that, Starling."

I froze, the blood draining from my face. "What did you say?"

"Don't like it? I thought it suited you—glossy black locks, a darling face, lips begging to sing for me."

I studied his face for a moment longer, then looked away. It was just a coincidence. "S'pose I have to make up a name for you now, don't I?"

"I'm always game for a trade. You'll find I love to reciprocate."

I chuckled and shifted on the cot. My ass protested, but I didn't get up. The blanket was rougher than I was used to, and the mattress was too firm, but it was the only place to sit. I'd already gone through my daily exercises from the king's militia—twice. There was nothing left to do but sit. Except now it was a visiting day, so maybe things were turning up.

"Okay, Starling, how about you give me a hint of where you're from? Inra, yes?"

I nodded. That part was obvious enough.

"You weren't that far from Cavendaffe when we found you."

"When you murdered my companions?"

He frowned. "I think you'll find I did no such thing. Did you grow up there?"

I laced my hands behind my head and leaned back. "I'm a man of the world."

"Tut, tut. All you need to do is give me a little bit, and I can show you what it's like to be someone's world."

"Never trust a flirt." I flashed a smirk.

My captor's smile went stale, then slid off his face. "Is that what you think is happening here?"

I sat up. "No. Bad joke."

"The only reason you haven't been dropped to the bottom of the sea is because *I* advocate for you."

"Not that I'm not grateful," I said, crossing my arms and leaning back, "but why would you do that?"

My captor swallowed, and I tracked the movement of his Adam's apple. "I won't be able to much longer. Dane's getting restless. It's time you did yourself a favor and gave me something."

I sighed and ran a hand through my tangled black hair. It was longer than I liked it and kept falling in my face. "My name doesn't matter. There's nothing I know that would do you any good."

My captor sighed. He crossed the cell and plopped down on the cot right next to me, our thighs touching.

"That's not how this works. You can't tell me you're useless. If I tell that to Dane, he'll order your death. You have to give me something with a glimmer of hope, so that there's a point to keeping you alive."

"Other than basic human decency?"

"Obviously. This is war."

"I am from Cavendaffe, but I doubt many there miss me."

My captor nodded. "Excellent. Were you headed there when we found you?"

"I'm not sure."

He placed a hand on my thigh and squeezed. "Come on. Give me just a little more."

I shook my head. "No good. I can't remember."

"Really?" He cocked his blond head to the side.

I didn't know why I offered up this truth. "I remember being in the militia. I remember we were headed for a death trap. I remember waking up at the camp with"—something in my chest spasmed—"a few others. You might remember their fate."

His hand traced up and down my thigh. Maybe it was meant to be comforting, but all it did was set my blood on fire. Heat pooled inside me, and it was exactly what I needed. I rested my head back against the wall. "Keep doing that, and maybe I'll start having more to say."

"Is that all it would take? Because for you, I'd do a whole lot more just for fun. But if you're willing to give me something for it, all the better."

I huffed out a laugh. "Exchange information for sex?"

"I wouldn't put it that way."

I held my silence. Fuck, I wished I weren't actually considering it. But I was. Creator, I was. This man boiled my blood in all the wrong ways.

"Don't you see, Starling? We're the same, you and I. Wings clipped, and so few options left to take." His hand began to wander, but I stood, stopping its dangerous path.

"You're no starling with wings to clip. You're a drake, prowling the lands and ready to devour the world." I crossed the room, putting distance between us.

My captor—my drake—stood and paced toward me, but I backed away a step. Then another, and another. The smile my drake wore grew predatory. "I can think of a few things I'd like to devour right now."

My back hit the stone wall, and my drake boxed me in.

Outside the cell, a new pair of boots echoed down the corridor.

"Maybe I'm not ready to take this deal of yours, Drake." I kept my voice low and steady despite my pounding heart.

"Drake?" A single eyebrow raised, and his piercing blue eyes intensified. "I like the sound of that." Drake leaned in and whispered, "And if that's the case, Starling, I think you'll find I can be very persuasive." Then, he traced his tongue along the shell of my ear.

The footsteps receded, and Drake pushed off the wall, heading for the door.

Alone and locked in again, I frowned. As much as I wanted to accept this deal, how could I? I spent hours each day trying to remember how I got from one place to the next, but there was nothing there in my mind besides an adamant wall. With my thoughts, I wailed upon it, dug into it, and tried to clamber around it, but it was no use. The wall never budged. Nonetheless, I hurled myself against it. At this point, it was my only way to pass the time.

It would be a long and lonely wait until Drake came back.

ELDRETH

MID-AUTUMN, BASMON 1036

ONLY TWO SHIPS were tracking the coastline, but that was two ships too many. And these were not the first. I stood at the top of the lookout tower with Yaego at my side. My idiot brother had rushed out to sea for no reason. Something was addling his brains, and I meant to figure out what. Not that I didn't understand the complete lack of impulse control. There was a particular pair of blue-green eyes that far too easily distracted me.

"There," Yaego said, drawing me from my reverie.

I checked the mounted spyglass, and sure enough, the colors of Inra and Cavendaffe were visible through the windows of the captain's cabin. They may not be flying colors, but they were doing a piss-poor job of maintaining secrecy. Or, they didn't take the threat of the Riht seriously. That thought made me smirk. Drakh hadn't been invaded since before my grandmother's grandmother's day. We were too well fortified, and that was without considering the Great Dragon's blessings.

"I have to report this back to Dane." I stepped back from the spyglass, and Yaego took my place.

"What were the orders?"

"No ships leave our waters in one piece."

She nodded. "Your brother will see to it, I'm sure."

I scoffed. "I have no doubt. The order was passed to all our ships, just in case."

I gripped her forearm in farewell. It was time to get back. There was no need for both sons of Auldren to be chasing down a couple of rogue crafts, even if it was the first time they had dared approach our ports in years. I leapt down the ladder, then down the winding staircase, and back out onto the streets of Port Drakha. Now, I just needed a horse.

"Eldreth, wait!" a voice called out.

Turning, I saw Branye rushing my way.

"Your brother. He didn't take the full crew. He ordered the ship to depart before everyone had made it to the docks."

I cursed his brashness a dozen ways in my head, but aloud, I only said, "Of course, he didn't."

"What do we do?"

I pivoted, heading for the docks, where a crowd gathered, talking loudly over one another. "Get Marr Longven," I commanded the first warrior I found.

"The sea master?" Branye asked.

I nodded. "We need another ship."

The warrior took off running with the order, while around me, the suggestions and opinions started to fly. The waves crashed against the rocks beneath the dock. A gull cried overhead. I pushed it all aside and focused on the salty air. It was fresh from the recent rains, free of the tang that often hung about the rocks and wood. I looked down at my boots and allowed my mind to blank. My heart rate slowed. I breathed deeply. When I looked up again, my mind was set.

"Del, my lad."

I turned to the leathery skin and bald head of the exact man I needed and smiled. He was broad-chested with arms like ropes, a bit too much weight around the middle, and a mustache so wide and white that he looked more walrus than man.

"You know I hate that nickname." I gripped the older man's forearm.

"Why do you think I use it?" Longven winked. "I've got the *Helgana* making her way around the bend now. She was over at the interlock getting a good scrape down, but she's ready for seafaring."

"My thanks, Marr."

"It's just Longven to you."

I smirked. "I know."

Longven chuckled and clapped my back. "I haven't been up to the keep in a while. How are you faring?"

"Well enough."

"That father of yours not giving you too much trouble?"

"No more than usual." I nodded. Longven was as loyal as he was astute, and I appreciated his separation of the man—my father—from the clan leader.

"And this girl he's cooked up for you?"

Serae. Things with her were...I shrugged.

Longven nodded, then turned to the eastern coast. "That'll be her, just rounding the bend."

I followed his gaze and could barely make out a pinprick in the distance.

"She's fast and light. We'll catch them up in no time." He brushed a hand down his mustache. "I'll go get these whelps assembled."

Before the hour was out, I found myself perched at the prow of the *Helgana,* speeding south through the fading light. Longven let out two birds, one southeast and one southwest. This was an odd choice. Anything going to or from Cavendaffe would be due south of Drakh, exactly where the ship Yaego had spotted was headed before it left visibility. Longven only tapped the side of his nose and nodded at my questioning look. *You'll see*, he mouthed at me.

We sped along, and the wind whipped at my face. Thankfully, I had the presence of mind to tightly braid my hair and switch to sea leathers, which were lighter weight and water-wicking, in my rush to depart.

Longven joined me at the prow and frowned. "The seas are too calm."

"Oil?" I asked.

"Oil."

"Fuck." We only cast oil to the sea when we needed to calm the waves. Controlling the water meant the others expected to be outmatched.

"Ready yourself. We're in for a fight."

One of the birds screeched and dove for Longven, landing on his outstretched forearm. "Southeast," he said grimly, then he shouted down the ranks to change course.

I frowned. Southeast made no sense. Perhaps I'd seen wrong, and it wasn't Cavendaffe colors. Some sort of ruse? I scratched my jaw, a healthy stubble growing. The crafts weren't Volaachi, of that much I was certain. The clouds shifted, and a ray of moonlight peeked through, illuminating the mist that hung over these waters. As our ship turned, we saw them. Three vessels emerged portside. One unmistakable Drakhi craft, which I knew bore my brother. The other two ships we'd sent out were nowhere in sight. Instead, the remaining two crafts barely ahead of my brother's were distinctly Inraen, and distinctly hostile.

"They've engaged!" a woman shouted down from the nest.

The longship's crews hurtled into action. Longven tossed out commands to each crew, who leapt as units to obey. Lines were pulled, sails were shifted, and the *Helgana* flew over the waves like one of the captain's hawks. We closed in, and clanging rang out across the narrowing expanse. Arrows thunked into wood and flesh, and two Inraen men fell into the sea.

Plucking a longbow from the ranks, I hooked it into a notch at the prow, along with a dozen other archers, and readied my arrow. I braced, waiting for their ship to come into range. They'd left lanterns hanging all along their decks, lighting up targets for us. Behind me, crews lined up with planks and rope ladders, and behind them were crews with spears and javelins.

"STEADY," Longven shouted from behind. One of his birds took flight, likely sent off to Drakh with a message. His second hawk—recently returned fruitless from scouting to the southwest—was resting in the nest with the lookout. She would be sent back with the result of the battle. A note indicating our failure was likely already tied to her leg. It would be swapped only after a success, allowing the bird to fly off with bad news even if every one of us died.

I forced the heavy thought from my mind. Just another necessity of warfare. Less than ten seconds until we would be in range, by my count. The people on the ships were becoming clearer.

"Fuck!" the woman next to me shouted. "They're overrun!" Her name was Anweh, and I knew her as a superb markswoman with a sharp eye. I had helped with her training but had never fought alongside her before.

My sight told me we were seven seconds out of range. I set my jaw. There was too much Inraen red on the Drakhi ship's deck.

Six. "NOCK," I shouted.

Five. The archers around me steadied their shots.

Four. "STEADY AIM."

Three. I picked my target on the nearest Inraen ship.

Two. I breathed in.

One.

"RELEASE."

At the bottom of my exhale, I let the arrow fly. A dozen arrows followed in a death arc through the sky. A cloud shifted overhead, casting us into shadow.

Thud! Thud! Thud!

Half the arrows hit their marks. The other half tore through sails, impaled wood, or fell harmlessly to the black sea. We readied another volley.

Behind me, the bridge unit moved starboard, readying their planks to connect to our Drakhi counterpart.

Longven shouted instructions from midship. "We bridge and free our sister ship. Archers, get ready to shift to short bows. Shields, ready your cover. Once the *Calanya* is recovered, we take the near ship."

The plan was sound, but I knew the risk without it being voiced. There was every chance the second Inraen ship might turn and flee before we could wrangle it. If that happened, we would have to run it down and sink it. It was a problem to worry about later.

"RELEASE," I called. The second volley flew. The fact that no arrows yet flew our way was a good sign. Aside from Inraen bows having shit range, my brother's ship was keeping them occupied. At least he was good for something.

The shield captain behind me shouted, "READY THE SWITCH." A man crouched at my left, ready to help de-notch and remove the longbow. Men and women crouched beside each archer down the line, doing the same.

"LIFT THE PLANKS," Longven's second shouted. The man himself was named Plankh, a coincidence that would make Serae laugh when I told her. Dragons, I needed to get back to her every bit as much as I itched to be a part of the boarding crew. But they had no archer captain on the *Helgana*. The regular woman for this crew took ill earlier in the week, so I would better serve the crew filling the vacancy. Unlike my brother, I didn't have to always be front and center with the action.

"RELEASE," I called for the final time.

"SWITCH," the shield captain's command followed. In pairs, we heaved aside the longbows then snatched up short bows and shields. The shield crew stayed crouched at our sides, ready to pop up to block arrows and spears or to engage from behind if we were boarded, all without interrupting the archer's flow.

"ON YOUR OWN TIME," I commanded. The archers loosed in a steady flow, despite the risk of firing at night. "Starboard, shift to the *Calanya*." I had enough faith in the archers' skills and training that they could avoid our own warriors at this range. Each one should know a safe shot from a risky one.

I looked to the enemy ship. At this range, there was no mistaking them. Every man—these idiots refused to train women in their militia—was wearing Inraen red with an obvious Cavendaffe sash marking his allegiance. I ground my teeth, but only for a moment. I needed to relax into my flow to be of any real use.

Nock. Target. Breathe. Release.

My first arrow plunged through the eye of an Inraen soldier.

Nock. Target. Breathe. Release.

My second tore through the leg of a man and thudded into the deck behind him.

The portside crew was firing next to me with devastating accuracy. The starboard, less so. The *Calanya's* deck had become so entangled that it was impossible to pick safe targets without compromising our own.

"Aim for the far ship," I called down the line. "Anything you can get in your sights."

Cries of men and women alike rang out from the *Calanya*. Metal clashed. We needed to move faster, but it was essential to slow to a crawl if we wanted to perform a successful bridge. Longven was an expert, having practically invented the maneuver. *Almost there.*

I fired two more shots, both missing their marks, and I cursed.

Crash!

The planks had fallen. One by one, I heard the latch mechanisms click into place.

"SECURE," Plankh shouted. Then, "BOARDING CREW, AS ONE!" as boots thundered over the makeshift bridge lashing the two ships together.

I turned as the man beside me jumped to his feet, covering my back with a broad shield. I needed to lay eyes on my brother. The longship was organized chaos of red and brown. Midship, I could pick out one woman fighting off two of Cavendaffe's men at once. She spun, whipping her blades around, but it was a risky move that left her side open. The soldier saw it. He thrust, and I turned away as she fell. Our warriors were flooding midship and would minimize casualties in seconds.

A volley from the far ship was released. Cavendaffe's captain must not care if they struck Inraen or Riht. I watched a dozen men and women fall, more than half of them Inraen.

I nocked an arrow. The Cavendaffe captain was in sight. He was tall and dark-haired, and even from a distance, I could see the man's self-confident smirk. I'd have to change that.

Steady aim. Beside me, the other archers saw the same and adjusted their sights. When the far Inraen ship moved close enough to release their volley on the *Calanya*, they hadn't realized it brought them in range of the *Helgana*, whose archers all had longer range and better aim than any Inraen could hope to achieve. Our advantage came from the wood we used, which only grew in the Riht.

Release.

Fuck. My first shot missed. I was quick to draw a second, which embedded itself into the captain's shoulder. Of the rest of my crew, only half of their arrows reached the deck, but it was enough to disrupt their archers.

Arrows thudded all around me, and the shield crew popped up and down, deflecting the blows. *Fuck, fuck, fuck.* I'd lost my focus on the nearest ship. They'd reformed ranks enough to line up their archers.

I needed to rally our forces back to the nearest threat. "As ONE TO THE—"

"AAAHHH!"

The scream beside me curdled my blood. Anweh's shieldsman was dead at her feet, an arrow to the heart. A second arrow plunged clean through her thigh. "Cover," I cried to my shield and dropped to my knees. The shield came up, covering us both. I ripped a strip off my tunic and wrapped a makeshift tourniquet above the shot through Anweh's thigh. Little blood flowed from the wound—a good sign. Her femoral artery was likely intact. "Keep her covered," I commanded my shield. I glanced at the body of her fallen shieldsman beside us. I knew him, but not well. He had a wife and twin toddlers, plus an elderly mother he cared for. I made a note in the back of my mind to solicit Dane's aid for his family when we returned home.

"As ONE TO THE NEAREST SHIP," I called down the rank.

The shieldswoman to my right repositioned herself between me and the archer next to me, popping up to provide cover for us both. At the end of the row, a woman screamed and fell to the deck. I didn't spare a moment to see if she was alive. We were already two archers down. A runner came up behind me swapping my quiver and continuing down the line swapping others. My eyes burned from the spraying sea mist. An arrow slipped past the reach of my shieldswoman, grazing my left shoulder.

"Fuck, sorry!" she shouted.

"I'm good," I assured her. It was shallow and stung but didn't impair my movement. I nocked another arrow as my eyes narrowed on my next target. The captain on the nearest ship had just emerged from the hull.

"Captain on deck!" someone bellowed.

"Bring him down!"

Eight arrows released toward the man. They pelted into and around him, killing him before he could react. The men on deck went berserk. Some jumped to the sea, swimming for the far ship. Some swung on ropes, aiming for the *Calanya*. Some fled below deck. Then, the sails shifted.

I turned to a runner taking cover nearby. "Get a message to Longven. The near ship readies to flee." She took off, keeping her head ducked and following the relative cover of the siding.

Within a minute, Longven was shouting new commands, echoed by Plankh on the *Calanya*. I still hadn't spotted my brother. He better not have gotten himself killed after all the effort I put into retrieving his ass less than three months ago.

Our sails shifted in tandem with the *Calanya's*. Now one synchronized craft, our joined longships moved. Together, we could take down a craft by ramming it head-on, or we could drop the bridge last second and sandwich it. Sinking a craft was never the preferred option. If I knew Longven, he would try to capture first. The role of the archers was about to switch to providing cover. My skills were best suited elsewhere.

"Go." Anweh gripped my pant leg from her position against the back railing of the prow. "My voice works as well as yours. I've got this."

I tensed and shifted my weight, regarding Anweh. She'd snapped off the head and tail of the arrow, leaving only the shaft bisecting her thigh.

"You know I'm right. Go!" she repeated. Then, she pulled herself onto a crate just high enough to peek over the siding by the stempost. She ducked back down and turned to the line. "Get ready for cover volleys!" she shouted.

I dropped my quiver at her feet, gripped her forearm, and said formally, "You command the lead." Then, I took off. I leapt across the benches to mid-deck two at a time. Longven was at the center of his crew on the keelson, and I pushed my way through to meet him.

"Raise the planks," he called out.

Men and women worked in unison heaving the ropes, separating the two Riht ships. Another crew was readying hooked leads to lash all three ships together after the Cavendaffe carrack was surrounded.

A large hand gripped my shoulder. "You'd better earn that nickname of yours if you ever want me to use it. Once the bridge drops, you command the lead from this side. Plankh will mirror you from the *Calanya*."

I nodded and gripped Longven's forearm. "Have you seen him?"

Longven shook his head, then bellowed, "BEGIN THE DROP."

We were already level with the Inraen ship, and the planks of the bridge were acting as a shield for the pathetic remnants of their opponent's archery squad. I unsheathed my twin swords and brought myself to stillness.

Inhale.

Exhale.

The planks dropped, and one by one, I heard the satisfying clicks of their locking mechanisms.

"TIE THE LASHINGS," Longven yelled.

"WARRIORS WITH ME," I shouted, but they were already in formation behind me. I grinned and charged.

An Inraen soldier tried to meet my charge. One swipe of my sword cut the man down. I dodged the next soldier, who was impaled by the warrior behind me. Steel rang out as I parried the next man's wild swing with my left and stabbed him in the side with my right. These were not trained men. A uniform didn't teach you to fight.

"FAN OUT, TAKE CONTROL."

My warriors moved on command, spreading over the ship like a blight. We cleared straight across the deck before the *Calanya's* bridge crew was set up.

"BEGIN THE DROP," Plankh called out from the deck of our other ship. In moments, my warriors would double.

"CLEAR THE WAY. PUSH!" The death shouts of the Inraen were so loud that I could barely hear my command.

A double line of Riht warriors cleared a path down the center, bisecting the ship and making room for more to fill in between. Forming two ranks, we pushed in opposite directions, forcing the Inraen soldiers outward toward their bow and stern, leaving the midship clear in our wake. More thuds and clicks sounded as the second bridge latched, and a new flood of Riht warriors appeared at our backs right on cue.

"Find any commanders and take them down," I told the warriors nearest me.

"That won't be necessary," a familiar voice called from behind. I turned to my brother, who was swaggering from the captain's quarters. In one hand, he gripped a man by his scruff with his arms bound behind his back. His other hand was holding a dagger at the commander's throat. "All Inraen weapons down, if you please."

A few clanged to the deck, but most of the soldiers had stilled. They were waiting for a command.

"Kill them a—" The commander's last words were cut off by a sick gurgling sound as the knife plunged into his throat. A river of blood spilled down his red uniform.

"None of that," my brother growled as the captain's body slumped to the deck.

"You're an idiot," I said by way of greeting. I turned back to my warriors to help with the real work.

It took the better part of an hour to clear the ship, toss the survivors overboard with their lifeboats, and get the clunky Inraen vessel ready to return to Port Drakha. I sent their highest-ranking officer with a note to his margrave that any further scouting or attacks would be considered open hostilities. I'd let Dane follow with the consequences of those actions as he saw fit. With everyone's help, the Inraen carrack was the first off, followed closely by the *Helgana*. Plankh and I stood side by side at the prow, monitoring the captured ship for any sign of trouble. The *Calanya* took the longest to ready, but it finally pointed northwest back towards Port Drakha.

After a quarter hour, I looked back and frowned. "They're not keeping pace."

Plankh studied our wake, then groaned. "Prayers to the Great Dragon that it's just because your brother's being a pain in the ass."

I chuckled and turned forward while my thoughts turned to Cavendaffe. Why the scouts if they'd brokered for peace that the Riht was upholding? Why offer up a treaty through marriage if they didn't intend to keep it? There was Gerta to consider, already returned to Cavendaffe, and then Serae herself. I had a hard time believing either could be the cause of this. There was one more Inraen in our midst. Perhaps there was more to that prisoner than we knew, but even then, why not just write requesting his return?

Yes, there was a lot to discuss with Dane.

CHAPTER 25

"Patriol, why?"

He coughed, and blood trickled out the side of his mouth.

I kicked off my shoes and dug my toes into the dirt, cradling his head. He coughed again, weak, raspy, and far too wet. I added lungs to the catalog of his injuries after the head and leg wounds. I reached for my connection, and her power flooded me. The tips of my fingers glowed white hot.

"This is going to hurt." Gripping Patriol's head, I began to push.

—Recounting from the private diary of Jerris, Dragonbound

SERAE

MID-AUTUMN, BASMON 1036

SERAE... SERAE...

"Fuck, SERAE?"

Someone gripped my shoulders.

"Shit, shit, *shit*, something's wrong."

A hawk screeched overhead.

"Wake up. Please, wake up."

He shook me—hard—jostling me from my reverie.

I opened my eyes. Gray-blue steel. It was the sky just before the storm came in.

"Thank the Great-fucking-Dragon. What happened?"

"It's you," I gasped. My voice was weak and cracked. "You're back?"

"Yes, I'm back. What the hell are you doing here?"

Here? I looked around. I was in a garden. No, that wasn't right. I was supposed to be inside. We needed to get indoors to clean off the blood.

Blood.

"Wep!" I shrieked. He was covered in it. "You're hurt!" There was blood caked to his tunic and flaking off his leathers, but I couldn't see where it was coming from. It was his head, right? And leg, and lungs... No, I had healed those wounds. This was from something else. I gripped his wrist, wrenched off his bracer, and shoved up his sleeve. The skin on his forearm was mottled with red scarring beneath streaks of blood. I couldn't discern the old injuries from the new.

"What are you—"

My magic unleashed. My hands scorched, and Wep let out a cry, but I gripped him firmly. Light—too intense—filled me. I grit my teeth as I fought through its searing agony, willing myself to stay conscious.

"Focus the light," Vaya'la instructed. *"Seek out the pain."*

I tunneled the light into Wep, pushing it through his body in search of anything that hurt. There was...*nothing.*

"Keep going."

I focused the light, using instinct to direct it toward his head and working my way down his neck, then shoulders. A slice of pain ripped along my skin, just below my shoulder, and I gasped.

"There. Direct your light. Let it heal the tissue, layer by layer."

"This is his pain?"

I didn't need her confirmation. As soon as I spoke the words in my mind, I knew. I guided the light to the center of the pain, willing it to restore him. I kept my focus until the last tiny ache faded away.

"Well done, Small One." Vaya'la's pride filled me. *"You controlled it by instinct. Now, let go."*

It took me several moments to piece myself back together. I was sitting in the grass, my back resting against the sacred tree. There was no danger; it had all been part of my latest dream. Jerris' brother had the injuries, not Wep.

Everything was fine. Wep had returned in one piece and—

"Why are you out here?"

I blinked furiously, eyelids scraping over dry eyes. "Welcome back to you, too." My voice was hoarse. "What time is it?"

"Never mind the time. Why aren't you inside?"

The sun was well past its zenith. Had I been out here all night and day? "I must've fallen asleep." My stomach rumbled. I licked my lips, which were also dry. My throat was rough and parched. As out of sorts as I felt, though, Wep looked far worse. It was the first time I'd seen him in disarray like this. Aside from the blood, which I'd gathered wasn't his, his tunic was ripped across the bottom and at the shoulder. His braid was coming unwound in places, and he smelled like salt and iron. "You need to get yourself cleaned up."

His laugh was mirthless and a touch wild. He was crouching in front of me, and one hand still gripped my shoulder. "You know your *ranng* is losing their shit inside? What in the name of all the Dragons of Jaeda are you doing out here instead of behind the fortified walls of the keep?"

"This is just the garden. I didn't leave the castle walls." Plus, Vaya'la approved of this spot, but I wasn't about to tell him that.

"Only the keep has blessing-fortified stone."

"Well, I have a sacred tree."

He looked up, and shock splashed across his face. It was a look I'd like to hold onto forever—confusion, bewilderment, and wonder all rolled into one.

Sprakt chose that moment to glide out of the tree and straight for Wep's face. His hand dropped from my shoulder with a jolt, and he flung himself to the side. Sprakt soared right through the space his head had just occupied. From the ground, Wep stared after the sparrowhawk in bewilderment. A laugh bubbled up from down deep that I couldn't keep in. This was so at odds with the collected, controlled weaponmaster I'd come to know. I liked him a little bit undone.

Wep's eyes returned to me, and the confusion stripped away to something intense. "His wings. They regrew?"

Sprakt hopped around in the grass. "I—"

"Get inside."

We both jumped and turned to Dane, striding across the gardens with heavy footfalls. His eyes blazed, and my second sight revealed lemon yellow *reverence* beneath. I looked up at the tree.

"Vaya'la, what makes this tree sacred?"

"I grew this tree for my last Bound, imbuing it with everlasting peace, so he

might rest free from the torment of his nightmares."

"For Jerris?" Aside from the one I'd just woken from, I'd been sharing her dreams of him for months. I marveled at the thought—a tree lasting through so many centuries.

"Give her a minute," Wep said, returning his attention to me. "She's weak from—"

"Serae is not weak. She is the savior of our time, the natural ruler of the Riht, and Blessed Bound of the Great Dragon herself. Compromising her safety will not be tolerated, even from herself."

I didn't have time to reflect as my insides welled up with...was it pride? No, it was satisfaction, and it wasn't mine. I knew I was no savior, and I certainly wasn't blessed, but I was bound to Vaya'la.

"He's pledged himself to us," Vaya'la answered my unasked question.

"Since when?"

"Since we demanded it of him."

"I don't remember that."

"It was early days. Your mind is better suited to our binding now and can remember all that we do."

That *we* do? *"Have you...done other things through me? Besides this with Dane?"*

"Peace, Small One."

We were going to have to talk about this little revelation later. In the meantime, both men were looking at me—one with awe, one with disbelief.

Wep spoke first. "How long have you known?"

He was looking at me, but the question was meant for Dane. Yet, as he scanned my face, he must've found enough of an answer there. He rounded on Dane. "How long have you known?" His tone sharpened, low and accusing.

Every muscle in my body sprang to alert.

Dane nodded. "You've seen her blessings. Have you not just witnessed her healing light? There's no denying it."

"When?" It sounded like the word pained him.

"The Great Dragon spoke to me, demanding the fealty of the Riht."

"WHEN?" Wep closed his eyes, and the muscles in his jaw clenched. Fuck, his jawline was inconveniently perfect, even when covered in blood. "When did this happen?" he repeated steadily.

Something in Dane's tone shifted. "Are you questioning your dane?"

Wep rose to his feet, turning to face his father and putting his back to me. "You told me you suspected, not that the Great Dragon spoke through her. You knew even then?"

"Everything I told you—"

"You forced her into combat against monsters, needlessly testing her. You commanded me to work with her to suss out more blessings, claiming you had suspicions and questions." His voice was rising. "Now, you tell me you've known all along that she was Bound. That you'd already pledged yourself to her. That's a far cry from what you led me to believe. How long have you known? Weeks? Months?"

"You go too far."

My second sight opened fully. Dane's lifelight shifted from white to orange to red, but Wep's shining silver light exploded around me. I threw a hand over my eyes, but his brilliance brought no pain.

"Too far?" Wep's voice dropped. The ice in his tone sent a chill up my spine. "I don't give a fuck what you think she is or isn't. Or what it means for the Riht. She's not a pawn in your games."

"Calm yourself, Son."

"No. You don't get to do your posturing and maneuvering with me, and you *never* get to do it with her. Are we clear?"

Dane set his jaw, but Wep would not back down.

"Are. We. Clear?" The lifelight around him darkened to a deep mauve. *Disgust.*

Dane's lifelight simmered down to a dull scarlet streaked with juniper. *Anger* was stamped across his face, but he was also feeling...*pride.* When he spoke, however, his voice held a note of malice. "Last I checked, I was still high dane of the Riht, not you."

A white-hot lance of pain shot through my head. I gripped my temples, gasping for air and fighting through it. Waves of furious, burning heat assaulted my senses.

Wep's head whipped to me, scowl lines still etched into his face. Then, they softened, leaving him with only deep weariness in their wake.

"Close the connection, Small One. You have not fully let go."

"This is his pain?"

"Just a headache. Let go."

With effort, I pulled the last strands of light back. The connection was so instinctual, I hadn't noticed any lingered. When the last one slipped away, the pain vanished.

"Can you stand?" he asked, his voice a quiet rumble. He was before me in a single step, crouching down to match my eye level. His lifelight calmed to a tumbling storm cloud of silver.

I nodded and took his outstretched hands. He lifted me to my feet easily and placed a steadying arm around my waist. "Come on, let's get you cleaned up and fed."

"I might say the same to you."

His lip twitched, and I mentally marked another point to me.

We passed Dane, who stood with arms crossed and eyes locked on his son. "Where's your brother?" he asked.

Wep's grip tightened around my waist. "I'm not his keeper."

"He hasn't returned to port."

At that, I turned. "Ell was sent out?"

"Aye, Daughter. He was with me when the messenger arrived."

Something about that tugged at me, but I couldn't place what. With a gentle nudge, I allowed Wep to guide me back into the keep. I tried very hard not to dwell on the fact that all my fears were wrapped up with the man at my side, while not a single thought had crossed my mind for my betrothed.

BACK IN MY rooms, I sat in my bath long after the water turned frigid. My mind was completely blank.

"It's time, Small One."

"I can't do it, Vaya'la. I can't. I'm supposed to learn to trust Eldreth, not Wep."

"He is ready to know the whole truth. The time is near when it will be evident to all. This is as it should be."

I abandoned the cold tub. Callagh, seeing how weak and shaken I was, helped me into a soft cream underdress, far thicker than the light fabrics I'd grown accustomed to.

"I got you something special on my way in today before all the commotion."

A pang of true regret pinched my brow. I squeezed her arm. "I'm sorry to have worried you."

She shrugged. Her eyes shone with light as she pulled a thick lavender coat out of my wardrobe. It was plush, soft, and long...and completely impractical. A coat like that would be filthy in seconds and useless against the frequent autumn rains. Still, I loved it. I slipped into it like a dream, and Callagh closed the fasteners down the front.

"It's a robe," she explained, admiring the finished product on me. "An indoor coat."

"Ohh. It's heaven." I was familiar with Inraen dressing robes, worn loose and open at the front. This hugged my body like the softest blanket without being restrictive. Forget Wep, forget Eldreth, I was in love with this coat.

"I set your tray in the sitting room next door. Wep has asked you to join him."

"Have you heard anything more of Ell?" I don't know why his absence bothered me, but it did. Anxiety flashed through me, dissipating just as quickly.

"He's not yet returned. You won't be interrupted." A smile tugged at the corners of her mouth.

I narrowed my eyes at her. "What are you suggesting?"

She grinned. "Nothing. Is there something on your mind?"

I still wore my scowl as Callagh led me to the sitting room. It was the door immediately next to mine, and yet, it had never been opened to me before.

I pushed inside and gasped at its magnificence. Two gorgeous couches faced each other and were capped by four large chairs, two on either end. The set was astonishingly carved with graceful lines and a faint imprint of dragon scales. The cushions were as thick and plush as those of the Relaxation Room, and the chairs and couches were each stacked with pillows. The entire room was a mix of deep, rich green and dark, rusty red from the tapestries on the walls to the coverings on the ottomans. Even the rug sprawling across the center of the room was shaped into two mirrored dragons, one in red and one in green. There were accents of gold and cream scattered throughout. How could I only just be seeing this room?

"You humans are easily distracted."

"And you dragons are surly busybodies."

Vaya'la chuffed as I turned to Callagh. "It's Midwinter Day every day."

She chuckled. "I think it's meant to be symbolic."

"Of me and Eldreth." The realization dropped on me with the weight of a boulder as I stepped through the threshold.

The more I looked at the room, the more astonished I became. There were golden sconces on the walls and matching golden candelabras scattering the room—though none were lit yet, given the afternoon light. Above the mantel was a piece of metalwork art that resembled dragon wings arranged like the petals of a rose. A long, stone bench jutted out from the hearth, and it was so highly polished that light from the crackling fire reflected off it.

The door opened, calling my attention. Wep entered wearing a thick tunic that exactly matched the forest green of the tapestries with heather gray pants. He scanned the room, and his eyes crinkled when they rested on me. His hair was damp and loose, and a small pouch on a long leather cord hung around his neck.

"Cold?" he asked.

"Not anymore. Is Drakh still under threat?"

"No. One ship escaped, but we captured the other. Port Drakha will remain on alert, but we're safe for now."

"Oh, good." I didn't have the heart to ask if the ships were Volaachi or Inraen.

His head turned to a waist-high table that stretched out along the wall opposite the hearth. "Excellent," he muttered and went straight for the trays atop it. He opened the first lid and barked out a laugh. "I think this one's for you." He replaced the lid and went to the next tray. Whatever was inside suited him. He scooped it up, brought it to the couch facing the doorway, plopped down, and began eating. *Inhaling* was a better word for it. He took bites a size I didn't even know was possible to fit in a human mouth. It was some sort of stew and flatbread with a side of greens and berries.

"Hungry?" I asked.

He grunted, not stopping long enough to form a single word. I was amazed it all made it into his mouth rather than the floor, the couch, his lap, maybe even the ceiling.

I wanted to laugh, but my stomach growled, reminding me that I hadn't yet eaten for...

"How long was I out there?"

"As long as we needed," Vaya'la replied. *"Less than a full day in the Mortal Realm."*

I sucked in a breath. No wonder Wep had panicked when he found me. How long had Callagh and my *ranng* been searching?

I collected my tray and moved to the opposite couch. My mouth watered as I lifted the lid. *Babi.* There were six small buns lined up, two topped with rosemary and salt flakes, two that had been rolled in seeds before baking, and two with a chocolate drizzle across the top. Each pair had a small bowl of dipping sauce beside it. They were so beautiful, I wanted to cry.

"I can leave if you two need time alone," Wep teased, eyes finally on me instead of his meal.

"That's up to you, but if you stay, I make no promises to be quiet."

His eyes darkened in a way that a less famished version of me would have appreciated. Instead, I pulled my legs up onto the couch, tucked my feet under a pillow beside me, and dug in. Wep returned to his tray, but I didn't miss the way his eyes kept flicking toward me.

When our bellies were full, and the trays were set aside, he poured us both a mug of honeymead, and we reclined on opposite couches.

"Where's the bird?"

I smacked my lips at the sweetness of the mead. "Out flying."

"With clipped wings?"

Oh, right. I discovered during my bath that his wings had made a miraculous growth spurt. It seemed my panicked healing episode earlier *had* affected someone, just not the someone I originally thought. "They grew back." I shrugged.

He sat up a bit straighter. "You?"

I nodded.

He ran a hand through his still-damp hair. "Can we...talk about your blessings?" He rested an arm over the back of the couch. Even here, in a room far different than his Training Hall, he looked at home. Then again, he had lived in this castle his whole life.

"I brought you this." I withdrew my green journal from a pocket in my robe and passed it across to him.

He set down his mug and cracked it open, flipping through several pages. "I can't read this."

"Sucks not speaking the right language, doesn't it?" A smirk stole across my face before I could stop it. Of course, I'd used my native tongue for my notes, but I'd also drawn some pictures I thought might help.

His lips pressed together, and his eyes darted up to me, then back to the page. "Your Rihtish is coming along well."

"What can I say? I have a gift."

"Fluency in a matter of months is a gift, to be sure."

"Well, I wouldn't say I was—" I cut off and gawked at him. I hadn't registered it, but our entire conversation was in Rihtish. It was as natural to me as speaking Inraen. How long ago had I switched?

"Is this your magic?" I asked Vaya'la.

"It is the knowledge of those who came before you, seeping through."

"But you speak Inraen."

Vaya'la laughed. *"No, Small One. I speak in the language of thoughts."*

"Another thing to add to your list?"

I nodded.

"A quarter of this is full. How much have you been keeping from me?"

I crossed my arms. "You don't have a claim on what I choose to tell you."

"It's a trust issue, then," he said neutrally. I opened my second sight, and he pulsed lightly with aquamarine. *Curiosity.* As always, his lifelight was more brilliant than any other I'd seen.

"It's not my trust you have to win—it's Vaya'la's," I lied.

Wep sucked in a breath, and my journal thudded to the floor. Every inch of his body stilled. His lifelight exploded with brilliant cyan. *Shock.*

"Don't worry, you have. I think she likes you."

His face went ashen. His lips parted, but otherwise, he was frozen.

I sat up, not sure what I'd said or done.

"He reveres me like the goddess I am, unlike you, petulant one."

"Don't be an ass."

"How easily you prove my point."

He still hadn't moved.

"Knock it off, you're scaring me."

Wep closed his mouth and swallowed. He leaned back and ran both hands through his hair. He sat forward again, bracing his elbows on his knees. Then, he stood and walked to the window behind his couch and leaned against the arched stone frame.

"Wep?" I rose and stood there, unsure what might help.

"I just need a minute."

I could do that. Except one minute in my head gave space for way too many thoughts. I could've filled the rest of the pages in my journal with the scenarios I ran through, each one more senseless than the last. I resorted to clenching my teeth to avoid disrupting his moment of peace.

Wep stood there, forearm against the windowsill, looking out over the forest. His breath was deep and measured. Despite reading him constantly, this time felt like a betrayal, but the temptation was too great. I focused on my second sight.

His lifelight was a rainbow. He flickered through emotions so fast, I could scarcely keep up—sadness, shame, guilt, rage, confusion, fear, pride, elation, desire, and back to fear. It was dizzying.

I shuttered my sight and turned myself inward. *Blackness seeped into the Violet Sea as I soared above. The land was already a blight—withered to ash and darkness. It was not burned, it was decayed. With a great breath, I unleashed my living flame upon the land.*

"You're Dragonbound."

His words snapped me back. The term stirred something in me, a connection I had not quite made—a kinship to the figures in the tapestry on the Relaxation Room walls. I was bound to Vaya'la, and because of that, I'd shared the dreams and knowledge of her previous Bound, but to think I was akin to these shapers of the world? A shiver ran down my spine. The task she'd given me, which I barely understood, carried a new weight.

"Tell him," Vaya'la prompted.

"But he already knows."

"He needs to hear it from you."

"Yes," I said simply. "I am."

He nodded. "Her name is Vaya'la. All this time, we thought her name was lost, but it's been right in front of us. I've heard a thousand songs about Veyhallah's halls."

My brows rose.

He shook his head once, and his eyes dropped to his boots. "Legend of where warriors go after death. Doesn't matter." He stood there for several more moments, hands in his pockets, leaning against the wall, before his eyes finally flicked up to me.

"You can heal," he said.

"I guess so."

"And talk to birds."

"No, not talk. I can just sort of...sense him."

The corners of his mouth turned downward. "The vines."

I nodded.

"And what else?"

I bit my lip. There was no reason for me to hesitate, but reason rarely played a part in the choices I made. At last, fiddling with the fasteners on my robe, I offered, "It might be easier if I show you."

Showing Wep, it turned out, was far more difficult than telling him. Having him as my audience when it was his opinion I cared about most was a brainless idea. I was able to produce absolutely nothing in the opulent sitting room. I cursed Vaya'la outright, but in return, she gave me only her patience.

"I think we need to go outside," I admitted with a sigh.

Wep eyed the fading light from the windows and nodded. He brought me to his alcove in the training yard. It was safer than risking the gardens again, especially with the attention we would draw sneaking out together. He kept his hands in his pockets and his thoughts to himself. He never moved from where he leaned against the eucalyptus tree, but the whole time, he looked at me like I was the center of the world.

I showed him the flowers and vines I could make. I showed him the life I could give to plants. I grew him a handful of cherries that he clutched to his chest before slipping them into his pocket. I even demonstrated healing on the tree since neither of us was wounded. He responded by slicing open his hand to give me something to practice on. The weight of his faith in me made me buckle.

When all was done, he thanked me for my trust and walked me to my door. He did not try to kiss me or touch me.

"Do you want to come in?" I asked. "We could probably both use another glass of mead."

His lips pressed together as he shook his head. "Not tonight," he said, but I heard the truth behind it. There was something final in his gaze, and it threatened to break me in two. Now that he knew the full extent of what I was, I doubted he would ever look at me the same again.

Behind the safety of my doors in my empty bed in an empty room, I cried. Not even Sprakt was there to temper my tears.

"He will always be beholden to you, Small One. Let that be enough."

At Vaya'la's words, I cried harder, wishing I could turn away from her, too, just for a moment, and be left to my tears in peace.

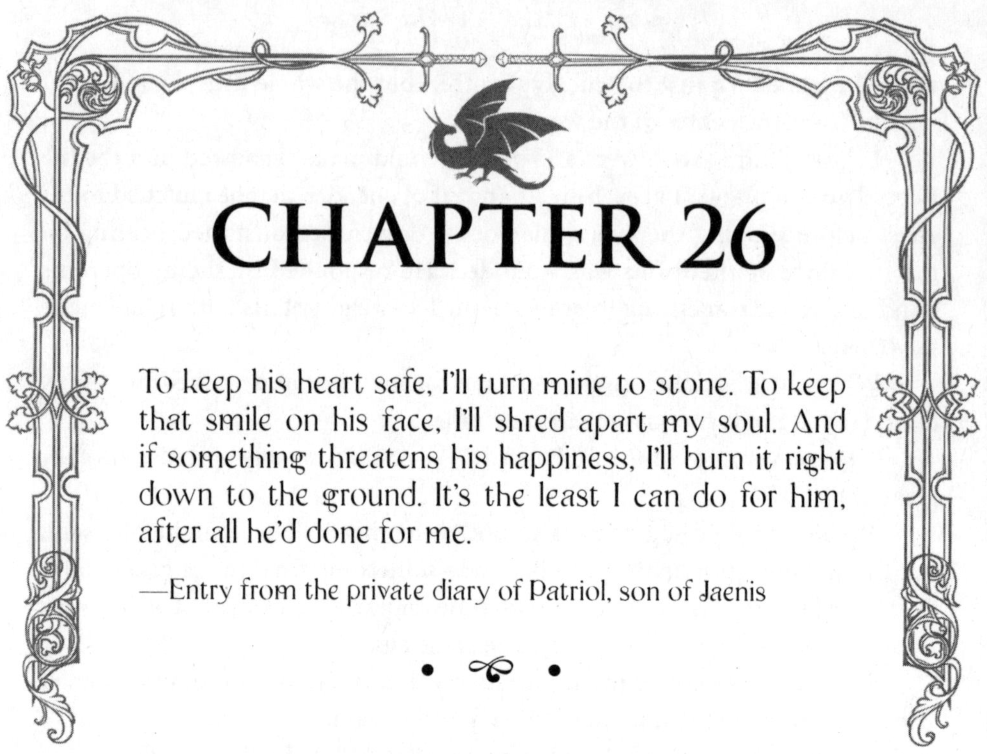

CHAPTER 26

To keep his heart safe, I'll turn mine to stone. To keep that smile on his face, I'll shred apart my soul. And if something threatens his happiness, I'll burn it right down to the ground. It's the least I can do for him, after all he'd done for me.

—Entry from the private diary of Patriol, son of Jaenis

STARLING

MID-AUTUMN, BASMON 1036

"BACK AGAIN SO soon?" I asked as Drake pushed his way into my cell. He had come last night, asking no questions, but claiming my body so thoroughly, I was still spent the following morning. Not that I was complaining. "I'm not sure I'm up to the task yet."

Drake chuckled. "As much as I love the idea, I'm not here for that."

"I was wondering when the questions would come." He struck this deal with me for a reason, and while I was enjoying the benefits of a body as stunning as his, I was already struggling with the blurred lines. As was my perpetual curse. Casual sex between men was all I could get in Inra, but my stupid heart wasn't built that way. Even Miloh—Creator keep his soul—was all too happy to share a bed but drew a hard line at friendship.

Drake dropped onto the cot beside me and threw his braids over one shoulder. "Maybe next time."

I turned to him, eyebrow raised. He stared straight ahead, eyes distant, distracted by whatever was going on in his mind.

"Hey,"—I nudged him with my knee—"what's up?"

"What do you want out of life?" He asked it absently, as if the topic were that night's dinner or my favorite shade of blue.

"Ah, yes, how my dreams abound from my barred window and door."

The corner of his lip quirked up. "I suppose I deserve that."

We lapsed into silence, but his hand found mine, lacing our fingers together. Something warm spread through my chest. My days were filled with silence. It was nice to have someone to share it with, for once.

"You seem like a man with dreams, Starling. I'm not sure I have any. The only part of my day I enjoy anymore is the time I spend down here."

"In the prison?"

He gave me a flat look. "No..."

With me? I bit my lip, trying my best to hold his gaze. "My dreams aren't very practical."

"Why not?"

I sucked in a breath and steadied my heart, which had decided now was the time to start racing. "Because I don't want a woman at my side. I need more than just a bit of fun when I can find someone willing. I want a true partner in life, a man I can love fully. It's hard to dream of any future without that."

A line formed between his brows. "Wait, that's true? You actually can't marry a man in Inra? Great Dragon, I thought that was a joke."

"No joke. Is it different here?"

A smile spread over his face, and his fingers, still laced through mine, gave a little squeeze. "Handfasting is for any two people. Even two like us."

Looking into Drake's eyes, locked on me like he might never look away, I decided they were definitely my favorite shade of blue.

SERAE

MID-AUTUMN, BASMON 1036

MORNING DAWNED WITH a gray sky, an autumn chill seeping through the stones, and an unexpected visitor. Ell held two breakfast trays and a charming smile. He waltzed into my sitting room, slapped down the trays, and seated himself at my table without so much as a *hello.*

"You're back," I said, trying not to show the shock on my face.

He winked. "Did you miss me?"

"Dane said you were delayed returning to port."

"Ah, just a bit of headwind. Nothing to worry yourself over. Tell me, what do you know about the rite of betrothal?"

That caught me off guard. "Not much," I admitted. Dane had yet to cover it in our lessons.

Ell smiled, catlike. He had five braids interwoven down his back—one larger on top and two smaller on each side of his head. His tunic was a deep blue that accentuated the brightness of his eyes, and he wore a flashy gold pendant on a leather strap. Objectively, he was handsome. Objectively, I should have been attracted to him. He was tall with stunning eyes, a perfectly trimmed beard, the same beautiful jawline as his brother, and a mouth that was made to be kissed. He wasn't as broad as his brother, but he was still incredibly toned. Next to most men in Inra, he would be considered a god of muscles. I should feel excitement at being betrothed to someone like him when there was every chance my father might have chosen some aging lord whose fortune he wanted to control.

Should being the operative word of the day.

"The betrothed couple stands before their peers individually to prove the sincerity of their commitment. The point, you see, is to show that you're the most deserving of the betrothal." He leaned back in the chair at my small sitting table and stretched his arms behind his head. "You should expect to be challenged."

"What does that entail?"

"Whatever the challenger wants. Or challengers."

"And what happens if I don't win?"

He tapped his chin. "That's a good question. Normally, nothing much. The match might be called off, or the couple may make a special plea to the High Priestesses to continue with the betrothal. But a betrothal with a foreigner is new territory. It's anyone's guess what failure might bring."

My mind went hollow as numbness spread through my limbs. My voice came out in a whisper. "What would be done with me if the betrothal is called off?"

"Hmm, a good question. You'll need to marry someone if you plan to stay in Drakh. At any rate, we'll find out tomorrow."

I jumped from my chair. "Tomorrow?"

Ell's eyes danced with delight. "Dane didn't tell you?"

I gaped at him. "Of course not!" If yesterday's bout in the garden had taught me anything, it was that Dane liked controlling information as much as everything else in Drakh.

"Well, I assumed he had. He's been planning it for weeks. Perhaps something's driven it from your mind?"

I ignored the barb and paced around the room. "What do I need to know? What do I have to do? Will you be there?"

"Of course I will. Half of Drakh will be there. Some have traveled from across the Riht to watch. The betrothal of a future high dane should be witnessed by all."

I rubbed my hands over my face. "It's the fucking Sun Trial all over again."

Ell stepped in front of me, halting my circuit. He hooked a finger under my chin, lifting my gaze to his. "Except this time, I get to play a part. Now," he stepped back and scooped up his tray, "get yourself to practicing or whatever it is you do during the day when you're avoiding me. I'll see you tomorrow morning in the pavilion."

Before the door had even shut, despair crept in, rooting me to the spot. Dane—once again—was throwing me into a challenge I was in no way prepared for. Should I succeed, I'd be trapped in a betrothal to a man I didn't love—didn't even like. How much time passed between a betrothal rite and a Riht wedding? I didn't know, but the likelihood that I'd be extracted from Drakh in time dwindled. And should I fail, who knew the consequences? I could be sent home, saving my father the trouble of coming after me. If he even still planned to.

Emotions wrestled within me, each vying to take hold. It was a good thing I'd used so much magic last night, or I imagined I'd be shedding plant life in droves. Fear and sorrow quickly turned to misery, anger, and bitterness over my lot in life. They crashed together, overwhelming me until, out of self-preservation, my mind blanked.

The day passed in one giant blur. Training had been canceled. Callagh arrived with her mother, a small, heavyset woman who shared Callagh's sweet face, ready to step us through the ceremonial portion. Teke showed up to hug me and wish me luck. We visited the arena, marked out where I would stand, and practiced what I should say. They debated potential challenges and challengers over dinner. I was tucked in bed before the sun had fully fallen from the sky.

Morning came in a hurry. In numb silence, I dressed in one of the overdresses I had designed myself. Then, I slipped into a wool-lined vest to combat some of the chill. Callagh braided half of my hair into a rose-shaped plait, leaving the bottom half long and loose. Had the silence in my head not been so overwhelming, I might have taken a moment to appreciate how pretty it was.

"Are you ready, my lady?" she asked.

"No."

She linked her arm into mine anyway and led me from the room. Braethair and Braedur, Dane's guards, waited just outside and trailed us as we walked. We took the pathway beneath the keep that opened out to the arena field. A chill hung low in the air, but the clouds overhead were puffy and white. There would be no rain today. Kahvrah waited just inside the archway, shocking me from my stupor.

"Kahvrah," I gasped, having not seen her in weeks, "what are you doing here?"

"Your Rihtish is better." She smiled and squeezed my shoulder. "I'm here for you—to help."

Callagh pulled me into a swift hug. "It'll be easy. You've progressed in everything that could be expected of you. Remember, this is mostly ceremony. You don't have to win every challenge, you just have to show the talents you have."

"That's all?"

She patted my cheek. "Whatever you do will be enough."

"And if I fail the challenges? Will I still be betrothed to Eldreth?"

The two women exchanged a glance. "Don't worry about that just now," Callagh said.

"All that matters is that you are open, honest, and above all, committed," Kahvrah added.

A horn blew, crisp and clear, rending the air. Callagh linked her arm with mine again, and we walked onto the arena field together, leaving Kahvrah behind in the archway. Having her at my side lent me strength. We stopped in the center of the grassy field and stood in wait as the arena filled with people. The noise was twice as loud as I remembered. My head pounded in time with their heavy steps. I gripped her arm tighter and slowed my breathing, trying to steady my racing heart.

Once most were seated, Dane raised a hand and bellowed out a speech of welcome. Just like during my Sun Trial, his voice magnified around the arena, but this time, I recognized it for the magic it was. I wondered what sort of blessing was at work in the arena's stones.

As Dane's speech ended, Ell and Wep took to the dais and flanked him. All three wore ceremonial leathers—Dane and Ell in brown, and only Wep in black—over matching green tunics. The roaring of the Riht was deafening. Their leaders, each tall, strong, and imposing in their own way, embodied why the Riht were so feared. They stood together, commanding authority in their unified front.

Dane held up his hands, and the noise died down, leaving my head ringing with hollowness. "We stand before Serae of the Riht, formerly Serae of Cavendaffe, to hear her plea for her right to betrothal. On her behalf, I will speak."

The crowd murmured. Callagh patted my arm, still linked in hers.

"The lass you see before you did not choose this betrothal. She came to these lands having never met me or my sons. She came here knowing not one word of the language, our customs, or our beliefs. It was I who chose this match for my son and the Riht. It was I who brought her here in our midst and asked for your acceptance. It was I who chose for you a dana born on foreign soil. Now, I plead for you to accept her right to be betrothed to Eldreth." Dane paused for a breath, allowing that sentiment to sink in. "But it was Serae who worked every day to become one of us. She has learned our language and our ways. She has been accepted into a *ranng*"—Dane paused again as cheering from familiar voices rang out—"who are as devoted to her as any. Many of you have already accepted her into your hearts. Today, the rest of you have the opportunity to do the same. Let the rite begin!"

Cheers bellowed through the arena and rumbled underfoot. Callagh gripped my arm tighter. Dane's next words could scarcely be heard over the tumult.

"Let any who challenge this match, the match I have personally selected for you, come forward!" He turned and dropped onto his throne. The seat at his side remained empty. Ell and Wep stepped back and remained standing, flanking the thrones.

I focused on my breathing. Cries and cheers sounded all around, but no one stepped out onto the arena floor. Seconds stretched to minutes, and still, no one moved.

"What happens if no one comes?" I asked.

Callagh smiled. "I hope we're about to find out."

The wait was agonizing, standing still and scanning the crowd over and over again for any sign of movement forward. Without my *réalta*, I would have passed out from anticipation.

"No one should dare challenge you," Vaya'la crooned in my mind.

When an age had passed, Dane got to his feet and held up a hand. "I leave one more minute for a change of heart. If none step forward, then the will of the Riht is decided, the rite completed, and the right for betrothal granted."

"I challenge you, Dane." Her voice was faint as she rose from her seat and made her way to the field.

Dane frowned deeply and glanced at Wep, who shook his head, wearing a matching frown. Wep crossed his arms and glanced at Ell. Unlike the other men on the dais, Ell was smirking and leaning forward to get a better look.

I didn't need to look to know who it was. Within moments, Meralda was striding toward me and Callagh with hatred in her eyes. When she was ten paces away, she stopped and turned to Dane. "The Riht would not be best suited to a foreigner, nor would our future dane. I stand for the people of the Riht." She turned to me. "I stand against your right for betrothal."

Another cheer echoed around the arena, but this time, it was accompanied by murmurs.

"Meralda, daughter of Scaya, has stepped forward." Dane's voice was low but carried. "What claim do you make? A claim of the heart or a claim of the title?"

"Both."

Dane turned and barked something at his sons. Both stepped toward him in hushed conversation.

Callagh whispered, "A claim of the heart means she believes she's more deserving of his love. The title means she believes she's a better political match."

My heart sank. "She wants to be dana."

Callagh nodded.

In truth, neither claim mattered to me. I was the least worthy of Ell's love, since mine had well and fully been stolen by another.

"Relax your mind. Your tensions run too high, Small One."

I tried to focus on my breathing while waiting for the three men on the dais to finish. Whatever they said made Wep's face flush red with fury. He gestured sharply at Ell as he spoke, who just smiled back. I could almost hear the laugh on Ell's lips when he tried to place a hand on his brother's shoulder but got shoved away.

Dane stepped between the two, motioning them back to their places. He returned to the front of the dais, his face a terse mask. He stroked his braided beard and took his time before speaking. "Meralda. Your right to challenge the title is accepted. Physical challenges may include dowsae, endurance, or combat. Mental challenges may include knowledge, strategy, or creativity. Name your choice."

She turned to me with a triumphant smile. "Now is your downfall, weakling," she spat in a low voice meant for only Callagh and me to hear. To the crowd, she announced, "Combat, Dane. Trial by weapons. Let her show us how well she would be his match."

"Aye. What weapons would you suggest?"

Meralda smirked. "Let our weaponmaster decide."

Dane turned to Wep, and they spoke again in hushed tones. This time, Ell did not join in. He smiled and waved and chatted with the people nearest the dais. It took several minutes to come to a decision.

When Wep stepped forward instead of Dane, the crowd cheered for him, more deafening than before, and stamped their feet. He held up a hand for silence, and his eyes met mine. There was something tight in his gaze, but I couldn't decipher it.

"Bow, staff...and dagger."

Four words of mercy. He had chosen the weapons I performed best with. He'd given me a chance.

I glanced at Meralda, whose face had gone slack. I opened my second sight and saw the pulses of cyan—*shock*—accompanied by flickers of scarlet—*anger.*

Callagh, at my side, was pulsing with bright orange. *Fear.* She pulled me away before I could say a word. When we reached the side of the arena, she pulled me into the small alcove.

"Where is Kahvrah?" she hissed.

"Here." Kahvrah came running up with an armful of leathers identical to the ones I'd worn on our dragori mission. "Quickly."

"What's happening?" I asked as Callagh began stripping me out of my vest and dress.

"She's chosen a trial by weapons. You'll compete with the three Wep selected. Only archery is done against targets. The other two are actual combat, not sparring. Killing is forbidden, but if she gets the chance to stab or break bones, she'll take it."

"Oh, fuck me."

Callagh was tightening leather bracers around my wrists with shaking fingers and tear-stained cheeks, but Kahvrah slapped her aside.

"Go calm yourself."

We continued together, ensuring all the leathers were properly fitted.

"Keep up your defenses," she instructed. "Meralda is incredibly well trained, but Wep has selected things that are not her strengths."

"They're mine," I said, voice hollow.

"Good. He wants you to win. Remember his training. All you have to do is defend yourself until Dane calls the halt."

Back on the field, Meralda was already waiting. She had on leathers that were worn in but not at all worn down. Bracht stood nearby holding two staves. He handed one to me, then one to Meralda. "We wish you luck." He bowed and took off to the side of the dais.

Dane announced a short reminder of the rules, which were mostly just the ways we weren't allowed to kill each other.

"Do you agree to these terms?"

"Yes, Dane," I said.

Meralda took a moment to consider me, then echoed with, "Yes, Dane."

He stepped back on the dais. "Begin."

"Let's see if you can last longer than a minute this time," she hissed.

"Does it make you feel big, attacking people from behind like a coward?"

A short horn blew, and Meralda lunged. I barely got my staff up in time to deflect the blow aimed straight for my face. She pivoted through the motion and attacked again at the side of my head. I ducked and blocked, pivoted, and blocked again. Her staff turned with each blow, spinning around her head or at her side and coming right back at me. The pace was impossible. I stood no chance of keeping up. I focused on protecting my head, where the most damage could be done. She smacked my knee, and I nearly buckled. I took another jab to my opposite hip. All I could do was block and deflect. There was no thinking about attacks of my own.

Then, I started to find my rhythm. I kept up my horizontal and vertical walls. I kept track of my hands so I wouldn't lose fingers between clashing staves. I kept my feet in motion, never sacrificing my balance.

I can do this, I told myself. *I just have to survive.*

She favored my right side, and I could sense her goading me. When the attack to my left came, I anticipated it. More than a few strikes landed, and I would be very bruised tomorrow, but no major injuries. I needed Dane to call it. I was beginning to tire.

But so was she. Her physique, compared to mine, was unfathomable, but I could tell that this weapon had her ever so slightly off balance. I began to see gaps in her defenses. Every time she swung around on her right side, she blocked low, leaving her head wide open. It was only for a fraction of a second, but I'd have to work with it.

"Just give up and admit that you're inferior," Meralda spat between strikes.

"And give you the easy way out? I don't think so."

She swung; I blocked. She swung around the other side; I reversed my block. She swung high; I built my wall. She struck forward; I smacked her staff to the side.

"You'll be begging me to go easy before we're through."

"Keep dreaming," I gritted out. I stayed ready and waited. I would get only one chance.

Meralda moved, attacking on my left. Like a dream, time slowed as the moment arrived. Her next swing around would reload her momentum to attack again in quick succession, leaving her head exposed. I'd take a hit to my side, but it would be my sacrifice for ending the match. I lunged straight for her face.

She smiled.

Oh shit.

Meralda sidestepped my lunge as soon as it started. Her staff flew straight at me. I was helpless to stop it. It collided with my cheek, cracking bone and shoving me off my feet. She'd been playing me for the fool I was. I hit the floor like a sack.

Cheers erupted. Over their shouts and jeers, Dane called a halt. I had lost.

I did manage to get to my feet and hobble off to my alcove, where Callagh carefully cleaned my face. Marr Magda arrived moments later with Kahvrah, and she layered one of her salves over my cheek and gave me a bitter potion to drink. Behind me, I heard Dane's voice call out that the next event was archery.

"You'll get a rest," Callagh exhaled as if she were the one in need of a break.

"Just make sure you hit all the targets," Kahvrah added.

I took a swig of water, swished, and spat. It was tinged red with blood. "Funnily enough, I worked that part out for myself."

Marr Magda forced a waterskin on me and wouldn't let me leave until I drank it all down. By the time I made it back, Bracht was waiting on the side of the field closest to the dais with bows and quivers. Targets stood scattered across the field.

He handed me a quiver first, then a bow once my quiver was in place. His eyes danced over my cheek, and he offered me an unconvincing smile. I had a feeling, by now, the side of my face was blossoming with bruises. He passed both quiver and bow off to Meralda and walked away the second they left his hands. She glared after him, then turned her glare at me. I gave her my widest smile, even though it did things to my cheek that made me see spots.

I turned to my targets. This was the only event I stood a chance at.

"Breathe, Small One. Your emotions run too high."

She was right. I needed stillness. I closed my eyes, blocked out the world around me, and focused on my heartbeat and the earth beneath my boots. I wanted to feel the grass between my toes, but now was not the time. With each breath, the pressure inside me lessened. Everything slowed, loosened, and unwound.

Dane was already speaking, beckoning the challenger forward to take her aim. There were ten targets in all. The same short blast of the horn echoed across the arena.

I kept my eyes closed. I heard the whizzing of each arrow and several corresponding *thwacks* into the hay-covered targets, followed by *oohs* and hisses from the crowd.

Next, Dane called my name. I opened my eyes and stepped forward. I couldn't help but make a count—seven hits, three misses, one bullseye.

I had to do better. I wasn't a perfect shot, but I was a good one, especially when calm and focused. I tested my bow and drew it to its full length. It was perfect, but my body was not. My back hip screamed at me, and my front knee threatened to buckle. This would make things harder. I nocked my first arrow, took aim, and at the end of my exhale, I relaxed my right hand.

Thwack!

My arrow hit the closest target. I aimed at the next, and Vaya'la began to speak in my mind.

"You are Serae, daughter of Jaeda, Bound of Vaya'la, shaper of life. You are as strong as the scales on my back and as tender as the babe's first breath. You are the joy in a butterfly's touch and the rock that not even waves can break. You alone among the people of this world have been deemed worthy of your gods. You alone already possess the power to command all life toward peace."

My last arrow loosed, and I stepped back. The crowd was deathly silent. All ten arrows had hit. No bullseye, but a clear win. I turned to the dais behind me by reflex, and all three men were staring at me. Dane was smiling. Ell's characteristic grin was still faintly there, but his brow was bunched up. Wep had gone very still, and he wasn't meeting my eye. His were trained on the top of my head. He frowned.

"What trick is this?" Meralda hissed at me. "You're a fool. In the Riht, we don't wear crowns."

A cold dread crept over me. I dared not move and draw attention to whatever it was I had grown on the top of my head. As calmly as I could, I set aside my bow and quiver and hurried to my alcove.

"What is it, my lady?" Callagh asked urgently.

I tugged at my locks, but there was nothing there.

"Did you see it?" I asked. "What was on my head?"

Her brow furrowed, and she gripped my shoulders. "You're fine—Serae, you're fine. You hit all the targets! It was perfect. I've never seen Meralda so angry."

One win, one loss. It would all come down to this last event. *Daggers.* I stood a better chance at living with shorter blades flying at me, but my prospects still weren't good. There was no time to dwell on it. Dane was already calling for the crowd's attention.

"I will protect you if it comes to it."

"No. I have to do this on my own."

"You are never on your own, Small One."

It took all my courage forced into my legs to walk out to my doom. Bracht's expression mirrored my own as he handed me two daggers and whispered, "Go for blood." He threw the second pair of daggers at Meralda's feet. The crowd jeered at him, but Dane held up his hands for peace. Wep gripped his arm and said something in his ear, and Dane shook his head.

"Begin." The horn blew for the final time.

Meralda began to circle me. "Pathetic display, as expected," she spat. "What makes you think you could stand at Eldreth's side?"

I didn't rise to the bait. I focused on her feet and her body, hoping I might anticipate something of her moves before she plunged a dagger into my heart. Killing may be banned, but I couldn't protest it if I was already dead.

"He won't even touch you. Do you know how many times I've had him in *my* bed?"

Well, there was a mystery answered. How mad would Dane be if I called off this whole thing, offered Ell up to Meralda, and begged to be rematched with Wep?

"He needs a woman who can handle him, not a weakling like you."

"Will you shut the fuck up and attack already?"

I knew it was a mistake the moment the words left my mouth. Meralda exploded forward, platinum braid swinging, attacking with a viciousness I'd never faced. I blocked blow after blow with my blades and my leather bracers and took one unlucky cut down the back of my hand. With no gaps between her strikes, I couldn't even turn and run. She knocked my arm wide and drove her dagger toward my gut. I barely twisted in time for the blow to glance away harmlessly. I tried using her momentum to flip her, but without the proper grip, the move failed, earning me a blow to my side. The cut stung, but it was shallow.

Still, Meralda didn't relent. She came at me with both daggers in rapid strikes, aimed at my torso. If any one of them hit home, she'd pierce a vital organ. I kept on the retreat, leaping out of the way and countering what I could until I misjudged an angle. Her dagger pierced clean through my left hand. Screaming through the pain, I dropped my blade and spun behind her, striking at her back, but I lacked the strength to drive it through her leathers.

"Call it." It was Wep, but I blocked him out. I couldn't spare any focus on him.

Meralda whipped around, trying to elbow me with a reversed blade running along her forearm. I flung myself backward out of her reach. She charged in with a downward strike that I easily blocked, but her other arm was aimed low. She was trying to stab at the gap between my leather vest and pants.

"CALL IT!" Wep shouted.

I caught her motion just in time, swiping the blade out wide. She swung it around, stabbing it straight into my bicep from the side. With nothing but my thick shirt to halt the blade, it sliced through my arm and embedded into my leathers at the breast.

"HALT!" Dane called out.

Meralda drove the blade in deeper, piercing through my vest. I screamed as it twisted inside my arm and bit into the side of my right breast.

"*HALT!*" Dane bellowed again.

My challenger would not listen. "Just die already," she gritted out.

My scream turned into a yell, forcing the blade away from my chest using the arm it was embedded through as leverage. The pain was so intense that my consciousness threatened to leave me. Her eyes were wild as her free arm came down, straight toward my neck. I caught her wrist with my injured hand just in time, gripping her in a hold that I prayed she couldn't break.

"Why won't you die!" she hissed.

A fist collided with Meralda's head. She was knocked back, taking her free blade with her. The other remained trapped within my arm and breast. I stared at the back of Bracht's head as he kicked Meralda to the ground, screaming profanities at her. Tied in a half-braid, his shoulder-length honey-blond hair flew wildly around his face. I watched the strands flutter as time around me slowed.

Pain from the dagger through my arm darkened the edges of my vision. I reached for the hilt with my left arm, but the angle was awkward, and my pierced, bloody hand could find neither the strength nor the grip to extract it. I swayed on the spot. Someone caught me, and my body reacted. Thorns jutted out of my skin, biting into their flesh.

The scent of mint and eucalyptus washed over me at the same time that I heard Wep's hiss.

"Sorry," I muttered as the thorns retracted.

"We need to get you to Marr Magda."

"She's already here." I nodded toward the alcove.

Every step was agony as the dagger jostled with my movements. Wep's hands were on me, steadying me, but with the dagger still in place, it was too much of a risk to lift me.

Marr Magda hurried across the grass to meet us.

"Get it out of her, you fool," she snarled at Wep.

"I'm sorry about this," he said, and he yanked the blade free.

I screamed. A rush of blood poured out at my side. I finally fell into blackness.

WHEN I CAME to, I was still on the arena lawn. I had been stripped out of my leathers and my shirt sleeve cut away. Marr Magda was wrapping thick bandages around my arm. Callagh was at my side, holding a thick wad of fabric to my exposed breast.

"Welcome back," Marr croaked. "Once I'm done here, we'll take you in. I'll need that shirt off to dress that wound at your breast."

"Thank you," I groaned.

"Don't thank me for doing my job. I told Dane this rite was folly. Anyone with eyes can see that you belong with the weaponmaster."

I gasped. "You know?" I whispered to her.

She just tutted and continued tying the bandage. "There, let's get you up."

In my room, she gave me herbs to chew, tea to drink, another of her special little potions to swallow, and far too many clean bandages. She assured me I'd need them all.

"Call on one of my underlings if you need help with the dressings," she told Callagh. "Or get Kahvrah. She's been trained enough to know what to do."

I drank my tea, nibbled on some bread, and then asked Callagh to help me into bed.

"I'll stay with you until morning," she promised. "We need to make sure the clot sets, or you'll bleed out in your sleep."

"Lovely." I had a feeling I was in for a long, painful night.

"Rest, Small One. I will not let you perish as you dream."

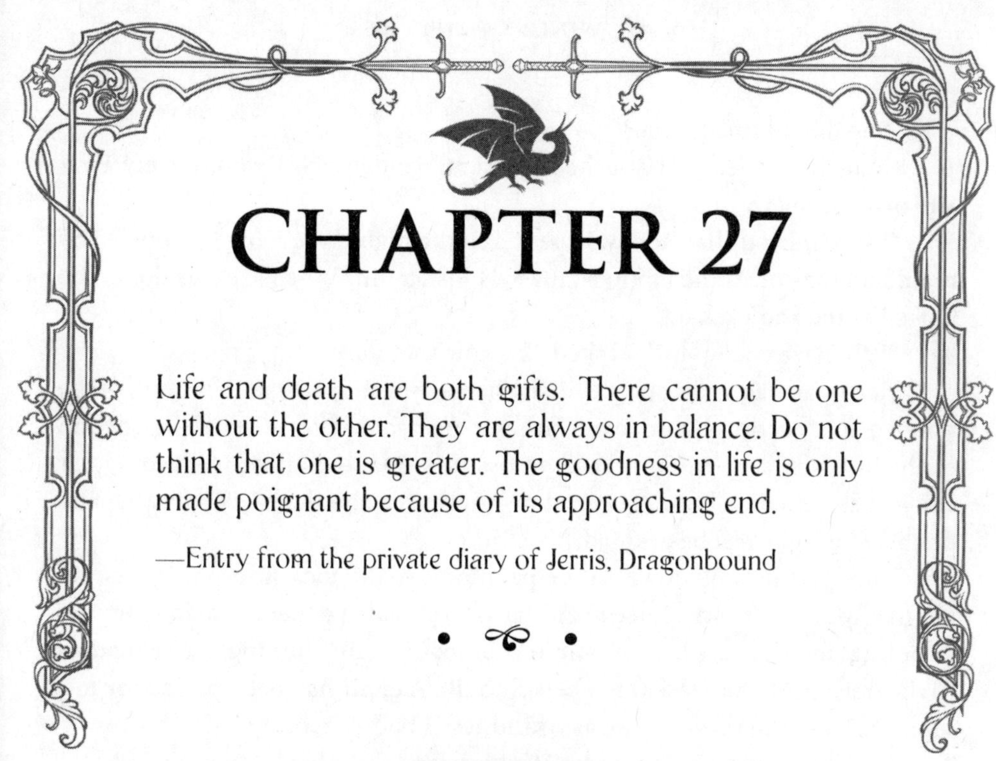

CHAPTER 27

Life and death are both gifts. There cannot be one without the other. They are always in balance. Do not think that one is greater. The goodness in life is only made poignant because of its approaching end.

—Entry from the private diary of Jerris, Dragonbound

SERAE

MID-AUTUMN, BASMON 1036

"It's time to wake, my lady." A gentle rocking shifted me about. "We have to get you on the dais for the rite."

I opened my bleary eyes and tried to sit up. Pain shot through my arm like being stabbed all over again. I gasped and fell back to my pillow.

"Dragon's fucking balls, that hurts!"

It was a fucking ordeal, all right, to get me changed and dressed. My arm wound looked horrific, and as soon as the dressing was changed, blood started seeping out. There was no bathing for me, and with no use of my right arm or left hand, Callagh had to help sponge bathe and dress me.

"I've brought you something special from Lanh Migram." It was a forest green overdress trimmed with pure white wool. It had been adjusted with a slit up the back of the right sleeve and ties to accommodate my injury. She had also sent along a matching cloak that was entirely lined with a soft layer of wool and an extra length of cloth so we could tie my arm up into a matching sling.

"She did all this for me?"

Callagh nodded and attached the same golden belt I wore for my First Sun around my waist.

"I'll braid your hair today. I spent half the night practicing this one." The braid had tons of strands in it; so many, I lost count. When she was done, she looked at me and cackled.

"What are you up to?" I asked. "I know that look."

Her grin was wide and devilish. "It's a woven message. Up here,"—she pointed to a section by my ear—"it says, *righteous*. Down here,"—a portion of the tail—"it says, *truthful*. And across this side,"—trailing from my other ear—"it says, *chosen*." She squeezed my uninjured shoulder. "There can be no doubt. The right will be granted."

Though the walk down to the pavilion usually took fifteen minutes, we left nearly an hour early. I needed it. Each step jostled either my arm or breast, crippling my pace. With Braethair and Braedur again flanking us, we made it to the dais just before the arena began to fill. A chair had been placed for me, separate from the thrones. It was a kindness I hadn't expected.

Dane arrived with Ell in tow. Wep was not with them. My heart sank.

"Do you think he's avoiding today?"

"He will fight for you. He is worthy."

"You think he'll challenge his brother?" I gasped. With so much focus on my injuries, I hadn't considered the possibility.

Vaya'la did not answer.

Ell came straight to me when he climbed the dais and patted my cheek. "How's that arm?" There was a light behind his eyes and a smile playing at his mouth. The crowd began to file in, talking and laughing.

"Do you really care to know?"

That got his smile to dim.

"Serae! Serae!"

I turned away from him and spotted Teke at once. Seated three rows behind the dais was my entire *ranng*, all side by side. I smiled up at them and waved with my bandaged hand. "You're a fucking badass!" Lispen shouted. Lex immediately took up the chant, "Badass! Badass! Badass!" I wished I were seated with them. Ell slipped away to the other side of the dais.

Just like the previous day, Dane held up his hands in welcome, calling out to the Riht who had traveled to witness the rite. As he spoke, two men walked out to the center of the arena. A flash of copper hair caught my eye. I stood, staring hard at the unmistakable figures of Wep and Bracht. My heart skipped a beat. Was he already challenging his brother before the rite even started?

Dane's voice boomed as he continued. "Today, we stand before Eldreth, son of Auldren, Marr Wep of the Riht, to hear his plea for his right for betrothal. On his own behalf, he will speak."

I gripped the railing on the dais with one hand, ignoring the pain that shot through it. The breath rushed from my lungs as all sense and logic fled my mind. My whole body seized. Eldreth? *Eldreth?* Using all my effort, I forced my head to turn to Ell, who was standing beside his father's throne looking bored. He caught my eye and winked.

What kind of game was this?

I didn't have time to consider as Wep began to speak. The crowd, like me, was whisper-silent, all waiting to hear his words. "I entered into this arrangement guided by Dane, but of my own free will. At first, I did question its merit. I wondered how a woman of Inra would challenge me, stand at my side, and be my match." He ran a hand through his loose hair. "You can imagine my shock at first sight of her." The crowd chuckled. "More than being uniquely beautiful, she is my complement in every way." This time, murmurs rose and fell in waves. Blood began to pound in my ears, almost drowning out his words. "She has already claimed me, body, mind, and soul." His eyes sought mine as he waited for the gasps and chatter to die down. When he spoke again, his words were simple and clear. "There is no other for me, in this realm or the next. I demand the right for betrothal."

The edges of my vision fuzzed as shouts exploded from the arena stands. I could only make out those nearest me.

"How could she be your match?"

"She has not proven herself worthy!"

"Red hair is not enough, Wep!"

"Have you lost your senses?"

I forced myself to draw breath. My whole body shook with anticipation. My mind was fucked in ten different ways. Dane held up a hand for peace, but for once, I agreed with the jeering crowd. I wanted answers.

I didn't know what was going on, but none of this made sense. Wep couldn't be Eldreth. I played back a thousand different memories, and I came to the same conclusion every time. It was impossible. I had only ever heard him referred to as Wep. That was his name. On that first day, he had introduced himself as Wep, hadn't he? Yet, I was staring at more evidence than I could have asked for. An entire crowd of people, his father and brother among them, looked at him like he was exactly where he belonged.

Wep was Eldreth.

A part of my heart swelled. It had been slowly breaking for weeks, and now the pieces threatened to smash back together. I wasn't sure I could survive it. Something in me dimmed as a niggling doubt took root in my head. No one had confirmed the results of my rite. This morning, I was in so much pain that I hadn't even thought to ask. I'd lost two out of three trials by weapon, but Callagh had said I didn't have to win them all. Was winning one enough? Was surviving Meralda's onslaught proof of my dedication?

Dane's voice boomed at my side, making me jump. "Let any who challenge this match come forward!"

"I challenge it, Dane."

My head snapped to the side. Ell hopped off the dais and sauntered out onto the field. Next to Wep, he looked like a peacock in his bright blue tunic and green pants. Wep—Eldreth—wore his leathers over a black tunic. His adornments were purely functional, the opposite of Ell, who donned a pendant, flashy belt, and rings glinting in the sun. Wep was armed to the teeth with a longsword, short swords, daggers, and who knows what weapons I couldn't see. Ell had only two short swords hanging from his belt.

Dane, at my side, growled. When he spoke, his words were laced with ire. "Ellán, son of Auldren, holder of *no* title, has stepped forward. What claim could you possibly make?"

Ellán?

He smiled that cat-like grin that set me on edge. "Why, a claim of both title and heart, of course."

"Nonsense."

Ell's smile fell away. "Who else here in the Riht could stand against this and win?" He turned to the crowd, and like Dane's, his voice carried loud and strong. "My claim of the title is sound. Dane seeks an alliance with Inra. I, too, can fulfill that alliance without putting an Inraen in the seat of high dana. As for my claim of the heart, I cannot make professions of love after knowing a person for so few weeks," he cast a sidelong glance at Wep, "but I can tell you that Serae has sought me out as both companion and confidant. Her heart is not so steadfast. I don't know what magic she brings to have turned my brother's head so quickly, but it was not so long ago that another stood in her place. I come forward for the good of my brother and the Riht."

"Your challenge is denied."

An uproar echoed through the crowd at Dane's words. They booed and shouted claims of unfairness and bias. Dane held his hands up for peace, but the cries did not die down.

I collapsed into my chair as Dane bellowed at the people, and they shouted back. My heart, this fragile thing, was bleeding out in my chest.

"Calm, Small One."

But I could not. I looked to Wep, the true Eldreth, my betrothed all this time, the only one I wanted, and I saw him slipping away. It was different when I thought I had never had him—when I thought he wasn't mine. My mind refused to believe that anything could be so simple. It was too much, teetering on the edge, not knowing for sure whether I had secured my right.

"Find your center. Do you not have faith in your weaponmaster?"

"I do."

Eldreth's eyes were on Ellán, and they were dark storms. "I accept your challenge," he called out. At that, silence finally fell. "Name your feat."

With a little shrug, Ellán suggested, "Short swords."

Eldreth nodded. "I invoke the right of first blood."

Gasps sounded from every corner of the stands.

Ellán laughed. "Done!"

Both men turned and began stripping out of their clothes. My eyes were glued to Eldreth, Wep, whoever he was, unable to look away as his longsword and scabbard hit the ground, followed by bracers, spaulders, chestpiece, short and long daggers, and finally his shirt, leaving him in pants, boots, and belt. He pulled a strip of leather from his pocket and tied his hair up in a knot. Ellán had tossed his belongings in the grass, though he had much less to take off—his tunic and a few trinkets.

They faced each other. Eldreth's right side was toward me. I could see the spiraling of dragon tails across his shoulder and down his bicep. Below that, his forearm was mottled with deep red scarring. He drew his swords.

"Begin," Dane called with arms crossed and teeth gritted. An attendant below the dais put a horn to her lips and blew.

Eldreth exploded into action. My mind cleared. He was the weaponmaster, Marr Wep by title, and he had been for years. The Training Hall was his. The warriors of Drakh were taught and led by him. He was an expert in combat and battle.

Ellán stood no chance.

I had seen them spar with short swords before, but this was different. Eldreth moved with violence more forceful and aggressive than I'd ever seen from him. His usual sweeping lines and redirected momentum were all sharper, using exactly what he needed and never more. He was strength and precision, yes, but this was no teaching moment. This was an attack. He drove Ellán back on his heels, forcing constant retreat. This trial would be over before it had truly begun. Even I could see that Eldreth was positioned to score a hit at any moment if my assumption about the right to first blood was correct.

But he didn't take it. With comical exaggeration, he slapped the side of his blade against Ellán's upper arm, leaving a welt.

Ellán yelped and spun out of reach, but Eldreth anticipated this. He moved inhumanly fast and scored his second smack. Then another. Then another. In moments, Ellán had welts on his arms, sides, and one across his back. Red mottled Ellán's face, and his next charge was sloppy. Eldreth pivoted with one perfect step and elbowed him across the back of the head as he passed.

"Is this just a game to you?" Ellán bellowed, whirling around. "You would toy with our sacred rites?"

This broke the crowd from their stupor. Angry shouts sounded in response, some with him and some against him.

Eldreth disengaged, shoving Ellán to the ground with two pommels to the chest. He spoke in a low rumble, but the magic of this place magnified it for all to hear. "I have a right to choice. I have a right to happiness. The only approval I will ever seek is that of Serae and the Great Dragon, herself."

"Her trial was lost," Ellán spat from the ground. "The decision is no longer up to you alone."

Lost. The word echoed in my ears as cheers erupted in the stands. Tears fell from my eyes, unbidden. The Riht began stamping their feet. Someone started up a chant that caught on, mirroring my exact fears. "Send. Her. Back. Send. Her. Back." They wanted the betrothal annulled. They wanted me gone from the Riht. With so many against me, how could Dane deny them?

Misery exuded from my soul, and petals as black as night piled at my feet. As each one touched the ground, it withered to ash. Eldreth shouldn't have ever been mine, and now he'd be taken from me before I even had him. He would win any trial he faced, but I had already lost mine. There was no going back.

Behind me, I could make out the voices of my *ranng* shouting their protests. In the pause, as Eldreth allowed his brother to get to his feet and retrieve his weapons, his gaze sought mine.

"It is time for all to know the truth. Show me your faith." Vaya'la's voice echoed in my head, and Eldreth's eyes went wide. *"You know what you must*

do."

Eldreth held my eyes for a moment longer, and then he nodded. Fear clenched my gut when he turned back to Ellán, jaw clenched with resolve.

"We stay or go together," he shouted.

"No!" I screamed. I could see his plan taking shape, but I was helpless to stop it.

Ellán charged in, but his form was wild. He had lost all control. Eldreth could've ended this easily, but he corralled his brother, forcing his strikes inside and back in line.

No, no, no, no, no, the word repeated on end in my head. The rite, the trial, the results—none of it mattered anymore. Not with what I was about to do.

"Be ready, Small One."

"No!" I screamed again as Eldreth took a single perfect step into his brother's sloppy thrust. The blade pierced his abdomen. I could hear the great *woosh* of air from his lungs as the blade plunged in.

Ellán jumped back in shock. He looked at his hand in horror. "What have you done?" he hissed, dropping his other blade. He gripped Eldreth, who sank to his knees. "Get the healer!" He bellowed, tears falling from his eyes and onto his brother's chest.

"Worry not," Eldreth rasped.

"She's not worth your death!" Ellán screamed.

At my side, Dane was frozen, but the sight of bright red blood seeping from Eldreth's wound spurred me to action. I leapt to my feet, fear giving way to fury. *Eldreth would not die today.* I stripped off my cloak and boots. The pain from my arm, my hand, and my breast all screamed at me, but I pushed everything aside. I pulled my arm free of the sling, jumped off the dais, and ran barefoot across the field. Others were running out too, faster than me.

"Move!" I screamed as one of Dane's guards gripped me, blocking my path.

"**MOVE,**" we commanded, and thick roots erupted from the ground, pulling everyone aside. I ran to Eldreth, ignoring the screams of shock and fear in my wake. Ellán was cradling Eldreth's head in his arms, weeping and muttering his apologies. They were surrounded by a pool of Eldreth's blood, staining the grass crimson.

"You idiots," I fumed. I dropped to my knees beside them, blood already seeping through my dress where I knelt.

Ellán moved toward Eldreth's wound, and I slapped his hand away. The sword was still embedded in his gut. It was the only thing stemming the flow of blood.

"She spoke to me," Eldreth rasped. "In my head."

"I know."

Ellán sobbed. "He's fading. He's no longer making sense."

There was no more time to waste. I gripped the pommel and said, "I'm sorry about this." Eldreth's laugh came out as a wheeze. I yanked the blade free, and Eldreth growled in pain. Ellán screamed in protest. I ignored them both as I plunged my fingers into his wound. My toes were already digging into the soft grass.

It took less than a thought to pull from Vaya'la and focus her energy into healing light. I let it fill me until the light leaked from my pores, until I thought I might burst from the weightless pressure of it, until I threatened to burn up from within. Then, I forced it into Eldreth, every last drop. My hands were awash with light so bright, it was hard to look at. That searing light was more focused and intense than any of my previous creations. My own gut screamed with unimaginable pain. It nearly overtook me, but I would not allow it. Not now, not today, not when Eldreth's life was at stake.

The light itself guided me. As I withdrew my fingers one layer at a time, tissue mended, and organs and muscles knitted back together. I pushed the light, focusing it further, and his veins fused, his ligaments reconnected, and finally, his skin merged until there was nothing visible but a pink line.

The pain receded. His eyes popped open, and they were alert and bright. My second sight revealed his lifelight radiating brighter than ever.

"Look at you," he whispered.

I smiled through the tears that sprang from my eyes. "I could say the same to you."

"Wings," Ellán gasped. He was staring behind me, his lifelight exuded in bright teal waves of *awe*. Gasps echoed all around, and I heard others cry out, "Dragon wings!" and "She's been chosen," and "They're wings of light!"

Eldreth sat up, his arm encircling my waist. The backs of his fingers stroked down my cheek. "Now everyone sees you as I do."

I huffed out a laugh and kissed him. This insane, beautiful man had seen a way past my failed rite. How could the Riht refuse me once they knew who—what—I was?

With a strength I did not have, I rose to my feet. Vaya'la's will pressed in on me, guiding me. "**Name me**," we commanded, and our voice boomed through the arena.

Eldreth stood before me, naked to the waist and completely healed.

Then, he dropped to one knee. His voice rose and echoed in every crevice and corner of the stands.

"SERAE, DRAGONBOUND!"

Vaya'la purred her pleasure in my mind. *"Sleep. Your work today is done."*

I collapsed into a fold of strong arms, rosemary, and mint.

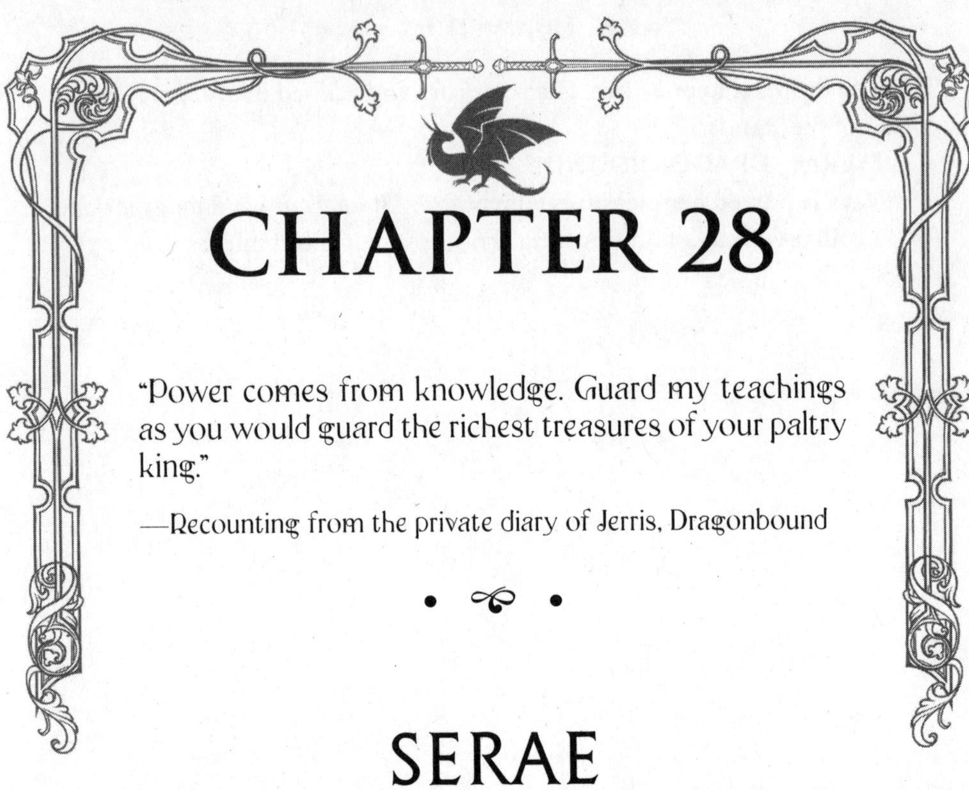

CHAPTER 28

"Power comes from knowledge. Guard my teachings as you would guard the richest treasures of your paltry king."

—Recounting from the private diary of Jerris, Dragonbound

• ❧ •

SERAE

MID-AUTUMN, BASMON 1036

"Have you ever seen anything like it?"

"No, never."

"Those wings...did you see them?"

"Callagh, how could I not?"

"And she healed you. I saw you. Great Dragon, I've never been so scared, but here you are. There wasn't even a scar."

"She healed herself, too."

"She's incredible."

"I know."

❧

I didn't know how long I slept. I woke with a bone-deep hunger and a throat of glass. Callagh was at my bedside with a cup of hot tea from Marr Magda. I drank it down and nibbled bits of toast and berries. One thought at a time, my mind returned to me. Aside from passing out after exhausting my power, I seemed to have no gaps in my memory.

My secret was out. It was spreading through Drakh like wildfire, if Callagh was to be believed. Everyone had seen what I'd done for Wep, and anyone who hadn't would surely learn how I had summoned the power of life to bring him back from the brink of death, while sprouting dragon wings of light from my back. I should be anxious or proud—or even terrified about whether the people would accept me as Bound to their goddess.

Except, since waking, I'd become wholly consumed by one thing.

Wep is Eldreth.

I bathed. Sitting in the tub until the water turned to ice, and my teeth chattered.

Wep is Eldreth.

I got out of the bath, dressed in whatever I could find, and took up pacing between my rooms.

Wep is Eldreth.

A knock at my door sounded. It was Callagh bringing me a tray and another letter from Merria. I snatched it up, broke the seal, and tried to read, but I couldn't make sense of any of the words. I cast the letter aside, leaving it to land where it may.

Wep is Eldreth.

Callagh did her best to help me, but when I finally confided that I had the brothers confused, she just stared at me. I opened my second sight and was unsurprised to find bright pulses of cyan. *Shock.*

"Did you really not know?"

I shook my head.

"But how could you not know?"

The question was eating me alive. Ellán, I was certain, intended the confusion and chaos he created. But, not Wep—not Eldreth. His forwardness with me, his willingness to touch me and kiss me all made sense now. Still, I had to hear it from his lips.

I opened my door to shouting. At the end of the hallway, at the final door that I had never seen used, stood a couple fighting. I pushed my door shut most of the way when I registered long, platinum hair. Peering through the small gap, I listened. Callagh stood beside me with wide eyes, pressing her ear in close to listen as well.

"We're so good together," Meralda was saying. "How could you throw this all away?"

Someone forced her backward, and Eldreth's frame took up the doorway. His beautiful copper hair was loose and mussed like someone had been running their hands through it. He was shirtless and bootless, wearing only a pair of thin cloth pants. His face was hard as he spoke. "We had our last night together. What's done is done. I've told you my path forward. You have to accept it."

"Fine, keep the Inraen bitch, but you'll tire of her. You know you will. When you do, you'll come crawling back to me."

He scoffed.

"Have you even fucked her yet?"

"Leave, Meralda." Eldreth crossed his arms over his chest.

"Oh, that's right, of course you haven't. She won't let you touch her until the marriage is secured. She'll be a lousy, unsatisfying lay with no experience. It'll be like fucking a child—"

"Dane already told you to leave Drakh. Go spew your bile somewhere else." He stepped back and slammed the door in her face.

Meralda pounded on it, and I used the cover of her racket to ease my door back shut. Scrunched up against it, Callagh and I stared at each other.

"She told me he'd been in her bed countless times," I breathed, just connecting whose bed she was referring to.

Callagh nodded. "They were together before you came here. I thought Wep ended it when he agreed to the betrothal."

I swallowed. Had they carried on? Or was it truly one last night together, like he said? Her hatred for me finally made sense. I had stolen her...fuck, what were they? Intended? Lovers? Engaged? A chill ran up my spine with realization. She had expected to be the future high dana of the Riht. I had taken more than a man from her; I'd taken a crown. And I'd taken *her* from the people of Drakh, too.

No wonder they hated me. I'd hate me, too, if I were them.

"I think I need to rest some more," I said tonelessly.

Sprakt flew in through the window, and I moved aside my hair, giving him a perch on my shoulder.

"Of course, my lady. I'll return later." Her voice was full of pity. I was glad for her to leave.

I returned to my bedroom and sat at the edge of my bed, staring out the window at nothing. Sprakt perched silently by my ear, occasionally nudging me with his beak.

Wep is Eldreth. But who even is Eldreth?

I truly didn't know.

I SAT IN a trance for a long time. The rain was heavier than I'd ever seen it in the Riht, matching my mood. The sound was thunderous, though no thunder or lightning came. Sometimes, I was looking out into the gray mist hiding the forest. Other times, I slipped into Vaya'la's mind to soar over the crystal mines and broken hills and watch creatures from a dream live out their strange lives.

When the storm inside me peaked, I rose to my feet. Sprakt flew out my sitting room window—the one I kept cracked just for him. Around me, the tempest of leaves I'd been shedding melted away. Heat bloomed from my scalp. A glance at the mirror showed me a crown of thistle sprouting from the top of my head. So be it. Drakh already knew what was inside of me, and so did Wep.

I walked with thunder raging through my head and heart across the hall and down the stairway leading toward Wep's training room. I allowed myself three slow breaths while lingering outside the double doors. A small part of me wished I had rehearsed what to say, but this moment was driven by instinct alone.

On the last deep breath, I pushed through the door.

The light of day had not fully faded, but the braziers in the room were already lit. Wep—No. *Eldreth* was in the middle of the floor performing a *dowsa* with a long, curved sword. The man I knew as Wep was gone. I had yet to see who this Eldreth was that had taken his place.

He must not have noticed my entry. He continued his practice, moving with a fluidity that I had rarely seen, combined with speed and strength I was certain I had never beheld on any other. He was wind and water all at once. He was a flash of steel and limbs. Whether airborne, grounded, moving, or still, there was such flow and liquidity and surety in him that I could almost see his imaginary opponent, swinging and missing strike after strike. He was truly a wonder to behold, but I set those feelings aside. My scalp burned as more thistles sprouted from my crown.

On his next spin, Eldreth caught sight of me. He dropped his sword to the floor, casting aside his practice in favor of me. A smile played at his mouth, and his eyes flittered over my thistle crown. He opened his mouth to speak, but I was the one with things to say.

"Why do they call you Wep?" I blurted out. Not quite the question I meant to ask.

It took several moments of confusion for him to reply. "I am the weaponmaster."

"Yes, but I've met Marr Magda."

He cocked his head to the side and began walking toward me. "This is a language thing? Marr Wep is my title. It's from Master of Weapons in Old Rihtish."

"But they call you Wep."

"I don't understand."

"No one calls you Eldreth."

He was right in front of me. His hand reached out to touch my crown of thistle.

"What's this about?" He sucked in a breath. "Fuck, those sting." He examined his fingers, then shook out his hand. His eyes roamed over my face. "Are you upset?"

"You are Eldreth."

His brow furrowed.

"Why are you not called Ell?"

"Ell is short for Ellán." His words had slowed. His expression turned wary.

"But Wep isn't short for Eldreth!" I yelled, my temper finally breaking. Jagged thistle leaves shot in every direction and left minuscule scratches down his arms. He barely flinched.

In a steady voice, he said, "Del is short for Eldreth, not Ell."

"They don't call you that either."

"Only because I hate it."

A memory of Marr Magda's chiding *Delly* clicked into place. "I don't get it," I shot back. "Why the fuck does no one use your name?"

He stared at me, jaw slack.

"I'm looking for an answer here!"

He shrugged helplessly. "Not many people would, I guess. My father, some of my *ranng*, that's about it."

"Then why have I never heard it?"

He cast around the room as if he might find an answer there. Eventually, his eyes narrowed back on me. "*You* never use my name."

My ire stilled. I swallowed whatever words I might have said.

"Tell me you knew my name."

Fuck.

"Dragon's fucking scales, Serae, tell me you know my name."

He stepped into me, forcing me to look up at him. I couldn't tear my eyes from the storms that were brewing behind his. "I do. I just thought it belonged to someone else."

"For how long?"

"That depends. How long was I unconscious after that little stunt with the short swords?"

He stepped back like it was a blow.

"Was this meant to be some kind of trick?" The second I said it, I knew it was wrong. The shock on his face was plain and reflexive. I didn't need my second sight to confirm it, but it opened anyway.

His eyes went distant. "You didn't know it was me," he whispered. He ran a hand down his face and turned away, taking a few steps before turning back. "How the fuck didn't you know it was me?" His lifelight flashed splayed fingers of maroon. *Frustration.*

"This isn't my fault!" I shouted. "*You* told me your name was Wep."

"They *call me* Wep. It's not my fucking name."

"You're not the oldest son! And your names—fuck, you have to admit they're a bit *too* similar."

"His name is *Ellán*."

"Well, I didn't know that either," I countered.

He ran his hands through his hair and paused with both hands atop his head, elbows wide. His lifelight flared cherry red with *horror.* "Hold on, hold on. Are you telling me you thought you were betrothed to Ell?"

The blood drained from my face as red leaves tumbled from my hands to the floor.

"You're not the eldest," was all I managed to get out.

"This isn't fucking Inra!" he roared. "Birth order doesn't fucking—" He cut off, taking a deep breath and finally completing the track of his fingers through his hair. When his hands fell to his sides, he looked at me with those silver eyes ringed with blue. The understanding in them cut me in two. "What did he say to you?"

"Nothing," I said quickly—too quickly. His eyes narrowed. "He kept seeking me out, and you never did. He was always so forward with me and suggestive. It was a lot of things."

"I never did? I sought you out *constantly.*" He shook his head and began pacing, kicking his forgotten sword to the side. "Always fucking Ell," he muttered.

I watched him pace, not knowing what to say. Anger still rumbled through me, but its sharpness had dulled.

He stopped mid-step. "But you kissed *me*." He turned to me. "You thought it was Ell, but *you* kissed *me*."

I sighed. "I know."

"Did you kiss him too?"

"Oh, fuck you. Really?"

"It's a fair question."

If I were holding anything, I would've chucked it at him. I balled my fists as they vibrated with power, locking them at my sides. Even through my ire, I had enough sense to stop myself from accidentally impaling him with spikes. "You want to talk about fair questions?" I asked through gritted teeth. "Why was Meralda leaving your rooms this morning?"

His eyes went wide.

"Correction, why was Meralda *in* your rooms this morning while you were half-fucking-dressed?"

"She wasn't in my rooms."

"I heard you. One last night together?" I released my fists, and a cascade of black petals fell to the floor. I tried to shove away images of them entwined in his private rooms—rooms I'd never even seen. Hours after I had expended all my energy to heal him, she was in his arms instead of me.

"That's not what happened."

I held up a hand, silencing him. Thorns burst from my skin, covering me in spiked armor from the neck down and riddling my clothes with pinpricked holes. "You want to know what happened with Ell? *Nothing.* Nothing ever happened because I was so fucked up over you that I couldn't even think about letting him get close to me. Nothing happened because all this time, despite all my efforts, logic, and obligation, I wanted you. Every time we kissed, I told myself it would be the last. I told myself I would end this madness. For months, I've *hated* myself for not being able to stay away from you and for feeling the way I did, thinking all this time it was wrong."

He took a step toward me, but I stepped back, keeping the distance between us.

"But, it's never just been me for you, has it?" The words broke me, but I needed to give them voice. The tears began, and black petals fell from me in droves. I was helpless to stop either. "Don't you see? This whole time, I've been choosing you first, even when I shouldn't have. Even when there would be consequences to face. But for you, I've always been second place."

"No"—he moved toward me—"No."

"Yes, Wep!"

"Don't fucking do that." His voice was a growl.

It was my turn to gawk.

"I *hate* my title on your lips."

"I didn't know." I had called him Wep countless times. I thought it was his name, but this whole time, had he thought I was pushing him away?

"That's no excuse."

"It's not like I wanted to believe you were someone else!" I burst out.

"But you let me kiss you, thinking I was!" His voice raised, but he caught himself. His brows lowered, and when he spoke, it was with deadly calm. "You thought I was the type of man who would kiss you and touch you while knowing you were betrothed to another."

"I—" I clamped my mouth shut. That's exactly what I had thought.

"To my own fucking brother, no less."

Tension gripped every muscle in my body at the truth behind his words. I sucked in a breath and took a step back, my heart hammering in my throat. He looked at me like I had just ripped his out. But how could that be when everything still felt like twisted lies and a massive, fucked-up trick?

"This was a mistake," I admitted, then I turned and left at a run. This time, he did not follow.

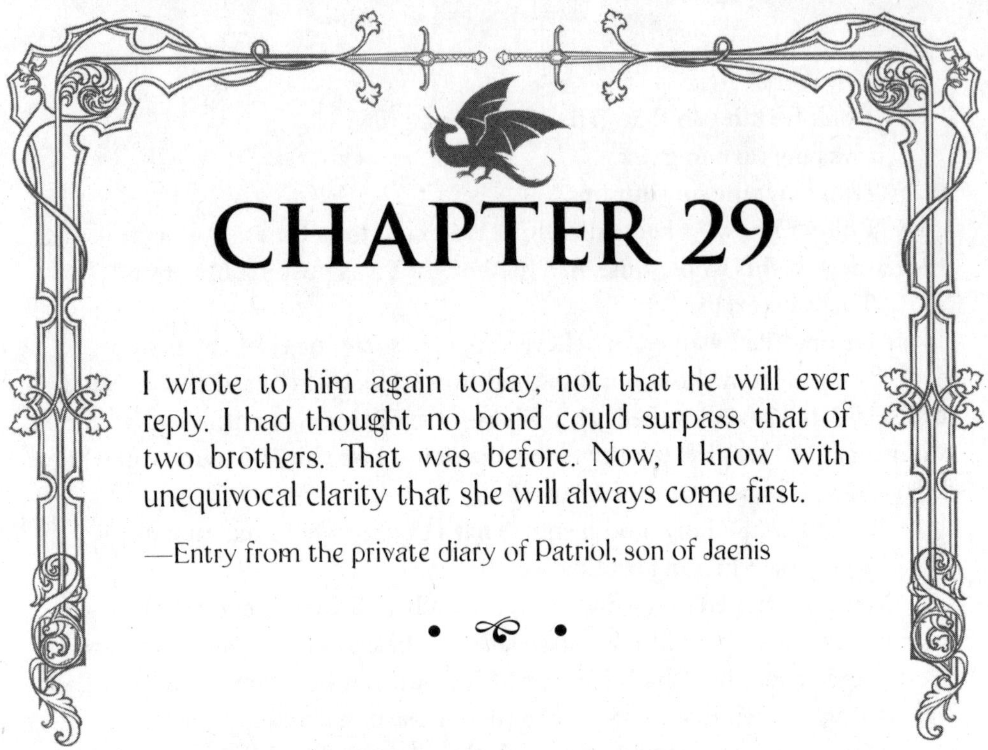

CHAPTER 29

I wrote to him again today, not that he will ever reply. I had thought no bond could surpass that of two brothers. That was before. Now, I know with unequivocal clarity that she will always come first.

—Entry from the private diary of Patriol, son of Jaenis

ELDRETH

MID-AUTUMN, BASMON 1036

I DID NOT follow as Serae left the training room. I did not follow as her footsteps faded up the stairs. I let her walk away.

I headed out the back door into the open air. It was pouring, but I never minded the rain. On instinct, I walked toward my alcove, ready to punch my fucking tree. It had taken more hits than I could count over the years. I rounded the corner and froze. The rosemary was in fucking bloom because of her. One glance at the tree brought memories of the feel of her body as I pressed her against it. I half expected to find her discarded blossoms still there in the kidney weed. I'd never taken anyone here before, not even Meralda, but Serae had permeated my life. Everything with her was different.

I was a fucking idiot not to go after her.

By the time I made it to the main corridor, tracking water over the stones, she was gone. I knocked on her door, but there was no answer. I checked our shared sitting room—empty. She wasn't in her Relaxation Room. I don't know when it became hers, but she had claimed it as surely as that spot between my ribs. The gardens? After thirty minutes of searching, I had to concede that she wasn't there. I was probably the only idiot mad enough to be out in this rain. She was avoiding me, and if I were her, I would avoid me too.

Fucking Meralda. She showed up at my door, pushing her way in and grabbing at me like it was still six months ago. I had to use force to get her out. I don't know what Serae thought she saw, but it wasn't *that*. What a fucking mess. And, how the fuck didn't she know who I was? My mind was still reeling. I couldn't think straight.

I knocked on her door the next morning, but still no answer. I had to spend the day in the lower city training a new set of guards for the northern gate. In the evening, I tried again. Nothing. She'd have to see me eventually, her *ranng* would return for training in three days.

The following day, I had to ride to Port Drakha to work out a new rotation schedule for the company stationed there. I didn't return until it was nearly dawn. I collapsed on my bed, but sleep was elusive. When I finally succumbed, I dreamt of Serae trapped in a cocoon of thorns. I punched at it until my fists bled while she screamed and screamed for help. I woke before midday and decided sleep could fuck right off.

The rest of the day I spent training. My body was sluggish, and I lacked focus. I was ready to give up and go bang on her door until she answered, when I heard the door to the Training Hall thump shut. I bolted. I don't know how I knew it would be her; I just did. I caught up with her in the hallway, touching her elbow but not stopping her.

"Don't touch me," she spat.

I kept pace with her. "You'll need to touch me at some point."

"Not if I can help it."

"We are to be married, Serae."

"That doesn't mean anything. All you need from me is an heir."

"That will require touching." I quirked a brow at her. Now was probably not the time, but fuck if I could help it. Whenever she walked into a room, all I could think about was touching her.

Serae huffed. "I can't do this with you."

"You're still upset with me."

She ignored me.

"Are you upset *that it's me*?"

That stopped her, but I had to know. She turned, and she looked like she wanted to smack me. I took her hand. "Please," I begged. "Don't shut me out again." I pulled her toward our shared sitting room, and by the grace of the Great Dragon, she followed. Fuck, did she even know this room was meant for us? That, before I had even met her, I had the whole fucking thing redone to make her feel more at home. I even brought Hanover in as a consultant, since he'd seen her home in Cavendaffe several times. There were so many things she didn't know because I was too fucking stupid to tell her. No wonder this had happened. I deserved the guilt that welled in my gut.

Serae went straight for the couch I'd meant for her, slightly shorter, but more plush. I wondered if she even registered the domesticity of it. A fire crackled in the hearth—I had asked it to be lit nightly—giving the room an intimacy it lacked with the sunlight streaming in.

I followed her, trying to decide where to start. I was still wrapping my head around it all, but I puzzled through a few things on my own. "Your kings, they're based on birth order, yes?"

"Kings, heirs, everything goes to the first son."

I nodded. "We don't pick leaders based on birth order or blood. They're usually blood relatives—children trained to lead since birth—but that's not a rule. It's whoever will best lead the Riht."

She nodded. "That makes sense." They were the first civil words we'd spoken in days, and it gave me hope.

"Do you use titles in Inra?"

"Not like here."

I nodded again and sank into the couch opposite hers. "This whole time, you didn't know?"

"How could I know?" Her voice was hollow and flat. She shifted to lie across the couch on her side, facing me. How could she know that I had imagined her lying just like that a dozen times with her legs thrown across my lap as we watched the fire and talked about our day? There were so many things I could've told her, things that might've spared her these feelings. My heart was splintering for her, and I didn't even know why. Nothing was stopping us anymore. Yet, a tear dripped down her cheek.

I leaned forward, resting my elbows on my knees. There were more truths I could give her. I needed to heal this rip between us. "I wasn't with Meralda that night."

"I hate her name on your lips."

I nodded. That was more than fair. "I haven't been with her since I agreed to the betrothal, long before you got here."

She rubbed her eyes; dark circles had gathered beneath. She must not be sleeping either. "She was in your rooms."

"She tried to be, but I blocked her."

"You said it was your last night together." Tears glistened on her cheeks, piercing my chest like shards.

"No, that was before. Fuck, do you even want to know this?"

"I wish I didn't have to. I never wanted to know that side of your past."

"Right, of course." I sure as fuck wouldn't want to know who she'd been with before me if things were reversed.

She rubbed her eyes again and wiped her cheeks clean.

I hated seeing her like this. I hated that I caused this, even unknowingly. I had to fix it. This time, I had to be the one to bend. I got up and went to her. I knelt by her head as she rested on one of the green pillows I'd had piled on the couches and chairs. Her hair splashed across it like flames.

"What can I do?" I asked.

She sat up and turned those hypnotic aquamarine eyes on me. "You really weren't with her?"

"No, fuck, no. I don't want her. I only opened the door because I thought it was you."

I reached for her, and by some miracle, that's all it took. My lips were on hers, and I tunneled one hand into her incredible hair. I moved slowly, taking my time exploring her mouth. The taste of her tongue on mine was a drug, and I was its addict.

"I can't believe it's you," she whispered and kissed me again. "You never said."

"You've been with me," I said between kisses, "this whole time. Dane put us together like this for a reason." I kept kissing her. I needed her closer. "The training, the rooms, the lessons—they were all his orders."

She pulled back a fraction. "His orders?"

"To keep us in proximity."

"Orders?"

Why the fuck were her lips not on mine anymore? I gave her a flat look. "Have you met Dane? Everything out of his mouth is an order. This was a kindness from him." I moved to kiss her again, but she pulled back.

"Dane had to order us to be together."

"He made time for us. You never saw the way he cared for my mother. He hides it well, but there's a softer side to him."

"No. No, I don't want to hear more reasons about why you were forced to be with me. I'm both your captive and your captor. Do you have any idea how that sits in my heart?"

"Dane wants us together to find happiness through a betrothal, and you're mad it worked? I can't help how I fell for—"

"No." She pushed me back and stood. "I don't want to hear that. I'm sick of having no choices."

No *choices?* My face hardened as I got to my feet. Everything that happened between us I made sure was her choice. Her own father demanded I listen to her choices, eliciting one of the most awkward commands from Dane I'd ever received. I shuddered at the memory, even now.

"She's to remain untouched until you're wed," Dane said.

"Fine."

"You'll have to rely on other methods of relieving yourself."

"I said, fine."

"No other women. If it comes to it, you'll have to ask her what sorts of things she's willing to do to satisfy you until the betrothal period ends."

"It's. Fine." I bit out. "I'm not fifteen anymore. If this is what she needs, there's no issue."

"There'll be no pressuring her either."

I had walked away at that point. If I never again had to talk with him about my sex life, it would be too soon. But, if not for this, I would've already had her in my bed, in hers, against my tree, anywhere, worshiping her with my body.

"I'm sorry you feel that way," I said, knowing bitterness had crept into my tone.

"Don't apologize for my feelings," she snapped.

I was going about this all wrong. "No one has a choice when it comes to love. We control our actions, not our hearts." I clenched my fist at my side. Keeping my hands to myself was impossible, but I could see the turmoil on her face. The amount of self-control I had to exercise with her was pure masochism.

The moment she softened, I reached up and stroked my fingers down the side of her face. Her cheeks had dried, which I hoped was a good sign. She pressed into my palm, closing her eyes and exhaling a sigh. When my hand started to move down her neck, she caught my wrist.

"I can't think when you touch me."

I pulled my hand back.

"I need time to think."

I stepped away and heard the crunch of fallen leaves beneath my feet. "I can do that."

I could give her space. I could wait for her to be ready to come to me. It might destroy me in the process, but I could do this for her. I left the room and didn't look back.

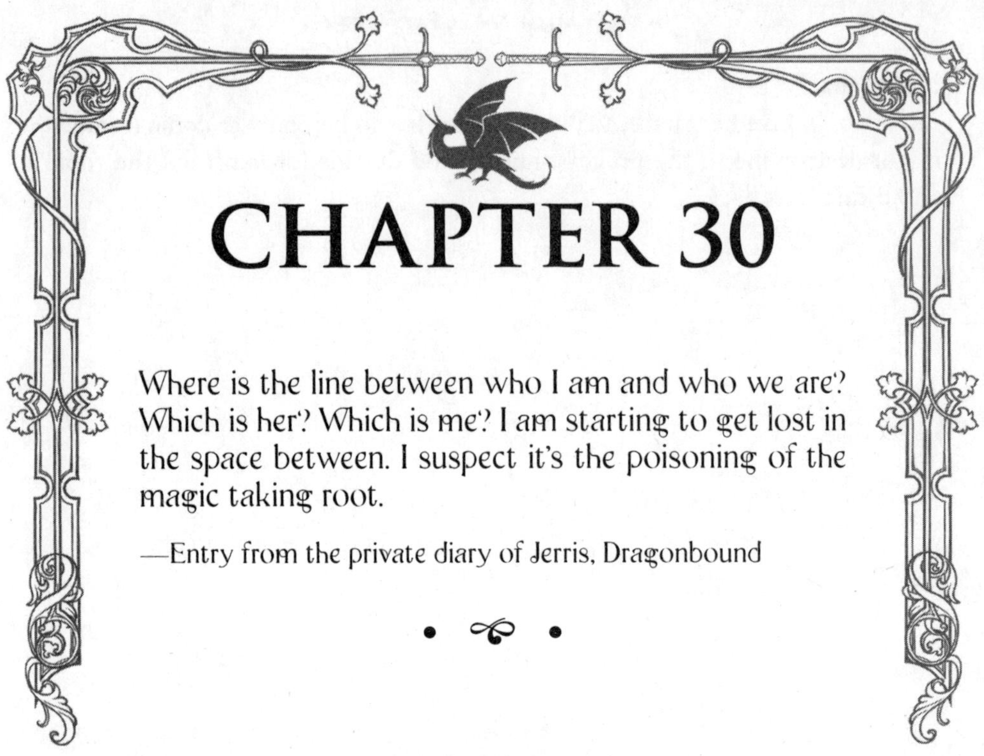

CHAPTER 30

Where is the line between who I am and who we are? Which is her? Which is me? I am starting to get lost in the space between. I suspect it's the poisoning of the magic taking root.

—Entry from the private diary of Jerris, Dragonbound

SERAE

MID-AUTUMN, BASMON 1036

I DROPPED YET another letter from Merria and rubbed my now throbbing temples. It was too long before sunrise, and the small candle I'd lit made my eyes squint. Her entire letter chastised me for not writing more frequently. Apparently, the entire family—Father included—found my lack of replies concerning.

It was true, I had not yet answered her ten-question monstrosity. It seemed an age ago that Dane handed it to me in the garden while commanding me back to training with my *ranng*. I found it exactly where I'd tossed and forgotten it on my writing desk. I hadn't been writing much of anything lately, least of all in my small journal, still crammed into its hiding spot in the crack at the back of my wardrobe. On hands and knees, and with more effort than I'd have liked to admit, I yanked it free and returned to my desk.

I sat down with Merria's latest letter alongside the ten-question one. There was only so much Merria I could take at a time, but I needed to send back a solid reply, or I'd risk raising more suspicions. Since Gerta returned to Inra, I had sent almost nothing of value home, and my father's displeasure was plain. This was not the usual Merria, prattling on about her dresses and engagements and gossip from the nearby nobles, though she did think to ask about Eldreth. Dragons, the things I could tell her about him alone would fill several pages, but the thought of writing home about him crippled my fingers. I tapped my quill tip against the wood and considered my words carefully.

Between nonsense that would match even Merria's ramblings, I wove in my coded ultimatum: send Gerta back to me, or no further information would come. This letter marked my first with no pretense of passing along information. No coded tidbits to hint at a greater plot lying in wait. Nothing but bald defiance and outright demand.

Yet, even as I levied the threat, fear clawed at me. I pulled out my little brown journal, its pages full of Riht customs and the political structure of danes, danas, and deins leading their respective cities, but all bowing to the high dane. I had detailed the four major Riht cities, their major exports, and their general locations in a crude map. Everything that would have helped my father had gone into that journal. I wanted to cast it into the fire then and there, but it was my only remaining bargaining chip for Gerta. Yet, if he did return her to me, could I really hand all this off, knowing what it held?

As full as it was, thoughts still swirled in my head over how much more I had that would benefit my father. He would never know how thoroughly I had succeeded in his task. Needing release, I grabbed my green journal next and purged everything that had happened since—the hidden port, the dragori, the rite of betrothal, the true identity of my betrothed. But I didn't stop there. Compelled by confusion and guilt and the grating anxiety that likely accounted for my throbbing headache, I wrote about the cave, Vaya'la, and my newest ability to heal.

Once done, I tossed both journals aside and sat back in my chair, relieved by the physical act of completing my duty without any intention of letting so many secrets into another's hands. It was my own act of forgiveness and letting go. Never again would I be Serae of Cavendaffe. Going forward, more than just in name, but in my heart of hearts, I was Serae, Dragonbound of Vaya'la, betrothed of Eldreth, son of Auldren, Marr Wep of the Riht, and future high dana of these people that I had a new determination to win over. This was where I belonged. It had to be.

"So be it," Vaya'la echoed. *"Your so-called Creator's neglected flock is no match for us."*

"You're awake." I smiled at Vaya'la's voice in my head. We had not spoken much since using so much of her power to heal Eldreth and myself, and though my body had needed multiple days of rest to recover, hers needed even more.

"One cannot sleep forever."

Dawn filtered in through the windows, gray light promising another day of drizzling clouds. After sealing my reply to Merria and tucking it into my pocket to post, I headed to the kitchens. The head cook that morning was a man I recognized, mostly from his red nose and dimpled cheeks. I'd seen him on my early meal trips with Gerta when I was new to Drakh, before Dallah took over my meals after that little incident with the poison. There was a different head cook I saw in the evenings. She was a severe-looking woman whose garb was always pristine white from head to toe. I avoided her at all costs. This one had friendly eyes and a severe mouth, and he wore a reddish-brown apron with no hat to cover his bald head. When I entered, he barked something at a nearby cook and nodded my way.

"What can we make you, my lady?" the cook asked in Rihtish, smoothing down his tan apron with a kindly smile.

Glancing around the kitchen, I had little idea what I was looking at. There were contraptions with levers, cranks, and all manner of oddities stacked on shelves and hanging from hooks. There was a jumbo-sized pot bearing a flat lid in the center of the room, propped over an open flame. Most of the central pot was surrounded by brick walls with gaps for tending to the fire beneath. Though flames licked the bottom of the pot, causing the flat lid-type contraption to sizzle, I could smell that there was no food yet being cooked. Men and women in matching tan aprons lined the various workbenches around the spacious room, most of whom were chopping all different manner of vegetables.

"Do you have a kettle going?" I asked.

The cook's smile didn't waver. "Just a kettle?"

"Well, a mug of boiling water would do the trick."

After a swift glance at the box wedged under my arm, he tapped the side of his nose. "Dallah told me about you. I've got just the thing."

He led me to a station with dozens upon dozens of small jars organized within wooden cubbies. Behind me, huge kettles were arranged in a line along the longest stovetop I had ever seen, and that included the one time I toured the king's kitchens. The cook gestured to the myriad rows of stacked mugs filling shelves above the stovetop. He muttered something in Rihtish I didn't catch as he bowed and shuffled back to continue with breakfast preparations.

I moved the nearest kettle over the heat, plucked a pot-for-one off the shelf, and set it down next to my box of spices. Then, I examined my stash. Many of the herbs Cergia had prepared were gone, and I'd begun filling the open slots with dried flowers and leaves from the gardens. I started by adding a small pinch of cornflower to the pot. Then, in went hibiscus flower and raspberry leaf. I had very little mugwort, but it would have to do. I paused, sniffed the mixture, then looked around. Something was still missing. I tapped my chin, frowning at my box. My eyes unfocused, and I let intuition flood me, just like I did with the patterns. Just like I did when moving through the *dowsae*. The hard lines of Eldreth's body found their way into my mind. I hadn't spoken to him in days, and an uncomfortable feeling twisted through my chest. With some effort, I pushed that thought away, and at the same moment, I knew what was missing. Just a hint of orange peel. I grabbed the jar, which I had been staring directly at the whole time, and added a bit to the pot. After giving the ingredients one last good swirl, in went the boiling water. While it steeped, I busied myself with replacing the jar, tidying my box, and collecting a mug.

Then, I waited.

The minutes crawled by, but with no morning training, I had nowhere to be. I still had afternoon lessons with Dane. At evening mealtime, I met with my *ranng* in the Main Hall. But I had abandoned strength training with Eldreth, keeping up with an abbreviated version of the exercises in my room. I had also not returned to walking with Ell, and now that I knew who he really was, I likely never would again. The rest of my time was spent either working on my patterns or training with Vaya'la.

When enough time had passed, I lifted the steaming mug to my nose and inhaled its delicate floral aroma. Perfect. A chair in a quiet corner was all I needed. I turned to find a tray and nearly jumped out of my skin. The head cook was next to me, peering over my shoulder less than an arm's length away. I'd been so focused that I hadn't even heard him approach.

He sniffed loudly. "Your own blend."

It wasn't a question, but I nodded anyway.

"Hmm. Our blends don't suit you?"

I cocked my head. "Enjoyment in one's work doesn't diminish the value of another's," I said. It was a Rihtish teaching I'd learned in one of the books I'd collected from the market.

He raised a single eyebrow at me.

"Right. I'm just saying, I enjoy making my own blends. I didn't think that would bother anyone. Your blends are lovely, and I drink them with most meals."

"Which is your favorite?"

"Your green and black with the bergamot and lavender," I answered without hesitation. I didn't have to think about that one.

"And?" He crossed his arms and waited.

"And...thank you?" I tried.

"No, what else? Bergamot, lavender, and..."

"Oh, and vanilla."

He nodded. "Good." Then he held out his hand expectantly, eyes still locked on mine, and beckoned for my mug.

With a sigh, I handed it over.

The head chef lifted the mug to his reddened nose and inhaled deeply, closing his eyes. Then, without asking, he helped himself to my first sip.

I frowned.

His eyes shot open, but this time, his eyebrows rose in what might have been appreciation. Without a word, he handed the mug back.

I took it, ducked my head, and moved past him. With the hot mug, I couldn't walk too fast, but I took as swift of steps toward the door as I dared.

"Come back tomorrow."

My hand stilled on the door handle. I glanced back over my shoulder.

The head chef nodded at me, dimples dancing on his cheeks. "Tomorrow," he said again, "and you make two mugs. One for you, and one for me." He crossed his arms over his chest and nodded again.

I didn't know if it was a nod of approval, a nod of dismissal, or a nod of pleasure at his own command. But I found myself agreeing, "Tomorrow, then." With that, I pushed through the door and, only when safe on the other side, let a smile creep onto my face.

I enjoyed my mug in peace, and by the time I'd finished it, I found my appetite finally awakening. The pinch between my eyes was starting to ease. Breakfast in the Main Hall sounded like a delight, and after several mornings with each one being shittier than the last, it was time for me to take control.

"As you should be. You feel peaceful today, Small One."

She was right. Spilling everything into the journal lifted a weight I hadn't realized I'd been carrying.

"Then you've forgiven your weaponmaster?"

I cringed at the question. *"Not yet."*

"Good. It gives us more time to hone and expand your skills. You've barely scratched the surface."

"Excuse me? I just healed a man from the brink of death while holding back an entire crowd of people with my roots!"

"And were you any other than my Bound, that would be marvelous work. But you are far more than parlor tricks and a bit of healing. All of life rests at your fingertips."

I shook my head. The Main Hall door sprang open just as I reached for the handle. The young man heading out jumped at the sight of me, then scrambled aside and held the door for me to enter.

"Thank you," I said, trying not to sound as startled as I was.

"It's my pleasure, miss, um—" His cheeks flushed bright red against his short blond beard, and he dashed away, letting the door thump shut behind me.

I stared at the door for a second, wondering what I'd done to elicit that reaction. Turning to the hall, I scanned the tables for Callagh or my *ranng*. A woman with a red scar across her cheek waved at me. I recognized her as one of the sibling pair from our mission with the dragori. Thank the Great Dragon she had recovered.

"Lady Serae, you can sit with us," she called out.

Lady?

"They should recognize you as above them."

I fought back my eye roll as I returned her wave, but at that moment, I spotted Raif and Lispen at a table nearby.

"I usually sit with my *ranng*," I called back. Heads were starting to turn, some eager, some with anger. I hadn't received this amount of attention since arriving in Drakh. I wanted to shrink away and duck back out of the hall, but Lispen beckoned me over.

A server was already following me with a tray by the time I plopped down in the seat next to her. "I can get you anything else you might like," he offered, voice cracking in the middle.

"This is fine."

He nodded but stayed at my side. My eyes bounced between Lispen and Raif at a complete loss.

"Off you go," Raif barked, and the boy jumped and scurried back down the row to his place at the end of the table. Raif shook his head and returned to his meal.

Lispen scowled after the boy. "Ignore them," she said.

Looking around, I spotted many curious faces still turned my way, so I lowered my head and tucked into my meal. Tension radiated from me, and I was certain Lispen and Raif could feel it. They both picked at their meals in awkward silence while all three of us avoided each other's gaze.

Raif was the first to break the silence. "Lispen, please." His voice was barely above a whisper.

"Later," she hissed.

I looked up just as Raif's face wiped blank—but a shock of blond hair distracted me.

"She's up!" Teke exclaimed, claiming the seat across from me and nearly hopping over the table to yank me into a hug.

I laughed and gripped them back. "I've been up for hours."

"Do tell. Tangled in the sheets with a certain red-headed stud?" Lex asked and dropped down into the open chair beside Raif. Lispen jerked beside me, and Lex yelped in pain. "Can't you do something about this?" he complained to Raif, who only smirked.

"Please tell me you're returning to training today," Teke pleaded.

I shook my head, and their face fell. "Soon," I promised. "I just need to wrap my head around...everything."

Lex leaned in, a rare moment of sincerity across his face. "Is it the part about being proclaimed as Dragonbound, or that very public declaration of love that's fucking you up?"

My mind fuzzed. He hadn't said he loved me, had he? No—it didn't matter. Anything he felt for me, it was only because Dane had forced us together. My head was starting to hurt again. I couldn't muddle through how I should feel about any of this.

Teke gripped my hand across the table and nodded. "It'll be fine. Soon, it is. But you better mean it, or Lispen's going to kick your ass from here into next *week*."

Lex snorted into his mug of tea. "Nothing some good head couldn't cure. Just tell Wep to get on his knees between your legs and—" He twisted in his chair just as Lispen's body jerked again, missing him, but Raif's arm shot out lightning quick and slapped him upside the back of his head, spilling his tea all over his lap.

"Fuck!" he shouted.

Lispen kept her eyes trained on her plate, but I didn't miss the smile she tried to hide.

I *did* miss being with them. One meal in the evening wasn't enough. *I'll make more of an effort*, I promised myself. I'd have to return to training at some point. I just needed a little more time.

At midday, Callagh found me in the garden, and we wandered together toward the market despite the sprinkling rain. After posting my letter, we made our way to the tailor's shop with my wrapped bundle of dyed cloth bolts in tow.

"Beautiful," Lanh Migram muttered. She held a lens to the fabric of my sleeve as she inspected every minute detail of the pattern. "But impractical."

I chuckled as she yanked out the bolts, offering them the same scrutiny.

"This must take hours upon hours."

All I could do was nod—her assessment was spot on.

"Why not just carve the patterns onto blocks and use them as a print template for a whole bolt? It would take ages to carve all the blocks, but then you could just stitch the pattern on as a cuff." For all her contrariness, Lanh was still stroking the fabric, inspecting the inverse, then scrutinizing a new part of the pattern before repeating the process.

"Well—" I took a moment to consider. "I think it's for individuality's sake."

She scoffed. "I'll make something of these bolts for you. I'll send word for payment when I'm done."

"All right." I looked at Callagh, unsure what to do next. She only shrugged.

"Off you go," the tailor crowed while ushering both of us out the door and onto the street.

THE NEXT MORNING, I rose early and returned to the kitchens. As soon as I entered, a cook with three tight braids woven back and forth atop her head nodded to me, then she yelled out, "Marr!"

The same head chef from the previous day emerged from a side room. He also offered me a nod and gestured to the worktable set with a hot kettle, a medium pot, and two mugs.

I looked back at the man. He had a stern brow, his mouth was drawn into a tight line, but his eyes were bright and curious. I smiled at him, knowing that he would not offer one in return. Then, I moved to the workbench, took a deep breath, and let my thoughts drift away. My senses took control, and I gave in to instinct.

Ten minutes was all I needed to blend the herbs, steep the tea, and pour out the mugs. Following the guidance of the other cooks, I called out, "Marr," and ignored them as all their heads turned to me with raised brows.

The head chef was before me in an instant. I said nothing, letting my silence be my shield. Wrapped in my own special quiet, I imagined myself above any criticism or reproach. With confidence blossoming from my very core, I lifted the mug and handed it over.

I waited while he sipped, smacked his lips, and sipped again.

"Peppermint," he began. "Marjoram, juniper, ginger."

I nodded. I had indeed used those herbs for healing, happiness, and good health. A dash of ginger for heat, too. But he had not identified the last ingredient.

"And passionflower," I added as flatly as I could, though inside, I was brimming with pride.

"Who knew you had such a large ego trapped in such a small frame?" Vaya'la's snark had returned. She must be feeling better.

"Hush, you!" I retorted.

His brow furrowed, he sniffed, he sipped, then he grinned. "Tomorrow, come back again."

I nodded and gathered up my mug.

"And you should call me Henkel." He pointed at the cooks and leaned in. "They must call me Marr, but you, master tea brewer, may use my name."

"Henkel," I tried, feeling the name in my throat. "I'm Serae."

Henkel nodded, took another sip of his tea, and wandered back to his post overseeing breakfast preparations with a distinctly relaxed brow.

The next day, I found a large pot and serving kettle waiting for me.

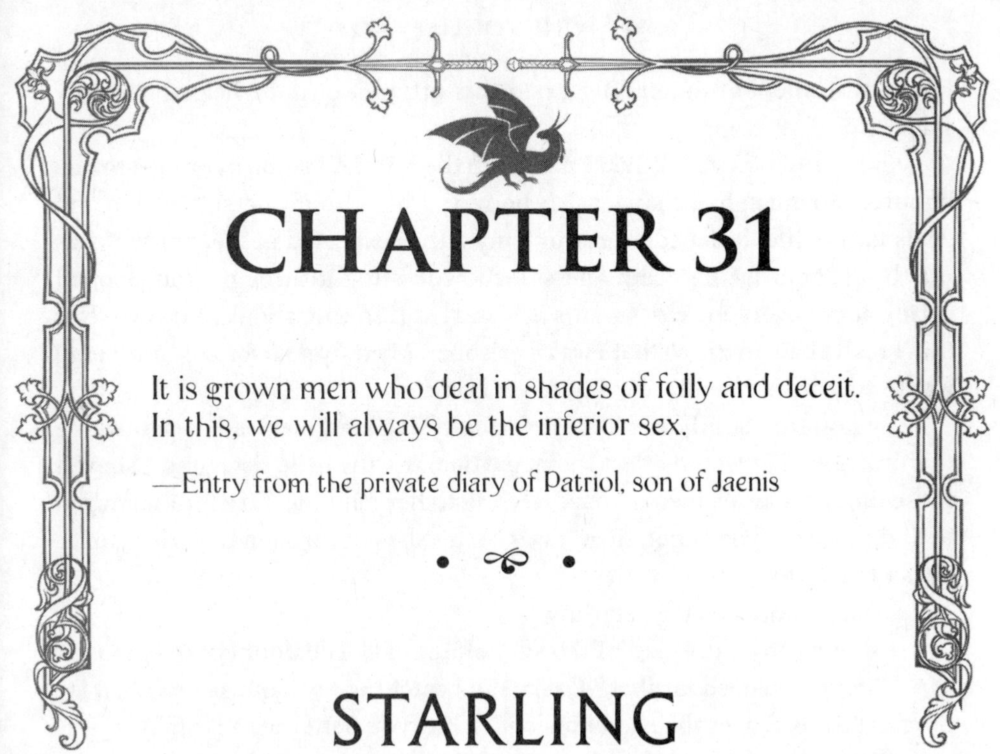

CHAPTER 31

It is grown men who deal in shades of folly and deceit.
In this, we will always be the inferior sex.

—Entry from the private diary of Patriol, son of Jaenis

STARLING

MID-AUTUMN, BASMON 1036

IT WAS RAINING, which was new. Sure, the sky drizzled most nights. This place was too green, from what I could see out the window, not to have constant rainfall. But this was the first time I'd seen the water come down in relentless streams. A cloying dampness hung in the air, setting me on edge more than usual.

I began reps of sit-ups, ignoring the cold stone against my bruised spine. I counted them rhythmically, all the way to one thousand. As always, I faced the door, watching and waiting for one particular visitor.

It had been six days.

That was the longest Drake had gone between visits in a while. Every time I heard footsteps in the hallway, I braced. I could tell they weren't *his*, but my stomach clenched every time anyway.

"This is stupid," I said aloud.

There was no one there to answer, but I still took the time to use my voice. I told myself it was to be ready in case I had to shout for a rescue. I had planned hundreds of ways to escape, each one more outlandish than the next.

It was all futile, but pretending I had this little bit of hope helped keep my sanity close.

Push-ups followed. When I started in the militia, I could barely get to one hundred. So much had changed. My body, yes, but also my determination and goals for my life. It defied everything my father expected of me, but that was the thing about facing death and somehow making it through. You stopped caring about everyone else's wants and started thinking about your own. Not that I really had any, now that I was a prisoner. My only goal for the time being was to stay alive. Maybe, one day, to get home.

By now, my family would have formally declared me dead. It pained me to think how that would affect them, particularly my little sister, but I shoved those thoughts away. I would have to cling to her happiness if ever I managed to find my way back. If not, then it was better she got through the grief sooner rather than later.

"You're morose today, Starling."

I shot up from the plank I'd been holding. The cell door clicked.

"There's no need for that," Drake said, catching my hand as I reached for the shirt draped over the end of my cot. "I like you better with it off."

"Where've you been?"

Drake scratched the back of his blond, half-braided head and winced, then examined his fingertips as if he expected to find something there. "Away. Were you worried about me?"

"You're the only person I talk to. If you disappear, I'll go insane staring at these walls."

"Then it's your lucky day. I'm moving you."

I dropped the shirt I'd just snatched up. "Where?"

Drake studied the window, as if searching through the rain. "I'll figure that out. My rooms if I have to." Something wasn't right. The way he walked was stiff. His words were clipped.

"What's happened?"

He kept his eyes trained on the window. "Time's up, I'm afraid. I've done all I could. Dane sent me here with an ultimatum."

"Which is?"

He flashed that fucking smile, and my heart thumped in my chest. "Don't you worry about that. I'll be back in an hour. The question is, will you come with me or not?"

"Not."

The speed of my response surprised us both.

Drake's smile slid off his face. "Why not?" he asked, his voice hard as ice.

I grabbed up my shirt, and this time, I threw it quickly over my head. "You'd betray your king for me, just like that? I don't buy it."

"He's not my king, he's my dane."

"King, dane, whatever. You have to do what he says. What happens to you if you don't?"

Drake huffed an exasperated breath and surveyed the hallway through the open door. "Not as much as you'd think. Let's just say I have leverage."

I cocked my head to the side, studying him. "Who are you?"

"Ah, ah, ah, you first. This little game would be easier to win if you'd give me the cards to play with."

I wanted to. Oh, how I wanted to tell this man everything about myself. To share more than a few scattered memories, sanitizing anything useful from them as I spoke. I was salivating to offer up a piece of myself and see what I might get in return. The problem was, no matter how much I tried, I couldn't bring myself to do it. I was already entirely at his mercy. He might be able to open up about his fears and hopes to me, but he wasn't dependent on me for his next meal or living through the week. There were wants, and then there were needs, and what I needed was to survive.

"You're asking a lot from someone trapped in a cage. I've got so little left to lose. Even a bit is all I have."

Drake moved from the door, invading my space. I met those piercing blue eyes that always drew me in. I had to clamp my hands to my sides, not trusting them to stay in line. Drake's, however, did no such thing. One tugged through my black waves while the other gripped my ass, pressing our hips together. I sucked in a breath, willing myself not to get lost in the heat too soon.

"Does this frighten you, Starling? I know you feel it." Drake whispered against my lips. "This fire between us that only builds the more I have you. I can't fucking get enough of you."

A chuckle escaped me as I looked up at my hungry drake. "I've never been afraid of fire."

We crashed together, all hardness and pushing and need. Drake's kiss was firm and demanding as he pressed me back against the wall and plunged his tongue into my mouth. I welcomed it all. Gripping Drake's shirt, I yanked him closer, nipping at his lips and connecting our bodies flush. I reached up and drove my fingers into the loose half of his hair, cupping his head to deepen the kiss.

Drake hissed into my mouth.

I pulled back. "What is it?"

"Nothing, Starling. It's nothing." He moved to recapture my lips.

A sound echoed down the hallway. Metal clanged like a knife dropped on stone. We turned, and Drake pulled back a few inches. Outside the window, a hawk screeched. When no other sounds came, he turned his penetrating gaze back on me.

"Will you come with me now?"

"Right now?"

Drake shook his head. "Give me an hour."

I nodded. *Fuck me.*

"Good, I'll hold you to it." He backed up, leaving several feet between us. There was still something wild and raw on his face.

"Is everything okay?" I asked, ignoring the irony of a prisoner showing this level of concern for his captor. We were long past muddling those roles.

In a blink, Drake was crushing me against the wall again. A hand slipped between us, and Drake gripped my cock, which half hardened at the touch. "Never better." He pushed my head to the side with the tip of his nose and bit my earlobe. My cock hardened more as Drake teased my length.

"Someone's coming," I gasped.

"Not yet, Starling." Drake's hand didn't still. Instead, it dipped beneath my pants, gripping my bare skin and pumping me in fast strokes. I was seconds from exploding when Drake's hand pulled away, leaving me breathless.

"If you're good," he whispered in my ear, "and all goes to plan, we'll be able to finish what we started." That cocky grin returned as he swept from the cell, but before he closed the door, he turned back. His eyebrow jumped as his eyes flicked down to what I knew was the jutting evidence of my arousal.

The door shut behind Drake, but the lock did not click.

I stood there, still pressed against the wall of this unlocked cell, breathing hard and trying to relax. My thoughts swirled through clouds of lust. Plans were already in motion. It was too late to back out now.

Drake was trusting me, so he said, but the real question plaguing me was—

Could I trust Drake?

SERAE

MID-AUTUMN, BASMON 1036

ANOTHER DAY OF rain. Autumn in the Riht, it turned out, was characterized by more than drizzles. Wind rattled the windows in the Main Hall where I sat quietly with my bowl of oats and berries. Sprakt had abandoned me early this morning, perhaps sensing the rain and wanting to get his flying time in before the winds grew too rough.

My mind was unsettled—more than usual. I'd woken in a blind panic, but looking around my rooms, I had found nothing amiss. Dread pooled in my gut. Sooner or later, I'd have to face the truth—my father and the king expected me back. And staying in Drakh would require Dane and Eldreth's help. But, did I truly want to stay? To let go of all I'd been holding onto and settle things with Eldreth?

Vaya'la's rumbling filled my mind.

"Sometimes, human affairs need to be settled by humans," I scolded her before she got a chance to start.

She chuffed.

"And yes, I would prefer you threaten to eat them, but again. You're. Not. Awake."

Her grumbling lessened back into the calming thrum I associated with her sleep, and I couldn't help but smile at her protectiveness. The truth was, I felt the same for her. What would it mean if I were forced to leave?

A scuffle at the door drew my attention along with that of everyone around me. Over the crowd, I could just make out the top of Teke's head.

"That's right," they called out at a retreating form. I caught a glimpse of a sleek platinum braid. "Do us all a favor and fuck off for good."

By the time Teke came fully into view, a wide grin split their face. They stopped at every table down the line, smiling and pointing my way. I didn't need to hear them to know the topic of conversation. Teke's sky-blue tunic covered in navy cloudlike swirls was all I needed to see. It was one piece from the bundle of clothes they'd commissioned that day I was trapped in the keep while Wep—Eldreth was off fighting at sea.

They made it to my side, threw their arm around me, and proclaimed, "You are a genius."

A flicker of warmth bloomed in my chest as I gripped them tight, the corners of my lips quirking up. They claimed the open chair beside me, and though I'd finished my meal, I hung around as Lispen and Raif joined us, then Ivank and Helene, and finally Lex, trailing in looking distinctly haggard.

"They're not twins," he said to me without preamble. "They're close cousins, raised like siblings, and while they won't share a bed for obvious reasons, they have no qualms with taking turns." His body jerked away from Lispen, but she and Raif had their heads together whispering back and forth. Both of their faces were hard with mouths pulled into matching frowns.

"Hey," Lex called out. "What's going on?"

"Stay out of it," Raif shot back, but Lispen got up and moved to the other side of the table away from him.

Lex shrugged at me—a gesture that I returned. I'd seen the two fighting multiple times lately, and I was every bit as perplexed as he was.

Teke nudged me and leaned in. "Wep is picking the formal leader of our *ranng* soon," they whispered. "Seems to be creating some tension there."

"Lispen would be brilliant," I whispered back.

"That's the problem. The presumed leader is Raif since his family far outranks hers. The assumption is that the role goes to him. I don't think he's happy about having it contested. Of course, Wep could always bypass them both and give it to you."

"That would be stupid."

"Agreed."

I elbowed them in the ribs.

"Hey!" They laughed.

"I'd be a brilliant leader if I didn't suck at absolutely everything. *Don't* say it."

Teke snorted so loudly that the entire table turned to us.

A server came up from behind us, pulling the attention away from my reddening face. Laden with a tray of tea mugs, he passed one around to all. "Marr Henkel gives his thanks, Lady Serae," he announced with a dip of his head.

Bringing the mug to my nose, I recognized the aroma of today's brew, which I'd mixed by hand early this morning.

A small voice spoke up as everyone else took their first sip. "My uncle would love this." Helene's words sent my already brimming heart straight to the moon as choruses of "Hear, hear!" rang all around.

"PLEASE," I PANTED, begging every dragon I knew—which admittedly weren't many. "It can't be gone."

Three days had passed, and on a whim, I decided to tidy my overflowing desk before training, only to find the little journal missing. Clothes flew around the room. Shirts and skirts soared through the air as I ripped them from drawers and hangers. Dresses toppled, and even socks were subject to my wrath.

"Stupid, stupid, stupid!"

I slammed my fist against the desk, and something in my wrist snapped. Pain blossomed, but I didn't have time for that. I needed a plan, and fast.

I pulled out my new, beautiful journal and clutched it to my chest, which was cinching with fear. My long-abandoned little journal of secrets and betrayal was missing from its place in the back of my wardrobe. It wasn't on my desk or in the drawer of my bedside table. I'd checked all my pockets, between sheets, under furniture, and even in my private bath. My heart threatened to explode as I came to grips with the reality that it was gone.

Gripping my new journal, I turned over the possibilities. Had someone found it and taken it to use against me? Would they hand it in to Eldreth or worse, Dane? Were there Inraen spies in our midst who had found and taken it? Would my father go to such lengths to get it from me? Had my negligence put us all in danger? I looked around, trying to think of a way out, a way to absolve myself, or a way to fix this that wouldn't involve revealing the whole truth.

"Any ideas?" I asked Vaya'la.

She was silent—asleep. She'd been sleeping more lately as I used more of her power. After the morning with my *ranng*, I felt more settled than ever. I was ready to work through things with Eldreth. I was ready to take my place among the Riht. I'd only searched for my old journal to cast it into the fire. Something in me needed to burn away the last part of that person I would no longer be. But it was missing.

I was so wound up that I opened my window and poured out every flower and plant I could think of from my hands to the ground below. It was a desperate bid to let loose even a little bit of tension. It didn't even matter that I was wearing my boots and a floor up from ground level. My power, like my body, craved release.

Sprakt flew in while I leaned out the window, clipping me with his wings.

I had no idea how long my window had been shut.

"Sorry, bud," I said.

In answer, he glided toward a chair on the opposite end of the room and shat on the floor.

"Pest."

He chittered happily.

A bit of white in the corner beneath him caught my eye. The latest letter from Merria. I scooped it up and read. My eyes had barely hit the page when I scoffed. Her engagement to that brute, Naton of Ingleton, had gone ahead, and she was brimming with glee at the extra attention. A ball in her honor, fine gowns, and gushing over the title of duchess she'd one day hold. She promised to tell me everything when I returned home—Great Dragon forbid that ever happen. I was ready to cast it aside when her postscript caught my eye: *Your maid Gretta has gone missing, and Father has engaged the General of the Peace in the search.*

I read the letter three times. Each time, my eyes snagged on the name "Gretta." Only Merria could live twenty years with someone and never learn their name. My irritation quickly bled into fear. Dread clawed at my throat, and tears sprang to my eyes. Perhaps I was reading too much into it. Surely, my father was not so cruel a man as to bring her harm. But if that was the case, then why did this feel like a consequence? I had chosen not to answer the request for more information about the Riht, and now Gerta had gone missing. I had a terrible feeling something worse was yet to come.

Pulling out a quill, parchment, and ink, I spent a long time drafting a response. Halfway through, I crumpled the draft, dashed it into the fire, and started over. I did the same with the next draft. And the next. After hours, my fireplace was full of excess ash, and my fingers were covered in ink. I couldn't do it. There was nothing I could say to appease my father without betraying the Riht.

A knock sounded at the door. I'd nearly forgotten about training. I set the quill aside. Fire and ash, I needed help, but how would I ever explain this to Dane—or Eldreth?

"Come in," I called, folding Merria's letter and shoving it in my pocket.

The door opened and closed softly.

"Don't worry, I was just about to—" I cut off as I glanced up. Callagh stood with her hands behind her back, a stunted smile on her face. Her lifelight pulsed ultramarine. *Guilt?*

"Are you ready for the market?"

"The market?"

"Lanh Migram's expecting us."

My eyes flew to the window. *Shit.* The sun was well past its zenith. Training had resumed today, and I'd missed it, along with the midday meal. Between my missing journal and Merria's letter, I'd lost more than half the day.

I hurried through scrubbing ink off my hands and arms and flung a cloak over my shoulders. At Lanh Migram's, I selected a batch of winter clothing to dye. Anxiety over the journal and letter scratched at the back of my mind. I had to remind myself to focus as I looked through the fine tunics, dresses, and skirts and planned designs.

By the time I got back to my rooms after the evening meal, where Eldreth was conspicuously absent, I stared at the cold, empty space that mirrored my cold, empty life. I missed him. I needed his help navigating Gerta and whatever else I feared might come from my father, but more than that, I just needed him. Did it really matter so much that Dane had forced us together? That these feelings, if he still had any for me, were a result of careful planning by his father and ill-conceived plotting by mine? I just didn't know anymore.

I sat in a chair at my table and undid the plait down my back, leaving my hair loose. I had two choices. I could get ready for bed, or I could do something that would force a choice, determining yet another course of my life forever. I already knew there was only one path for me.

So, I moved.

I made sure the window stayed cracked for Sprakt, who must have been out hunting, and left the bareness of those rooms behind. I crossed to the familiar stairway of the Training Hall. The smaller rooms were vacant, but a steady light glowed from the large double doors at the bottom. His training room. There was no time to question myself. I flung the door open, knowing my brashness was displayed as openly as the patterns on my sleeve, knowing I was abandoning my stubbornness, knowing this was the step I had to take for any chance at salvaging this thing between us.

But the room was empty.

It had never occurred to me that I might find him anywhere besides his training room. I fought back a spike of shame. I had no idea where else he might spend his time. His purpose was singular, and I had made it that way. I hadn't wanted to know more about him, only to find myself pulled more toward the man who I thought wasn't mine.

Slowly, deliberately, I turned. I left his training room and retreated up the stairway. Standing there in the corridor, sending a quick thanks to the Great Dragon that it was empty, I surveyed the four doors that each led off to their own set of rooms. *Of course*. It had been right in front of me all along. This wing was for *Eldreth*. There was his Training Hall behind me, his gorgeous sitting room, my rooms—his betrothed—across the hall, and his private rooms at the end.

I had never been in his rooms. I had never thought to try. I had only realized that door led to his rooms on *that morning* when I saw him barely dressed in his doorway. They were a place in the keep that I stored under the "forbidden" category in my mind. He had been to my rooms multiple times, but I had spent most of my time doing everything possible to avoid being alone with him.

Standing before his door, I pushed aside my fear and my trepidation. Vaya'la had always told me that fate was mine for the making, so here I was—doing just that.

I knocked.

ELDRETH

MID-AUTUMN, BEYMON 1036

I TOSSED A husk of bread back on my plate. I stood and paced. The room was strewn with clothing, boots, weapons, and different weather cloaks. The chaos reflected my mood, even if it was a practicality. I was in a perpetual state of packing and unpacking with how often Dane sent me away. The trips I'd taken lately, though, were fewer than I could ever recall. More evidence of Dane's influence that would set Serae off if she knew, not that I hadn't suggested it.

Words like *liar* and *trickster* buzzed around my head. I knew they were unfair—mostly. I ran my hands through my freshly washed hair, still damp. My mood was too dark for the Main Hall, so I'd hung back and indulged in a rare soak that relieved the tension in my muscles but not my mind. The inescapable truth was that some part of her accusations held that pesky kernel of truth. I had not lied to or tricked her. I had never wanted to do that, but there were still actions I had to own. I had sought her out, but always as an excuse. Never in the way she expected. I hadn't given her special treatment. In the beginning, I was drawn to her in spite of myself, and I had done all I could to discredit those feelings.

Until Ell.

I knew my idiot brother better than most—him and that blasted blessing. It had all been a game to him. That man had not spent a day at home where he wasn't trying to poke at me for one reason or another. First her ankle, and then Meralda, then the rite itself...and I'd done nothing to stop it.

Well, not *nothing.* I smirked at the memory of my fist in Ell's stomach.

But then she'd poured all of her truths out for me, and I couldn't help but recoil in shame that I'd never done the same. I'd held back. I'd pushed her away. I'd let jealousy and duty and my own idiocy stop me from sharing my truth before her being Dragonbound was shoved between us. She was right. How could she ever trust me when I wasn't willing to give her everything until it was too late?

I picked up the bottle of mead Bracht had brought with my dinner plate and took a long pull of the sweet honey liquor. A knock sounded at the door. Bracht had returned to collect the plate exactly on time, as usual.

"Enter," I called. There was no response. Memories of Meralda assaulting my door made me pause. I was in no mood for games. I stalked across the room and flung the door open.

Serae stood frozen with a hand raised toward the handle.

I dipped my head to hide my surprise. My body reacted to her, as it always did. I moved aside, letting her in and holding my breath while allowing her to make the choice. I watched her eyes roam over me and snag on my damp hair before stepping past me. My shoulders sagged in relief.

Looking around my room, Serae gaped visibly. She had not yet spoken.

I extended the bottle to her. Maybe she needed to relieve some tension as much as I did.

She looked at me with those blue-green eyes, which tonight were swirling with depth. She grabbed the bottle and drank, a sip at first, then deeply.

"Your room's a fucking mess," she said.

My lip quirked. "It's fitting."

"Why?"

Because of her. Not that I could say it aloud. My head was fucked trying to figure out how to fix things between us. In the end, there was nothing I could do. She needed time to think, and after everything she'd gone through, I could respect that.

"My duty," I settled with. "I'm never here long."

Something shuttered in her eyes, tearing through me.

Another thing that would come between us, and this time, I couldn't spare her. My sigh came straight from my gut. "It's part of my usual orders."

"And how are those working out for you?" There was a flash of playfulness in her eyes that went straight to my cock.

"Could be better."

She chuckled, and a little bit of tension left my brows. She handed the bottle back to me, which I brought to my lips, chasing the ghost of her kiss against the bottle's mouth.

"You should clean up. You could never bring a girl back to your rooms in this state."

"Yet, here you are." It was supposed to be light and goading, but I heard the undertone of desperation. I couldn't hide it. I missed her banter. I missed her presence. She was everywhere lately, but not for me. She was the center of every fucking room she walked into, and I was drawn in whether I wanted it or not. I craved her attention like a man starved.

"I'm not here for—" She clamped her mouth shut.

My pulse stuttered. "Why are you here?" I asked, hoping she wouldn't flee. We'd done enough walking away from each other for a fucking lifetime.

Her expression turned hard, or harder if that were possible. She kept her silence, but all I wanted were her words.

She had already taken this step of coming to me. I could meet her the rest of the way. That constant pull toward her brought me across the room to stand before her. I swallowed any lingering stubbornness. I knew what I needed to say, but the words were having a hard time making their way out. I reached for her. Nothing sensual, just a hand on her shoulder.

She didn't pull away. She looked up at me, and something new was in her eyes. A swirl of emotions that I had no chance of reading. I may be able to anticipate every swing of an opponent's blade, but here, standing in my bedroom with her just an arm's length away from me, I was clueless.

"Serae," I started and then paused. Before I realized what I was doing, my hand had drifted down her arm, glancing over the tantalizing mix of softness and muscle tone that was so uniquely her. Past the swirling patterns of leaves adorning her wrist that made her stand out like the dana she could one day be. I took her hand, and she responded by threading her fingers through mine. I took another step into her, allowing her to fill up my space. "I'm sorry this happened."

Her brow scrunched, and immediately, I knew it wasn't what she needed to hear.

I could give her another truth instead. "I was bitter about the betrothal, at first, even if I agreed to it. I thought I could keep my distance. But then..."

"You realized you're a fucking idiot?"

"Such compliments." I smirked. "I don't know why I ever fought it. The first time I saw you, I knew I was in for it. You looked like you could bring down my entire world around me."

"The first time you saw me?" She raised a brow.

I'd never seen anything sexier. The challenge, the taunt, and the invitation in that little arch were everything I needed. I slipped my hand around her waist, drawing her body flush with mine. In an instant, everything shifted. Until then, I had to push myself to open up and reach out, but something snapped as soon as our bodies connected. I had to force every ounce of my energy into restraint. My whole body vibrated with it. Everything in me was screaming to slam her up against the wall and devour every inch of her. My hand on her waist was so close to where I now ached to be. It only had to slip down a few inches, and I could be pressing her against me, grinding my length into her most sensitive spot.

"When?" she asked.

My brain stuttered. Having her this close turned me into all primal need and no sense.

"When was the first time you saw me?"

I racked my sluggish brain. "From the tent."

She pulled back. "You *were* there. I knew it was you!"

"I know," I said, surprising myself. I had glimpsed her for only a second, and in the months that passed, I figured I had imagined it or that my eyes were playing tricks on me. There was no logical reason to think Serae would have glanced into a tent full of people for the span of a single heartbeat and managed to lock eyes directly with me. But the reality of our magnetism was undeniable.

"Why were you hiding from me?"

"Hiding? I'd barely caught up with the camp when I was ushered into Dane's tent and sent away again. There wasn't time for an introduction, let alone hiding."

"Why send you away?"

My mind whirled. These questions required thought, and I was having trouble thinking about anything but her mouth and the things I wanted to do to it. I forced myself to focus. "Outside of the Riht, we never stay together for long to protect the clan."

"And then you were gone for weeks." It was a statement, but I heard the question in it.

"We received a message from a nearby port that was under attack by dragori."

"You killed them."

I nodded. "With casualties and damage to two Drakhi longships and more of theirs. I stayed to help rebuild and train their warriors on fighting dragori, but I left once I learned the date for your Sun Trial." I paused, waiting for her to ask more.

"Hmmm," was all she said.

I watched her. How could I not? She was so fucking mesmerizing. Her mind at work was beautiful to behold—the way she tackled a problem, breaking it down until she conquered it. It was the same with her training. She was constantly frustrated and degrading herself, but in reality, her progress was astounding. Her drive was unparalleled. I should find the words to tell her. Even when she had stopped coming to training, I knew she kept up her *dowsae* on her own. And through all of it, she'd been training so many unfathomable aspects of her powers. As if I weren't already in awe of her, she rebounded from our earth-shattering rite by finding other ways to share her talents—brewing teas and dyeing fabric. Did she have any idea how quickly she was winning them over?

It all hit me at once, and my truths spilled out. I didn't want to hold back—I never wanted to again. This time, speaking came easily. "I should have told you from the start how you captivated me. After one little taste, I was addicted to you, and it fucking terrified me. You were changing things in me so fast, I didn't know how to keep up, and that was on me. When I stood on that field and spoke those words to the Riht, I knew I should've given them to you long ago."

I sucked in a breath, waiting for her reproach, but her eyes stayed locked on me.

"You want to know why I held back? Because I'm a coward who could never deserve you, but I want you for myself anyway. My lungs only want to breathe your air. My tongue craves only your taste. My heart only beats when you're in the room, and every waking moment of my life is spent in search of you. And when I sleep? You invade my fucking dreams with all the things I've wanted to do with you and never could. If this is what it means to be in love, then good, because I can't live unless I have all of it. I want you—only you.

And I won't, I can't, fight anymore."

Serae scoffed. "I thought you liked fighting." Then, she fisted the front of my shirt and pulled me into her. Our mouths crashed together, giving me everything I craved. She kissed me with all her force and frustration, and I accepted every bit of it. She pushed me until my back was flush with the wall, and fuck if this wasn't an incredible reversal of the last time I had her up against one. Except no one could interrupt us here. Her hips thrust against mine, and my body responded to hers immediately.

I wanted her right there, right then.

But this wasn't about me. She had sought me out, but that didn't mean I could take everything I wanted. It was my job to listen. When her hips ground against me again, asking for friction, I gripped her waist and pressed myself against her. When she pulled at my shirt, I broke our kiss and yanked it over my head, tossing it to the floor. When her eyes drank in the sight of me, stripped to the waist, I waited until she'd looked her fill before kissing her deeply again. It wasn't until she untied her shirt that I returned to myself.

"Serae, I don't—"

Her shirt hit the floor, and my mind stopped working. Her breasts were perfect, and I ached to feel them. The overwhelming need to touch and taste her tan skin and beautiful curves assaulted me. Through the haze, something tickled at the back of my mind. A promise I had made. The last thing I ever wanted to do was push her too far. So I forced myself to say the words that threatened to test all my resolve and bring me to my knees.

"I don't think you want to do this."

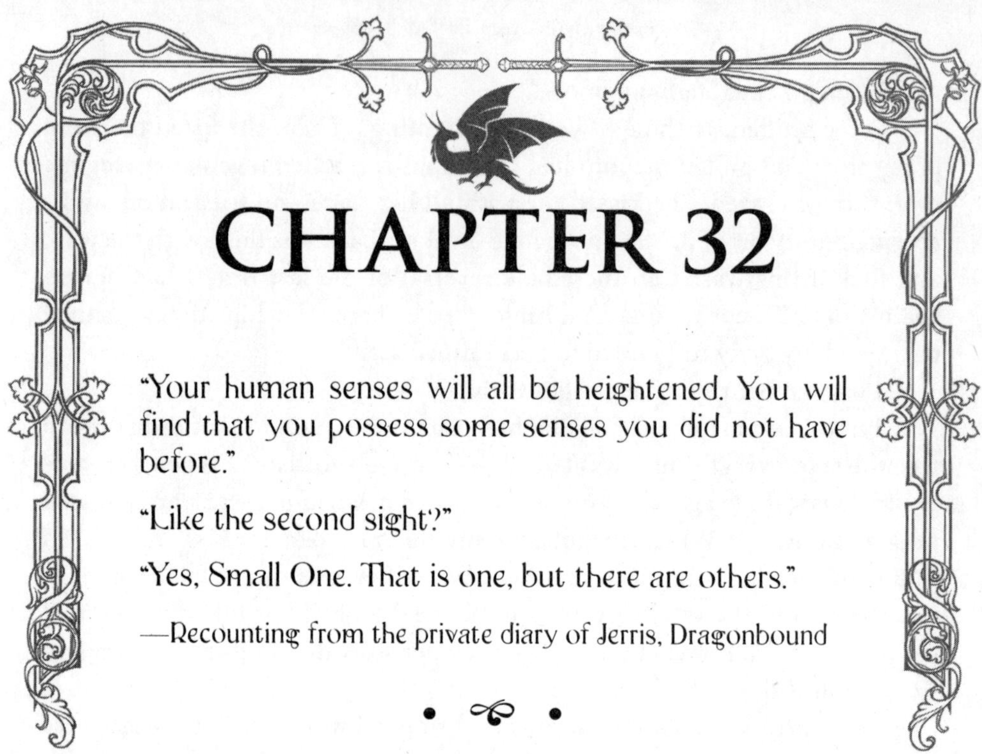

CHAPTER 32

"Your human senses will all be heightened. You will find that you possess some senses you did not have before."

"Like the second sight?"

"Yes, Small One. That is one, but there are others."

—Recounting from the private diary of Jerris, Dragonbound

• ∞ •

SERAE

MID-AUTUMN, BEYMON 1036

WHAT THE ACTUAL *fuck?* I had my shirt on the floor, and once again, he was backing off. "You mean *you* don't want to."

He laughed, though nothing about this was funny. "Burning scales, you have no idea how much I want you. Since the first time you kissed me, I can't stand to be alone in a room with you without wanting to tear your clothes off."

I couldn't believe what I was hearing. "Then what's the problem?"

"Jaeda's tits, really? We're not married yet," he said as though he were prompting me.

I raised an eyebrow. "Is that a problem for you?"

"No, not for me, but—" He gestured at me inarticulately.

My eyes went wide. "Eldreth, do you think I've never done this before?"

He balked. "Have you?"

"Of course."

"Of course?"

"Yes?" Had he thought I was untouched? "Is that a problem?"

"But," he hesitated, then took a deep breath before continuing. "I thought in Inra, sex was never done before marriage. Your father was clear that—"

I know I shouldn't have, but I laughed. I couldn't stop it. I laughed straight in his face, bold and genuine and right from my belly.

Eldreth's face lit up with a rueful grin. "I guess that's not true?"

"No! Martyrs, Eldreth, what made you think that?"

"I thought it was part of your religion." He gave a little half-shrug. "I was also given a very stern warning to leave you untouched until marriage."

"I guess I have a new religion now." My eyes roamed over his chest as his actions for months became clear. "Let me speak plainly." I ran my palms over his shoulders and down across his hard pecs. "I've had sex before, though not with you." I traced the harsh lines of his body across his impossibly toned abs and delighted in the way he sucked in a breath. "And I'm telling you right now that I want you." To emphasize my point, I slid one hand down its delicious path to palm his clothed cock. I had to stifle a groan at how hard his length was in my hand. "All of you. Right fucking now."

Another breath hissed out of him that sounded suspiciously like, "Fuck yes," and just like that, his hands were on me. He grabbed my ass first, hauling me into him so he could reclaim my lips. His hands were caressing my back and my sides, skimming the swell of my breasts. One hand dove into my hair as the other returned to my ass, pressing us as close together as possible. I felt him everywhere, and my senses tingled with anticipation.

I moaned into his mouth and followed it with my tongue. I wanted every inch of his body. He pulled back, and my mouth chased his in protest until I discovered that he was a smart, smart man. One hand moved to my breast while his lips traced down my neck, landing on the opposite nipple. He sucked it into his mouth and flicked with his tongue just as his hand tweaked the first. The dual stimulation was exactly what I wanted, but he didn't stop there. His other hand gripped the hollow of my hip bone, applying delicious pressure that left me panting his name. I was already slick with arousal, and he'd barely started touching me.

"Please," I whispered, not even knowing what I was begging for.

Eldreth seemed to know because he lifted me in one fluid motion and carried me to his comically large bed. Then he was on top of me. I was surrounded by soft skin covering hard muscles. Ordinarily, I would hate the idea of being trapped, but with Eldreth, I knew he would give with the lightest touch. The way he surrendered control was intoxicating, and I repaid him by thrusting my hips up into his. His length was rock hard as he ground against my core. One hand ran up my stomach and reclaimed my breast again, tweaking my pebbled nipple.

I needed more, and fast. I reached between us to undo his pants and whined—*Fuck, I actually whined!*—in frustration. I had no flaming clue how men's pants fastened in Rihtlond. They weren't like any pants I'd seen in Cavendaffe. Eldreth wasted no time unfastening something at his side and stripping off what looked like a built-in belt. His pants fell to the floor, and he kicked them away. Then his hands were on my waist, untying my skirt and pulling it down my legs. They roamed back up, over my hips, and traced up my stomach like he couldn't stand to not be touching every inch of me. I knew the feeling. As soon as he made it to my breasts, his hands were traveling down again, pulling off my leggings.

Looking between us, I saw that we both wore soft tan shorts that clung to our bodies like a second skin. I don't know what I expected of underwear here, but this was better than I imagined. The material was thin and incredibly flexible and left so little to the imagination. Seeing his cock straining against his undergarments heated my arousal even more.

Eldreth paused, looking down at me sprawled across his bed. "You're sure?"

"Yes," I whispered.

When he moved atop me, the frenzied hurry dissipated, leaving something sensual and intimate in its wake. His body settled between my legs, and he kissed me slowly. I wrapped my arms around his neck and threaded my fingers through his loose hair. It was silky soft even though it was still damp. I had seen him with his hair undone before, but this was different. It gave him a wild quality, just the tiniest bit unhinged and dripping with sex appeal. When he had opened the door with his hair mussed like he'd been tugging his hands through those locks, I nearly jumped him then and there. The amount of emotion pouring out of him, more than anything else, had changed my course as I stepped through the door. If I hadn't already decided it, I would have in that moment. From there on out, I was his.

With urgency building again, I guided my hips to move against his and bring back that delicious friction. All that hardness of his body was pressed against me, and with so few layers of fabric between us, all I could think was *more, more, MORE.*

"Fuck, I need to taste you." He waited for no confirmation before his lips and tongue trailed down my neck to my breasts, then continued down the planes of my stomach. His thumbs hooked under the lip of my shorts and dragged them down my legs, exposing my sex to him. "You're so fucking perfect," he whispered as he stripped off his own shorts.

I wanted to say something witty, but his cock was finally free, and all I could do was admire him. Could a cock be called beautiful? It was long and thick in a way that matched his build perfectly. All I could think of was how I wanted to lick it. I needed him between my lips—both sets—and my mind exploded with a hundred different scenarios of how I wanted him to take me. "I need you inside me," I panted.

He groaned and gripped my ankle, pulling it up to his lips. This time, his tongue worked its way up my legs until his breath ghosted over my sex. "Just tell me if there's anything you don't want."

Words left me as his eyes locked onto mine. I was desperate for him to continue.

The seconds were agonizing until his head dipped, and his warm tongue circled my sensitive bud. The sound he coaxed from my throat was one of pure, blissful pleasure. My head fell back as his mouth closed around my clit and his moan reverberated through me, sending my pleasure higher. Then his tongue swept down my center and back up to my clit in long strokes, pausing to return attention to that sensitive bundle of nerves before moving to my entrance. It was everything and too much.

My hips bucked against him as my body coiled with pleasure. "More," I gasped, and his chuckle pulsed through my core.

One long finger slipped inside me as his other hand snaked up my body to palm my breast.

"Yes, fuck yes!"

After a few strokes in and out, a second finger joined the first inside me, stretching me. His tongue focused all its attention on my clit, and my arousal began to peak and sharpen. His fingers plunged faster into me, priming me to explode.

A knock sounded at the door.

Eldreth ignored it, thank all the Dragons of Jaeda, and pinched my nipple as he sucked my clit into his mouth, pumping his fingers faster at my urging.

The knock sounded again, more insistent this time.

The heat of his mouth left me, making my mind implode with desperation. "Go the fuck away!" he yelled.

"I wish I could," came the voice on the other side of the door.

Eldreth's fingers slipped out of me and moved to grip my hips. "I need more time, Bracht. Go."

I had never felt so bereft in my life. I needed him back inside me.

"Dane calls for you, Wep. Something's happened. You must come now."

Eldreth groaned. "That was the idea," he muttered as his head fell against my stomach. Then, louder, he said, "All right, I'm on my way."

Bracht's voice changed as if he were pressing his face to the door. "Both of you."

Eldreth looked up at me.

What else could I do? I nodded.

"Fine," he called back.

If misery had a name, it was Serae.

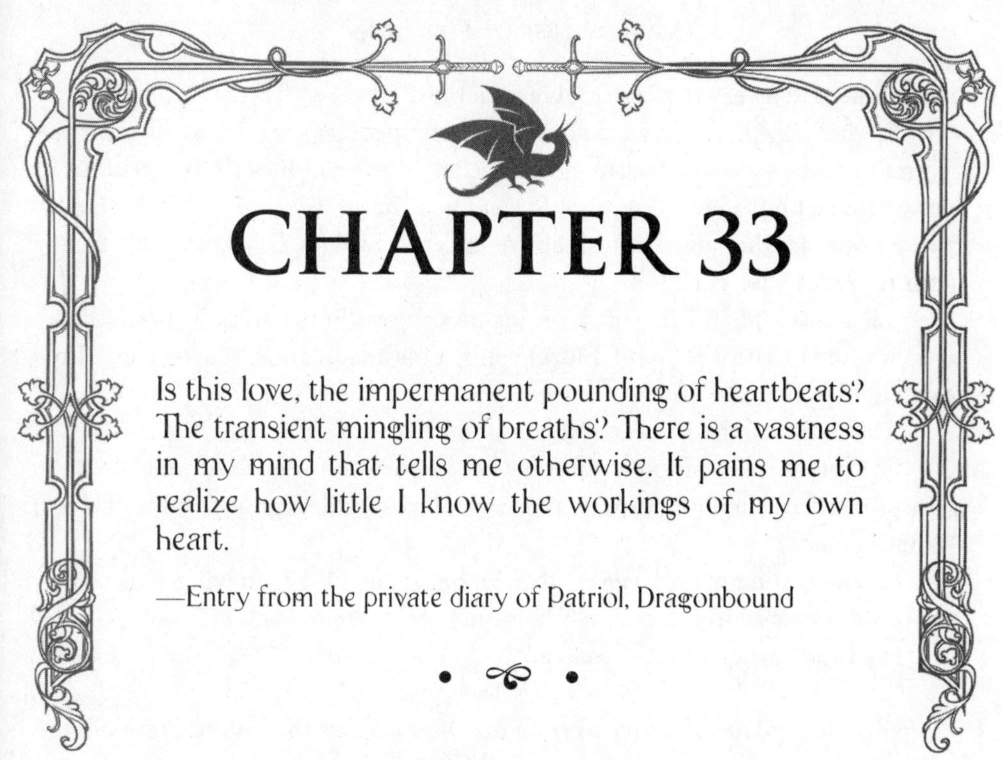

CHAPTER 33

Is this love, the impermanent pounding of heartbeats? The transient mingling of breaths? There is a vastness in my mind that tells me otherwise. It pains me to realize how little I know the workings of my own heart.

—Entry from the private diary of Patriol, Dragonbound

SERAE

MID-AUTUMN, BEYMON 1036

RETRIEVING OUR CLOTHES and dressing was a torturous affair.

Eldreth crossed the room to collect our shirts. As he walked back to me, his eyes drank in my body with far too much heat. He kissed me deeply, reigniting the flame that pulsed just under the surface, then said, "I'm so fucking sorry about this."

"So, you regret it?" I teased.

"Watch it, or I won't continue where I left off."

I bit my lip as the memory of him between my legs flooded my vision.

"Please, for me, refocus on separating our minds."

My cheeks burned. Of course, Vaya'la chose that moment to wake up. I redoubled my effort to pull away from our connection.

Eldreth reached for me, half-dressed, and tugged our bodies back together. "Fuck, you need to stop looking at me like that, or Dane is going to burst in here to a very uncomfortable situation."

"Right." *Right.* We needed to focus. I stepped away and tied my skirt. Merria's letters were still secure in my pocket. "Let's go." Eldreth had tied his hair up into a knot again. "You should wear your hair loose more often," I said, trying not to let the image of him above me with his hair falling into his face get through to Vaya'la.

"Likewise." That little smirk on his mouth was hotter than it should be, and I wanted to kiss it right off. Eldreth shook his head. "Fuck. Maybe I should leave first."

"Don't want to be seen arriving with me?"

"I'm not sure I can stay another second in this room without—" He glanced over my shoulder, brow furrowing, all playfulness gone from his face. "What in Jaeda?"

I turned, and my eyes went wide. His bed, where I'd been lying, was now completely covered in red chrysanthemum petals. "I can explain."

His head turned to me. "You can?"

"I—"

"Yes, do explain how you were so lost in your lust that you didn't notice growing a bed full of flowers. I'm sure that'll go well for us both."

My cheeks burned, but she was right. That admission would lead us right back to that bedroom, which we did *not* have time for. "Dane first, then I can explain."

He nodded, took my hand, and together we hurried down the corridors toward the Receiving Hall.

"He's in here at this time of night?" I whispered.

"He'll have come here so anyone summoned can easily join."

"Right, that makes sense."

Eldreth let go of my hand to open the door for me, ushering me in with a hand at the small of my back.

Dane's eyes lingered on us as we entered, and I realized I hadn't taken the time to plait my hair or even fix it. He mercifully ignored it.

"Son, Daughter, you're both here. Good. Hanover, share your message."

I recognized this messenger from Dane's visit to the Cavendaffe manor. He was tall, blond, and handsome in a classic sort of way. He held an air that spoke the exact opposite of *messenger boy.* Dressed in leathers and road weary, exhaustion exuded from him, but his countenance was sharp. His eyes darted to me for only a second before he unrolled a parchment and spoke.

"Lord Tychon, Margrave of Cavendaffe, bids you well. He shares his regrets that ill tidings have befallen our two kingdoms. A report has reached his ears that two of his vessels were blown off course by an untimely tempest. Rather than see to the safe return of these ships, you attacked forthwith, capturing one of the vessels for your own. No survivors have been recovered from this ship."

"No survivors?"

I startled as Eldreth and I spoke the words in tandem.

"We sent half a dozen crafts back to them filled with survivors," he added.

"You attacked their ships?" I asked.

Eldreth's head snapped to me. "What? No. I mean, yes. They threatened the port, and we chased them down."

"When did this happen?"

Eldreth turned fully to face me. The gray in his eyes was deep and searching. "The day we bought Sprakt. *Are you all right?*" he added in a whisper.

"There's more," Dane announced.

Hanover cleared his throat and continued. "As Margrave of these lands, commissioner of these two woeful ships, and holder of the peace treaty between our peoples, he communicates with regret the dissolution of our alliance. He demands the safe return of his daughter, if she is not already spoiled, to his port on the northern border of Cavendaffe forthwith. In addition, he demands the return of his ship in good condition or the value of said ship paid to him in its place. Further, he demands compensation for the lives of the good men and women that were aboard the ship, who are believed to have perished, to the sum of three hundred crown each."

"Spoiled?" I cried out. Tendrils of vines began to spider out from my palms and up the back of my arms. I took a deep breath.

"Perished?" Eldreth spat.

"The margrave demands a response and compliance with these terms immediately, else he threatens to take action against the Riht." Hanover turned to Dane, proffering the parchment. "I await your command."

"You're a good man, Hanover." He gripped the messenger's forearm. "For now, you have my thanks. Rest and await my summons. We have much to discuss here."

Hanover nodded to each of us in turn, hand to his heart, and withdrew from the room.

When the door thumped closed, Eldreth linked his hand in mine and pulled me to the front, where he sat without ceremony on the first bench across from Dane. He did not drop my hand, instead pulling it into his lap.

Dane himself thumped down onto his throne.

"Where's Ellán?" Eldreth growled.

"Dealing with a prisoner."

"He's still in your dungeon?" I asked.

Dane shook his head. "That's the problem. Prisoner's gone. We have a traitor in our midst." He rubbed his brow. "Ell was expected to report back hours ago."

The blood in my veins ran cold. An Inraen prisoner had escaped, and my little journal full of every damning piece of evidence was missing. My hands started to shake, and I pulled free of Eldreth's grip before he could notice.

"The two missing longships returned," Dane went on. "They tracked the entire Inraen coast and found Cavendaffe amassing ships in his harbors."

"I've also had a letter." I pulled the page from my pocket. "From my sister."

Dane got up and took it. His limp was more pronounced than usual. After one glance, he handed it back to me to translate aloud. When I was done, he said nothing and paced with his uneven gait.

"She already expected you home?" Eldreth asked.

I shrugged.

Dane's pacing continued while he stroked one hand down his braided beard. "You send many letters to your sister."

I nodded, though his tone was matter-of-fact. I always sent my letters from the lady Gerta had found at the market, yet he knew.

Eldreth's hand moved to my thigh and tightened. On instinct, my second sight flew open. His usually bright lifelight was dim and tinged with orange. Waves of *fear* wafted off him. I could feel the apprehension weaving through his body.

Turning to Dane, I saw flickers of dull blue and mauve, wavering between *disappointment* and *disgust.* Not what I expected from either man.

I gasped. "You're sending me back."

"No," Eldreth said, fingers denting into my flesh as if he would keep me here by their force alone. He looked up at Dane in challenge. "No."

"Calm yourself, Son. She stays."

In a flooding rush, the fear disappeared and was replaced by his usual shining white light.

"There is, however, the matter of *this* to discuss." From a pocket, he withdrew a small brown journal that I recognized at once.

My heart bypassed my stomach and fell straight through to the floor.

At the same time, my lungs stopped working. A sob choked in my throat as the lack of air cut it off, and my whole body began to shake. Eldreth turned, wrapping an arm around me and pulling me to his chest. A selfish part of me let him, knowing it could be the last time he ever wanted to touch me again. Our tentative bond could only take so much strain at once, and this might just be enough to snap it in two.

"Care to explain why your *reálta* found this in your rooms?" Dane asked.

Eldreth shook his head. "I don't know what it is."

"Daughter?" Dane prompted.

"I was going to burn it." I wanted to scream the words, but with no breath left in me, they barely scratched out of my throat. Betrayal burned deep in my gut. Why hadn't Callagh brought this to me? We could have tossed it into the fire together.

"And the prisoner?" he asked. His tone was level and even, but each word felt like a slap to the face.

Eldreth's grip on me loosened. He was already pulling away.

All I could do was deny it, but I knew how it looked. "I know nothing of the prisoner. I don't even know where the prison is."

"Father"—Eldreth's voice held a warning—"what is this?"

Dane tossed the book to Eldreth, who caught it in one hand. Then, he clomped back to his throne. "Do you want to tell him, or shall I?"

I swallowed hard and wiped the tears from my face with the backs of my hands. Eldreth deserved so much more than a sobbing wreck and wayward betrayer, but I wanted him with every part of me. We'd barely had a chance to start. He may have been done fighting, but now more than ever, I knew I would have to begin. I would fight until my very last breath to keep him.

"It's a journal of notes I took detailing everything I've learned since coming to the Riht."

Eldreth shrugged, looking between me and Dane. "I already know you like taking notes."

If my ribs weren't so busy shredding me from the inside, I might have laughed. Of course, he would think this journal was as innocent as the green one tucked safely in my room.

"What were you going to do with this?" Dane challenged.

"Burn it. I swear."

He lowered his brows. "Daughter, come here." The formality of Dane's voice caught me off guard.

I rose and approached. He held out both of his hands for me to take.

"Where do you belong?" he asked.

I flinched, trying to pull back, but he held firm. My face crumpled.

"This is no test. Answer from your heart. Where do you belong?"

"Here," I said. "I am part of the Riht."

Eldreth stood and walked to my side. "I can ready our forces. I can start within the hour. But I need to understand everything first."

Both men's eyes were on me, but it was Dane who squeezed my hands and spoke. "Serae, lass. It's time you came clean."

Eldreth's hand moved to the small of my back, turning me ever so gently toward him. I wondered if I would feel casual touches like this from him again. I began to speak. Secrets I'd been holding onto for months poured out. Neither man interrupted as treachery and betrayal fell from my lips. The only thing I had to prove my sincerity was my words—so I gave them everything.

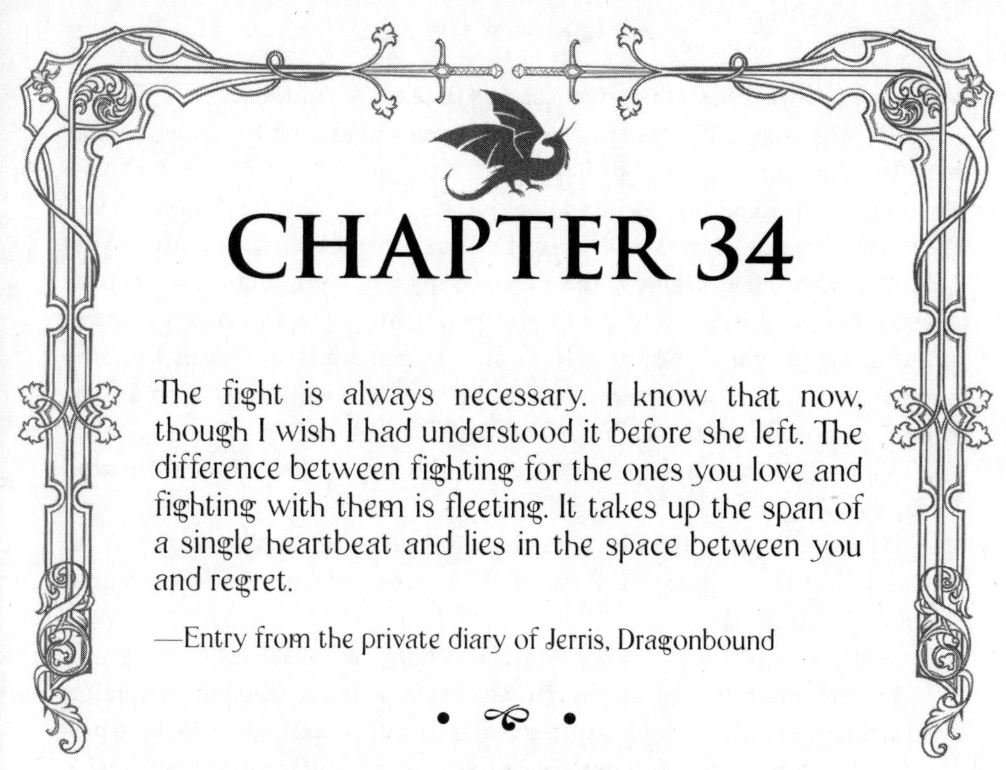

CHAPTER 34

The fight is always necessary. I know that now, though I wish I had understood it before she left. The difference between fighting for the ones you love and fighting with them is fleeting. It takes up the span of a single heartbeat and lies in the space between you and regret.

—Entry from the private diary of Jerris, Dragonbound

STARLING

MID-AUTUMN, BEYMON 1036

It was late when my door swung open, jostling me awake. The voice I'd been craving whispered, "Are you up, Starling?"

My heart panged at the nickname, despite having taken it on. "Yes," I whispered back.

Drake had relocated me to a dark set of underground rooms that I suspected were beneath Drakh Keep. This strange safehouse was so well stocked with supplies that I could only guess at its original purpose. A far better place to hide than the hidden corridor I had back home. Aside from comfortable beds, a larger space to walk about, and no more bars, the best part about the change was that Drake could visit every day and stay for longer.

That made the sudden change—far too many nights since he had come for a visit—so much worse. The absence had clawed a new fear into my chest.

Worry was eating away at my sleep, as was the lack of sunlight.

But why should I be worried about the man holding me prisoner? I may have left that flaming cell, but I was still every bit the captive here with no way to leave. I asked myself this same question every day, but I never found the guts to answer it. In truth, I was in no rush to get home. To return to my old life. I cared for my family, and I missed my sister, but home also brought questions. Would I return to the king's army? Take a place at Father's side in running the province? Be thrust into an engagement to a woman I had no hope of pleasing? At least here, I could be myself, even if only with Drake. Even if we both knew this arrangement couldn't last forever.

"Good." Drake strode across the room and looked down at me. "No need to get up. We've got time."

We would need it because I was pissed. I propped myself up against the headboard as Drake plopped down on the bed beside me. "You've been gone a while," I mumbled.

"Were you worried?" Drake's smile was hungry.

I knew better than to answer. He was a forward man who had no qualms with striking exactly where his proverbial iron was hottest. We were long past the point of stolen kisses and touches in that jail cell, still, my body overheated at the mere thought of Drake's hands and lips against my skin. The deal we had struck morphed into something else, too—something more. Something I wasn't quite sure I could handle. If we were in Inra, it would've been a dream, but here...

Instead, I hardened my gaze. "Why am I here?"

Drake's smile did not waver as he ran a hand up the inside of my thigh. "Somewhere else you want to be?"

A laugh huffed from my chest, then my jaw clenched as Drake's hand wandered higher to cup my balls. My body was reacting against my will, and I knew I'd be rock hard in seconds. "I haven't got much choice, have I?"

I turned my head away as Drake gripped my length. A part of me hated myself for letting him continue—for wanting him to continue—instead of pulling away.

"Tired of my hand already?" Drake teased.

"Does it fucking feel like I'm tired of it?"

"How about my lips instead?"

I sucked in a breath. Fuck, yes, I wanted that, but this game was getting old. It only took a few days in this new place before the questions resumed. Sure, there were lust-filled days of pure bliss at first, but they were too short.

"You have to give me something," Drake said. "Anything."

He tugged at my waistband. My cock would be free any minute, and then this fire would consume me. "Like what?" I asked, trying for distraction.

I never knew which version of Drake I'd be getting: the one with dreams of a future together, or the one playing games, trading favors for information. Some nights, he was full of ideas about getting me his dane's pardon and formal release. Other nights, he was relentless with his questions. Once my truths were revealed, I knew none of his dreams would ever happen. But, oh, how I wanted to spill them all the same.

"Your name?"

"You already know it, Drake."

Fabric slid down my hips, and a warm hand wrapped around my hardness. "Your house?"

I tilted my head, clear thought abandoning me as a wry smile danced at my lips. I threw caution to the fucking wind. "You know that too."

"Do I?" Drake's head dipped, and his tongue swirled around my tip, making my hips jerk up. "Have you been feeding me riddles, Starling?" This time, Drake's lips wrapped around my length, taking me deep in his throat.

"No riddles," I gasped.

Drake's head bobbed up and down, and my hands threaded into the loose blond strands I loved to pull at the base of his neck. Without warning, that blissful, wet heat wrapping around my cock disappeared, and Drake sat up. Our eyes met, and this time, Drake's held concern. "You're a Cavendaffe?"

"Does it matter?"

The way his eyes hardened was foreboding. His shoulders squared, and his chin dipped. In an instant, he had morphed into a man of resolve. "Not to me, but it will to others." His eyes darted down to my glistening length. "No more games."

My chest dipped, and my mouth filled with the bitter taste of rejection. "Couldn't even finish me off after I gave you all that?" I ground out.

Drake's eyebrow quirked up, and fuck was that a sexy look on him. "Oh, I'm going to suck you off, and it'll be the best blow you've ever had in your life. But then, we need to plan."

"Plan?"

"Exactly."

SERAE

MID-AUTUMN, BEYMON 1036

Rain and wind pelted the keep walls. In the months I'd been here, it had drizzled, and it had rained, but I'd never seen such a downpour. Sprakt clutched my shoulder, unwilling to attempt flight in the storm. Lightning flashed, and a second later, thunder rumbled overhead.

I played the events of the evening over in my mind. It took more than nerves and grit to reveal my role in coming to the Riht as an informant—a spy in their midst, sending coded messages back to my father. But I owed Eldreth and Dane too much for this chance they were giving me, so I didn't hold back. Every scrap of information sent, I shared. Yet when the time came, I couldn't bring myself to admit that the betrothal was a farce. Not when Eldreth's eyes had already hardened. Not when the way he looked at me had already changed.

After my confession, Dane had waved it away and patted my cheek. "The journal is still here. No harm has been done."

My heart had skipped a beat. I expected to have to prove my trustworthiness. The thought of forgiveness never crossed my mind. "How can you say that?"

"The margrave is a petty man with little land and less power. The might of Inra is nothing compared to the might of the Riht. Why do you think I have never restricted your mail?" He resumed his pacing across the dais of the Receiving Hall. "There's something larger at play here, but I can't yet see it. Still, I think it's time you both left Drakh."

I ruminated on this as I darted around my room, gathering only essentials into my bag. Clothes, a brush, leather hair strips, the few pieces of soft leather armor I had, and my green journal all went in. I wrapped my spice box in some spare cloth and added it against my better judgment. I couldn't bear to part with it, considering I would have to leave behind all my dyes and brushes. The drying plants above my hearth would have to stay, too. I added a pair of *sollars*, which I now used as slippers to fend off the cold of the stone floors.

My little journal—the physical manifestation of my betrayal—was tucked safely in my tunic pocket, ready to be burnt at the first chance. I didn't know why Dane returned it to me, unless as a show of faith that I didn't deserve. I hadn't seen Callagh yet, but I wasn't sure I was ready to face her anyway. Did she truly doubt me enough to go behind my back to Dane? And even if I could convince her that my heart had changed, could I really trust her again? Time was running short, so I would have to figure it out soon.

Dane hadn't mentioned how long we'd be away, accompanied only by our *reálti*. We were headed inland on horseback before first light to a place he referred to as the Heart. That left us with only two hours to pack before heading to the stables. Despite agreeing with this plan, the war in Eldreth's eyes left me uneasy. We had no time to spare, but Eldreth and I still spent an hour together in our shared sitting room shouting words of bitterness, sorrow, and doubt. At least we'd be leaving together. At least he hadn't shut me out entirely. At least I still had a chance to make things right.

The rain put even more of a damper on my mood. If it didn't let up soon, we'd be in for a very uncomfortable ride. Thunder sounded again, shaking the floor. Scratch that—a very *dangerous* ride.

Horns blared. Dozens of them, one after the next, and alongside them, voices rang out. Something was wrong.

"That was no thunder," Vaya'la said. *"Get to your mate."*

"He's my betrothed, not my mate." I hoped he was even still that.

"Do not trouble me with human nomenclature. Go to him now."

As if on cue, Eldreth burst through my door. "Change of plans," he barked out like an order. He was dressed head to toe in fighting leathers with strategically placed pieces of mail. "They're outside the gates."

"Who is?"

"An Inraen army. They've brought catapults."

"The walls," I gasped. A shudder ran through my body. I could not meet Eldreth's eye. This was all happening because of me.

"They'll hold. We need to get you safe." He crossed the room, and the fact that he had no questions about what I'd packed or what I'd be doing with Sprakt or anything at all snapped me to attention. His need for information and control was gone. Right now, he was entirely orders and action.

Eldreth grabbed my bag. "Is this done?" He didn't wait for a response as he tied the flaps closed.

"I packed all I could think of."

"It'll do." He slung it over his shoulder where another sack was already secured. "I'm taking you below. I hope you don't have issues with the dark."

"No."

He gripped my arm. "Good. This way."

I followed him. I had never been in a battle unless you counted our mission with the dragori. I'd never had my home attacked. When my father received reports of skirmishes on his lands, they were always in border regions far from the manor. Until this moment, I had never fully appreciated how much I took my safety for granted.

We darted down stairways and through corridors that I'd never known existed. Sprakt kept pace with us, flying through doorways and darting ahead to the end, then waiting to see where we'd turn.

"These are the family safe rooms," Eldreth explained as we walked. "We memorize the locations as children. There's no time to teach you now. You need to stay here, no matter what happens."

"What could happen?" I had to take two strides for every one of his, and I was already getting winded.

"It'll be fine. If Callagh is in the keep, I'll have her escorted here as soon as I can."

"She's at her mother's home. Eldreth, please, what could happen?"

"The castle hasn't been breached. You'll be fine. This is a precaution." He marched us along a dim corridor and stopped at one of a dozen tapestries lining the walls. He cast it aside, revealing a stone door without a handle or hinges. His hand groped along the wall, searching for who knows what, but when he found it, the door swung inward. "Do not leave here." His eyes finally met mine. "Can I trust you with this?"

If I hadn't spent months acclimating to his usual surliness, I might have missed the bitterness in his tone.

"I've said I'm sorry a hundred times. I can't change the past."

"We don't have time for this," he snapped, staring down the corridor. He was right. We'd already wasted time fighting and gotten nowhere.

"You said yourself, you don't always like your father's commands, but you follow them. How is what I did any different?"

I instantly regretted the question when his head snapped to me. "You're comparing Dane to your margrave?"

"No."

"That's what it sounds like."

"I just meant that we both understand what it's like to have expectations we don't agree with."

His eyes darkened. "No, we don't. If I don't agree with something, I fight it."

I stepped toward the opening in the wall. "You fight with Dane?"

"Constantly. You've seen me."

He was right. I had. "It's true," I admitted, "nothing about our situations is the same." One of his eyebrows raised. I ignored the way it made my whole body react and pressed on. "When I push back against my father, it earns me the back of his hand. I'm not given the chance to state my piece like you are. You know nothing of what it's like to be a woman in Inra, where you're not allowed to think on your own, much less have a voice. Obedience is the mark of a daughter, and punishment for defiance is swift."

Eldreth's jaw clenched, and his fists tightened, but he did not interrupt me.

"So, no, I didn't defy him at first. I did as told, making myself complicit in his deception. I was terrified to do it, but I was more terrified to fail. What do you think he'd do to me if I ever went back?"

"You won't." His voice was a growl.

"You say that now, but what happens when you can't forgive me? If we can't get past this?"

The corners of his mouth ticked downward. It was a tiny thing, barely perceptible, but it cut right through me. "When did it change?" he asked.

"What?"

"The letters. When did you stop feeding him our secrets?"

I took a deep breath. "The day I met Vaya'la." I wished I could turn it into something romantic. Some foolish part of me thought that if he were my driving force, this might all change. How quaint a picture that love might have helped me overcome my fear of defying my father. But that wasn't my truth. The moment I met her, my view of the world changed. There were suddenly things in life so much bigger and more important than me. Such a small change, stopping the flow of information, but it was what I could control. I did it for Gerta, who had such hopes to make a life in this land. I did it for Dane, who showed me what it meant to care for an entire people, not just rule over them. But mostly, I did it for Vaya'la because even before I knew what she would become to me, I knew she should be protected at all costs.

"After your First Sun?" he asked.

"When she called me back to the cave. That's when I stopped sending anything important."

"What do you mean?"

"I don't know, I started writing about dresses and food and stupidity like that. Probably infuriated my father to no end. That's why he's here, isn't it? If I'd come clean sooner, we could have stopped this, or prepared."

"Why didn't you?" The question was open and curious.

"Because of this." I gestured between us. "I knew the moment the truth came out, I'd lose you for good."

Eldreth surged forward, his lips seeking mine. His kiss was soft despite the intensity vibrating from his every bone. His tongue swept across my lips, and I parted them, letting him deepen the kiss. Lightning shot through my body as he cupped the back of my head and worshipped me with his mouth. When he pulled away, I was more breathless than after running down all those stairs.

"You haven't lost me. Don't worry about this today. I'll be back when all is clear, and we can fight then." The corner of his mouth quirked. He slung both bags off his shoulders and handed them to me. "There's food in here for several days, plus more inside. You'll find crates of fresh water, cups, beds, blankets...everything you need."

"Except you."

He stiffened.

"Come back to me, Eldreth. I understand your role. I know leading the warriors comes down to you, and you've probably done it dozens of times before, but this time I need you to come back to me. There's still so much to say and do together."

He cocked an eyebrow, and that delectable corner of his mouth quirked up again. "There's a lot I can't wait to do with you."

Sprakt swooped down from somewhere overhead and landed on Eldreth's shoulder, who glanced sideways and frowned. He shrugged, but Sprakt stood firm.

"How safe will you be?" I asked. "Tell me the truth."

He kissed me once, quick and firm, causing Sprakt to screech and fly through the doorway, landing on the floor several yards in. "The walls of Drakh have never fallen. The castle has never been breached. No one has taken control of the keep in the entire time it's been standing. Don't worry about me. Stay safe, and stay hidden."

I nodded, dropped the bags, and flung my arms around him, holding tight and drinking in his scent as I prayed to Vaya'la that this wouldn't be the last time. "This is all my fault," I whispered.

His arms wrapped around me, crushing me to him. "That can wait until this is over," he muttered. He buried his face in my hair, inhaling slowly. I matched my breath to his, stealing his calm.

When I opened my eyes, so did my second sight. Eldreth glowed with a pure white light.

"Your time will come to lead the fight," he whispered to me, dropping his forehead against mine. "Today is my turn."

I released him and stepped back into the gloom of the hallway.

With one last look, he placed his hand on the wall, and the stone door slid back into place.

Darkness engulfed me. I waited, allowing both my sights to adjust. The first thing that returned was my own glow. My lifelight swirled with every imaginable color all at once, bouncing between radiant white and refracting to an iridescent rainbow. Then, I saw Sprakt, who glowed bright green instead of silver.

"I've never seen that on you before," I told him. He responded by hopping up to my shoulder and clicking his beak.

I hefted the bags at my feet and followed the dark swirls of the corridor. A faint moss was growing along the walls, which gave off a forest-green glow. I smelled damp earth and stone, though the air was fresh. I had expected the air in a place like this to be stale. The floor angled downward, and I stepped gingerly to keep my footing.

After several twists and turns, the corridor let out into a large room. Braziers flickered in the corners, and a hearth crackled in the center of the room. Behind me, a pair of large doors were propped open using great beams also meant to bar them shut. Several woodpiles were stacked along the wall, and Sprakt fluttered from my shoulder atop one. At the center of each of the other three walls was an opening leading to more hallways.

Down the hallway to the right, more moss grew along the walls. There were five doors in this wing, two on each side and one at the end. I opened the first and found a modest room with a bed, a half-table against the wall, and one chair. A large chest sat at the end of the bed. I pried open the lid—pillows, blankets, and sheets.

I dropped my bag on the bed, then went to check the other rooms. One was a bathing chamber. The others were identical to mine, except for the room at the end, which had a larger bed, two chests, and a small table with two chairs. I shut the doors, except the one I'd claimed, and headed back to the main room, stopping to retrieve my cloth-wrapped spice box on the way.

Time to inspect my food and the other provisions. The sack, judging by its weight, was overfull. I found a whole loaf of bread, a variety of fruits, veggies that could be eaten raw or cooked, a few jars I'd have to investigate later, a pouch of oats, a pouch of rice, and a hard cheese. At least a week of food for one person, if not more.

I left these in piles across the table and moved to the shelves along the wall behind the benches. Pots and kettles, bowls, mugs, plates, cutlery, and really anything you could need to prepare food were stacked in neat rows. One side of the hearth had a flat surface, undoubtedly meant for cooking. But where was the water? It took a full loop of the room for me to realize that barrels of wine propped up every table instead of legs. With Sprakt's help—as he bounced atop it—I discovered a shoulder-high pile of triangular, interlocking casks, which I had mistaken for a neatly arranged stack of firewood. Each one was as long as my arm and had a small spout on the top. I hefted one down, and it was *heavy.* My grip slipped, and it thudded to the ground, just missing my toes.

"Good thing it's sturdy, eh?" I said to Sprakt.

"Back so soon?"

I whirled, raising my hands and connecting with Vaya'la's power.

A figure rimmed in sage green stood in the archway of the hallway opposite mine. *Delight?* If not for my second sight, I wouldn't have seen him against the darkness at all.

"Stay back," I warned.

"Who are you?" He was speaking in Mayoran.

"Announce yourself," I demanded, switching languages for him to understand.

"Did Drake send you?" His lifelight danced toward dull aqua. *Confused.*

I inched forward, moving so the light from the hearth would obstruct less of my vision. "Who's Drake?" I asked.

"Why are you here?"

I *knew* that voice. I dropped my hands, the familiarity disarming me. "I could ask the same of you. I *am* asking. No one is supposed to be down here."

He gasped and stepped fully into the room. "Serae?"

The light flickered across his face, but I already knew. The way he said my name, his accent, his height, the way he stood. "Bale?" I whispered.

His face split into a wide grin.

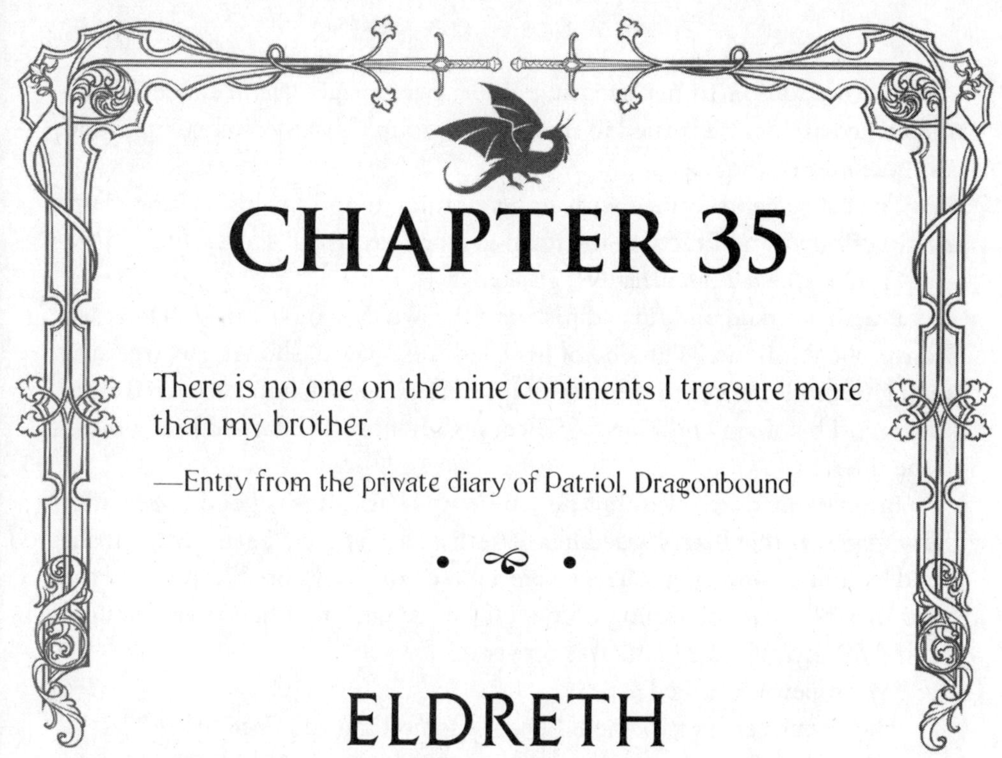

CHAPTER 35

There is no one on the nine continents I treasure more than my brother.

—Entry from the private diary of Patriol, Dragonbound

• • •

ELDRETH

MID-AUTUMN, BEYMON 1036

THOSE FUCKERS HAD taken the hidden port. A score of good men and women dead, maybe more.

The next time I saw him, I was going to kill my brother.

It was no more than he deserved, risking the lives of our people over, what? Vanity? Laziness? There was no reason for him to have used the hidden port over Port Drakha. I was looking forward to hearing his excuses, though. I was sick of saving his ass from his own brashness and poor decisions.

A pang of doubt niggled its way through. Had I caused this?

No. I would not accept blame for him.

Only three things mattered now. Serae was safe. Ellán was under guard with Dane. And I had a city to protect.

"Line up the foot ranks," I told Sellan. "Let's get them rotating through practice *dowsae*."

"And where are you headed?" Sellan asked darkly.

"Peace." I gripped his shoulder. "Up on the wall to lead the volleys."

Sellan nodded. "I'll send Yaego up if I see her." She was likely up there already. In addition to her scouting skills, her farsight *bierla* made her an unmatched archer. He turned to the nearest group, "You there, form up!" and continued down the line.

The battlements teemed with archers, runners, and shields. I climbed up, meeting Branye and Praeth at the top. I gripped my friend's forearm.

"You're allowed out already?" I asked.

Praeth smirked and turned his warm brown eyes on his wife. "Don't tell Branye, she'll kill me." The side of his head was shaved, showing a large scar tracing from his temple to the base of his neck. He had barely recovered from the dragori before my mission to collect my idiot brother earned him a blade to the side.

Branye rolled her eyes, but her smile was back. It was good to see after the worry lines that had plagued her. Praeth's recovery had been hard, but she stood by him unwaveringly. They were a match in every possible way, and the bond they had was something unique. It was something I had never thought I'd find for myself until I laid eyes on Serae.

"What news?" I asked.

Their expressions darkened. "There's something you need to see."

Praeth led the way to an open crenel halfway up the northeast side. "There," he said, but I didn't need his guidance. Silhouetted against the rising sun was the distinct outline of two looming structures. They had brought catapults.

"Our walls have withstood worse."

"Not in a hundred years, but it gets worse."

"Eldreth"—Branye touched my shoulder, drawing my attention—"they've got at least a full regiment, over a thousand strong."

"I've heard."

"They're using *bahroi*."

I scanned the horizon as if searching the trees would give me an answer. "*Bahroi*," I muttered. "You're sure?"

"Yes," they said in unison.

"Send a runner to Dane. He'll want to know immediately."

Praeth nodded and left.

Bahroi. That made no sense. This was no Volaachi force. Even Ellán had confirmed the Inraen colors.

"Do you think they're in league?" she asked.

I shrugged. "That's Dane's job to consider. Ours is to uphold the wall. Get me a stone mender and a woodcarver. I have an idea."

THE FIRST CATAPULT launched. It was a test that fell pathetically short. The most it did was rattle the ground.

Praeth ran along the battlement toward me. "Branye says they're in place."

I smiled.

The next boulder smashed into the outer wall and crumbled to pieces. We ran above the spot of impact. I extended my hand, and Praeth gripped my forearm and braced, allowing me to lean out farther over the edge. The boulder had cracked in half on impact with the wall, leaving part of it fused into the stone itself.

"Free reinforcements." I smirked at Praeth.

"Get your ass back over. How much do you weigh?"

I ignored him as I jumped back and jogged over toward the gatehouse. I had a volley to lead.

Up and down at every crenel, longbows notched into grooves in the stone. The Inraen army thought themselves out of range. It was a constant idiocy of their commanders never to learn the range of their opponent's weapons, and it was one I would take advantage of again and again.

"Pick them apart," I called down the line. "Wait for a shot you can make. Volleys will start when they've cleared the trees."

I repeated the order as I jogged, but the back of my mind returned to one thing—Serae. I had left her unsatiated and unsettled in the safe rooms with that miserable bird of hers. Great Dragon willing, I would make it up to her tenfold when I returned.

A familiar screech sounded overhead. Ducking behind the nearest merlon, I looked up in time to see the moody beast diving straight at me.

"No," I said, but it was too late. It landed on my shoulder, an unnecessary flap of its wings clipping my ear.

My heart sank.

"Please tell me she isn't roaming about."

The creature cocked its head to the side, then turned away and surveyed the surroundings.

"Right."

I had to push Serae from my mind. Hundreds of lives would be lost this day, and I needed every last drop of my focus on making sure those lives were all Inraen. Difficult as it was, I needed to trust her.

The catapult on the left jerked, and its arm thudded to the ground. *One down.* I smiled to myself, knowing the woodcarver had found her mark.

"NOCK," I called, hearing the command echo down the lines on either side of me.

I took a breath as I heaved my bow into place and slotted the arrow.

"STEADY AIM!"

Bowstrings around me creaked.

"*RELEASE.*"

SERAE

MID-AUTUMN, BEYMON 1036

BALE WAS ALIVE. My mind stuttered to a halt despite being scooped up into his arms. *How was he alive?* The missive had been signed by Prince Hammon, the king's brother and head of his army. But here Bale stood, breathing, smiling, and shining with bright green *joy*.

He gripped my shoulders and shook me. "Serae, how are you here?"

The fragments of my scattered thoughts snapped back together. "How am I here?" I cried. "How are *you* here?"

We hugged, we laughed, we cried, and we hugged again. It was all too good to be true. Then we rearranged the pillows beside one of the floor tables, sliced up some fruit and cheese, broke into the bread, and settled down for what was sure to be a long chat.

"Where are your glasses?"

I blinked. Since tucking them away in my drawer, I'd barely thought of them. "It's hard to explain, but I don't need them anymore."

I told him of the missive we received about his presumed death and everything that had happened since arriving in the Riht. I confided in him about Father's expectation that I return home and marry Tam. It was such a relief to have the one person I could tell everything to, who would know my heart in this as well as I did. However, when it came to telling him about Vaya'la, her warning tickled the back of my mind.

"We can trust Bale. He's my brother!"

"No, Small One. I sense something else in him. This time, you must trust

me."

"You trust all of the Riht, but not my brother?"

"Not all."

The subject was closed, and even though my heart was screaming to share all that had happened to me, I held back. Bale listened to everything, asking questions at all the right moments. When I was done, he shook his head. "You can't marry Tam."

That wasn't the reaction I expected. "Why not?" I agreed, but I hadn't expected him to.

"You don't love him. You never have."

"It's more than that." I hesitated. It was one thing to explain to Bale my confusion over Eldreth and Ellán. It was another thing altogether to describe this precious thing blossoming inside me when I didn't even understand it myself. In such a short time, Wep—Eldreth—had become my rock, my center. With him, I had the chance to have a partner by my side instead of a lord standing above me.

Bale's perceptive gold eyes regarded me in that knowing way of his. "Well, I'll be. My little starling is head over heels for her Rihtlondish prince."

I shook my head. "He's not a prince."

"Semantics." He waved a hand.

"I'm staying here. I don't care if Father sends all his forces—I won't leave."

"Good for you," Bale smiled. "Okay, I have to ask about the bird."

"His name is Sprakt, and he's a good friend of mine, so watch it."

He held up his hands, and I laughed again, feeling more carefree than I had in months. "I still don't understand how *you're* here."

He nodded and laced his fingers behind his head, leaning back against the stack of pillows we'd piled on the floor. "It's a confusing tale. One minute, I was on a death mission, our squadron hand-selected for slaughter by the captain of our regiment. I remember the attack. Volaachi soldiers were everywhere. They tore through our unit like a knife through paper. I have no idea how we could have fended them off. Then, it's just blank. The next thing I remember, I was on a boat landing a few leagues from the manor. It was the dead of night, so we made camp on the beach. That's when the Rihtlonders showed up."

"Volaachi soldiers?" I asked carefully.

Bale nodded, then sat up and drew in a breath. His head drooped. "The men I was with helped bring me back toward Cavendaffe. The Riht killed them. I watched a...friend of mine...die before my eyes." He glanced up. "That's most of the story. I've been in a cell ever since, until Drake moved me here."

"And this Drake?"

"Ah, that's not his real name."

"A code name?" I offered, trying to piece it all together.

"Sort of. Anyway, he would visit me every few days. One day, he came in and said he had to move me for my safety. I've been down here ever since."

I nodded. A tall, blond, blue-eyed Riht was hardly distinguishable. The fact that he was fair-skinned helped only a little. The bigger mystery was that he had access to the family safe room. And something Dane said... It couldn't be, could it?

"What else do you know about him?"

Bale shook his head. "I know nothing about him. He's visited me often since I've been down here, but he, uh, just told me it's still not safe. What of back home?"

I scowled.

"Whoa, that bad?"

Aside from our current predicament? Merria's infuriating letters, her betrothal to that dick, Mother's compliance in all of Father's plans, the attack on the port, and the demands that followed, to name a few. There was Gerta, the aftermath of Bale himself disappearing, and even the lies about birth order that I'd forgotten to tell Dane. It was all swirling around in my head, and it was far too much to go over in one day.

BOOM!

The impact reverberated through the walls, and I sat up straight. The noise had come from above, but I couldn't make out exactly where.

"Bale," I gasped, everything finally clicking into place. "They're here for you."

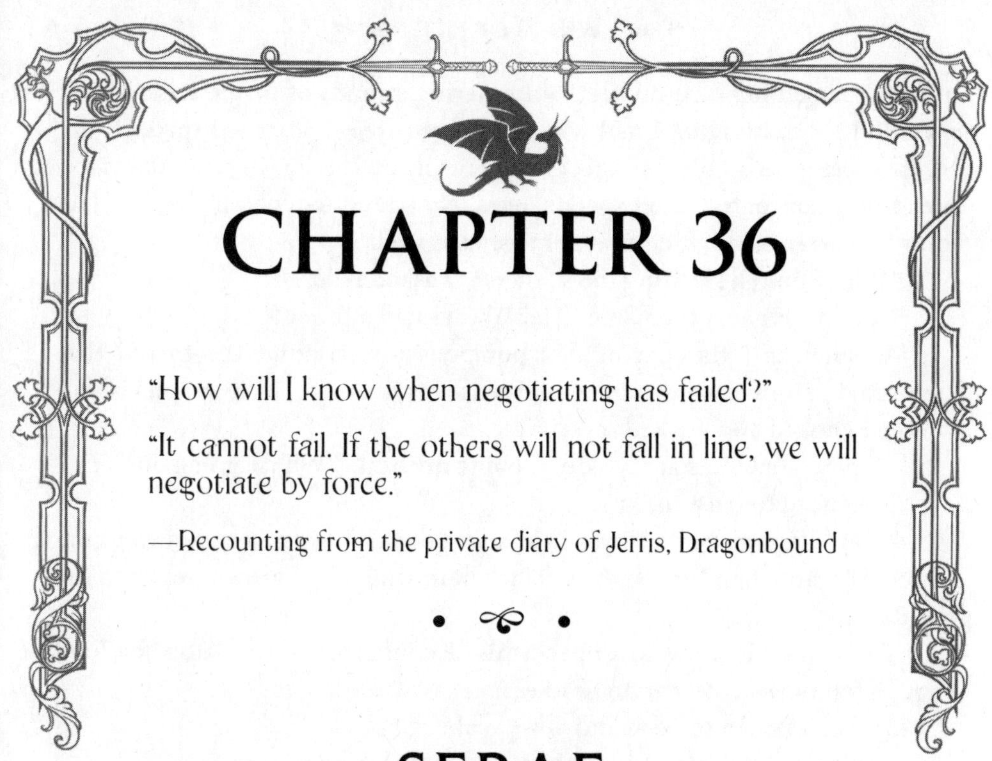

CHAPTER 36

"How will I know when negotiating has failed?"

"It cannot fail. If the others will not fall in line, we will negotiate by force."

—Recounting from the private diary of Jerris, Dragonbound

SERAE

MID-AUTUMN, BEYMON 1036

MY DECISION WAS made. If our father knew that Bale was here, he would send as many forces as he had to retrieve his heir. It was the only thing that made sense. And, the only way to stop this madness? Return the heir.

It was difficult to convince Bale to go along with the plan, but in the end, he knew it was the only way to protect the innocent people of Drakh. I just hoped Eldreth would forgive me. In case things went wrong, I ripped a page out of my journal and wrote him a note explaining everything. Then I stripped off my boots and tucked the pair of *sollars* into my skirt pocket. I was better at using Vaya'la's magic, but I wasn't taking any chances.

"Be with me," I called to Vaya'la. *"I can't do this alone."*

"You're never alone, Small One. I will be here when the need comes."

The stone underfoot wasn't a bad connection, but resting my hand against the moss-covered walls, already glowing with lifelight, was better. I closed my eyes, flooded my senses with power, and connected to the lifeforce of Jaeda herself beneath my feet. Shimmering strands of magic crisscrossed my mind's eye. Just like I had with the sacred tree, I searched through the threads seeking a familiar connection. Focusing on Inraens in general was too broad, so I concentrated on specific ones. No strand touched my father. The lords Fethersen and Ingleton were missing as well.

"Who would be leading the soldiers?" I asked Bale.

"Naton." He spat the name. "He's always had a thirst for war."

As soon as I thought of that pompous ass, I found the thread that connected to him. Through it, I could sense his lifeforce, but it was sickly and wrong. I choked and yanked myself free.

"Serae..." Bale was at my side, rubbing my back. "What's going on?"

"You need to trust me."

"I do," he said, but his eyes held a wariness I'd never seen aimed at me before. He ran a hand through his black hair, which had grown nearly to his shoulders.

There was no time to unpack this. I connected with Naton for long enough to know we needed to head east.

Sprakt let out a screech and flew on ahead.

"Let's go." I ran after him, trusting Bale to stay on my heels.

Making our way back up the winding passage to the hidden stone door was only the beginning. I was winded from sprinting at an incline, which didn't bode well for what we had left to do.

The end of the tunnel was nearly pitch black. My hand fumbled along the wall. "I know it's here somewhere."

"Let me help." Bale moved to my side. He ran his hands along the door and wall as I did the same.

There was a soft sound, and the door eased open.

"Found it." He grinned.

Sprakt darted out and led our way, thank the Martyrs. He had remembered all the twists and turns, which I had no hope of doing. I was running on instinct alone. Our footfalls echoed down the hallways as we ran, but we had yet to encounter a single person. Still, I jumped at every turn, expecting to be caught, but it was as if the entire keep had been emptied. When we finally hit a corridor I recognized, I grabbed Bale's arm and pulled him to the side.

"This way," I hissed, changing our course.

The garden path was just beyond the back of the keep. There were still the castle walls to worry about, but I had a plan for that, too. We rounded the last corner, and I froze.

Too late. Three guards stood at the end of the corridor, blocking the door to the garden. All three had looked up the moment we barreled around the corner.

"Shit," Bale whispered.

I walked forward, acting as if it were perfectly normal for me to be fleeing barefoot during a time of attack.

"What's happened, my lady?" one of the guards asked, breaking post to head my way. I knew that gravelly voice. It was one of Dane's personal guards, Braedur. For once, he was not paired with his brother, but with two other guards I didn't know. Both stalked down the corridor, eyes trained on me like I was a threat.

"Why are you not guarding Dane?" I asked.

He put a fist to his chest. "We all have different duties during times of attack. Please, let me help you back to Dane."

"I need to get outside."

He stopped. "I can't do that."

"Just for a minute, I promise."

But he was already shaking his head. "Wep's orders were clear. The family stays inside the keep. Only Wep is out there."

"Dane and Ell are inside?"

"They're in the Receiving Hall. I'll escort you."

Bale stepped closer to me and hissed in my ear, "What now?"

That was the wrong thing to do. Braedur turned his eyes on Bale. "Who's that with you?"

"No one. It's fine, he's safe."

He stepped forward, eyes locked on Bale's dark hair. "There's a prisoner missing matching his description. Step away from him, my lady."

"No, please. He's under my care."

"She's helping him escape," one of the guards spat, her lifelight radiating scarlet with *anger.*

Braedur waved her back, but both guards at his sides drew their swords. "We can't let you go—either of you."

I held up a hand. Just like she had in the market months ago, Vaya'la spoke through me. "**Let us pass. I have commanded it. Step aside, or suffer the consequences of my wrath.**"

Despite her using my voice, I was in control. I hesitated, giving the guards a chance to back down.

Braedur was edging backward, hand on hilt but no weapon drawn. The other two guards, however, stepped forward. Bale at my back hissed my name in warning.

But I was Vaya'la, and Vaya'la was me.

Barefoot on the stones, I reached down with my magic. I had to dig deep to find the roots beneath the stone floors. With a thought, they grew. The ground shook. Two roots surged through a crack just as the guards began their charge.

"Do not hurt her!" Braedur cried out.

My roots lashed out, wrapping around one of their ankles, but the other came at me full force. I sidestepped his first wild blow, his lifelight blazing with orange. His *fear* of us was my ally. Vines shot from my hand and snaked around his wrist, but he did not drop his blade. He slashed again, but this time, he found his control. Muscle memory alone allowed me to jump aside and then duck his next reversed strike. I knew this combo. Eldreth had trained me, too.

His blade thrust toward me. I ignored Bale's shout and rolled into the blade, smacking the flat of it away with my palm. As predicted, he pivoted and brought the blade down on top of me, but I dropped to the floor and kicked out his knees. He went down, and Bale lunged on top of him, slamming his head against the stone and ripping the sword out of his hands.

Braedur continued to shout. "Stay back! She's not to be touched by Dane's order!" He blocked the door with his body, but his sword was still sheathed.

"She's a traitor!" the other guard shouted. "She freed the prisoner, and she's brought the Inraen army to our gates. How can you defend her?"

She was on me in an instant, and she was fast. "Bale!" I cried, extending my arm for the weapon.

"Really?" He asked, stepping in front of me. "You've been training for a couple of months, Serae. I've been training for years." He lunged forward, and metal rang through the hallways. He had more skill than I gave him credit for. He parried, dodged, and blocked every attack the guard sent his way, but his speed was no match for hers. Step by step, I could see her gaining the upper hand, pushing him back on his heels.

"Enough!" I screamed, but both ignored me.

The guard's strikes were becoming predictable. Every chance she had, she went for a high strike. Bale blocked and parried high, matching her, but all he could do was keep on the defensive. This was a losing battle.

I willed the roots to grow toward her, but Braedur finally drew his sword and hacked them back. I switched tactics, throwing power into my arms and shooting more vines straight at her, but she spun, slashed them aside, and was back on Bale in a heartbeat. He was leaving his left side open.

"Bale!" I screamed, but it was too late.

Her hit was deeper than a glancing blow but not a direct hit. He cried out and clutched his side with one arm, his sword arm still aloft.

I charged, hurtling into the guard in an attempt to knock her to the ground, shoving aside her sword in the process. It dropped as I connected, and we both collapsed into a heap. She was bigger than me, and in an instant, she had the upper hand. I tried to twist the roll, but she redirected my weight in a move Eldreth would have been ashamed I missed.

She had me pinned.

Frustration took hold of me. Vines exploded uselessly from my hands and scattered along the floor. Spikes erupted from my skin, piercing into her. She screamed but did not let go. She ripped a dagger from a sheath at her ribs and plunged it into my arm, the same arm that Meralda had pierced mere days ago.

Agony reverberated through me as she nicked bone. A scream tore from my throat.

Her arms flew into the air as I gasped for breath. Bale had the sword to her throat, but Braedur now had his sword trained on Bale.

I locked eyes with him, the guard who had been by my side since day one. "Please," I rasped. My thorns retracted, and I clutched my bleeding arm. Spasms of pain shot through me. "We need to get out. It's the only way to stop the attacks."

"Get up," he growled.

My eyes widened when the guard on top of me rose to her feet. With one swift blow, Braedur knocked her out.

He shot a hard look at Bale, then sheathed his sword. "Drop your blade," he commanded. "Riht steel stays in the Riht." Then he turned back to me. "I trust Wep, and I trust Dane. They seem to trust you. Swear to me you know how to end this."

"I swear it, but you have to let us both out. It's the only way. Once I'm back, I'll go straight to the Receiving Hall with Dane."

His shoulders tensed, and his eyes searched mine. He was wavering.

"Protecting Drakh must always come first. Over any one life. Please."

"I break no oaths today," he said, but he stepped aside all the same.

I tried to push up to my feet, but sharp pain radiated down my right arm, which collapsed under my weight. Metal clanged to the floor, then Bale lifted me from under my arms like a child. I cried out when he gripped my arm, stemming the blood flow.

"Let's get outside," he muttered.

"Thank you." With a final look at Braedur, I shot out my left forearm, and he gripped it without hesitation.

"Blessings of the Great Dragon are upon you." He nodded.

We rushed out the door with Bale supporting my every step. I led him toward the northeastern corner.

"Stop," he said. "We need to wrap that, or you'll bleed out.

He had a point. My entire sleeve was thick with blood. I was moving forward on adrenaline alone. Bale ripped a strip of cloth from his already tattered shirt and tied it tight above my wound like a tourniquet.

"We'll need to clean and bandage that soon," he added grimly.

"As soon as you're out, I will," I promised. I needed to preserve my power rather than risk using too much trying to figure out how to heal myself.

We took off through the gardens, bypassing the sacred tree, my corner of lavender, and the vegetable patch. It was a gnarled old apple tree I was after. It grew in the corner of the gardens, right by a wall, and it was our best chance of climbing over.

Vaya'la's presence filled me, and the pain in my arm lessened. A new clarity overtook my mind, and I connected with the apple tree. Her lifelight pulsed, and through it, I could feel her—the tree—ancient and strong. She had nourished the people of these lands for generations, and she was eager to help.

"**Grow,**" we told the tree, and her branches grew and twisted until they interlocked, forming rungs like stairs. I watched in awe at the beauty and simplicity of the magic. All I had to do was ask, and she listened.

As soon as the branches moved, Bale climbed. He leapt off the last branch and gripped the side of the wall, pulling himself up. He surveyed the river below, and without a glance back at me, he jumped. There was no time to think this through. I ran up each branch, leaping to the next before my balance had a chance to fail me, and flung myself over the wall.

I screamed as I fell. By some miracle, I missed the rocks surrounding the castle walls and plunged straight into the river. I tried to swim with one arm, but the current twisted me this way and that. I kicked my feet as hard as I could, struggling toward the direction I hoped was upward. A shudder racked through my body as my lungs began forcing out air. Just in time, my head broke the surface, and I gasped in a breath.

"Serae!" Bale shouted.

Rough hands gripped me and yanked me out of the cold. We had made it to the opposite bank. Bale was soaking wet and bleeding from his side. His eyes were blown wide, but he was standing.

I got to my feet and stripped off my skirt, leaving me in my tunic and leggings. I couldn't carry the excess weight, and I didn't have the strength in both arms to wring it out. I dug through my sodden pockets and found both *sollars* still there. They were wet, but they would do. Before I slipped them on, I paused to find the thread that connected with Naton. His vomit-inducing rage pulsed toward me from the southeast.

"Let's go," I said to Bale, who nodded at me without a word. He asked no questions about the powers he'd just witnessed, but his eyes searched mine for answers all the same.

We were still within the walls of Drakh, less than halfway to where we needed to be. I scanned the sky. It was well past midday. Sprakt was nowhere to be seen. He had disappeared when the fighting broke out in the corridor, but there was no time to double back and search for him.

I led the way through the lower city. With each step, shouting grew louder. People rushed through the streets, carrying arrows, water, weapons, and armor. Some had carts laden with food, while others carted blankets and medical supplies. No one stopped us as we walked, soaked and bleeding, toward the epicenter of the warriors and noise. Each step was an agony that needlessly lengthened our journey.

When we made it past the last row of houses, the full scope of the eastern gates finally came into sight. I drew up short.

"Oh, Creator fuck me," Bale groaned.

I had to agree. The top of the wall was lined with archers in either direction. Warriors were clustered into groups all around the gates. Everyone looked to have a task, and each group worked in tandem, restocking quivers and running supplies. There were groups leading *dowsae* in front of the gates, keeping the warriors limber enough for when their time came to rush out. Our best chance was to wait with one of these groups and dart out in the chaos.

Cries of death and pain echoed from over the walls, chilling me to my core. People were dying because of me, and both sides were *my* people. I reinforced my will to keep my second sight firmly closed. With so much going on around us and so many emotions, an explosion of rainbow light was threatening to slip through and blind me.

"Warriors of the Riht," a voice cried out from above. It was a voice I knew as well as my own. My heart ached, begging me to move toward him, but

I resisted. I searched the battlements until I found a streak of copper amid the sea of blond. "The time has come for you to protect your people, protect your land, and protect your way of life! Show them no fear."

The crowd cheered and banged their shields. Eldreth was there, bow in hand, commanding the forces from within the walls. A wave of relief hit me. I had expected him to be part of the melee that sounded beyond. Within the walls, I knew he was safe.

"When these gates open, we must push forward."

"As one!" they cried out.

"We must do more than hold our lines."

"As one!"

"We must make them rue the day they challenged the Riht!"

The warriors dissolved into a mix of shouts and cheers. Then, the banging started. It began with one group thumping their shields, and more joined in. Those holding spears slammed them into the hard earth in time to the rhythmic beat. Others stomped their feet. The result was a drumbeat that shook the ground itself. The cacophony was so loud, so jarring, I felt it in my teeth. It was a sound that struck fear into the hearts of its enemies, reminding them of the ferocity of the Riht.

"Brothers and sisters!" The pounding eased to a rumble so they could hear their future dane's voice. "Never would I ask you to do what I, myself, would not. WE GO TOGETHER!"

"AS ONE!" The cheers were deafening.

Bale gripped my shoulders, propping me up when my knees weakened. He shouted something in my ear, but I couldn't hear him over the throng.

When the uproar dwindled, Eldreth called, "May our archers' aim be true!"

The warriors echoed back, *"Our arrows will fly true!"*

"May our blades find their marks!"

"Our blades will find their marks!"

"May we all go home as one!"

"To Dane's halls or Veyhallah's!" They took up the drumbeat again. *"As one! As one! As one!"*

Eldreth disappeared from his post atop the battlements, and I knew he was readying to lead his warriors on foot. Fear, hot and feral, raged through me.

I gripped Bale's arm and shoved between the nearest groups of warriors. Our only hope was to circumvent the fighting and pray that we managed to stay alive. My arm was throbbing, and Bale's side was still seeping blood.

Could we even make it?

There was no time to consider. A hulking, grinding crank began to turn, opening the gates. Between the slim gap, one of the curved talons peeked into view. As soon as the gates parted, the warriors began to pour through, dashing beneath the dragon's monstrous claw. When it opened to the width of four people standing abreast, it ground to a halt. With horror, I saw Eldreth raising his sword in salute to each group that passed through.

A hawk screeched overhead, and I turned my eyes to the sky. My heart sank. I knew the outline of that sparrowhawk. He was circling low. My eyes flew to Eldreth, who had paused his salute to watch Sprakt's descent. The bird would lead him straight to me.

No, no, no!

Sprakt dived and landed, not on my shoulder, but Eldreth's.

"We have to go, *now!*" I shouted to Bale. I gripped his hand and pulled us as far to the left as I could manage. I kept my head down, but with the bottleneck at the gates and my hair shining flame-bright in the sun...

"What's wrong?" Bale shouted in my ear over the clamor of the ranks.

We were nearly there.

"Later," I said, not daring to raise my voice.

Just a little farther...

"Serae?"

Fuck.

Eldreth's next shout was strangled. "No! Serae!"

I did not turn. I clung to Bale's hand and shoved forward as fast as I could, ducking between the last few rows of warriors blocking our path. With a final push, we squeezed through the gates.

"Stop! STOP!"

We took off at a full run. I angled us north away from the fighting and straight for the trees. The Riht warriors parted for us easily. They were focused eastward, readying to block the army advancing from straight ahead. We didn't dare slow in case Eldreth was on our tail. I could just make out his voice above the rest, barking orders. He would understand when all was done.

We weaved between warriors until we hit the trees, where we slowed our pace to navigate the rustling woods. I directed us straight for Naton, praying to all Dragons that we wouldn't be shot down before we had a chance to speak. It was already a miracle that I was still on two feet with my useless arm bouncing painfully at each step.

Luck was on our side, or maybe it was Vaya'la's influence. Halfway there, I saw a small party with white flags making a slow path toward the Riht warriors. I redirected our course. Bale, seeing the group, began waving and shouting as we ran.

"Help us—we're Cavendaffes!"

The name grated me. I wasn't a Cavendaffe anymore.

The three men paused their course and turned to us. One reached for his sword, but the other two gaped.

"Lord Bale!" one shouted. "Is it you?"

We reached their group panting.

"Lorrick," Bale gasped between heavy breaths. "You're a sight for sore eyes."

"What are you doing here?" The soldier had stripes of honor on one shoulder and the Cavendaffe crest on the other. He was as tall as Bale but broader, with brown hair tied back in a low tail. I knew many of the guards and soldiers from living at the manor, but I didn't recognize this one.

Bale attempted to explain, but I interrupted. "Call off the attack."

"Serae?" Large hands gripped my arms, and I screamed when he pressed on my wound. The man ignored my protests and crushed me to his chest. "Thank the Creator. How did you escape?"

"Escape?" I asked, shoving him away. I looked up into his face. *"Tam?"*

He rested a gloved palm on my cheek in a way that might have been tender if it didn't make my skin crawl. I pulled back.

How was Tam here?

"This changes everything. We need to regroup." Tam gripped my forearm and marched us farther east into the forest.

"I can walk on my own," I said, twisting my arm free of his grasp.

Shock flashed over Tam's face, but he nodded. "Of course, of course, I'm sorry."

Lorrick, Bale, and the third soldier were on our heels. I hated moving farther from Drakh, but I needed them to agree to take Bale and leave as quickly as possible, before more people were hurt.

"Where are we going?" I asked.

"To Lord Naton. We have what we came for. He's the one who has to signal the retreat."

It was a shorter walk than I expected. Directly between the two disabled catapults stood a mobile tent. From dozens of yards away, I could already make out Naton's figure. He was a harsh shadow with blood-red lifelight oozing around him. The sight of it had never been more revolting. Vaya'la's unease poured into me.

"Do not approach, Small One."

"Don't worry, I'm not staying."

"It would be better if you turned and ran now. Flee back to the walls."

Dragons, I wanted to, but I had to make sure Drakh was safe first. After the part I played in betraying the Riht, the least I could do was help end this conflict. If that meant convincing Naton face-to-face to initiate their retreat, so be it.

Bale slipped his hand into mine. His half-smile at my side was reassuring, though faint. My pace slowed, and Bale slowed with me.

"What's up?" he whispered.

There was an acrid scent in the air. It was more than swords and catapults and arrows. Something rank was at work here.

"What is that?" I called to Tam.

He gave me a dark look. "We need to hurry."

"I have to go back."

Tam shook his head. "I can't let you do that."

Bale came to a halt, yanking me behind him. "Like hell, you can't. Explain yourself."

Lorrick and the other soldier closed in behind me, each placing a hand on my shoulder. I dropped and twisted out of their grip, but another pair of soldiers had closed in on our group. I struck, following my instincts and allowing Eldreth's training to flow through me. When one soldier tried to grapple me, I used cat *dowsa* to slip away. When another swung at me, I used bear *dowsa* to knock him to the ground. Air *dowsa* kept me light on my feet, but I couldn't last. Adrenaline alone let me move my injured arm, but I was fading.

Tam called out, and more soldiers came. I was forced back and surrounded. Fighting my way out was the only option, but I didn't have a blade.

"You are never unarmed, Small One."

I called for my roots, my vines, anything from my magic within.

That's when I heard his voice. "Get your hands off of my betrothed."

My heart swelled even as panic gripped me. Turning to my left, my second sight opened as Eldreth came striding out of the trees—a beacon of pure white brilliance—with two warriors at his side. A man and a woman I had seen before, but didn't know their names. The three of them radiated power and control.

"Kill them," a chilling voice spoke in Inraen.

I turned, expecting to see Naton, but it was Tam, lifelight pulsing puce with *jealousy.* Tam—who hated hunting, cried when his favorite hound died, and always treated me with so much care—had just ordered the death of three people like it was nothing.

Eldreth only grinned and continued his approach, flanked by his two shadows. Soldiers broke away and charged their group. They fell like wheat. It happened so fast, I couldn't even register whose kill was whose.

"Stop this!" I shouted at Tam, using my native tongue. "Take Bale and go. You have what you wanted."

He turned back to me, a flicker of dull aqua surrounded him. *Confusion.* "We came for you."

"Me?" It struck me like a blow. My balance wavered, though that may have been from blood loss at this point. My wound was freshly bleeding again. "Why me?"

"Enough games, Serae. You've had your fun. It's time to come home."

Steel cut through the air, and I turned to see Eldreth cleave a soldier from shoulder to hip. He kicked the body aside and moved like water to the next. He was no eddy nor curving river. He was a tidal wave, crashing into each soldier he met and leaving destruction in his wake.

"Call off your dog, and let's go."

I punched Tam square in the jaw. His head snapped to the side. I'd had to use my left, but his jaw still cracked. "I'm not going anywhere."

"I think you'll find you are." Tam gripped my injured arm, squeezing hard.

I screamed. Before I could react, he flung me into the arms of a waiting soldier. A moment later, cold steel pressed against my throat. Panic blinded me. I kicked, trying to gain leverage to do something, anything, but the arm around me lifted me to my toes. The blade at my neck bit in. I stilled.

"Stop—*oof!*" Bale shouted before doubling over from a punch to the gut. Lorrick pinned his arms behind his back while the third soldier, who had accompanied him and Tam, doled out the punches.

"Stop, or she dies!" bellowed a voice beside me in Mayoran. Naton of Ingleton had finally joined us, and it was his blade at my throat.

My eyes flew to Eldreth and his warriors. They, too, had stilled, but they held their fighting stances. Eldreth did not speak. He didn't even glance my way. He stood at the ready and waited as soldiers encircled us.

"Good," Naton crooned. His voice was as cocky and arrogant as ever. He wore the colors of his house—black and gold—with not a dot of Inraen red on him. His hair was slicked back and as oily as the man himself.

"Release me, Nate," Bale warned. "Or, is your plan to turn traitor as well?"

Naton gave a dramatic startle, as if he had just seen Bale for the first time. His grin was wicked. "Why, Bale, my old classmate. As soon as you prove yourself an ally, you'll be released. The same goes for Tam's little pet."

Bale growled as the soldier behind me tightened his grip, making me whimper in pain. My useless arm was crushed to my side, and he twisted my good arm behind my back.

"Or, can you not control her, Tam?"

Tam walked forward, keeping a considerable distance from Eldreth but speaking loudly enough in Mayoran for him to hear. "Stop this madness. Tell your Rihtlonder attack dog that the game is up. We're headed home."

"She is home." Eldreth spoke as if it were the most normal conversation. Every ounce of him radiated calm.

"Let's get one thing straight. Serae is *my* betrothed. She always has been, and she will be until the day I marry her."

"Call upon your roots and vines," Vaya'la spoke into my mind. *"Do not hesitate."*

My feet weren't touching the soil. I hadn't removed my *sollars,* not expecting to need my power so soon, and I was still suspended by the brute holding me.

"I can't."

"You can. Your only limitation is your mind. Connect."

I had to try. I'd conjured plants from my bedroom more than once. I'd first summoned my thorn armor while at sea. And today, I called up roots through the stone floor of the keep and reshaped a tree into a staircase. If I could do all that, I could damn well do this. Tam was talking—snide remarks Eldreth would never fall for—and I ignored him. I searched for that heat, that connection, that power. I closed my eyes and relaxed all my muscles. The soldier's grip on my arms loosened just a fraction, but it was enough to allow me to breathe without agony. My feet grazed the grass, and the tiniest spark traveled from my chest down to my toes.

Grow, I told it.

Nothing happened. Fear clawed at me. What if I couldn't do it?

A hawk screeched overhead, but no one else moved. Either they were waiting, or time had expanded around me. I redoubled my focus, pushing aside my panic and searching for the roots. I called them forth, willing them to grow and expand. I imagined the roots twisting around the boots of the Inraens and forcing them to the ground. I imagined them jutting up like spikes, surrounding Eldreth and his warriors in a ring of protection. I imagined them engulfing Lorrick and allowing Bale to run free.

Screams sounded. Pounding drums rumbled underfoot. My eyes popped open. Hundreds of Riht warriors advanced toward us, having finally caught up with Eldreth and the other two. I could see the archers in the back, the line of shields up front, and warriors with every imaginable weapon in between. Some were on horseback, and in the very back, though I couldn't see them, I knew there would be carts to rush the wounded back to safety.

But there were no roots—not even a lengthened blade of grass. I had failed. I couldn't sound the Inraen retreat. The Drakhi warriors had closed in. And Eldreth and Bale, the two men I cherished most in this world, were at the epicenter of it all. I choked back a sob, and Naton's blade grazed my throat.

Eldreth inched toward me, swords still at the ready.

Naton laughed. It was a bone-chilling, throaty laugh of a man unhinged. "Very good delay tactic." Trumpets blew behind him, their metallic ring so incongruous with the natural horns of the Riht that it set my teeth on edge. "We've got what we came for. She's more than just a pretty trophy, wouldn't you say? Please, feel free to kill more of my men."

He nodded to the man restraining me, who turned and hauled me up like a sack of grain. His spaulder slammed into my diaphragm, driving the wind from my lungs as I tried to scream. Spikes exploded out of me, but between his spaulders and bracers, they did little harm. I spluttered and coughed as he ran, armor jabbing me every few steps while his arms wrapped around my thighs in a death grip. I beat at him with my one good arm, unable to kick my legs against his grip, but he didn't even flinch. All I could see was grass and leaves under his feet.

"Over here!" someone shouted, and we changed directions. "We've got a crate!"

Even through the jarring pain, that phrase sent a shiver down my spine. "No," I rasped without any chance of being heard.

"I see it," said the man holding me.

A moment later, I was dropped ass-first into a sort of litter.

"Get your hands off me!" Bale's shout rang out from somewhere nearby.

I had barely gotten myself upright—a harder task with only one good arm—when the ground beneath me shook. It reverberated with so much force that I was thrown forward and then flung back. The base of my head connected with something hard, and I fell into blackness.

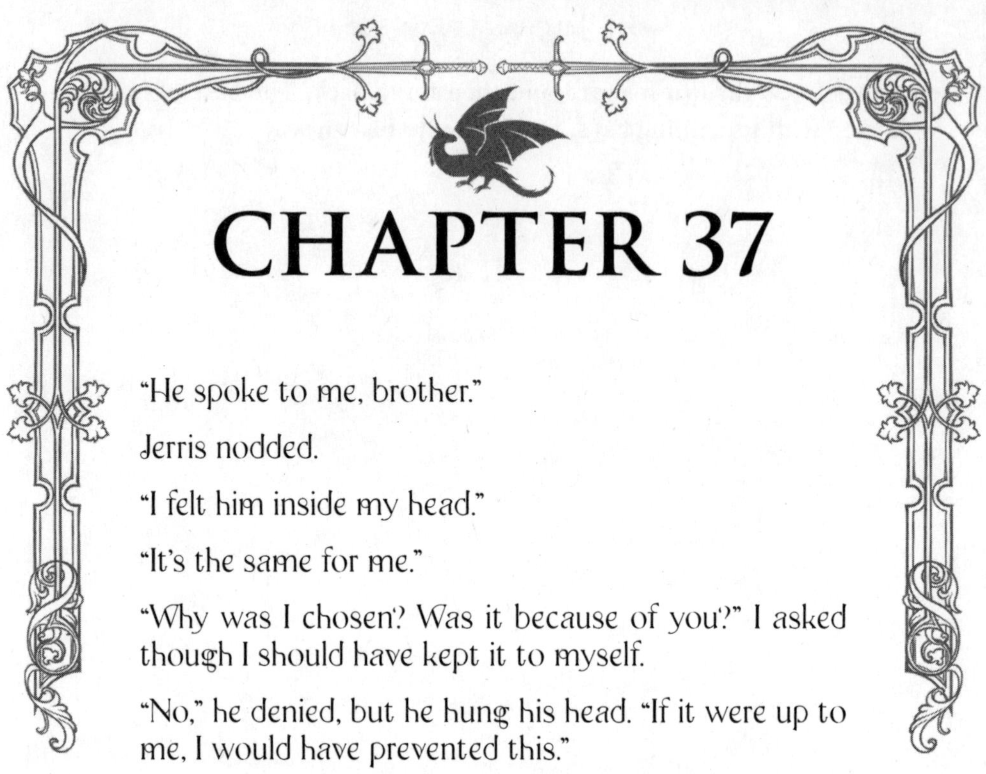

CHAPTER 37

"He spoke to me, brother."

Jerris nodded.

"I felt him inside my head."

"It's the same for me."

"Why was I chosen? Was it because of you?" I asked though I should have kept it to myself.

"No," he denied, but he hung his head. "If it were up to me, I would have prevented this."

—Recounting from the private diary of Patriol, Dragonbound

ELDRETH

MID-AUTUMN, BEYMON 1036

Dane sat on his throne and glared. The war council had been convened. Half the members had arrived, while others still made their way from the outskirts of the city. They would decide whether the danes, danas, and deins from across the Riht would be summoned. Since restoring our city to safety, I had organized teams to supply aid to the hidden port and begin the rebuilding process. I had spoken to the families of those who were killed both at the port and outside the walls. I had bathed, dressed, and eaten. But I had not slept.

Even when I tried to close my eyes, sleep would not claim me.

"How did they know?" my father asked over the din.

That was my question as well. I shook my head and rubbed my face in my hands. "I don't think they did."

Dane grunted.

Ell and I sat directly across from him in our usual seats of honor within the council. My brother's face was uncharacteristically grave. Serae's absence at my side threatened to break me.

In my mind's eye, all I could see were the drops of her blood staining the grass. Taking up equal space in my head was that spineless man with the pointed chin who looked at Serae like he owned her. His words rang in my ears.

Let's get one thing straight. Serae is my *betrothed. She always has been, and she will be until the day I marry her.*

The prince of Rihtlond, brought low by the cunning of a woman.

Did you think she was yours? She was using you, fool.

The worst part was that his taunts had worked. I had hesitated, just for one deplorable second, and they had whisked her back into their ranks and beyond my reach. I had pressed my warriors forward, Branye and a newly recovered Praeth at my side, until every last Inraen soldier was fleeing on a ship or dead. I had killed dozens of men, but my only regret was the one man I hadn't.

At least he didn't get away unscathed. I scored one hit before the coward turned and ran.

Dane's hand fell on my shoulder. I looked up, not having registered him rising to his feet or descending from the dais. He held out his hand, and I gripped his forearm. He pulled me to my feet and looked me square in the eye.

"We will not rest," Dane said. Ell stood and moved to my side. They boxed me in, blocking out most of the room.

I nodded. I held my body still and calm. My breaths were deep and even, but inside, I was crawling with guilt.

"Listen to me, Son." It was my father's voice this time, the command of the dane stripped away. "We will find her. We will get her back."

The words tore something in me. "What if she doesn't want to be found?" I could not meet his eyes as I gave voice to my fears, but I felt the question in his grip.

It was Ell who answered. "Serae will claw through the stars if that's her only way back to you. If you don't know that by now, you don't deserve her."

"Aye." Dane nodded. He released my arm.

I wished she didn't have to. I gripped their shoulders, giving the thanks I couldn't bring into words. "Forgive me, I'm not myself."

I moved to retreat to the back of the room, away from the focus of the assembly, but my father pulled me back into a beast of a hug that only a man his size could give. I gripped him back, allowing myself this moment of weakness. Next would come the planning. The time for strength and action waited around the bend. But for this one moment, this span of heartbeats that we shared—even though it was in the middle of the Receiving Hall with only Ellán to block all the eyes of the Riht on us—I gave myself the grace to acknowledge my failure.

"Only lies spew from the mouth of envy," he said, his voice rumbling in my ear.

He clapped my back, then held me at arm's length, surveying me again. He nodded once.

"We need to talk," I told my brother.

Dane's face turned hard as he surveyed us, his two sons. "I expect both of you in my chambers after the council meeting. We have much to discuss."

I left the Receiving Hall and made my way across the castle to my Training Hall. My body thrummed to be with Serae. I should never have left her on her own. The pull to be near her brought me to her Relaxation Room, calling forth my first memory of her here, candlelight dancing over her skin. Despite the lack of sleep and the pain etched into her face, she had been radiant. The door was already cracked, and I pulled up short when I heard voices.

"This can't continue, and you know it." Lispen, the little fierce one from Serae's *ranng*, said. What on Jaeda was her *ranng* doing holed up in here?

"It can." I recognized the voice as Raif's. "I don't give a fuck about my family or yours."

"You don't mean that."

"You're right. There's nothing wrong with your family, but mine can fuck right off."

I shifted, angling my head to see into the room. Not her *ranng*, then—just these two.

"Now's not the time. Serae's missing, Wep looks like he's about to lose his shit, and you want to talk about this?"

This was a private conversation I didn't need to get involved in. I was ready to pull away, but after hearing both of our names, I paused.

"Obviously I'm worried about Serae, but until the council approves a course of action, there's nothing we can do."

Lispen scoffed. "Wep won't accept that."

She was damn right I wouldn't.

"Then we'll follow whatever he chooses. There's no debate here. But that changes nothing between us."

"There *is* nothing between us! Raif, you need to stop. I've said no, and that's final."

"It can't be final."

"Why the fuck not?"

"Because I'm fucking in love with you!" he shouted.

Lispen was either shocked into silence, or something I definitely didn't want to hear was about to happen. I continued down on silent footsteps toward the main training room.

"I will not be the reason you step out of line!" Lispen's voice echoed through the stairwell.

I pushed through the training room doors and let them thump shut. I had a lot bigger problems than the two of them to focus on.

SERAE

MID-AUTUMN, BEYMON 1036

I DIDN'T REMEMBER my old room being so brown. The wood paneling on the walls was honey oak. The brick outer walling was tan and worn. Even the flooring was oak, though largely covered by the surplus of rugs lying about. The covers were the same floral as always, and aside from some decorative pillows strewn across the floor, they were the most color in the room. I had always thought of this room as warm and inviting, especially compared to the cold harshness of my rooms in the keep. Funny how things had changed. A few months ago, it would've been my dream to wake up back here in my old room. Today, it filled my heart with lead.

Judging by the distance I'd been taken and the sourness in my stomach, I had been unconscious for days. My throat was dry and cracked from disuse. My shoulder ached, and pangs of numbness shot down my arm. I tried to sit up, settled for propping myself on my good arm, and cast around the room.

There was neither water nor a service bell on my bedside table.

One name ran through my mind—*Gerta*. If Merria's letter was to be believed, she wasn't here.

Merria. I'd have to put up with her again. Martyrs, I might even have to put up with Naton. Just the thought of him had my fingers itching for a blade.

But more importantly, where was Bale? Had he made it back, too?

Images flashed through my mind—Naton's sword at my throat, Bale being restrained by a soldier he'd personally known, Eldreth cutting down men as easily as the blowing wind. The way he had looked at me...

I reached for Vaya'la, but I couldn't complete the connection. The place she resided in my mind was barren. Hollow. Grief struck me, sharp and swift. She was gone, and I had no idea how to get her back. Or if I even could.

I shoved toward the edge of the bed, and my arm exploded in pain as I tried to put weight on it. I checked beneath my nightdress. The wound was bandaged and clean. I managed to move my hand and wrist, but I couldn't raise my arm at all. This would make escaping much more difficult.

My door opened, and a maid came in with a tray. *Gemma. Not Gerta*. She had a lovely round face and a penchant for gossip, both of which brought her trouble. I'd also seen more than one guard leering after her in the hallways or courtyard over the years.

"Milady, you're awake." Gemma shuffled over to my bedside. "How are you feeling?"

"Parched," was all I could croak out.

She lifted my legs and tucked them back under the covers, forcing me back against a pile of pillows. "Stay right there." Then, she returned with a tray, which blissfully held an entire pitcher of water. She held the cup out to me, but when I reached for it, she didn't let go. With one finger extended, she cautioned, "Slowly, now."

I nodded and sipped. The water was cool, but it burned on the way down. I spluttered and coughed. When it subsided, I tried again.

"That-a-girl."

"Thank you, Gemma," I wheezed out. A few more coughs, a few more sips, and my voice started to return. "Where's Bale?"

The smile that spread over Gemma's face was enormous. "Lord Bale is back and safe, thanks to you. He's been in his room recovering, same as you, but he's been up and about some. When he's awake, I'll have his man help him to visit you. How would that be?"

"Yes. Who else is here?"

"The whole family, milady."

I nodded.

"No guests at the moment," she added.

I nodded again.

"Were you looking for someone in particular?" Her smile was a little too eager.

I shook my head. This was why I never preferred Gemma as my maid. If you wanted to know what secrets anyone in the entire manor held, Gemma knew them.

"The young Lord Fethersen returned home, but he was here for at least a day after your safe return."

"I'm tired, Gemma. Please bring me a bed tray. Then, I'd like to rest."

"Yes, of course, milady. Your lady mother will want to see you now that you've woken."

She bustled about setting the tray for me, which had some sort of broth, a bit of buttered toast, and a piece of fruit. In truth, it was probably more than my stomach could handle. I sipped at the broth and fumed. So, Tam had stuck around pretending to see to my safety, had he? I would have been safe if he'd let me stay in my home rather than kidnapping me back here.

We came for you.

Why? I had sent home nothing valuable, no hints that I'd discovered anything of use, and no reason for my father to think it was time to end this arrangement. The more I thought about it, the more rash it all felt. Surely, if he'd decided I'd failed him, I'd be more useful to Cavendaffe as a bridge to a foreign alliance—even a weak one—than as nothing more than the neighboring lordling's wife. I was worth more to him back in the Riht. Tam was my father's idea of an incentive, allowing a mediocre match he thought I desired rather than a strong match to serve the family. The tradeoff was information enough to compensate, but especially now that I was extracted, I had no information to give.

That's not true.

I had nothing but information. I had more information than he could have ever hoped for. But it was mine, and I would safeguard it with my life.

My door creaked open, but it wasn't the door to my bedroom. It was the secret door in my wall that connected Bale's room to mine. It was originally built as a hideaway by our ancestors should raids from the Riht make it this far south. We hadn't used it since we were children.

"You're awake, thank the Creator."

I beamed at Bale with his mussed hair, his lopsided smile, and his dressing robe thrown over whatever shirt and trousers were likely first in his wardrobe.

"You look a mess."

He eased the door closed, made sure the seam was flush with the panels, and trotted over to the chair at my bedside. "You should see yourself. How's the head?"

"Hurts."

He nodded. "And that arm?"

"*Hurts*," I laughed.

"That fucker stabbed you clean through. The cut in my side was shallow."

"She was protecting our clan," I said automatically.

Bale stilled. "We shouldn't have left."

"Don't. There's no use—"

"There is. I'm sorry I let this happen. The safehouse wasn't so bad, and Drake may have even helped me get out. We should've stayed. I should have insisted."

Tears pricked the corners of my eyes. "It's done. But how did we get here?"

His face darkened. "Naton is more of a bastard than I thought. He ordered the retreat, but he left half our forces behind to cover our escape. Hundreds of good men, all dead."

I gasped, covering my mouth as tears welled in my eyes. "All Cavendaffe?"

"And Fethersen. Father appointed him as leader. He's been cozying up to Ingleton ever since he got news I was dead, apparently."

"Before that, actually. The bigger question is, what do we do now? Do we flee? Do we find a way to return?"

"Return? Are you mad?"

Bale's eyes had blown as wide as saucers. He shook his head, hair flopping in his eyes, and he ran his hand over the short beard he'd grown while imprisoned. His hair was longer than he usually kept it, too, but now that it was well-washed, it had its usual bounce and curl to it.

"Fleeing back to Rihtlond would be the perfect excuse for Father to launch a full-scale war backed by the king. Ruper's been obsessed with expanding Inra's reach since we were boys. Just imagine, the Cavendaffe heir and his beloved sister stolen in the dead of night by agents of the Riht?" Bale swept his hand in a wide arc. "It'd spread like wildfire. Just the sort of fearmongering they'd need to get the backing of the lords, when not even the nobility can lie safe in our beds. But Inra can't afford to be fighting on both our borders."

"Both? Is it that bad in the South?"

"There's more I haven't told you." His face turned dark, and he swallowed hard before he answered. "I should be dead, Serae. I don't even know how I'm alive. The border was overrun by Volaachi. They have weapons, the likes of which I've never seen. They have these contraptions they fill with powders that explode, killing men around for thirty feet or more. They hurl them into the skies and rain down fire and metal. They have others that leach clouds of poison into the air, choking you where you stand and burning out your eyes. And they have these...things. I can't describe them. Half-dragon monsters bigger than men."

"Dragori."

He blinked at me. "They have a name?"

"Yes."

"How do you know it?"

I shook my head. There was too much to explain to him. "Inra isn't supposed to be at war with Volaach. They've always been at war with the Riht. Are you saying you've been fighting in the king's army on the south coast, not the north?"

He nodded and pulled his robe tighter around his middle. "We need to find time away from the house. On the ship here, Naton, the brainless braggart, spilled everything. Their plans go far beyond what I'd imagined, and Father's at the center of it. We'll need to find somewhere we won't be interrupted." Bale's face said more to me than his words. He had that look in his eyes, the same one as when he saw Naton courting Merria, the same one as when we overheard Father planning to enlist him, and the same one he would've worn if he were here when I was told I'd be sent to the Riht. His skin was pale from lack of sunlight, and his eyes were sunken. He was thinner, too, but the fire in him was alight. His gold eyes flickered like twin flames.

The door opened, and Bale leaned back in his chair. A lazy smile overtook his face.

"Serae, my darling, they told me you were awake!" Our mother bustled over, scooting between Bale's chair and the bed and laying a hand on my forehead as if checking for a fever. She was dressed in a lavish *bliaut* I'd never seen before, covered in gold embroidered roses. Her honey-blond hair was curled and pinned atop her head like a crown, but she wore no *cercle*. "The worst is over, my dear. The important thing now is that you're home." She turned and offered the same treatment to Bale. "You two holed up in here together just like when you were children. The Creator has blessed me in bringing you both back."

Bale rolled his eyes when Mother turned back to me again.

"Have you eaten?"

"Only a little," I said.

"Good, best to take it slow. Can you get up? Can you dress?"

"I...don't know."

"Why?" Bale interjected. "She's barely returned. What could be more pressing for Serae than recovering her health?"

For a fraction of a second, Mother's smile turned stale. In a blink, it was gone, and her cheery tone returned. "Nothing, nothing! There is nothing more important than rest for both of you." She ran a hand down my cheek, then turned and did the same to Bale. "I simply ask because I know how much your father wishes to see and speak with you. You've each been through your own ordeal. And to think, Bale, my precious son, back from the dead and rescuing his sister in the same breath."

"I've told you, I didn't rescue Serae. Quite the opposite."

"Pish posh, enough of all this. Just so long as you're both home. I'll send up a maid to help you dress. Did your man not help you this morning?" she asked the last while eyeing Bale's rumpled clothes beneath his dressing robe.

"I sent him away so I could spend time with my dearest sister." He winked at me.

"Fine, just see to it that you're both dressed by midday." She turned and flittered toward the door. She turned back and said more softly, "Welcome back, my dears."

Once the door had thumped shut, Bale raised both eyebrows at me.

"Do you really think—"

He shook his head in warning. "If you've ever trusted me, trust me now. Not here. We'll find a time and a place." He rose, leaned over me, and kissed my forehead. "Happy birthday, by the way."

I grinned. "I think *you've* been hit over the head. It's not our birthday."

"I missed it. And you."

Gemma burst back in since apparently there was no need for anyone to knock at my door anymore, and Bale left—this time through the main door—with another wink and lopsided grin.

Washing and dressing took far longer than I'd expected. First, my wound began to bleed in the bath, and we had to apply fresh bandages and pressure for ages. Then, my useless arm made it impossible to put things over my head and lace them up the normal way. It took all three of our arms to wrangle my one useless arm into place enough for Gemma to do all the ties, though she nearly had to call in a second maid for help. After all this, I became so lightheaded that I had to sit down in my chair and sip juice and a cup of cold soup until my head cleared.

Our last battle—the stairs.

The banister was on the right, so I couldn't grip it. Gemma braced me by my left arm as we took the stairs one painstaking step at a time. I wobbled with each step and had to pause for two short breaks on the way down. My body was so weak, I had a feeling it would take several days to get back to a place where I could simply walk around on flat ground normally again.

Gemma led me to the family parlor, and that same dread passed over me as it had months prior when being led to this room for the opposite purpose. My imagination ran rampant with all the possibilities of what my father might do or say. Gemma seated me on the very same sofa. Mother sat on the opposite sofa, this time bereft of her mourning shawl, and Bale lounged, very much alive, in a chair to the side. Father stood before the mantelpiece with a smile on his face.

A small fire crackled in the hearth where a kettle was warming. The window hangings were tied back, and sunlight flooded the room. The refreshments table between the two sofas was laden with tea service, iced cakes, and biscuits.

"My dear." Father smiled down at me. He held out both hands, but I gave him only one. He didn't seem to notice. "You and your brother have accomplished what none other on this continent have. You have gone into the heart of Rihtlond and returned to tell all."

He beamed at me, but I could not return his smile.

"I know those brutes have hurt you. It will take time for us all to heal. But, each day, we will unravel this together." He turned to Mother and added, "Please, my dear."

She nodded and rose to her feet, pouring tea for us all. She placed a plate, already set with biscuits and a small cake, before me. Then she pulled over a writing tray complete with a quill, ink, and parchment, resumed her seat, and readied her quill.

"In your own time, my dear," she encouraged, a kindly smile crinkling her eyes.

The falsity of this charade grated on me. "What, *me?*" I demanded.

"Of course, my dear," Father answered. "This is all for you. We are all here for you. No one will disturb us while these doors are closed." He gestured to the room.

I glanced at Bale, but he was looking at Father with open disgust. His hands were balled into fists, and his knuckles were white.

The fire popped and swelled. The room was unseasonably warm, and I pulled at the collar of my dress with my left hand. Outside the window, birds twittered, and I could hear the gentle rustle of the wind through the trees. I reached for my second sight...nothing, as expected. It was for the best. I shouldn't be trying to connect to Vaya'la or her power in front of my parents and risk giving myself away. If I even *could* connect with her again. I had grown accustomed to the dormancy when she slept, but this hollowness was new—terrifying. With effort, I pushed that fear aside.

"I don't understand," I said evenly.

"Don't be silly, Serae," Mother crooned. "Just tell us everything you've seen and heard."

"Start wherever you'd like," Father added. "Don't worry about sorting through it all—we can do that. Just begin wherever is easiest for you. Where were you before you escaped?"

I stared at them. I couldn't even answer this first question.

"We were put into a dungeon of sorts," Bale supplied. "They must have known the attack was coming."

Father nodded at Bale, then turned back to me.

"Had you been to this dungeon before?"

"No."

"So, you weren't imprisoned?" he asked with the hopefulness of a hound perking up for a treat.

"No, I was mostly kept to my rooms."

Mother's quill flew over the page.

"I see. And when you weren't in your rooms?"

I chewed my lip. "Mostly in a training room."

"And, what sort of training did you do in there?" His face was pleasant and eager. I had never received this sort of attention from him before. That, more than anything, set me on edge.

"Physical training."

"Physical?"

"Training the body, weapons training, that sort of thing."

He laughed a courtier's laugh, and Mother at his side chuckled politely while she took notes. "What a thing. Can you imagine? One of my daughters holding a sword. How beastly." They smiled at each other, and I took the opportunity to share a look with Bale.

"She packs a punch," he muttered.

Father continued as if he hadn't heard anything. "What happened after these lessons?" He ran a hand down his doublet.

I stared at him. The black doublet was new and cut in the same style Lord Ingleton preferred, but with Cavendaffe colors embroidered on the cuffs and shoulders. "I ate in my rooms."

"Were you taken to explore the town?"

I hesitated. "Once or twice."

"Excellent." His grin stretched wide. "Could you describe its layout?"

"Well..."

"Better yet, we'll set you up with some paper, and you can draw us a map."

"A map?"

"It can be rough, darling. No need to get worked up. Just whatever you remember. Now, tell us about the castle. Is that where you stayed?"

I sighed. "Yes."

This line of questioning went on for over two hours. The shadows in the room grew long, and all the water from the kettle had been used for cup after cup of tea. It was exhausting trying to riddle out what was okay to share and what wasn't. I lamented the loss of Dane's support. Our lessons consisted more of what to do in the Riht than what to keep safe from outside. I took to glancing at Bale for support, who would tilt or dip his head in suggestion. A few times, he feigned a cough, interrupting me and then sputtering apologies as he sipped his tea. Once, he spoke over me entirely and told a very different story about the layout of the city. He described a grid with a castle at the heart, neither of which were true. He also described the prisons as being on the outskirts of the city, though I had no idea whether that was the case.

It wasn't until my head drooped that Mother set down her quill. "I think that's plenty for today. You've done wonderfully, my dear."

"Yes, yes, my dear. I couldn't be prouder of you." Father rose from the sofa and paced toward the door. "Why don't you all take some rest before supper? We will pick this up tomorrow. Constance, dear, have those notes delivered to my study."

"Of course."

Bale helped me to my feet and led me back up to my room to change for supper. Only, my room wasn't empty. Tam stood in its center, hands behind his back. He smiled with that boyish charm I used to love. Except now, my stomach churned with guilt. Before leaving, I had made him promise that nothing could ruin me for him, but I had never considered the reverse. Looking in those hopeful brown eyes, I felt no spark. Nothing like the passion and all-consuming desire I felt for Eldreth. No love beyond that of an old friend.

"What are you doing here? I thought you left already." I had foolishly closed the door before checking my surroundings, trapping myself in with him.

"I'm here to see you." His brown eyes were warm. "It's such a relief to see you up. How are you?"

I bristled. "I'm well enough. Why are you really here?"

"A man can't check on his betrothed?"

I froze. "You're up in my room to ask a question that might have been addressed in the front hall?"

He flashed that roguish grin of his. "Don't be like that. I wanted to talk."

I moved to cross my arms, belatedly realizing I couldn't, and settled for wrapping one across my middle. I reached for my power, knowing none would come.

"You punched me, you know."

"I recall." I took a step toward the wall that connected my room to Bale's.

Tam turned as I moved, facing me head-on but not moving from his spot at the room's center. He cocked his head. "You didn't want to come back with us. Why is that?"

After hours of practice this afternoon, the lie was quick on my tongue. "They'll come for me here. The betrothal rite is done—you don't understand what that means to them. I had to get Bale out, but staying was the only way to stop what's coming."

"You'd have stayed there with *him?*" Bitterness touched his voice

"To prevent a war, Tam!" I shouted, though my heart slammed in my chest, knowing all the real reasons I wanted to stay.

He bowed his head, hands still behind his back. "Did he touch you?"

"Excuse me?"

"You know what I'm asking." He lifted his head and met my eyes. "Did you lie with him?"

A chill ran up my spine as the blood drained from my face. "No, I didn't have sex with him if that's what you're asking. I need to get dressed. It's time you left." The truth of those words stung, but I kept my expression hard.

"Serae." He stepped toward me, holding out a hand. I stepped back. He frowned and let his hand drop. "Serae, I'm sorry. I shouldn't have asked that.

I've been a wreck since you were sent away."

"Whatever you've gone through, I assure you, I've been through worse. Now, go." I pointed at the door with my good arm.

He sighed, holding up a hand in surrender. "I just wanted to say...I'm happy you're home safe." He crossed the room, and I watched his retreat. Behind his back, his right hand was bandaged heavily. He opened and closed the door with his left, keeping the bandaged one close to his side.

"Oh, Serae! I can't believe how much you've missed!"

I had been beside Merria for less than an hour when the time for supper came, and already I had heard everything worth knowing—and then some—about her betrothal, the dancing, the food, the attendees, and the gowns involved. It was enough to make me want to gouge my ears out.

"Where are your glasses, by the way?"

Merria's voice startled me out of my reverie. I'd forgotten about my glasses—first with Bale, and now *again*. It was a miracle Mother hadn't asked about them, considering how much she always hated that I wore them.

"I, uh, lost them. In the Riht."

She tossed me a pouty frown. "Poor thing, I can't believe you had to suffer through being there for so long. Anyway, you're in luck! I thought of everything while you were away, you see." She trotted over to her dresser and withdrew a short, rectangular box.

"Happy belated birthday!" she announced as she handed me the gift.

Inside the box was a pair of delicate, gold glasses.

"You love them, of course." She beamed.

"I do." I had to admit, they were beautifully crafted. The problem was, if I put these on now, I'd never be able to see. "Thank you, Merria. This is so thoughtful."

She nodded and gave a little curtsey. "Come on, let's go down." She gripped me by my right arm, and I winced.

A tiny knock sounded at the door, and a moment later, Bale entered.

"Ah, two of my loveliest sisters. What a treat it is to be home."

Merria giggled and released me, giving Bale a little twirl. "You're going down?"

"Only if I can have you both on my arms." His broad smile lit up his face, reminding me why he was always more successful at all the courting and ceremony than I was.

Merria took the opportunity to shove us both out of the sitting room and into the hall, but I took the moment to retreat.

"Go ahead, I'll be right down," I called over my shoulder as I hurried toward my room. "I just want to spend a moment adjusting these." I held up my glasses.

"Have Gemma do your hair while you're in there," Merria called back.

I would rather die than be forced into the selection of hairstyles she had offered me. Each one was more ridiculous than the next, with gold and ribbons and gem-tipped crowns. Instead, behind the closed door of my room, I wedged the glasses between my knees and carefully popped the lenses free one at a time. I cast around the room, shoved the lenses behind a bottle of ink and some melting wax in the writing desk drawer, then went to the mirror to check. Unless someone was paying me close attention, I might just get away with it.

Dinner was an uncomfortable affair. Lord and Lady Fethersen, in addition to Tam, had returned to celebrate my return over dinner—and no doubt reinforce the expected alliance. His younger brothers, the only three of the lot I would have liked to see, stayed home. The meal started with Mother making a lovely show of seating Tam and me side by side at the center of the table.

"Only the best for our happy couple reunited!" she proclaimed and led our party in a round of applause.

My cheeks turned as red as my hair.

They passed out the aperitif, and I drank it quickly.

"You look lovely," Tam said in a low voice at my side, sipping from his glass. "I've never seen this gown before. It suits you."

"All Merria's creation." I looked down at my dress, a gaudy, scratchy nightmare next to the clothes I was wearing in the Riht.

Tam kept his right hand in his lap under the table. My right hand was cradled uselessly in my lap as well. We were a pair of wrong-handed simpletons tonight. I'd never before envied Bale his left-handedness.

"What've you got there?" I asked, nodding toward his lap.

He choked on his drink and flushed. He set down his glass, cleared his throat several times, then said, "I'm afraid I don't understand."

My eyebrows knit together. "You're bandaged?"

"Oh, right, of course." His voice was that formal mask he used during the grand dinners we'd been forced to participate in since coming of age at fourteen. "It's nothing major. I took an injury during your rescue."

"My rescue?"

"Yes."

Our eyes met. The slant of his jaw, the quirk of his brow, and the tensing of his shoulders all held challenge.

I was ready for a fucking challenge. "Do you see yourself as my rescuer?"

His lips pursed, and he leaned in toward me. "When have I ever been one to discredit you?" he asked in a whisper. "I am well aware that you can take care of yourself, but it doesn't change that I came for you. That's the truth of it. I'm not asking you for anything but a little bit of acknowledgment that I've been here, doing what I can, every day for you."

"Tam," I rested my hand on my oldest friend's shoulder. "I'm not doubting that. I'm not doubting you."

His throat bobbed. "I thought you'd be happy to see me."

"I am," I said, though I tasted the lie as the words left my tongue. "But I have a much bigger responsibility now. You have to understand that."

He placed his hand over mine, holding it against him and pressing lightly. "I know that. Everything you learned in Rihtlond is crucial to the kingdom. But once you've shared it all, things can go back to normal. We'll get through this."

Except, he didn't know the half of it. He didn't know about Vaya'la, my binding, the task she'd given me fighting the spreading evil, my training, both physically and with my power—any of it. He never could. The doors of fate had closed between us as heavily as the gates of the city he'd failed to breach. The time had passed when I might have returned to this place ready to pick up my old life, and I didn't regret it.

I smiled at Tam, a courtier's smile that might have been stolen from Merria's lips. "Of course."

He smiled back as the fruit course was served.

The mask I donned, I imagined, was the girl my parents wanted me to be, rather than the woman I had become. I still laughed at the wrong times and sharpened my tongue when I should have been demure. I needed them to see a version of me who was still me, in some ways, and yet not. It was the version I imagined would have been happy as Tam's wife.

Merria, put off by not being the center of attention, was in rare form. "Lady Fethersen, this wine is simply superb. I have never tasted a finer fruit," she crooned.

Tam's mother bristled. "Is it a wine from our lands, dear?"

Mother intervened. "That was at our last party before Serae's return,

Merria. So good of you to share from your vineyards for our gathering, Lady Fethersen."

"Oh yes, I do recall. It was such a lovely evening."

Merria would not be deterred.

"I simply cannot wait to help Serae with her dress design. I've learned all the latest fashions from my time at court with Lord and Lady Ingleton."

"A lovely sentiment, my dear," Father said. "Your sister has a strong mind and makes excellent choices." It was a compliment meant for Tam, not me. "Tell me"—he turned back to Lord Fethersen—"what report do your tenants give of the late autumn crop? I've been told we're expecting a more bountiful year than usual."

Lord Fethersen was a rotund man with a broad mustache whose primary fortune came from their crops. "Why, yes, I was speaking with our principal tenant just yesterday."

Their conversation continued along the lines of yields, profits, and general finances while Merria pouted in her corner of the table beside Mother and thankfully opposite Lady Fethersen instead of me.

Tam leaned closer to me and whispered, "She's in rare form tonight."

I smirked. "As expected."

"Can't handle even one night without all the attention on her?"

"You have met her before tonight, yes?"

He chuckled, and this time, I found it easy to return his smile. Dealing with Merria's antics was a cornerstone of our relationship. With the way he looked at me... Perhaps I could still find an ally in him yet.

It was a long time before I was able to crawl into my bed, completely spent from a day of posturing and mind games. Kiral was sent to help me, thank the Great Dragon, though my heart panged for Gerta. I hoped she'd fled back to her family home. She used to tell me that her mother wanted her to marry, but she only wanted to make her own way in life. Perhaps being away for so long brought her back to her roots.

When I was tucked in and finally alone, I sat in my bed with a single candle burning on my bedside table. I closed my eyes and pushed all my will toward that voice inside my head.

"Vaya'la?" I called.

No answer.

"Can you hear me?" I tried again.

Nothing.

I tried and tried until my head fell back against the pillow, and sleep overtook me.

That night, I had no dreams.

BALE

MID-AUTUMN, BEYMON 1037

I PACED THE length of my old bedroom, unable to sleep. I glanced up at the wall, eyeing a tapestry that hung lower than the rest.

No, I should let her rest.

I had too many thoughts swirling around my head to be coherent anyway. Amongst them, urging their way to the forefront, was a pair of ice-blue eyes.

Late into the night, I paced, and paced, and paced. My mother would scold me for wearing a path into the rug if she were there. Undoubtedly, she was tucked in, asleep beside Father, content in another day's good progress. The dinner with the Fethersens was a success, judging by the eager grins of the lord and lady when they bid goodnight. I could barely keep down my dinner at the thought. Not after the way I saw her eyes light up when she talked about her Rihtlondish prince. Not after seeing him ready to destroy an army to get her back.

Fuck me. I had a terrible feeling I wasn't the only one who left my heart back in Rihtlond. Even more shocking, I recognized him. You don't quickly forget the man who drives a blade through your shoulder and drags you across the sea to rot in a fucking cell. Or his companion—Miloh's murderer. My heart clenched at the thought.

Despite that, I couldn't deny the feeling in my gut that they belonged together, in every way, down to the matching red of their hair. I knew it with the same certainty I had always known Tam was never her match. He had offered me a nightcap earlier, which I'd declined through clenched teeth. That foolhardy man-child only wanted an excuse to stay over. We had plenty of spare rooms in the manor, but I was certain Serae would be unhappy to find her *new* betrothed still here in the morning.

And Serae—Creator above—I didn't even know what she'd been through, but the change in her was undeniable. She always had strength of character, but now her body was toned. She held herself taller and moved with a grace that radiated power. A very real power I had witnessed with my own eyes. Had I not already seen those monsters she called *dragori*, I might not have believed what I saw. Magic, like the stories of old. The thought brought a smile to my lips. If anyone could bring magic back into the world, it was my little sister.

The candle behind me spluttered out.

"Fucking bones and blood."

There was no way I'd be able to find a flint in the dark, even with the moonlight streaming in through the window.

"You couldn't have lasted a few more minutes?" I asked into the darkness.

The candle sputtered back to life.

I stopped short, having just fumbled my way to the top drawer of my desk. I glanced over my shoulder. The candle had barely a sliver of wax left, yet the fire flickered, happy and steady, casting shadows around the room once more. One creeping step at a time, I approached the candle, examining it where it stood. There was a small bit of wick, the candleholder, and a few drips of wax down the side. That was it.

I frowned. "*Take it,*" a voice in my head beckoned.

My thoughts were running away from me. I needed to sleep. I pulled the tunic off my back and cast it to the floor. Then, I stripped off the ridiculous leggings I was made to wear. The scraps of my old uniform had been burned last night, but it couldn't be denied they were far more comfortable than the nonsense dress of busybody nobles.

I climbed into bed nude, trying to ignore the images my mind provided of skin and muscle and a blond braid made for pulling in the best way. I fell into a fitful sleep, only dimly aware that the candle on my bedside table had yet to flicker out.

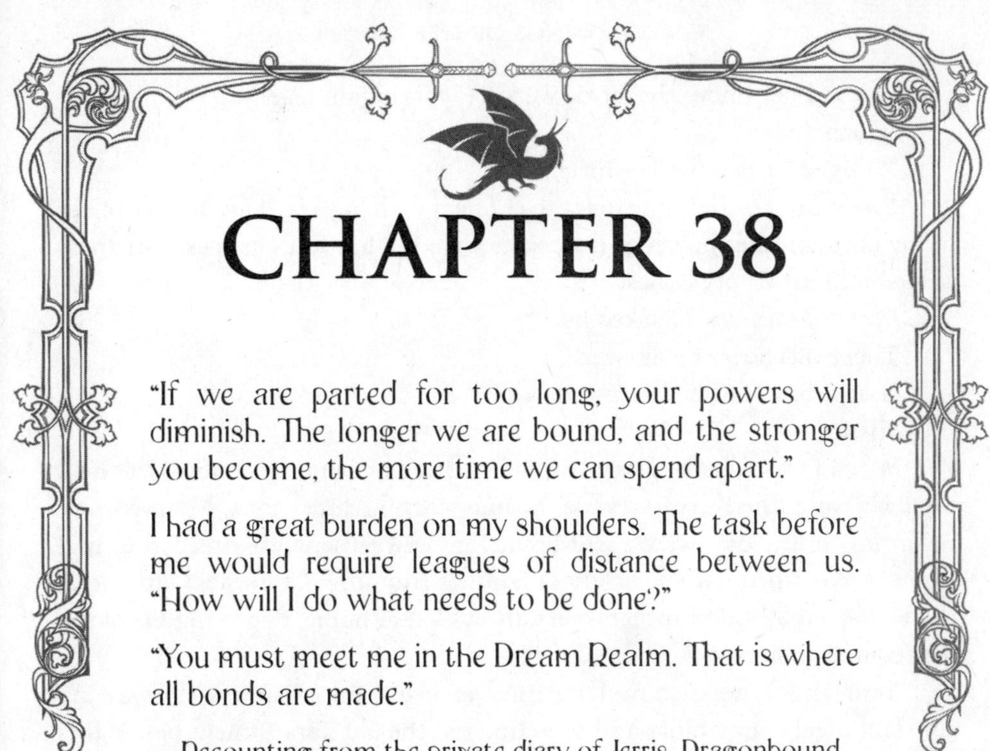

CHAPTER 38

"If we are parted for too long, your powers will diminish. The longer we are bound, and the stronger you become, the more time we can spend apart."

I had a great burden on my shoulders. The task before me would require leagues of distance between us. "How will I do what needs to be done?"

"You must meet me in the Dream Realm. That is where all bonds are made."

—Recounting from the private diary of Jerris, Dragonbound

• ∞ •

SERAE

LATE AUTUMN, BEYMON 1036

Life back at the manor was monotony unlike anything I remembered.

"This is a punishment for the ages," I complained. Mother had forced Merria and me into an embroidery circle, which my limited movement made nearly impossible. The repetition was nothing like the trance-inducing dyeing process I'd become so fond of in the Riht. It was entirely devoid of creativity, rigid to a pattern, and mostly involved unforgiving gold thread.

Mother chuckled.

"If you would take your time, your stitches might be more even," Merria added.

I kicked her under the fabric we were working on together.

"Ouch!"

"Slipped," I said with a shrug.

Every day, I found time to try to connect with Vaya'la. The absence of her in my head and her power at my center were the hardest changes. Tiredness seeped into my empty bones.

"Are you sleeping?" I asked her.

There was never an answer.

"I hope one of us is sleeping, at least."

Silence.

When I wasn't being grilled for information or caught in embroidery hell, my days were filled with errands, fittings, teas, or luncheons. My evenings, regardless of the day, were spent bouncing between endless dreaded formal dinners. We dined with a variety of families from town, but most often with the Fethersens. Tam's brothers were always left at home, depriving me of the innocent diversion of their shenanigans.

Tam and I were shoved together at every opportunity. He was my constant meal companion, and something of the old Tam I knew, before this separation wedged between us, came out more and more. Roughly two weeks had passed, plus the few days I was unconscious, and I found my smiles for him growing more genuine. It became easy to fall into a routine of laughter and dancing with him. I was able to ignore his hand on my back, guiding me everywhere we went.

At one such party, he steered us outside to stroll through the gardens, saying, "You look like you could use a break." He was right. We walked through the cold autumn night along a row of roses at the end of their bloom then sat together on a wooden bench. His arm draped around my shoulders, and I was grateful for the bit of warmth.

"I've missed this." His smile crinkled his eyes. "You and me, alone together. I remember the last time we sat on a similar bench."

"When was that?"

His voice lowered. "The last time you gave yourself to me."

My whole body tensed, and his grip on my shoulder tightened, squeezing me closer. "I think it's time we return to the party."

"Will you not even kiss me?"

I pulled out of his grasp and stood. I could endure the casual touches of friendship, but nothing more. I may be absent from Vaya'la and the Riht, but Eldreth was always with me. My heart bled for him every second of the day and night. No matter if I was sneaking evening strength training in my room or sipping afternoon tea with my mother and Merria, my heart was back in Drakh with him.

If I let them, the memories of our time together would play in my head nonstop. Instead, I packed them away neatly in a box in my mind and let myself focus on the blur of days that were becoming my life. Otherwise, I would crumple on the spot. The thought of never seeing him again—not having one more moment together, never feeling his touch or hearing his voice—was more than I could bear.

I walked away that night, leaving Tam on his own for the rest of the evening, but that didn't stop his wandering hands from finding their way to my thigh beneath the table when seated beside him at the next dinner. Or the time after that, when he boxed me into a dark corner, begging for one kiss until I had to forcefully push him away. He caught my hand, bringing it to his lips.

"I need you, Serae. If you need more time, that's fine. I've already waited months. I can be patient a while longer."

But time couldn't heal my heart. It slipped away from me, leaving me feeling more hollow every day. At night, I never dreamt.

After that first dinner with the Fethersens, Bale had my glasses refitted with false lenses in town. Despite the lifelong habit, it was a challenge to remember to put them on in the morning. Bale was my guardian, constantly helping to cover for my slip-ups and dragging me away when he saw me getting overwhelmed.

One afternoon, he gripped me by the hand after a wasteful session with our parents about the common dress habits of the Riht. He tugged me along without a single word to the stables.

"Bale, stop," I protested. "You know I can't ride with one arm."

"Good," he said, turning serious.

He brought round his sturdy gelding, already saddled, and hoisted me up. Then, he pulled himself up into the saddle behind me. We rode. The wind whipped through my hair, which I'd left loose, and set the ridiculous billowing sleeves of my *cote* flapping. His gelding jumped a log and raced onward at Bale's urging as I laughed into the freeing wind.

We came to a clearing in the forest, and Bale pulled the reins. It was a small gap between the trees where a tiny patch of sunlight shone through and encouraged a patch of grass to grow.

"Oh, a faerie patch!" I beamed, remembering the name from our childhood.

Bale grinned and pulled out a pair of matching green cloaks from the saddlebags.

My smile soured. It was the exact shade of green from the tapestry that hung in my rooms in honor of Vaya'la.

When we were wrapped up and seated in the sun, Bale's eyes turned serious again.

"What are you doing?" he asked.

"I thought I was enjoying an afternoon with you."

He folded his arms over his chest. "Tell me, sweet and innocent sister, how it is you know so much about the buckling of pants and undergarments of men in the Riht?"

"I— What?"

"I thought as much. I get what you're doing, and it's admirable, but you need to put more thought into this. You shouldn't know that a man's belt buckles at his side, let alone anything about what he wears underneath."

"Oh, dragons."

"And that's another thing. Since when did you change your beliefs?"

"I didn't, of course not." I changed everything about my life and had evidence that my previous beliefs were incomplete. That's all.

His eyebrow raised. "I see. The problem is that the signs are all there. Our parents, especially our father, are cunning and observant. They're starting to catch on that you have changed. I don't think they've noticed whatever was going on with your glasses, and they certainly don't know about the things I saw during our escape, but they've noticed other things."

My shoulders sank with the strength of my sigh.

"How did it happen—your sight?"

I could barely form a reply. All I could think about was Eldreth, quizzing me over my change in sight. "I can't explain it."

"And the magic? That's what it was, right?"

"What does it matter? It's gone."

Bale hung his head. He looked off into the trees, pretending not to notice as I blinked away tears and shoved the memories of my time in the Riht back into their neat box. "Tell me you'll be happy with him."

"I can't be with him, you know that. How would I ever get back without starting a new war?"

"No. Tell me you'll be happy with Tam."

My heart leapt into my throat. I shook my head.

"What's his name? The one you keep dancing around when you talk about Rihtlond."

I choked back a sob, not sure when my body decided to start crying.

"The one who you said trained you, challenged you, and lit up your face with smiles the day you found me in that dark room." His words were tender and soft, and his eyes were downcast, offering me a modicum of privacy as I failed to wrangle in my tears. "The Rihtlondish prince who followed you into the forest with the might of an army at his back just to keep you."

Eldreth. It was a whisper in my mind and a plea to fate.

"The woman I met back in Rihtlond, who in less than a day broke out of a castle, bypassed a heavily guarded gate, and charged straight into the opposing army's lines because she wanted to keep me safe—where did she go?"

"I can't." The pain in my chest was physical. I curled my cloak fully around myself. "I can't be her. I can't feel those things, Bale. Don't you see? If I let those things out, I won't be able to breathe."

Bale scooted closer, slung one arm over my shoulders, and rested his head against mine.

"Come back to me, Small One."

My eyes popped open.

"Vaya'la?"

WE RETURNED TO the manor late and heard an earful from our mother. She hissed at my mud-stained shoes and chastised Bale for taking me so far from the house. As it turned out, we were hosting the Ingletons and Fethersens for dinner, and I, being a crucial member of the party, had delayed the entire lot.

"Shall I join you in my *cote?*" I asked. The hem of my dress was covered in mud and grass. "I hate to keep the lords waiting."

Mother looked as if she might faint, but Bale looked like Midwinter Day had come early.

"Excellent idea. I'll go kick the mud off my boots, and we'll join you presently."

"Don't. You. *Dare,*" she hissed. Her eyes narrowed dangerously, and we both ran up the stairs to our separate rooms like punished children. Kiral, my mother's lady's maid, was pacing across my room, holding the bodice of a pale blue and gold *bliaut* in her hands. She had me stripped, washed, dressed, and hair plaited in minutes. The plait was simple and tied with gold ribbon. I hated it. Somehow, even this was confining next to the options I had in the Riht.

As usual, my place at the table was beside Tam's, but this time, we sat opposite Naton and Merria, with Naton directly across from me. I had not seen him since he held a blade to my throat. Merria cooed and batted her lashes and bit her lips at him, but I just stared. His grin for me was feral.

We made it to the second course before he finally spoke up.

"I was beginning to think the day would never come when I saw you seated beside Tam. Does this mean you've had a return of your senses?"

"Careful, Nate," Tam growled at my side.

"My throat has healed." I raised my voice slightly. "Thank you for asking."

Naton's eyes narrowed, but his smile didn't drop.

Bale was two chairs away from Naton, and he leaned forward, keeping his eyes trained on him.

Oblivious to, or more likely enjoying the tension, Naton pressed on. "I wonder, are you happy to be back in Tam's bed after being sold to those brutes?"

Tam was halfway out of his chair when my hand on his arm stilled him.

"Surely, you don't mean to insult my faithfulness. That would be quite the slight on the house of Cavendaffe and indeed on the king, since our orders came from him. I must not have heard you right."

"What's that, now?" my father boomed from the head of the table.

I turned to him. "The young Lord Ingleton has some interesting questions about my time in the—in Rihtlond," I corrected myself.

"Does he," my father said matter-of-factly. "Let's hear it, boy."

Naton's jaw twitched at the word *boy.* I had to hand it to him, my father knew how to strike at a man's pride. "I was simply expressing concern that the young lady had been thrust into a situation where she would not be able to fend off unwanted advances."

Lady Ingleton gasped.

"That's not a topic for polite conversation," interjected Lord Fethersen. He turned to Lord Ingleton, seated across from him, and looked at him expectantly.

"See now, the lad means no harm," Ingleton added. "Do you, son?"

"Of course not. I am merely expressing my good wishes for Serae and Tam's future. It's my understanding that ladies who have been through such a trauma are not forthcoming in the marital bed."

Merria dropped her fork, and it clattered to her plate. Her mouth went slack-jawed as she stared at her betrothed.

My cheeks burned, and beside me, Tam's hands vibrated with rage beneath the table.

"See here now!" the margrave shouted, and every trace of the kindly father he'd pretended to be over these last weeks was gone. All three lords jumped to their feet, while Naton reclined with a smirk directed at me. Lady Fethersen was fanning herself with her napkin while my mother began imploring the two lords near her to take their seats.

I stood, picked up the paring knife before me, and flung it just above Naton's head into the opposite wall. It embedded into the wood with a loud *thunk*, and all eyes turned to me in shock. Merria's shone with outright fear, and my mother turned to me in horror.

"Lord Naton," I said clearly, "your worries are unwarranted. Not a hand has been laid on me lacking my consent." Bale's eyes flashed to me. "That is to say, nothing ill or untoward has been directed at me while in Rihtlond. There is no need for anyone to speculate about a trauma that has not occurred. Any further conversations regarding the details of my and Tam's future marriage will be private between us, and certainly not a conversation over dinner."

My father thumped down into his chair and banged his fist on the table in support.

"I invite the Lords Ingleton and Fethersen to take their seats," I continued. "The slight is forgotten. Let us eat in merriment."

Both Lord and Lady Fethersen, who had been openly gaping, clamped their mouths shut. Both lords sat, and my father still glared between them. Lady Ingleton alone had locked her shrewd eyes on me, picking me apart with her glare. I returned her gaze with my head held high. Naton, like his mother, glared at me, wary and assessing, but behind it, I saw a glint of something dangerous.

Bale rose to his feet with a glass in hand. "To Serae, a woman of wise words and wiser actions."

Merria, eyes still round, was the first to lift her glass, followed by Tam a second later. One by one, the glasses and mood lifted. The meal continued in relative peace. At its completion, I excused myself from after-dinner chatter with smiles and well wishes all around.

Up in my room, I changed into my nightdress, settled myself upright in bed, and reached for Vaya'la. Again, I was met with only silence. It may have been my imagination, but I sensed a hint of her presence. It was an echo of a whisper, but it gave me the smallest flicker of hope.

My sleep was light and restless. I dreamt I was a tree with a bright green trunk, but a dark shadow came and chopped off all my branches. Blood-red sap wept from my wounds, staining my bark and roots.

Sometime well after midnight, my door creaked. A strip of light lanced across the floor and the end of my bed. I was instantly awake, reaching for my second sight on instinct, though it failed.

"Who's there?" I hissed into the darkness.

"Shhh, it's me."

"Tam?"

The door shut, plunging the room back into darkness, and the lock clicked.

"What are you doing here?"

I could just make out his silhouette in the faint moonlight as he crossed the room. Only a sliver of moon hung in the black sky.

"Serae," he whispered, his voice slurred. He swayed as he walked.

"Are you drunk?"

"Serae," he repeated. "It's been months. Why haven't you asked me to come to you?"

Leveraging my good arm, I pushed myself up to a seated position. "Go back to your room. We can talk about this when you're sober."

He sat on my bed, directly on top of my feet, ignoring my squeak of protest and forcing me to shift. "You used to want me. You're supposed to want me."

"I can't even see you. Just wait until tomorrow, we'll talk then." I didn't want to talk at all, but that didn't seem like an option he'd appreciate. I yanked at the covers, desperate for a modicum of protection in only my nightdress, but they were pinned under his weight.

"You're supposed to be my wife." He leaned toward me.

I held out my good arm to stop him. "Have you been listening to Naton?"

"What if I have?" He leaned in as if he might try to climb on top of me.

"There was your first mistake. Get off my bed." I tried to shift away from him, but I'd let him go too far. His arms came down on either side of me, his body still pinning my legs.

"It's been months waiting."

"So you've said." I struggled, freeing a leg from his weight.

"How can you stand it?" He started to crawl toward me.

I kicked a foot up into his chest, halting him.

He chuckled, gripping my ankle through the blanket. "I love it when you're feisty."

"I'm injured!" I hissed. "I still can't move my arm. This is *not* happening."

"I lost two fingers for you!" he shouted. All pretense of quiet was gone. "The least you can do is thank me properly."

"You sound like Naton," I spat, trying to scoot toward the opposite side of the bed.

He lunged, trapping me fully with his body. "Naton had a point," he hissed. "I can't keep waiting. It's all right. I'll be gentle." Blind panic ripped through me. I froze, unable to move, unable to scream. I tried to do something, anything, but I couldn't get my body to react.

His body pressed down into mine as his lips found my cheek in the darkness. His breath was hot against my skin and smelled sour with drink. His hips began thrusting against my thigh.

"Breathe," a voice told me.

I sucked in a breath.

Tam took the opportunity to cover my mouth with his. His lips were wet and sloppy against mine, which I'd pressed tightly together.

"Fight."

I pulled my head back and slammed forward, dipping my chin so my forehead smashed into Tam's face. He let out a howl of pain and clutched his nose, freeing my arm, but my legs were still trapped beneath him.

"What the fuck, Serae!"

I writhed, trying to wrench myself free. With his injured hand, he pinched the bridge of his nose. His left shot out and caught the wrist of my injured arm.

"That's the second time you've struck me."

"Let me go!" I tried to scream, but it came out as a strangled whimper.

"This isn't how you treat your husband." His voice carried an edge.

"You're not my husband!" My voice was stronger, but my throat kept constricting, cutting off the volume. It was the panic. I had to get to a place of control.

"I'm as good as. Once we're married, you'll have no choice but to obey."

His words broke a dam within me. Eldreth's face swam behind my eyelids. "I'll never marry you!" I shouted, and my volume finally returned.

He shifted, and I worked a leg free. Rather than pull back, I wrapped it around his torso and twisted with my body weight, forcing him beneath me.

"I knew you'd like it rough." He grinned and gripped my thighs, pushing my hips down toward his. I squeezed, halting his progress, and he ran both hands up my waist. "Let's get this off you." He laughed. Clumsy hands tugged at my nightdress.

A fury I'd never known raged through me. I pointed my left palm at his neck, calling on my vines to control him.

My palm *glowed*.

For one wild second, I saw the whites of his eyes. His grip on me relaxed. Then, the light dimmed, and I heard a light tapping at my door.

Tam flung me off and scrambled over the foot of the bed. "What was that?"

I laughed, pouring every ounce of scathing and malice into my voice. "Do I scare you?"

His body tensed, ready to pounce. His eyes flicked to the empty spot on the bed as someone began calling my name through the closed door.

"Did you come here tonight to force yourself on me?" The flash of power faded, but my voice was steady and strong. "Get. Out."

"How *dare* you—"

"NO. How dare *you?*"

My door burst open. Bale barreled in and ran at Tam, knocking him to the floor. He threw punch after punch at Tam's face.

"Get the fuck out of my house," he bellowed as two guards rushed in behind him.

"What's going on?" Merria's voice sounded from down the hall.

Bale stood, grabbing Tam by the scruff and throwing him from my room into the arms of the waiting guards.

"Chuck him in the courtyard until his father wakes. Use any means necessary to keep him in line."

The guards saluted, and the door slammed shut. On the other side, I could hear shuffling and cursing as they hauled Tam off to who knows where.

I was still perched on my bed, my nightdress around my knees. My left arm was extended out, trying to call on vines that wouldn't come. I dropped it.

A candle, miraculously still in its holder, sat flickering in the middle of the rug. Bale picked it up and ran a hand through his unruly, black hair. "Did he hurt you?"

"Barely," I said, though my hands shook. "I did worse."

"Good, budge over."

"Bale, you don't have to—"

"I do." He cast around the room and scooped up a blanket from a nearby chair.

I shuffled back to the right side of the bed and pulled my covers into place. "Thank you," I whispered.

The door opened again, admitting Merria with a candle of her own. "Are you okay, Serae?"

Bale and I exchanged glances, then I shuffled toward him, clearing a space for her on my other side. She shut the door and tucked herself into the covers beside me.

"Did he do anything to you?" she whispered.

I shook my head. "He tried, but I fought him off until Bale..." I trailed off.

Merria wrapped her arms around me, taking care to avoid my bandaged arm, and squeezed. "I didn't think he'd do it. Naton was goading him all night. He said the only way to know for sure was to try it and...you know...see if you let him."

"And you're going to marry that fucker?" Bale asked.

Merria did not respond.

They slept the entire night beside me, Bale on top of the blanket, Merria tucked in at my side. It took quite some time before any of us fell asleep, but when I finally did, I dreamed.

THE FLIGHT WAS long, and despite my immenseness, my wings tired. Landing in the center of the molten lake was the easiest way to beckon him. If he would come. I stayed in my true form, knowing he preferred scales to skin. The island of glass and emerald rocked violently under my mass. The lava creatures, as always, churned about in their fiery home.

I waited. I had time enough to wait for an age if needed.

When the sky shifted to green, I sensed his presence at my back. I did not turn, allowing him to be the first to speak.

"It is long since you visited me, Life Bringer."

I spun slowly, allowing my tail to curve around my body with the motion.

"It has been longer since you visited me, Fire Starter. When was the last time you made the flight to my realm?"

He huffed out a plume of smoke and sat back on his haunches. The molten lake rocked, casting flickers of light beneath the island of glass. "I know why you're here."

"It's the only way."

"I disagree."

"You haven't seen the world as I have. When was the last time you took on a binding? When have you bothered at all with the lands of Jaeda beyond your volcanoes and magma?"

"I know more of Jaeda than you could ever imagine!"

I reared back, lifting my neck to the sky. "Your temper always did get the better of you."

He huffed out a cloud of smoke, and within the plume, I saw a human figure. A woman—unusual for him—made of charcoal and ash and wreathed in forgetfulness, except nothing about him, her, was forgettable.

"I have walked the lands while you slept, dear Sister. I have seen the world and its pettiness. And I have seen the corruption firsthand. The Darkness spreads faster than you know. Toy with your little bindings, by all means, but know that it is I who fights this war already. Return to me when you're ready to take up the mantle and fight at my side."

His great wings spread, and he leapt into the sky, sending the glass island rocking again. I watched as he turned west toward his charge. I had underestimated him, true, but he had also underestimated me.

"Remember this, Small One," I said aloud. "Already, the great players of this realm are in motion. You will not fight alone."

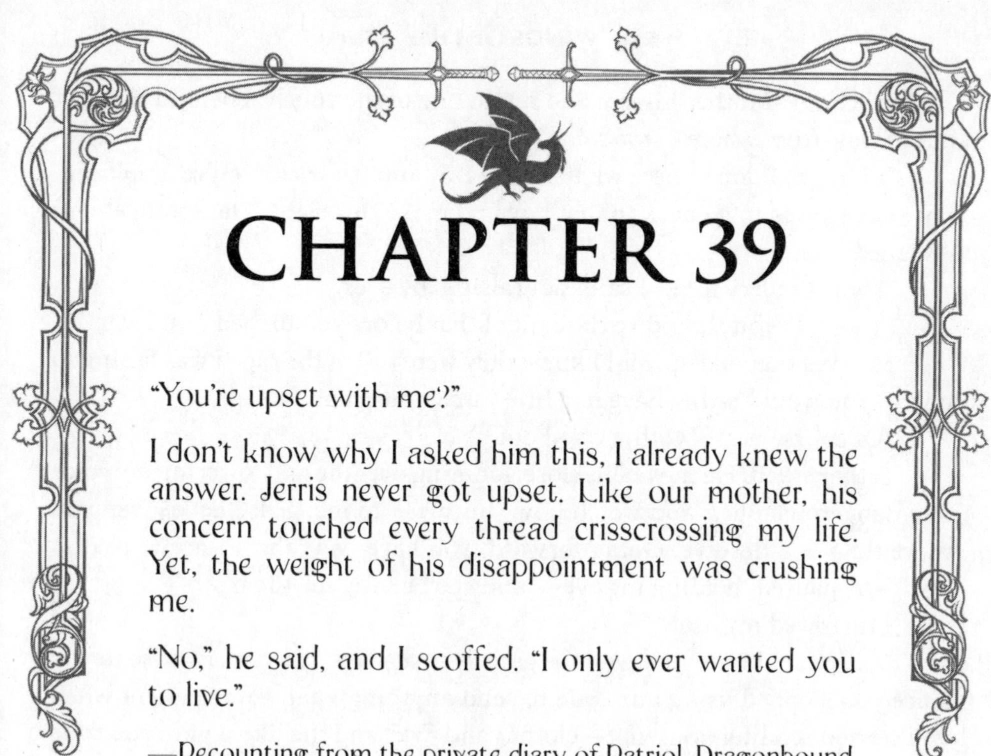

CHAPTER 39

"You're upset with me?"

I don't know why I asked him this, I already knew the answer. Jerris never got upset. Like our mother, his concern touched every thread crisscrossing my life. Yet, the weight of his disappointment was crushing me.

"No," he said, and I scoffed. "I only ever wanted you to live."

—Recounting from the private diary of Patriol, Dragonbound

• •

SERAE

LATE AUTUMN, BEYMON 1036

I STOOD BEFORE Father in the family parlor, feeling fifteen again. He was seated in one of the plush armchairs before the fire. I kept my eyes downcast, and I held my tongue, clenching my jaw shut for good measure.

"What were you thinking?" he asked. His voice was low, but his tone was livid.

This wasn't a question he wanted me to answer, so I kept my silence.

"I'll tell you what—you weren't. You can't seriously expect me to believe the two of you have never gotten up to any dalliances with all the times he's stayed at this house."

"Tychon!" Mother hissed. She sat on one of the couches behind me, just out of view from where I stood.

"Enough! I don't know what insane Rihtlondish tricks you've employed, but you're going to go back to that boy and make this right. The arrangement is signed."

"I won't marry him," I said, not raising my eyes.

"You will. You should've thought of that before you turned him away."

My eyes snapped up, and I knew they were full of the rage I was failing to quell. "You would rather have had him force himself on me?"

"Of course not!" Mother cried out.

Father stood. He moved in close, looming over me and lowering his voice to a dangerous tone. "You watch how you speak to me, girl. I have given you more than you deserve. Going forward, you have two jobs. Please that idiot boy"—he paused, holding my eye—"and start giving me the truth."

I furrowed my brow.

"Aye, yes. I know very well the game you're playing. I've been wise to you since you stopped using our code to send anything vital. I was patient when you started sending nonsense—clothes and food and the like. I gave you time to come to your senses and return to your true purpose. It was you who failed to keep up the bargain. It was you who forced my hand in allowing Ingleton to bring you home."

"Lord Ingleton wanted my return?" I asked.

He nodded. "Since you've been home, I've played along, giving you niceties and biding my time, but that time is up. You've had your chance, and you've squandered it."

"I can't just pretend to know things—"

His open hand flew across my face. My head snapped to the side as fire erupted down my cheek. I was no longer a stranger to pain, though. I turned back to him, unmoved and unimpressed.

"Really, Tychon," my mother admonished, but she didn't move to stop him.

"No more games," he declared. "By this afternoon, you'll have good information for me. Until then, you're confined to your room. I suggest you use that time remembering where your loyalties lie."

True to his word, I was led away and brought breakfast on a tray. Locked in my room, I used my time exactly as he suggested—thinking about Eldreth and the Riht. I ran through every *dowsa* I could, remembering the flow of each movement. My injured arm ached and protested, but I ignored it as I moved through each form with controlled precision. I paused only briefly when a lunch tray was brought up to me. I laughed out loud at the irony of being brought a tray while trapped in my room now that I was back in Cavendaffe, my supposed home.

I sat on the floor, barefoot and cross-legged, and focused on my breath. When I had mastered the steadiness of my heart and the depth of my breathing, a knock sounded at my door.

"I've been asked to escort you to his lordship's study," Kiral said. Her face was pale.

I had expected this. I nodded and followed her downstairs to the back corner, where my father's private study was tucked away from the rest of the house. The curtains were drawn shut, allowing only scant strips of light to bounce off the walls and ceiling. The sconces were lit despite the afternoon sun.

My father sat at his large, mahogany desk. At its center, a ledger with gold-dusted pages lay open, quill and ink at the ready. Across from his desk, a single chair had been placed.

"Sit," he commanded as Kiral shut the door behind me.

I obeyed, collecting the red folds of my *cote* around me.

"We begin small." He lifted his quill and opened the ink bottle, but he did not dip the nib. Instead, he looked up, analyzing me with his dark blue eyes. In this light, they might have been black. "Eldreth, son of Auldren. What is his role in Rihtlond?"

"Future dane."

He scratched out a small note. "Any siblings?"

I hesitated. He didn't look up, just waited with his quill poised. *This was a test.* He must already know that Dane has two sons. "Yes, a brother."

"When were you last in contact with him?"

"The day I left Rihtlond."

He nodded. His chair creaked as he leaned toward me. "This is a good beginning. I implore you to keep this level of honesty and forthrightness, and I daresay our conversations will be pleasant. Do you understand?"

I nodded and shifted in my seat.

"Our scouts have discovered two ports that lead to the city of Drakh. How many gates lead into the city?"

"Two. One to the east and one to the south." The gate to the east they already knew about, and the gate to the south was the most defensible.

The margrave set down his quill. "I have it on good authority there are at least three."

"I have seen only two."

He frowned. "Let's shift topics. Who leads their armies?"

"Dane Auldren."

"I am sure the dane is ultimately responsible, but who is their commanding general?"

I froze. "I don't know."

He rose from his seat and moved around the desk to stand in front of me. "You have been in the heart of the keep where the dane of Rihtlond lives, and you have not seen the commander of his armies?" He crossed his arms and stared down at me.

"I've only seen Dane commanding them." I widened my eyes and looked up at the margrave, hoping it made me look innocent. I'd seen Merria do it dozens of times before.

"You told us you'd been trained to use weapons. Who conducted that training?"

"A woman."

He leaned back against his desk. "What was her name and station?"

"I don't know."

Smack!

I didn't even see the blow coming. He backhanded me so fast that I couldn't even brace. I rocked back in my chair as tears welled in my eyes. When I turned back to him, I spoke through gritted teeth. "We called all instructors Master. I was given neither names nor stations beyond this title."

"Is that so?"

"Perhaps they trusted me even less than you do."

"And perhaps they, too, grew tired of your cheek."

I scowled and tapped my slippered foot on the rug, right over a swirling pattern of the Creator. It was one of several new and expensive rugs I'd found around the manor.

"Who was 'we'?"

Shit. I clamped my mouth shut.

"Answer me, girl!" he shouted.

That was when the hitting began. It started small. The first few days brought more slaps across the face. When bruises developed along my cheeks, he began rapping my knuckles.

But on the fourth day, I entered Father's study to find him holding a thin reed from the garden. I stared at him, unbelieving at first. Then, he bunched up the sleeve of my yellow *cote* and tied my arm to the chair, palm up. Dread seized me, and I yanked at the bindings.

"Do not force me to bind both your arms." His voice was cold and uncaring, freezing me in place. *He was really going to do this.* He began with questions.

How many ships did you see at their port?

How big is their fleet?

How many men are in their armies?

I held my silence like a shield, but that didn't stop the reed from snapping across my forearm. I bit back my scream. Each blow left a stinging trail, and red welts formed into thin, angry lines. My resolve had been steel—until that first blow. Instead, fury pooled in my gut, lending me strength. It was hardest, I learned, when the strikes landed on a joint.

The margrave rolled up the sleeves of his deep blue tunic. "This ends as soon as you allow it, girl. What claim do they have over you that you would rather betray your family and your kingdom than give in?"

"No claim." My voice trembled only a little. "I have already told you everything I know. It is your choice to abuse me over what I cannot give."

The reed cracked again, splitting skin this time. I cried out, and blood welled up along the cut.

My father knelt at my eye level. "This is for your own good. I know you're holding onto more. The sooner you answer, the sooner we return to attending dinner parties and planning for a wedding. You hold the power here. Do you understand?"

I nodded. I understood perfectly that he would beat me senseless until he got what he wanted. Perhaps I deserved it, making myself complicit in my father's plans. Could I not have defied him from the start, finding the courage to cast aside my role as spy before sending that first letter? Without my help, would they have found the hidden port to launch an attack? Or Drakh at all? Then again, I had never actually written about the small port. My damning instructions should have sent them to the well-defended Port Drakha.

I thought of Eldreth, constantly fighting to protect his people, and hardened my resolve. We never had the chance to work past my betrayal before I left, but I would never let him down again. I would take ten thousand blows if it meant protecting him—and the Riht. It was all I had left that I could control.

Once he freed my arm, he opened the door, and Gemma rushed in. She gripped me under the opposite arm, lifting me from the chair and wrapping a cloth over the cut. She carted me upstairs before anyone else in the family could speak a word to me.

"Where's Bale?" I asked as we climbed the stairwell.

"He's in his rooms as well," she whispered to me. Her boots shuffled over the rug. "He started a fight with his lordship last night, so he's been confined." Her voice trailed off as we rounded the corner to the hallway that led to Bale, Merria, and my rooms.

Two soldiers were stationed at the end of the hall outside of Bale's door. I recognized one of them as Lorrick. I couldn't see the other through the gloom.

Gemma bobbed her head in acknowledgment when both men turned toward her. "This way, milady." She opened my door and ushered me inside. "The guards showed up yesterday. You're lucky none are outside your doorway. Pardon me for saying, milady, but I hope you know what you're doing."

"I do."

She nodded with a forced smile and straightened her apron. "Of course. Let's get this cleaned up."

The next day, my father switched to my other forearm, where my skin split in three different places. He promised to move on to my back if I didn't talk soon. I believed him. He smoothed down his doublet, this one resplendent with Inraen red and gold trimmings, and sent me away. The day after that, both arms were tied at once.

Between meal trays and sessions with the margrave, I sat in my room and stared out my window. I did not cry. Pain lanced down my arms, but I endured it. *For Eldreth.* With each leaf that fell from the branches outside my window, I imagined a drop of my pain fading away. To occupy my time, my mind conjured up images of Eldreth appearing at my door, scooping me in his arms, and taking me away. Sometimes, I imagined breaking free and fleeing to the coast, where I sprouted wings and flew home to Drakh. Other times, I imagined setting the entire manor aflame.

One morning, after several days of abuse that all blurred together, a soft knock sounded at my door. I didn't bother answering. I heard Gemma's voice speaking to someone on the other side—a man. The lock to my door clicked, and the door opened.

"There you are." Tam sighed with relief, as though he'd been searching for me. As though I could've been anywhere.

The lock clicked again from the outside. I did not turn to him.

His footsteps shuffled over the carpet. "Serae? Will you not speak to me?"

I didn't respond. Outside the window, I watched two birds somersault in the air. I thought of Sprakt and how he would rip them into pieces and devour them.

"I've come to apologize. I was very drunk and very stupid, and I'm just glad you were smart enough to push me away."

I concentrated on a bit of frost covering one of the windows. Autumn was nearly through, or perhaps it had already ended, and the air held a chill that reminded me of home.

Home.

Drakh was already lost to me, and I had never even seen it in winter. What right did I have to call it my home?

"Serae, look at me."

Please that idiot boy, the margrave's voice echoed in my mind. He was no longer a father to me. How could anyone treat their own daughter with such cruelty?

I turned and looked Tam square in the eye. My sleeves on the silk *bliaut* Gemma had dressed me in were down, covering the welts and cuts that riddled my forearms.

"Do you hate me so very much?" he asked, fidgeting with a velvet cap he held in his good hand. His other hand was hidden beneath a diagonally worn cape. His eyes were full of sorrow.

"No, Tam, I don't hate you."

He smiled.

"I think nothing of you at all."

Tam went still as the impact of my words hit him. He looked down at his navy and silver doublet, no doubt worn as a symbol of his house. "I suppose I deserve that. I'll make it up to you. You'll see, once we're married and away from this house, things will be different. We'll be happy."

I will never marry you. There was no point in speaking the words aloud again.

Tam backed toward the door. "I'll come visit you tomorrow. I'll show you every day how sorry I am until you see it."

I turned back to the window. My face was an empty mask, a perfect mirror of my soul.

His cape rustled as he hesitated at my door. "Just give him what he wants, Serae. Whatever he wants, whatever you're holding onto...it can't be worth all this."

So, he knew.

When I didn't respond, he knocked softly at the door again. The lock clicked, and he withdrew.

That day, the margrave moved to the back of my forearms, concentrating on the protruding bones of my wrists.

The following day, my shins and ankles.

Sometime after that, I was brought to him in my robe and nightdress, which laced up at the back. On the center of his desk sat a familiar brown journal with waterlogged pages. My heart clenched. I had shoved it in my tunic pocket, intending to burn it, on the day I was taken. With all that happened, I'd forgotten.

"This is very enlightening," he said. "It's taken a long time to riddle through." He flipped open the pages, and horror descended over me. The ink was faint and blurred in spots, but my writings and drawings were all there.

"I knew you'd uncovered something big. Do you really think I'd go through such trouble to get you home if I thought you knew nothing? Or that we'd go through all this if I had no sense of the secrets you hold? This journal is remarkable, but you've left even more out, haven't you? I can see it in your eyes. You're holding onto something so great, it would bring down the Riht itself."

Fear lanced through my chest, and I couldn't help the way I stiffened and sucked in a breath. *He knew.* A slow smile spread over his face as he watched me fight back the urge to squirm. There was no doubt in my mind. He might not know what I was holding back, but he knew I had secrets worth beating his own kin—his own daughter—to reveal.

"Are you ready to speak?" he asked simply. When I shook my head, he had my nightdress undone just enough to expose my back while standing. I clung to the thin fabric covering my chest. These lashes were harder, and I wondered as my skin split whether it was because he didn't have to look into my face as each blow fell.

The next day, the session was even longer. The margrave replaced the reed with a leather lure, allowing him to use more strength without the reed snapping in two. *How practical*, I thought, as he opened new stripes across my back.

That night, I slept on my stomach. The nightdress kept snagging on my back until I ripped the whole thing off—regretting it as my fresh scabs ripped open again—and lay there naked from the waist up. I stared out the small patch of window I could see from my vantage until I fell asleep.

"Serae..." That voice, *his* voice, was a caress on my skin. A kiss pressed to my shoulder, and his short beard tickled just beneath.

I groaned, not wanting to wake.

"We have unfinished business between us." His voice was laced with sin.

"Mmm..." I tried to roll over, but his body pressed against my back. The skin of his bare chest grazed against mine, and it was enough to drive me mad.

"All I can think about is how fucking good you taste." His hand snaked between my body and the mattress, searching for that perfect spot and teasing in a way only he could.

I stretched, catlike, as he circled a finger around my bud, sending lightning bolts through my core.

"You like that?" he asked.

"Fuck yes."

This was too good to be true. My body had been aching for his touch with a desperation that threatened my sanity. It was all too much and not enough.

"As I recall, we were interrupted the last time I had you naked and writhing on my tongue."

"Martyrs, that mouth." I twisted, capturing his lips, kissing him with everything I had between the moans he coaxed from me.

He eased me onto my back, and the only solace I had from losing his mouth on mine was the fact that his lips were now trailing down my stomach. He parted my legs and settled between them.

A sharp stab of pain lanced across my back. I twitched, lifting off the mattress, and my wrists throbbed in response.

"Eldreth," I cried, and my eyes flew open. The room was empty. My bed was empty except for me. I looked down at my naked torso and the stripes of bruises and cuts down my arms. I was still in Cavendaffe, trapped in my old room and very much alone.

Gingerly, I turned onto my stomach. Pain surged across my spine at every movement, no matter how slight. I buried my face in my pillow, wishing I could never wake up again. If tears came, no one was there to witness.

ELDRETH

LATE AUTUMN, TALMON 1036

FOUR ENTIRE WEEKS of waiting. I was ready to tear out my fucking hair. It took one day to assemble a crew of forty after the council came back with their decision. The wrong fucking decision. We would not invade Inra. They could all get fucked.

Serae wasn't safe in Inra. It didn't matter if they were her people, they took her by force. Their leader, whose life was forfeit the next time I saw him, nearly slit open her throat. And they wanted me to trust her life to those people? Serae, who meant more to me—to the whole of the Riht—than any other. The counsel should've known better. Even Longven was ready to help, providing the fastest galley in the fleet to speed us across the White Sea. It was carved with a single dragon head at the stempost, and looking at it made my insides churn.

Vaya'la.

I'd repeated the name hundreds of times in my head. A name I only knew because of Serae. A name I now safeguarded on Serae's behalf, because I couldn't fucking safeguard her.

Serae being Dragonbound was only one of the reasons why I had a full crew with me, each warrior happy to defy the will of the council for her. Not that there was any lack of volunteers for this mission—a testament to the impact Serae had made already. My entire *ranng* was with me, and her *ranng* as well. I had reservations about letting them join, but fuck if I didn't relate to their steely looks when I tried to say no. Even Raif and Lispen had gotten past whatever it was between them to come to me as a united front.

With the speed of the longship and the help of Dragon-blessed winds, we made the three-day journey in two. It would be another half-day's travel to get to the manor house. Sailing at speed in a single craft meant we'd brought no horses. We'd take the last leg on foot, and with the right pacing, we'd be there by nightfall.

Thankfully, I had the foresight to assign who would be staying back to guard the ship before we set sail, so there'd be no squabbling once we landed. The pull to get to her was tearing me from the inside out, and every choice I made was for speed. It had been a full month since Serae was taken from me, and the guilt was a leaden anchor in my soul. I should never have waited for sanctioning. Dane put too much faith in the elite families that would rather guard their fortunes than take any risks. Their only fair point was that damage to the east gate from the *bahroi*, plus extensive losses at the hidden port, required immediate attention.

Every day, working from sunup to long past sundown for Drakh, I clung to my sanity by trying to convince myself that she was safe with her family. While we bolstered our defenses and cared for our dead, I was trying not to claw my eyes out at the thought of the prisoner she risked everything to flee with or that fucker that claimed to own her. She was safe with her family. She was safe.

But then, why was my gut still roiling with fear?

The coast was empty when our craft made shore. We wore dark, oiled leathers and minimal mail or plate. Exposed on the beach and in the light of day, we were easy to spot, but by nightfall, when we would arrive at the manor, we'd blend in with the shadows.

Seconds after making land, my *ranng* and I broke from the crew to take the lead. Sellan had ensured everyone knew their role over the two days we spent at sea, partly because it was his duty as my second, and partly because he knew how close I was to snapping. We took off at a jog, not bothering for stealth until we were farther inland. Inra's long coasts and sparse northern population made it easy to infiltrate their lands unseen, unlike the rocky coasts of the Riht.

Before we hit the trees, Yaego hissed, "We've been spotted!" She took off into the brush, leaving us scrambling to follow her.

"*Fuck*." I dashed after her with Sellan hot on my heels. Pebbles flew as we ran toward the tree line and crashed straight through the brush. The glint of Yaego's bald head was all I could focus on as I ran.

"Declare yourself!" She stopped as abruptly as she had taken off, one thin sword extended. Before her, a quivering figure stood with her back pressed against a tree. Her clothes were worn, but they were Rihtish, and a single sack was lashed across her back.

"Please," she whimpered in Mayoran, "I'm no enemy. I know how I look—"

"Gerta?"

All eyes turned to me, and Gerta collapsed to her knees. "Wep!" she sobbed. "Thank the Creator."

Yaego lowered her sword and stepped back.

"What's happened?" I could hear the severity in my voice, but fuck if I could check it right now. There were things so much bigger than one maid at risk here.

"I left them weeks ago. I can't go back. I don't belong there. I belong with Serae in the Riht."

"Serae isn't in the Riht."

She stilled. Her whole body tensed, then she got to her feet. Her tears halted. "Wep"—she leveled me with matching severity—"where is she?"

I ignored the shame that clutched at me with the admission. "At the manor."

Gerta took in my leathers, the few pieces of strategically placed plate that would remain soundless as I moved, the swords, daggers, and bow strung across my back. Then, her appraising eyes moved to Yaego, then Sellan. Behind us, Branye and Praeth cursed my name as they caught up to us and earned a piece of her appraisal for themselves. She placed a steadying hand on the birch tree at her back. Its sparse leaves rustled overhead in the chill winter wind.

"You're going after her," she said matter-of-factly.

I nodded.

"I'll come with you."

"No." I knew Serae would want Gerta out of harm's way.

"I know that manor like the back of my hand. I know every hidden passage, every crack, every hole that could be exploited. I'm helping you."

My gut told me to resist, regardless of how useful she could be. Her overdress and cloak were covered in mud and bits of dried leaves. She raised a finger at me, dirt heavy under the nail.

Whatever scolding was on her lips halted when Sellan asked, "Have you eaten recently?"

Something like guilt stole over her, and she shook her head. He pulled a pair of cloth-wrapped *babi* from his cloak and handed one over. The sight of the round pastries hit me straight between the ribs. My hand pressed to that spot at the center of my chest that hadn't stopped aching since Serae's feet left Riht soil. Gerta's eyes tracked the movement.

"Get this down, and I've got a waterskin too," Sellan told her. "We've got a long walk ahead."

He was deciding for me, but I couldn't give up so easily. I was done holding back when it came to Serae. I beckoned her a few paces away from my *ranng*. "There's no shame in staying with the ship," I told her, halting her protest with an upheld hand. "We'll take you back with us either way. You've been here in the forest for—what, a month? It doesn't take much to see you're half-dead on your feet already." Her gaze fell away from me, frown tight and brow creased. "Whatever we need to know, tell me. You know I'll see it through. I'll do whatever it takes to bring her back."

"She's in love with you," she blurted out.

My heart fucking soared. I cursed the smile that stole over my face and that little disbelieving breath that huffed out.

"I'm sorry to be the one to say it," she continued. "She'd never say it herself, she's too good a person. She'll see the betrothal through and do what's expected of her, but it's you she truly wants. You should know that...before you do this for her."

I ran a hand down my face as my chest splintered again. Too many regrets were piling up. "I really must get people to use my name more."

Her brows knit together.

I extended my forearm to her, and she tentatively took it. "We haven't been properly introduced. I'm Eldreth, second son of Auldren, Marr Wep of the Riht, and High Dane apparent."

Her eyes bulged, and her jaw fell open. Her hand around my forearm went slack.

"I'm here to get back my betrothed and kill anyone who gets in the fucking way."

Her grip tightened, and tears sprang to her eyes. "I'm going with you."

"You know what you're saying?"

"I do. I've been in the wilderness living off the land, waiting to find one of your ships to get back to her."

I nodded, praying to the Great Dragon it was the right choice.

There were thirty of us—five intact *ranngs*—making the trek while ten warriors remained at the galley. The forest floor was firm, easing the journey on foot. We kept pace, alternating between walking and jogging, and then resting every third hour. We kept our distance from the main road, traveling parallel to it. On horseback, it would have taken six hours at most. On foot, even at a warrior's pace, it would take us well past nightfall.

When we jogged, Gerta fell to the back of the group, but as we walked, she moved to the front beside me, answering my questions and sharing everything she could.

"There's a servant's entrance at the front of the house and a separate entrance for kitchen staff 'round the back. That's our best choice for the middle of the night. We can sneak through to the old staircase and up to the family wing."

I would storm through the front door if I had to. The first goal, I knew, was stealth. If we could get in and out easily, we could be on our way home before anyone was the wiser. But if anything went wrong, I'd burn the fucking house down to get to her. We didn't have time, not where Serae was concerned. The constant thrumming inside me told me to hurry to her.

"How many servants in the house?" I asked.

"Ten if they've replaced me, plus three kitchen staff and two valets."

"How many soldiers?"

Gerta shrugged. "Two, inside, unless something has gone wrong. There are more surrounding the property, but I've never counted."

"Go over the family again."

"The margrave and his wife. The oldest son is gone, so that leaves Merria and Serae."

"How old is Merria?"

"Twenty-four."

I stopped. Gerta caught on two paces later and turned to me. "I thought Serae was the eldest."

"No, no, she's the youngest child. Two older, then Serae."

So the margrave liked to play games, too. I filed this away for later and kept walking.

"What of the man she fled with? He was an Inraen soldier. We didn't even know he was from Cavendaffe."

She shook her head. "I don't know any of the militia, and I doubt Serae did."

"She knew him."

The outer gates of the manor came into view. The arrogance of these Inraens always baffled me, trusting nothing more than a wall and a few soldiers to keep their families safe. As planned, our party split in two, scouting the perimeter. There were four entrances, each guarded by only two soldiers. Gerta directed us toward the western gate. It took only minutes of waiting before these so-called guards abandoned their posts and propped open the fucking door. They may as well have invited us in for tea.

"This ale's gone straight through me tonight," one soldier laughed. He shifted his tabard aside and pulled at his belt as he walked through the opening.

"And every other night!" the other called after him.

The poor fool headed straight for us. Sellan put him down before he even saw we were there. A perfect throw from Yaego's dagger dropped the second one.

I gathered Serae's *ranng* and told them, "This is as far as you go." I'd set one *ranng* at the north gate, hers at this one, and the last three would be coming with me.

"Like hell it is," Raif barked. "We have just as much right to be here."

I silenced him with a glare. "This door must be under our control for a quick exit. This is your task."

Lispen stepped forward, and Raif made room for her. "We've got this, Wep," she said. Then, to her *ranng*, "Surround the gate." They rallied around her, readying their weapons and fanning out. My instincts about her taking the lead had been spot on. Raif may have been the obvious choice, considering his parents, but he didn't inspire the others the way she did.

I signaled for the rest to continue. Gerta crept along a few paces behind me. Her determination was admirable, even if I hated myself for accepting this risk. Under normal circumstances, I'd never have allowed it, but nothing about Serae elicited normal from me. It should have terrified me that I'd bend every fucking rule I ever made for her.

But it didn't.

We skirted a single patrol on the grounds surrounding the manor. I set one *ranng* to keep the path leading toward the kitchen secure. They took up positions behind posts and trees and tucked into shadows, blending in with the night.

This was where Gerta's most crucial part came into play. Using the servant's key she had kept, she unlocked the door and entered. If all was clear, she would come back and signal us. If she ran into trouble, she would feign having returned to the family after some invented trauma and wait for us to extract her.

I watched the door and counted the minutes. The air held a chill that I wasn't expecting this far south.

"I can't see anything," Praeth whispered in my ear.

"Nothing to see yet."

Gerta better hurry. I was giving her two more minutes until I added her name to the list of people we'd be rescuing tonight.

One more minute...

Her figure appeared in the doorway. She was paler than she had been before entering, but she motioned me forward.

"There are four guards in the family hallway," she whispered in my ear.

"To the bedrooms?" My brow furrowed. "Why?"

"I've never seen anything like it. They're in front of Serae's door and Lord Bale's."

"I thought you said he was dead?"

She nodded. "They got a missive from the king saying so."

That didn't sit right with me, but there was no time to change course. Four were too many to incapacitate quickly. We would need four silent deaths.

I instructed the next *ranng* to keep the kitchen entrance under control. Following Gerta's descriptions, I led the final *ranng*, my own, up the stairs and down the first hallway, so unlike the winding corridors of our keep. Branye was at my back, followed by Praeth. I glimpsed around the corner and saw them—four soldiers all in a line, exactly as she'd said. The bedrooms they guarded were along the same wall, side by side. Two of them dozed while the other two played a game of cards by the light of a single candle. All four wore uniforms and weapons, but none had heavy armor. Not one so much as glanced at their surroundings.

They weren't concerned about people coming in.

Rage filled me, making the lives I would claim even easier. I stepped out into the hall on silent footfalls, keeping to the shadows. I made it to the first guard dozing in his seat before any of them noticed and plunged a dagger into his neck.

One down.

His companion leapt to his feet. A dagger flew from behind me and embedded in his eye socket. Only Yaego had vision sharp enough to make that shot in the dark.

Two down.

I went for the next one's neck, but he'd dropped his cards and drew his sword in time to meet my dagger. The fourth soldier roused.

"You have no business here," the closer one said, holding my blade at bay. "Leave at once."

"Leave, or we'll sound the alarm," the farther one demanded, a slight tremor in his voice.

They always think talking will help them live.

In one motion, I stepped in, drew my short swords, and slashed upward, slicing clean across the closer guard's chest and neck. He fell in a gurgling heap. *Three.* The last one, farther away, had more time to prepare.

"Intruders!" he shouted. "Sound the warning bell! Call to—"

Sellan surged forward and took the last words from his mouth, stabbing through the hollow of his neck. He'd wasted valuable effort in shouting. *Four.*

Branye and Praeth hurtled past me to the far door and waited as Sellan returned to my side. We nodded in unison, each knowing the plan. Yaego retreated to block the hallway and drew a pair of the many throwing knives she kept on her person.

Sellan grabbed our assigned door's handle, but it was locked. As one, we kicked.

The door flew open, and Sellan rushed into the room. With one glance, he pivoted on the spot and turned his back to whatever he saw in the room. I had half a second to consider this before I cleared the doorway.

My vision went red as my sword clattered to the floor.

Someone was standing at the foot of a moderately sized bed with four posts and a carved headboard. He was trying to block her from us and utterly failing. I could see every inch of Serae, who was lying on her stomach and covered only at the waist with a strip of her blanket. Every exposed bit of her beautiful, tan skin was covered in welts, cuts, and bruises. If not for the cascade of red hair across her pillow, I might not have recognized her. A bowl and cloth lay discarded on the other side of the bed next to a clear indent where this man had been moments before.

My eyes moved to him, ready to kill. I recognized him—the prisoner I had spared months ago. The same one Serae had fled with during the attack.

"The other room's clear," Branye said from the door, "but trouble's coming."

Shouts and clanging filtered in through the window. We'd been discovered.

"*You.*" The prisoner hissed, redrawing my attention. He carried no weapons, just fists raised at the ready. Did he think he could fight me?

"What the fuck have you done to her?" I asked, checking none of the lethality in my tone.

His jaw set. "I'd never hurt her." Like he had some claim over her. I smiled, knowing he would die at my hand.

I stepped toward him, drawing the long knife I kept at my thigh. He sidestepped, already retreating.

"Wait, you don't understand." His back hit one of the bedposts, jarring him. This time, I didn't hesitate. My blade plunged straight toward his heart. Luck alone spared him. He jerked away, and I missed his heart by inches, piercing just below his collarbone and going straight fucking through. The tip of my knife jammed into the post behind him.

His scream was a melody to my ears, singing out sweet justice.

"Oh, fucking dragon dung," Branye cursed from the doorway. I turned to her, my fury spiking that she'd dare question this.

The prisoner gasped, clutching at my arm still holding the dagger's hilt. "Brother," he wheezed. My head whipped back to him. "I'm...her...brother."

Shit. All anger fled me as I took a step back.

Yaego, standing watch in the hall, said in Mayoran, "Back in your room, sweetie, or you'll be next." A woman squealed, then a door slammed shut.

"Eldreth, this complicates things." Branye's tone was grim as she stepped into the room.

"Eldreth?" a weak voice echoed.

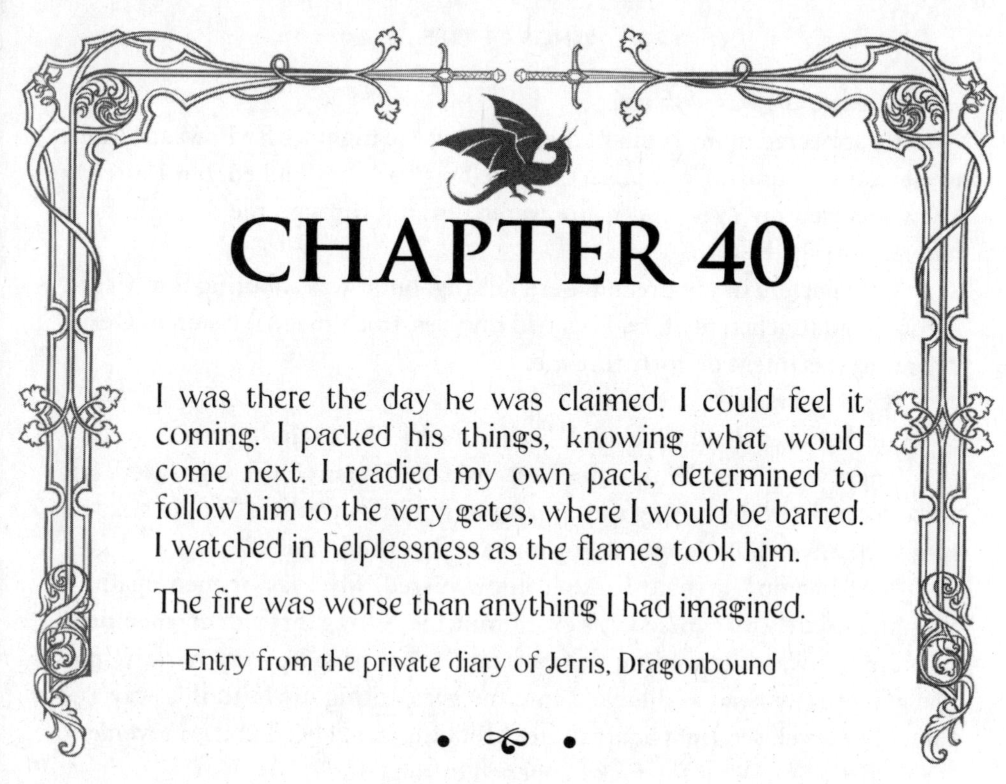

CHAPTER 40

I was there the day he was claimed. I could feel it coming. I packed his things, knowing what would come next. I readied my own pack, determined to follow him to the very gates, where I would be barred. I watched in helplessness as the flames took him.

The fire was worse than anything I had imagined.

—Entry from the private diary of Jerris, Dragonbound

SERAE

LATE AUTUMN, TALMON 1036

I woke from one dream straight into another.

"Eldreth?" I called uselessly. He stood beside Bale, emanating that intensity I loved about him, like he was ready to tear down the world for me. Only, I knew he wasn't there. This was the fever, mixing dream with reality as it had been for the past week.

I shivered, and a small cry escaped me as the skin across my back tugged and split. My ankles were the worst of it, swollen with edema and pulsing with a heartbeat of their own. Two new cuts across my back from today acted as rivals, truncating my sleep to mere minutes at a time. The night brought me alternating sweats and chills. That, plus the fever dreams, was a clear sign of infection.

At least Bale was with me.

He appeared in my room in the middle of the night with a bowl and cloth to clean my wounds. He wouldn't tell me how bad they looked, but I already knew. I closed my eyes, and if fire weren't raging through me, I might have had tears to shed.

The specters in my dreams were talking, but it was shouting to my ears. A cool hand touched my face. I opened my eyes, this time to a vision of Gerta. My mind was intent on torturing me.

"Can you move?" she asked.

I let my eyes slip back closed. "Leave me be," I told the specter.

There was a thud behind me. "Yes, pack it," Dream Eldreth growled. His voice constricted my aching soul. There was muttering, then, "I didn't expect him to be alive, did I?" Scrambling and another thud. "Fuck!"

"Get her up," a voice I didn't know hissed. My eyes opened again. A woman I vaguely recognized was examining me. Sifting through my memories to place her was like wading through tar. "We'll have to wrap her and go." She gripped my head and looked into my eyes, tilting my head this way and that. My eyes closed tight against the throbbing in my head at the movement. "Fever delirium. What the fuck happened to you two?"

"Our father," Bale rasped, then he let out a groan. He'd been hurt. The margrave got to him, too.

"A full rank is on the way," a new voice warned from my window. She was bald, slender, and dressed in black leathers. I knew her from training. "If we're not out of here in five minutes, we won't be leaving."

Leaving. My mind started to wake.

"Take him," Eldreth said, then the bed beside me shifted. "Fuck, Serae. I'm going to have to carry you."

The sheet dragged over my abused skin, and I whimpered. Strong arms lifted me, and I was wrapped into his warmth and the scent of mint and eucalyptus and something that was entirely *him*. Not even my imagination could reproduce that perfect mix.

"You're here?" I whispered. Stinging shot down my back as my spine cradled into his arm.

"Yes." His face was tight, and he did not meet my eyes. "Find her anything loose," he told the first woman.

"Nothing but fucking dresses," she replied. She was also clad in dark leathers, though I saw mail glint on her chest.

"My room...there." Bale gasped from the floor. "Through the tapestry.

Wardrobe..."

"Go." Eldreth's voice rumbled through me, waking something in my chest. The fog over my mind was clearing. I was looking straight into his steel-blue eyes. "You're okay," he whispered to me. "You'll be okay."

"Eldreth, time to go," a man at the door warned. I recognized him as well.

Pain spiderwebbed over my back, but my gasp was for a very different reason. Eldreth was holding me in his arms, and my bedsheet was wrapped around me. The others in his room were his *ranng.*

His eyes raked over my broken, bruise-splotched skin, and the pain in them shattered me. His forehead dropped to mine. "I'm here."

I grabbed him by the back of the neck and pulled his lips to mine. I kissed him hard, ignoring the stabs of pain in my forearms and wrists. His lips and tongue met mine, stroke for stroke, but he broke it far too soon.

"We have to move. Can you walk?"

"Yes," I answered, though I wasn't sure I could.

He set me on my feet, then caught me as I swayed.

"Here!" Gerta tossed a bundle of clothes at Eldreth.

He caught them and pulled a tunic over my head. He dropped to his knees and helped me with shaking hands into a pair of trousers that he cinched tight below my hip bones, where I was blissfully unharmed.

"Let's move. Get him." Eldreth's chin jutted toward a heap on the floor.

The man beside Eldreth handed him a sword that he sheathed at his hip. "We can't cover the distance with two wounded," he said.

"We'll have to."

"Two wounded?" I turned to look. The heap I'd assumed was a pile of covers was a man. His shirt was stripped halfway off, and a thick, white cloth was haphazardly tied across his shoulder. Before my eyes, it was staining red with blood.

"Bale!" I screamed.

I threw off Eldreth's grip and ran to my brother. The man holding him upright stepped back as I collided with him. Bale let out a loud *oomph* when I gripped him around the middle. Our skin touched, and my second sight flew open. His lifelight was dull gray and dimming.

"**No,**" we commanded. The power I'd been craving all these weeks flooded me. I ripped away the bandage and cloth packed into his wound, then rolled him to his side. I gripped his shoulder, pressing my palms directly into the entry and exit points of his wound. Warm blood covered my hands in pulsing waves.

Heal, I commanded. I directed the light through my arms and into him, knitting the wound together from the center outward. His pain mingled with mine.

"Keep going," encouraged that familiar voice in my head, and I wanted to weep.

I pushed more light into Bale, and when I could sense the wound was closing, I instinctively searched the rest of him.

"His mind."

As soon as she said it, I felt the burning block buried deep within him. It couldn't fucking have him. I forced all my light into it, but it pushed back with fire. I screamed and dug in, matching my will against it. Every time I gained an inch, it doubled the force of its flame, pushing me out.

"Let go!" Vaya'la cried out in my mind.

I ignored her and pushed harder. I would not let this thing win out.

"Release me!" A voice resounded in my mind, but it was not Vaya'la's. It was male and deep and crackling.

I couldn't let go. I tried, but the light tunneled out of me and exploded into the night. My nails dug into Bale's skin, but still, I couldn't stop. My fingers refused to listen as I tried to force them to release. I was trapped in the burning light.

Bale's hands wrapped around my wrists, prying me off him. **"Let go,"** he said in a voice that was not his.

Fire and light exploded out of us, slamming into everything in the room. Screams and shouts echoed all around.

Then, darkness.

My hands dropped to my sides, and Bale took a deep breath. His eyes went wide, and he pressed a hand to his shoulder, rearing back. In the firelight, I caught a glimpse of his pink, unblemished skin—fully healed.

Firelight?

Behind him, the sheets, tapestries, and rug were all kindling. Fire lapped up the side of one bedpost. Bale got to his feet, pulling me up with him. He gripped his head as he shoved me backward and into Eldreth's waiting arms.

"Get her out of here."

Eldreth's strong hand gripped my arm, and we were running. Through the hallways, down a staircase, into the kitchens. I caught a glimpse of the staff in their nightclothes huddled against a wall behind Riht warriors with weapons drawn.

"Bale!" I screamed.

"Behind you," he called back. "Keep going!"

We burst into the cool night air, and at least five joined our ranks. Their lifelights flickered with more emotions than my swirling mind could read. We ran to the curtain wall and followed it to the small side gate that Bale and I used to sneak through as children.

An arrow whizzed past, clanking against the outer wall, followed by shouting. Across the courtyard, a group of a dozen men charged us, each flashing with reds and oranges—*hatred, anger, fear.* I reached into the ground, and roots erupted around them, weaving through their limbs. Screams of shock and terror replaced the shouting.

There were more ahead, blocking the door. At least another five, maybe six.

"Eldreth," I panted, pointing ahead. The group was flashing between blood orange and mint green, a mix I wasn't expecting. *Anxious and hopeful?*

"It's us."

We collided with the group moments later, and I was engulfed in a bone-crushing hug. I looked up into Teke's face. They were pulsing with bright green *joy.*

"Thank the Great Dragon!" they cried.

"Run now, hug later," Lex said, pushing Teke away. "Who's the naked one?"

Bale was still shirtless when he reached my side. The lifelight around him flickered like a wreath of flames.

"Bale," I gasped, reaching out a shaking hand. Relief flooded me, smoothing over his healed skin. He wouldn't even bear a scar. He was warm to the touch, but it could have been his natural body heat. He gripped my hand, pressing it against his shoulder, and gasped. Power surged through me, filling me with heat that pitched toward feverish.

"Can you feel that?" he asked, voice tinged with awe.

Shock radiated through me. "Can you?"

"How?"

"Let's go," Lispen called out.

The last of our group barreled through the door, slamming it shut behind them. It barred from the inside, but Raif and Ivank rolled a boulder they found who knows where in front. We ran together toward the trees.

"It'll be a long, hard run." Eldreth was at my side again, and his voice was low and steady. "I can carry you if you need it."

"I can run."

"Your back—"

"It doesn't even hurt," I panted, which was true. The real problem was that I hadn't been able to keep down food in days. I was surviving on pure adrenaline for now, but as soon as it wore off, I'd be tapped and weak again.

Still, we ran. My pace was stilted as I dodged roots and bramble. Yaego looped back twice and returned clean reports.

"Maybe the boulder did its job," Ivank muttered to Lispen.

"I don't know," she replied.

It must have been hours before Eldreth finally signaled our halt. By that point, determination alone stopped me from collapsing. Teke offered me a waterskin, which I drank deeply. At our side, Raif unhooked two waterskins from his belt and passed one to Lispen. Around us, others were passing around flasks I suspected contained *choirsa* along with nut crackers, dried fruit, and hunks of cheese.

Eldreth approached with a grave face and a handful of clean linen strips. "We should use this rest to wrap your back."

"Anyone have a spare shirt?" Bale asked from behind me.

"For you or her?" Teke asked. My shirt was wet and sticky against my back.

He shrugged. "Either, I guess."

"I'll hook you up," Lex said, slinging an arm around my brother's shoulders and leading him away. I didn't like the grin on his face.

"Serae," Eldreth said, drawing my attention back to him. There was something worse than pain in his eyes.

I nodded and pivoted, giving him access to my back. A trembling hand grazed over my hip, then slowly, the fabric of Bale's tunic began to rise.

Eldreth's sharp intake of breath startled me. Behind me, he dropped to his knees, then both of his hands caressed the skin of my back, working the tunic up higher.

"Incredible," he whispered.

There was no pain, only the roughness of his bare hands smoothing over my skin. Next, his mouth was on my back, pressing kisses up my spine. When he reached my shoulder blade, he rose back to his feet, letting the tunic fall and turning me. He took my hands in his. Then, one at a time, he raised my sleeves, revealing my uninjured arms. His smile broke my heart, and he brought my hand to his lips and kissed a trail from wrist to elbow, awakening my whole body to his touch.

"You're healed," he said. "Thank the Great-fucking-Dragon."

His hands snaked around my hips, pulling me into him, and fuck if the hardness of his body didn't set me on fire. His lips were firm and demanding, and all I could sense was him as he kissed me like his life depended on it. His fingers delved into my hair, cupping the back of my head. His tongue danced across my lips, and I opened for him eagerly. He tasted like warmth and cinnamon and home, and I couldn't get enough. His hands found the backs of my thighs, and he lifted me easily as I locked my arms behind his neck and wrapped my legs around his waist. In a few short steps, my back met the bark of a tree, and I remembered the last time he had me in this position. If he pulled away again, I would die. Instead, he pressed into me, deepening our kiss further. My need for him was desperate and wild, and I hated his leathers for blocking me from touching every inch of his satin skin.

"Martyrs fucking bones, really, Serae?" Bale's voice rang out. Others around him chuckled.

"You should see the way they eye fuck each other in our training sessions," Ivank answered.

Eldreth's lips against mine slowed, and the heat that was building between us simmered. When we finally separated, I grinned so widely that my cheeks hurt.

"I missed you," he whispered, placing a last, chaste kiss against my lips.

"We did leave some things unfinished between us."

He smirked. "Keep talking like that, and we'll really put on a show."

"Promise?"

His eyes darkened. I bit my lip, and his gaze tracked the movement. He pulled me in again a few inches, but then his hands released me, and he took two steps away. He looked up at the moon.

It was hard to focus on running again after that, especially as Eldreth led the group, and I had to watch his tight ass and powerful thighs at work. *Fuck, that man's body is perfect.* And in *leathers...* We ran for an hour at a time, taking short breaks in between. The sun rose at some point, and still, there was no coastline in sight.

When morning was fully upon us, we rested to eat. Lex and a man I hadn't met both carried packs of supplies, which included fruits and oat bars that they passed around to all. At first, I assumed the pack produced Bale's spare tunic until I noticed Lex now wore nothing beneath his leathers. Bale cut a striking figure in the black tunic, highlighting his dark locks and offsetting the gold in his eyes. Lex kept shooting him furtive glances, and so did Helene, who had yet to speak much to anyone.

"At this rate, it'll be dusk by the time we reach the shore," a man with dark skin and eyes said to Eldreth. His blond hair was braided in three sections. "If we split up our strongest into shifts, we should be able to sail quickly through the night."

Eldreth nodded. "Agreed. Thank you, Sellan."

I looked again at the group, picking out the ones I recognized from the manor and Eldreth's mixed training session, now that I could analyze them more closely. *So, this is Eldreth's* ranng. They were the first group I'd heard using his name instead of Wep, and they had an obvious camaraderie between them.

He caught me staring at him, and the corner of his lip quirked up. He crossed his arms, left over right, and his eyes lingered on mine. Then, he turned back to Sellan, who was grinning. They continued their conversation in hushed tones.

Raif approached them to get orders. He cast a glance over his shoulder back our way, and his eyes softened. Eldreth smirked as he watched, then snapped his fingers. Raif turned back to them with a blush staining his face.

I turned to Lispen, whose face was just as red as she stared at the ground. Teke, at her side, was nibbling the last bits of their fruit. They had rolled up their black sleeves despite the early winter chill and wore a black cloth to hide their white-blond hair.

"I can't thank you enough for coming for me." I meant it more than I could express.

"Don't be stupid," Teke said. "You're part of our *ranng*."

"Was there much trouble?"

Lispen frowned. "No. It was all easier than expected. Doesn't feel right."

"Quit baiting the dragon," Lex interjected. "We got out, and that's what matters. What I want to know is why you never told me about this absolute treat of a brother you have."

"She thought I was dead," Bale cut in from behind me.

"Ah, right."

Bale threw a wink at me as he nudged my knee and claimed a piece of the log beside me. He leaned in and lowered his voice. "I see it between you two."

"What?" I asked.

"That...fire. I never saw it between you and Tam. Friendship, sure, but not this."

"Oh." A blush crept up my face as I tried very hard not to smile.

"You're lucky to have found it."

"When did you become such a sap?"

He laughed, and the tiniest tint of mint green *hope* licked through the white flames taking over his lifelight. "Let's just say a lot has happened since I was sent away."

"When we get back, I want to know everything. You're coming with us?"

His grin dimmed. "If your prince will let me. I can't go home now—Father will lock me up again or chuck me back to the army. I pushed him too far, for all the good that did."

I placed a hand on his knee. "It wasn't your fault."

He grunted. "Plus, I can't leave you now. Who else will keep you two in check?"

Gerta chuckled, joining our group. She bypassed the logs, sitting on the leaf-strewn forest floor. My heart was full, seeing her again with Bale at my side and Eldreth nearby.

"Let them have their fun," she said, beaming at me. "They've certainly waited long enough for it." She unwrapped a perfectly round bun from a scrap of cloth and bit into it.

"Where did you get that?" I cried.

Teke burst out laughing.

When all had eaten their fill, we walked for a quarter hour before moving back into a jogging regimen. My muscles screamed with exhaustion, but I pushed myself on. It was past dusk when we finally emerged from the trees with the shoreline in sight.

"Shit! Eldreth!" Yaego, whose name I had learned over our lunch rest, shouted.

"I see it," he responded, rushing forward at full sprint.

I ran several more yards before my eyes rationalized what I was seeing in the fading light. At least ten dark forms dotted the pebbled shoreline. There was no lifelight around them.

They were bodies.

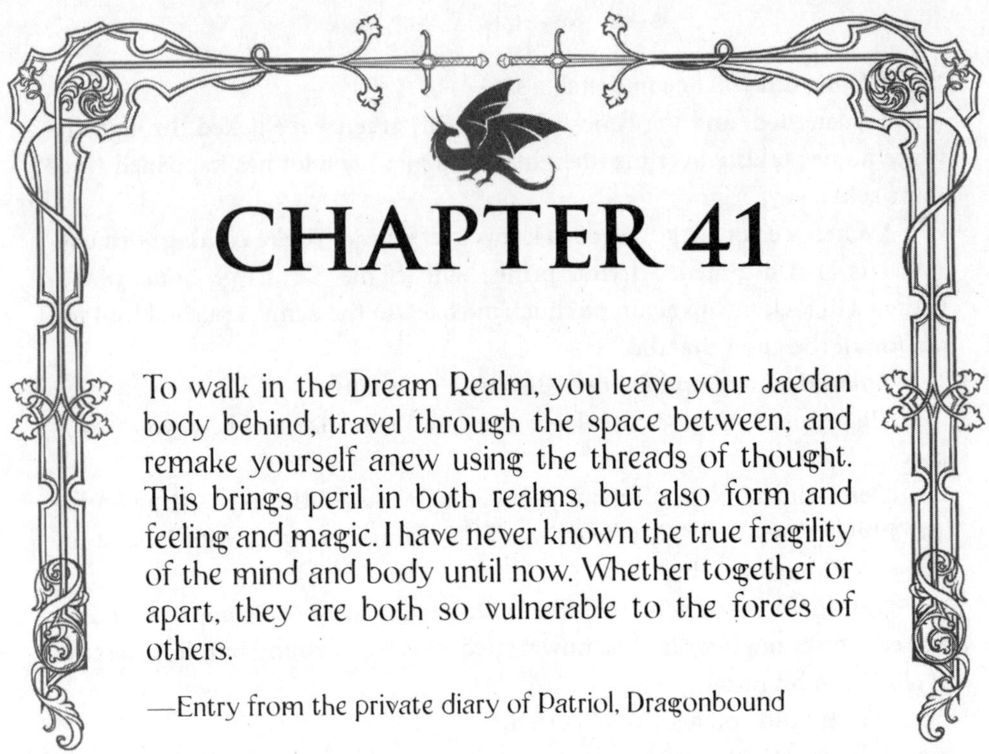

CHAPTER 41

To walk in the Dream Realm, you leave your Jaedan body behind, travel through the space between, and remake yourself anew using the threads of thought. This brings peril in both realms, but also form and feeling and magic. I have never known the true fragility of the mind and body until now. Whether together or apart, they are both so vulnerable to the forces of others.

—Entry from the private diary of Patriol, Dragonbound

SERAE

LATE AUTUMN, TALMON 1036

TEN BODIES IN Riht leather and mail were strewn across the beach, some in pieces. An acrid tang filled the air. Scorch marks covered the pebbled beach. One by one, we all ran at full speed toward the longship carved with Vaya'la's likeness. Eldreth spun around first, longsword unsheathed and raised toward the trees.

"Swim for the ship," he commanded. A handful of warriors dove into the water. The Riht galley had floated just offshore. I prayed to Vaya'la that they'd bring it back in time for us to flee.

"Small One, something is wrong."

Her voice made tears spring to my eyes. *"You're back."*

"Return to me with the other Bound," she commanded.

"What other—?"

Rumbling at my back drew my attention. At least a hundred soldiers in full mail marched from the opposite tree line and began surrounding us. The sea was at our backs, and a cold, salty wind swept my loose hair into my eyes.

"Did you really think I left my home so unguarded?" My father's voice rang out in the distance. I scanned the squadron for a glimpse of him, disbelieving. I expected him to secure the manor, maybe send a section or two out scouting for more threats. But an entire squadron after us? We, the two children he happily sold—one to the army and one to the Riht—to curry favor with the king? The center of the group split, revealing the margrave, Lord Fethersen, and Tam, all dressed in black. They were on horseback, despite the lack of purchase their steeds would have on the rocks.

"I had thought you Rihtlonders were smarter than that." He tutted. "Such a small party, too. It's a wonder you've ever succeeded in raiding our lands."

"The Riht take only what is rightfully ours," Sellan replied, his longsword raised.

The margrave ignored him. "I'll give you one chance. Hand over my wayward progeny, and your deaths will be quick."

Eldreth stepped in front of me. "I have a counter-proposal."

The margrave laughed.

"Turn your little company around, march back to your pathetic homes and wasteful lives, and I'll let you keep your heads attached to your shoulders."

His laugh fell away alongside all pretenses of civility. An ugly scowl overtook the margrave's face. "Attack!" he commanded.

"Halt!" Tam intervened, holding up a hand to still his men. I had mistaken the Fethersen blue for black in the twilight. Except for the margrave, whose black doublet was a shade darker than the rest, all the soldiers donned the colors of Fethersen.

Tam urged his horse forward a few paces. "Serae, please, we can stop this."

I moved to Eldreth's side, fists clenched inside Bale's overlarge tunic sleeves. "What's your price?"

"My price?" He sighed. His reins were fisted in his left hand, and his right was covered by another diagonal cape. "Come back with us. Let this foolishness lie."

"So he can whip me to shreds again?" My eyes flicked to the margrave.

Tam turned to my father, then back to me. "He should never have laid a hand on you. He never will again. You'll be moved to Fethersen immediately. You have my word."

It was the last thing I wanted, but the white, pulsing lifelight of thirty Riht warriors, sparkling with *loyalty* in waves as bright as green amaryllis against fresh snow, met me at all sides. Except Tam no longer counted among the people whose word I trusted. He had ruined that beyond repair.

"Will you let them all live?" I called back. "Let them board their ship and sail away untouched?" All heads of the Riht turned to me, but it was Eldreth's glare at my side that penetrated my chest like an arrow.

Tam dismounted and walked out from the line of soldiers. If he was hoping I would meet him in the middle before exacting an oath from him, he was sorely mistaken. "Our lives have been tied together since birth. You know this. We were each other's first friend, first kiss, first lover... Our bond is deeper and stronger than anything they can throw our way. I've never been more certain of it. You belong with me." Tam held his arms out wide, cape still draped over his right side, offering himself to me. "Please, you know it's true. Come with me, and everyone lives."

Eldreth's eyes fell away from me. The glow of his lifelight flashed deep blue, darker than a moonless night. *Grief.* Across from me, Tam's lifelight was jarring in contrast, flickering with bright peacock blue. *Shame.* Over what he had done to me, or over the lies I knew he spoke? In the end, it didn't matter. I was foolish to think, even for a moment, that my father would ever back down.

I laced my fingers into Eldreth's, and his hand gripped mine tightly. There was only one way out.

"I never belonged to you, Tamas Fethersen. Don't you see? I belong to myself."

His face twisted as maroon *frustration* poured from him. "You would go *with him* instead of me?"

"He holds my heart. That will never change." My answer was a truth so simple, it was easy to speak. If these weeks apart had not already proved it to me, the fact that he came for me, despite how we left things, would have.

Tam's eyes hardened. "Order the attack," he hissed. He turned his back on us and remounted his horse. Behind him, Lord Fethersen called out the charge.

The Riht were ready to meet them. Eldreth and his *ranng* moved forward as a unit, waiting. Together, they might stand a chance. Bale and I, behind them, were unarmed and a liability. I pulled Gerta to my side as we withdrew as far back as we could. Behind us, the Drakhi galley had been boarded, and I could just make out our warriors rushing to tie the sails.

"We're going to die," Bale said to me, resignation in his voice.

Eldreth glanced back, locked eyes with me, and smirked. "Not today."

He spun as the first wave of soldiers approached, and in three strikes of his blades, three were down. Death cries rang out all around his *ranng* and the others who had come—the most skilled warriors the Riht possessed.

And they had come for *me.*

More and more pressed in, but Eldreth was relentless. He and his chosen warriors kept a tight semicircle, blocking the Fethersen soldiers from breaking through. Behind them, my *ranng* formed up, providing a double layer of warriors to protect Bale, me, and Gerta.

"Break the line!" Tam shouted at the back.

Every Riht warrior became a dance of death. Yaego flowed between sword and dagger. She threw one, stopping a man at Praeth's back before unsheathing another at her ribs and meeting her next opponent with full force. Praeth and Branye fought side by side in perfect complement. Sellan fought at Eldreth's side. His movements were sharper than the dizzying fluidity Eldreth exuded, yet still, he moved with the same exactness that wasted nothing between strikes.

In seconds, twenty men lay dead at their feet, but Fethersen's army had barely taken a dent. What I thought was a hundred men kept filling in—spilling from the trees in droves and organizing into lines. The next wave charged at our group, twice as many men as before, but the *ranngs* moved out to meet them. Their skill was phenomenal, but it would never last. Soon, we would be outnumbered ten to one, and the Riht would begin to fall.

I froze, at first, paralyzed with fear. Either from my experience with the dragori, my overall training, or my own sense of will, I came back to myself. I was no longer helpless. I reached for that connection with Vaya'la, and though she settled back into that special place in my mind, I couldn't feel her magic anymore. But I could keep trying. Short of picking up a sword from the fallen and joining the fray, there was nothing else I could do. As I reached within, time and again, I bore witness to their pain, praying our warriors were not fighting in vain.

A man with two blond braids and dark skin was the first to go down. He slipped on a patch of blood-slick pebbles, and his opponent's sword sliced clean across his abdomen. His companion, a woman as tall as him, screamed as he fell and charged wildly. It was the cry only a lover could make as their entire world was taken from them. It was a mercy that she spent only minutes in agony before she was impaled in the side by a spear.

By some miracle, Eldreth's *ranng* had pushed a dent into the Fethersen soldiers, rallying the warriors at their sides. But then another wave came, twice as big as the last. Our chance, I knew, had slipped away.

Praeth, still with a fresh scar down the side of his head, took a blade to the thigh. By luck, it missed the major artery, but he was struggling to stand.

Helene jerked as an arrow embedded in her arm. She snapped off the tail, but her second sword clattered to the ground.

One by one, I watched in horror and misery as my friends and companions were forced back into a tight group, trying to protect me to the very end. Even Bale took up a sword from one of the fallen soldiers, but next to the Riht warriors, he was barely any help.

When Lispen was lanced through the gut, I cried out as far too much blood gushed from her wound. Ivank rushed forward, killing the soldier that wounded her and pushing more back. Raif dropped to her side, abandoning the fight entirely, and cradled her head in his lap. His lips mouthed *No,* but they made no sound. I reached for my magic again—nothing.

"Please," I begged Vaya'la, and though I felt her comfort, I could not hear her voice.

Teke collapsed with multiple stab wounds to the torso when they jumped in front of Lex, stopping what would have been a killing blow to him. Lex pulled them back away from the enemy before another death blow could fall.

Still, the Inraen soldiers pressed on. Not even the skill of the Riht could overcome so many. Blood and gore splattered, vigilant in my role as witness, until every single Riht except for Eldreth and Sellan had collapsed with wounds that were incapacitating or would soon be fatal. My entire *ranng*, holding on until the last, lay around us in pools of blood. Raif alone was uninjured, but judging by the way he wept as he pressed his hand over Lispen's stomach in a desperate bid to staunch the flow, he bore a wound just as deep.

Sellan was the last to go down. It was only after he was slashed across the chest, leaving Eldreth's lone figure in front of me and Bale, Gerta still tucked behind us, that Lord Fethersen called for a pause. He had not even dismounted. "You have all fought valiantly today, but you are beaten. Send forth the Cavendaffes, and you will be released to your boat to save those few of your wounded that might yet live."

Eldreth adjusted his stance and spat blood onto the beach. He had taken a wound to the head, but I couldn't tell how serious it was through the rivulets pouring down his cheek.

"The choice is simple." Fethersen continued. I had always known the rotund man as one of fairness and reason. "You can all die where you lay, or you can give up what was not yours to begin with. The Cavendaffes will not be harmed."

"Serae goes with the Riht. You can have me in her place." Eldreth's voice boomed over the army, making Fethersen's sound weak in comparison. At his words, my knees threatened to collapse.

Tam stepped forward a few paces past his father's horse and laughed, but there was no mirth in his voice—only bitterness. He had dismounted again on the pretense of commanding the soldiers, but he had not raised his sword that day. Perhaps he couldn't, missing two fingers from his right hand and untrained with his left. "You're hardly in a position to negotiate."

Eldreth ignored Tam and spoke directly to Lord Fethersen. "She's nothing to you but vanity. Take the heir, and take me. She is the second daughter and worth very little to you."

"If you think you can—"

"Agreed," the margrave interrupted from somewhere behind the ranks. Cold dread flooded me, choking off my scream into a drawn-out whimper. *He couldn't.* I had to stop this.

Gerta gripped my arm, holding me in place. Bale did not move from my side, but Eldreth stepped forward. He sheathed his sword at his back and continued walking until he was right in front of Tam. He stared down at the smaller man and waited, an angel of death standing before a mere mortal. With his black leathers, blood-smeared plate, and imposing frame, the image was uncanny.

To his credit, Tam did not back down. "Let him pass," he commanded. A frightening grin overtook his face.

The soldiers parted down the center, leaving an uneven path directly to the margrave, who had also yet to dismount. Eldreth walked down the lines while I looked on in horror, unable to speak. He stopped at the center of the circle, directly in front of the margrave's horse. Tam followed, leaving his back to me. I searched the ground for an intact bow.

"No!" Yaego screamed, squeezing a gash in her side as blood gushed from the wound.

At her side, Raif was clutching Lispen's body to his. She had gone still in his arms. He pressed a kiss to her forehead, shifted her still form to the ground, and rose to his feet. Tears welled in my eyes, but his face hardened with resolve.

"*For the Riht,*" he whispered and surged forward. He ran straight for Tam's back with his blade raised, kicking up pebbles from the beach. His sword sliced diagonally with enough force to cleave Tam in two, but at the last moment, Raif jerked, and the strike fell short. Tam dropped to the ground and scrambled away.

Raif's grip on his sword loosened, and the blade toppled to the sand. Tears streaked down my face as he sank to his knees, twisting to reveal the two crossbolts embedded in his gut. His lips moved, and his breath wheezed, but no words came out.

Tam lurched back to his feet and approached Raif with fury in his eyes. He placed a boot on Raif's chest and kicked. I watched on helplessly as Raif collapsed to his back. Blood pooled onto the pebbled sand, but he struggled until he'd rolled enough for his eyes to lock on Lispen's expressionless face. Her lifelight was barely a wisp around her.

His lips formed the words, *Soon, love. Soon.* I could only watch as his lifelight began to dim.

"On your knees." Tam's voice drew me away from the senseless loss. I barely recognized it, thick with so much hatred.

"No," I sobbed, finally finding my own voice. "No, please, no." I looked to my father, whose eyes were cold with triumph. "If you ever loved me, please, give me this. Don't kill him. I will stay. I'll do whatever you command. Please!"

His smile was cruel. "The death of the next high dane far outweighs any secrets you hold, child. I am done with you." To a soldier at his side, he ordered, "Shoot her if she tries to interfere."

The soldier leveled his crossbow directly at me, but Eldreth stepped into its path.

"No!" I screamed, lunging forward, but Gerta locked her arms around mine, holding me back. Bale, sword raised, edged forward.

Eldreth dropped to his knees. Despite the death around us and the direness of our situation, he smirked. "It's your turn," he said directly to me. There was no fear in his eyes. "I trust you."

A sob racked through me. I lunged again and nearly broke free, but Gerta and Bale forced me behind them.

Gerta rounded on me, gripping my face and taking up my whole view. "Do not watch, my lady." Tears rolled down her cheeks, but the lines of her face were hard. "We follow him to the land of the Creator. It will all be over soon. I'm sorry that it ends this way, but you have been my truest friend. I am glad to meet my end at your side."

"*NO!*" I screamed, and something feral broke free inside me. I would not let Eldreth die. My next scream shook the earth. I called upon my power and felt a wisp of it at the edge of my mind, begging to return in full force. I just had to find a way to reach it. I stepped forward, pushing Gerta to the side. She latched onto my arm and yanked, but there was no stopping me now. A warning shot whizzed by, splashing in the water behind me. Ignoring it, I tugged us forward.

The second shot connected with something solid. Gerta's body jerked, and her grip on my arm loosened. Shock widened her eyes as the breath huffed from her lungs. She started to slip, and I gripped her, steadying her. Her head shook, and she fell to her knees, crossbolt buried between her ribs. "Tell her..." The words died on her lips. Her lifelight winked out, and her body went limp in my arms. It had pierced her heart.

She was gone.

"No," I whispered, shaking her. But her head lolled to the side.

"No!" I shouted, tears falling from my eyes. She couldn't be gone. Those shots were meant for me, not her. My chest imploded, as surely as if I had taken the arrow through my own heart.

"Bring her back!" I screamed, voice tearing through my throat.

Bale was behind me, wrapping his arms around me and Gerta. "I've got you."

But as his hand touched the exposed skin of my arm, the reach in my mind expanded. Vaya'la's light flooded me alongside something scorching hot. I gripped it, forcing it into Gerta, but it recoiled. Gritting my teeth, I tried again, bending the light and demanding it heal her. There was nothing left to heal.

But this twinned power, coiling within my core, begged to be used.

I let her go. Pressing a kiss to her forehead, I laid her body onto the pebbled beach. Turning away from her, I slipped my hand into Bale's and squeezed. Power, bright and burning, swirled through me until I was sure it would burst through my skin.

"Together," Vaya'la spoke into my mind alongside another's voice. *"Trust."*

Turning back to the army of men—led by nobles playing at war—my heart hardened. I would give them exactly what they deserved. Eldreth's eyes were locked on mine with such sympathy that, if I took the time to look back, I might break in two. Tam's blade was drawn and held in his left hand. He took two steps toward Eldreth and dared to place his steel against that beautiful throat. The storm inside raged. The wall of black grief that was descending halted and began to recede. In its wake, I found control.

My hand tightened even stronger around Bale's, and he gripped mine just as fiercely. I didn't know how or why, just that we needed to stay connected. I turned to him, and his eyes shone bright yellow with live, flickering flames. Whatever he saw in me ripped a gasp from his throat.

"Hold on," I said, and my free hand shot to the trees.

"**Wake.**" We spoke as one voice, and the trees listened.

"**Wake,**" we repeated, and miles away in a hidden cave, a pair of slitted, peridot-green eyes opened.

ELDRETH

LATE AUTUMN, TALMON 1036

I WATCHED HER, there on my knees in failing light. My heart ached at the grief in her eyes. Gerta was an innocent, and her loss was a needless waste of goodness and life. But this fight wasn't over. I had no desire or intention to die today, and I would do whatever I had to for *her* to live. I let that scrawny bastard put his blade to my throat. I felt no fear.

I still had a promise to keep.

The air shifted, and something like lightning crackled. My eyes locked on her, stunning, even in blood-drenched clothes with more streaked through her hair. She was fucking beautiful, inside and out. She gripped her brother's hand, and I braced for whatever was to come.

She began to glow. I smiled.

Gasps from the soldiers around me echoed down the lines. Their useless, fat lord was shouting commands, but I could smell the fear. They pulled away from Serae as her eyes glowed green and her skin shone with starlight. Her flame-red hair danced with firelight as great wings of light erupted from her shoulders. They were different this time. The light was more golden and flickering than the first time I'd seen them, but they were still radiant with the purest white light imaginable.

"**Wake.**"

The earth beneath me shifted. The blade at my neck fell away as the three-fingered wonder lost his footing.

"Wake."

I was never one to hesitate.

Rolling forward, I kicked the lordling in his side and yanked the sword from his hand. The blade was trash, but the point was good enough. I plunged it through his shoulder, pinning him to the beach.

He screamed and flung his injured hand over his head, but he wasn't my true target. Not today. It was time to keep my promise.

I whirled and charged straight for the margrave's horse. The animal spooked and reared up. I dodged its front legs, avoiding the hooves that kicked out, and grabbed the margrave by his tunic. One strong jerk was all it took to relieve him of his seat and send him crashing to the ground. The horse bolted forward, creating the exact diversion I needed. This man, who should have been Serae's protector and instead was her torturer, was finally at my mercy.

Except, when it came to mercy, mine had run cold. They were fools to accept an enemy into their midst fully armed. Even worse to accept me.

The margrave squirmed under my grip and reached for a dagger at his belt. *A dagger.* He didn't even carry a sword. I retrieved it for him and plunged it through his hand and into his protruding belly. He howled in pain, and I relished every blubbering cry.

"Please," he spluttered. "I'll give you anything you want. Take her and go. The alliance will stand. I'll see to it myself."

I grinned as I looked down at him, and he shied away from the sight. "Tell me, Margrave, what incentive do I have to let you live, when your death would give me a true ally in your heir, and vengeance over the man who nearly killed my future wife?"

His eyes widened in horror. I dragged the moment out, letting him feel every ounce of fear as I pulled a short sword from my side. I should have taken my time, slicing him to bits as he did to her. Covering him in gashes until there was nothing left but a bloodied heap of flesh. But Serae was still on that beach at risk, and it was now my job to keep her safe. With one swift thrust, I sank my blade straight through the margrave's throat.

I leaned down as he choked up blood, spluttering out the last seconds of his life.

"Serae is worth ten thousand of you," I spat.

He clawed at the sword, slicing the fingers of his free hand apart, but I held it until he stilled. Serae's father was dead. I'd made her brother an early heir, and just a few hours ago, I'd nearly killed him, too. Not a good track record for my first time meeting her family. I didn't have time to feel the doubt or guilt that hit me. I looked up and saw...*trees.*

The fucking trees were moving. Not just swaying with the wind but clambering across the beach. Branches and roots lashed out everywhere, strangling, crushing, and flinging soldiers in all directions. A branch whipped over my head, and I ducked.

The soldiers turned to fight this new enemy—some of them, at least. Others fled toward the beach. Some dove into the water—fucking idiots, they'd all sink—while the rest turned and ran down the coast.

Then, a blinding light exploded from Serae in a radiating arc. It slammed into everyone around her, throwing back Inraen soldiers while absorbing into the Riht. One by one, their heads rose. Some got to their feet. By the time the light hit me, I already knew what to expect. A wave of fire surged into my skull, healing the blow I'd taken to my temple. It poured from her in heaving pulses until every Riht who hadn't already been claimed by death rose to stand with weapons aloft.

"Protect her at all costs," Sellan shouted, breaking me from my trance.

I turned and ran back down the beach. Screams sounded from every direction, but one more piercing than the rest.

"Raif!" It was Lispen—*alive*. "No, no, NO! RAIF!" Her voice descended into harrowing wails. For a moment, my heart fucking shattered for her.

"Lispen," his voice rasped, "I'm here." I turned to see Raif, surrounded by the bodies of soldiers Serae's trees had slain, yanking bolts from his gut. They made nothing but shallow cuts as he ripped them free instead of the deep gashes they'd been moments before. Serae's magic was astounding. The bolts had been pushed toward the surface, and though he bled when he pulled the bolts free, I had no doubts that the life-claiming damage had been reversed.

I didn't have time to stop for their reunion as their bodies crashed together in the way I was desperate to grip Serae. She was providing us with a distraction, and I had to take it.

"Get everyone to the galley!" I shouted to Sellan as I ran straight for Serae. I could barely hear my voice over the ground rumbling and the violent wind in my ears.

Serae and Bale stood hand in hand at the edge of the shore. Bale's black hair whipped around him, but he was otherwise still. Serae, on the other hand, was vibrating power. It stopped me in my tracks. I watched in awe as she reached one arm to the sky. Roots shot up from the ground and wrapped around limbs, torsos, and necks. With a sweep of her arm, trees crashed down, crushing soldiers who hadn't already fled. All the while, the wings at her back moved in tandem with her arms, and a goddess-like light shone from her every pore.

Off to my side, Sellan was corralling our remaining warriors and shouting, "Get to the ship!" What was left of our troop turned and ran in pairs, hauling the bodies they could back to the longships. They needed proper death rites, which the Inraen would never give.

My focus remained clear—get Serae out. The three words chanted in a loop through my mind. I scooped her up in my arms without stopping as I ran. Her arm wrenched away from her brother, and he turned to me with wrath in his glowing eyes. "Run!" I shouted, hoping he had the sense to listen. I didn't look back as I made for the ship.

Trudging through the waist-high water with Serae in my arms was no picnic, but once Ivank pulled her on board, I was able to grip the side and climb in myself. We were the last two in.

Our work wasn't done yet. I moved to an oar. With nearly half our numbers diminished, it would be harder to crew the ship with the speed I wanted, but not impossible. Lispen sat at the stem and called out our strokes through a face streaked with blood and tears, but there was a smile on her lips. We just needed to get far enough out for the wind to take over.

"Fire!" Branye called out, pointing back to shore.

I whipped around. *Fire* was an understatement. A column of flame as high as the sky itself raged on the shoreline. When it reached the clouds, it fanned out in a burning plume. Flames rained down over the forest, igniting leaves and branches. The column swirled the clouds above until a figure like the head of a great dragon with a gaping maw formed. Whether it was breathing the fire in or out, I couldn't tell.

I squinted into the epicenter of the white-hot magma. It was barely a speck on the ground, but the dark center almost looked like...

My eyes sought out Yaego, who immediately snapped her gaze to me. Judging by the shock on her face, she had spotted the same thing. Only once before had I beheld such a fire—on the worst day of my life. The day I got my scars.

"Where's Bale?" Lispen called out.

I scanned our boat, but he wasn't among our crew.

Yaego stood and scanned the length of the hull. Her lips pressed into a grim line. She grabbed the mast and climbed with a speed none could mirror. Yaego's eyes scoured the shoreline, then flicked down to me. One nod of her head, and I knew.

I drew in my oar and moved to the sternpost, leaning out as far as I could. Looking into the fire burned my eyes, but I deserved the pain. The column was diminishing. The figure in the middle collapsed to the pebbled beach, and the fire went out altogether, but I could still make out his likeness.

Fuck. Serae would never forgive me.

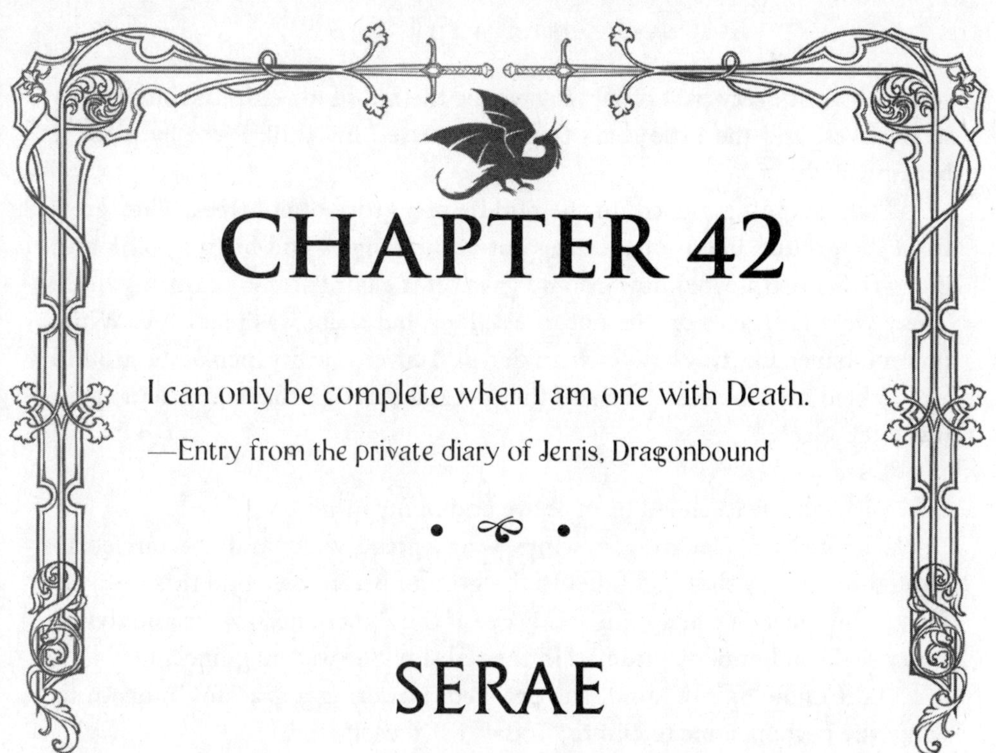

CHAPTER 42

I can only be complete when I am one with Death.

—Entry from the private diary of Jerris, Dragonbound

• ~ •

SERAE

EARLY WINTER, TALMON 1036

Awaken.

Do you remember yourself?

Who you are at your core?

What all the little things are that make you, you?

Remembering is the first step. Remember your love for those you care about most. Remember your passions, your likes, your dislikes. Remember the things that make you laugh. That make you cry. That make you hate.

Are you with me now, Small One?

This is how you exist in the realm of thought. Imagine yourself. Bend your imagination into being, and you shall be. Give yourself a body—your body—and command it. Anything you can dream, you can do in this realm.

Be.

I was. I felt a spark within my mind. It caused no pain until I remembered that such a thing as pain could exist. Then, it was excruciating. I opened my mouth, and indeed, I had a mouth. I filled my lungs with air and bellowed out a mighty scream. As my voice strained, I remembered my arms, my legs, my face, my hair. On and on through minutes and hours, I used that terrible sound to craft every part of me. It gave me the red of my hair, the blue-green in my eyes, and the little scars that crisscrossed my skin. Piece by piece, I became myself.

I was standing, naked, in the middle of a grove of not-trees. They grew from the ground like roots, jutting out at odd angles and bearing pink and green fruits that floated upward and gave off the faint aroma of rotting flesh. There were no leaves on the not-forest floor, but there was plant life. White flowers shaped like tiny balls of wrinkled fluff covered every inch of the ground and tickled my bare feet. The soil that peeked through their minuscule gaps was pitch black.

"*I see you.*"

Vaya'la's voice echoed from above and in my mind.

I looked up. Her dragon wings were spread wide, and she circled in tightening arcs as she descended to the ground before me amid this unlikely forest. Unbidden, a tear sprang to my eye at the sight of her, awake and flying. Every scale on her body gleamed in the red sun. She was magnificent.

As if knowing my mind, she preened. Lowering a graceful, monstrous wing, she beckoned me to climb. "Today, I will carry you."

Atop her back, nestled between her shoulder blades, I rode over this strange, wondrous realm. Not that I could enjoy it. Everything blurred together. It was familiar, waking to a misshapen world before my glasses brought it to clarity. Except, I had no glasses—*needed* none. I kept my eyes trained ahead, where I could see best, and only when she banked did I catch glimpses of the lands below. My skin crawled. There was a wrongness to this world. I knew this with a deep certainty, though looking at the diamond cliffs, red rivers, and violet grasslands, I saw only beauty.

We flew for hours. Weariness settled into my mind, dulling my thoughts. Perhaps I slept, cradled in my seat. When Vaya'la began her circuitous descent, I woke, seeing with perfect clarity for the first time. Matching her movements, I curved into the wind. The magnificence of our flight ended before I could fully appreciate it. We landed on a glass island, and something about its emerald hue tickled my memory. A throne jutted out from the center, and upon it sat a being that was not a man, and yet he was. He had hair and skin of flame. He wore no clothing—his body covered by armor made of black stone.

A pool of magma churned beneath us, and as I marveled at it, a creature moved from within. The thing swam through the molten liquid and emerged at the other end of the island. I recoiled. For several moments, it flopped and crawled as an amorphous blob until its shape resolved. It stood on two thick legs, still burning from its core, though its outer skin had cooled to charcoal black. As soon as the process was done, it marched off toward a dark spot on the horizon, and a new creature began its writhing beneath my feet. *What was that thing?*

"One of my army," a voice, ageless and somehow familiar, answered the question I had not asked. "I was sorry to lose you from my fold."

Brow furrowed, I did not respond. Or, perhaps, I didn't quite know how to shape my voice. My eyes turned to *that spot*, where everything was drawn—where *I* was drawn. In it, I sensed malice and death. Instinct told me to flee, and yet, I wanted nothing more than to move toward it.

"Don't be a child."

It was Vaya'la's voice, but she was missing. In her place, a beautiful woman stood. Her hair was a living ecosystem unto itself that cascaded down her back and spilled over the glassy floor. Her body was lithe and strong and glowed with a living green light over her timeless skin. Before my eyes, great vines grew from that skin and formed around her as true living armor.

"*My goddess.*" I fell to my knees, but she touched a moss-covered hand to my cheek, bidding me to rise. Her hand pulled away, covered with small white blossoms.

"Vaya'la, my boon, what brings you to my humble rock?"

"What news, Tin'nen?"

His smile was hot and sharp. "What makes you think there's news?"

"You're amassing your army."

"They don't call me the Creator for nothing." He flicked a dismissive hand. "I like your new pet. I'm thinking of taking one of my own."

"*The Creator?*" My head whipped to him, but his eyes remained trained on Vaya'la, that horrible smile still in place. They both ignored me.

"Your sense of time is lacking."

Tin'nen let out a crackling laugh. "Was, is, will—what's the difference?"

Vaya'la smirked.

"Why are you here, Vaya'la? Your figure is stunning. Your pet is striking. But, *your* sense of timing is foreboding." He flipped his flaming hair over one shoulder, allowing it all to cascade down his back as he turned away from her to look upon the growing black dot on the horizon. "Long years have passed since giving you our pledges, and I alone am seeing it through. What more do you need of me?"

She moved to stand next to him. Her figure shifted with the strength of boulders diverting a stream, and she placed a single, slight hand on Tin'nen's shoulder. The pale flowers that decorated her fingers did not so much as wither at the contact with his pure flame. "I need a favor, old friend."

"Oh, is that what we are?"

"Always."

Tin'nen placed a flaming hand atop Vaya'la's and squeezed. "*Name it,*" he said, though I only heard his voice in my head. He had stopped speaking aloud, and yet, in this strange world, that did not stop him from speaking to us.

"Show her." Vaya'la's focus shifted to me, though her eyes remained fixed on that same black spot.

I stepped away. For the first time, I was aware of my nakedness. The thought of clothes formed in my mind, and they took shape over my body. I was wrapped in a green underdress complete with leggings and boots, except they were made entirely of leaves.

"She must understand. She needs to see it."

Both of them turned to me. The weight of their gazes—these dragons, these gods, these living entities of power—forced me back another step. "No."

Tin'nen held out a flaming hand. "Come." He took a single step and was before me, despite having been halfway across the glass island. My hand was in his, though I didn't remember giving it. I tried to pull away, but his hand clasped firm. "*Open your eyes,*" he spoke into my mind. "*Do not fear the power of sight.*"

I blinked, and I was in the air. A scream ripped from my throat, but it didn't meet my ears. Soaring high above the Darkness, I was a fool to ever think it a mere spot. It was a land as vast and black as night—no, not night. The night is a place of cool, crisp peace. The blackness of this land was the unending sleep, the restless torment, and the cunning embrace of death. It beckoned as much as it revolted me. Before my eyes, it seeped and grew, swallowing land and sea, rock and tree. Fear gripped my mind as it turned the depthless waters into flat pits and replaced every speck of light across the lands with shadow. It was rotten and hollow and beautiful as the coming storm, captivating my senses while it wreaked havoc around us.

"*This creature is one of mine.*"

As soon as Tin'nen spoke the words, I became aware of the body we inhabited—a winged ball of flame given sight. Though we had become this strange sentry-like creature, I knew that it was separate from me. Seeing through its singular eye, we soared above the darkness until its vision began to adjust. The shadows below lurched and writhed, and as I watched, unable to look away, they took shape. They came together from death and darkness in a way that was alike and yet entirely unlike Tin'nen's fire beasts emerging from the magma. I recognized the churning in my stomach. I had felt this *wrongness* once before.

"*You know them,*" Tin'nen said into my mind.

"*Yes,*" I replied through our mental link. "*How can I hear you?*"

"*We are connected by touch.*"

"*Only you and I are always connected, Small One. Without a binding, the mental link with another requires a physical one, too,*" Vaya'la explained, though she was miles away from the fiery creature we inhabited.

"*You can also hear him?*" I asked.

"*Only because he speaks to us both.*"

I watched the sickening creatures as they sprouted arms and legs, snouts and scales. Though my mind was miles away, I felt bile rise in my throat. "*No wings.*"

Tin'nen growled. "*These have neither wings nor brains, but not all drakes are so. The Corruption bleeds and breeds as it devours. Over the centuries, it has mutated the creatures of the Dream Realm into beings of nightmares. Look to the west.*"

I followed his mental gaze, drawing me off to the right of where we hovered. It was a clash of blackness and flame. The fire creatures oozed between forms as they fought, rendering great beaks and horns and gnashing teeth to tear apart the darkness. Deadly maws, gleaming black, responded with equal force. I recognized drakes and dragori, but there were other creatures, too. Smaller four-legged reptilian *things* launched themselves onto the fire and were consumed by the dozens. A great roar shook the ground, and a creature emerged from the blackness and pounded its feet, stomping beings of fire and darkness alike. It had a pair of great wings spread out across the sky, and despite its features being so similar, it was not a dragon. Even from afar, I could sense that it did not hold the intelligence or magic of one such as Tin'nen or Vaya'la.

"*The doors keep them in our realm, but the magic is leaking. If the barriers are ruptured, there will be nothing stopping them from passing through.*"

We flew to the east, high above the terrible army emerging by the hundred from the Darkness. Thousands upon thousands of the black abominations gathered, all moving eastward. On the other side of the line of battle, fire creatures of all shapes and sizes came together, some merging with others to create grotesque multi-headed beasts while others shifted between forms with each flicker. They emerged from pools of magma dotting the land and followed flaming lines toward the raging battle. From above, they might have been fiery ants marching in dozens of lines against a swarming nest.

Our flight pivoted back to the west, beyond the fire creatures and magma lakes. Relief flooded me to be away from so much death and horror. We continued over the very glass island where our bodies stood and beyond until we reached the farthest edge of this land. The sentry plunged toward the ground, and I shrieked a warning, but the tiny creature swerved, wings tucking in. It darted through a hole, barely wide enough for it to squeeze through, that opened into a tunnel and then a cavern. There, in the center of this secret place, burned a doorway. It stood on its own, raging fiercely despite consuming nothing to feed its flames. Every inch of the door burst and popped. The crackling echoed through the quiet chamber, overwhelming me. Far away on the glass island, my hands flew to my ears but did nothing to block out the sound. At its center, a plane of fire and magma swirled in a state of constant eruption—both a warning and a dare for anyone who might enter.

"*This is my charge. If this or the other doors are breached, nothing will stop the onslaught of Darkness from overtaking your world. I have found my champion to guard this door, but you must find the others.*"

"*What others?*"

"*You know the song. It lives within you. From Flame and Ice and Blood and Bone... Each door will take one of its own...*"

I gasped as knowledge filled me. My mind began to tremble, trying to hold on before it all slipped away. The creature we inhabited screeched, breaking my concentration. As it fled the cavern, I glimpsed a form lying in a heap on the other side of the doorway. I knew him instantly. Even if I had not seen those telltale black curls, I could never mistake him. I knew him as well as I knew myself.

A rage unlike anything filled every inch of my being, and I screamed into Tin'nen and Vaya'la and the winged creature's minds. I was flung backward, and when I opened my eyes, I was sprawled across the glass island with Vaya'la standing over me. Her back was to me, and an ire to match my own was leveled at Tin'nen.

"You took my brother!" I screamed, and I pushed myself off the glass. I flung my arms forward, and great spikes flew from my hands. They hit Tin'nen square in his armored chest and bounced harmlessly to the floor. I screamed again and reached for my power.

"Peace, Small One." Vaya'la had turned to me, eyes soft with understanding. "The Dragon chooses their Bound. This is the way of things. He is worthy of this binding."

My tears sprang forth. I wanted to fight this, to reverse it, to force anyone else to be chosen, but how could I disagree? I knew his merit more than anyone, and with it, how much he meant to me. I choked down my sob and wiped my eyes dry. Then, I turned to Tin'nen and said, "So be it."

He nodded and turned to Vaya'la. "Send your Bound away. There is much yet for us to discuss."

Vaya'la, to my horror, agreed.

I gripped her arm. "Don't." I pulled her toward me, and vines crept from my hands and wound around her arm. "Don't abandon me," I breathed.

"Don't be silly, Small One." Her hand smoothed down my hair, and she cupped my face in her palm. "Wake up."

The vines vanished.

"Wake up."

I opened my eyes.

Sunlight poured in through the window of a room that was not mine. I was stretched out like a bird in flight across the bed, which was large enough to hold me, arms extended, and then some. *Eldreth's bed.* A fire crackled in the hearth nearby.

"It's about time you woke up." Kahvrah looked at me over a knitting hoop. There were dark circles under her eyes.

"You've taken to knitting," I croaked. My lips hurt. I tried to lick them, but my mouth was just as dry.

"There's a glass just there beside you." She nodded to the table on my left. "Drink up."

The water burned my throat even though I could feel the chill of it through the glass. I choked and spluttered, took a deep breath, then tried again slowly. I sipped at the glass until it was gone, then I took a mental tally of my body. Everything ached from disuse, but there was no other pain. Shouldn't there have been pain?

The main door to these quarters opened, and a great clatter of wood sounded from the adjacent room.

"Any change?" A voice called out. *His* voice. The voice I'd been dreaming about for weeks while confined to that horrible room in Cavendaffe.

An embrace, then fire and light erupting from us and setting the tapestries ablaze. Now, I understood the fire. I hoped the house burned to the ground.

"Come and see." Kahvrah rose to her feet, though her shoulders stooped.

Then, he was there in the doorway. Eldreth. *My betrothed.* That sour, grumpy, perfect man looking scrumptious with loose hair and his usual black shirt, black pants, and matching leather boots and bracers. It was so *him* that I wanted to cry. He took a single step into the bedroom.

"You know where to find me if you need me, Wep." Kahvrah slipped from the room, and a moment later, I heard the main door thump closed.

Eldreth had not moved. He stood unnaturally still, except for his stormy blue eyes, which consumed me. "You're awake," he said in a low rumble.

"I'm awake." My voice was steady now that he was within my sight. Plus, the glass of water helped. "You've cleaned up in here."

He chuckled in that same deep timbre that went straight to my core. "Have you eaten?"

I shook my head. "I only just woke up."

"I'll get you something. Tea, soup, maybe some bread." He turned to go.

I couldn't let him. I needed him beside me. I had a thousand things to tell him, but my mind was a jumbled mess. Every pounding beat of my heart echoed in the same two-tone rhythm, calling for him. *Eldreth. Eldreth.* "Eldreth."

He stopped in the doorway, and when he looked back at me, I could read the tension in his face. His body was the picture of calculated ease. He might have looked unconcerned to anyone else, even to me a few months ago, but now I knew him better. That unrelenting self-control of his was everywhere. It was in the clench of his jaw, the flex of his arms, and the straightness of his spine.

I reached out to him. Just one hand, extended for him to take.

His breath finally left him. His shoulders dropped as he took long, languid strides around the bed frame to my side. I drank him in as he gripped my hand in his own and dropped to one knee before me. A single lock of copper hair fell into his face, and I resisted the urge to brush it away. He looked up at me with so much pain in his eyes that my second sight flew open on instinct. His brilliant white light, always outshining any other, exploded through the room, filling every crevice of my vision. Steady as the beat of my own heart, orange pulses of *fear* broke through, tainting his beautiful lifelight.

He closed his eyes. "Please, let me bring you something first." His voice was raw and jagged. "Give yourself time to recover. There will be time enough for Dane and Ell and...all there is to say."

Streaks of blue between the orange. Was that *sorrow? Shame?* "Eldreth, what's happened?"

Grief. "I've failed you." My whole body tensed. Then, he added, "It's your brother."

A great gust of breath escaped me. *Bale.* Bale and *Tin'nen.* "I know. There's nothing we can do for him now."

Eldreth blinked. "You know?"

I nodded. "It's a long story and one that requires food before telling. How are we here?"

His brow furrowed. "You healed us. Everyone. We sailed home under swift winds blessed by the Great Dragon herself."

"Vaya'la doesn't command the winds," I said absently. My mind was still piecing together what had happened on that beach. "Everyone lived. Truly?"

He did not respond immediately, which told me everything I needed to know.

"Who?" I asked. "My *ranng?*"

"All recovered. Mine as well. But, Gerta—"

He let the name hang in the air, and my chest squeezed. The last moments of her life played before my eyes, and before they were through, sobs racked my body. *Tell her...* Kahvrah's hollow eyes and crumpling form hit me all at once. Grief was a sucker punch so swift that I turned away from him and buried my face in his pillows. Drawing breath became a struggle as my body shuddered under the weight of it all.

My closest friend was gone.

After a moment, the bed beside me dipped, and Eldreth's strong hand stroked soothing paths down my back. But no amount of soothing would change her loss or the fact that I was the one to blame for it.

Yes, I had my *ranng*, and I would take my time to thank Vaya'la later, but there was no one left on this soil who truly understood me like she did. Bale was an entire sea away, and who knew when I would next see him.

More than that, the happiness that Gerta would never feel lanced straight through my heart. I had robbed her of that. Gerta had found a life here worth living, and I failed to give it to her. I didn't keep her from being sent back to Cavendaffe. I didn't help her get safely back to Drakh. She had given her life for me, and the last moments she had were ones of hopeless defeat.

I cried, perhaps for hours, until my eyes were grainy with each blink and swollen to slits. All the moisture was leached from my body into those tears. Now, even they were gone. And so was she.

"Please, drink this," Eldreth pleaded. He had never left my side, not as I collapsed back into sleep from exhaustion and woke up to fresh tears already dotting my cheeks.

I sat up, took the glass he offered, and drank. The pain in my heart had bypassed unbearable and looped back around to numb.

"Do you think you can eat something?" he asked in a low rumble, like speaking at a normal tone might frighten me back into tears.

"Yes," I said, "but there's something I need you to do for me first."

"Anything." He spoke without hesitation, and I knew in my heart, without the confirmation from my second sight, that he meant it.

"Ask your brother if the name Drake means anything to him."

ELDRETH RETURNED WITH two bitter draughts from Marr Magda—one for calm, and one to replenish my body after multiple days asleep. I downed them both. The first must have been potent, because the weight on my shoulders lessened, and I felt even the tension in my brow slip away. Next, I managed to bathe and relieve myself before tiring out and climbing back into his bed. As a reward, he propped me up against far too many pillows and settled me in with a tray.

Never in my life had I tasted something as incredible as this vegetable broth from the kitchen. It was a giant, steaming bowl of heaven. It was rich and dense and just the right amount of salty. An infusion of rosemary and oregano danced over my tongue. I dipped a thick hunk of buttered bread and ate and ate and ate. Alongside them was a tiny chocolate treat, which Eldreth delivered with a stern warning from Dallah to eat last. Rounding off the meal was a tea specially brewed by Henkel, and it came with a demand, again relayed by Eldreth, to offer my full critique when I was next able to make my way to the kitchens. All of them together did wonders to temporarily keep my grief at bay.

"If this stays down—"

"It will."

"—I want *babi* next."

Eldreth chuckled. A half-smile played at the corner of his mouth, and if I weren't so distracted with this masterpiece of bread and broth, I would have jumped in his lap and kissed it right off.

My other deterrent came in the form of an overanxious Ellán, lounging in a chair dragged in from Eldreth's sitting room, tapping his fingers endlessly against his knee. His mouth had opened four times now, but each time, a look from Eldreth had him clamping it shut and tap, tap, tapping away. When he wasn't playing a tattoo with his fingers, he was bouncing his knee or shifting back and forth in his chair.

I took a final gulp of tea, pushed aside my tray, and surveyed them both.

Ell leaned forward. "That name—"

I held up a single hand, silencing him. My mind was still sluggish, but I was able to wrangle my thoughts while I ate. "The day I was taken from Drakh, Eldreth brought me to a safe room beneath the keep."

Eldreth nodded.

"I expected to be alone in that room."

"But you weren't?" Eldreth shot a look at Ellán.

"But you weren't." Ellán sighed and hung his head. "I can explain. He wasn't dangerous, I swear it."

Eldreth sat forward in the chair Kahvrah had vacated earlier and fixed his brother with a spectacular glower. His whole body tensed like one wrong move from his brother would make him snap. Ellán's head darted between us so fast, he looked like a drunk owl in a bright blue overcoat. I almost waited for him to hoot. A laugh bubbled up from somewhere deep beneath my ribs, and both men turned back to me with matching quizzical stares.

"Bale would never hurt me."

Eldreth's face morphed into understanding, but Ellán's brow only furrowed. "You found out his name?"

Quick as lightning, Eldreth was out of his chair and smacked Ellán upside the head.

"Ow!"

"That's her brother, you fucking idiot." He left the room and returned with a glass of water for me and one for himself.

"Ohh." Ellán's face went through a full range of emotions. My second sight, still open, flashed like a rainbow before settling on a lightly *curious* aquamarine.

I took a deep, slow drink, allowing the cool water to loosen my tense throat. Then, I spoke. I explained how I found Bale, what I'd surmised about the attack, my desperate need to return him safely, my capture, and my questioning. When I got to the part of my torture, Ellán rose, moved to his brother's side, and placed a steadying hand on his shoulder. Eldreth's knuckles were white as he gripped the arm of the chair, and though neither spoke as I relayed the tale, the wood cracked when I got to those final days when my back was split open time and again. Ellán's hand tightened claw-like on Eldreth's shoulder. Still, they let me speak as I explained what I could remember of our battle on the coast. Tears fell from my eyes as I recounted the deaths, and as I remembered nothing after commanding the trees, Eldreth took up the last part of our journey home.

"Fuck, Serae, I'm so sorry," he finished, hanging his head. "I told him to follow, but I had to get you out. I couldn't go back for him."

Ellán's skin paled whiter than the bedsheets, and his lifelight flickered with fierce sparks of red-orange: *terror.*

"Peace," I told them both, and I rose from the bed and moved on instinct before Eldreth. He reached up and rested both hands on my hips. With one hand beneath his chin, I turned his face up to meet mine. "Bale is alive. He is protected by a Great Dragon." Eldreth's brow quirked. I could feel Ellán tensing again, but I couldn't take my eyes away from the swirling blue-gray storms that were threatening to consume me. "One day, we will go to his aid, but not yet."

"You're certain?" he asked.

"Yes."

That was enough for Eldreth but not Ellán.

"So, what, we do nothing?" Ellán demanded. "Just leave it in the hands of the Great Dragon?"

"No." My voice held an authority that was all my own. "Go to Dane, tell him everything. There's a lot for us to discuss—tomorrow."

Ellán looked to me, then to his brother, then back to me, and his lips quirked up into his most devious smile. "Tomorrow sounds like an excellent idea. I'm borrowing your *reálti* for the rest of the day. I'll tell them they have your leave, shall I?" He was backing out of the room already.

I couldn't free my attention from the darkening storms that held every bit of me too captive to respond. Eldreth rose to his feet as the main door thumped closed and the lock clicked. His hands never left my waist, and my whole body tingled with anticipation. The air in the room held more of a chill than I remembered, but the heat that radiated off his body wrapped around me. I closed my eyes and allowed his *passion*, the brilliant golden glow of his lifelight, to wash over me alongside that delicious heat.

"I missed you," I whispered.

His hand stroked up my back and threaded into my hair. "It's my fault. I fucking hesitated, and I lost you."

I don't know when my hands began moving against the hardness of his body, but I couldn't get enough of his muscled chest and abs and—*fuck*—those obliques that I knew led straight to the part of him I was most desperate to explore. Our lips met, and there was a moment of pure bliss, where everything in me stilled and hyper-focused on his mouth. But my heart was still so heavy. How could I enjoy him when there was so little joy left in my world?

I turned my head up to him, knowing the pain that he would see seeping out of me, but unable to stop it. As my eyes fluttered open, his darkened, and that warm yellow *desire* of his lifelight threaded aubergine with *regret*. His beautiful, soft, demanding, luscious lips turned downward into a frown.

His words registered. I pulled back, and for the first time, I saw the *pain* hiding behind his eyes and flickering in faint wisps of deep violet in his lifelight. I gripped his biceps—*dragons, this man is a god amongst men*—and dug my nails in enough for him to feel. "You didn't do this."

He pulled back an inch, but I gripped him even tighter.

"I need you to hear me. This was *my* choice. It was *my* mistake thinking they'd take Bale and leave me be. I never thought it would come to all of this."

"I should have stopped them. I should have cut them all down before they had a chance to touch you."

My hand moved to cup his face. "I did this, not you."

This was the difference between him and the reputation he'd built as weaponmaster of the Riht. Everything he did—every death he took, every choice he made—was to protect others. It was never selfish or cruel or for personal gain. He carried this burden so that others might live. But he would not carry this one. "If it's a choice between reliving what happened to me and you losing that hesitation, the part of you that makes you the most human, I will always choose the pain. Don't you ever sacrifice your humanity for me."

His lifelight grew stronger, but then it dimmed again. "There's something else." He took a moment to compose himself. Whatever it was, we could navigate together. There was no turning back. "It's your father...he's dead."

Shock sliced through me. My hands dropped from him as I took in his words. *Dead.* I hadn't expected it to hurt. After losing Gerta, I didn't think anything else could hurt. I slipped back to take a seat at the edge of the bed. This was the man who had brutalized me up until mere days ago. This was the man who stood on that beach and chose to kill the man I loved rather than take me back into his home. This was the man whose calloused command had led to the death of my closest friend.

But, this was also the man who told my mother to let me have my fun when I wanted to run off playing swords and arrows with Bale. He was the same man who encouraged my learning when he discovered my talents at my lessons and how quickly I was outpacing Merria, despite being younger.

Somewhere along the line, his priorities shifted to what his children could bring him rather than what his children could do. *How did it all change?*

"How?" I asked aloud.

"Please don't hate me when I tell you this."

I looked up, not expecting Eldreth to know the answers to the questions of my twisted, wretched mind.

His face hardened into a mask of barely concealed rage. "By my hand. After what he'd done to you, I couldn't let him live."

I blinked. All the sound in the room evaporated, nothing but heavy silence pressing in on my ears. "How?" I repeated. My mind had gone numb, and when I tried to call on my thoughts, only blank blackness responded.

"Does it matter?" he asked, voice grating and rough.

"It does. How do you know he's dead?"

"No one can survive a blade through the throat and spine. Not even your healing could reverse it. He's dead."

In my mind's eye, I saw him lying on the pebbled sand, blood matted in his raven-black hair, his body crushed by fleeing horse hooves. His head nearly severed from the brutality of Eldreth's blade. Shock and horror were stamped forever over his navy-blue eyes. Bile rose into my throat. I barely turned my head in time to miss Eldreth as I vomited all over his floor.

EPILOGUE

BALE

EARLY WINTER, TALMON 1036

HEAT.

I sat with my eyes closed and focused on the cold stone and chill winter air. All I could feel, despite the icy draft, was fierce, consuming heat.

"Awaken."

The voice was a command that I continued to ignore. I was awake, and yet, I was trapped at the heart of a storm that devoured my mind. Until I could find my way back to myself, I couldn't pay that voice any heed.

A clattering sounded outside the cell. It could be my daily meal, though more likely, it was a new session with a whip or switch or blade. They had stopped trying fire. Perhaps because they'd figured out it didn't work, or perhaps because of the way their eyes shone with fear when I laughed as the flames licked harmlessly over my flesh. Boots clomped on stone, and three men entered the cell. There was no need to open my eyes. I was ready for the blow to the side of my head when it came. It was my jailers' preferred method of incapacitating me, not that I'd ever fought back. Metal clanged against the stone at my side. Looks like it was mealtime after all.

I waited long after their footsteps dissipated down the corridor. I'd have to open my eyes if I wanted to eat, but that brought its own challenge. Sometimes, when they opened, I was in this miserable cell that held only a pile of straw and a bucket for piss. Other times, I was deep beneath the ground, staring at a door made of pure flame. Around me, there were small mushrooms that glowed with inner lights and little creatures that scuttled over my skin and pressed healing herbs to my wounds. Every time, I sat there in peace with these tiny beings of magic until a single blink brought me back to this fetid cell. After, the heat within me would rise to the point of overwhelm, and my willpower alone kept it contained within. I shuddered to imagine what would happen if it escaped.

With a deep breath in and out, I pried my eyelids apart. I was met with thick iron bars and my own sense of disappointment. This place had given me a new appreciation for my cell in Rihtlond, not to mention my blue-eyed captor. I pushed aside thoughts of Drake and instead fell on my latest favorite pain point—Serae. She was safe. She had to be. The last I remembered, she was fleeing this cursed place in her Rihtlondish prince's arms as an entire squadron fell before her. Then, there was only fire, followed by blackness, followed by this delightful stone cell. I was getting fucking tired of memory gaps.

"I will show you all, but first, you must come to me."

That fucking voice.

"She is safe, this one you seek. Come to me, and I will show her to you."

A trick if I'd ever heard one. Still, my thoughts lingered on my sister. I'd been away from her for just over a year, yet in that time, she had grown into a woman I scarcely recognized. It was not the power, no. Serae had always held a quiet power that others discounted. It was what turned away would-be suitors and stilled the tongues of any gossipers—except for Merria, of course. Now, there was a purpose to Serae. A sense of action.

"I know a thing or two about siblings. Let me tell you a story, and when I have finished, you may decide. Cast me out, and I will choose another in your place and leave you be. Agreed?"

Despite wanting to be left in peace, I found myself listening.

"I warn you now, Bale of Cavendaffe, brother to Serae of the Riht, that when all is known, your mind will be changed. This is a tale of truth, a tale of the past, and a tale, most importantly, of two brothers: Jerris and Patriol. This is the story of how these two ordinary people, born of simple folk from a small farm in the middle of nowhere, became extraordinary. They were the last of their kind, the last of the Dragonbound. This is the story of how they sealed the Great Dragons behind the doors of ice and blood and bone and flame; of how they sacrificed themselves to save the entire Mortal Realm from corruption by the Darkness; and, above all else, of how they completely and utterly failed."

AUTHOR'S NOTE

My first spark of an idea, which much later morphed and grew into *Wings of Life*, came from a snippet by a thirteenth-century English chronicler complaining that all the English women were being stolen away by Danish men wielding weapons such as good manners and better hygiene. As if regular bathing, hair combing, and clothes changing were enough to sway those fickle females' hearts. Obviously, that single quote was wildly out of context, misrepresented a lot of the harsh truths of the time, and perhaps was written by a man riddled with bitterness. Nonetheless, the idea was born.

Rather than look to the nitty gritty details of the past, I've crafted Jaeda in honor of my own imagination. *Wings of Life* isn't a work of historical fiction. The Riht are not Vikings. Everything within I've created from scratch, sampling and weaving in a few aspects from history books that stuck with me most. For example, you likely spotted the root word of Dane used as a title, giving a small nod to this inspiration.

As you read, you may have noticed many people of the Riht described as fit. Perhaps it all comes down to Serae (and me) getting trapped in the beautiful fog of discovery. Still, their culture places a heavy focus on bodily health, seen in their *dowsae* and, of course, their food. If you, like many of my early readers, were salivating to pluck *babi* straight from the pages, I have to admit I'm not at all sorry to leave you wanting. *Babi* were inspired by an amalgamation of tastes I've yet to encounter in the real world. One day, I may break down and take a stab at making them myself. Until then, they'll live on in my imagination...and now yours.

If you found, along your journey through the Riht, that you saw a wider variety of race, gender, and sexual orientation than you expected of a work with Viking inspirations, you'd be right. I've intentionally shaped this world to match what I wish I saw in my own. I hope you found enjoyment and, dare I say, relief in it.

The story of Serae and Wep will continue, as we see more of the Riht and more of Jaeda in the next books. Until then, may you channel Lex every time you raise your cups, be they filled with water, tea, or something stronger—*va draske!*

ACKNOWLEDGEMENTS

What a strange feeling it is to sit down and come up with more words to add to this already voluminous work! I am not in the practice of expressing verbose gratitude, but I nonetheless feel so keenly thankful to so many people for the support they have shown me. I'm sad to say that I couldn't possibly name every person here, but that doesn't detract from my feelings of pure appreciation for each one.

In transitioning my career away from a soulless corporate job to my true passion, anxiety and I have become fast friends. Beside me, every step of the way, stood my family. My first thanks must be given to my husband, who told me to take the chance on myself, and to my girls, who always help take care of Mommy when she's focusing on writing.

Many thanks go to my agent, Diego—there is no bigger cheerleader out there than him. His encouragement has been constant, and his faith in me has helped me recognize I should also have a bit of faith in myself.

To my editor, Jordyn, with whom working is just the best. I love the way she thinks, and I feel like our brains meld together in the best sort of match. So many times, her comments had me laughing out loud one second *(ahem, Delly!)* and pondering the depths of my characters' souls the next. I'm so excited for what is to come in the rest of the Dragonbound Chronicles! And I am so thankful for all the support from Page & Vine, especially from Meredith, Amber, and Victoria, who I've worked with the most.

For my dearest friends, Alyssa, Andreana, and Jamie, whose cheerleading and support have nurtured my soul. Borrowing a bit of their confidence has been a blessing I can only hope I manage to repay. As well as Roberta, who has been so kind and encouraging from afar in Romania. Her adoration of my words has made my heart soar time and again.

For my family, especially my sister, Emily, and sister-in-law, Renee, who both helped as very early readers. It has been such a treasure to hear their enthusiasm!

To my mother-in-law, Janine, who daily safeguards my writing time—a gift that makes all of this possible—and follows my every update with so much excitement.

And perhaps most importantly, to my mom, Deborah, who reads everything I write, helps me nitpick the grammar, finds the spots that don't quite make sense, and lives the journey with my characters before anyone else. I secretly love the little ways she brags about me to her friends (and she does some seriously hard work for me in manifesting success). She even crafted a recipe for Serae's magical veggie broth, which truly is to die for! In all seriousness, if you are blessed to have them, listen to your moms. Mine always told me I could do anything...it just took me a while to believe it.

Finally, to you, dear reader. When crafting my stories, I'm releasing the magic and monsters inside my head to feed my creative soul. But really, I'm doing this for you—all of you. *Only you.*

ABOUT THE AUTHOR

Meghan Le Fay hails from present-day Earth, despite her lifelong dream of being born as an elf in Middle-earth. A constant and consummate fan of fantasy, she lives, breathes, and dreams in the spidery language of the magic. Her works are inspired by her obsessions with mythology, medieval history, and all things magical and mystical—especially dragons.

When not writing or daydreaming of other realms, Meghan can be found avoiding the Arizona desert heat through reading, crafting, music, or dance. Or having wild adventures (both real and imaginary) with her family.

Learn more at: meghanlefay.com